# SUPERNATURAL VIGILANTE

# SUPERNATURAL VIGILANTE

## SUPERNATURAL VIGILANTE SOCIETY BOOKS 1-4

D.R. PERRY

Supernatural Vigilante (Supernatural Vigilante Society Books 1-4) is a work of fiction. All of the characters, organizations, and events portrayed in this novel are either products of the author's imagination or are used fictitiously. Sometimes both.



LMBPN Publishing
PMB 196, 2540 South Maryland Pkwy
Las Vegas, NV 89109

First US edition, October 2019
ebook ISBN: 978-1-64202-530-9
Print ISBN: 978-1-64202-530-9

# BE COUNTED

## SUPERNATURAL VIGILANTE BOOK ONE

*Life sucks, and then you die. Sort of.*

*Valentino Crispo loves Mom's Italian cooking, sun on the beach, and working for the Cranston Police Department. He loses it all after getting vamped. Now, he's the newest vampire in Providence.*

*When a hitwoman apparently shoots his dad and one of Cranston's Finest on the same night, Tino stops letting vampirism bite him. He'll mix supernatural and PD skills to solve the crime, but he hasn't got the hang of being a vampire yet.*

*The mystery of whodunit and why is tied up with Tino's turning. The Providence vampire elders hate nosy vamps almost as much as new ones. Will Valentino stand up and be counted, or add to the body count?*

# CHAPTER ONE

I barely know anything about vampires, even after I got turned into one. Yeah, I know. That makes me sound like a walking stereotype. At least it didn't happen in High School or before I quit my job at Cranston PD to hang out my own shingle as a PI. But now everything's different in new and special ways. In other words, it sucks. Pizza and beer are right out of my diet plan. So are long walks on the beach at sunrise. I can't tell anyone I'm a vamp, so it gives me no extra cool factor with friends or game in the dating department, either. Which is bad enough anyway for a twenty-seven-year-old dude like me.

Sunday dinner with the folks isn't the same as it used to be, either. And that's where I am, in my parents' downstairs bathroom glaring at an empty mirror while I try to figure out a fourth excuse about why I'm not at Mass every Sunday morning. Forgive me, Father, for I have been vamped. It's been a whole month since my last confession because I can't set foot inside Church. I used to be an altar boy, too.

"Tino?" Dad's knocking at the door. I've got to answer him. He's my father, and we're Italian Catholics. Honoring our parents is just what we do. It's the same way for my best friend, Maury even though he's Jewish.

"Yeah, okay." I run the water and rinse my hands so Dad doesn't get grossed out. It's not like I need to because I don't actually use the john anymore. All the blood we drink goes to fuel spiffy vampiric powers I haven't learned yet.

I come out of the can, doing the switching places shuffle with my old man and then swoop out of the way as Ma almost brains me with a plate of broccoli rabe, heavy on the garlic. It used to smell delicious, but now it only makes my eyes water. With blood. I hope she doesn't notice. Yeah, we don't cry regular tears without using one of those powers I mentioned earlier. She stops and blinks so hard I run one hand through my hair and then pat down the front of my shirt. When Ma looks at me like that, I always think I got something in my teeth even though I haven't bitten a veggie in a month. I look at my shoes so it's harder for her to see my eyes.

"You've been hitting the gym hard, huh, Tino?" Ma whisks the dish away, and I know her rhetorical question is as much of a front as that wiener joint in West Warwick used to be. Not the one you're thinking of, that other one down past the Dunkin Donuts with the burnt-tasting coffee. Anyway, she knows something's up with me. Mothers usually do.

"Yeah, Ma." I head back into the kitchen because I know that if I don't, she'll just give me a guilt trip later on for not offering to help cart everything out to the dining room.

I don't understand why the three of us have to eat in there on the hoity-toity glass table when the beat-up wooden hand-me-down from Grandma did just fine while I still lived at home. I didn't start the unliving thing until after moving out, which is good since Ma's practically psychic. Or maybe she's got honest to goodness psychic powers. I'm still not sure if that's a thing. What do you want from me? I'm new, okay?

"Thanks, Tino." Ma hands me some hot pads I wish were thicker or maybe the size of Texas. "Please take the eggplant out of the oven. You're a good boy."

You're probably wondering why I don't have a problem with her calling me good boy like that. Italian Mamas sometimes talk the same way to their grown sons as they did when we were little. And yeah, we have tempers like you think but never really stay mad at family.

Anyway, Ma clicks away down the hall on high-heeled shoes she wouldn't have worn a few years ago when I still lived in the basement. My eyes roll as I pile forks and knives on some napkins. The cloth kind, which are in the same drawer with the rest of the hot pads. But the only kind in there are those dinky flat ones, not the kind that actually go over your whole hand. The sound her shoes make in the tiled hall stops at the edge of the carpet in the dining room.

And that's it. I can't procrastinate any longer. At that point, I have no choice but to stick my extra flammable vampire arms into a hot oven. Ma expects me to, so I'll do it. It's the decent thing to do, and I don't want to blow my cover. I holler back to the dining room, "Ma! Where're the long oven mitts?"

"Use what you got!" I hear a tinkle of glass and a muffled thump and assume Ma knocked over a wine glass in the china cabinet or something.

I'm bending over the oven, and all I smell is eggplant. And garlic. Which means I have to stop myself from sneezing. All I feel is three hundred and sixty degrees of heat, which could make me blister like a white Russian on the Riviera. Why they don't make oven mitts that go up to the shoulder, I'll never know. Oh, yeah. Because vampires don't cook. Or maybe they do if they were Gordon Ramsey before getting turned, but what do I know?

I reach in with the little square hot pads and grab the pan, thanking God that the vampirism makes me extra graceful and fast, even if I'm not breaking the sound barrier like that guy in red on TV. I get the pan to Ma's fancy-pants dining room as quickly as I can while still seeming human like my parents. After that, I set it down on the trivet Ma always puts out for bakes like the eggplant. God, I miss being able to eat them.

Remembering the breaking glass sound, I look around. But I don't see Ma or any evidence of broken glass. I'm a little confused, but my mother's always been like a ninja with cleaning anything up. It's kind of unnerving sometimes. I shrug and leave the dining room.

On the way back into the kitchen, it happens. I smell blood. Ma never cuts herself, and she hasn't this time. I see her going through the doorway from the parlor, carrying those fancy linen napkins and the utensils I piled up on the counter before. The blood smell comes from the bathroom where Dad is. So I stop outside the door. Not much else I can do, being a vampire and all. We smell human blood, and it stops us in our tracks for a second or few. Hunger is something we've got to be careful about, you know.

And after a few, it occurs to me that Dad has no business bleeding in the downstairs bathroom. He always shaves upstairs, and besides, I don't smell any of his Barbasol. Another thing being a vampire tells me is how much someone is bleeding, and my father is definitely doing too much of that for something like biting the inside of his cheek or trimming a hangnail too close. I open the door just as Ma clicks up behind me.

Dad is on the floor between the sink and the john, clutching his right arm with his left hand so hard Ma thinks he's had a heart attack. She calls 911 while I'm stuck staring there, realizing he's been shot. I know right away the bullet's still in him, too, although it smells odd. Also, I know he got shot from a distance and through the window, which now has a hole in it. My vampire senses help with that, but really it's the police experience that gives me knowledge of ballistics. Yeah, I used to be a cop. Quit when I didn't make detective, hence the going into business for myself thing I mentioned earlier.

And a couple of other clues I notice; Dad was either on the can or just getting up when they hit him. His pants are around his ankles, and there's a deuce in the bowl with some paper. The indignity makes me narrow my eyes and curl my lip in anger. My fangs get extra pokey with a side of wanting to bite whoever did this, too. I can't stand here and let someone get away with shooting up my parents' house.

I don't step foot in the can, don't want any of my old CSI buddy Raph Paolucci from the Cranston PD to find evidence of vampires on my account. But I have to know who'd dare do this to my Dad, and I'm fast enough to catch them, maybe. I run out the back and around the side of the house, then look both ways like I'm considering crossing the street to cover the fact that I'm looking for witnesses. After that, I jump two stories up to the roof of the house I grew up in.

Being a vampire isn't all blood-thirst and sun allergies. We get strength and speed like something out of those superhero shows you see on TV. We get to see like hawks, hear like German Shepherds and scent like bloodhounds. Exactly how good we are at that varies on an individual basis, but we're all leaps and bounds above regular people in those departments. Anyway, the bonuses seemed lame to me before tonight. Dad gets shot, and now I feel like they're like some kind of freaking miracle. Except for the fact that undead vampires are definitely not welcome at Saint Mary's. I run across the roof without even worrying about balance or anything and leap to the one next door.

I don't see the sniper, but I smell gunpowder across the street and three doors down. So I follow it, springing off Old Man Fitzpatrick's roof to land on a tree branch the width of my wrist. Hurtling through the air, I tap the gutter with one toe to get some extra lift. It groans but holds, and before you can say blood I'm on the apex of the roof, looking down at the back of a head covered by a ski mask. The body has a petite build with wiry strength. The sniper is latching what looks like a saxophone case but smells like a gun cabinet. I leap.

As the sniper's head turns, I catch a whiff of something perfumed. I'd know it anywhere, the scent my old High School girlfriend Kayleigh used to wear all the time; Anais, Anais. The eyes in the ski mask go wide. I can only just barely see them, though. I smell more oil and gunpowder and realize the sniper's drawn on me. A side-arm because shooting a dude at close range with a sniper rifle's stupid. This hitwoman's smart. Yeah, okay. So that's a huge assumption. I know it's right almost immediately.

I'm dodging before I know it because if I hear the shot, it's already too late. The sniper might not know I'm a vamp, might not have holy water or wooden shrapnel bullets, but I like my hide in one piece. This is my dad's would-be killer I'm stalking here, and I don't want to make a stupid mistake. The cops probably don't know about us undead people, but the less lawful organizations just might and keep it under wraps.

But the sniper doesn't aim for me. The gun isn't loaded with ammo to hurt supernaturals, either. Instead, it's a different kind of special round. The bullet hits about an inch from where my feet were before, but the flash-bang it makes blinds me all the same. My vision's more dazzled and star-struck than that one time I saw Taylor Swift on Misquamicut beach. By the time it clears, the shooter is gone.

I bare my fangs and hiss up at the sliver of moon in the sky. I'm not being melodramatic; it's instinctive, okay? Fire is something we vampires freak out about, and that light show sure looked like the beginning of a barbeque. I take a deep breath I don't need because there's just something refreshing about that. And then I look down to see if anyone's watching so I can jump down from the roof already. Someone is, of course. Because my luck sucks to match my vampirism, of course.

There's a lamp on in an upstairs window at Old Man Fitzpatrick's place, and the twitch of curtain just before that light goes out means the old guy might have seen everything. I remember that he wears the dorkiest round bifocals in the known universe. That and the fact it's dark out probably means he doesn't know it's me up here. But I get my undead ass down from the roof just the same. The police are coming and I don't want them to find me up there. I realize I'll have to disguise myself just like that sniper did if I want to do rooftop chases in the future. The bright side is, I love costumes. But I hate masks with the passion of a thousand fiery daystars.

I jump down between the house I was on top of and the one next door, landing neatly and mostly silent behind a forsythia whose yellow blooms are converting to green. Before you go getting the idea I'm a wuss because I know flowers, I'm telling you Dad's a florist. It helped my popularity with the ladies in High School, but apparently not his with whoever was trying to bump him off. He's supplied funerals for a handful of underworld types over the last few years.

I check my shoes for roofing shingles and brush off my pants and sleeves just in case. After that, I round the corner of the house and head back across the street. I look down out of habit because I always used to trip over the curb on our side of the street before the vampination happened. Then I fall on my ass on the asphalt because I bump into someone.

"Thanks, Tino." I hear the scuffle and plop of a flip-flop on pavement and look up.

"Thanks for what, Scott?" I blink at Old Man Fitzpatrick's teenage grandson. At least his name's not Patrick Fitzpatrick because that'd just be obnoxious.

"The good old knock-about." He's standing, but he hadn't been just a few seconds ago. Scott sticks a hand out to help me up. I wonder why he's wearing flip-flops and shorts with no shirt. It's got to be too cold for that out here even though it's May.

"Thanks." I wrinkle my nose.

Teenagers literally stink, especially to vampires. Which is why most of them think the recent book and movie trend of vamps falling for teens is hilarious. Something about all the crazy hormones and rapid growth they're going through gives them an unappealing aroma. But Scott's off the charts odorous. I hope he'll just let me go, so I don't have to gag my way through a conversation.

"So, what were you doing— Woah." Scott jerks his chin at the corner where an ambulance careens around the corner before shrieking to a halt in front of my house.

"Yeah, it's my dad." I shrug, trying to hide the fact that I'm wiping my hand on my pants after letting go of his. "Gotta go."

"Hey, you need help?" Scott calls after me.

I want to get away from his stinky teenage miasma, but think maybe the stench would help me keep from slavering like a mad dog over all the blood in my parents' house. Jumping rooftops makes me thirsty, and I don't mean for wine. The vamp in charge will kill me if I go nuts and try to eat a house full of emergency personnel.

"Yeah, maybe. Come on!" I focus on not running at top vamp speed. Even though I jog faster than I used to on a good day as a human, Scott keeps up. Teenagers. They're going to save the world, I tell you. If you don't believe me, go to the movies.

I go around the side and in through the kitchen door. Scott just stops next to the fridge and sniffs, rubbing his nose like he's got allergies or a cold. But I don't care. The paramedics have Dad on a stretcher. He's unconscious. There's a blue band of rubber wrapped around his right arm next to his shoulder, above the bullet wound. He looks way too pale. One of the EMTs drops an IV kit on his chest. He meets my eyes.

"Blood type," says the EMT.

"AB positive." I know these things now, wouldn't have a month ago. I realize vampires could probably be pretty decent doctors if they kept themselves fed enough. Ourselves. I keep my mouth shut after that, feeling my fangs pricking against my lower lip. I even take a step backward toward stinky Scott. Thank God that smell coming off of him helps kill my appetite.

The EMT gives me a thumbs up, then barks Dad's blood type into the speaker on his chest. Then, the EMT and his lady partner wheel Dad out of the house through the front door. Mom is weeping and wailing and following. The lady EMT nods at her, and Mom gets bustled into the back of the ambulance with Dad. I turn around.

"Why didn't you tell me your Dad got shot?" Scott rubs one hand down his face, and I notice he looks like he's barely got himself under control, just like me. I listen for his heart, and it's thumping away. Good. He's not a vamp too, then.

I feel how he looks, so I'm not sure how to answer. Old Man Fitzpatrick's always been a good neighbor even if he's the world's biggest gossip. I used to look up to Riley, Scott's dad, back when I was a tiny tot. But I'm not sure I can tell the man's grandson about the sniper or how I got on the roof to confront a lone gunman in the first place. As I try to decide, a sharp new scent rises up over hormonal teen. This one's coffee and cigarettes, and it's at the door the EMTs left open behind them. I turn.

"Hey." A mop of curly hair tops a thin face with a hawkish nose in the middle.

"Weintraub." I nod at my oldest friend. We survived everything together, from toddling around the playground to the theater department back at Cranston West. And he used to be my partner back when we were beat cops, too.

"Crispo." Detective Maury Weintraub grins. He's way more intimidating than he used to be back before he got the promotion I didn't.

"Uh, I gotta—" Scott mumbles something about a curfew.

"No." Maury shakes his head. "This is my case, and you're not leaving. Not until you both answer a few questions."

# CHAPTER TWO

I'm standing there with Scott Fitzpatrick, trying not to gag on a stench coming off him that only I can smell. I hope, because it looks like the kid's in aromatic distress himself. I'm worried he's about to toss his cookies all over the detective on the scene who just happens to be my oldest and best friend in the world. What do you want? It's Rhode Island. The state motto here should be, "I know a guy."

"Okay, questions." I nod, trying to look like I don't know what I'm talking about even though my old buddy knows better.

"Fine. I'll start with this." Maury pulls one of those blister packs out of his coat pocket. I know it's Nicorette before I even see the printing on the silver side he pushes the gum through. He pops one chicklet in his mouth and chews away. Nicotine gum is maybe half as pungent as Scott. "Why did you leave the house, Tino?"

"Saw the broken glass in there." I jerk my chin in the general direction of the bathroom door. "Thought maybe I could catch whoever hurt Dad." I play dumb because it's easy, and Maury always buys that. "What was it that hit him, a rock?"

"A bullet. Shot." Maury stops chewing. "Someone shot your dad, Tino. And you mean to tell me you went out there and then bring the first guy you see inside like you don't suspect him?" He snorts. "No wonder you didn't make detective."

"Um." I turn and notice a uniformed officer behind Scott. "This is just Scott Fitzpatrick. He's the neighbor's grandkid. And look at him, Maury." I jerk a thumb at the kid's face. "Green around the gills like this, and you think he's the attacker?"

"If it were my dad, I would have popped the first person I saw outside in the mouth, green kid with tummy troubles or not." Maury sticks another piece of gum in his mouth and goes back to chomping away, unaware that by saving his lungs, he might be damning his heart. I hear it racing. Or maybe he's just nervous while on a case with people he knows. Or excited. I'll take Things I Never Wanted to Know About Maury Weintraub for two-hundred, Alex.

"Well, maybe my temper is better than yours." I shrug.

"Except I know that's not true, Tino." Maury stands with his hands to either side of his hips. Next to, not on. Like he thinks he's some kind of gunslinger. And he's right on both counts.

"Well, okay. So when I got outside I hollered a blue streak."

"Um, yeah." Scott nods, then puts one hand over his mouth and glances at the sink for a moment. I can't believe he's backing me up without any clue of why I'm acting so dodgy. "Yeah, I heard Valentino yelling and came to see what was going on."

"And you don't have a busted schnoz because?"

"I hollered right back." Scott cracks his knuckles but thinks better of it and rubs what passes for his gut instead. Kid should be in Planet Fitness ads. If I sound jealous, it's because I am. "And I'm a big guy. Scary, don't you know?" Scott waggles his eyebrows.

We look at each other. I can tell Maury's trying not to bust his gut laughing out of respect for Dad. I nod and let the moment pass. Everyone's back to serious business for now.

"So, did you see anything?" Maury's eyebrow goes up, peeking above the rim of his wireframe glasses.

"Just Tino." Scott's voice carries a little lilt that reminds me of his grandpa. "And the ambulance after that."

"And how about you, Tino?" Maury turns and leans in the

doorway sideways, just like he used to while on the lookout for teachers when we prepped pranks back in High School. I wonder what he's watching out for this time. Then I realize what's missing from this picture. Maury's here alone, without a partner.

"It's Sunday, so I came over for dinner with the folks." I sigh, running a hand across the back of my neck. "It all starts like any other Sunday since I moved out, too. Except that I hear something after Dad went to the can." I explain everything. In human terms, of course.

"Hmm." I don't like the conniving look on Maury's mug one bit. "And you say your mom called Emergency services after you figured out your dad got shot?"

"No, Maury." I roll my eyes because I know this repeat-the-question trick. "You heard me the first time. I said I thought some punk threw a rock through the window. Ma thought he had a heart attack because she rushed off so fast she missed the glass and blood."

"So, how did you know what she said all the way out here?" His smile reminds me of a shark's. Maury's looking at the phone. Yeah, my parents still use a land-line, and it's on the kitchen wall farthest from the hall with the bathroom.

"Huh?" I blink. There's nothing in my eye. Maury must wonder how I heard Ma on the phone from outside at the curb. There's no explanation I can give him without revealing what I am, either. Maybe he'll think I'm secretly from Krypton.

"Weird." Maury shakes his head, dropping the predatory act. "Something doesn't add up about the timing of events here, but I don't see how it's possible for you to be the cog in this machine."

"How do you figure?" Scott turns his head, giving Maury the fisheye.

"I know all of Tino's tells." My detective friend chuckles. "We don't just go back. We go all the way back."

"Really?" Scott's still rubbing his tummy, but he grins, anyway. The kid's as much of a gossip hound as his grandpa. He knows Maury and me were tight but not for how long.

"Yeah." I nod, wishing the chuckle over fond memories could shake itself loose from my throat. "Our moms were in the same Lamaze class. We were born three days apart."

"The joke is, Tino's mom tagged mine into the maternity ward on her way out." Maury sighs and deflates like he's been running on half the sleep he needs. He looks pretty bad now that I see him without all the investigative posturing. "Whoever did this to your dad, Tino, we'll catch him."

I nod, choke out a thanks, and doubt him. Maury Weintraub is only human, after all. And he doesn't even guess that the perp's a woman. I listen to him breathe, hear the crackle of imminent pneumonia or something worse in his lungs. His skin's dull, too; yellower than it was last time I saw him. But I don't smell any drink on him, not even the sick-sweet Kosher wine we always used to sneak from his parents' sideboard. Instead, Maury smells dry, like something out of a museum. And I don't like it, not one bit despite my jealousy about the promotion, but I can't place it. I file the information away in my brain for now.

I look at Scott again. Kid stinks to high heaven like a bucket of locker room towels but looks healthy as a horse. And I'm standing between the two of them, undead. It starts feeling too much like the start of a really bad Dad joke, the kind where you know the punch line will be one of the worst puns you've ever heard, but you just can't stop your buddy from delivering it. And then it all adds up, so I ask the million-dollar question.

"Hey, Maur?" Not that.

"Yeah?"

Here it is. "Don't you got a partner since making detective?"

Maury sighs and turns his head. In profile, his face looks even more pinched, the dark circles under his eyes more pronounced. His head bows like someone settled a barbell on his shoulders.

"Larry's dead, Tino." Maury tucks the pencil into the wire spiral and then sticks his unused notepad back in his pocket. "Found in his unmarked car in a parking lot downtown early this morning."

"I'm sorry." I reach out with one hand before realizing it'll feel too cold and Maury will notice. But he doesn't take it.

"You couldn't have known." My pal peels himself out of the doorway, then heads past Scott and me without an upward glance. "Anyway, call me if you see or think of anything else."

And just like that, Maury Weintraub has left the building. I remember Detective Larry Tierney from the Precinct, too. He was pretty sharp and well-connected, but always had time to make nice with the beat cops like me. If they're having a wake, I realize I want to be there. But then I hang my head, remembering how Larry had no family. I wonder who's going to make the arrangements or if he'll just go in a pauper's grave alone.

"Woah," says Scott. "Heavy."

"Ain't that the truth." I sigh and lean against the counter. After making sure I'm not too close to the oven. Thing's still on and you know, vampire. Flammable. Ugh. I reach out and shut it off.

"So, why aren't you calling your friend back then?" Scott's still there, and I suddenly wish he wasn't.

"Just get out of here, Scott." I wave a hand, not even looking at him because I hope that'll seem more dismissive. I push people away when stuff upsets me.

"Look, I know there's something you're not telling him."

"You don't know nothing, kid." I stand up straight, put my hands on my hips. If dismissive isn't working, then my defense mechanism decides it's time for aggressive. "Except the way back to your house."

"Sorry." Scott turns, heads for the door he came in by. For whatever reason, I think of a kicked dog, tail between its legs and all.

When the door shuts behind him, I realize I'm alone in my parents' house. I don't live there anymore, and the one thing I've got to have isn't here. And that's important because I need blood. Badly.

The only blood at the Cranston house is on the floor in the john. My father's blood, and I made myself a promise never to sample that vintage if you know what I mean. And even if I hadn't that's tampering with a crime scene. Hell to the no to the way.

I leave, thumbing the lock on the doorknob before closing the side entrance behind me. I think my old two-seater beater will be a haven from the smell of the only thing that does my body good anymore.

But you probably know by now that I'm a big fangy idiot with sucky luck.

Some of the blood got on my shoe somehow. I spend the entire drive trying not to put my foot in my mouth. Literally. The fact that it has to be on the pedal helps like a band-aid on a sucking chest wound. Which my father might have for all I know.

The streetlamp outside the triple-decker I rent in Rolfe Square is one of the old sodium deals. It's a "retro neighborhood" or "revival" or something. But whatever they call it, the vintage lighting makes everything look orange. I hate that color. My pale skin looks spray-tanned under it, and that makes me bitter. I used to turn a golden olive color at the beach in summer, and now I'm facing down my very first one allergic to the sun. Happy undeath day to me, I guess?

I go up the stoop, open the door and head down the building's shared hall. A set of narrow stairs leads up, and I take both flights. My apartment's the whole third floor, which isn't saying much. There's not a lot of usable square footage with all the slanted ceilings and dormer windows. I call it "the Belfry," because vampire, bats, belfries. It's a good name for an inconvenient space. I got a good deal on the rent, though.

I get away with foil over the windows to keep things sun-safe and hope no kid ever chucks a rock or bats a thousand through one of them at high noon. It's unlikely for kids to play ball on a street this busy during the day, at least.

I'd find a basement apartment and move, but breaking the lease makes me lose my deposit, and the rents skyrocketed last week. If only the fangs and thirst for blood came with millions of dollars like it always seems to in the movies. I'd buy the building and get steel shades put up inside all the windows. Maybe in five years I'll have saved up enough to find a more sun-proof place.

I toss all of my clothes and the shoes into the bathtub and run the cold water over them. My sneakers might be ruined, but whatever. At least I'm not in danger of eating them now, which would also wreck them. I have no idea what else got blood on it besides that one shoe, so it's better to be safe than sorry. My pajamas are a cozy change from the Sunday dinner polo and khaki wardrobe. And what's wrong with that, anyway? It's okay for a vampire to like wearing flannel and fluffy bunny slippers.

A bag of blood from the fridge tides me over, but I take another one out and warm it up on the burner in the coffee maker I bought for that purpose. Random acts of parkour make vampires hungry. Who knew?

I think about how much of a wreck Maury is, wonder if I should call him up, say something comforting. Maybe even tell him to get to a doctor. But I can't think of a way to say any of that without giving my new unlife away. I mean, what am I going to do, call him up and say, "Maur, you smell like death and your ticker sounds out of whack?" He's got no idea I'm a vampire. No one is supposed to find out, either.

The world doesn't know, and the old vamps will kill to keep it that way. Sure, random people find out by accident on occasion, but those get branded as crazies. There are rumors about new vampires vanishing, too. Folks like me, who are new to all of this and can't keep their mouths shut. Their human families, also, sometimes.

I go my whole life staying out of trouble, keeping my nose clean, avoiding the life of crime my impeccably Italian background could have let me in on. I get experience as a cop, quit when they shun me out of detective, go about planning for my own PI business. And then some random chick at a bar puts the bite on me and I'm inducted into something even more secret and harder to get out of than Organized Crime. And potentially as deadly, too.

I'm not sure what to do with myself for more than the short term, either. It's only been about a month, just long enough for me to get the instruction manual basics and meet the vampire King and his bigwigs once. And I can't go forward with officially hanging out a shingle as a PI until I clear it with the vampire authorities, either. I haven't felt this clueless since starting Middle School.

I'd do what I did then, stand in the bathroom and ask myself a bunch of questions. But that's impossible. Vampires can't look at themselves in the mirror. All I can see are my clothes, hanging in midair like they're on an invisible mannequin. Or the Invisible Man. Can't see other vamps in the mirror, either. Maybe it's supposed to be a way for us to recognize each other. And it's definitely the reason so many vampires wear hats. Those make it easier to get past a mirror without people noticing if you walk fast enough. On the other hand, we can hear heartbeats or the lack thereof as a way of identifying each other. The mirror thing is just plain stupid.

I go over to the bathroom, mostly a waste of space for me now except the whole washing off blood exercise I performed earlier. Then I turn to look at the john, flushing it so the water doesn't go moldy and start to reek. I contemplate filling it with potting soil and transplanting my Christmas Cactus into it. It'd save space out in the big room that makes up the rest of the apartment, so I decide it might actually be a practical idea.

"Hullo, Valentino."

I jump nearly out of my skin at the voice, husky and low. Its owner got the drop on me partly because the flushing sound hid every move she made, but mostly because she's undead like me.

"Stephanie, what the Hell!"

# CHAPTER THREE

The vampire who turned me stands in my apartment, uninvited. Which is perfectly within the rules for our kind since that whole invitation thing is fake news anyway? I would bounce her out the door if it was in my power to do so. Not because she poses me any danger but because she is and always will be a giant pain in my neck seven ways from Sunday.

"That's a nice way to greet a friend, Val." Steph tosses a lock of wavy brown hair over one shoulder.

"Don't call me that, Stephanie. I told you, it's Tino."

"Very well, Tino." She saunters to the one comfy chair in the apartment and drapes herself on its arm. She manages to do this with class, like practically everything else. But somehow she's like this without being even a tiny bit sexy. Go figure. Stephanie's a special kind of high-brow.

"I'm here to offer my support."

"Huh?"

"About your father." Stephanie studies her fingernails, which are glossy with silvery polish. "Shot, wasn't he?"

"Like it's any of your business." I don't bother asking how she knows because she won't tell me until she feels like it. All the same, I take a whiff of the air. No Anais Anais perfume, plus Steph is more, um, angular than the assassin in a couple of places.

"You're my business." She keeps her head down, looks up at me through her eyelashes. Stephanie seems wholesome and innocent, even though I happen to know those impressions are completely fake. I get the idea that nobody knows the real Stephanie McQueen, and she likes it that way.

"Yeah, I know." I reach into a cabinet to get down a mug for the blood in the coffee maker. "Your responsibility, all that Vampire Court compass respect bullshit."

"Language, please, Tino." A matronly clucking sound comes from her pouty, youthful mouth. "You weren't this uncouth when I turned you."

"Well, yeah. Might have helped with my attitude later on if you'd told me that's what you were doing at the time."

She'd pulled some serious chicanery on me that night, acting like she needed me to escort her out of Dusk because of the sudden arrival of a violent ex. I wish I could say I don't hold grudges, but it's hard not to when I don't know the answer to my biggest question. Which was "why me," of course. But she'd said nothing, and probably wouldn't unless she absolutely had to.

"We've discussed this *ad nauseum* since then." Stephanie talks like a lawyer half the time, slinging Latin like she just passed the Bar Exam. She stands, then heads back toward the door. "I came here to help, but if my mere presence causes you this much distress, I'll leave you with your thoughts."

I let her hang because I think she deserves it. Waiting always gets to me, though, especially after I became technically dead. The idea of an eternity waiting alone freaks me out, so I cave. Nobody wants to be alone and Steph is one of the only vamps I've met that I can tolerate having around. After all, I can use a second opinion from someone who knows more about my new state of being. And my mistakes are still on her head, like she said before.

"No, Stephanie." I shake my head. "Wait a minute."

I pull a chair away from the breakfast table in the dinky and mostly useless kitchen and wave a hand at it. She sits again, less comfortably this time. I hunker down in the other seat and lay the entire story on her, warts and all. She rolls her eyes at my trouble going to church, having dinner, and the oven. But when I get to the part about the window and the gunshot and the roof, she narrows her eyes, which get a little red and glowy. But when I mention stinky Scott Fitzpatrick, she opens her mouth and laughs.

"What?"

"Oh, Tino." Stephanie grins. "You've met your first werewolf. The Fitzpatricks have one in their family every generation."

"So, the boy next door is Teen Wolf?" I shrug. "I'd say there goes the neighborhood, but they've lived in it longer than my folks. Is it their territory or something?"

"Essentially, yes. And you may find this family of wolves quite useful if you play nicely with them. They're good people."

"Good people?" I pour warmed blood into my mug, then gesture at the pot while looking in Stephanie's direction. She shakes her head. "Play nice? What do you mean?"

"Nicely." Stephanie loves her some grammatical correction. "And by that I mean play all hands you deal them honorably. Oh, and remember not to feed on them or turn any of their kin."

"Okay." I wrinkle my nose. "Don't want to anyway, they stink to high heaven."

"That's fine and well, then." She folds her hands and sets her chin on them, grinning. I'm reminded of silent film ingenues. "Continue."

I talk about the paramedics and then the cops, including my old pal Maury Weintraub. Stephanie sits up and purses her lips, tapping her cheek with one silver fingernail. But then she moves it away and in a circle so I know she wants me to keep on talking.

"But that's it, Stephanie. After Maury left, I came here."

"Hmm. The chippie on the roof, you said she smelled familiar." See what I mean about how Stephanie talks? She can't even insult a bitch without sounding like a class act.

"Well, it's a super common perfume." I bite my tongue before adding something about how it's common in this day and age. I don't want to accidentally on purpose insult her.

"Ah, I see." Stephanie makes her thinking face, which is opening her mouth and tapping her right fang with her tongue. It's kind of cute in a mom-friend sort of way. Oh, God. I have a vampiric mom-friend. What's next, a manic pixie dream girl or a magical girl?

"So, what do I do now?" I ask so my mind doesn't turn into some kind of Tumblr meme.

"Visit the scene of the murder."

"Um, but my dad's alive."

"I'm talking about your friend's partner." Stephanie snaps her fingers absently. I wonder whether she's faking this sudden case of absent-mindedness. "Weinberger?"

"Weintraub."

"Yes. You need to have a look at what happened to him." She stands, then claps her hands. "Whatever are you waiting for? The night's still young. Chop-chop, Mr. Crispo."

I sigh and roll my eyes so hard they almost fall out and bounce on the floor. Maybe I'm lucky. She could be snapping her fingers like I'm a butler or whistling like I'm a dog. I grab fresh clothes and go back into the bathroom to change into them. We're undead and don't reproduce sexually, but I'm keeping my modesty, thank you very much.

After that, it's to the kitchen to shut off the coffee maker and chug the rest of my bloody beverage. I head to the door and grab a coat because I like having lots of pockets year-round. I'm a freaking vampire now, and it's not like we sweat in the heat or anything. Our beards don't grow, either. I save a chunk of change on Speed Stick, razors, and Barbasol, too.

"You coming?" I've got my hand on the doorknob.

Stephanie stands there, finger running along the shelf where I keep my books. That's where all of my ill-gotten Speed Stick savings go. Books. They're in storage cubes lining the half-walls I can't do anything else with. Eternity sucks, and good stories don't. I understand why Stephanie might find them appealing, too.

"Excuse me?" She raises an eyebrow.

"You said you're here to help. You know, earlier. Before I, um, insulted you." I gulp. "Sorry, by the way."

"Accepted. Yes, I came to lend my support." She tips one volume toward her, then eases it out from between its shelf mates. "And I did by advising you on your next course of action. Now I believe I'll curl up with some tea and the incomparable Richard Adams."

"That book's about a bunch of rabbits, you know." Shifting my weight from one foot to another, I wonder how to motivate her to come with me.

It's not because I think I need help to check a crime scene, either. I just like my privacy. But I can't make her leave my apartment just because, or even ask her to. Not even while I'm gone. She's like my warden or legal vampire guardian or something. I'm an adult by human legal standards but a minor according to the vampire brass. Or nobility. Because that's a more accurate term for them. I mean, our leader calls himself a king for crying out loud.

"Yes. Rabbits are violent little creatures, and this book is supposed to give a well-researched portrayal. I've been meaning to read this for decades." For all I know, she means that literally.

"But—"

"Val." She closes her eyes and corrects herself. "Tino. You've got the right mindset to navigate modern issues in this era. I'm afraid my theories and conjecture would only muddle your take on what you find."

"Look, I don't want to be out there skulking around alone in Providence. That's one sure-fire way to get myself caught and vampires revealed to the world."

"Oh, Tino. If you're truly this worried, perhaps you'd do well to construct a disguise, like the Scarlet Pimpernel."

"Um, what?" I'm not sure whether she's insulting me or not.

"The Scarlet Pimpernel." Stephanie peers at the lowest shelf on my bookcase. "Ah, here. Put this at the top of whatever stack of books you're currently reading through. It's a classic and might help you besides. And this." She points at a copy of The Murders in the Rue Morgue.

"I read that one last month." I pause by the fridge to pocket a couple of bags of blood just in case. "All the hard-boiled investigator stuff, too. I was a cop, remember? Anyway, I'd better get going. There's a stop I've got to make first."

"At Rhode Island Costume?"

"No, to get investigation supplies. I have any costume I could possibly want in my parents' basement." I don't tell her that I own several boxes of costumes from Halloween and the Community Theatre productions I never manage to find time to audition for anymore. But maybe I'll grab some pieces along with my old crime scene supplies while I'm there.

"I see."

I'm almost out the door, tucking the blood into my jacket's inside pocket. Stephanie clears her throat. I turn.

"Have fun." She's already back on the comfy chair with my favorite fleece throw draped over most of her body. It's like she wanted me to see her settling in and getting comfy. I haven't mentioned that Stephanie's tiny, probably has to shop in the kid's section, might even need to sit on a booster seat to drive a car. Usually with vampires, the smaller they are, the longer they've been undead. People weren't so big back in the day.

"Fine." I shut the door, locking it behind me on the way out. Not that locks ever seem to stop the vamp who turned me. Maybe someday the same will apply to me. A guy can dream, right?

In the car on the way, I drain the bags. Back in the 80s, Gary Numan sang about how being in a vehicle makes people feel invisible. Invincible too. I've heard of vampires who can actually be either or both of those things by burning some blood. But either I'm not one of those or too much of a noob to do it for now. I force down the cold blood. It's not pleasant or even satisfying to my palate, but it does the trick, so I'm not lusting after every neck in the universe. God, I miss Chianti.

At my parents' house, I almost grab a box of costume stuff just for kicks. I pass it all by and take the small case of crime scene supplies I'd purchased the day I quit the force. Having them on hand was supposed to be my motivation to start PI work right away. And I would have done it too if it hadn't been for that pesky vampire. After that, I get back in the car and head out of Cranston.

I drive into the City. Providence isn't as lit up as Times Square at night, but it's almost the same difference. Maury mentioned a parking lot. If a dead cop goes unnoticed all night, it has to be in an unmanned one. Providence has a handful of those. I drive to the nearest one, across the street from a titty bar, and roll my window down.

Not a hint of gunpowder or blood meet my nose. Mostly, I smell a miasma of mingled perfumes, Axe body spray, and jizz. It's gross, I know, but that's life outside a strip club in downtown Providence. And there's no hint of blood or death this time, so I move on.

The next unmanned parking lot is at the edge of the nightclub district. I used to get the best sausage and pepper grinder in the universe across the street at the Haven Brothers truck, but vampires can't eat sausage or any other kind of sandwich, so I try to ignore the aroma. And there it is, underneath the motor oil and spices. Day-old blood.

"Bingo." After parking, I open the door and get out of my car to walk around the lot.

I'm rewarded for my efforts by a few scraps of tape backing and a discarded vinyl glove that almost declare "CSI Was Here." I shut my eyes and let my nose do the walking. Someone shot whoever bled out here, and the wound was a geyser. I taste the gunpowder residue and recognize it. Same kind of rifle as before. Of course. There's a conclusion in sight, so I jump to it.

"The bitch of a hitwoman was here, too."

Maybe I'm insulting bitches by calling the assassin who killed Larry and tried to off my dad one, but if you have a problem with that, I'm sorry. I call them how I want, and this is my story. I'm not sure what else to call a chick who kills for hire anyway, but if you've got another suggestion, I'm all ears. Literally. Vampires hear practically everything, you know.

I open my eyes only to see a rotund figure move away off in the corner of the lot. I follow it but not at top speed because regular plain old people might see. Whatever I'm chasing either doesn't care about that or sticks to the shadows. When I get there, the noun has left the vicinity. I rely on my nose, ears, and eyes for more clues.

Footsteps moving with a longer stride than the typical human head away down a dark alley. Their owner isn't alive but smells wrong for a vampire. There's a pungent odor, too. Not like Scott the reeking werewolf, and not of perfume like Sniper on the Roof, but something new and different. A burnt sort of spicy. My skin's tingly. Intriguing. I follow.

Halfway down the alley, a glittering green fog rolls in. Everything I hear and smell melts away in it except the tingly feeling. I wonder whether I've been whammied by some chemical. Visions of the Joker dance in my head, but that feels all wrong.

Maybe this is more like one of Batman's smokescreens than a mind and body-warping attack. Except as magical and green as the Wicked Witch of the West. Whoever I tailed gives me the slip. And I'm okay with that for the moment. Resistance means I'm on the right track.

When I get back to my car, there's a faded yellow post-it note stuck to the driver's side windshield. I pull it free and peer at the fat-fingered scrawl. My fingers tingle.

"What the fuck is this?" I blink and shake my head.

The inked missive is sloppier than a Jackson Pollock painting and might not even be in English for all I know. I can't even begin reading it. Whether it's a clue, warning, or bad example is beyond me. But at least it's on paper and more indelible than lipstick on a mirror or some other lame method of hastily done communication. I pocket it and get into the car to head home. Except I remember I can't do that until I make a stop first because inconvenient vampire rules are inconvenient.

On the way toward the highway, I take a few turns and stop at The Arcade. Across the street from there, in a building everyone who's really alive thinks is boarded up, is the place I have to go and check in.

It sucks, but it's something I've got to do every time I go east of I-95 inside Providence city limits.

I lock my car and jog across the street. Around the back of the building is the door where I'm obligated to knock four times in a circular pattern. The doorman inside hears it and decides whether it's right or not. Of course, it is, so he lets me in. I head downstairs and prepare to do the necessary. When I enter the long, dark room, I bow in the general direction of a throne whose occupant sits in shadow.

"To what do I owe the—" The gravelly voice pauses, and I hear a sniff of disdain. "Unexpected pleasure?"

"A murder, Sir." Even with the chilly reception, I do my best to behave properly. And fail miserably.

"How many times must I insist, Valentino, child of Stephanie?"

"A murder, your Majesty." I twist my hands together behind my back. "A human's."

"Very good. You'll make performing monkey any night now." The new and brighter voice belongs to the figure emerging from the darkness to the right of the enthroned one.

"Thanks, Raven." I try not to grin because I know they don't like that. Raven keeps track of all the vampiric social engagements, like a who's who columnist except not in a newspaper.

"Coming to meetings regularly is the key to a proper recovery." Raven bats their eyes. "Our Monarch wants your attendance to improve."

"And I'm here." I keep my head and gaze low as befits my station among these people. "I aim to do my best."

"But this isn't one of the meetings His Majesty means. So, you'll be at the next Blood Moot, I assume?"

"I understand that, Raven. And I'm sorry. I promise to make it the next time."

"Then we'll see you tomorrow night."

"Okay. See you!" I try making a mental note of that, but I suck at keeping dates. That isn't something I want to whine about in front of the vampire king of Providence. He'll probably cut off my head if I piss him off too much. I don't let my inside voice call him King Decapitate instead of King DeCampo for nothing.

I wave and then turn, trying to measure my strides as much as formal vampiric decorum will allow, but the tap of long fingernails on the king's ebony armrest tells me I won't make it out that easily.

"You uttered the word 'murder,' child of Stephanie." The king's voice stops me undead in my tracks.

"Yeah, I did." I don't turn around. If King Decapitate's going to make good on his name, I'd rather not have him go all Edward Scissorhands on my neck while I watch. Yeah, one of his special talents is turning his hands into claws when he wants to. Creep city.

"Who?"

"Detective Larry Tierney. He was a police officer from Cranston, where I live. Friend of a friend."

"A mortal associate?"

"Yeah." I don't want to say anything else about Larry or mention Maury to the king, not even their names if I can help it. But my old friend's luck is apparently better than mine when it comes to not getting King DeCampo's attention.

"Well. I must ruminate on how interesting it is that the youngest vampire in my territory has already taken an interest in cultivating his mortal assets." The king's remark makes Raven gulp. The word interesting is doublespeak for something a vampire wants to keep their eye on.

"Uh, thanks?" I think that means King Decapitate believes I'll be manipulating the Cranston PD with all the vampiric powers I don't know how to use yet. I don't bother correcting him.

"Be aware that others have tried and failed at making inroads there. We believe this is due to another sphere of influence outside our control exerting its force on Cranston's Finest. Perhaps the victim you are investigating has displeased someone whose allegiance does not lie with this Court."

"Wow, Sir." I blink, glad the king can't see my face. He just gave me a key piece of information. "I mean, Your Majesty. Thanks for the tip." But nothing's free, apparently.

"Please inform Miss McQueen that my debt to her is paid. Raven?"

"Noted."

"Um—" I shut my own mouth around the protest. Stephanie is going to be pissed about me cashing in her chip without meaning to. "Thanks again, Your Majesty."

"You may take your leave, Valentino."

I do exactly that and spend the entire drive home wondering how to explain this to Stephanie.

# CHAPTER FOUR

I take back roads instead of the highway back to my apartment. My old work bag comes upstairs with me. Stephanie's still there. When I walk in, she closes *Watership Down* around my favorite bookmark and tucks the volume into the giant handbag she brings with her everywhere.

When she stands, the cozy throw drops to the floor. She picks up my favorite coffee mug, drinks the rest of the blood in it, and sets it in the sink. After that, Stephanie raises an eyebrow at me. I put the investigation bag on the counter, open it. She shakes her head and sighs.

"I told you, you will need a disguise."

"I know. But really, I blended in better downtown wearing my regular clothes."

"So you did go to Providence, then?" She leans against the sink, taps her foot. "You paid your respects?"

I blink at first because the whole way over, I'm thinking about Larry Tierney and how my own father almost ended up like him. I've got to find out when and if he's got a wake because that's a totally different and just as important type of respect I've got to pay. Maybe someone at the PD will make the funeral arrangements. But I can't call the precinct in the middle of the night for something like that. I put my mind back on vampire problems, and that makes me cranky.

"Yeah, had a nice little chat with King Decapitate." My inside voice escaped. Oops.

"Valentino Crispo, watch what you say!"

"What? I mean, it's what he does to the bad guys." And supposedly the good ones who make mistakes but I don't say that. I roll my shoulders, glad my head's still attached to them.

"You never know who's listening." Stephanie tilts her head at the window over the sink. "You can't afford to let anyone hear you refer to King DeCampo that way. He commands respect for a reason."

"Okay." I fiddle with a box of blue gloves. "Speaking of affording things, his Majesty might have given me a tip about the Cranston PD."

"He gives nothing for free." Stephanie saunters toward the front door, then leans against the wall next to it. "So what do you owe him?"

"It's more about what he doesn't owe you anymore."

"Tino." She shakes her head, then hangs it. "Well, I suppose it can't be helped. Some of our future tasks will be more difficult, but I'll simply have to handle the extra work. Your investigation led you into his personal territory, and you are still my responsibility until you can prove to the king that you've learned enough to be a full member of vampire society."

"How about I try to do that tomorrow night?" I bend over and pick up the throw she left on the floor. "There's a Blood Moot, you know." I'm surprised to have actually remembered that. But Stephanie speaks again before I can head toward the kitchen and mark it down on the dry-erase calendar I keep on the fridge.

"I'm not sure you'll be ready by then." She puts her hands on her hips.

"I'm ready now." I fold the cozy square of fabric, lay it over the back of the comfy chair.

"Prove it." Her foot's tapping behind me.

"Uh." She has me there, and she knows it. I turn around to find Stephanie hanging her head again. I feel almost as bad as I would if I'd kicked a dog. Not that I'd ever do something like that.

"Well, it can't be helped for now." She straightens almost like a marionette when the puppeteer lifts its strings. "Not with your father's situation. But you'll attend tomorrow night, then?"

"Yeah, I already told Raven I'd show." The gravity dropping in my stomach is familiar. Guilt. It turns out it affects me the same way whether I'm disappointing my Ma or the undead equivalent. Who knew?

"I suppose that's a bit of good news. Shall I meet you here before you head over?"

"No, how about we just meet there?" I'm not sure where the investigating I'm hoping to finish in the earlier part of the evening will take me, and I don't like the idea of Stephanie hanging around here without me. Vampire rules give her that right, but my lease says one tenant only. She knows this, but my creator's nosy. Or maybe clingy. I'm not sure which.

Stephanie steps back over to the comfy chair. She stares at the now neatly folded throw like she's considering bringing it with her. Instead, she shrugs. At least now I know what to get her for Christmas. Then she slips on her shoes and picks something up from the side table. On her way toward the door, she sets it on the counter next to my box of gloves. I stare at it.

"See you at midnight tomorrow, Valentino."

She closes the door behind her and on my thoughts. The Scarlet Pimpernel sits there like an unspoken reprimand. Even the man on the cover glares at me, half his face hidden by a leather-clad hand. The square-cut ruby in his ring reminds me of the brooch Maury wore in Cranston West's production of *Dracula*. He'd played the leading role while I stalked him as Van Helsing. I chuckle at the irony.

Even if DeCampo and company aren't testing me tomorrow, I ought to brush up on the rules of unlife, according to King Decapitate. So I leave *The Scarlet Pimpernel* on the counter and head for the little alcove where my bed is. The last tenant used the space for a closet, but the fact that there wasn't a window in there sold me on repurposing it. Yeah, that's right. I sleep in the closet. The double layers of light-blocking curtain hanging across the double-door threshold are my last line of defense against the sun if a window breaks during the day.

I keep a notebook full of observations about being a vampire under my mattress, along with the little handwritten booklet of Society notes Stephanie gave me to study on my second night. Both of those are in Latin so the average person can't read them without extra time and a computer. Thanks, Google Translate.

There are only four rules, and following them is called "Honoring the Compass." But they're confusing and hard to remember because directions don't have the same kind of connotations now that they used to back in the day. And they'll never change over to a new system. Because old vampires are crusty and hidebound.

The first and most important rule is to Honor the North. They expect everyone to understand that North means oldest. The king over any territory is always whoever's the most ancient creature with fangs. All the other vamps have to report to them and do whatever they say, no matter how crazy. King DeCampo supposedly has his living origins back in the golden days of Greece.

I guess the idea is that if a vampire lives that long, they must know what they're doing. The flaw in that logic is that times always change. King DeCampo of Providence might be ancient, but he doesn't even know what a smartphone is. His age gives him the right to tell me exactly what I can do with mine. But because of the rule I can't say that his ignorance on technology means that half the time I'm in his presence I want to shove my iPhone up his ass. Sideways. At least I can be sure he knows how to follow the second rule.

Honor the South is easy because it makes total and complete sense. All that means is to be secret about vampires. We can't use powers in front of regular people. Vampires should avoid making a spectacle out of ourselves by doing things like catching fire out in public at high noon. Because the king is old-school, he thinks killing humans who find out is the best idea in the world. Like I said, he's behind the times. Fortunately, Stephanie's teaching me a bunch of better track-covering techniques.

The last two get trickier, and I always mix them up. East and West have to do with making new vampires and keeping promises made to vampires or others in the supernatural community. I try to remember which is which without looking in my notebook. But I can't. So I try flipping a coin. But when I check the notebook against my guess, I'm wrong. Even the odds can't give me a break tonight, apparently.

East is about keeping promises. Between vampires, money doesn't mean much. We need way less cash than living people, so we end up with decent chunks of change in relatively short amounts of time. Our word has value instead, so favors are the only currency that counts. That's why I'd better make it to the Blood Moot. Which is important in part because of the fourth rule.

West is all about making new vampires. You can't get turned and then go inviting your family and all your besties into the vampire club. Half the world would have fangs, and the other half would be running for their lives nightly if it worked that way. Instead, a vamp's got to get permission at a Blood Moot or similar gathering. I bet you can guess who gets authority over that kind of hefty decision. Bingo. The same guy who doesn't know how to use a phone.

I drop the notebook. It occurs to me that I can't think of a single reason Stephanie would have asked for permission to turn me specifically. I'd never met her until the night it happened. But if she hadn't asked, I would still appear in mirrors and churches all over Rhode Island. She'd gotten the go-ahead from DeCampo himself, somehow.

Even more mysterious is why the king allowed an unknown guy like me to get turned. I get off my bed and pace because that helps me think. It feels like I'm wringing everything I know about vampires out of my brain, and still I come up empty. There's nothing, no good reason I can imagine.

But finally, there's one tiny idea. A bad reason, from my perspective, at least. I stop in the middle of my apartment and blink. It's all wrapped up in what King DeCampo told me about Cranston.

I'm a replacement for whoever used to be the big vamp on campus in my town.

Maybe whatever matter I'm investigating now killed the vampire DeCampo mentioned. If an older and wiser vamp couldn't get through it, my chances are at a snowball in Hell levels. I give up trying to figure out why Stephanie specifically got to do the honors. The only reason I can think of for that is, since the king just got out of debt with her tonight, maybe he owed her even bigger favors before he let her turn me.

It's getting late. No, it's getting early. Whatever. I'm a month-old vampire, don't expect me to have all this straight, police training or not. This is like a whole different world to learn. I hang my head, tired of being what I am and wishing it could all go back to the way it was before my severe sun and garlic tandem allergies. But that's not happening unless Djinni are real and I somehow find a lamp. Fat chance.

I face the foiled-over window on the east side of the building in defiance of the flaming death-orb that's getting ready to hang out in the sky for over twelve hours. And I recite all four of the rules without looking back at the notebook on my bed. When I check, I find I did it right.

"Take that, King Decapitate."

It doesn't matter one bit that Stephanie warned me not to say that out loud if I could help it. DeCampo's just a vampire, not Lord Voldemort. Anyway, this is my apartment, and I'm the oldest vampire in it. Technically I'm the king in here. And who knows? Maybe DeCampo might surprise everyone some night and reveal an actual sense of humor.

"Respect that, bitches."

I go into the bathroom and splash some water on my face. After that, I change into my pajamas again, finally. It's a habit but also a precaution in case anyone breaks in here and sees me. If I'm lying in bed with all my street clothes on, it'll look weird. And before you ask, I should worry about what a potential robber thinks, thank you very much. I'm Respecting the South by sleeping in pajamas. All they'd think is that I work the graveyard shift, not that I'm an undead blood-drinking creature of the night. Most human people want to keep it simple, which makes it easier for non-human people like me to keep on going bump in the night.

Staring at the ceiling while trying to fall asleep is nothing new to me. I had insomnia while fully alive, too. According to Stephanie, it gets easier to zonk out at daybreak the older you get. I'll believe that when I experience it. I'm not sure how long it's been, but I'm just starting to drop off to sleep when I remember the thing I forgot to back up: a reminder for the Blood Moot tomorrow.

"Siri, set an alarm for—"

I fall asleep before I hear the computerized chick say okay. This does not bode well.

# CHAPTER FIVE

The phone wakes me up at ten in the morning. That's like two in the morning for a vampire. I'm out of it when I answer but perk right up when I identify the voice at the other end.

"Dad!"

"Tino." He lowers his voice. "They've got me in the hospital with a policeman at the door."

"That's good." I sit up in bed. My right eye is refusing to open because I slept on it funny.

"No. That's bad," he whispers.

"Why?" I put the phone in my lap and switch to speaker so I can rub my eye.

"They think it was a hitman that shot me."

"Um." I happen to know the police misgendered the shooter, but don't say so. "Wow. So how's it a bad thing to have a police detail protecting you?"

"Because the doctor says it was a sniper rifle that hit me. What if it's the Caprices who ordered it?" Leave it to my old Dad to worry about Cranston's own crime family.

"Geez, Dad." I try not to yawn, and tell myself it's just a bad habit because vamps don't need air. "Maybe you shouldn't say this on the hospital phone."

"I'm not. Your mother got me one of those Go phones." His admission tells me he's developed a case of paranoia severe enough for Ma to humor it. I can't decide whether it's unhealthy or not.

"Oh. Okay. But the Caprices? Really?" I open and shut my right eye, which is fine now. Then, I scratch my head because I don't get it. "You're just a florist. Why those guys, and why now?"

"I don't know." Dad's sigh reminds me of the only time I brought home an F. "I supplied a funeral a month and a half ago and saw some of them there. They weren't too happy with the wreath. I was hoping you could find out."

I stop, head spinning. My dad's got Maury Weintraub working his case, and he wants his non-detective-making son snooping around instead? It makes no sense to me because Dad trusts Maury as much as I do. Maybe more since my father doesn't have to hide any vampirism from friends and family. But probably he wants me on the case because I'm his kid. Guess that means he's proud of me. My face gets all fuzzy and tingly because I haven't been able to blush since I got turned.

"Tino? You there?"

"Yeah, Dad." I rub my cheeks, wondering whether unlife will ever feel normal.

"Look, I think you might be able to find stuff the police will miss."

"Huh?" I freeze. The only reason my guts don't follow suit is that I'm not really alive anymore. Does he know what I am? Besides a PI, of course. I don't dare ask. And I was thinking Dad was paranoid.

"Those Caprices can smell cops from a mile away. And everybody knows you up and quit the force." Now I get what he's implying. He thinks I can pull off an undercover job.

"But I'm your son." Dad's logic has a serious hole in it. "They didn't get you. And they might decide to use me for leverage."

"No, they won't." I hear my father swallow over the line. It's one of his tells. He's feeling big-time guilty.

"Dad, what are you not saying here?" I say a silent prayer that he'll get himself to a Priest as soon as he can. Maybe prayers on my own behalf won't work, but it can't hurt if I do it for someone else, right?

"Son, I've wronged you." The silence on the other end is broken by a monitor beeping. "I complained where everyone can hear about how you haven't been to church, not even on Easter."

"Oh." This makes more sense now. The Caprices had a huge falling-out with the new Father at Saint Mary's Church, and they all stopped going. For all I know, they might think I'm angrier at Dad than the Cranston PD. My father's smarter than I give him credit for. Probably most grown-up kids realize that at some point.

"So, can you forgive me?" His voice has a strange pitch to it, higher, like something hurts. I realize I left him hanging like a jerk.

"Yeah. I forgive you, Dad. I'll go and check on the Caprices for you."

"Thanks, Tino."

I open my mouth and let my feelings out before he can hang up. It's way easier to do with my dad in the hospital than at Sunday dinner. Holding back the feels isn't optional when someone you care about almost dies.

"I love you, Dad."

"Love you too." The feeling is mutual then. I'm glad I said it and got to hear it back. Even with armed guards, the hitwoman might try again.

Dad hangs up after that. I can't help but feel like the world's biggest shithead for not being able to set foot in a church. It's not easy. Guilt's part of being Roman Catholic like drinking blood's part of being a vampire. So maybe you see now why it sucks extra for me in particular. I got to deal with both.

I lay down and try to go back to sleep. All I get for my trouble is a pack of daymares featuring a horrible smell, a creepy doll, and the itchiest rug in the universe. When I wake up, I pull a composition book off my daystand and scrawl everything I can remember about my dreams. After that, I close the cover and set it aside.

It's almost seven in the evening. I check the app on my phone that's linked to the camera. I hung it under the eave outside one of the

Belfry's dormered windows when I moved in. It gives me a view of the front stoop and the skyline. And fortunately, vampires can tolerate looking at sunlight over a video feed. The sun's making the sky pink and orange all the way down to the west, which reminds me of a creamsicle. I miss those. I know that overhead it'll be that cobalt blue that means it's almost safe for me to go outside.

In the bathroom, I splash water on my face more out of habit than anything else but also to wash away all the bad dreams. The call from Dad means I have something to do besides moon around. There's a place I can check out, a location the police couldn't investigate without a warrant. I wonder whether Stephanie's right and I actually do need a disguise. I trust Dad, but he's got to be on meds after a gunshot wound. Probably he's not thinking straight enough to be completely reliable.

I don't go to the hospital. Instead, I head to my parents' house and let myself in by the door out back, the one that goes into the partially exposed cellar. In the basement, I turn on the light and rummage through all the old boxes and bags I left behind the night before, unearthing the spirits of Halloweens and theater productions past. Any box or bag I think might be what I'm looking for goes into a pile. I don't care how big a heap I end up with because vampires can lift a ton. Literally.

Even though the weight's no problem, I still have trouble getting them through the door and down the back path to the driveway. I drop bags as I go, like Hansel leaving breadcrumbs. But when I get to the car and pop the trunk, there's someone standing there, ready to load them in. I can smell who it is right away.

"Scott?" I set the boxes down.

"Yeah?" He smiles.

"What gives, my dude?" I grin back. Thankfully he's not as pungent as last night. Maybe it has something to do with the moon, I don't know.

"If it were my dad in the hospital, I'd want help. So I'm giving it." He holds out the bags.

"Anyone ever tell you you're too friendly for your own good?" I load one of the boxes into the Miata's tiny trunk and play Tetris with the other.

"Yeah, but so what? Mr. Rogers is my Sensei."

"Oh, boy." At least Scott doesn't say he's a Boy Scout.

"Don't dis Mr. Rogers, man. He's a goddamned saint."

"You know how ironic that sounds, right?" I mutter a word that rhymes with itch at the second box as I dent a corner trying to get it in.

"Helping people in need is sort of a tradition for my people." Scott shrugs like the teenager he is. "Anyway, I don't care about irony."

"No, I guess you wouldn't about something like that."

"Words are words." He loads a bag into the trunk, stuffing it on the side of a box.

"Yeah, and water's wet." I grunt, pushing on the box. It's at a bad angle for leverage, okay? "Your point?"

"Anyone ever tell you you're an ingrate?" Scott shoves on the opposite side of the box, and it goes in.

"Yeah. And the nice thing was after that they left me alone."

"I live next door." He passes me a bag.

"So?" I stuff bags into the now cramped trunk.

Why am I being such an absolute asshole to this kid, anyway? The main emotion I feel for Scott right now is anger, despite his helpfulness. I realize it's because he's a liar who never bothered telling me he's a werewolf. But then, I think about how I never bothered telling him I'm a vampire. I'm new at undeath but not so much at life. Absolute assholery goes both ways.

"Look, I'm qualifying for the Jerk of the Year award. I'm sorry. Thanks for the help."

"You're welcome." He sticks his arms out when he says it, like a Disney character. Yeah, I watch Disney movies. I like musicals, okay?

"But I'm going to tell you something." I lean toward him, lowering my voice. "I'm in a dangerous situation here, and I don't want you getting in trouble because of it. Or worse."

"Okay. And?"

"There's no 'and.' That was a warning, Scott." I try to close the itsy-bitsy trunk, but it won't go. The bags fill it and then some. But they're full of clothes and air. Something's got to give.

"Huh. Because it sounded to me like you maybe had another thing to tell me."

"This whole business I'm in is dangerous. I'm getting into situations that could kill a regular person."

"Okay. I'm not regular, Tino. I'm a werewolf." He digs one toe of his sneaker in the dirt. "Woulda told you sooner but didn't have permission."

"Oh." So, there goes my whole reason for being pissy at Scott.

I turn my back shoving on the bags trying to deflate them. Judging by my track record with this exercise in packing, it won't go well. Like this whole conversation. But Stephanie practically told me werewolves were on-limits allies as long as I didn't try to turn them.

"You can say anything to me, you know."

"What is this, one of those old 80s movies?" I lean on the trunk, trying to close it. Fail. "Are you going to stand outside my window with a boombox next?"

"No." He's looking at me with the same puppy eyes he used to make when he wanted to tag along with Maury and me when we were fifteen and he was five.

"Okay fine." I push the trunk with more than human force and dent it. Oops. "Look." I indicate the dented metal. "I'm a vampire. You happy?"

"I'm mostly happy, generally speaking. But thanks for telling me. And just so you know, you can put some of those bags in what passes for a back seat in this thing."

"Fucking a." I do a face-palm.

"I know, right?" He hefts a half-dozen of the puffy plastic bags and hauls them toward the passenger side. Somehow, he manages to open the door.

"Fucking b."

Scott bends over, laughing as he slaps his knee. Bags fall around him like petals off a daisy. I roll my eyes, then open the driver's side door. After that, I shovel bags inside bench in back just like my newly outed wolfy pal.

I start to think that maybe Stephanie's right. Working with a werewolf might give me the edge I need to keep my head above the water that drowned whoever had this gig before me.

"Do you want to take a ride with me?"

"Okay." I remember now that the kid's always been easy-going and chilled out. I wonder whether that makes him good or bad at being a werewolf.

We get in my car. I watch Scott bend his knees, noticing how tall he was already. A sixteen-year-old kid without his full growth still barely fits in my little old Miata. If we team up more often, I have to consider getting a bigger ride.

"There goes the Speed Stick book fund."

"Huh?"

"Never mind."

I drive us back to my apartment building. Peering up at the tiny windows, I find them dark. No Stephanie then, which is a good thing. I try to remember why I know she's not dropping by tonight but come up with nothing. There's some reason hiding at the back of my mind, but it's sticking to the shadows for now.

I take a chance and grab as many bags as I can. Scott imitates me like he always did as a little kid. I guess the two of us, next-door neighbors and only children, have a bit of an unintentional brotherly vibe going on. Those two guys on the CW program with their Impala surface in my mind, and I banish them. I used to like that show, but now the idea of those dudes scares me. Brothers who kill monsters aren't half so entertaining after you actually are one.

I unlock the door and go into my rented place. Nobody waits in the dark for me except my unread copy of The Scarlet Pimpernel on the table. I pick it up, leaf through it. Then I gesture at Scott to shut the door.

"Welcome to The Belfry."

"Cool." Scott nods then sets his bags down in the small living room. "Why did you want all this stuff, anyway? The clothes, I mean. Don't you have something to wear to Larry Tierney's wake?"

"Oh, shit." I blink. "That's tonight?"

"Yeah. Gramps was talking about it all day. It's at Michellino's."

"We'd better go there first, then." I drop the boxes I'm carrying near the cozy chair.

"You were going somewhere else?"

"Yeah, my first PI investigation. But I can do that stuff later. Wakes don't wait."

"Okay."

"So let's go."

"Um." Scott points at the fluffy bunny slippers I'm still wearing. And the pajamas. Definitely not a fashion statement. Not a good look, either. Guess I'm not a morning-equivalent vampire. Madonn.

"Oh." I go into the bathroom and change into black pants, a black polo, and loafers.

Scott's already wearing black jeans and a black t-shirt, so he's all set. We head back downstairs and get in the car. I think about stopping at CVS to get some condolence cards, but I have no idea who to address them to. I sigh.

"What's wrong, Tino?"

We're stopped at a red light, so I jerk my thumb over my shoulder at the drugstore we passed. I tell the kid my failure of an idea about the cards.

"We all knew Larry. Every beat cop at the precinct. Enough to know he had nobody. This sucks. I don't even know who's paying for his wake and the whole nine yards."

"I do. Anonymous donor."

"Huh. Weird." I've got my ideas about that, but keep them to myself for now. It's still unclear to me exactly how much I can reveal to a werewolf about vampire society.

We ride the rest of the way in silence, which doesn't take long. Rhode Island's tiny, remember? I pull the car into Michellino's depressingly barren parking lot. I've seen the place packed enough for cars to line Park Avenue on both sides before. But Larry, well-known to police officers, with the anonymous donor and all, barely has anyone here.

The emptiness is downright weird. The only car I recognize is Maury's. Not even the captain is here. There are only two reasons I can think of for nobody to show up to a detective's funeral. Reason A, some big SWAT is going down. Reason B, most of the brass and all of the grunts on the force think Larry Tierney's corrupt. Maybe they even think that was why he got killed. I wonder about the hitwoman and my dad. If they're connected and Larry's dirty, Maury could be the next target. He might even get hit right here and now.

"You ready?" The kid's question snaps me out of my pessimistic thought spiral.

"Yeah, okay."

We get out of the car and make the short walk up to the doors of the funeral home.

# CHAPTER SIX

Only one viewing room is open, and the sign out front has Larry's picture on it. He's grinning, eyes bright with that twinkle they get when he cracks one of his dad jokes. No, I mean got. And he was never anyone's dad, no matter how much he tried to act like one to every rookie who walked through the precinct's door.

Here's the one thing I can say for sure about what Larry's damage was: loneliness. It's not an excuse for disregarding your co-worker's personal time and space, but it's an understandable reason. I banish contemplation of my own self-induced solitude before walking in there to look at the face of a man whose eyes won't open, let alone twinkle again.

I pick up my feet as I walk. It seems like a weird thing to do, put a spring in your step inside a funeral home. But I came into this viewing room just two weeks ago after helping Dad with a delivery and know from personal experience that the new carpet's pile is high enough to trip me. Falling on your face at a wake is a mistake you don't want to make twice in one month, believe me.

Why was I even here before? I went to a random wake for a lady I didn't even know. I forget her name. Mainly, I figured I was dead, sort of, so maybe I ought to go someplace to contemplate mortality. And you know for a vampire, doing that at Church is out of the question. In case you haven't noticed, I'm still a walking fanged disaster. My idea didn't have the effect I'd hoped either. The whole visit to that poor old woman's wake didn't do me any good as far as coping with being undead goes.

And this wake isn't doing me any favors, either. It's got me down, as much as when my grandparents passed, even though Larry Tierney was way less important in my life than they were. It's not him, it's me. Maury's sitting up by the front, and now I'm second-guessing myself for coming here. My oldest friend is going to know something's wrong, and I don't want his nose up in my vamp business.

But I'm here. So's Larry, with nobody else. I realize I can't abide this nearly empty room. My heart tells me it's wrong to leave, loudly enough to shout down my head. That's rare, so I go with it. I let that too-springy step ferry me to the front of the room, where I give a golf-wave to Maury without turning to look at him.

Beside the casket, I kneel to pay my respects. Genuflecting only stings a little.

Looking at Larry close up, I see all the laugh and smile lines around his mouth, on his cheeks. There's barely any next to his eyes. I bow my head, trying not to shame Larry's lost clown tears with my own basic, bloody, and eternal ones. Basic because I'm not just crying for him.

Loneliness sucks. Its possibility is the single most terrifying prospect of potentially unliving forever. Right now, I'm focused on all the people I'll end up losing when they die, and I keep going and going like a blood-addicted Energizer Bunny. I think of my fluffy bunny slippers and consider burning them. A hand drops on my shoulder. I look at it, stained with nicotine and dry like a manila envelope. Maury.

"Thanks for coming, Tino."

"Hey, he was your partner." I unfold my hands and stand, turn to face good old Maur. "And practically a fixture, you know?"

"Yeah, I know." Maury holds out a hand, intending to shake.

But ain't no human got time for keeping a distance like that. Like sands through the hourglass, all they are is dust in the wind. I hug him instead, closing my eyes to banish the illusion that it's my best friend in that coffin instead of Larry Tierney. His shoulders quake and he sniffles, so I know Maury needed one of those more than a dumb old professional handshake.

When I open my eyes again, I see a veiled figure in the back. It's small, like kid-sized, but a little too big. And the crazy veil goes practically all the way down to loafer-clad toes so I can't even figure anything else out about them. I try to remember whether Stephanie said anything about Faeries, but it's a no-go.

I lift one hand off Maury's back to point at my nose while looking at Scott. He gets the idea, and I see him sniffing the air. He blinks, so I know we'll need to have a chat later, but for now, the rest of this excursion is Maury's show. I'm going to focus on him until he goes home.

He lets me go, then straightens his jacket. His face is dry, but his eyes are red. I realize that even though I hugged him on a not totally full stomach, his blood didn't make me hungry that close up. But is it unappetizing because of the medicinal odor of formaldehyde coming off Larry's body or Maury's mystery illness? I'm about to ask Maury how his health is when the funeral director pokes her head in to glance around the room.

The small person in the veil heads out, garnering a nod and sympathetic smile from the too-perky blonde lady at the door. She wrinkles her nose at the three of us then glances at her watch. I get the message. So does Scott. Maury is another story.

"Hey, you want to grab a coffee?" I figure the siren call of caffeine might motivate my buddy to get out of this depressing dodge.

"There's still fifteen more minutes, Tino." He sits back down again in the front row, center this time instead of the aisle.

"Yeah, Maury. Okay." I take the hint and sit next to him.

He's not budging, and neither will I. Scott's a trooper because he either understands or plays along. The kid gets up there and kneels to pay his respects, says some kind of prayer in Gaelic, too. After that, he sits on the other side of Maury. And we stay the whole time, immune to the constant impatient tapping of the funeral director's foot.

And I'm glad about going even though this errand comes with a side dish of existential dread. Maury's going through it too, in his own actually alive way. And somehow, that makes it easier for me. As we finally head out to the parking lot and go our separate ways, I hope he's thinking the same thing.

---

Scott doesn't know what he smelled, and neither do I. All we can agree on is that it's mostly human but with a hint of something cobwebby and dusty. It doesn't seem dire, so I file looking into that after all of the assassination business is done. I don't drop Scott off at his house. He says he'll help me with the next thing I have to do this evening. Once we're back in the Belfry, we tackle Stephanie's homework assignment by unpacking the bags and boxes of costume stuff. But the kid still doesn't know why.

"Are you going to run a fashion show or something?" Scott scratches his head.

"No. I need a disguise." I hold up the book. "Like this guy."

"Oh, cool! That's the first classic I ever read, you know. It's about a masked vigilante back in like the seventeenth century. They say it's the first superhero story ever written."

"Nah, that's The Epic of Gilgamesh." I point it out for him on one of my shelves.

"Gilgamesh doesn't wear a mask, though." Scott shrugs. "He's like Hercules; lets everyone know who he is. Was. Whatever."

"Good point." I know Stephanie pointed Pimpernel out even though she could have given me Gilgamesh. I understand. The mask must be the difference. "One of my friends wants me to hide my identity. It's just what vampires do. Big secret and all."

"Makes sense. I mean," Scott puts Gilgamesh back on the shelf. "It's what werewolves do, too."

"Did." I shrug. "You came out as a wolf to me like one of those snakes in the fake can of nuts."

"Yeah." He chuckles. "But I already knew you got yourself vamped, Tino. That's so last month."

"Huh?" I open one of the bags and pull out a purple wizard robe and hat from when I was ten. I look at the kid and shrug.

Scott taps his nose then points at me. He sighs. "It sucks for you, too. Almost everything you like or want to do just doesn't go with vampirism."

"True story." I drag something red from the bag. It's a Santa hat. I shrug and toss it at the pile with the wizard stuff.

"Hey, check this out."

Patrick has a collar with ruffles all over it. I remember the piece from a High School theater production and set it on the table.

"I remember Grandpa taking me to see that at the High School. You were Rosencrantz."

"Yeah. Fun times." I didn't mention that I couldn't have managed performing in that play if Maury hadn't been up there with me as the other friend of Hamlet's with a funny name. And then I remember the title of that one-act play. Rosencrantz and Guildenstern Are Dead. That's only halfway ominously prophetic, right?

"Hey, how about this?"

Scott holds up a red opera cape, something from Maury's stint singing in a medley from *Phantom of the Opera* for a talent show that I perma-borrowed one Halloween. I glance at the book Stephanie recommended earlier and then think about that 80s graphic novel, The Watchmen. The older characters talk about a guy who died because his cape got caught in a door and choked him. But I don't need air, and the cape hides my build. It's not just your face that gets you recognized. Besides, the costume piece is gorgeous and has pockets.

"Yeah, probably. Put it with the neck thingy."

"Cravat?" Scott scratches his head. "No, that's not right. Dickey."

"Don't ever call any part of my costume that again." The last thing I wanted to be was synonymous with a dick of the non-private variety.

Or a different kind of private, anyway. This hangup is brought to you by the letter D and my guilt over being a tool to just about everyone recently.

"No problem."

We go back to rummaging, and it's all a blur. I swear, the clothes in the bag just fly through the air like so much confetti, pieces landing as fate dictates. Eventually, I end up with a pile half my height and realize that I'll have to try stuff on. I bring it all into the bathroom and come out a few minutes later wearing a combination.

"It's too bright."

Scott's right. I stare at the mirror where my clothes hang in what looks like thin air. The white dress shirt I've got on under the opera cloak and over the frilly thing-a-ma-bob stands out like the Beacons of Gondor. I go back into the bathroom and replace the pants, shirt, and belt with other stuff.

"Dude." Scott crosses his arms and shakes his head. "You're fighting crime, not going to Goth night at Dusk to get your flirt on."

"Okay." I check myself again. He's right, the vinyl pants are both too shiny and too tight. Like I need a dance belt. They squeak a little when I walk, too. And even if they were dead silent, I always thought the whole superhero in tights thing was awkward. I mean, you're carrying distressed people out of fatal danger and displaying your package at the same time? The last thing I want to do is rescue someone and then get slapped with a harassment complaint. And the boots with pointy toes and slippery soles aren't going to do me much good in chases on foot. I set the clubwear aside and try different options.

"That might work, Tino. I think you've got it."

I feel good. Comfortable and ready for almost anything. I look down and see the frilly collar stand out against a black button-down, red vest, and the opera cape over all of it. I stick my arms out, revealing the red interior. Scott smiles. I do, too. I mean, come on. It's got pockets.

"Okay. But what about my face?"

"Here."

I look at the mask. It has white lace edging that extends up over the forehead and down the bridge of the nose. I remember it unfondly from Halloweens past. Itch city. I tear the frills off and put it on. Even without the lace, it's driving me crazy.

"Be honest." I'm hoping he'll honestly hate it as much as I do.

"It works." No luck. "People will look at that instead of your jaw."

"Makes sense." I nod, wrinkling my nose. But there's one way out of the stupid mask. "Can you do me a favor?"

"Sure."

"Take a picture."

Scott gets his phone out and does it. I try not to blink at the flare of bright light, which is hard because, in some primal part of my undead brain, it reminds me of fire. Fire bad! Pretty much for everyone, getting literally burned sucks, but it's a rage-inducing proposition for a vamp. I'm glad the flash is mostly harmless, though. No, I'm not talking about that red speedster from DC comics, for crying out loud.

When Scott turns the phone around, I see a hero staring back at me. Well, mostly, but I'll get to that in a minute. I can hardly believe that photo's not from somewhere else, of another person. Because I sure as Hell don't feel like a hero or even someone who can sleuth out the clues to solve a crime. I sigh and bite my lip. After that I wince. Fangs suck.

"I like it."

"Really? Because you're making a face like—"

"It's just the mask, Scott. I might do something else, but the rest rocks."

"Okay."

"And anyway, you should get yourself a disguise too if you're going to run around with a vampire vigilante."

"Already got one." He grins like, well, a dog.

"Really?" I raise an eyebrow.

"Yeah. I wolf out, remember?"

"Not really." And I don't. Remember, that is. Because he's never done it in front of me.

"Okay. Well, you will when you see it. Trust me, it's memorable, and I look completely different."

"What if you have to do something that requires opposable thumbs? Like opening a door?"

"I've got thumbs when I shapeshift."

"Oh, really?" Do werewolves turn into actual wolves or wolfmen like Lon Chaney in *Werewolves of London*? I don't want to ask, afraid I'll inadvertently utter a slur bad enough to start a vampire/werewolf war. My pessimistic imagination gets out of hand sometimes. I settle for stating the obvious. "But you're not going to be wolfy all the time, right?"

"Hmm, forgot about that." Scott shrugs. "I'll figure something out. The thing is, shifting ruins most of our clothes. Except for family heirlooms or enchanted stuff."

"Well, do you have any wearable hand-me-downs?"

"Maybe. But I have to check at home."

"Fine." I glanced up at the clock on the wall. It's after eleven-thirty. "Um."

"Yeah, I get it." Scott chuckles. "Almost my curfew. I want to turn into a wolf, not a pumpkin."

"Sorry, I can't drive you home." I forget why because I can't think of anyplace I need to be. I glance at the calendar on the fridge. There's nothing on it. Why do I think there should be?

"That's okay, it's a nice night for a run. See ya, Tino!" Scott smiles. After that, he lets himself out the door. I look out the hall window, watching him walk across the postage-stamp of a lawn in front of my building. When he's out of the direct beam from the orange streetlight, he starts jogging. Well, it looks like jogging, but the kid has to be going at least fifteen miles per hour. I try not to blink so I don't miss anything, but it's hard. I wonder how he can just run faster than the Boston Marathon winners like that. And does it hurt him to just do it? One thing's clear. Nike's got nothing on Scott Fitzpatrick, teenage werewolf from Cranston.

When he's gone, I go back into my apartment and grab a bag of blood. I didn't do anything vampy, but sometimes we get hungry just from being awake. It's impossible to go about regular business without drinking the stuff, so I do. But why I feel like there's no time to heat it up like a civilized vampire is beyond me. At least for the moment.

I'm changing out of the costume while contemplating my pajamas and a book when my phone beeps. I ask Siri to read the message. After hearing the robotic voice read what Stephanie sent, I speed the rest of the way through changing.

Instead of pajamas, I put on one of my two suits, the tan one. I'm a Millennial, what do you want from me?

I'd almost forgotten about the Blood Moot. And now I'm going to be late.

# CHAPTER SEVEN

The ride in the car doesn't wrinkle my suit that much. As I'm about to thank God for small favors, I step in a puddle on the way across the street and soak my wingtip. I try to tell myself the aroma of mud and sour seawater won't make the wrong impression. I'm going in to see vampires, not werewolves who I'm pretty sure I have the better sense of smell. Mostly, vamps don't freak out unless you smell like fire or blood, but that doesn't mean they won't be silently offended and lash out in inconvenient ways later.

I get to the door and make with the secret knock. It takes longer than I expect, but eventually the knob twists and I'm let in. The dude at the door wears a cloak with a hood that hides his face. I only know it's a male vamp because I've already met this guy. Everybody with fangs in Providence has heard of him. He's notorious, like his best buddy.

"You're late."

"Shadow, nice to, um, see you." I've never actually laid eyes on the guy's face. Rumor has it the only people who have seen it don't live to talk about it.

"Shut your mouth and get in there. Walk softly."

I do as he says. Shadow's not known for making nice with the peanut-gallery denizens like me. He's one of the king's enforcers, something like a spymaster. I'm just glad the other enforcer, Hargrove, isn't answering the door. If Shadow's a scalpel, Hargrove's a sledgehammer. I nicknamed him Hardcase in my head with good reason. That guy's nothing nice.

After I get down the hall, I take a right and hug the wall. The king's on his throne as usual. What's not so typical are all the other vampires from out-of-town standing in front of it and him. They almost look like an eyewitness lineup from a criminal investigation at a ComiCon. Most older vampires get anachronistic with their wardrobe choices, especially when they go to Blood Moots. Maybe I'm lucky Stephanie's an exception to that rule. She has other age-related faults, though.

The shortest out-of-towner's in the middle, wearing a pale trilby hat and a pinstripe suit in white with thin black stripes. Something about how this person stands is familiar. A long ponytail hangs down their back. I don't recognize them from the rearview and they don't talk, so there's no chance to recognize them that way.

The trilby-wearer is flanked by two of the biggest vamps I've seen. One is tall enough to play pro basketball, and the other's wider than a linebacker. They both look female and dress that way too.

The tall one's wearing a get-up like something out of Buffalo Bill's Wild West show, with a bandoleer full of bullets and everything. It smells like she's packing loaded heat, too, though I can't see any guns on her. Some vamps develop the power to hide items they're carrying from view, so I trust my nose. The broad one's got on a twill skirt and a pink cardigan. Librarian City. She's also got a satchel full of books slung over one shoulder.

A strapping fellow in a tan trench coat leans on air like there's someone I can't see next to him. My nose tells me nothing's there. Finally, there's a young lady with an afro in torn jeans and an off-the-shoulder sweatshirt. She's the only one who looks normal. Just watching her stand there makes me want to smile because she's probably younger than everyone like me. Like I said, old vamps dress weird, and this one is wearing normal clothes.

I almost bump into Stephanie. She shoots me a pointed glare and taps her watch. I nod to let her know that I get it, I'm late. But the king's pretty well occupied anyway, so I don't sweat it. Maybe if I act like it's okay, everyone else will too. Part of dealing with other vampires is showing them that you're confident.

"So, what brings you to Providence this evening?"

"You're having a Moot, and we've got business." Trilby's voice is a flat alto, faintly accented and familiar again. "Specifically about our intentions toward the island in your bay. Your Majesty."

Did he just sass the king while asking to move in on Newport? Oh, yeah, he did. Just as I think I like the cut of the trilby-wearer's rebellious jib, that ever-present pain in my noodle, Raven, makes their appearance.

"King DeCampo already knows all about you, Whitby." Raven looks down their nose at the whole group of them. "I just love telling cautionary tales with you in the leading role."

And there's the accent I recognize. Whitby's stance reminded me of Raven. I wonder whether the resemblance comes from it having been fashionable during the same bygone era or a past history. Maybe both.

"Raven. What a pleasant surprise." Whitby's tone tells me they think it's opposite day at King DeCampo's Blood Moot. "I've never cared much for what you think, as long as it's about me."

A low chuckle ripples, and I blink when I realize where it's coming from. The king. He thinks this new animosity, sour enough to erupt into violence in front of his throne, is funny. I take a step so my back's against the wall, wondering when my king will start unliving up to his head-severing reputation, but I'm spared the spectacle of sliced necks, blood, and ash. For now.

"You five visitors are welcome to mingle and carry out any traditional business for the duration of this Moot. I shall make my decision about Newport at next month's meeting."

The mood breaks. Or the tableau or stage blocking. Whatever you want to call it. One of the things I never get used to was how conspicuous vampires can be while trying to act in a normal-for-them fashion. It looks like something out of a green room at a movie set.

Whitby breezes by me, so I try to stop him and say hello. It seems natural to me that the frenemy of my frenemy might end up being a decent friend.

"What do you want?" The accent and inflection remind me of good acting in a bad BBC show.

"To introduce myself. I'm Valentino Crispo, and I'm new around here, too." I stick my hand out and don't bother mentioning exactly how new I am or in what way. In a society where value is based mostly on how not new you are, advertising that I'm a month old is the opposite of good.

"Whitby. I'm Raven's brother, though I know they never mention me here." He shakes my hand. It's colder than mine, and he grips it with a strength he doesn't look like he should have. I make a mental note not to underestimate him.

"Raven loves talking about anyone but themself." Yeah, cattiness is natural for me. I'm a recovering performance artist, what do you want?

"I know. It's been the most obnoxious thing about them since back in our mortal days."

"So you were turned by the same vampire, then." I grin.

"We had the same living mother as well, but you'll never hear Raven admit to it." Whitby makes air quotes. "They would just as soon have let me rot. But there's nothing better than being a creature of the night. The thrill of the hunt and all." There's a gleam in his eye that disturbs me. "Siblings are more burden than joy."

We're not supposed to hunt humans the way Whitby implies except in absolute emergencies because it could get us discovered. There's nothing about what he says or how he says it that makes me think he's talking about hunting deer out in Chepachet or Coventry. I fall back on Stephanie's old standby. Yes, she taught me social navigation before explaining what things smell like or blood abilities. Nobody's perfect. But anyway, that's how I know how to use a technique she calls the vague compliment.

"Huh, interesting." I don't make the mistake of saying it's cool.

Some of the older vampires think the word cool is an insult. Apparently, back in the day, it was one. Go figure. "I've got no siblings."

"Lucky." Whitby winks then tips his Trilby over my shoulder. "Be careful what you don't wish for." He looks at something over my shoulder. "Milady."

"Whitby, you bad boy!" Stephanie breezes forward and upstages me. She holds both her hands out, and he takes them. She locks her elbows, keeping him at literal arm's length. "It's been entirely too long."

I watch her make Cheek-kissing greetings with Whitby, who might be an old friend of hers. Or something. She blends in so much better than he does. Better than most of the other vampires often seen at these Blood Moot shindigs. They all have this way about asserting their individuality in a too-conspicuous manner.

On some of them, like Hargrove and DeCampo, it's scary. On others like Whitby, Shadow, and Raven, it borders on absurd. I can't imagine any of those three being able to do something routine like gas up their cars or buy a pack of smokes without freaking the norms. But Stephanie manages. I'll have to ask her some night what she does to keep up with the mundanes. Because I don't want to look like a misfit in the twenty-second century if you know what I mean.

"I hope I get staked and left on the beach before I ever get that bad at acting human."

You know when conversation breaks in a room, and there's an unintentional moment of silence? It happens all the time at Blood Moots. My hand goes over my mouth too late.

Everyone. Heard. I close my eyes and wait for both shoes to drop. There's no way I'll get out of this with just one piece of anachronistic footwear falling to the floor.

"What to the who now?" The woman from Whitby's contingent, the young-seeming one with the big hair and the sweatshirt, blinks at me.

"Um, nothing." I smile, more out of nervous habit than anything else.

"You sound like how my brain thinks." She tilts her head to one side and smiles back. "It's refreshing."

"Huh?" I blink, my face frozen the way your mother tells you it will when you pull undesirable expressions.

Her face has this quality that's engaging. I don't want to look away from it even though I should be making my apologies to Stephanie and walking out the door right now.

"No matter how many times I tell them to tone it down, they don't listen." She shakes her head, chuckling a little. Then she leans on the wall next to me and turns her head toward my ear. "Old vamps can't dress even worse than white men can't jump."

I press my lips together, trying not to laugh but don't dare shut my eyes. She tilts her head back, and I watch her shoulders shake. Somehow, this lady has mastered the art of silent laughter.

"I'm Tino."

"Maya." She shoots a glance in Stephanie's direction. "She turned you?"

"Absotively." I roll my eyes at Whitby. "He turned you?"

"You could call it that, in one sense of the word." Half her mouth turns up. "At least she has fashion sense."

"Yeah, one bright spot in the dead of night. Which we're confined to." I turn my head and side-eye her. "Sucks, doesn't it?"

"Not all the time, but yeah, it can." The smile's gone, replaced by what I think is her face-at-rest expression. Determination. And flawless mahogany skin.

"How do you deal with it?" I manage not to sigh. Which is a good thing because I don't know whether that impulse comes from exasperation at my elders or something else.

"Don't have much free time to worry about it, spend most of that trying to find sun-proof accommodations. I talk to the nice living people because the rest of them fail at it. Except for Roger, sometimes." She jerks a thumb at the guy in the trench coat. "He calls himself Peligro, though. Believe it or not, he's great with kids, old folks, and animals. But he's got his own special hurdles."

"So that's why Whitby's asking for Newport." I nod. "You can set up for good."

"Bingo."

I kind of want to offer Maya my place, but that's way too forward for polite vampire society. Okay, it's forward in any type of society. I'm thinking she's got a special ability, the kind that affects people's moods. It's hard for me to think in a line that doesn't lead to some charming feature of hers. Maybe it's something she can't help but she might be doing it on purpose. Nah, it's got to be unintentional. I've got negative rungs on the vampiric ladder, so she isn't trying to bilk favors out of me.

"Can't you guys just stay here?" I clear my throat and clarify. "In Providence?"

"Well, that's a problem. On account of what happened the last time King DeCampo let an out-of-towner try to make his own way in this city."

"I never heard that story."

"Really?" Her smile's like a necklace of diamonds, sparkling in the sun. Her eyes are clouded, though.

"Truly." I manage to smile back at Maya. She's a bit intimidating. No, that's a lie. She's downright incredible, and I'm having a hard time untying my tongue around her. I decide to tell her the immediate truth. "I'm happy to just stand here and listen to anything you feel like telling me."

She throws back her head and laughs out loud. I'm more dazzled than the time the guys in the High School lighting booth turned the follow spot on me by accident. If I'd known a goddess would grace the Blood Moot that evening, I'd have been hanging around outside before the sun was all the way down.

"We should find a place to sit down if you really want to hear it. Because it's a long story."

I let her lead me to a loveseat off in the corner opposite from where we were standing. After that, I listen to her talk. And watch, of course. Focusing on what she's saying is a challenge because Maya's something like *The Most Interesting Man* except female and a vampire. I manage.

The gist is that I'm not Stephanie's first turn. I'm a replacement, as I suspected. It's a good thing Maya's telling me this because just watching her talk is a distraction that keeps me from freaking out about the whole thing. When she gets around to naming the guy it must show on my face because she stops.

"What was that, Maya?"

"I said his name was Tierney. Tino, are you okay?"

"Irish?"

"That's right, he was." She sets her elbow on one knee and leans her chin on her hand. "That means something to you."

"It does." Maury's murdered partner has the same last name. But he worked a rotating shift, so there's no way they were the same guy. Probably related in a mortal way. "Hey, Maya?"

"Yeah?" She's gazing at me. I don't know why. Maybe she can see the hamsters turning the wheels in my brain.

"I think I owe you for this conversation." I glance toward the king's corner of the room, spot Raven, and prepare to flag them down to formally record a debt.

"Wait until I finish the story."

"Okay." I don't tell her that I could listen to her recite bad infomercials for seventy-two hours straight and not get bored. Instead, I just let her talk. Her story's more enlightening than an entire room full of Christmas lights. The LED kind. She mentions who took the rap for killing Tierney.

"Is that why the king owes Stephanie?"

"I don't know. Maybe you should ask the king's Attaché." Maya has a point. The king in any given territory delegates that kind of thing. But I'm not happy with her suggestion because I don't like the owner of the job here.

"Ask Raven?"

"Ask me what?" Apparently, they saw me looking and ambled over already.

"Did Stephanie's other kid get killed?" I raise an eyebrow, challenging Raven to harp on my slang for someone who got turned. They don't bother. I manage not to blink as they answer my question, all straightforward and everything.

"Yes, he did."

"How?"

"You wouldn't be asking if you didn't know. But since you asked, he died by vampire claw."

"Any chance you could tell me who the claw belonged to?"

"If I have to look it up in here, it'll cost you." Raven taps their little black notebook.

"Never mind. I'm a Private Investigator, I'll figure that out on my own." I grin.

"Your brain is growing, Crispo." Raven smirks.

"Yeah. Learn something new every day. And I owe Maya a small favor for her time, so make a note of that, please." I figure using the magic word mitigates the risk of waving Raven off. "Now, if you don't mind, I'm trying to enjoy the lady's company."

"Be careful, you crazy kids." Raven notes my debt down in the book. With a feather pen.

"The king told Whitby and his folks to mingle." Maya drops Raven a wink. "I'm mingling."

"True." They look back at me. "Keep on feeding your head, Crispo. Some night you'll even figure out how to tie your own shoes." They saunter off.

I turn back to look at Maya, and she's blushing. I blink, then listen for a heartbeat. There is none.

"How do you do that?"

"Nice parlor trick, huh?" She winks. "It's great for blending in and not freaking out the norms. Most of the others don't care about that, but you're different. This is a skill I think everyone should learn, so I'll show you how for free."

Maya spares me twenty minutes of her time and teaches me how to pop a fake blush on demand. It's harder than I expect, but she must be a better teacher than Stephanie because I manage to do it once. She thinks I'm a natural and tells me to keep on practicing. We're laughing about something or other when I get the feeling someone's looking over my shoulder.

"Ahem."

I don't look at whoever said that. I'd rather watch Maya sigh because it's clear that our time together is coming to an end for now. I figure she's got to be relatively new for a vampire but not anywhere near as young as me. She's a good person to know. So I hand her a business card.

"You really are a PI." Maya drops me a smaller smile this time, but it seems just as genuine as her bigger ones from earlier.

"Don't be a stranger."

She giggles. "I won't."

The interrupting vamp strides past me and escorts her away, linking his arm through hers. It's Whitby himself. How could he possibly be her sire? I wonder why she implied that he turned her but shake the question off. Sometimes, it's an extremely personal question. I can ask another time.

"You can leave if you want to now, Tino." Stephanie steps into the space Maya left. "You showed, mingled, and I saw Raven noting your attendance. I know you've got things to do."

"Yeah. One of those things is getting some information. And we should talk about one of the things I learned tonight. About Tierney."

"You're right." Stephanie wrinkles her nose. "But unfortunately, I still have demands on my time and a few small but important tasks to finish here. Why don't you go about your outside business, and I will meet you at your apartment in the wee hours?"

"You have tasks here?" I turn my head and look at her out of the corner of one eye. That always used to intimidate people before I undied, but it's not so effective now. Probably my being the equivalent of a fifth-grader has something to do with it.

"Yes." Steph's looking away when she finishes explaining, which makes me think she's understating things. "The king's territory is growing with these new arrivals, which always comes with more busywork for the rest of us."

"Well, the last thing I want is for you to get on his bad side."

"I know, Tino. But don't worry about me." Stephanie turns her back on me, mostly because as my elder and better in this place, she can.

"See you later," I say to her retreating form.

And I do worry about her. Because she said nothing about staying on King Decapitate's good side now that she doesn't have a debt to leverage against him. Whitby might not be as old or powerful as DeCampo, but he's got numbers. And if that crew is here for a benign reason, I'll eat Whitby's stupid hat. After the upheaval at Cranston PD that led to my resignation, I know a political shift when I smell one.

## CHAPTER EIGHT

After I get home, I pick up all the costume selections I made earlier with Scott. Some of them need to get familiar with the business end of my Febreze bottle. So, I get that from under the sink. My parents' basement is musty, okay?

After that, I put some blood into the coffee maker's carafe and turn the burner on. I twist the dial on a plastic kitchen timer, too. That's a lesson learned the hard way. Leave blood in there too long, ruin a perfectly good carafe right along with my dinner.

As I put the clothes on hangers from my closet, I sigh. If the world knew about vampires, maybe there'd be a Mr. Blood machine, something like a Mr. Coffee but with a shorter timer. My imagination runs off, dreaming up a world where all the human conveniences have vampiric counterparts. Why can't we all just get along?

Now I'm dreaming of a special sunblocking suit that'd let me vacation in Fiji. With the cat I don't have yet. Probably they won't invent technology like that until after they make sentient holograms and perfect space travel though. The timer ringing startles me out of my reverie.

The mug I drink my blood from isn't up in the cabinet. It's sitting in the sink, right where Stephanie left it the night before. I shut off the coffee maker before rinsing it. The blood pours like maple syrup. After I set the carafe in the sink, I turn the tap on to run water over it. Once I'm sitting down with my mug, I tap the app on my phone to see the evening news.

"An alleged Organized Crime associate was apprehended last night in Roger Williams Park, based on an anonymous tip to WPRI. The official joint statement by Cranston and Providence Police says that they have no alleged associate in custody and ask that any citizen with information about the death of Cranston Detective Larry Tierney call either department." The phone numbers for both duty officers flash at the bottom of the screen.

I don't have time to wait for those details, so I set the WPRI app to send alerts to my phone about that story. The weather, too, because that's good to know. I figure I might end up outdoors for part of the evening so that kind of information could come in handy.

The costume now passes my sniff test, so I put it on. I go into the bathroom and have a look in the mirror. That's when I realize the whole idea sucks. There's no way I can go out there and talk to people with my reflection the way it is. Even with the itchy mask, it looks too weird. People are going to notice. I shake my head but only see that mask and the shoulders of my opera cape shimmying a little in the stupid vampire-unseeing glass.

I look like The Invisible Man dressed up for a costume party. Everyone can see my clothes in the mirror, but not any part of me that's exposed. Putting on gloves solves the problem with my hands. But I realize that I have to do something about my face besides the mask.

My medicine cabinet is empty. When I got turned, I emptied it out in an impulse-driven balancing act of denial and affirmation. I open the linen closet and find the box with my old stage makeup kit in it. Could greasepaint solve my mirror problems? Maybe.

I open it, ready to go to town. But there's no tube in my flesh-tone because I used it all up. I try blending red and white, but there's not enough of that either, so I add some yellow and blue. What I end up with is a ghoulish mix that's between green and gray. It doesn't do much for my eye area, so I use a pencil to color in my brows. I get fancy and change their shape into something more dramatic, too. I don't worry about sweating the stuff off because that doesn't happen to me anymore.

Color contact lenses lend an eerie effect of floating pupils, but upon inspection, that's only a problem extremely close up. Most people will only get a glimpse of me in a mirror and think my eyes are perfectly normal when looking directly at me. I definitely have to order more of this stuff. I'd just use Maybelline, but that won't give the coverage this does. Greasepaint doesn't come off in the rain, and it's bad enough that the sun keeps me indoors. I need to be able to work in a downpour if one happens.

My new reflection makes me chuckle, but then I blink. Because it works. The irony is that I look like everyone's idea of how a vampire should appear, based on stage and screen representations. They believe so strongly that we don't exist, there's no way I'll blow my cover even if I flash fangs or get blood-lusty red eyes. They'll just think it's part of some vigilante gimmick. Like I'm a pro wrestler or something.

I'm almost ready to go, but as I approach the door leading out of my apartment, I understand that I'm forgetting something fundamental.

"Shit. I don't have a freaking alias."

But I've got no idea where to start, which means my time's shorter than I'd like. I have to damn the torpedoes and head out anyway.

"You can make it up on the way, Tino," I tell myself. "Think of it as a nickname."

Talking to yourself is a sign that your sanity's in need of a few small repairs. And going out unprepared should be number one on the top ten list of things not to do when you're a vigilante. But I know nothing, so I think everything's going to be peachier than a Georgia springtime.

I'll probably end up embarrassing myself for all eternity because that's just how I roll.

Providence and the surrounding areas have one thing in abundance that most people don't think about. Old factories. Most of those are renovated into space. I'm talking about the kind you can rent, not the place past Earth's atmosphere that's about as high as the totals of construction and real estate racketeering.

And I just happen to know that the Caprice family owns a handful of those. I also know that the only one that's not on the king's turf is over by Broad Street, right on the Cranston Line near Roger Williams Park. It's okay if you can't make sense of my directions. I'm a Rhode Islander, and we all get it. You kinda have to live here or visit frequently. And if you haven't, you should, because the food here rocks. Not that I can enjoy it anymore.

Anyway, I could run across rooftops like Hollywood's favorite nocturnal cape-wearer, but I don't. Instead, I stick to the sidewalks and the shadows. This has the bonus of keeping me away from reflections and the city's recording devices, some of which still use silvered mirrors. I'll be in trouble with the monarch and his buddies if I get caught on tape, and that's the last thing I need.

When I get to the actual shadow of the old converted mill, most of the lights are on. It's also loud out here, probably because nearly all the tenants are bands with screamy vocalists and heavy distortion on their guitars. All the windows on the first floor have a reinforced steel screen over them to keep people from making like I was going to and breaking in. I walk most of the way around the place before I see a window I can jump to that's dark.

Before I try it, I lean against the brick wall and glance around. I'm not in the line of sight for any cameras, so it's a go. I leap and catch the line of bricks just above the window. Once my feet are on the sill, I squat and pull the pane up. Also, I grudgingly thank Stephanie for the reflexes and extra dexterity that come with being a vampire. At least this part doesn't suck so much.

I shimmy inside and close the window behind me. Leaving it open would only make the tenants lock it in the future. This current setup is way too convenient for me to scuttle it because I forgot something so silly. I'm chuckling and wiping old mortar crumbs off my hands when I trip over something on the floor like a stupid oaf. Whatever it is feels cool and rigid but eerily squishy. It reminds me of the last thing I want to find. A corpse.

In seconds, I'm at the light switch on the opposite wall next to the door. After flipping it, I lean beside it. The light reveals a rubber dummy dressed in old clothes and decorated with obviously (to me) fake blood. The floor said dummy is sprawled on would usually have a carpet, but it's been rolled back. That's not strange, but what is are the weird shapes inside circles chalked in green across the polished concrete. There are jars of what looks like green glitter on half the available surfaces in the place. My feet feel all tingly, too. It's like when the Novocain wears off after a trip to the dentist.

"Crap on a crap cracker." I wonder whether this is some kind of magic, but I'm not sure whether that actually exists. My mind comes up with a list of more questions to ask Stephanie.

I stare at one of the lines. Well, it's not really a line anymore, exactly. I stare at the Tino-sized footprint on it. I lift up my right leg to examine the sole of my gumshoe. Yup. I smudged it and fudged it, but fudge has a way of still coming out good as long as you smooth it over before it goes solid. Can spells solidify? Is fudge magic? It sure tastes like that. Tasted. I miss chocolate.

On a rolling cart off to the side of the circle, I see the box of chalk. It's easy to find a matching green piece, so I grab it and step carefully back to the line I mussed worse than Kayleigh Killarney's lipstick at the Homecoming dance. I fix it.

Once the line's filled in, I tread carefully again and drop the chalk back in the box. There's a rag next to it so I use that to dust off my hands and my shoes. Leaving chalky footprints in the hall would suck more than the industrial vacuum in the corner by the window.

"See ya, weirdo lab," I say to the empty, silent room.

Because that's what this place looks like, a laboratory for people learning stage or movie special effects. Or magic if it's an actual thing. I'm not sure what I literally stepped in exactly, but I know it's not as important as the reason I came here. The Caprices. I shut off the light.

I open the door and head out into the hall. Everything's so loud out there it almost stops me undead in my tracks. It was half as loud outside the building, but practically silent in the room I just left. It makes no sense, but again, I came here for a murder mystery, not a magical one. Once I get some dirt on the Caprices, I can check The Weirdo Factory out if it still bothers me.

But I can't help myself. I can't leave the room behind until I have a look at the door. There's no sign on it, not a flyer or poster or anything to indicate that the tenant runs a business that they want to advertise to the bands in the other spaces here. But there's something on a card pinned under the room number, just one word.

"Solomon?" I scratch my head. "Whatever."

My curiosity on the matter curls up like a cat in my head. On the comfiest seat, of course. I can't let my thoughts rest, but I can pick up my feet, so I do. Down the hall at the junction of three corners, the sounds blend to make an ear-numbing cacophony smoothie. I have to shut my eyes and try to tune some of it out, which takes magical vampire powers. I'll be hungry later on, but it'll be worth it.

The band singing *"murder death kill kill, Lord Satan gets his fill"* gets damped down. So does the cover of *I'm Not Okay* by My Chemical Romance. Love the band, but now's not the time to wax nostalgic for my emo listening days. I mute a handful of others before the noise gets intelligible to my vampy ears. Once that happens, I head down the stairs to the first floor.

There's a sick bassline coupled with a kicking drumbeat. It's like an orgy in the rhythm section, and I don't want to ignore that one. Whatever band is playing that has real talent. It pops and kicks along in the auric background because I can listen to the other stuff over it. And said stuff is exactly the kind of conversation I came here to hear. I look both ways to be sure there aren't cameras or observers then do a vamp yard dash in the general direction the heavily accented voices come from.

I stop between the doors to the restrooms, across from another door marked Office. It's close enough for supernatural hearing to make out every word, and the door marked with a male stick-figure covers me if someone happens by.

"I ain't paying her." That voice comes out of a mouth that must have smoked two packs of cigarettes a day. "She didn't do it."

"We already gave her half." This one sounds smoother than butter. "It's dangerous to stiff the hitman."

"Hitwoman." Cigarettes chuckles. "And I'd stiff her in more ways than one if you know what I mean."

"You're crazy," says Butter. "You ain't even seen her without that mask on. She might have a horse-face or worse. Anyway, she's got enough kills under her belt to make a Silver Anniversary. You'd have a hard time turning her into a stiff. I'm telling the Boss we ought to pay, anyway. I mean, she hit Crispo even if he's still sucking wind."

They're talking about Dad. I clench my fists and my jaw, trying to control myself. The last thing I want to do is go into a vengeance rage in a building this busy. And I want them to finish their conversation about stiffing a hired gun with over twenty-five kills.

"No kill, no cash," says Cigarettes. "And that's what I tell the Boss."

"You're going to get us all iced."

"She'll kill the messenger, whoever it is. After that, she'll be dead meat for sure."

"And you're sure that messenger won't be you?"

"Absotively." His chuckle hides a cough. "I've got friends in low places."

"I wish I shared your confidence."

"You'll die before you match it."

I hear a metallic sound, recognize it. Drawn pistol. I can't blame Butter for drawing on Cigarettes. That sounds like a threat, even to me. I debate busting in fangs blazing, but someone comes out of the ladies' room. A chick, apparently normal, and definitely a little older than me. The only thing odd about her is the leather jacket she wears in the summery weather. I wonder whether this is their hitwoman, but it can't be. No Silver Anniversary assassin would come in plainclothes if she wore a mask at her "interview." She knocks on their door.

"Put the piece away." Cigarette's voice is soft enough that the woman at the door won't hear it. "We got company."

"Who the hell comes here at this hour?" I hear Butter holster his piece. "It's after three in the morning."

"Rent money, probably."

"You're lucky."

"You've got no idea, pal."

The chick holds up her right fist to knock again, but the door opens. The guy looks maybe ten years older than me. He slaps on a big old smile that reminds me of reptiles in sewers.

"Hey, Esther." I can tell by the voice, it's Butter. "You got your rent this time or just an excuse?"

"Fucking rent." Esther thrusts an envelope into Butter's hand. "Back and current."

"Nice. You staying another six months?"

"What do you think, jerk-off?"

"Pay on time from now on, or we start putting your stuff in the Lost and Found, we clear?"

"Crystal."

He slams the door in her face. Esther doesn't even flinch. Instead, she forks her fingers at the steel in an all-too-familiar gesture. It's the ward against the evil eye, straight out of grandma territory. I blink. She turns on her heel and stalks toward me. Without looking up, she stops.

"Nice fucking costume." She raises an eyebrow. I notice a few lines on her face, which make me question my original guess at her age. I can't decide whether she's in her early thirties or even older.

"Thanks." I wring my hands. "I'm in a band," I blurt.

"Yeah, you and every other dick-owner in this crappy frigging place." Esther continues down the hall, holding up her left hand in a gesture of farewell. There's a glove on it. "Stay out of the fucking Mafia. They suck hairy donkey balls."

"Yeah, I'll do that."

As Esther takes her attitude away with her, I realize I now have the perfect excuse to get my eyes on the room the mobsters use for an office. I step over to the door and knock. I cross my fingers, hoping they don't have any mirrors in there.

This time, another guy opens the door. When he smiles, I know for sure it's Cigarettes. Even if I hadn't seen Butter already, the teeth, yellow and cracked like old tombstones, give him away before he says a word. I grin just in case my fangs are out from fine-tuning my hearing. Or, you know, the fact that these guys were involved in taking the hit out on Dad.

"Hi. I'm looking to rent some practice space."

"Huh. Okay. We've got a few vacancies, but they're all on the third floor."

"That's cool." I nod. "I want to see them."

"Fine." Cigarettes steps out into the hall and closes the door behind him. All I see is the corner of a tan counter.

It occurs to me I haven't heard a peep out of Butter since he slammed the door on Esther. But maybe they take turns at that or something. I try putting my unease out of my mind, but it acts like a cat when you try to put it in the bathtub. It knows the water's coming eventually. I follow Cigarettes up the stairs, keeping on guard.

When we get to top of the third flight, Cigarettes turns around on the landing. I'm still a couple of steps down. He's got one hand in his pocket and it has nothing to do with an old '90s song.

"What kind of band are you in, anyway?"

"Oh. We're sort of like um, a theatrical mashup," I fib. "Like GWAR but more Emo." At least I know how to talk that talk even if I can't play an instrument to save my life. My hands are in my pockets, too, fingers crossed.

"You'll fit right in on the third floor, then. There are a few um, theatrical acts up here." His raspy chuckle carries no hint of good nature.

He doesn't know the half of it.

# CHAPTER NINE

For a moment, I think Cigarettes has seen right through my ruse and will push me down the stairs, but he turns and opens the door to the third floor instead. He lets it fall instead of holding it open for me, which I'm okay with. Because he doesn't have to be a gentleman, just show me the damn room for rent.

It's down at the end of the hall, on the same end as the Weirdo Lab that I used to break in. Some people call that kind of thing a coincidence or kismet or fate. But in my opinion, luck's just as blind as justice and way less of a righteous babe.

I let Cigarettes turn on the light before I go in. It's just a room, maybe a half-foot too long on one side to be exactly square like the one below it. That sticks in my mind like broccoli used to in my front teeth. I can't put my finger on what's making it stick because my gut's screaming at me like tweens at a boy band concert. Not the literal gut that wants blood, the kind that people associate with their psychic friends.

"I'll take it." My gut settles down like a baby after a good burping.

"Cool. It's one Benjamin a month. We control the heat to keep it cheap, so don't bitch at us if you get cold. No air conditioners allowed. What kind of amps do you guys have?"

"We practice with headsets."

"Huh." Cigarettes peers at me. "Well, whatever. We don't handle noise complaints. Neither do the police in this neighborhood. Understand?" He means that if people think you're too loud, they'll bust in and take your amps. But I don't have to worry about that because I'll never actually be in a band. I think.

"Yeah, I get it. Thanks."

"Come on down to the office, and I'll give you the paperwork. You gotta pay cash for everything, every time. If you don't have that much on you, bring it back tomorrow night or afternoon, like at three or something. We ain't morning people here."

"Don't worry, neither are we." I'm checking the walls and the window. Is that circle by the window a dent from moving stuff or a bullet-hole?

"What do they call you? Your band?"

"Yup." I'm only half-listening, so I answer like a moron. After that I fictionalize. "Uh. We're still trying to agree on that."

"You coming or not?"

"Sure."

I follow him, mentally kicking myself. Down on the first floor, Cigarettes goes into the office and shuts the door in my face. I stand there wondering why, so I go out of my way to sniff things out. There's no scent of blood, but it smells like someone's taken a leak in there, maybe in a bottle without a lid? Or huffed some super-stinky glue? I can't make sense of what my nose picks up, so I quit on it.

Cigarettes steps back out, waving a clipboard at me. I take it, and accidentally-on-purpose drop the pen that goes with it. I can't see anything but an old sofa behind the manager/mobster. After straightening up, I look at the form. It's got the room number scrawled on a line at the top, 319. I start filling it out, relieved that the space on the form for a name says "Business or Act" in front of it. They don't keep records of real people here.

In that blank, I write the acronym for the name I plan to use for my PI business. Hey, maybe I can write this expense off on my taxes next year. I pull my billfold from my right front pocket. There's a couple hundred in there in various bills. I slap five twenties on the clipboard and hand it and the pen back to Cigarettes.

"Here are your keys. No propping or holding the goddamn door out front. We don't want riff-raff street people sleeping in the halls here."

"No problem."

Cigarettes drops the keys and shuts the door. I catch them with my crazy vampire reflexes before I'm technically out of his line of sight. He doesn't give any sign that he notices. It's not until I'm about to walk away that I realize there's only one clear heartbeat behind the office door now. Butter could have left while we were upstairs. Or he could be dead, killed in a bloodless manner that my nose either can't detect or identify.

But the whole reason for renting a space in this place is to get information about the Caprices and this hitwoman they hired to bump off my dad. So I chalk it all up to a part of my investigation and head upstairs to the room leased out to SVS, also known as Shadow Vanguard Sleuthing. I think it's a cool name.

As I climb stairs, I wonder what Cigarettes would think if he knew he'd just leased space to a PI masquerading as an Emo act. Maybe I should order some business cards for the fake band from Vistaprint. I shrug and unlock my new door. I wonder whether the neighbors here are as nosy as the Fitzpatricks back by my parents' house.

Thinking of the old neighborhood puts me in mind that maybe attempting all this alone is a big mistake. I get the idea that maybe some help would be nice. Stephanie already made it clear that she's worried about trouble for or with King Decapitate of the City of Hope. Now there's more of an oxymoron for you than a D minus average High Schooler using anti-acne products.

The thought of High Schoolers reminds me of Scott. I whip my phone out and call him.

"Yo, Tino! "He answers awfully fast for someone up way past his curfew. I check the time. It's four in the morning, which is actually early enough for him to legitimately be out for a morning jog.

"Yo yourself." I figure that's a hip enough response.

“What’s up, my dude?”

“Um, I just rented us some practice space in a Caprice Family-owned building.”

“Us?” I can practically hear his eyebrows gain altitude. “You mean we’re a thing? I can help?”

“Yeah, sure, Scott. You can. But make it snappy because the sun coming up sucks for me.”

I give him the address, and he says he’ll meet me over here in less than fifteen minutes. I know that's true because that’s how long it takes to get somewhere in Rhode Island from anyplace else. We’re small on space but big on quirkiness here. Visit sometime, and you’ll see what I mean. What other place on Earth has coffee milk? Not that I can drink that anymore.

Just as I get to the point where I think Tino, you're a moron because now you have to buy furniture that has to work for a band or a PI firm, my phone beeps. There's a message from Scott. I read it.

**Dude dragging something that smells like a body out of here. WTF do I do?**

"Shitballs." I open my window and stick my head out. Sure enough, Cigarettes has a dolly with a rolled-up carpet on it. Six feet tall and too stiff for something that just ties the room together, too. I open my nostrils and know Scott's right. I’m starting to hate that.

And why am I so much more upset about teen wolf being right than I am about a dead body in the building? I make the disappointing realization that it’s hard to get busted up over a guy who helped hire someone to shoot my dad. And what am I going to do, call Maury? He doesn’t have a warrant and Cigarettes will get rid of blatant evidence before Detective Weintraub can get here.

**Nothing**, I text back. Leaving the window, I head downstairs to let Scott in. He follows me up, and on the landing at the second floor, Esther almost knocks us over.

She's coming through the hall door like a bat out of hell, so fast and angry I think she's a vampire too for a second. But her racing heart and the bile I smell in her throat assert her essential humanity.

"Waffle-twatting ass-clowns!" Esther doesn't even notice we're there, let alone that she could have killed us. Well, Scott, anyway. Stairs don't kill vamps, even if we break our necks on them. Maybe they don't kill werewolves either unless they're made of silver, but what do I know? I'm new, remember?

"You okay?" Scott calls after her.

"Those shitfaced cock-masters broke into my space again!" She throws her hands in the air. "Uncle-fuckers!"

Something green shimmers in the space over her hands, but when I blink, it's gone. Scott wrinkles his nose, so I scent the air. I smell something like the incense Mom and Dad burn when they're using their medical MJ. I wait until I hear the first-floor door slam shut behind Esther to say anything.

"Did you see that?" I wave my hand like I'm at the end of a jazz dance routine.

"I don't know, but I sure smelled it." He waves his like he wants to get rid of a bad smell.

"Come on, let me show you the new digs before we talk about it."

We get to 319. Scott chuckles at the door.

"What?"

"You don't listen to Prince, huh?"

"Should I?"

"Definitely. Or maybe not." Scott gestures at the room number. "That's one of his songs, *319*. It's like the kind of cheesy Easter egg a pulp writer would leave lying around in their book."

"Well, you can play it for me some time, I guess."

"Okay."

I open the door. Scott walks in and stops in the middle of the floor. Once I close the door, he's on the polished concrete, nose to the fake stone. I lean against the wall by the light switch, watching him until he stands up.

"That woman from the stairs rents the space under ours."

Well, crap. I realize the weird circle I'd stepped in earlier was Esther's. So much for being a good neighbor. How do you recover from that kind of faux pas against a potentially magical person, anyway? Bring cupcakes over? Or maybe beer? I had to hope she didn't know how to conjure fire or anything.

"How do you know it's hers, anyway?"

"That smell from the stairs? It's coming from the floor."

"What do you think it is?"

"I don't know." Scott shrugs. "Gotta ask Grandpa."

"Maybe it's not such a good idea to tell him too much about this."

"Why?" Scott scratches his head.

"He's only a huge gossip."

"Nah, it's a front." Scott shrugs. "He gabs about which neighbor lady drinks during the day and which ones tip the mailman so he can avoid talking about werewolf stuff."

"He knows you're a werewolf?"

"Yeah. He's one, too."

"Seriously?"

"He taught me everything I know about being one before the first time I changed."

"You're lucky," I blurt. "Uh, forget I said that."

"Um, okay." Scott paces to the window, peeks out, then turns back around. "That's a pretty good vantage point. You can see the dumpster right under us and the parking lot on the diagonal."

"Yeah. I wasn't planning on renting the place but just had a feeling it was the right idea to do it, anyway."

"Cool. So, where are we going to put all our musical instruments?"

"We're not playing music, we're investigating crimes. Leave the tunes to the actual acts in here."

"Why?" Scott cocks his head like the RCA dog. "They're not that talented. Well, except that one percussion duo."

"I know, right? Anyway, we are definitely not as good as them. I'm a vampire, not a musician."

"I saw you in the High School Theater productions. You can sing." He shrugs. "And as far as the vampy stuff, you seem to know what you're doing. Covered your ass in front of good old Maury and all."

"Well, but I just got turned last month. Bet you've been wolfing out longer than that."

"For about two years."

"See? And you're not even fully grown yet."

"Okay, you have a point." Scott shakes his head. "But I'm gonna bring in my drum set and my guitar so we fit in. And if we're investigators, we still need a few things. A computer, desks, maybe stuff to sit on."

"Expensive."

"Not really." Scott shrugs. "It's May. All the college students move out of their places this time of year. We can pick some furniture up down by PC where the off-campus students rent."

"Good idea. But how do we carry it?" I point out the window at the tiny car Scott already knows is mine.

"I drove Dad's truck over here. So let's go!"

"I can't. Sun's going to come up before we're done." I realize that I've got a curfew too, even though I'm not a teenager anymore.

"Okay, so we go tomorrow night. I'll drop by your apartment at sunset. Let me just bring that drum set up now before we leave."

"You don't waste any time, huh?"

Scott doesn't answer. We go downstairs, where I wait at the door to open it for him. I don't want to break the door-propping rule on my first night in the place. My dude Scott has a drum set and the guitar he was talking about. There's a stool and a stand, too. We lock the instruments in there and head out.

As Scott gets in his dad's truck, he waves. I return the gesture, then take a jog around the side of the building to peek in the dumpster. There's nothing in it, so Cigarettes must have gotten rid of Butter's body some other way. So much for my idea about calling the Cranston PD with an anonymous tip to inconvenience some Caprices.

On the way back to my apartment, I wonder whether Cigarettes killed Butter under orders from higher up. The only alternative to that is Cigarettes is already on the upper tier of authority in Caprice family business. I'm not sure who to discuss this with besides Scott, and that'll have to wait for tomorrow.

Stephanie's in my apartment like she said she'd be. But instead of being in shape to discuss anything she's sprawled across my bed, fully dressed with her shoes kicked off. Sleeping like a baby. Her face is paler than usual, so I figure she used powers during the rest of the Blood Moot that I haven't learned yet. There's enough blood in the fridge for both of us when she wakes up.

I let her sleep and go have a shower. The greasepaint isn't easy to scrub off without cold cream, which I do not have. So I leave my face unwashed and change into my pajamas. With Stephanie in the bed, the only place for me to sleep is the comfy chair so there's no risk of smudging it while I'm out for the day. I recline it and snooze.

## CHAPTER TEN

I'm waiting by the coffeemaker, listening to the water running in the bathroom while Stephanie washes her face. I'm not sure whether it's a habit or an excuse, her reason for going in there. Maybe both even though she's way older than me. One month's acquaintance is nothing compared to my still human friends, who I've known for as long as I can remember. She's the vampire I've known the longest, but it's hard to decide whether I can trust her. Then again, maybe she's in there acting human to put me at ease.

The blood's warm now, so I pour it into two mugs and set them on the breakfast table. I take the seat facing the front door. Dad always called it The Paranoia Chair. Stephanie walks out of the bathroom wrapped in my terrycloth bathrobe. Before I continue, here's a little four-one-one on Steph.

Usually, the woman who vamped me looks more alive than most humans. She's somehow larger-than-life, comes across like she's six-foot-something and not someone you want to meet in a dark alley despite the lipstick and fashionable clothes. She's posh, polished to a high-gloss like literal brass balls.

I blink because I've never seen her like this before.

She looks too short without her pumps, almost an entire foot shorter than my high opinion of her vampiric prowess elevates her in my mind's eye. My robe dwarfs her frame, hangs longer down her legs than her usual slightly below the knee skirts. But it's worse than that.

Steph's face is as white as the pancake I put on my own mug last night. That includes her lips. Her eyes don't have their usual twinkle; instead, they're flat. Even her chestnut hair lacks luster, sticks in limp clumps to the beige cloth under it. She sits in the chair across from me and curls both hands around the mug of warmed blood.

"You okay, Stephanie?"

Instead of answering, she lifts the stoneware to her mouth, steadily swallowing until it's all gone. Her shoulders droop as she sets the empty cup down. Instead of getting up for the refill I can tell she needs, Stephanie looks at the coffee maker like a puppy being left behind at an animal shelter. The kill kind.

"I got that." I reach for her mug, and she lets me take it.

Up at the counter, I pour her the rest of what's in the carafe. I empty two more bags into it and turn the burner back on. Once she's got her refill, I sit down again. She stares at her hands before wrapping one around the handle.

"Thanks, Valentino."

"It's no problem. About the blood and the crashing, I mean. But I still want to know if you're okay."

"I've got to be, and so I am." She holds the mug close to her lips and gazes at the blood inside. "Just fine. Thanks for asking."

It's clear that she's not, but I let her cover it up. For now. Stephanie isn't telling me the truth, and the contrast between all her little tells then and now illustrates how she's been mostly honest with me all along. Something happened the night before, but if any of it is my business, I'll have to trust that she'll tell me when I need to know. No matter how counterintuitive that might feel for me.

"Okay. So, last night, you said we'd talk about Tierney."

"Yes. What do you want to know?"

"Am I his replacement?"

"To King DeCampo, yes, you are." She closes her eyes. "But for me, nobody could replace Edwin Tierney. He was my best friend."

I don't want to put my foot in my mouth, so I sip my blood and wait for her to say more. My patience pays off.

"I told you about how we sleep sometimes when the years start weighing too heavily. The allies who should have been there to assist me when I woke had perished, so it was their mortal associate Edwin who found me and helped me learn the ways of the Twentieth Century. I got permission to turn him in the days leading up to the Second World War. He died one week before I turned you."

"Jeez, Stephanie. I'm sorry." I turn the cup around in my hands. The aroma of the blood calls me like it always does. But just like the night my father got shot, I hold myself back from it. "There's a rumor that the king was responsible for his death. Is that why he let you turn me?"

"It's part of the reason, yes." She takes a long pull from her cup. "But not how you think. I don't believe His Majesty killed my friend. But he couldn't disprove it, so he took on the burden of punishment."

"Okay, then." I narrow my eyes, my stomach turning at her evasion. "But you didn't answer my question. Why me?"

"I'm not entirely sure. You see, Edwin had King DeCampo's permission to turn a new Detective at the Cranston Police Department. You were supposed to get the promotion that was denied you. And then, you would have been put on the night shift. Edwin would have turned you and been responsible for everything I'm trying to manage teaching you now. I'm fulfilling a dear friend's last wishes."

It's not typical to transfer turning permission like that. I already know there's more than Stephanie's telling me. If she's not volunteering the info there has to be a dangerous reason. Maybe the king really did kill Edwin with his own hands. Or claws, as the case may be. "So you didn't choose me. Edwin Tierney did. And he never told you why."

"Correct." She says no more. Morbid curiosity makes me wonder who she would have picked, what she thinks my shortcomings are, whether she even wanted to turn someone in the first place. But I have to stay focused if I want to stop the murders.

"So, I didn't get my promotion because your Edwin was pulling strings at the PD, and when he died, I got cut off."

"Yes." Stephanie's lips curve up, but her eyes stay flat and serious. "Over the last month I've come to understand the potential he saw in you."

I don't get what she's saying. It doesn't take a genius to put two and two together. Maury, with his natural talent for everything, would have been a better pick for Edwin Tierney than little old me. I try to think about what I've got that my best friend doesn't. It takes me a minute, so I finish my blood.

"I'm Italian. Like the Caprices. And half the people in the state of Rhode Island."

"That is a contributing factor. But you were a good cop, Tino. And you'll be an even better private investigator because of all the setbacks you're facing now."

"I wish I shared your confidence. And anyway, we need to talk about how Edwin Tierney's absence might be connected to Detective Larry Tierney's death."

"I can't say. And after last night, I realize I couldn't help you with it even if I knew. But one thing I noticed when I awoke this evening is, you're making more connections with the werewolves."

"Um, yeah." Stephanie's words are almost a blatant statement that she knows something but is bound by oath not to talk about it. I let her change the subject. "Scott's been a buddy for a while. I hope that's okay?"

"It's more than okay. Connections with the other supernatural groups will be an advantage others don't dare try to make."

"Groups?" I get up, take the mugs for another refill. "You mean there's more than us and werewolves?"

"What is it that the aliens with the pointy ears said on that television show? The one with that spaceship Industry?"

"Infinite diversity in infinite combinations," I recite without bothering to correct her. Even if Steph was more modern, she probably wouldn't be a geek.

"Exactly so. I'm far older than you, but even I don't have many answers about what exists in the world and what does not. However, I can tell you that some mundanes have extra senses, and others experiment with more than science."

"Magic?"

"Perhaps. I've not seen it with my own eyes. Raven knows more than I do."

"Then I'll have to ask them what they know."

"Be prepared to—"

"I know. Pay the piper."

Stephanie stands, leaving her empty cup on the table. When she heads back into the bathroom, I take it to the sink. The water's running in there again but this time only minutes pass. I drink the rest of my breakfast and wait for her. She emerges looking like her usual self this time, in her clothes and with her face made up.

"Tino, thank you for your hospitality." Stephanie grips the doorknob and pauses. "It's impossible for me to repay you now, formally speaking. But when you finally go through your Trial and prove you know the ways of vampiric society, I'll make sure everyone knows that I am in your debt."

My mouth opens, but no sound comes out. The door shuts behind her. It takes a few minutes to compose myself after the strange experience of seeing what amounts to my vampiric parent with her walls down and masks off. I glance at the clock and see that I've got enough time to walk down to CVS for some cold cream to take the greasepaint off my face. How Stephanie managed a straight face, let alone a straightforward conversation with me in ghoulish stage makeup, I'll never know.

The night air is nice and balmy, which is good because it's Rhode Island in May, and you never know what weather you're going to get until mid-June. Stretching my legs down the block is refreshing even though people are looking at me funny on account of my full face of makeup. There aren't even any Goths in the Rolfe Square neighborhood for me to pretend to blend in with.

I'm willing to bet that vampires up in Salem, Massachusetts have it way easier than us here in the Ocean State. Maybe someday I'll move to a place where being an oddball is more common than here. Nah, who am I kidding? This state gets its hooks into a person, even the ones who weren't born in it. And I was, so I'm pretty much a goner for Rhode Island. I hope that doesn't end up being literal and permanent someday.

I'm in the store trying to find where they keep the stuff for washing faces. But this is the third time they changed the layout in here over the last year. I get it; merchandising and marketing are important, but so is being able to find whatever the hell you're looking for. Just as it starts to seem like I'm on the right track to hunt down some cold cream, my phone rings. It's an unfamiliar number, but I'm too curious for my own good. So I answer it.

"Hello?"

"Hi, Tino."

"Maya!" I glance around, then use my inside voice to tell its outside counterpart to settle down. "Good to hear from you. What's up?"

"Oh, thank God. You don't say stuff like," she lowers her voice in a fine mimicry of Whitby, "'What does Milady need help with this evening?'" She giggles.

I snicker. A little old lady farther down the aisle gives me the stink-eye. I glance around one more time for the cold cream but fail to spot it. That's okay, I'd rather talk to Maya than wash my face, anyway. I head out of the store, intending to go back to my apartment and finish the conversation there. I can always go back to CVS and ask an employee for help. But that's not what happens at all.

Listening to Maya, it's easy for my mind to go back in time and imagine I'm chatting with one of my old High School theater friends instead of a fellow vampire. She mentions how it was fun to finally meet someone modern. Apparently, the other vamps in Whitby's group are seventy or over. She asks me what's fun to do around here because Providence feels so much smaller than New York City or even Boston.

"Well, a couple of things I still like even after I got vampinated are movies and concerts." I grin even though she can't see me. "Live theater, too."

"How about dancing in a club? Do Rhode Islanders do that?"

"I'd imagine, yeah." I'm not a good dancer unless I'm wearing tap shoes and practice with a choreographer. Wait, human me wasn't, but that doesn't mean vampire me can't bust some improvised moves. "That might be something to go out and try in the real world some night instead of just imagination."

"Maybe dancing's even better than before since we've got really great reflexes now." Maya doesn't just share my line of thinking, she takes it a step further. "I can't wait to try it."

Clearly, she isn't as in hate with having fangs as I am. And somehow she hasn't had a chance to dance yet. I wonder why but figure it's personal, a topic to talk about some other time. For now, I want to enjoy basking in Maya's optimism. But I can't because no vampire calls another out of the blue just for fun. Not after the kind of night I know Stephanie had and Maya must have witnessed. Some serious blood-fueled powers got thrown down and around after I left the Blood Moot.

"So, you must have called for a reason besides chit-chat of the social fun variety. So what's up?"

"Oh, I wanted to ask if Stephanie's okay." Her voice lowers, not exactly a whisper but close enough. The concern in it comes through, anyway.

"She is now." I blink, realizing that no matter how bad I thought Steph looked this evening, she must have looked even worse before resting last night. "I just saw her maybe a half-hour ago."

"Good. After you left, we had a little chat about a few things. I like her."

"Cool. But why are you asking if she's okay? What happened last night?"

"She didn't tell you?"

"No, just said something like her duties wore her out is all."

"Oh, wow. Tino, be careful."

"Huh?"

"Things are getting shaken up like a can of soda on a hot day." The phone is muffled, but not enough to cover the sound of a door opening and closing in the background.

"Yeah, I gathered that." I remember how well-informed she seemed to be in matters regarding the king of a city she hasn't been to.

A gal so charming and easy to talk to must hear all kinds of things. I consider that maybe she and I share a common problem; knowing too much. And I think about the line of vampires standing in front of the king, more like a challenge than a presentation. That line included Maya herself. I lean the back of my head against cool brick. What if she's not just being friendly? Without her physical presence, the wheels in my head turn in directions they hadn't the night before. Why did Whitby bring his crew here, anyway?

"You be careful, too." If the king accepted responsibility for Edwin Tierney's death, maybe Whitby and his crew were in town to challenge him over it. Penalties for ending another vamp's life usually include either death or a long sleep. But did DeCampo actually commit murder? If he didn't, some vamp with abilities to rival the king's is walking around free and might strike again to discredit the current leadership. I try not to panic at Maya's sudden silence. "Maya?"

"I will. As much as I can." She's being cagey. After how we talked the night before, I realize that's not like her. She can't speak plainly, either because of where she is or who she's with.

"Can you say more about what we're being careful of, Maya?"

"No, not right now."

"Can you meet me later on?"

"Okay, I can pick that up. You said it was where now?"

I give her the address and room number at the Broad Street studio. Her voice carries some of the relaxed good-will it had last night when she thanks me. We say goodbye and hang up. I'm just about to head back to CVS when a pickup truck honks at me. The driver's Scott Fitzpatrick. I'm fresh out of time for face-washing, apparently. Crossing my fingers, I hope I'm not all out of luck, too.

But with a Mafia assassin and a clawed vampire killer around, any luck I've got left is probably bad.

# CHAPTER ELEVEN

Scott's dad's truck is a faded blue metallic color with that fake wood paneling painted on the side. All the trim at the borders that tried to make it look like real timber has fallen off, though. Rust dots the fenders, which have a primer coating some scratches and a few dings. The chrome on the boxy bumpers still shines, and the tires have nice, thick treads. When we get in, I can feel that the suspension's nice and tight. It looks tacky and is the opposite of inconspicuous, but the Fitzpatrick vehicle seems safe enough.

We're heading out to the neighborhoods between Providence College and Rhode Island College to find discarded furniture for the office-studio mashup. While riding in Scott's truck, I tell him all about Stephanie, how she looked this evening, and a less personal version of what she told me. The theory about some sneaky vampire trying to frame and discredit the king goes unspoken. I wait and watch for his reaction.

"The deaths don't sound like they're linked, but maybe I'm wrong." Scott tilts his head, slowing the truck as he takes a right on to Pembroke Avenue. While we're stomping around in Providence, we're west of the highway, so I don't have to check in with the king. "Would you have been Maury's partner if you'd both made Detective at the same time?"

"I'm not sure. Larry Tierney was a department fixture, though. He had community connections, so maybe one of those was Edwin. Larry knows all the ins and outs at the precinct. And usually they like to put rookies together with more experienced detectives. In all likelihood, he could have been my partner instead."

"Well, that tanks my idea. I thought maybe the hitwoman was supposed to kill Maury's partner without specifying who that was exactly." Scott chews on his lower lip. "Maybe Larry was a vampire's associate, pulling strings at the department. It could be either of those that made him a target. Or both. If the Caprices know about vamps, you could still be in danger. If they don't, they could be cat's paws, and Maury might be the next target."

"You sound like you know more about assassins than I'd have guessed." I side-eye Scott because he deserves it for being so precocious. "You may be right. But you may be crazy."

"Back at you, buddy." Scott cracks a smile and winks.

"Look, if we're going to work together sleuthing out the bad guys, we shouldn't have to second-guess each other all the time." I cross my arms over my chest. "How do you know anything about this at the tender age of sixteen?"

"Gramps. Werewolves find out loads of stuff just because we see and hear more than the average person thinks we do. But I gotta run almost everything I find out by my grandpa first. He won't let me keep working with you if an outsider knows more about threats to our community than he does."

I blink. This is not the reaction I'm expecting from the kid who used to hero-worship me. "Outsider? Scott, I was there the day you were born."

"Yeah, but not the night of my first change. And Gramps runs all the wolf stuff. They've got rules. I'm just a kid and answer to the adults, whether they're on two legs or four at any given time."

"Okay, that makes sense." I open my mouth, about to tell him about how I'm not a free and clear agent myself. It occurs to me that I'm not sure if that'll get me murdered by King Decapitate. "We both got things to learn. I can live with that."

"Hey! Look at all the chairs!"

Scott stomps on the breaks and throws the old truck's transmission into park. The beastly vehicle jerks to a stop that would have given me whiplash if I'd still been technically alive. I get out to help with the chairs and whatever other things we'll find along that street. I forget all about the reason I was in CVS earlier until some random person makes sure I remember.

"Halloween's next year!"

The chick shouting out from the third-floor window at number fifteen can't count. It's May, not November. I ignore her and try going about the business of shouldering the mismatched but solid chairs into the back of the beastly truck.

"Hey, buddy! I'm talking to you!"

I turn to the window and see the young woman leaning out her open window, red plastic Solo cup in her hand. A sour hoppy scented liquid sloshes out and down. I was never that obnoxious in college. I roll my eyes and keep on keeping on. Scott's found a computer cart and a shelf.

"Can't you freaking count?"

She's drunk enough to think seeing a vampire outside her building was either a bad dream or a drug trip. And I'm made up like a Haunted House vampire, so why the hell shouldn't I have a bit of fun with it?

"I am the freaking Count! One! One drunk chick! Ah-ha-ha!"

She laughs so hard at that, she drops her cup and falls. Inside the house, thankfully. Of course, if she'd fallen out the window, I would have caught her. I'm supposed to be a hero, even though I can't keep small priorities like removing makeup from my mug straight, you know?

"This is the last time I go stuff-collecting without washing my face."

"Never say never, buddy." Scott snorts. "And you know, 'The Count' has a nice ring to it."

It ends up being a short hunt, thank God. The pickup's full enough to make me reconsider my original opinion of the truck's suspension. Although I think we might want to take another spin around the off-campus neighborhood, we did pretty well.

Unloading the truck in the dark isn't so bad. Finally, a literal bright side to being a vampire turns up. I can see like it's twilight instead of half-past ten. Scott also doesn't seem to mind hustling furniture out of a truck and up three flights, but whether that's because he's compensating with his sniffer or for some other reason, I don't know.

We leave it all in a cluster a few feet from the door and head back downstairs. Scott parks his truck in the lot, and I stay in the vestibule to open the door for him when he gets back. I'm not about to break the rule about propping the door after suspecting Cigarettes the building manager of murder. I don't have an undeath wish.

"You got a motherfucking death wish or what?" The voice behind me sounds familiar, but not enough for me to place it immediately. "Move your damn carcass out of my way before you ride this wood like a hooker on a carousel."

I might not have immediately known the voice, but the creative cuss-out is unmistakable. My downstairs neighbor is here, and I forgot about bringing over cupcakes and beer. Or whatever. Dammit.

"Esther, hi!" I step aside.

"I fucking wish I was high." Her glance lingers on my face, and she snorts. "What in Balthazar's bastardly ballsack are you supposed to be again?"

"Um, my band is emo."

"I'm sorry." Esther rolls her eyes at the door. "Clear it, asshole."

I get the message and go to open it, but stop. She's carrying one of those shoji screens, which could come in handy.

"What the fuck, man?"

"Are you moving that screen or throwing it out?"

"Are you sure your band's not Junkyard or some shit? Throwing it out. Why? Do you want it?"

I nod.

"It'll cost you one Yuppie Food Stamp." Esther balances the screen on one hip somehow and holds out her now-free hand. It's got pink marks on it where she's been holding onto the wooden edges. My hands don't do that anymore. Vampire is sad.

"Fine." I cross her palm with a twenty-dollar bill.

"Peachy as Valkyrie tits." She stuffs the bill into her right front pocket and tosses the screen in my general direction. I manage to catch it. After that, Esther turns on her heel and stomps back through the door into the stairwell.

"You're welcome," I say, even though she probably can't hear me by then.

"I fucking heard that. Asshole."

Scott's knocking on the door, so I forget about getting into a shouting match or cuss contest with my surly downstairs neighbor. I'd lose anyway. I let the werewolf in and head back into the hall with him, taking my sweet time. Scott elbows me and points at the door leading into the stairwell. I don't see it until I blink. Green glowing glitter hovers in the air.

"We've gotta find out what's up with that Esther lady." Scott wrinkles his nose.

"But we have more important things to do first." I jerk a thumb over my shoulder at the office door. "Remember?"

"Yeah." Scott pulls open the door to the stairwell and heads up. He's still talking, so I follow fast enough to hear him say, "Maybe we should talk to Maury."

"But I don't want to involve him in this." I turn the corner at the landing carefully and manage not to drop the Shoji screen. Go, me.

"He already is, though."

As we walk down the third-floor hall to 319, I think about that. Scott has a point. It's hard to believe he's only sixteen sometimes. Maury might be a target of whoever offed Edwin Tierney, killed his partner, and shot at my dad. Once we're in the studio space it occurs to me that I might be going at this all wrong.

"I think we have to start with the weakest link." I set the screen down in the far corner and start unstacking our other furniture.

"Huh?" Scott puts me at ease by acting and sounding his age for once.

"I'm talking about tracking down our hitwoman."

"Thought you said you didn't see her face. Also that she wore one of those common and heavy perfumes."

"I did. But I know somewhere else she's been. In the office downstairs. How long does it take for you to catch a scent, Scott?"

"Maybe a minute." He cracks his fingers.

"Takes me about the same." Not really, but I'm competitive, okay? "So if we go and talk to our landlord maybe we've got a shot at it."

"Didn't you say he was a Caprice, and you think he killed his underling?"

"I did. But I have the perfect excuse to go down and see him. You."

"Uh, what?" Scott scratches behind one ear.

"I'm going to ask him for a spare key. He'll ask why. I'll introduce you. Chat with him about our fake Emo band or something. I'll sniff around literally. After that, I deal with any deposit or information he needs while you have a go."

"Tino, this is the craziest thing I've ever heard. And I get werewolfery lessons on the regular." Heh. He said, "werewolfery."

"Hey, what could possibly go wrong?" I smile, fangs and all. It's kind of a relief to be able to let it all vamp out.

"At least let's finish setting this place up." We both glance at the clock and see that it's still pretty early.

"That's cool by me."

We're not masters of Feng Shui by any stretch of the imagination, but we manage. There are two small desks, several extremely mismatched chairs, a rug, two clamp lamps, and a busted click-clack futon.

We tuck the futon in one corner and set the screen up to block that off from the rest of the room. I tell Scott I plan on foiling over the back of that screen to make it into as sun-proof a shield as possible. After that, we set up the desks in a clear line of sight to the door. One lamp clips on to the side of each. Scott's drum set and guitar are in the corner by the window, opposite the screen and futon. Since the drums have a stool that came with them, we put the two dented folding chairs near the guitar.

I grudgingly give Scott the bigger of the two office chairs we scored. He's taller and stockier than I am already, and he's only going to get bigger. For the prospective client's seating, we're left with a barstool and a hot pink saucer chair.

"Dibs!" I reach for the stool, reacting fast enough to snatch the more dignified seat before Scott gets his hairy mitts on it. Almost as fast, the stool goes in front of my desk, perfect for anyone who seeks my PI services. "Ha!"

"Whatever." Scott shrugs and sets the ridiculous novelty seat in front of his desk. "Hey, Tino?"

"Hmm?" I'm looking around the room, realizing that while it needs detail work and a measure of refinement, the place is fully functional. No, it's not anatomically correct. It's a freaking studio space, not an android from Star Trek. Get your mind out of the gutter, okay?

"What do you plan on doing about that?" Scott's pointing at the one feature all remodeled old mills share.

He means an abundant natural light source, also known as a giant window, of course. Here Comes the Sun is every vampire's least favorite song. I sigh, feeling my shoulders droop lower than an old man's jockstrap. Don't ask me where that thought came from. Maybe it's your fault, what with conjuring anatomically correct androids to my imagination and all that.

"Curtains, Scott." I gaze up at the property-value-increasing view and give it a glare worthy of Superman's heat vision with zero results. I'm a vampire, not a Kryptonian. What do you want from me?

"Yeah, curtains to prevent it being curtains for you." The teenage werewolf paces the area of wall under the window. "I'll find you something and rig it up tomorrow during the day. If we get that extra key from the landlord, that is."

"Sounds like a plan. And speaking of the key, let's go downstairs and get it already. I'm about done here for the evening if it's all the same to you."

If that comment seems a little bitter and laced with disappointment, it is. Maya never showed. I rethink our last conversation and the bitterness changes to curiosity. If she isn't hanging out with vamps her own age, what does she do on a typical evening? That's a story for another time, probably.

"What do you want to do if we manage to pick up the assassin's scent, Tino?"

"If that happens, we talk about it in the truck on the way back to the Belfry."

"Cool beans." Scott grins. He's almost too laid back. But maybe that's part of how he hides the existence of werewolves. By acting opposite of what people expect from a wolf-man. Or maybe he's a Hufflepuff, I don't know.

We step into the hall, and I lock up 319's bare door. I'll get a sign if and when we slog through the current danger. With the office-studio set and mostly secure, we head downstairs to begin our killer-catching adventure.

# CHAPTER TWELVE

I'm the one who knocks on the door because I'm not sure whether Cigarettes has silver ammo in whatever heat he's packing. I'm certain he's got a gun because I can smell gunpowder, metal, and oil like I did on the rooftop across the street from Dad's house. That smell sucks almost as much as being a vampire. Also on the schnoz menu for scents I don't like is cigarette smoke. So our crime lord landlord is definitely in.

My knuckles hit the door four times. We don't wait long, and when it opens, I remember to grin instead of full-out smile. Last thing I want to do is fang out in front of a mobster. Who in the world would want monsters in the Mafia, anyway? Harebrained idea, if you ask me.

"Whaddaya want?"

"A second set of keys for my bandmate here." Something useful has changed since I got vamped. I'm a halfway-decent liar because I only blush when I'm thinking about it now.

"Huh." His mouth grimaces, but his eyes twinkle and crinkle. "Good on you for coming here instead of wasting time at the hardware store. They know better than to copy the keys to my building."

Cigarettes steps inside, somehow managing not to fully turn his back on us. Scott and I walk in. This room's the same size as ours, but it has more windows. They're covered, and at first I wonder why. But if Cigarettes is used to doing things like killing dudes in here with his bare hands, no wonder he's got curtains to draw.

Scott sits on a loveseat. Smart idea since just about any scent sticks to those. I follow our unlovely host toward an open cabinet where a pegboard hangs on the wall above the counter. His hand hovers over pegs labeled with room numbers. I notice most are empty, but a few have one or two sets of keys hanging from them. He takes the only remaining set from the 319 peg. Under it, I see that the 219 peg still has one set. Esther's working in there alone, then.

"Thanks." I hold out my hand, but it stays empty.

He shakes his head. "I want to hand them to the guy who's gonna use them."

"Makes sense." I back off and let Scott take my place.

The kid's not saying much, but Cigarettes is talking more at him than to him. If we're lucky, maybe he'll say too much. As they chat, I head toward the counter. It's got some papers scattered across it, but the one that catches my eye has been discarded and crumpled on the floor halfway under a trash can.

I boost my speed to pick it up and briefly see a list of familiar names, including Tierney and Solomon. And Crispo, of course. Tierney's the only one with a line through it. Good thing I didn't put my actual name on the rental form after all. That list gets stuffed in my pocket faster than Esther pocketed my money. Now, why's her last name on there? Coincidence? I don't believe in that when it comes to crime investigation.

I glance at the sofa and see the monster's still talking to the mobster. Lame idea in real life, but come to think of it, a book or movie about that subject might be intense. Anyway, I try not to listen to Cigarettes ask Scott about running errands for him and focus on my nose. It's not the easiest thing.

For vampires, living smells are stronger than dead ones. I don't know exactly how it works, but when a person's alive, their scent lingers longer than someone's who died. This happens even when said dead human didn't get killed where I'm catching the scent, like the way it must have gone this time.

Stephanie says it's because we're magical creatures, so we just know if someone we're on the trail of has died. Blood from a dead person doesn't do as much for us as stuff from someone who's still alive, even if it's stored in a bag. Hunting down an already-dead person isn't productive for a vamp, but it works in a weird way, like most supernatural stuff.

Smoke, alcohol, and old blood are all easy to filter out. But Cigarettes is alive, and has so little blood in his nicotine stream I can't help but pick that up. There's also the guy he bumped off my first night here. And yeah, Butter has been killed, all right. His scent is on stuff, though that's more faded, which is exactly right for a dead person.

There are two other living people's scents in here, more feminine. One of those puts me in mind of glowing green stuff and drunken sailor curses. Esther Solomon, who is on the kill list, but Cigarettes lets her suck wind and pay rent. Maybe he doesn't want to get his hands dirty killing a paying tenant. Or maybe she's so cranky because one of her relatives got murdered recently. And then, there's the other woman's scent. It would be intimately familiar to me even if it wasn't all mingled with Anais Anais and rifle oil.

Bingo. That's my sniper. Also known as Kayleigh Killarney, my old high school girlfriend, who'd been responsible for most of my adolescent firsts. Her dad didn't want us dating anymore on account of me being in the Drama Club. He thought I was gay and using her to cover for it. Which I guess seemed like the case at the time even though that's not exactly true. So she broke up with me. We stayed the sort of friends who drift apart the second they walk away from school with diplomas. I don't know where she lives because the Killarneys moved a few years ago. But with both a vampire and a werewolf on the trail, we're going to find her.

"You got your keys, now scram already." Cigarettes is shooing us out of the room.

Scott's got a wild and ferocious gleam in his eye. He shoots me a look like he's asking my permission to attack the murderous mafioso instead of following his instructions. But when I comply with Cigarettes, so does the teen wolf. In the hall, I put one finger over my mouth. Scott gets it and follows me down the hall and out of the building. When we're in his truck with the door closed, I speak.

"I got a couple of leads. Thanks, Scott. Tell me if you recognize any of these names."

Taking the list out of my pocket is tricky to do while sitting in the truck, but I manage. I read the list silently and then out loud. Scott shakes his head at each of them except mine. His eyes widen when I tell him Esther's last name is Solomon. Then, I mention how Tierney is on that list. Larry. He sighs.

"I got one thought on my mind about that list, and you're not going to like it."

"You mean that this is a list of people the Caprices have hired Kayleigh to kill?"

"Yeah." Scott pulls out of the parking lot. "It must suck to know that your ex-girlfriend grew up to be a hitwoman. But on the bright side, I guess you vamps have decent tracking skills."

"I'm going to have to run this list by someone else."

"Esther?"

"No, I want her out of this until I learn more about dealing with magicians. Because that's what I think she is." I make a mental note to call Raven about that after we leave. And I don't care about owing the attaché if it means saving a life. "I'm talking about showing this to Maury. And one of my fangy contacts."

"Okay." Scott nods like a determined kid protagonist in an anime. "You want me to ask Gramps if he knows any of them?"

"That's a good idea. It's a long shot, but if he does know any of them, there might be a juicy gossip bonus round from him about these people."

"You want to go back to the Belfry or your parents' house?" He turns the key in the truck's ignition.

"Belfry."

"Yeah, I get it." He pulls out of the parking lot. "You don't want to mix the vamp family stuff with the human family stuff."

"Pretty much." I lean against the door. "Also, they're still at the hospital."

"It must be hard for you. Not having the natural and supernatural sides all mixed in together, I mean."

"I was just thinking the same thing about you, man." I chuckle. "Or the opposite, or whatever."

Scott lets out an honest to goodness belly laugh. He even slaps the steering wheel. But thankfully, he's a good driver. Or maybe the old rust bucket truck is just that sturdy. It doesn't weave or wobble us out of the lane. I jot a copy of the list on the back of an envelope that once graced the passenger-side floorboard. Writing the name "Tierney" reminds me that even though two of them got killed, the name's only on this list once, so which one was Kayleigh's target? I might not get a chance to ask her, but I could pump Stephanie for more details.

When we get to my place, I remind Scott about the curtains and hand him the copied list. The passenger-side door doesn't shut on the first try. It probably needs some oil on the hinges, but I don't mention that because it also means I need a drink. It shuts on the second try, after I put my hips into it like when you swing a golf club.

Upstairs, there's no sign of Stephanie. I call her while making my mug of blood, but the phone goes straight to voicemail. Staring at the name Solomon on that hit list, I try Raven. That gets me an answer.

"What do you want, Crispo?" They sound more curious than annoyed, thank God.

"Stephanie told me you might have information." I tap the phone to put it on speaker because I forgot to wash my mug.

"She also told you it'd cost you."

"Yeah." I don't say more because some of the blood is caked into the bottom of the mug, and it's a bitch to scrub out.

"That wasn't a question."

"Okay." I keep scrubbing because if I just leave it, the whole fresh cup will be soured.

"So ask, already. I don't have time for you to waste."

Finally, the stupid cup is clean. I shut off the water and reach for a towel to dry it and my hands. After that, I put the cup next to the coffee maker and pick the phone back up. Raven can wait until I'm done. They're old, so maybe a minute feels like a second to them by now.

But where was I in the discussion? I forget, so I just say the first thing that comes to mind. "I was thinking we could negotiate a price."

"Listen well, Crispo. I'm the king's attaché. I don't haggle like a street-market salesperson. Besides, does it make sense for me to name a price before you've asked?"

"No, it doesn't." I close my eyes.

"Because you're new to all this, I won't demand payment for the insult of wasting my time."

"Insult?" My eyes go wide. That's one thing I'm good at, and if Raven thinks this is all I've got, they're absolutely wrong. "Trust me, if I'd meant to insult you, you'd know."

"I'll keep that in mind the next time I'm in the mood to own another vampire."

"Harsh, Raven." It occurs to me that I could make a mint selling tickets to a dis-slinging contest between Esther and Raven, but those two would probably team up to stake-and-ash me right afterward.

"Did you call with a purpose other than this unlovely conversation?"

"Um. Yes." I clear my throat out of nervous habit. "So, I met a woman recently—"

"Congratulations."

"Uh, thanks." My blood's warm, so I pour some into the mug, then sit down with it in the comfy chair. "Anyway, there's something weird about her."

"Maya's a perfectly normal vampire."

I almost drop the phone. Was I that obvious? Do I dare ask Raven what they're on about, assuming I want to go into debt for information about Maya? Maybe I do, but that isn't the reason I called. I take a deep breath and let my thinker work. Raven's trying to get me to ask them for more than I intended so I'll rack up more debt with them later.

"I'm not calling about Maya. It's a mortal neighbor. She's got this odd scent with green light and sparkles around her."

"Hmm." In the background, I hear Raven's fingernail tapping on something. "Are the special effects all around her entire body, or mostly the hands?"

"The hands." I close my eyes, conjuring an image of Esther in my mind's eye. "One time around her head. And she leaves it behind on her stuff sometimes, too."

"I see. If I tell you what I know about this brand of human, you will owe me a set of small favors."

"Okay, that's fine." When it comes to vampire favors, a set is three, and small is stuff like picking up the dry cleaning. A fair price. "Lay it on me."

"It sounds like she uses one of the three forms of human magic. Alchemy, specifically."

"Should I avoid her?" I take a sip of my blood.

"Answering that will cost you another set."

I shake my head. So this is how Raven haggles. "Go on."

"Alchemy isn't about things like calling fire or making the sun shine in the middle of the night. You should be safe around this alchemist, but remember that extended use of this form of magic often comes with severe consequences for the practitioner. They have a way of losing things and inflicting property damage beyond insurance coverage limits. If you become allies or even friends, keep this downside in mind. Alchemists always end up getting hurt one way or another. And never let her work any of her magic directly on you. It's not something vampires ought to get mixed up in. It's got a few nasty side-effects."

"Wow, Raven. You really know tons about magic." I figure a little flattery never hurts.

"I learned the hard way before I got turned." Raven chuckles over the line. It makes no sense until I realize that sound wasn't in the same hemisphere as a laugh. I'd made the king's attaché cry or something like that. Oops.

"Thanks for talking to me about this. I appreciate it."

"Show me your appreciation by actualizing your potential so your debt to me increases in value. And try not to get staked and ashed. Or worse."

"I'll do that." Before I can thank them again, Raven hangs up.

I plug my phone into the charger and head over to my journal. Leaving all that valuable information inside my noggin seems like a bad idea. While I write it down, I wonder where Stephanie is and what she'd make of it.

I try phoning my vampy mom again, but she still doesn't answer, so I send a text saying we need to talk. And there's no way to procrastinate anymore. I've put it off long enough already.

"Time to call Maury." I tap the green button on my phone next to his name. It rings twice before he answers.

"Weintraub." I can hear over the line that he's at home, not the precinct. Good.

"Hello, Maury."

"Tino. You got information for me?"

"I hope so."

So I tell my former bestie about this list I found and all the names on it, but I change the mysterious Tierney to Edwin Tierney specifically. I've got a hunch he'll do everything in his power to take it from me if he thinks his partner was on it. No matter how much he insists, I don't tell him where I got it or how. He wants it for evidence, and I say maybe, partly because I want to check with Stephanie about whether I'd leave evidence of vampires on a piece of paper for CSI to find. But mostly because this is my case, dammit. I saw it first.

"This list is a big deal, Tino. But I can't do much with it or even help you unless it's actually in my possession for me to show to the captain."

"I understand, and I want to give it to you." I wrack my brain for how I can explain without revealing the secret of vampires. Then, I remember my PI business that I just rented office space for. "It's from a case for a client, so I need to wrap that before sending it to you."

"Tino." Maury's sigh has a rattle at the end of it that reminds me he's ill, maybe without knowing it. "While I'm glad you're getting business, you still need to share things like hit lists with me. Otherwise, I can't be your contact on the force."

"Look, I want to present it to the client first." I close my eyes, hating the fact that I'll always have to lie to Maury. "Maybe their reaction will give even more clues that I can share with you."

"That's a good point, Tino."

"Thanks. Now, I called so we could help each other, so what can you tell me about the names on this list?"

"That Edwin Tierney character. He was a lawyer and consultant friend of Larry's, no relation. They found his house burned down just over a month back. All Forensics found was his ashes. Raph had a hard time with the ID, too. And I met him a couple of times." Maury takes a breath that I know comes with a drag on a cigarette.

"Edwin was more straight-laced than most consultants I've met, old-fashioned, too. But oddly open-minded when it came to other people's lives. Like someone who's a fiscal conservative but has a live-and-let-live attitude about social stuff. An odd duck."

"Do you have maybe an example or anecdote you can tell me about him?" I get up to pace because it helps me think. "I never heard of him when I was on the force."

"He seemed like the kind of guy who'd be intolerant, you know, cracking your grandpa's uncomfortable jokes and that kind of thing. But he wasn't like that at all. Ed Tierney kicked a beat cop out of a meeting for making remarks about Jews and ovens even though I wasn't there. And he had a couple of weird people doing research for him, but he didn't treat them like crap for just being who they are."

"Weird people?"

"Yeah. One of them was this huge librarian-looking lady. Ms. Kent. He said she was an archivist or something. And there was the Enby."

"Enby, like in Non-Binary?"

"Exactomundo. Dressed in all black, white hair, some kind of hippy name to do with birds, too."

"Raven." I stop pacing in the kitchen.

"Yeah, that's it. And then, about two months ago, Ed Tierney shows up with the strangest one of all."

I get a weird feeling. It takes me a second to remember what it is. I'm nauseated. My gut intuition, which is enhanced by the instincts vampirism gives me, is in such high gear I can barely move. It's like having the wind knocked out of you while in the throes of illness from norovirus. Don't ask me how I know what that feels like because it's a long and unrelated story with a messy ending. Anyway, I know what Maury's going to say before it comes out of his mouth.

"This guy wore all white, a suit like something out of the Roaring Twenties. I can't remember his name or his face exactly. And you know me, Tino."

"Yeah, you never forget a face." And he doesn't. Remembers names almost as well, too.

"Anyway, I saw that guy twice. That was right before Edwin Tierney's place burned to the ground with him in it."

"That sucks." I'm leaning my forehead against the fridge because it's colder than the wall. Opening it is out of the question. Vampires sicking up is bad news. There are rumors we can end up knocked out for half a century or even die if we puke too much because eventually what comes up isn't food or even blood, but bits of our insides.

"Yeah. I kinda miss the guy." Maury takes another drag on his cigarette. "You would have liked him, Tino."

"I bet." I know for sure that Stephanie did.

"Anyway, I notice that your name's on this list. So you get it over to me as soon as you're done with your client, Tino. Don't make me come to your door with a warrant."

"I won't, Maury." And just like that, the gut feeling's gone. "Thanks, buddy. I owe you one."

"Listen, I'd rather go grab a coffee or a beer than call in a favor."

"We can do that. Maybe in a few days."

"Yeah, sure. Talk to you later, Tino."

I let Maury hang up, then dash over to my notebook again. I jot the words down, then look at them.

*Whitby's behind this. Can his face be forgettable?*

I realize he's put a ton of roadblocks between him and me that I'll have to contend with before I can touch him. I barely know a thing about Whitby except that he's connected to Maya and is double related to Raven. But that's okay. I'm a vampire, and we can wait.

But of course, Whitby's a vamp, too. And way older than me.

I'm so screwed.

# CHAPTER THIRTEEN

I decide to take the makeup off my face, but CVS is closed by now. There's a bottle of olive oil in the salad set Mom gave me as a misinformed housewarming gift. Even though I'm not sure that'll work, at that point, I'm willing to try. I plug my phone in and am about to see if I'm right when the damn thing rings. I tap the green square.

"Hello?"

"Tino, thank goodness it didn't go to voicemail."

"What's up, Scott?" I blink, trying to remember what he'd be calling about.

"Are we going to track Kayleigh or what?"

"Yeah, we're going to. But I had to call my contact first."

"Oh, right." Scott clears his throat. "What did they say?"

I tell him everything I know about alchemists, including that unfriendly neighbor Esther is one. Scott whistles.

"Well, we can avoid dealing with her for now because I passed that list of names to Gramps, and he told me a few things."

"Okay, lay the wisdom of old werewolves on me."

"Only three people on that list got shot. Gramps has either heard of all of them or knows them personally."

"But our Caprice family landlord mentioned something about a silver anniversary's worth of killings under her belt."

"And I'm not saying she didn't kill that many people." Scott sighs. "I mean Gramps says the Irish girl could have lied to the Italian Mafia. Or she could have told the truth. But if she killed twenty-five people, they were folks not on this list. And there have been enough deaths in the supernatural community to account for it lately. Not all suspicious, but that's hard to determine for reasons."

"All of that makes sense, actually." Now that my mind's back on our hitwoman issue, the facts fall into place. "Would the Caprices hand Kayleigh a list of people to bump off if they thought she had no experience?"

"No. And all the more reason to figure out where she is so we can stop her.'

"Exactly."

"So, let's do this."

"Where should we meet?"

Scott laughs. "At her house, of course. Race ya!"

Before I can say we should do this more methodically, he hangs up. Yup, he's got that typical adolescent invincibility mindset. Obnoxious, overzealous teenage werewolf with his childish race. Now I still can't wash my damn face. I'd face-palm, but the greasepaint would just smear.

I grab my opera cloak because it has pockets and hides my frame, and it's not like I'm going to overheat. Then I put my phone in airplane mode and tuck that away in a cloak pocket. Throwing it on over my clothes, I head out the door and get in my car. It's not far to my parents' house in Western Cranston and the lights stay green for me. I even remember to keep to the left at the intersection with the cockamamie right turn only lane.

Once there, I park around the corner to walk down the street and turn my back on the house I grew up in. I'm thanking God that it hasn't rained. Then I look up at the roof where this all began, remembering how everything smelled and sounded the night my dad got shot.

I have to walk between that house and the one to the left of it before picking up a scent. It's faint but there, and I look up at the sky, glad that the New England weather is atypically constant for now. In May, it has the potential to be more unpredictable than a game of whack-a-mole.

Following the trail is pretty easy, making me wonder how Kayleigh could have known to put flash-bang rounds in her holdout pistol and not realize a supernatural opponent could hunt her down with enhanced schnoz powers.

I'm walking through the old neighborhood near Cranston West High School, taking shortcuts I haven't thought about since middle school. It's not a trip down memory lane because there are no lanes, only backyards and cut-throughs.

Kids today don't use these old ways. I refuse to blame that on them, though. As a former law enforcement officer, I know that it's not legal for the parents to let children under thirteen run around without adult supervision. I'm not blaming the lawmakers, either. It's the fault of all those American psychos who snatched kids off the street when my age was in the single digits.

I guess I just might have something in common with some of those sickos myself now. Not in a literal sense, but I can't fight the suspicion that supernatural people have contributed to the missing person caseloads in densely populated areas. As our numbers grow, so do the missing people. No wonder vampires have a rule to limit turning.

With my eyes closed to catch Kayleigh's scent again, I realize I should do my part in preventing that sort of thing in the future. Not the part about Honoring the West in our rulebook. Something new about feeding more carefully, or having more accountability toward protecting humans. Maybe I can pitch it to Raven as a modern method to keep vampires secret. Or even the king. Nah, DeCampo's too scary. That's why Raven's the attaché.

I find the rifle-oil-laced floral-scented thread again on the ground and in the shrubs. Following it isn't as hard as trying to imagine how Kayleigh, who'd been the sort of girl to insist on free-trade organic everything and went vegetarian at age fifteen, became an assassin. Something must have happened that I don't know about.

Eventually, the trail lets out in a cul-de-sac south of Cranston West High School, not far from Meshanticut Lake and its surrounding park. I know which house is hers the second I lay eyes on it. This is not because of some identifying factor on the building or by way of recognizing a car in the driveway. Scott's already outside it, and I smell him sitting in the bushes. Dammit. The little varmint beat me here. He had a head start, remember.

Sneaking over there is easy enough. The black cloth on the outside of my cloak is useful for hiding in the darkness. If I plan on making this sort of activity a habit, maybe I'll ask Shadow how he does his vanishing trick. The dude's practically invisible half the time. But that'd probably get me into serious levels of debt with him, so I forget the idea.

"Shh." Scott's heard or smelled me coming. Possibly both. Of course.

I nod. We're looking straight into the back of the house through one of those bay windows half the houses in this neighborhood have. Kayleigh is sitting at the dining room table with her dad. They're cleaning a small arsenal's worth of guns, but it's the ammo that catches my attention. Boxes of different rounds sit on the table in the window, close enough for my sense of smell to take an inventory.

Wood-tipped, silver, dragons' breath, rock salt, and even some with inscriptions sit ready to load into clips, barrels, or magazines, depending on the firearm in question. On the other side of the table are the ever-popular flash-bang grenades, more with salt, and others that smell like they've got garlic in them. One box of round glass bottles is stamped with a crucifix. A rancid smell comes off those bottles, like rotten eggs. I realize it's Holy Water. A second set of glass containers is clearly labeled Silver Nitrate. Nasty stuff to use against werewolves.

"They're not playing around." I realize I'm not the only one who's considered the role of supernaturals in human disappearances. And they've prepared more to deal with it than I have, to boot.

"The Killarneys are monster hunters, Tino." Scott's got to be the world champion of stating the obvious.

I don't have a comeback for something like that. Instead of arguing, I watch Kayleigh pick a paper up and check over it. When she turns, I see it's a copy of the list from the Caprice office in my new building. So the Caprice Family Mafia did hire her after all.

"Crap on a crap cracker." I put my hand over my mouth.

Mr. Killarney glances up and out the window. Over our heads, thank God, but something about his gaze bothers me. It's almost like he knows something lurks out in his yard without using his hearing or eyesight. Which would be Scott and me, of course. I wonder whether he's another type of magician or a psychic. If a guy is a monster hunter and gets to be Kayleigh's dad's age, he's got to have an edge, right?

It's about time we get ourselves out of there. The last thing I want is to get caught lurking outside my ex's window. That was bad enough the couple-few times it happened when I was Scott's age. And I'm not sure whether the embarrassment or the potential to get slain by a hunter is going to be worse.

I elbow Scott to catch his eye, then gesture away from the house. We head out, and I lead him back the way I came. When we get back to my little car, I open the doors so we can sit and talk about all of this.

"So obviously we can't just ambush Kayleigh in her own house." I wave one hand at the armory disguised as a suburban single-family home.

"Yup." He fiddles with the radio until he finds Thunder by Imagine Dragons. Ugh. I don't want to imagine any giant scaly fire-breathers at this juncture. The prospect of psychics, magicians, and hunters is bad enough.

"We'll have to keep eyes on her somehow and then get her alone." I tap my palms against the steering wheel.

"Since she's not nocturnal, I'll have to do it." Scott side-eyes me. "Unless you can think of another way."

"Maybe, but I have to make some calls." I lean back against my seat and close my eyes. Lately, it feels like I'm always on the phone. I'm sick of peopling already. Haven't these older vampires learned how to text yet? I'll bet the hunters do it. Which brings my thoughts back around to Kayleigh's out-of-character killing spree. "Do you think all the people she killed were vampires and werewolves?"

"Probably." Scott's voice is low, sad. It's time to get his perspective on this change in our old friend. "Considering what Gramps said."

"I wonder why, though. I mean, you remember Kayleigh from when she dated me and lived down the street, right?"

"Yeah. She wouldn't have hurt a fly back then. I'll talk to Gramps again, see what he knows about the Killarneys."

"Ditto for my contacts, kid."

Scott's phone rings.

"Dude, you didn't turn that off while outside the monster hunter house!?"

"Sorry." He shrugs with one shoulder. "Thought it was a regular-person house before we got there."

"You could have gotten us killed." I'm about to read him the riot act about how having no sidekick is better than tolerating a shitty one, but the phone keeps on ringing. I take mine out and turn off airplane mode. Sure enough, there's a text and a voice mail from my mom.

Scott holds up one hand and answers the phone with the other. "Hello, Mrs. Crispo. No, you didn't wake me. I go for a run every morning at five, and was already up getting ready."

My own phone rings. It's Maya. I answer and try explaining that I'm busy. She goes quiet, though, and I realize she's able to listen in on Scott's conversation. I'm about to hang up but realize I don't mind, even if she's in Whitby's crew and he just might be the big bad in all this.

After setting my phone in the cupholder, I listen to Mom on the other end of the line, excitedly explaining that Dad's been cleared to go home. Today. At high noon. Scott explains that I'm on a case and will be pounding the pavement covertly all day.

"How do I know?" Scott glances at me. "Well, Tino asked me to help him with his new PI business. Answering email and phones, that kind of thing, because it's hard to do that while he's in the field investigating. Yeah, he's paying me." Scott smiles. "My dad's got the day off from work, though. I'll ask if he can help you two get settled back in. You're welcome, Mrs. Crispo. I'll see you later." He hangs up.

"For Christ's sake." I reach across Scott and push the passenger-side door open. "Get out, Boy Scout. I've got to go home. Four-thirty's too early for me to stay out. It's not sun-proof at Mom and Dad's."

Scott exits the vehicle. I tell him I'll send a text when I get to the Belfry. I would have thanked him for the excellent cover story because it more than makes up for him spacing on silencing his phone, but he told my mom I'd pay him, so I have to. With funds I'm running short on after paying two rents. And only fictional cases.

"Shitballs," I say as I manage not to leave tread marks on the street. Don't blame me, it's the sun's fault. I've got to race it home now. What do you want from me? At least my car is fast.

"Tino? Are you still there?"

"Um..." I almost hang up again but can't stomach doing that. I click the button to put her on speaker. "Yeah, I'm here, Maya."

"Are you okay?"

"Yeah, just trying to make it back to my place before sunrise. What's up?"

"Just that I heard you discussed magic with Raven."

"Yeah, I bet they're bragging about all the favors I owe them."

"No, actually. I just happened to be there at the time. Raven's keeping your chat under wraps for now, and I got paid a set of small favors to keep quiet about it, too."

"Huh, that's interesting."

"Yeah. They said I can only talk to you about it."

I wonder what Maya means when she says "they." Is it Raven's preferred pronoun, or was someone else in on the favor-granting? There's no time to ask.

"And you want to discuss magic this close to sunup?" I pull into my building's parking lot. A glance at the sky tells me I made it with just enough time to get inside.

"No. I just called to tell you about that favor. Thought you'd want to know about the super-formal tactics they're using to handle this. I can't tell anyone else. Not any of the people I traveled to Providence with. You get what I mean."

"Wow, Maya. Thanks." I throw the car in park, wondering where a nice girl like Maya learned Mafia-speak. "What do I owe you?"

"Nothing. I just like having you around is all." Wow. Maya's not ominous at all. That was sarcasm, by the way. "Anyway, I've got to go. Listen, if you need any help with your dad, let me know. I've got the feeling things are going to get hairy for you in the near future."

"What are you, psychic?" I unlock the downstairs exterior door.

"Yes, actually. And that's one of the reasons I got turned. I'll talk to you later, Tino."

She hangs up, leaving me with a lot to think about on my way up the stairs and back into my apartment. The attaché wants the subject of magic off the social topics table, possibly with the king's agreement, or even on his orders. But why? I think about Raven's chilly staring contest with Whitby. I remember that they look more than a bit alike in the facial features department and my theory that they're mortally related. Wait. My memory's on the fritz. They're siblings but different as night and day from what I've seen so far. But that's something to investigate after the immediate threat to the people on that list is squashed.

Maya's part of Whitby's entourage, and though she seems generally contented with her vampirism, she's clearly seeking other company. Why else would she hang around the king's building with Raven and the Enforcers? Why else would she keep calling me? The former could be explained by assuming she's a spy, but I've never been much of a hit with the ladies, so both of those points together don't make sense for spy behavior. She hinted at being psychic, so maybe she's seen that I'm mostly harmless.

But if Maya's psychic, maybe the Killarneys are, too. Mr. Killarney probably is. There's yet another thing for the new guy to learn about. But I doubt I'll manage to study up on that before I have to face one or both of the hunters in combat. With weapons specially designed to ash me and perma-kill Scott.

"Oh, Madonn. What have I gotten myself into?"

After hanging up my cloak, I stand in the bathroom, staring at the greasepaint that's all I can see of my face. It's been smudged now, probably from leaves on my way through the old neighborhood trails. The bottle of oil is there on the corner of the sink, and I finally have time.

For the record, olive oil can clean greasepaint off faces. I get a washcloth and go to town, removing it all. After that, I scrub my skin with plain old soap for good measure. It's what I used to do after my high school plays, and it feels just as good now as it did back then.

Once my face is clean, I take my stuff out of the opera cloak. Next time I put it on, I'll be fully suited up. I go into the closet with more of my old police stuff. There's a Kevlar vest in there, so I hang it with the frilly shirt. I'm not sure whether it'll stop dragons' breath rounds, but the first couple of wood-tips might shatter on it instead of staking me. There's a spare, but it's too small for Scott. I send him a text, advising that he should take a spin by Surplus Provisions over on Pontiac Ave for some gear. He texts back with a dog face. Right. I forgot he can't wolf out in tac gear.

I plug my phone in, shower, put on pajamas, get in bed, and draw the curtains. Once there, I jot the new stuff down in my composition book. Exhaustion catches up with me, and I fall asleep right in the middle of a sentence.

## CHAPTER FOURTEEN

My phone's beeping like crazy. At first, I think it's ringing, but I discover that there are just so many texts the chime sounds like a ring. When I check, I see that it's a series of messages from Mom and pictures from Old Man Fitzpatrick. Apparently the old werewolf thinks I want a photo documentary of Dad's arrival home from a nosy-neighbor's-eye-view. It's about three in the afternoon, which is equivalent to the middle of the night for a vampire. I yawn and roll over, prepared to go back to sleep.

Someone knocks on the door.

I sit up and stare at the spot on the curtain that the door is on the other side of. I don't bother wishing it were see-through. If someone does open the door, the sun won't fry me with these curtains. I hear a scratchy noise against the wood. It's creeping me out because I've got no idea what it is. And then, there are voices in the hall.

"Oh, no, don't leave a slip." It's a woman's voice, bubbly, and with a cheesy fake Valley Girl accent. I don't recognize it. "I'll bring it in with me."

"But you don't look like a Valentino." This voice is male. "I can't leave a package with anyone but the resident."

"Like, I'm practically one." A manic little giggle ripples through the air. "This is, like, my boyfriend's apartment, you know?"

Now I'm almost freaking out. I don't have a girlfriend, and if I did, she wouldn't sound like that. Or be hanging around outside the door in broad daylight, either. Whoever's in the hall wants to steal a package from me, and I can only think of one thing I've ordered off Amazon Prime. It's my new greasepaint set, which I need for tonight. I get out of bed and head to the door, standing on the side, so it shields me from the hall window sunlight when I open it. I unlock it and turn the knob, standing in a patch of shadow cast by the slab of wood that's the only thing between me and sunlit doom. Now that I'm by the door, I smell who the mystery girl is.

"Come on in, Esther." I stay perfectly still, waiting as she walks across the threshold so I can close the door behind her. She's got my package under her left arm. We stare at each other, waiting for the UPS man's footsteps to get all the way down the stairs before speaking. I'm about to welcome her to the Belfry and ask what I can do for her. I might be a blood-drinking monster, but Mom, Dad, and Mr. Rogers taught me to be a good neighbor. Esther speaks first.

"Hey, asshole, you broke into my crappy frigging place." She brandishes her right fist, her leather-clad forearm reminding me of armor. I guess I'm not the only person who goes around dressed too warmly for May weather.

I shake off my empathy. I'm fed up at this point. Esther wakes me up in the middle of the day, nearly turns me into a crispy critter, and almost walks off with gear essential to protecting my identity. The alchemist has just made my shit list, and I want her to know it. I narrow my eyes, hoping I can tell her off harshly enough to make her run away in tears. Or at least leave my apartment without making any trouble or asking too many questions.

"Back at you, bitch." Impostor syndrome clubs me upside the head. I'm no drunken sailor. Gosh darn it. I can't match the level of cussing Esther is accustomed to. Some fake boyfriend I am.

"I'm only here because I tracked you from my studio." She steps forward, getting in my face. "Where you stepped on my seal and fucked up my spell, you undead toilet-circler."

"Look, I'm sorry. I put it back the way I found it." I blink and step back. "Wait. Undead?"

"You made my fucking squared circle worse, shit-for-brains." She takes another step. "Badass alchemists like me can sense vag-pire perma-death and your fleabag fuckboy's distemper like flies smell shit."

"So you know I'm a vampire?" My back's against the counter by this point.

I don't know if Esther's going to kill me or kiss me. Either possibility absolutely terrifies me. It takes everything I have not to flinch. I put my butt on one of the stools at the counter and yawn because daytime makes me zonky. She rolls her eyes, puts the package next to me, and then her hands on her hips. Her left shoulder is a little crooked, sitting lower than the right.

"Why in the name of Lazarus's ever-living anus do you think I came here in the fucking middle of the day, dumbass?"

"I don't know jack shit about magic." My brain flails for a witty comeback, but her talent for cussing is downright biblical, and I'm exhausted. "Dammit, Esther, I'm a vampire, not an alchemist."

"Damn straight." She sits on the stool beside me. "You fucked my spell worse than an industrial sander up the ass, but vampires are creatures of their word. I expect you to fucking pay up."

"And I will." I lean my elbows on the counter. "But I've got a couple of psychic hunters trying to kill me and my perfectly normal human dad at the moment. Once I handle that, I'll make up for being a clumsy asshat, okay?"

"Hunters?" She raises an eyebrow, lowering her voice in both pitch and volume. It's scarier than the Killarneys' weaponized dining room table. "I. Fucking. Hate. Hunters."

"Yeah. They're armed for overkill, too." I'm not going to say that her name's on a hit list. She's scary, what do you want from me?

"Fine. You can pay off maybe a tenth of a percent of your debt to me by telling me about them."

I oblige, mostly because it's a relief to have Esther's anger facing away from me and toward the enemies. Maybe it's a side-effect of her magic, but Esther's emotion emanates from her like heat off fresh blacktop in the summer. I'm willing to bet Tolkien knew an actual magician from the way he wrote about Gandalf, Saruman, and the rest.

"Listen, I'm gonna let you finish this beef with the hunters." Esther cracks a grin. "I'll fucking brew up a few things that might help you kick their asses. It'll fucking cost you, but not an arm and a leg."

I decide to just take Esther at her word. She seems to know what she's doing even if her execution seems unstable. Maybe all the cussing is a weird form of punctuation. Who knows?

"The entire city of Providence is going to own a piece of me at this rate." I head toward the kitchen to heat up a bag of blood since sleep isn't going to happen. Then I look over my shoulder at her before opening the fridge. "I owe someone pretty high up."

"I don't give a rat's ass." Esther's grin turns into a full-on smile. It's almost as scary as contemplating direct sunlight. "I want the fucking hunters out of the damn picture. They don't like magicians any more than bloodsuckers. And I don't want to risk my fucking investment by letting the assholes kill you. I fucking know how the hell vampire debt works. If one of your dead-alive butt buddies stakes your ass, they fucking pay your debts."

"Well, I was going to make a plan to confront the hunters but can't without knowing what kind of support you're supplying here." I smell the AB+ to make sure the donor hasn't died before dumping it into the carafe.

"Tell the Amazing Dog Boy to get his ass over here and we'll talk about it. I can do a fucking location spell if you've got any of their shit lying around."

When I call Scott, I put the phone on speaker and tell him an Esther-friendly version of the situation. When we hang up, I think about whether I've got anything that belonged to my ex. I do. It's one of Kayleigh's old love notes from High School. Admitting I kept that would be embarrassing, but it's not easy to feel too bashful around an alchemist with a bad case of potty-mouth and an attitude.

I sit around reading The Scarlet Pimpernel and drinking blood while Esther draws a chalk circle on the floor of my closet. She's using symbols straight out of an astrology chart and geometric shapes like I've seen in Masonic Lodges. It's some kind of prep for the location spell she'll do when we're ready to leave. After that, she ransacks my kitchen.

Scott gets to my place about an hour later, after he's done helping with Dad. He's also picked up a list of ingredients Esther asked him to grab on the way over. We've got just over three hours before sundown to prepare our supplies and strategy. I'm not sure we'll come up with much until Esther goes to work literal magic in my kitchen.

"I don't get why Stephanie wanted me to read this book so badly."

"Why? What's the fucking book about?" Esther sprinkles some yellow powder into a simmering pot. It smells like rotten eggs.

"Basically, there's this vigilante who helps refugees escape from Revolutionary France. Somehow, the dude keeps people from knowing his secret identity for thirty-one chapters by acting like a fool." I snort. "Can't believe anyone would fall for something like that."

Esther turns around and stares at me. I hold both hands up and shake my head. She points at the book. I show her the cover so she can see the title. She rolls her eyes, but in the smiley way that I'm starting to realize means she thinks something's funny.

"What is it?"

"Whoever the hell gave you that homework assignment is a goddamn fucking genius."

"Huh?" I scratch my head.

"Because you fucking come across as a harmless shitbrain, you idiot." Esther turns back to her work, stirring the concoction that's got to be ruining my only saucepan. Not that I'll use it at any point in the near or distant future. Her tone tells me she's not angry despite the cussing. The casual f-bombs and nonchalant insults are her version of normal conversation.

Whatever. For all I know, it's a way to prevent casting spells by accident. Maybe all magicians talk like this. I can accept a non-binary vampire Attaché, so I can handle an alchemist whose vocabulary would shame sailors worldwide without a problem. At least I hope so.

"I do kind of see Esther's point, Tino." Scott yawns and stretches, refreshed after his wolf-nap on my bed. I hope the stench doesn't linger, even if I'm slowly getting used to it. I can't tell him the bed's off-limits, or I'll sound like I'm anti-werewolf. Jeez. Wait a minute. Did he just insult me?

"Um, you agree with her?"

"Well, yeah." Scott stands up and shuffles off toward the bathroom. "You're less Broadchurch and more Brooklyn 99. At least you were while you worked at Cranston PD."

"Holy shit. You were a pig? Shoulda fucking known." Esther chuckles.

"Uh, thanks?" I set the book down and get up. "I guess I should go put my game face on."

The box with the greasepaints is on the counter. I wrestle with the tape until Scott ambles over and slices through it with a fingernail. Showoff. Newbie vampires can't pop out object-shearing appendages like King DeCampo, but apparently two-year werewolves can. Just one more thing that sucks about being a bloodsucker.

I'm in the bathroom, thinking about how ironic it feels to put on exactly the same makeup I'd been so desperate to take off just the night before. Maybe I could make a full mask someday, one that won't itch or smudge while sneaking or fall off if I get punched in the face. But masks have their own issues, including limited peripheral vision and removal by enemies, so I just apply the damn greasepaint, already.

Back out in the kitchen, I find Esther barking vulgarity-embellished orders at Scott. He's holding a small bottle while she steadies her hands to pour some of the saucepan concoction into it. I interrupt even though Esther's clearly in a fouler mood because her hands are shaking. One breath through my nose tells me why.

"Wait a minute, guys." I point at the saucepan. "Put that down. There's a funnel in the cupboard under the sink. Something to take the edge off for Esther, too."

"Edge?" Of course, Scott doesn't get it. He's not the type of teenager to get hammered at a house party.

"Fangy fuckboy to the rescue!" Esther sets the pot on the stove and opens the cabinet.

The alchemist goes straight for the jug of rum I haven't touched in over a month. Vampires can't get drunk because fuck you, that's why. Um, Esther's vocabulary seems to be contagious. Excuse me.

As I was saying, we only get intoxicated if a person we drink from is three sheets to the wind. That's risky for both, so only the most hardcore alcoholic vamps try it, and they leave a trail of bodies outside bars whenever they go on a bender. According to one of Raven's most popular officially unofficial rumors, the king has alky vamps put down before that happens.

With the funnel, the alchemist and the werewolf manage to fill two dozen bottles. Esther corks them, then melts wax to seal them all. I fill up on blood while Scott just lounges around. Must be awesome to have all your supernatural powers at your fingertips instead of needing to consume the blood of the living in order to function at a more-than-human level.

The sun's still a hair too far over the horizon for me to risk going outside, so Scott loads everything we need into the truck. After he's done, Esther fires up the locator circle in my closet without getting chalk or anything else on my stuff. I thank God that she's not a giant klutz. The spell involves dangling a crystal on a string over the art project. More of the glittery green stuff surrounds her hands. Scott sneezes three times, and then Esther says it's done.

We get downstairs, where we decide on travel arrangements. Yeah, Rhode Island's a small place, but you kind of need a car everywhere except the downtown areas of Providence and Newport. I want to go with Scott while Esther takes her car by herself, but we have stuff that has to ride up front with him, and I won't fit. I steel myself, mentally preparing for a thankfully short ride with an abrasive person.

Esther hangs the crystal on the rearview as I expected. But when she turns over the ignition, the stereo's on. Cranked to eleven or whatever. And emanating from her speakers are the bass beats and tinny lyrics of a musical act from the 1990s. Aqua. You remember them, right? They're the people who gave the world *Barbie Girl.* Genius, I know. A truly astute contribution to humanity's musical repertoire. You can't see me, so you don't know my eyes are rolling like dice on the craps tables down at Foxwoods Casino.

I listen to bubbly pop songs the entire way to Western Cranston. Esther makes no apology or even a sign that she cares what I think of her musical tastes. I'm so stunned by this unexpected facet of her personality that I'm speechless all fifteen minutes in the car. I'm stunned enough to forget that she shouldn't have been driving after drinking half a fifth of rum.

Maybe alchemists have a hard time getting drunk, too. Or she's a functional alcoholic. I don't have time to ask because we're there already. Esther pulls into a spot at Meshanticut Lake Park, and Scott takes one a handful of spaces down. We get out and go over to the truck. Scott hoists the duffel from the front seat on his back. I get a hip bag full of potions.

"No need to pull any pins, just throw. But make sure you're clear when you do." Esther buckles on two bags of her own. One jingles, and the other rustles. She pulls a watch on a chain out of her front pocket and checks it, then pushes a button.

Before I can ask her why, she holds up the string with its crystal. She glanced at it the whole time while driving over here, but I couldn't figure out what she was looking at. I still can't. But it's telling her something only a magician can see apparently because she walks with it wrapped around her hand. It's like she's following its lead or something.

She turns down one of the trails I took last night. We're getting close to the hunter's house, and Scott taps me on the shoulder. I don't want to grab or tap Esther. Like I said, she's more than a little bit scary in the volatility department. Raven says she can't summon fire at the drop of a hat, but I don't want to take any chances.

That's why I push through the bushes to the right of the deer trail we're on. I hold up one hand where Esther can see it and pull a leaf out of my hair with the other. She stops, puts one hand on her hip and shrugs.

"This leads to the hunter house. If she's in there, we're outgunned."

"Of fucking course." Esther jerks her chin at the path ahead.

"It's still early. Probably why they're still home."

"We should get a little closer." Scott gets ahead through the same shrubs I did. Not a leaf on him, of course. He winks. "Let's silence our phones."

We do that and then continue.

Esther stops us farther back from the spot we hid in the night before.

We wait.

# CHAPTER FIFTEEN

When Esther's crystal moves, so do we. But the first thing we see is Kayleigh Killarney emerge from her house. She doesn't get into her car. I wonder if maybe she's out on mundane business at first. She's wearing a long jacket and carrying a small case that almost looks like a handbag, but the scent coming off her is metallic and deadly like the stuff on the table last night. She's planning something, then.

We follow through backyards. From her posture, I can tell that Kayleigh walks with purpose. I hear her heartbeat, too. It's faster than usual but not by much. Wherever she's going, trouble's a possibility but not an absolute expectation. She stops at a double-decker, takes a deep breath, and heads up the front stoop.

The cuss words exiting Esther's mouth as Kayleigh picks the lock and goes inside rush out as fast and evil as demons through the gates of hell. The alchemist's teeth grind, and I sense when she's about to leap out from behind the trash can enclosure. Burning blood to outrun her, I grab her under the shoulders and hold Esther back. Her left arm feels funny, but I forget about that in a hurry.

"That cunt! That's my fucking apartment. I'll tear her tits off and shove them so far up her ass they come out of her felching mouth!"

"Holy. Shit." Scott's jaw might as well be on the lid of the trash can. His eyes look like the moon phase that supposedly makes him wolf out.

I hiss. Scott growls. But neither of us can stop Esther's tirade. That's a huge big deal because vampires are pretty scary, and werewolves are exponentially worse. All we can do is weather it. She's swearing even more hardcore than her initial reaction, but the words are garbled and high-pitched enough to be cats rutting. Or bears. I'm not sure which. And I can hardly blame her.

Sometimes you've got to lose your shit, or you end up full of the stuff. I was due for that myself, all things considered. If it were my apartment, there'd have been a Category 5 shitstorm named Hurricane Tino. I'd have rushed in already and gotten ashed. Neither Scott nor Esther are fast enough to stop me. Moving quickly is my one advantage. My wits are pretty speedy too, so I get an idea.

"Well, she's not at her house, surrounded by weapons. Let's kick Kayleigh Killarney out of Esther's apartment."

I unleash the alchemist. The hound follows. I bring up the rear on purpose so I can replace the blood I used stopping Esther. This bag of AB smells wrong, but I drink it, anyway. Whoever donated it is really most sincerely dead. I don't care because I'm just topping off. Down the hatch it goes. I tuck the empty sack of plastic back in my coat. What? I'm a vampire, not a litterbug.

Esther's place is the whole first floor. When I get to the door, everyone's inside, Mexican Standoff-style. Kayleigh's got pistols with silencers on the ends, pointed at Scott and Esther. My nose tells me they're loaded with silver. Awesome. For me, anyway. No wood.

I have a plan. I hoist the hip bag up to my Kevlar-enrobed chest and take a breath I don't need. But Kayleigh's a slow, still a live person. How slow? I don't know, but I can't stand there waiting. I'm dressed for bullets. I burn blood and run for it.

By it, I mean straight at my ex-girlfriend. She turns the pistols on me. I smile. She squeezes the trigger. Scott takes Esther to the floor behind me. Glass shatters before my ribs. Even with the Kevlar, that fucking hurts. My smile turns upside-down.

The stench is magically undelicious.

Kayleigh drops her weapons and clutches her stomach one-handed. The other goes on her mouth. One pinkie lifts like she's drinking tea. Elegant. Instead of acting high-brow, she pitches a hurl. I stand and wince, reaching to subdue her. Flashback to Homecoming. She sicked up Dad's stolen limoncello exactly like this.

"What the fuck?" Esther's yelling from the far doorway. Her voice is muffled.

I turn my head. My friends are standing in the kitchen. They have dishcloths over their mouths. Kayleigh doesn't. They aren't puking. Kayleigh is. I'm with her. Oh, shit.

Retching hurts almost as much as the bullets. I can't stop it this time. I barf in misery and company. The world is pain, radiating from my brightly burning busted ribs down to a dull ache in my gut where dead muscles spasm. Ma would still say it hurt less than childbirth. The last dregs of that AB come up, and that's when it happens. My Gift reveals itself.

Vampires get a set of talents in common. Speed, strength, frowning at bullets instead of screaming and bleeding. With time and training, we learn stuff like invisibility. We get better senses than anything but werewolves, too, and then there are the freaky Gifts. These are individual and obscure skills. Nobody can predict what they'll be until they happen.

And what's happening now is that I'm getting visions from dead blood. When I puke it up. Awesome with a side of suck sauce. Shh, I'm trying to watch the movie in my mind.

It's the office at the Broad Street studio, and my perspective is from the floor. Cigarettes is tamping one out that's almost down to the butt. After that, he kicks out with one foot, and I'm rolling. Scratchy woolen fabric plagues my skin like a poison ivy rash.

"Just want you to know, it ain't personal." Cigarette's voice is raspy as ever. "Like the poet says, nobody beats a rug. It's the dust inside they want."

"The Boss will kill you for this. He's got ways to make it look like misadventure."

"Just so happens there's someone more important to me than him. Them's the breaks."

Cigarettes lays down another rug, then rolls me again. After that I can't talk because there's something cottony in my mouth. And then I can't see. The rug gets beaten. And that's why I didn't smell blood. I spill something about the fishes getting revenge for everyone we dump on them. After that, the mind I'm goes empty and everything fades in a fog.

And I'm back to myself. Sort of. I'm still spewing but aware that it's chunks of ash now. I try to stop but can't. It's from Esther's potion, which is everywhere, but mostly all over Kayleigh and me. I can't stand, so I crawl toward the kitchen.

"Jesus, Mary, and Joseph—" Esther slaps her hand over Scott's dishtowel-covered mouth before he can say my name.

I can't speak, so I hurl again. The potion's on my clothes. Esther grabs the sprayer in the sink and hoses me down, washing away the nauseating stuff. I feel like a wet Vampire Retriever. Maybe I look like one too, I don't know. But the improv shower works. I stop puking.

Before I get up, I chug all the blood bags in my opera cloak as fast as I can. I burn most of it to heal the sections of gut I lost in the unintentional purge. Esther's magic watch beeps, the signal that the puke bombs have worn off. We get back into the living room to find Kayleigh and her guns gone, but I can smell her in another room. So can Scott.

"Wood this time." Scott taps his nose, then unzips the duffel. He can tell what the ammo is through walls. I try to be grateful instead of jealous. I fail because I suck at beating down envy and let him go first. Taking turns at being inhuman shields was part of our plan, anyway, but the plexiglass riot shield he's now carrying doesn't hurt.

Down the hall are a bedroom and a bathroom. I already know Kayleigh's in the bedroom, so I point. I hear a rustle of paper behind me as Esther takes something yellow from a pouch. She slaps it on the wall. It's a sticky note with her wonky alchemic writing all over it. That script is almost like the Post-it I found on my car, but spidery instead of fat-handed.

And I watch the wall dissolve. I shit you not. It's almost like watching lights come up on the opaque side of one-way glass, except completely different. A cop in interrogation knows that'll happen. Kayleigh isn't expecting this.

She's reaching for the shelf over Esther's bed, a row of trinkets and keepsakes. Her eyes go wide like the time we rescued a flipped-over turtle that turned out to be dead. I open my mouth to ask her why. Why murder? Not every kid has to go into the family business.

But Esther dashes through the hole in the wall. She hip-checks Kayleigh, knocking her off-balance so she can't draw her pistols. It's like her right leg weighs more than it should. And then alchemist reaches for the last thing I'd have expected—a creepy little blonde doll. It's got that glittery green glow around it, too, like Esther's hands when she does magic.

Kayleigh regains her footing and uses it to aim a kick at Esther's head. I'm blocked by Scott, who charges through the door. Except I don't know it's him at first because he's got a wolfy head and hairy paw-hands like Michael J. Fox in Teen Wolf. I can see them through the riot shield.

"That's why!" Kayleigh aims at Scott and lets silenced bullets fly, toasting the shield. She glances down at her pistols, nose wrinkled. She drops them and pulls two more from a line of holsters under her coat. It's like something out of *Boondock Saints,* a movie Kayleigh couldn't watch without covering her eyes.

That was then, this is now.

I know she'll shoot silver this time. I get in the way again, even though I'm fresh out of Kevlar and blood.

"Why, Kayleigh?"

The bullets hit me. One, two, three. Punctures punctuate syllables. I hiss. Her eyes narrow. Lines at their corners draw me closer. She draws another set of guns. I step, grab, and throw, a move from my days at the Academy.

She's a brick, falling slowly. Her back hits a dust- and marble-topped antique vanity table, mirror included. Bullets chew through the wall over Scott's head. Reflective shards fly, silver-backed, bad luck city. I open the opera cape and they patter against it, then tinkle on the hardwood. Scott growls behind me. I raise my hand and kneel beside Kayleigh.

Her legs aren't moving, but her forehead's got that crease. You know the one. No, you do. It's the line between the eyes, the one that says, "I'm doing the thing." But this time, it's saying, "Why won't the thing work?" Kayleigh's gaze turns up, cutting through mine. It could cut diamonds, it's so sharp.

"Fuck you, Valentino."

"So much for my disguise." I shrug with one shoulder.

"You better not have broken my back." Kayleigh shuts her eyes. When they open, tears stand at the corners like guards. I don't know how she's managing to talk because she's got to be in ten worlds of hurt.

"I'm sorry. Didn't want to. Couldn't let you shoot my friends."

"You're monsters."

She's right, we are. But she's also wrong because I'm learning that being a monster is less about your physical details and more about how you decide to use them.

"I know. But we're still, well, ourselves, so I hope you'll tell me why. Why shoot us? Why shoot my dad? And Maury's partner?"

She blinks. Her tears shimmer, threatening to fall and unleash an army of their fellows, but she holds them back somehow.

"I never killed Larry; he's human. I did the other Tierney, though. And you were my target, not your dad. Why can't I move my legs, Tino?"

"I'm sure it's only temporary." I'm not, but I have a crazy idea as usual. I know nothing about the long-term consequences. I hesitate.

"Bullshit."

"No, really. I think you'll be okay, Kayleigh, if we can figure this out. But you're getting into stuff, setting yourself against people you can't possibly take on alone."

"So the vampire ex-boyfriend is doing all this for the girl's own good? What is this, a *Twilight* movie?"

"You can't fucking reason with shit-for-brains hunters." Esther's pointing a finger at Kayleigh. Her other hand holds a glowing green Post-it. I already know what those do. "Get out of the way, bloodmunch."

"No."

"Come on, only good hunter's a dead one."

"You can't kill her."

"She broke in here and tried to trash my place." Esther has got to know she's done more to break stuff in here than Kayleigh. What was it that Raven said about property damage and alchemy? But it's her apartment, after all.

"This isn't Florida, and we don't have Stand Your Ground."

"Fuck you sideways with a chainsaw."

"Yeah, okay, in a minute. I'm just trying to figure out why a vegetarian whose childhood dream was joining the Peace Corps goes into the wetwork business."

"Fair enough. But you can't make allies out of hunters, Tino."

"I'll remember that, Esther."

"You told her my name, asshole."

"I knew it already, Ms. Solomon. And where you live." Kayleigh sticks out her tongue.

I can't help it. I laugh. A series of canine snorts from behind me indicates that if I'm crazy, Scott's along for the ride. He's a good guy to have around, I guess. Or a seriously effective enabler. I'm not sure which.

"So Kayleigh, are we talking here?" I look in her eyes and almost melt. Almost doesn't count. Instead of an old memory about Kayleigh, my mind conjures up Maya. Huh.

"Okay, we're talking." She closes her eyes. The line between them eases, but its ghost sticks around. "I was a teenage rebel. It's the family business."

"Assassination?"

"Hunting."

"Oh." It's my turn to blink. "But why for the Mafia, and why now?"

"Because we need the money." She cuts her eyes away. "No, not me and Dad. We as in me and my fiancé, Calvin. He's in a coma, and that's expensive."

"Oh, shit, Kayleigh. I'm sorry."

"It was ruled an accident. Brain injury. We'll run out of money to keep him on life support if I don't do this Mafia infiltration thing."

"Wait." I straighten, staring down at her. "Infiltration?"

"Yeah. The money will keep Cal alive while I get revenge on the vampire who fucked him up in the first place."

"What vampire?" I think I already know, but I want to hear it from her.

"I don't know, but he's pulling the Caprice's strings, and me and Dad can't touch him because of that." She shakes her head. "He made the hit list. It's hard to describe him. Average everything, would go unnoticed if he didn't wear white zoot suits like a moron."

"I know that guy, and he sucks." I take a leap of faith and make an offer I hope she won't refuse. "You want me on the case?"

"Tino, I'm supposed to kill you." She slows down like someone explaining things to a kid. I let that slide, trying to cool my jets.

"Yeah, and if I fix this problem, you don't have to."

"Look, it's not just the hit list. My entire family thinks monsters should die, even if they're behaving themselves. I still don't agree with that, but I'm the newest hunter, and my opinions don't count for much."

"Man, I know how that feels." I shake my head. "Anyway, I'm going after Mister Zoot Suit for other reasons. Might as well pool resources."

"Fine, but Calvin's problem isn't going away. Even if you distract or off that vamp, you can't fix it all."

"Maybe he fucking can." Esther can't even be hopeful without tossing in a four-letter word. Of course.

"What do you mean?"

"So fucking typical." Esther shakes her head. "You know my name, my damned address, and you don't know jack or shit about what an alchemist does."

"I think Esther's got an idea about the other half of your problem."

"I can fix your man if the vampire and the werewolf help."

"Really?" Kayleigh doesn't seem to mind that Esther spaced on the finance detail. Being in a coma is expensive.

"Fuck, yeah."

"What about my legs?" She clenches her teeth. "Still can't move them."

"Here." I turn so she doesn't see me bite my wrist and will blood into the bottle I swiped from Esther's supplies. Ironic, using my blood to heal someone who made me spill so much of it. I hand the vial to Kayleigh.

"What is it?" She tries to lock gazes with me, but at that moment, my will is blue steel.

"Health potion. Doctor Horrible's Leg Tonic. Pan-Galactic Gargle Blaster. Just drink it." I can't tell her the truth because she might refuse it, but even I'm not sure exactly how it works or what side-effects she'll experience. It's not the kind of medicine with an FDA-approved list of side-effects.

She uncorks it. "Down the hatch." After drinking, she makes a face, the one everyone pulls when they suck the lime after a tequila shot. "Ugh. What was that?"

"You don't want to know." My blood has healing properties when used quickly enough. I wonder if Esther's plan for fixing Calvin involves it, too. I clench my jaw, trying not to breathe so I don't get hungry.

I'm all smiles as Kayleigh wiggles her feet and stretches her legs. She sits up and holsters all the guns she dropped faster than I expect. After brushing bits of glass out of her hair, she stands. It's awesome because she was almost paraplegic. I remember her running bases at the old lot we played stickball in. Hope for a good ending in all of this conjures Maya's optimism to my mind again. Maybe she's right, and it's not so bad, being what we are. Kayleigh tells us what room Cal is in at Kent County Hospital and that his last name is Kelley. Esther nods.

"This truce between us is only temporary, Tino." I already know it is but I have hope she'll break rules and change minds in the hunter community. After all, I'm trying to do the same thing on the vampire side.

"You decide terms when it comes to me, Kayleigh. But leave my friends out of it."

I hear a murmured "Fuck, yeah" from Esther and something like "aroo" from Scott because he's still wolfed out. What did you expect me to do, anyway? Leave my friends hanging? No way. I told them I'd look out for them, and vampires keep promises.

"They're not on my list, so fine." Kayleigh pauses at the hole in Esther's bedroom wall. "But this deal is just with me, remember."

"What?"

"The Caprices only gave me one of their lists, and monster hunting is a family business." She takes one last look over her shoulder. "Don't get in Dad's way. You know what he's like."

Yeah, I do. Ornery with a side of mean. "I'll remember that." The words come out garbled because my fangs won't go back in.

I need blood, and there's none in Esther's apartment that's not inside my friends' bodies. There are only so many more minutes I'll be able to control myself. No, seconds is all I've got. Kayleigh has left the building, but Esther and Scott are right there in my path. And this time, even Scott's gamy scent isn't putting me off. They both smell delicious.

I open my mouth, about to quip something like "You won't like me when I'm hungry'" but the joke gets lost in the slipstream around the sound of their hearts pumping blood. When I try telling them to run, I hiss instead. The edges of my vision go red.

I thirst.

# CHAPTER SIXTEEN

Esther sprints out the bedroom door, which makes sense. She's running away. Scott plays the typical teenager card, Bad Idea. He runs toward the hungry vampire, growling. I rush at him, fangs forward.

We clash. I bite. Tufts of fur fill my mouth, and my fangs can't dig in. I spit it out. Old hand-to-hand muscle memory kicks in, and I sweep his legs. We fall. He grabs me around the waist and kips us both up. I strike like a cobra, aiming for the jugular.

I make contact, but get a mouthful of fur again. A chiming sound from the next room comes with the scent of burning herbs. I spit fur again. Wolfman Scott's got a bald patch on his neck now. I lunge again. It's growing back before my eyes.

Scott's weird hand-paw thing ends up in my mouth. I splutter, but he's got me. It's like the time me, Ma, and Dad got hopelessly lost on vacation in Florida and ended up at a gator-wrestling show. The old dude put a metal pipe in the alligator's mouth vertically. Scott's paw is so huge, I can't open my mouth wider to dislodge it. Just like that poor reptile, I'm captive. Or at least my fangs are.

I can't burn blood to get faster now because I'm out of everything but what keeps me awake. If anything, my strength increases. I unleash a flurry of punches on Scott's midsection, but it's like werewolves are the ultimate holdback friend for vamps. You know what I mean. The buddy you have who, when you've got to punch a dude on principle, holds you back so you don't get arrested. Anyway, Scott's making a noise that sounds more like laughter than screaming.

But we're at as much of a stalemate as when Kayleigh had her guns out. Except no, we're not. I'm going to run out of steam in a minute and zonk. Not good. Vamps going unconscious from lack of blood oversleep on an epic scale. If I don't get blood or have someone to conk me out soon, I'm not waking up for years.

Scott's taking the punishment I can dish out pretty well, but it's got him on the defensive. He can't knock me out or fully subdue me. I hiss around his hand and wish I could pray instead. I might be a vampire, but I was raised a good Roman Catholic boy. What do you want from me?

The chiming sound from the other room turns into humming. I'm not talking about the noise a fridge makes or that tone when someone hangs up on you. This is like a person, a little girl maybe, doesn't know the words to a song but wants everyone to hear the tune.

The humming's right behind me now. A hand curls around my arm. It's not one of Scott's. It's bigger, and it has no claws. I try to shake it off, my body responding by hunger instinct instead of the way my higher brain wants it to. But the hand doesn't budge.

I shake my head, hissing as I try to dislodge Scott's paw. I don't have to. He moves it and steps back. That humming creeps me out. It doesn't sound human, and at first, I'm not sure why. It's a voice directly behind me, but no breath moves my hair. And something else about whoever's back there isn't human either.

No heartbeat.

I snarl, using the same weight shift that ended with Kayleigh's broken back, but the thing holding me doesn't flip. It's too heavy, like Esther's leg. Instead it turns me around so I can look in its face. After that, the fight goes out of me like air from a deflating balloon.

It's a doll's face, the one Esther grabbed off the shelf earlier. Except its fake plastic features are human-sized with creepy doll proportions.

It's like a toddler she-Hulk with blonde hair. The skin is pink, overlaid with a pale green with a sparkle to it, like all the rest of Esther's magic.

"Be good and take your nap." The mouth doesn't move. There can't be vocal cords in its neck, but the words are clear as anyone else's. Just inhuman sounding, like the hum.

I open my mouth, bare my fangs, hiss, and claw at the frilly green dress it's wearing. No dice. The doll can't make a real fist, exactly. Its fingers aren't jointed that way, but that's enough for it to bop me on the head, like it's the Good Fairy from that song and I'm Little Bunny Foo Foo. A Post-it sticks to my nose as green glitter fills my vision. I only just make out that the script on it is fat-fingered.

And just like that, I'm out.

---

I wake up in the back of Scott's truck, which makes sense. My head's in a lap, which doesn't. I flare my nostrils, but all I smell is blood. Don't freak out. It's in the bag a set of cool, pale hands holds out toward me. I open my mouth, and the business end of the bag goes in it. As I drink, more becomes clear.

Stephanie peers down at me, her eyebrows closer together than usual. The moon is high, and about half-full. I wonder what's got me so optimistic until another air-temperature hand wipes my face with a cold-cream-coated cloth. This one's not so pale, though.

"Maya? Stephanie?" I start thinking in tropes.

"Yeah, it's us." The Vampish Pixie Dream Girl removes more greasepaint from my cheek. "We went by your dad's house to keep some extra eyes on him for you."

"And you left?"

"We did." The Vampire Mom-Friend holds out another bag of blood. "Your mortal allies are there now, which is for the best since they'd only put you in hunger rage again."

"Is that what happened to me back in Esther's apartment?" I feel hungover.

"Yes." Stephanie shakes her head and clicks her tongue. Mom Friends; everyone has one, right?

The rages are things that kick off a vampire's instinct. There are three kinds; hunger, fire, and vengeful. Stephanie told me about all of that after she turned me, but understated it by a country light-year. Well, now I know from first-hand experience. Hunger rage feels like being a Power Ranger stuck inside a malfunctioning Zord. I have to hope the other two aren't so bad that I need Esther to summon her creepy doll again.

I down a second bag of blood, wondering whether the dolly was some kind of blood-deprivation dream. The whole thing's surreal, like a real-life version of some kid playing with a pile of random classic horror film action figures and their kid sister's baby doll, with an action sequence straight out of a Kaiju movie. I shake my head.

Something crumples in my right hand. I look down to find the Post-it, dingy yellow now. It's got alchemy script of the fat-fingered variety, like the note on my car. So, the doll exists, and it can do alchemy, too. I try contemplating how that's possible, but can't even begin without learning a truck-ton more about magic. Well, maybe I've got time.

"Hold still, Tino." Maya's fingers tighten on my hair. "You can't go in to see your dad looking like that."

"Or without more of this." Stephanie hands me another blood bag.

I want to talk to my dad now that we know who shot him and why. Maya and Stephanie are only here for moral support. I ask them to stay outside. I tell them it's because Dad needs protecting from other attacks, since who knows what else the Caprices will try. But really, I don't want to explain their presence to Ma. Or to Maury, whose car is in Dad's driveway.

I take a few more minutes to get full and cleaned up, but I can't walk in there looking like Percy Blakeney. Because Stephanie is right. That's who I'm like, doing this night gig to hide elite supernatural people from the mundanes who'd just as soon see them dead. Yeah, werewolves, vamps, and magicians are powerful, but we're the minority by a lot.

Anyway, I've got to look like Tino now, not some Count whose name rhymes with macula. Taking off the opera cloak and stashing the frilly cravat in one of its pockets helps me look normal enough except for one problem.

"These bullet holes, though." I poke a finger through one in my shirt.

"Oh." Maya shrugs, tucking greasepaint-streaked cloths into a trash bag Stephanie's holding. "I don't know."

"I do." Stephanie points at a duffel bag bungeed under the truck's toolbox. "He'll have to change before meeting with the king this evening, but for now, what's in there will do. Werewolves always keep spare clothes handy."

I free it, unzip, and look inside. There are t-shirts, pants, socks, underwear. Two pairs of sneakers, too big for me, but that's okay. I only need a shirt, and wearing an oversized tee is nothing I haven't done in front of my parents or Maury. This truck belongs to a family of werewolves who probably splits more seams than Lou Ferrigno. Fishing out a shirt and putting it on is too easy and too convenient. I wonder what the catch is.

And that's how I end up in my mother's kitchen with Maury Weintraub for the second time that week, wearing a t-shirt that says I do grate things with a picture of a cheese grater on it. At least it doesn't have any four-letter words on it. I don't want to end up putting Dad back in the hospital with a heart attack.

"You boys need to eat something. You're so skinny, you look like a couple of stakes for tomato vines." Ma sets tea saucers loaded with homemade biscotti next to steaming mugs of Autocrat coffee. She put on the good stuff for us, and I can't eat it.

"Yeah, Ma." I can't look at her.

The stake comment makes me wonder whether she's guessed what I am already. It'd be a whole lot safer for her to figure this thing out on her own than for me to tell her, just like when she found my condoms. I remember her face, redder than the Christmas tablecloth. Maybe I just don't want her to know, okay?

"Thanks, Mrs. Crispo." Maury's manners always make Ma's day. Or night, as the case may be.

He beams at her. Well, he tries, anyway, but doesn't manage anything so bright. That's because his teeth have a slight tint from too many coffees, cigarettes, and long nights. But it's not just that. Whatever's been wrong with my friend healthwise is getting worse. We wait until she's out of the room before racing to steer the conversation. Maury wins.

"Tino, you've gotta give me that list."

"Okay. I've got it right here." I reach into my pocket and push the folded paper across the table. I don't mention the other list Kayleigh hinted at. For now, that's only a rumor I need to investigate later.

"Thanks." Maury taps his fingers lightly on the crumpled-then-smoothed surface. "That was easy."

"Yeah, I should wear a red button on my chest, maybe open an office supply store." I grin.

"No, Tino." Maury pockets the paper without looking at it, a sign of trust. "You're going to do great as a PI. I'm not saying I'm jealous, but..." He lifts one shoulder.

"Thanks." I set my face to undeadpan. I can't afford to let Maury see my fangs, not now. Of course, he thinks I'm mocking him.

"Wow." Maury shakes his head, then tilts it like a crow contemplating something shiny. Except the little glint that's always been there the whole time I've known him is missing.

"Okay, my turn." I lean back in my chair, crossing my arms over my chest. "Go to a freaking doctor, Maury. I mean, Jesus Christ."

"Nice Prophet, but you know my people are still waiting for the Messiah."

"Yeah, yeah." I flap one hand, dismissing our old Judeo-Christian banter. "I'm serious, Maur. You look like crap. Get checked out."

He leans back in the old kitchen chair. It doesn't even creak on account of all the weight he's lost. "What if I don't want to?"

"I'm not giving you any more tips." I put my hands flat on the table to show him I mean business.

"Woah, you're serious." Maury blinks.

"Nah, I'm Valentino, not Harry Potter's godfather." I lean forward. "Doctor. Tomorrow. Go."

"Tino—"

"No more excuses." I push my saucer of biscotti across the table toward him, then pretend to drink some coffee. "You look like you need these more than I do."

Maury's eyes go wide. He's staring at the twice-baked cookies like they're the jackpot in a lottery. No, not like that. More like a plate full of french-fried spiders. He makes a run for the bathroom and my jaw drops. I feel like the shittiest friend in the universe, pushing food at him like that just because I can't eat it.

I don't need to get up. I can smell it from the kitchen, now that Maury's emptying his stomach. Cancer. I wait for him to come back, thinking about Esther and the stuff she's brewing for Kayleigh's man. I've got to hope she can make more than one batch, and that it'll work on whatever's eating Maury Weintraub. But I know he's not eating cookies after losing them, not any more than I am. So I pocket two handfuls of the biscotti, leaving crumbs on both our napkins so Ma will think we ate. I slosh some coffee from both our cups into the sink too, for good measure.

Maury notices what I've done, of course. He doesn't miss a thing, which is why he's the one who made detective. Except now I'll never know how much of that was vampire fuckery and how much was honest talent and achievement. I swallow that bitterness, and it almost makes up for the fact that I can't drink coffee anymore.

"Listen, Maur. I was way out of line, and I'm sorry."

"Okay." He rubs the bridge of his nose, pushing up his glasses so it almost looks like they're perching on his nose like a vulture. That image is too morbid for even me, so I set the coffees back on the table. "Anyway, I'm already seeing a doctor, Tino. We're doing what we can."

"I'm not going to push anymore." I pat his shoulder, which feels bony under the padding in his jacket. "But I'm here if you want to talk about it."

"Tino, your father's awake!" Ma doesn't even come down the stairs to tell me this. In true Cranston-Italian-mother fashion, she hollers it from upstairs.

"Listen, Tino. We still gotta talk about the list and some other things." Maury heads for the kitchen door. "Don't call me, I'll call you."

"That's fine, Maury." I gesture at the doorway leading to the stairs. "Look, thanks for being here. For Dad. And me."

"Just protecting and serving, Tino, like we always said we would growing up." He opens the door and steps out. Before it closes, I hear him mumble, "You're welcome."

I'm pressing my lips together as I head up the stairs, not sure what to make of that entire conversation with Maury. Even though I know the skeleton of our friendship exists, it's shifted shape as surely as Scott and his family. I'm not sure what its final form will look like. I shake off my misgivings. Dad's home from the hospital. The doctors think he'll be okay.

I focus on that for now.

# CHAPTER SEVENTEEN

Ma passes me on the stairs, no mean feat since they're narrower and steeper than the Italian Alps. Or at least, that's what Ma always says. I've never been there. I nod a silent thanks and head down the upstairs hall to my parents' bedroom.

"Dad, hi."

"Get over here, Tino."

I do. We hug.

"Sit."

Dad holds out his left arm. The right one's still in a sling. He's sitting up, television and the radio on, with the Providence Journal open on his lap as usual.

It's exactly the same, but completely different. If it weren't for him being in bed and the sling and the nostril-stinging tartness of antiseptic, it'd be any other night at home since as long as I can recall. Just before making the mistake of smiling at him, I remember the other difference. I'm a vampire.

Almost a week ago, I thought that was the worst thing in the world. Looking at Dad, I know it's not. Losing him would have been worse. If I wasn't a vampire, I couldn't protect him. I wouldn't have friends who could help with that, either. There's only so much a human cop can do, even one as talented as Maury. They're frail and uninformed. I'm still a little bit guilty of the latter, but getting better.

The voice in my head says Dad wouldn't have been shot by accident if I hadn't been turned. I give it my best Esther impression and tell it to shut the fuck up. The Caprices have another list, and I'll bet bitcoins to blood bags that Maury's on it. I would be too if I wasn't a vamp. Bad guys come in all states of being.

And so do the good guys. I sit with Dad and Ma, chatting like we would have over Sunday dinner if Kayleigh's misguided assassination attempt hadn't interrupted us. It feels good to be with my family. Because finally, I'm not focusing on how I'm going to live forever and they're not. My head's in their game, on the thousands they're batting at hobbies and jobs. I've never been so contented to listen to Dad talk music and Ma babble about book club. Even the workaday gripes I listen to sound like pearls from heaven.

Perspective is important for everyone. That night I realize it's exactly what I need to cope with becoming a vampire. But I'm not out of the tunnel yet even though I see the light at the end of it. It's going to take work and time. I'll screw up, backslide. But that's all right. Everyone does.

This is the first time in years I can feel okay with that, though. For now, I bask in that feeling as much as parental love and company. People care. What's more important is, I do too. Maybe too much but nobody's perfect.

After an hour, Dad's nodding off. I go downstairs to be with Ma, where she's clearing all the coffee things Maury and I left behind. I work beside her, tidying in tandem. After the dishes are all in and the washer's running, I just know she's going to address the elephant in the room.

"Tino, you know I love you."

"Yeah, Ma. I love you, too."

"So why aren't you telling me what's up with you?"

"It's hard, Ma." I shake my head. "I don't want anyone to get hurt."

"If you're worried I won't love you anymore once you come out and say it, you're wrong."

"Um." I swallow past the lump in my throat. Here's the woman who birthed me, standing in her dressing-gown in the kitchen, declaring love I think she can't possibly maintain. Vampirism is a pretty heavy and unexpected circumstance. I'm about to explain it, too, but she interrupts.

"Listen, kiddo. I'm gonna love you forever, no matter what. And I'm sorry about all the times I've harped on you about giving me grandbabies. I'm an auntie, and that's enough for now. And these days, anyone can start a family. They come in all shapes and sizes."

If I'm this obvious, then every human I know is going on King DeCampo's hit list, and he's scarier than the Caprices. How did she find out? Did I screw up and get fangy in front of her? My heart crashes and burns like a downed jet. Were my hopes, dreams, and ideas really that lofty upstairs? I've all but signed death warrants for my parents.

"Wow, Ma." I blink, shaking my head. How will we recover from this?

"Wow, yourself." She puts her arms around me. "Have I ever done anything to make you think I'd disown you because you're gay?"

"I'm—" My denial and apology die on my lips. It doesn't matter what my sexuality is because I'm a vampire now. I'll never have kids, even if I do fall in love and settle down. There's only one way to respond to a person who just said they'll accept you no matter what. "I love you, Mama."

"Oh, Tino." Ma pulls back and looks up at me. Her eyes shimmer at the name I haven't called her since I was a tiny tot. "My little boy's grown into such a good man."

"If you think so, Ma, I can believe it, too." I pull out the blush trick Maya taught me. It's the least I can do at this point. Apparently, honest to God tears are part of that package. And here I thought I'd never be able to cry anything but blood again.

We stand there hugging, with the tears running down our faces. It's not pretty, but that's life. It's more than worth the mess.

And then the alarm on my phone goes off.

"I gotta go, Ma."

"Work?"

"Yeah." I'd feel bad for lying, but I'm not. The shindig Stephanie wants me to attend *is* work, in a vampiric manner of speaking.

"If you're investigating this shooter at all, there's something you need to know." She pulls a Kleenex out of her sleeve and dabs her face with it.

"Okay, Ma."

"The doctors said that the bullet in your dad had wood on it. They gave it to the CSI guy."

"Which one?"

"Raphael Paolucci."

"Oh." That's a mixed bag for me. What sucks is, Raph Paolucci is the sharpest forensic pencil in Cranston's box. The bright side is that he's clean as a whistle and won't be working for the Caprices or Whitby. "Thanks, Ma. I'll call him if I need to."

I give Ma one last hug and a kiss on the cheek, then I'm out the door and squeezed in the cab of Scott's truck with him, Stephanie, and Maya. Up in the window next door, I see Old Man Fitzpatrick, keeping watch over my parents. An unmarked car's across the street, too. My parents won't be alone.

Scott drives Maya to her car, and me and Steph back to the Belfry. After that, he's got to go home. Curfew. I tell him he'd better get that extended, which makes Stephanie laugh for some reason. Upstairs, I change into my suit. I can't wear a t-shirt to see the king, no matter how great a pun it is.

Downstairs, I get into my car with Stephanie. She's quiet, so I break the ice.

"How come I never see you drive?"

"I never learned how."

"Seriously?" I take the on-ramp for I-95 North. "Then how do you get around?"

"Since vampires take pride in age, a lady must maintain other secrets. This is one of mine."

"Okay."

We drive along in silence until I take the downtown exit. Circling to find parking gives me time to wonder what this meeting with vampire royalty is all about, anyhow. But maybe that's less secret than Stephanie's favored mode of transportation. I put on my blinker and wait while a bald and hunched little man with a limp and a walking stick gets into a sedan. He smells like the ocean.

"What does King DeCampo want with me tonight, anyway?"

"Oh, nothing much."

"If it's nothing, you can tell me, right?"

"Very well." Stephanie puts one hand on the lever to open the passenger side door. "It's your Testing Trial." She gets out before I can say anything else.

Well, this is less than great. The penalty for failure is death, and I haven't even studied.

# CHAPTER EIGHTEEN

A nice Italian boy walks into a vampire club… Sounds like the start of a pretty bad joke, right? But it's my life, and it's now or never. Tonight determines whether I get the chance to live forever. Yeah, I rhyme. I'm a poet and don't even know it. So sue me.

Hargrove lets Stephanie and me in. We don't go to the big throne room where the Moots happen, either. I can hear the usual suspects in there, though. Peering through the doorway as I walk past, I spy Maya. She drops a wink while giving me a thumbs-up. Whitby turns his nose up at me. The rest of his crew stare like stone statues, except for Roger the trench coat guy. One corner of his mouth twitches, and he wrings his hands. Raven raises an eyebrow, then marks something down in their little black attaché book.

At the end of the hall is a door I never knew existed. It's got the fanciest compass rose I've ever seen on it, so it's obvious what this place is for. Hargrove holds the door open, and I enter Testing Trial Central alone. Almost thirty years as a Catholic aren't enough to prepare me for the dire air of ceremony this room holds.

It's a circle with two alcoves. The floor is marble, polished to a high-gloss finish, and inlaid with a compass rose that's somehow more ornate than the one on the door. I'm standing in one of the alcoves, just two steps away from the letter S. Each letter representing the cardinal directions is inlaid with a different gemstone. North is onyx, South is garnet, East is lapis lazuli, and West is moonstone. A faint sparkle hangs in the air above each of them, like magic, but not Esther's kind.

In the alcove directly across from me stands King DeCampo, for once out of his throne and standing in full light. I only just manage to keep my jaw from dropping because I've never seen him before. His Majesty is a striking figure.

He's maybe a hair taller than Stephanie, but other than that they're different as day and night. The king's skin is ebony, and his hair hangs in long rows of braids, bound at the ends with silver beads that match the pointed jewelry on the tips of his fingers. His nose is wide, but has a distinctive point that reminds me of paintings on Etruscan pottery. I realize that he's not old like I thought. King DeCampo is downright ancient.

I feel like a gnat facing down a giant.

"Valentino Crispo, youngest in my territory, I call you to Trial this evening." A tingle descends on me along with the sound of his voice, as though he's invoked the tradition of ages down on my little head. Which, to be fair, he absolutely has.

His voice booms, even though I know he didn't raise it. This room has the best acoustics I've ever heard. So good, they just have to be enchanted. I want to know how and would have looked at the ceiling, but I don't dare offend the king. I bow my head instead in deference to his age and power.

And that's when I notice the ashes. Ominous little heaps line the edge of the circular room as though the people they used to be were found wanting and then swept neatly aside with a grudging sort of care. And I'm at risk of joining them.

Others have failed at the Testing Trial over the years. They tried to go big and never went home. The evening's earlier moments with my parents might be the last. I try to swallow past the lump forming in my throat, then realize it's not physiologically there.

All of these physical human affectations are psychological,

happening only inside my head. But like the wise man said, the stuff in your head can still be real. I need to set these human vestiges aside if I want to think like a vampire and walk out of here.

I close my eyes, trying to remember all four points from my notes and how I mean to deliver them. At least I get to start with one I know. South is easy, right? And North is practically a gimme with the king standing right next to it. Maybe he wants me to ace this.

"Your Majesty, I am prepared." My voice takes on that same booming quality, and an itchier sort of tingle follows it. Oh, yeah, there's magic in this here room, the kind that feels like it's going to screw me over big-time if I don't stick to the words I say in it.

"Then begin. Make your vows to honor our rules." The king looks on, unblinking.

I step forward, placing my feet at the bottom curve of the S. There are two spots inlaid with pink marble for me to put my feet on and everything. I close my eyes, trying to visualize my composition book. Instead of just how it looks, my memory brings everything about it back. Its weight, the dry feel of its paper, the scent of black ink filling my nose when I fall asleep with it against my face.

And at that moment, I realize I know more than I think I do. And I think of exactly what to say for the southern point on this compass of rules.

"Your Majesty, I have a previous vow to protect innocent humans, and I have no intention of breaking it. However, I believe my old obligation to be in accord with this new one. So, I vow to honor the South by keeping our existence secret from humans in order to protect and serve both them and you." I feel a twinge of magic, warm like the bygone taste of cinnamon.

"Proceed." The king inclines his head at the white W. He didn't really need to since there's a trail inlaid in the floor for me to follow.

I pace along a pink marble trail outside the circle around the compass rose until I reach the next direction. And here's my moment of truth. The two directions I always get mixed up are East and West. As my feet come to rest on the spots below the W, I take a deep breath and let it out. If I'm wrong, I'm dead, but the same goes for if I stay silent.

"And here is another new vow that works alongside my old one, your Majesty. In my admittedly limited experience, becoming a vampire hurts. I promise not to turn any human unless I am under direct orders to do so from my king." I close my eyes, praying I got this one right. When the magic comes, it almost tickles, and it sounds like folding fresh linens.

"Continue."

I open my eyes but missed where DeCampo wants me to go next. Luckily, the pink marble path guides my way, and I follow where it leads. The blue E at the eastern point of the compass. And I've got it cold now; I know I'm going to remember them all.

"No society can exist without trade, Your Majesty. I vow as a member of the vampire community to honor each of my debts and obligations to its other members. But I'm taking on an additional responsibility. I will also honor my debts to others in the supernatural community, provided that they act with honor toward vampires and humans." This magic smells like a salt breeze fresh off the ocean.

"Interesting. And appropriate." King DeCampo nods. "Complete your Trial."

The path can only lead to one place—directly in front of the oldest and scariest vampire I know of. The marks for my feet on the floor put me on the opposite side of the letter N from him, turned so that we face each other. The foot of height I have on the king makes no difference. Even an uninformed bystander would know immediately which of us was the more powerful and who commanded true respect.

"Your Majesty is the most powerful being I have ever encountered. I vow to honor you for your age and experience, and promise to give my best effort on any task you assign me." I try to stop them, but the words flow from my mouth anyway. "Unless the other vows are violated. This I swear." That last word of mine resonates in the room's acoustic perfection. The magic now is the feel of your fingers in the first deep snow of winter.

The silence hangs between King DeCampo and me. I got all of the points right and made my vows. So why isn't he saying anything? What's stopping him from granting me full status as his citizen? I stand, looking at a spot on the bridge of his nose because I can't bear the weight of his gaze. But I realize I have to. It's part of the Trial, and if I don't look the king in the eye, I will fail. We lock gazes.

He blinks. Irises like midnight pools change to a glowing red.

"I see."

For an unmeasurable space of time, I feel like a bug pinned under a microscope, scrutinized. And then I'm surrounded by flickering light and heat. Fire. I get the feeling those flames are waiting, watching to see how I'm judged. I want to squirm and wish to flee, but I'm held there, paralyzed like Kayleigh's legs were after I broke her back. Guilt over that action presses down on me, threatening to grind me into dust and ash. Maybe it's karma. I drop to my knees.

Or maybe the king's gaze and all this fire are part of the test. I made protecting regular people part of every vow I swore in this room, and I'd hurt Kayleigh this same evening. It didn't matter that I'd healed her minutes later. The fact of the injury was enough, along with any unknown consequences the healing method might have. I close my eyes and bow my head, waiting to feel DeCampo's claws sever my head from my body or the flames to burn me up. But the light and heat vanish, and the king speaks.

"Rise, Valentino Crispo, a full-fledged vampire."

I do as I'm told because that's what I promised. He could tell me to hop on one leg and bark like a dog right there on the compass, and I'd obey.

"The weight of your guilt over past actions is balanced by your refusal to let even me break the other vows. Now, be burdened by the lighter but no less significant heft of responsibility."

King DeCampo reaches up, holding out a blood-red stone on a chain. His eyes return to their original color. I recognize this or something like it. Stephanie wore one the night after she turned me when I got presented to the king for the first time. I forget what it's called.

Something amulet. But I reach out to take it anyway. Its inner light glows like the fire, but it's cold to the touch.

"Thank you, Your Majesty."

"Your Lazakhar amulet binds to your person and will only be visible on the most formal of official occasions, but you must wear it always or risk being considered as you were before your Trial. Never lose it."

"I understand, Your Majesty."

"Good." He holds out one hand to indicate the door I came in by. "Spend the rest of your evening as all others to come, in accordance with our laws and your will. Be well, Valentino Crispo."

I bow my head to him because it seems weird not to, and then I get out of there and hope I never have to go through this again. The Testing Trial room is a hinky place, and I'd prefer not to see the inside of one for a handful of centuries. Maybe more. The second I'm out in the hall, I hear a voice.

"Hullo, Tino."

"Stephanie! I did it."

"I knew you would." She's grinning. "Now come and mingle. Everyone will want a moment of your time this evening."

And they do. And for once, it doesn't suck.

# BODY COUNT

## SUPERNATURAL VIGILANTE BOOK TWO

*Something's fishy in the state of Rhode Island.*

*Tino Crispo's investigating something big and nasty in Rhode Island. Trouble is, nobody's talking, even with murder and abduction connected to rival magical families.*

*Tino was just sinking his fangs into unlife as a vampire and a PI, when Stephanie, his old and powerful vampiric sire, gets body-snatched.*

*With his usual crew sidelined, Tino's help comes from unconventional sources. An old enemy, a psychic 'tween and her pet, and a scapegoat are the Ocean State's only hope to beat back the horror lurking beneath the bay.*

*Can they stop the body count from rising, or will they go out with the tide?*

## CHAPTER ONE

"Get him!" I raise my voice for the first time tonight because there's no way any of us will catch the bastard if I don't. Unfortunately, that means the prey Scott, Esther, and I are stalking gets spooked.

"Aroooo!" Scott can't use his words right now because he's a six-foot-tall furry monster with giant clawed paws. He swings and misses. Yeah, my big scary pal is a teenage werewolf.

"Waffle-twat!" Esther's right leg goes out from under her in a shower of green sparks. She's a magician with no four-letter word filter. And apparently a klutz.

"Fine." I burn blood to turn on some speed.

Right now, you're wondering, "burn blood? Is he a pyromaniac? What the hell does he mean by that? Who is this guy, anyway?"

I'm Valentino Crispo, PI. And I also happen to be the newest vampire in Rhode Island. So yeah, I'm using blood to boost my speed because that's one of the things we can do with it, and it's one of two vampiric abilities I actually have the hang of. I'm using my powers to finish my case. You got a problem with that? That's what I thought. Keep reading.

Dashing past Esther and Scott is the easy part. Pouncing on the bastard isn't hard either, but getting a grip, man, that is damn near impossible. He's one slippery customer.

That shouldn't have surprised me. I knew what we were getting into when we took the job. I'm speedy enough to get around and corner him, so that's what I do. He looks up at me, blinks, and starts climbing up the smooth sealed cement wall. I see my chance and take it.

Whipping off one of my gloves, I scoop the little guy up in it. "What?" you might be wondering. Or maybe, "How is that even possible?"

Said guy is a missing pet. A salamander, to be specific., and I'm holding him captive in an article of clothing that I wear to keep people from noticing that I don't show up in mirrors. This victory wouldn't have been possible if I were still human because nobody wears gloves in Rhode Island during the month of June.

"Case closed."

"Nah." Scott's adjusting his clothes. The stuff he usually wears is stretchy so it doesn't shred, but it gets all out of whack when he wolfs it up. I hand the glove with the amphibian inside to him.

"Can't a fucking lady get a goddamned hand over here?" Esther's sitting on the floor, pounding on her right leg with her left hand.

I oblige by reaching down. She hauls herself off the flagstones. I notice that her right leg's pretty stiff around the knee. Looking her in the eye isn't easy, but I do it anyway. She turns her glance away, face reddening. But I smell it. Shrapnel. It's under her skin somewhere, though not in the leg she's favoring.

"When did you serve?" Yeah, I have a bad habit of pissing powerful people off.

"Fucking-a. I don't want to talk about it." She practically pushes my hand away, tossing her head so her jet-black hair obscures her face.

"Okay." It was a pretty personal question. "Shouldn't have asked."

"Don't do it again, Tino, or I'm cutting the hell out of every goddamned fucking thing you've got going on."

"I said okay, Esther." Usually, I'd smile at someone while backing down. Not Esther and not after my foot's crammed that far down my throat.

I know it seems weird for a vamp like me, even though I'm new, to make nice to what's essentially a human with magical mixology powers while she's cussing me out. But like I said before, Esther's four-letter-focused vocabulary is normal for her. She even does it when she's in a good mood. I think it stops her from accidentally casting spells or whatever, so I don't mind that.

"Um." Scott's holding the glove up. "I think we all want to give the lizard back and get paid."

"Kid has a fucking point." Esther rolls her eyes. "But it's a salamander, shit-for-brains."

"Okay, then." I hook one thumb over my shoulder in what I think is the direction we parked. "To the, um, wolfmobile?"

We head out of the tunnel next to WaterPlace Park in downtown Providence. It's been full dark for maybe three hours, which means it's eleven o'clock because it's June. This is one of the sucky parts of being a vampire. The nights are pretty short over the summer. But right now, it only motivates me to get stuff done faster.

I'm wrong about where the car is. I forget other things sometimes, too. But that's why I have a team and try to write everything down. Scott easily finds the big old rust bucket of a truck his dad lets him drive. The werewolf schnoz is a thing. They can track faster than just about any other creature on the planet.

"Fucking shotgun." Esther means that she's called dibs on the window seat, not that she spotted somebody getting frisky with a double-barrel. The truck's a regular cab with a bench seat, not extended. She pulls open the primer-spotted door, rolling her eyes at the imitation wood panel painted on the side.

"Joy." I climb into the truck and put the lap belt on. What? I'm a vampire, not Superman. Besides, if we get pulled over, I don't want Scott to get a ticket for driving without everyone buckled in.

Esther gets in and pulls the door closed behind her. Scott hands me the glove with the salamander in it and hops into the driver's seat.

They both buckle up, too. He turns the key in the ignition and then puts it in gear.

"Hold your fucking horses." Esther holds her hand out at me then glances at the flimsy glove.

"What?"

"Little guy can't wear a belt, but he's dead if we get in a wreck." Scott shrugs. "I guess she wants to make something better for him."

"Fucking a." Esther brandishes a permanent marker.

"You owe me a new pair of gloves." I hand it over.

Esther mumbles something about buying stock in a glove-making company while marking her alchemical symbols on my garment. The green glittery aura that always goes along with that magic surrounds her hands, the marker, and then the glove. When she hands it back, it feels like metal mesh instead of fabric and doesn't change shape in my hand. I can hear the salamander moving inside and peek through the small hole in the top. It eyes me back.

"What's so special about this lizard anyway, Scott?" I ask him because he's the one who arranged this missing pet case.

"Dunno." He turns the wheel and pulls out on to the street.

We ride along in silence until we're almost to the highway. Then I realize my mistake.

"Shitballs."

"What the fuck?" Esther blinks.

"What? I can't cuss?" I shake my head. "Um, I forgot to, uh, check in with Stephanie."

Yeah, I'm lying, and it's possible that Scott knows it. Esther seems clueless though. My partners in private investigation and the occasional technically heroic crime know about the vamp who turned me. They don't know that the vampires have a king I'm required to contact every time I'm in the city limits.

"Can't you just call her?"

"Oh." Scott's right.

I can phone instead of drop by. That's one of the fringe benefits of passing my Trials and becoming a full member of vampire society last month. But I don't want to do it in the truck where they can overhear anything. I'm allowed to tell people like Esther and Scott that I'm a vampire but supposed to keep details about our ways secret from the other supernaturals.

"Um, but there's something kinda, uh, personal that I—"

"Get the fuck out." Esther opens the door.

"Woah, holy shit!" Scott's usually the chillest person in any given group, but even he can't relax when the alchemist opens the door of a moving vehicle.

The werewolf pulls over while the magician cackles like a Golden Age Silver Screen witch. I just roll my eyes. Once the vehicle stops, I unbuckle the belt and hand the glove to Esther again. Then I climb over her lap to get out.

And there is definitely something unnatural about her right leg. Her left arm, too. They're colder than they should be, for one thing. For another, the pulse in them is slower and stronger than the ones in her other two limbs. Does she have some cockamamie kind of magicked-together prosthetics?

I promised I wouldn't ask her again, so I let it ride and focus on getting my feet on the pavement. The phone in my pocket buzzes before I can even get it out. There's a text from Ma, but I let it sit while I dial the number at what's essentially vampire HQ in the city of Providence. It rings three times before I hear the voice on the other end.

"Valentino."

"Raven." I'm glad it's not King DeCampo on the other end of the line. Raven's annoying, but way less intimidating to talk to about official stuff.

"I'm, uh, in Providence." I cup my chin with my free hand and the phone to cut down on road noise.

"Why?" I can almost see Raven arching their eyebrow. And no, the king's attaché isn't two people. Whenever anyone asks what gender Raven is, the eternal answer is vampire. When we first met, I took that interaction a step further and asked for pronouns. Hey, if I can get my brain around the idea that vampires are real, accepting that one happens to be Enby is no biggie. And Raven's at least as influential as

Stephanie, the vamp who turned me. Probably more even though I think she's older. It's a good idea to stay on Raven's good side.

"On a case," I answer. Honesty is easier than making up a story I'll only forget.

"Murder?"

"No. Missing, uh, person." The last thing I want to do is admit to the vampire nobility that I chase amphibians through Providence's old tunnels.

"Some night, I hope you'll tell me what an uh-person is. Because even I've never heard of one before."

"It's a long story." The last-ditch utterance doesn't spare me from Raven's curiosity.

"We're vampires, Valentino. We've got all the time in the world for that."

The blast on the horn would have scared the piss out of me if vampires still had that bodily function. I glare back at the big blue clunker to find Scott trying to shoo Esther's hands away from the middle of the steering wheel. She flips me both birds.

"Hurry it up, asshole! I need a fucking cheeseburger!"

"Go cheeseburger yourself!" I flip her one right back. It's impossible to keep up with Esther's foul language, so I never bother. One-finger salutes are another story.

"Where are you again, Valentino?" Raven's chuckling on the other end of the line. The king's attaché seems to enjoy my distress way too much.

"Near the Mall. By the highway exit."

"Oh, God, don't get hit." Raven's tone carries more genuine concern that I expect. "People would discover what we are if you total someone's car." Yeah. That concern? Not for me. It figures.

"Yeah, trying not to cause wrecks. But this influential vamp I'm checking in with keeps asking me a million questions. You know how it is."

"Fine, you're in the clear. But so help me, if letting you off the hook ends up biting me in the ass later, you'll owe."

"Sure thing."

Raven hangs up, so I pocket the phone. Climbing back into the car is just as awkward as before. I have to flat-out ignore Esther's weird left arm and right leg, which sucks because I'm one curious dude. Which is a good thing, what with me being a PI and all. Anyway, as Scott drives away, I'm relieved. We got the salamander and managed not to piss off the vampire royalty.

But I know better than to count my five-hundred-dollar share of the fee before it's paid. There's something about this simple case that's got my gut instinct in a twist. Staring out at the hypnotic dashes painted on the surface of I-95, I do my best to shake it off.

How much trouble can one little amphibian be?

I hope those aren't famous last words.

# CHAPTER TWO

I prop the door on the way in. Not only is it good for business, but it's also an act of rebellion. The guys who own the building hate that, and I don't like them either. They had a hit list with my name on it, after all. But I got their hitwoman to quit, rented a space in their building under an alias, and have bugs set up to make sure I can stop them if they manage to hire another one. And now, I'm breaking their petty slumlord rules like some punk kid instead of a creature of the night. Maybe that's why I chuckle all the way up the stairs to the third floor.

We're in the studio space that's also our Private Investigation firm's office. Which the Caprice crime family I mentioned before knows nothing about. It's complicated. Anyway, Scott gets on the phone, dialing the client's number who hired us to get her lizard. Instead of asking us to hang on to him she wants to come over to the office right now and pick him up.

I'm surprised but not upset. This means we get paid quicker. It also means we're getting our first actual guest in the office. This is nerve-wracking because the decor and furniture are all junked or abandoned items we picked up during off-campus college move-outs last month. What do you want, it was free, okay? But that makes our space look and feel less than professional.

I'm pacing and wringing my hands. Esther grumbles something about amateurs and heads downstairs. I don't bother trying to decipher her words or actions, which is why I'm surprised when she comes back up maybe a minute later.

"Get off the chair, you son of a bitch." She's brandishing a piece of chalk and talking to Scott, who's sitting at his desk.

"Hey!" He stands and puts his hands on his hips. "My dad's the werewolf, not my mom!"

"Boo-fucking-hoo." Esther points her chalk at Scott's posterior. "Move your candy-ass!"

Scott's probably one of the most laid-back people I know despite being a dude who does a furry hulk out when things get dangerous. Or maybe he's chill because nobody likes him when he's angry. But I don't blame him for scuttling out of the way.

We've seen Esther bring down literal walls with a fistful of alchemical Post-it notes, wrecking her own apartment during a battle with the hunter who broke into it. I haven't seen her place since then, but she delivers epithet-laden descriptions of the contractor's lack of progress with repairs on a regular basis. She says she won't fix it with magic because it's too much energy on a place she doesn't own.

The surly alchemist chalks out a circle on the back of the threadbare office chair and mumbles a few words sans cussing. Glittering green haze shimmers in the air around the cast-off seat, and before our eyes, it changes.

I'm so busy staring at the shiny new poshness now gracing the area behind Scott's desk I fail at watching Esther work more of this magic around the room. When she's done, the place looks like we spent ten grand on decking it out.

Scott's blinking. I'm standing so still my undeadness is showing. Esther's brushing off her hands and stowing the chalk in her pocket. She looks at me, then the teenage werewolf. After that, she pulls the chalk out again and marks the glove. It turns into a fishbowl with a plastic mesh lid. I shake my head.

"What?" Esther sets the bowl on my desk. "I'm a goddamned fucking alchemist, and you expect me not to do any fucking Alchemy?"

"Um—" I'm about to mention my now missing glove and how I kind of need it, but her narrowed eyes make me think better of saying all that. Her next statement proves my wisdom.

"You've got to be shitting me."

"Thanks!" I give Esther a big friendly smile then put my hand over my mouth because I just basically fanged out at her. It's worse than flipping the bird because I kind of tried to eat her once. And Scott, too. I totally didn't mean to, and still feel bad about it. My friend Maya says not to worry about turning into a monster until I stop feeling sorry. So I apologize.

Esther just rolls her eyes, which is normal for her. She stalks over to the door and opens it. A kid's standing there, fist raised, green eyes wide. Rust-colored brows dip down as she lowers her hand and scans the room. This girl can't be a day over thirteen with a room full of particularly scary adults staring at her. But she makes a face like she just caught the ice cream truck before it left her street. Her mouth transforms from a flat line to a smiling Cupid's bow. She only has eyes for the lizard. Salamander. Whatever.

"Sparky!" She dashes across the threshold, ducks under Scott's arm, dodges my hand, outstretched for a handshake. "I thought you were a goner."

The kid pulls the mesh lid off the fishbowl. Instead of scooping the little red amphibian up, she sets her hand against the glass rim, and the salamander hot-tails it up and out of the container. She giggles as he climbs her arm to put one little foot on her cheek.

"I missed you, too." The girl boops him on the nose. "Get in." She opens a pouch strapped across her shoulder, kind of like a cross between a handbag and a shoulder holster.

Sparky scrambles down her shoulder and into the bag. A moment later, he sticks his head out and winks at me. I shit you not.

The kid walks right up to my desk and mouths the three words on the swanky little placard that came with Esther's alchemical redecorating. Her eyes glance from Scott to me and back again because neither of us is behind that desk. She shrugs at Esther.

"Which one of you is Mister Crispo?"

"That'd be me." I cross over to get behind my desk. "Hi there."

She pulls wads of ones and fives from pockets in her pants and the hoodie she's wearing. A few twenties join the mix. Then she takes off her left shoe and slaps a handful of Benjamins down in front of me.

"Crap." The girl shakes her head. "I'm short."

Scott's standing frozen, blinking at me as I uncrumple and count every bill. I put the money in piles, the stack of ones dwarfing all four of the others. Esther's mouthing something like "What the fuck" at me. I don't care. Kid or not, she's a client. And unless she's standing here crying or bleeding, which she's not, I'm going to let her pay by whatever means she has at her disposal.

"It's only two dollars. You can owe me, okay?" I grin.

"Are you sure, Mister Crispo? It's just that Sparky's, like, the most important thing in the world right now, and I should pay what my Baba told me it cost."

"Absolutely." I'm not sure what a Baba is, but she's too old to be talking about a baby bottle. Maybe it means Grandma, like "Nana" does in my family.

"When do you want the money?"

"Take your time. I can wait a year if you need."

"Wow, Mister Crispo. You really are a nice guy, just like my Baba said you'd be." The kid turns and heads back through the room. This time, none of us try to get in her way. Once she's at the door, she looks over her shoulder. "Thanks!"

"Oh, any time, Miss—" I grin. "I didn't catch your name."

"I'm Leora Kupala."

"Well, it's good to meet you, Miss Kupala. Call us if you need help again. We give discounts for repeat customers."

"Kay, thanks, bye!" Leora dashes out the door and down the hall.

Something's off, but I can't put my finger on it. I split the bills into three nearly equal dollar amounts, then give the two full shares to

Esther and Scott. I pocket the stack that's short by two dollars. That's when my face hits my palm.

"Did the two of you also hear Leora tell us her friend hired us for her?"

"Yeah."

"Fuckin' A."

"Shitballs."

"Why?" Scott scratches his head.

"Because she's maybe thirteen, and out past curfew for any kid that age, even though she says her grandma's the one who hired us. And paying us in scrounged bills." I put both hands on my desk and lean forward. "What's that tell a good investigator, Scott?"

"You're a fucking sucker for helping critters and kids?" Esther's eyes are rolling like dropped coins.

"Is your name Scott?" I roll my eyes right back.

She shuts her mouth and shakes her head. But Esther's grinning, so we're good. It's all part of our continuous snarkfest.

"Well, it could mean a couple of things." Scott leans one hip on his desk.

"Such as?"

"Leora's adult supervision can't get here?"

"Go on." I turn my finger in a circle. "Tell me why."

"Disabled. Agoraphobic. Can't do stairs?"

"Occam's fucking razor, shit for brains." Of course, Esther knows way more than Alchemy. Which is a good thing, and explains why she looks like a fish on a bicycle whenever I'm teaching Scott this stuff.

"Oh, yeah. The whole keep it simple thing." Scott stands. "Something happened to the nice lady who called us and Leora's on her own."

"Bingo!" I tap my nose with one finger. "Ten points to Wolfenpuff!"

"So let's go after her, then."

Scott grabs his keys and sprints for the door. He's got a point, but blood-drinking vampires like me who get toasted by sunlight can't put little girls up in their apartments. Neither can Esther because her place is still trashed.

But a pack of benevolent werewolves might be willing and able to protect Leora Kupala. I let Scott go since he knows more about that possibility than I do. Though I wrack my brain for a backup. Maybe my mundane and in-the-dark about supernaturals bestie, Maury could help? Nah. I've got nothing, not even by the time Scott returns a handful of minutes later.

"Can't find her."

"Huh."

"No trace of the kid's scent, either." Scott's eyebrows try to meet in the middle. "That makes no sense. It's been over a month since I had any problem catching a scent."

"When was that?"

"Funeral home."

"Oh, yeah." I try to hide the reflexive wince I make over my forgetfulness. I was supposed to ask Scott what was up with the strange veiled figure standing in the back at a murdered police detective's funeral. But I spaced.

"It was weird, but Gramps said not to worry about it." Scott shrugs. "Anyway. I don't know what to do now. Do you guys?"

I grab my phone and dial back the number that called us earlier. But it goes straight to a voicemail that says the Inbox is full. I set the phone down and stare at it. But that's no good. I have to do better.

"Well, we tracked the salamander." I pace a couple of times behind my desk. "And it definitely didn't act normal for its species. So my theory is, she's not a regular kid."

"No shit, Sherlock." Esther's holding one of her rocks on a string over the stack of bills I handed her. There's a smudge of red on one of the Benjamins that smells faintly of something sweet. "Alchemists don't need our fucking noses to find people. Blood and the right tools do the fucking job."

Maybe a minute later, she huffs and puffs, then chalks a small circle on the floor. After drawing lines and the weird symbols she uses inside it, she puts the money in the middle and tries again with the pendulum.

"Can't fucking track the little shit, even with blood on the bills."

Esther stows her pendulum and the cash, then heads out the door. "Need my fucking lab."

"Ahem." I clear my throat, pointing at the chalk she left all over the middle of the floor.

Esther stops in the doorway and snaps her fingers. The chalk blows away. She slams the door behind her, and Scott sneezes. I know she's in a hurry and wants to get downstairs to the Alchemy lab I'll forever think of as the weirdo factory, but that's no excuse for leaving chalk everywhere. At least the one time I made a mess in her lab I tried to put it back. And made her botch her spell in progress. But that's a story for another time.

I sit at my desk and pull the top drawer open. Inside is a tray of writing implements, a stack of Post-its, and a legal pad, which was exactly what I put in there before Esther magicked its appearance. I pull out the yellow pad and slap it on the desk's surface. Then, I grab a pencil and let my thoughts go to town.

"Huh. I wouldn't have thought of that." Scott's reading over my shoulder.

"Shush, kid. I'm thinking here."

"Okay."

Scott leaves me with my brain-to-paper-exercise. I'm jotting words from left to right and leaving space in case more ideas come from me or the others later. I flare my nostrils, trying to remember how I managed to count all that money without noticing bloodstains on any of the bills. I smack my forehead, nearly staking myself in the eye with the yellow number two pencil.

"More shitballs, boss?"

"No, just one big dumbass." I remember that sweet scent from my days of human living, so I tap my phone to wake it up. "Siri, call Esther."

It rings once. "I'm elbow-deep in shit, so this better be good. What the fuck do you want?"

"Esther, that's not blood on the bill you're trying to track Leora with."

"So what the hell is it then?"

"Raspberry something."

"Can you be any more fucking specific?"

"No."

"So why the fuck did you call instead of coming down here, dickface?"

"Hey, I know my Roman nose is big and all, Esther, but it definitely doesn't look like a dick, okay?"

"Shut the fuck up and get your goddamn asses the hell down here before I drag you both through the hall by your ballsacks."

"Yes, ma'am." Scott wastes no time heading for the door.

It takes me a few seconds longer because I take my pad and pencil and bring the keys to lock up.

# CHAPTER THREE

I head down the echoing stairwell, trying to resist the urge to take two steps at a time. Esther sounded scared, and she's a tough bird, not the type to get the vapors over nothing. If she's worried, then there's got to be a good reason. Or a bad one, depending on how you want to look at that.

Scott follows with less urgency. Either he's not afraid of anything Esther might find threatening, or he's conserving energy. Probably the latter since I haven't seen the teen wolf eat anything in over eight hours. That's a long time for a normal kid his age to go without food, let alone one with a werewolf metabolism who wolfed out in a tunnel less than an hour ago.

On the second floor landing, there's a scene. Don't worry, it's got nothing to do with my alchemist partner's lab space. Well, almost nothing. It's only happening right outside her door.

"If I told you once, I told you a million times." The guy with the bushy beard pushes the fellow he's talking to. Well, pushes him away, like he doesn't want a hug right now, thank you very much. The guitar srapped to his back tells me he must be in one of the bands that practice here.

"Um, whazzat again?" Said fellow's words are slurred like he's drunk, except I know he isn't because I don't smell a drop of alcohol on him or in his bloodstream. Instead, he's got a watery odor, like he spent the entire day next to a fishing pier. His hair looks all slicked back with some sort of gel, too. Or wet, maybe.

"Stop getting drunk and staggering around my building. I can't deal with your drama anymore, which is why we broke up in the first place. You look like something the cat dragged in. Smell like it, too. Get out of here."

Normally, I don't get involved in messes like this one, but this guy's personal misfortune is directly in my path. Also, if they start trading punches, they might bust Esther's door down, and that'll make her blow a gasket for sure. The guy's mumbled apology is almost unintelligible even to my ears. I manage to decipher it all the same.

And that's all thanks to that spiffy enhanced vampire hearing that comes with the bloodthirst. The bearded dude gets in the not-drunk guy's face again, grabbing him by the collar of his faded black tee shirt. The poor sap cowers, trembling so hard that his gel-soaked hair is shaking.

"'M just here to see Esther, not you."

"Look, he said he's sorry, leave him be." I hold my hands out in what I hope is a gesture showcasing my intention of peaceful intervention.

"Yeah, sure, fine, whatever." Beard man drops his not-drunk ex-boyfriend. He turns his back and delivers his parting shot as he opens the door across the hall, pausing before slamming it. "Just get outta my sight, Frankie."

"Hey." Frankie looks up at me from his spot on the floor. "Thanks, mishter. You're nice for a vam—"

"Shhh!"

"Izza secret, amirite?" He blinks, shakes his head like he's trying to clear it and stop talking like an internet meme. Maybe it even works. "Sorry."

"You'd better be." Scott's eyes are an alarming shade of yellow. Something about Frankie has him on a sharper edge than my dad's straight razor.

"Look, pal." I hunker down next to him. "It's late, and you're having a bad night. Why don't you call a Lyft and go home?"

He garbles more words about wanting to see Esther. But that can't be right, can it? I fall back on what I always try to do in this type of situation.

"Look, maybe you're in the wrong place. Maybe you should just go home and sleep the, um, whatever it is off."

"Magic, Tino." Scott snarls. "From a creature, too. The worst kind of mojo I've ever smelled in my life. He totally reeks of it."

"Oh." maybe I'm the mistaken one, and he really is here to see Esther. Alchemists might know how to take the bad out of mojo. Or maybe not. I know next to nothing about what the three kinds of magicians can do, which is why I work with Miss Pottymouth Rhode Island in the first place. "I'll see what I can do."

I loop one arm under Frankie's shoulders, across his back, then try to help him stand up with me. It's not going so well. The guy is floppier than overcooked pasta and almost as slippery.

Frankie's also more cumbersome than the average guy. For whatever reason, he's throwing my balance off like nobody's business. Maybe it's the mojo Scott mentioned. One moment he's top-heavy, and the other his torso feels light as a feather. His face is pressed against my chest while I try to hoist him up by the back belt loop on his distressed black jeans. It's not a pretty sight. So, of course, that's when we suddenly gain another spectator.

"Get your fangs off my fucking uncle, Crispo."

"Um, Esther. Hi!" I try waving, but almost topple over with Frankie under me. Not a good look.

"This dude's your uncle?" Scott's upper lip curls like a surfer's ideal wave. I can't blame him for the doubt. Frankie looks younger than his niece. But I can smell the similarities in their blood. Complicated as it looks and sounds, my nose doesn't lie. They're definitely related.

"Just get him the hell inside already until we figure out what to do with him, okay?"

"I'd do that, but—" I try to shrug and fail miserably. "A little help here would be nice."

Esther rolls her eyes and ducks back inside her studio for a moment. She comes back out with a shaker like one you might see in my mom's kitchen with Parmesan cheese inside, except this one is full of sparkly yellow dust instead. It's got to be magic. A moment later, Esther confirms my hunch.

She turns it upside-down over Frankie's head and shakes seven times. I figure it's some kind of Alchemy she's cooked up in there. Turns out I'm right. It's the levitating kind of magic. Handy thing to have in a sprinkle jar. Frankie lifts far enough off the floor so only his toes touch it. After that, it's an easy thing to guide him through the door like a partially deflated helium balloon.

After we're inside, Esther closes the door and positions Frankie over a bean bag chair in the corner. She flicks him on the cheek with one finger three times, then presses down on the top of his head. The floating effect wears off immediately, dropping him on his rump into the middle of the bean bag. Frankie's head lolls back, and his eyes close. But I wait until I hear a faint snore before talking.

"So, he looks a little young to be your uncle."

"It's complicated."

"By that, she means some magician family trees are more like wreaths." Scott's studying his fingernails.

"Fuck you, distemper poster-child." I don't blame Esther one bit for the insult.

"Well, it's what everybody I know says. And I said some, not all."

"Look, I asked you guys to come down here to talk about the raspberry tracking thing, not the uncle fucker."

"Okay." I'm cool with leaving Frankie in his niece's care. "So lay it on us. Everybody knows it's raspberry jam now."

"Good. But what you couldn't know is where those raspberries are from."

I blink because it's hard to believe Esther Solomon actually said a sentence without any words that would give a censor a coronary. She takes that as a sign to continue, which is good because I'm totally speechless.

"This jam was made of raspberries from the brambles on Baba Yaga's house. Same old lady in all those Russian folk tales."

"So you're telling me that Leora's dear old Baba is some kind of legendary magical paragon?"

"I can't fucking say. But whatever asshole gave the kid that stack of cash is in good with the old bag. She doesn't give that damn jam to just anybody. Or the witch actually handled the money herself."

"Correct me if I'm wrong, but isn't Baba Yaga unable to leave her house?" Scott scratches his head. "The stories I heard said that's the reason it's on chicken feet."

"I've got no clue." Hooking a thumb at my chest, I continue. "Italian, remember? Not a drop of Slavic anything in these veins. And Ma kept the scary stuff out of my bedtime stories."

"Go read a fucking book or surf the web and leave me the hell alone. I don't have time to give your lazy ass a mythology lesson here."

"Well, can you track Baba Yaga's little buddy or not?"

"Yeah, but like I said, I need some fucking alone-time to do it, without you assholes hanging over my head like Damocles with his overcompensating sword of fucking dick substitution." Esther means that affectionately. I think. But there's one problem I can see with her logic in telling us to get lost.

"You're not alone with him around." I point at Frankie.

"You're right." She hands me the yellow sparkle dust shaker. "I can't risk having him in here with the shit pile he's stepped in. He might fuck up all the energy I'm using. Take him off my hands, and I'll have some kind of fucking tracker for you by sunset tomorrow."

Esther's cussing again, but not her usual blue streak. I sprinkle the levitation dust over Frankie's head seven times like she did before. Scott doesn't complain or ask any questions as he drives us back to my apartment in Rolfe Square.

All the same, I can tell my teenage werewolf sidekick is angrier than a nest of hornets because he doesn't help me get Frankie out of the car or up to my apartment. He burns rubber peeling out and drives off instead of hanging around like his usual tag-along self. Probably he'll wash down the inside of the truck he borrows from his dad. I guess bad mojo is extraordinarily funky to a werewolf's nose, even if I can't really smell it. Frankie might just smell as bad to them as they do to me.

So that leaves me alone with the unluckiest man alive. Maybe. I mean, if you've read as many of the Dresden Files books as I have, you might beg to differ on the question of who's the guy with the worst fortune.

Helping a partially levitated and functionally drunk man up three flights of stairs is harder than it sounds. Okay, maybe it's exactly as hard as it sounds if you know anything about floating objects and wrangling almost unconscious people.

Frankie bumps into the banister, the wall, the light fixtures, the ceiling, and the door to one of the second-floor apartments. I freeze, afraid the occupant will wake up and be angry about a seemingly drunk man knocking on his door at zero dark thirty in the morning. I pick up the pace. If we're both gone before that happens, he won't have anyone to complain to.

I maneuver Esther's wayward uncle to my apartment door, but it's much trickier getting him inside. Well, it's unlocking and opening the door without him putting his eye out by floating into the wall sconce or all the way up to the vaulted ceiling that's really the problem. The last thing I want to do is use the powder on myself. As I fumble with my keys one-handed, an unexpected solution to all my navigation problems presents itself.

My door opens.

I don't freak out because coming home to an uninvited guest in the apartment I call The Belfry isn't unusual. At least not for me. There's only one person it could possibly be at this hour, anyway.

"Hullo, Tino."

"A little help would be nice, Stephanie."

"Hmm? No, thank you." She steps aside. Again, I'm not surprised.

Stephanie is the opposite of helpful as a general matter of course when it comes to anything physical. Has been for the entire two months I've known her. She's single-handedly responsible for most of my own personal issues, beginning with the fact that I'm a vampire.

As the one who turned me, she has the right to enter my house without an invitation. Technically she owns everything in it, including me. Yes, this is true even though a couple of weeks ago, I got my status as a full member of vampire society in a bizarre Trial ceremony thing I don't have time to explain right now.

Did I just say she wasn't helpful at all? I'm wrong. She's got a pot of blood on, and I'm thirsting like woah. Fortunately for me, Frankie smells about as appetizing as a piece of paper, which is to say, not one bit. He doesn't have a foul odor, but what I can smell of the blood pumping through his veins reminds me of reptiles or maybe even fish. Vampires get the most out of blood from mammals. And maybe marsupials, too. I have no way of knowing, but if I ever make friends with an Aussie vamp and hear first-hand stories about being able to live off drop bears and kangaroos, I'll be sure to let you know first thing.

Anyway, while thinking about vampires in the land down under, I managed to wrangle my hinky house guest into the cozy chair reserved for my incurable reading habit. Which Stephanie happens to share. This gives me a small dollop of satisfaction because I can tell Stephanie was sitting in it just before she opened the door. As I repeat the gestures Esther used to make Frankie stop floating, I notice the book sitting on the side table beside the lamp. She's got it marked about halfway through.

It's *Shadow Over Innsmouth* by H.P. Lovecraft.

The idea of that one creeps me out so much I've never actually read it. Why she's got it out is a mystery I won't bother trying to solve. Everything my sire does is cryptic, which makes sense on account of us being born in different millennia. I head straight to the kitchen for some blood from the coffee maker, past where Steph sits at the dinky breakfast table that still takes up too much room in here. Yeah, it's a studio apartment. Luckily, my bed's in the closet with a light-blocking curtain where the double folding doors used to be, so at least I get some privacy and extra safety from the sun.

As I pour warmed blood into my second favorite mug (she's drinking out of my favorite one, of course), I sigh and shake my head.

Last month, the book Steph had me wrapped up in like melon slices in prosciutto was The Scarlet Pimpernel. I ended up confronting and stopping a masked assassin. If she's currently recommending horror by Lovecraft, I don't want to ask what she thinks might be in store.

Still, there's nothing better to do, so why not have a chat about a classic of the horror genre?

But she doesn't give me the chance.

# CHAPTER FOUR

"Why are you storing that in here?" Stephanie's eyebrow isn't in any danger of touching the ceiling, but that's got more to do with her being five-foot-nothing than how far it's migrated up her forehead.

"Um, what?" I can't even imagine what she's talking about. The Belfry isn't a storage unit, and I didn't bring anything in with me.

"That." She points at Frankie. I realize she's engaging in dehumanizing speech and calling him a thing. Uncool.

"Oh, he's Esther's uncle." I shrug. "You know, my magician friend with the cussing and the Alchemy?"

"Is that all she told you?" Stephanie makes a clucking sound. "Oh, Tino. You're so naive."

"Yeah, well, she's got no reason to lie." I'm not in the mood to hear one of my friends trash another, especially when they haven't even met.

Stephanie turns her head, looking at the wall for half a moment. She doesn't do anything so juvenile as rolling her eyes or as crass as snorting. She's been classy with a capital C the entire time I've known her. Well, except for the part where she referred to a down-on-his-luck human being as a thing just now. But that should only serve to make me pay attention. Any time my sire does something outside the realm of normal for her, it's been followed by some serious shit going down.

"Okay, so Esther's exactly as trustworthy to me as I am to her." I lean back and take a long gulp from the blood in my cup. "Which is like, almost microscopic."

"Microscopically." There's good old normal Stephanie again. Correcting my grammar. "And that's why you ought to be extremely careful in your dealings with her." She wrinkles her nose. "I'll bet young Master Fitzpatrick has as much apprehension about that thing as I do."

"You know, he's got a name." I emphasize the pronoun. It's not right to talk about a human being like they aren't one.

"That's all part of its appearance." Stephanie's giving me the fishiest eye that ever resembled a fish.

"Look, Frankie was staggering around the studio building like a drunk, trying to ask his niece for help. According to Scott, it's not alcohol, it's magic. So somebody hurt the guy. And Esther's doing Alchemy for a case we're on so I'm watching him until she's done. That's all."

"Hmm. I suppose you are a product of your time and generation." Stephanie turns her head and looks at me out of the corner of one eye. At least the gaze doesn't come down her nose. "My comments stand, regardless of what you might think about their delivery."

"Do they have anything to do with your reading material?" I glance at Shadows Over Innsmouth and then back at her face again.

"Astute, Valentino." She grins.

"So, what are we looking at here?" I set my cup on the table, figuring she can't be giving me a hint that's literally about fish people. But I've heard the book has more subtle themes. "Cults of personality? Mass hysteria?"

"What happened last time I recommended a good book to you?"

"Um, I had to read it? And take notes." I lean back in my chair. "It helped me figure out what to do in the end."

She drains her cup, then stands. "I've got no stomach to stay and chat while—" She snaps her fingers, as though searching for something other than the right word she doesn't want to use even though nothing else in the English language fits Frankie. For once, she fails. "He remains. Please contact me when you've no longer got this houseguest."

My sire leaves without another word. Also, without even putting my favorite cup into the sink. And she had the nerve to complain about the dude who's asleep. Except he's not sleeping. Not anymore.

Frankie hasn't moved his body, only opened his eyes. It's a bit creepy, the way they follow me. Well, no. That's not really true because this reminds me of *Scooby Doo* and other cheesy horror or mystery shows with the goofy paintings that have people hiding behind them. And I'm a vampire, so I've got no reason to get creeped out by something so campy. It's supposed to be other people getting creeped out by me.

As much as I try to do something constructive with the biological changes that make me into a monster, I still am one. Only technically because I still feel guilty and say sorry when I screw up. But anyway, being a monster means that when it comes to dealing with potentially dangerous humans, I'm allowed to act totally fearless. I've really got to start owning that.

"So, Frankie," I say. "What the fuck is up with you, man?"

He doesn't reply or even blink, but his mouth drops open, and he lets out the most heinous croaking belch I've ever heard or smelled in either of my lives. It's as though with one eructation, he turned the atmosphere in my apartment into a fish market operating in late afternoon during the hottest day of the year.

I wrinkle my nose. My eyes would water, too, but since I'm a vampire, that doesn't happen so much. "Let's get you into the bathroom, buddy. Can you stand?"

"Tryin'." His feet are on the floor, but when he tries putting weight on them, the rest of his body threatens to follow the bottom of him down.

I get an arm under the poor unsteady guy and remember that tendency Frankie has to be off-balance. It's puzzling as all get out, too.

How does he function if he has no center of gravity? And whoever heard of a human who defies the laws of physics this way. Or at least seems to. I'm not well-versed in the scientific kind of laws, just the kind police enforce. Maybe it has something to do with what happened to him, the bad mojo. Or the smell. Or both.

One good thing about living in a studio apartment is that it takes only a handful of steps to get from one side of it to the other. Frankie's in the bathroom before I can lose my balance too and tumble us both on to the floor. Once he's in there, the man does the most natural thing in the world for a human.

He drops trou.

I turn away because it's a dick move to stare at a dude while he's on the can. And also out of a sense of superstition. Last month, my unlife-threatening troubles began with a man in distress while on the john. Supernatural creatures don't generally believe in coincidences.

Even though I give the guy a little privacy, that bad luck feeling has overruled any ideas I might have had about walking out and shutting the door. This means my ears get a front-and-center listening experience as he does his business.

My inside voice doesn't break free with any of those thoughts, thank goodness. When Frankie's done, I hear a flush and a rustle of clothes. Thinking it's safe to face him again, I do. But as it turns out, that's a bad idea.

Frankie's in the altogether. By that I mean, he's wearing his birthday suit. Catching a breeze around his knees. Bare-ass naked. His clothes sit in a sad and faded black heap. I look only at his face because the last thing I want to see is Esther's uncle's skinny backside.

I'm about to exit stage left, but he groans in genuine pain. His hand is on the side of the shower, and his eyes are wide with some sort of hurt and red-rimmed with an impending deluge of utter misery. And that's when I see them—the marks and the other stuff on his body, things that don't make sense.

And that's why I do everything in my power to stop my naturally inquisitive mind from going down any dark paths. Instead, I let my body act, reaching out to turn the shower on and draw the curtain after the poor young man gets in. I pick up his discarded clothes and leave the bathroom because no matter where I go in my apartment, I'm still close by in case he falls down or whatever. I'm fast enough to get in and help him, even by vampire standards. Turns out, I'm speedier than all of my vamp peers, and even some of the elders.

As I bag his shirt, pants, shorts, and socks in a large evidence sack, my brain turns back on now that Frankie's busy in the shower. It's easier to think about what's so horribly wrong with him now that I don't have to look at it. He's in rough shape, and it has nothing at all to do with inebriation from alcohol. At least that's what I gather, so I sit on my bed, trying to take stock of everything I saw.

Half-inch cuts covered most of the poor guy's belly, upper thighs, stripes across his back, and some of his chest. A slimy glistening substance either covered or oozed out of them, deep purple where blood should have made a ruddy tint. That's probably what was in his hair, the stuff I mistook for gel. The indigo slime almost completely covered Frankie across his groin. Gunmetal gray scales clung to that, some sticking either into or out of his flesh. And all of this clung to his body without much smearing even through the clothes and his misadventures in the studio and on the way here.

Snagging my notebook out of my nightstand, I jot all of that down. Since I'm so new to the idea that anything other than regular people even exist, this is stuff I'll have to look into with those in the know. But I think I understand now why everyone's flipping out about poor Frankie. And I'm not likely to get far unless I can find some friendlier sources.

Whatever left him such a mess is a type of creature so universally reviled, both vampires and werewolves are reluctant to even speak words describing or naming it. Either that or there's some sort of compulsion. Or maybe a little of both. Out of my three closest supernatural contacts, only Esther seems remotely tolerant. And she still kicked her own uncle out of her working space the moment she had the chance.

So, I either need to chat up a magician who's not busy cooking up spells, or a vampire with less prejudice against even the victims of whatever the slime-covered scale monster is. I grab my phone and send out a text. It's getting near dawn, so I don't expect a response, but that's fine by me. I don't want to ask directly about Frankie's trauma while he's here recovering from it, probably posing both stupid and upsetting questions in the process.

I put the notebook away and my phone on the charger. Then, I rummage through my dresser and the coat closet, trying to find a change of clothes for the supernatural rape victim trying to get clean again in my shower. At least he's leaner than I am so everything should fit. Once I have a shirt, gym shorts, boxers, and socks set on the bathroom vanity, I sit down to drink more of the heated blood from the coffee maker.

It's going to be a long day.

## CHAPTER FIVE

The first thing I do when Frankie emerges from the bathroom, fully dressed in a t-shirt and my now-totally-useless gym shorts, is offer him my bed so he can catch some winks. Instead, he lowers himself into the seat across from me at the little breakfast table, rubs his eyes, and mumbles something about not wanting to owe a vampire because he knows we trade in favors.

"Look, Frankie." I set the cup down and lean on the table, striking my best good-cop pose. "The whole fangs and blood gig is new to me, but I'm an experienced investigator. I'm in business with my partners for plain old cash to help people like you, no vague future favors required."

"People like me?"

"Yeah. Folks who are just going about their business and get caught in a supernatural shitshow."

Frankie puts his hands on the table, palm up. On his left wrist are a web of scars; horizontal, vertical, diagonal. A semicolon, stark black, is inked over the convergence of the attempts he survived. He takes a deep breath and hangs his head. Tears rain on the table's green faux marbleized veneer.

"Been caught my whole life."

I'm silent, unable to think of something comforting to say. Part of this comes from the fact that I had a good life coming up as a regular mortal kid. The other part is straight out of Catholic dogma. Suicide's a mortal sin, and I can't imagine any good Catholic attempting it once, let alone as many times as there are scars on Frankie's wrist.

But he's Esther's uncle. That means he's probably Jewish like her. I'm not well-versed on the nature of sin according to the older faith, but that doesn't matter. What's important is that I stop making assumptions about Frankie's situation and just give him the space to speak. Or breathe, cry, or scream if he has to.

I burn blood, using my vampiric speed to nab the box of Kleenex Scott left on the kitchen counter last time he was over. Once they're on the table next to Frankie, I gulp down the remainder of the warm blood in my mug. I'm going to need a refill now but wait until he reaches out with one trembling hand to ease a tissue past the plastic barrier on top of the box.

Papery rustles echo in my ears as I carry my cup back to the coffee maker. The slow, deliberate action gives him time to compose himself with relative privacy. I pour the last of the warmed blood into the mug, then get a new bag from the fridge along with a bottle of water, another one of Scott's recent additions.

This whole situation must have me more shaken up than I expected it to because I almost pour the water in the carafe instead of my bagged blood. Once I correct the impending mistake, I sit back down. When I place the water within Frankie's reach, his left hand shoots out, grabbing my wrist.

"There's nothing to investigate." He looks up, amber eyes gleaming from above his hook nose and under his mop of freshly washed jet curls. He reminds me of my best friend, Maury Weintraub, about ten years ago. I realize Frankie isn't much older than Scott, not some strung-out guy in his late twenties. More like of age to enlist in the Army but not to buy a beer.

I don't ask him for clarification or try to naysay him. Instead, I go with the hunch that comes at me from that fleeting moment of recognition. Some people need prompting, structure, interrogation. But my instinct tells me Frankie isn't one of those. He just needs a chance to say his piece, something I've got the suspicion he hasn't had for most of his life.

He opens his mouth again. And of course, that's when my phone beeps. I ignore it, keeping my gaze on Frankie, my wrist unflinching in his grip. Even though this guy isn't a Hallmark movie tween who lost her pet, my desire to help is just as strong for him as it was for Leora. I realize at that moment, I don't even care if I have to work his case alone in order to do it without pay. He deserves to have someone on his side for whatever my sympathy might be worth compared to older and more experienced vampires.

"Listen. I knew my whole life that this would end up happening to me. Everybody did. In fact, they made a deal on purpose so it'd happen."

"Who's they?"

"Mother and Father."

I search my mind for any scrap of information it might harbor about magical families. The only thing it comes up with is that there are three kinds, and one of them is Alchemy. There's nothing I can ask or even say, so I wait again.

"That's just the way things are in our house. It's the Pickering way. Always has been, for as far back as memory goes. One mundane son gets sacrificed every generation to keep up our end of the bargain. And it's not a blood sacrifice, either. They take us for breeding. Almost every time, they kill us afterward, too."

"So, you're not a magician like your niece?"

"No, I'm completely normal, except for my upbringing." A throaty sound somewhere between a bark and a chuckle escapes his throat. "It took me years to figure out that my family's twisted as a cyclone. Not normal. They treated me like an appliance. I can't even remember them hugging me. They already sold me to a gang of perverted monster women, so why bother getting attached? Today, they refused to take me back when I ended up surviving. There's nothing you can do for me. I'm stuck, like I said before. Always have been."

But if that were true, poor Frankie would have been in his grave a long time ago instead of battling through his depression despite knowing his eventual fate. There's got to be something he lived for. No. Not a thing. A person he's protecting.

"Maybe I can help someone else, though." I go with a hunch, reaching out with my free hand to run my pointer finger along the tattoo on his wrist. "So. You did everything you could to escape your fate. But at one point, you quit that. Why?"

I expect a one-word answer, a name.

"Levi. My kid brother."

"He's got no magic, just like you."

"He's only thirteen. All we had was each other for his whole life. I wanted to off myself so bad, meet death on my own terms. But I couldn't let it be him instead of me. And that's what would have happened. If I'd succ—"

"Completed. Completed suicide, Frankie. There's no such thing as success in that."

"What are you, Catholic?"

"Yeah." I grin just wide enough to let him see the tips of my fangs. "Well, I was. No more church for little old undead me."

Frankie blinks. The dregs of his tears seep out at the corners of his eyes. Then, they multiply. Finally, he throws his head back and guffaws. He's still got my arm in a vise grip, so I shake right along with him. We're laughing in tandem.

Some pain cuts us so deep through the heart after the fact. At the point where we just can't bleed anymore. And that's when we've got no choice but to laugh. I was there just over a month ago, the last time I tried to go into my church. But I went through that mostly by myself, unable to tell my parents or friends, and surrounded by older vamps who assumed I'd screw up and get myself killed. But Frankie shouldn't have to go through his physical and mental shitstorm the way I went through my spiritual one.

He takes a few hitching breaths after the fit passes. "Tino, you might not be a Lamb, but you're a pariah just like me. Outcast. Unclean. Alone." I've got no idea what he means by "Lamb" yet, but that doesn't matter. I understand exactly what he's saying and the fundamental element he's missing.

"Wrong on one count. I'm not alone. And neither are you. Not now and not going forward, either." God help me, I'm making a new friend. Thought that sort of thing stopped happening after college.

"I guess you learn something new every day." Frankie sniffles. He lets go of my wrist to snag another tissue.

"I guess so." I grin, without the fangs this time.

"Did it hurt?"

"You mean, getting turned?" I blink. This wasn't the question I expected, and nobody's thought of asking since it happened. "Yeah, when her teeth went in. It was like bee stings. I got dizzy, passed out, woke up here. Got the facts of unlife talk from the sire, plus an apology. She was ordered to do it. And she's still a pain in my neck. You know what's fucked up? It hurts more that I can't go to church than it did when she bit me." I take a breath, hoping my light description doesn't spook him. "How about you?"

"I—" Frankie blows his nose. "When they told me about it, that actually hurt more than when it happened." He glances at his tattoo and the scars under it. "They always treated me differently from my little sister, Sarah. She's the middle child, the one who got the magic. I was five. That's when they laid it on me. The fact that I'm the Lamb this time, the sacrifice. I'm surprised the monsters left me alive. So were Mother and Father. Doesn't usually happen that way."

His revelations are halting, disorganized. Natural for someone who's never spoken aloud about their damage. I've had practice. I'm hoping Frankie will give himself time to get his own. But as we gaze into each other's eyes, I understand that his entire existence is precarious. Supernatural beings like their masks and will kill to keep their privacy. Now that he's talking, Frankie needs what little protection I can offer. But he's got to agree to it first.

"So, are you going to let me help you?"

"Don't know." Frankie's mouth stretches in a cavernous yawn. The whites of his eyes are veined with red. "Should sleep on it."

"Do what you've got to." I glance up at the clock above the kitchen sink. "The sun's coming up. I can't make sure you get out of the building safely." I stand, head to the curtains over the closet door, and open them, revealing the bed. "So you should stay here."

"Okay." He shuffles past me and gets in. Frankie's breathing turns long and even only seconds after it hits the pillow. I grab my notebook and close the curtains to let him sleep.

I jot down all the new information before I forget it. After that, I need to clear my head, so I wash the dishes. Two mugs and the carafe aren't much, so when that's done, it's my turn to shower. I grab some pajamas and bring them into the bathroom with me. The notebook, too. My guest knows about vampires, but I'm not sure how much. Even though it's all in Latin, I can't assume he hasn't studied that language. The notebook has some sensitive information in it. That's an understatement.

I didn't get too messy in the tunnels we chased Sparky through, which is a relief. But when I take off my shirt, I notice a stain on the back. It's slimy and glistens, even though the fabric is dark gray. That patch bothers me, so I run out to grab another evidence bag. It can't hurt to have that checked too. Even if it's got nothing to do with Frankie's problem, it might give us insight into Leora's.

While I'm out there in the main room, my phone beeps again. I bring it into the bathroom, where the steam from my shower obscures the screen. Oh, well. Whatever it is, it can wait until I'm done.

Vampires don't need showers, but every vamp I've ever had the chance to ask loves them. It's about the only way we can change our body temperature. Some vampires can do things like fake a blush. One of them, the amazing Maya, taught me how that little parlor trick works. But it's not the same as a shower hot enough to make you feel a just a little bit human for ten minutes or so.

I get out, dry off, dress, and bring the phone and my notebook with me as I go out. In the daytime, I usually like to sleep, but my bed's occupied, and I don't want to give Frankie the wrong idea. Or freak him out, which is way more likely. The last thing he needs is another monster invading his physical space.

I get in my comfy chair, drape the plush throw over my legs and check the phone again. No word from Esther on Leora yet, but that's to be expected. She said sunset, and she's always on time.

I find a text from Maya, the one vampire I've met who doesn't feel like a perpetual frenemy. She's asking how my night went because I told her about the Sparky case. I send back a quick reply, then do the redundant thing and ask if I can ask her something. It never hurts to be polite when dealing with other vampires, even if Maya and I get along like tomato and mozzarella.

While waiting for her reply, I check the other one. It's Scott, apologizing for bailing on me like that. I accept that olive branch and am about to pick up Shadow Over Innsmouth when he replies.

**Gramps wants to talk. Can I bring him over?**

**Only if he's okay with Frankie being here.**

**Nope. Better come by here at sunset instead.**

**Still going to be with Frankie.**

**Your meeting's outside, then.**

**Fine. See you later.**

I can't get my brain around all the cockamamie victim-blaming here. But then again, I'm missing information about exactly what my new friend's family sacrificed him to and what they get in exchange. Well, I can guess at that. It's got to be power. I look down at the book in my hand and shudder because an entire flock of geese walks over my grave. Canadian ones. And they're wicked pissed.

I tap out another text, this one to Maury Weintraub, the Cranston PD Detective I've known literally my whole life. I compose it carefully because he knows nothing about the supernatural, and I'm required by vampire law to do everything in my power to keep it that way.

After hitting send, I glance at the evidence bags on my kitchen counter. I'm not sure if I want Maury to succeed in pulling the string that'll let me get the slimy substance analyzed by Raphael Paolucci, the best CSI in the state. Results will help. Raph getting nosy won't. But Paolucci's a busy guy. He probably has no time to do side sleuthing on Maury's cases.

I hope.

# CHAPTER SIX

I can't send Frankie's clothes to the lab until I get any ID he's got in them out first. With gloves from my evidence kit covering my hands, I open the bag and reach in. His wallet is in the front pocket, along with a keyring, the kind that has a church key on it for opening bottled drinks. There's a phone, but it's both shattered and water-logged like it's been dropped in a puddle and stomped on.

Scott is my tech guy, not because I'm some stereotypical vampire Luddite, but because I've never been good at dissecting hardware. I put the phone in my pocket, so I don't forget to bring it when I visit the Fitzpatrick home later. Hopefully, the kid can either salvage something from it or knows a guy who can. It's Rhode Island, knowing a guy is just part of how we do things here.

Frankie is sleeping soundly, so I figure it won't hurt to have a look inside his wallet. Maybe get a little more information about the asshole family who literally threw him to something way worse than the wolves. Scott's family would never have done something so horrible to this poor guy.

He has a Rhode Island State ID, not a driver's license. His given name isn't a nickname, it's really Frankie. Last name is Pickering, as he mentioned, not that it means anything to me yet. And I was right about his age. He's turning nineteen next month. There's an address, of course, in Warwick on the border with Cranston by Pawtuxet Village. In case you haven't been there, that's an area that's heavy on the hoity with a healthy helping of toity.

Frankie's family aren't just assholes. They're rich assholes.

Only one vampire I know has been willing and able to answer my questions about magicians. Raven. But I owe them a ton of favors already. There has to be another way. I flip through my notebook, back to the scrawls made the night I went into major debt with the king's attaché. And there it is, the tidbit my brain reached for but couldn't quite find.

*Three types of magic.*

But unfortunately, my notes don't name any of them except Alchemy. If I want to know what Frankie's family is packing in the magical department, asking around is unavoidable. But at least I have a name. I turn around in my chair and snag my laptop off the bookshelf behind me.

Searching the address gives me a map of its location, and checking up on the Pickering family gives me an eyeful. They were one of the first Jewish families in Rhode Island, here even before Esther's. I read about how they took the name Pickering before coming over from Europe to the Colonies, something that was common enough during the Inquisition. Mundane records on the Pickerings show that they came here to finally live as Jews again and escape religious persecution for being themselves. Ironically, Rhode Island didn't consider them full citizens until decades after the Revolutionary War.

Italian families like mine went through our share of issues coming to this country. Back in the early twentieth century, immigration got restricted in part because US citizens were scared of organized crime imported from Sicily. Jewish people from southern and eastern Europe dealt with the same sort of bias. Several in both groups became natural associates and later allies. What the Pickerings went through and how they were treated when they got here is depressingly common, even in later times.

But Frankie's family has no excuse for casting him out the way they did, after emotional neglect and setting him up to be a victim his whole life. A reason, maybe, because monsters are powerful, scary, and their demands seem absolute. But I can't understand why they'd still shun their kid after the fact, even if he's not magically talented.

I'm going to have to phone a friend. But this time it can't be Raven. I can't afford the price because enough small favors add up to big favors, eventually reaching life-owing proportions. I don't want to owe the king's attaché my unlife in my second month of vampirism.

The phone beeps again. It's Maury, getting back to me. He'll bring my evidence to the CSI lab, but he wants to know what kind of case I'm investigating. I fire back a message about how it's an assault, possibly sexual, assailant unknown. A minute later, the phone rings. I get up and take it in the bathroom.

"Tino, is your client a little girl?"

"A kid? No, Maur. It's a guy, adult even though he's on the young side. From a wealthy family, too." I give him that bit so he won't insist I send Frankie directly to him.

"Okay. Well, no wonder he wants to keep things discreet."

"You got something about a kid?" I lean back in the chair, knowing that if it still beat, my heart would have skipped a few, worrying about Leora. Why didn't I insist on Scott walking her home? Esther wouldn't have had to bust her behind making a tracker from raspberry jam if I'd done that. Apparently I've got some work to do in the logistical planning department.

"Yeah, we do."

"What can you tell me about that?"

"Missing person cases. A mom and her little girl. The landlady reported them missing yesterday evening but thinks they've been gone for weeks now. We found the mother's body, and it ain't even in the same universe as pretty."

"Oh, shit, Maury." I close my eyes, shake my head, do the right thing. "Leora Kupala."

"You've seen her?"

"Yeah. Just did a case for her, found her missing pet."

"So the girl's missing, the mom is dead, and she hires you to find

Fido?"

"It was a lizard, Maury, not a dog. A salamander."

"Salamanders are amphibians, Tino."

"Whatever." I sigh. "I caught the critter, gave him back, and she paid me."

"When was this?"

"Um…" I check the clock and see that it's five in the morning. "Last night."

"If you have any of the bills she paid with, read me the serials."

I do that. As I'm reading off alphanumeric codes, something occurs to me. I stop in the middle of one of them.

"Leora's not a suspect."

"Can't say, Tino."

"She's definitely not." But I don't really know. I might be able to find out if I can get her mother's blood. I've got a painful but useful ability to see all the gory details about how a dead person met their end by drinking some of that.

"Look, I have information you don't about this." Maury's telling me this because he probably can't share it, but I take the long shot and ask, anyway.

"So help an old friend out."

"I'm already helping you by sending your evidence to CSI."

He's got a point. I can't really argue with it, either. The only thing I can do is try to track Leora down and get the story from her before Maury does. But I'm just a nocturnal sap with two weird partners while my bestie has the entire Cranston PD on his side. It's unlikely I'll outpace him, especially while I'm protecting Frankie. But I'll try my best. In fact, I even know a guy who might be extremely interested in protecting a human kiddo from monsters. Well, sort of a guy. But not really.

"Tino? You there?"

"Yeah. You're right, Maury. Sorry I asked. It's just a little too easy to forget that our professional relationship has to be quid pro quo."

"Look, if I were a Captain, you'd get what you want. I'm sure that you're in business to help people. But I'm just a rookie detective who lost his partner last month. If you need info, you've got to find a different source. You know what I'm saying?" Maury means that he won't stop me if I try to snoop around at the crime scene. If I can find out where it even is.

"I understand, man."

"When can I pick that evidence up? And from where?"

I tell him to meet me at my mom's and dad's house a half-hour after sunset. That'll work because the Fitzpatricks live right next door.

"See you later, Maury."

"Later, Tino."

We hang up. I immediately send a message to Kayleigh Killarney. She's my ex-girlfriend from high school and also a hunter. Normally that'd mean we're automatic enemies, but we've got a truce going on because I got the bright idea to include protecting the innocent in my Trial ceremony, proving I'll be a nice, compliant vampire. Oh, also I'm working with Scott and Esther to mix up a magical cure for Kayleigh's fiancé who's in a coma. Esther says it'll be maybe another week before it's done.

My old flame will want to help Leora stay safe for sure. She always loved kids, and as a hunter, it's sort of her duty to protect regular humans from the supernatural set. But it's way too early to get in a conversation with a human whose job makes them stay up during my usual hours. She'll get her rest before getting back to me. And that's okay.

Back in the apartment's main room, I listen for any sign that Frankie's been woken up. There's nothing but even breaths. I stare at the phone, wishing there was someone I could call at this hour just to hear a friendly voice.

Well, there's Maya. She's awesome, but I already sent her a text, and she hasn't replied. Five in the morning is like two for a vampire. She's probably asleep. And maybe that's where I should be, too.

A charging cable for the phone is right on the side table by my reading chair. I set the alarm for a few minutes before sunset and put it down on top of *Shadow Over Innsmouth*. Pulling my favorite fleece throw around me, I settle into the comfy chair for a nice little sleep. But it's not restful at all. I have a daymare because, of course, I do.

My dreams are dank and echoing like I'm in a humid drainpipe, or maybe a cave. Then I'm out and soaring through the air. My vision resolves into a reeking low-tide puddle, where I get a bird's-eye view of a body so maimed it barely looks humanoid. Except I know who it is. An old friend.

A squat hut is near her body, its foundation raised slightly off the ground, windows lit and doors closed. I sense that its occupant won't welcome me, so I drop the item that'll get the message across where it'll be seen if I don't make it back. But the dawn is coming and I want revenge, so I swoop down on leathery wings toward the drain pipe.

A hand, webbed and slimed over in something, curls around my fragile body. Wings crushed, I can't escape. Bones, skin, and hair transform as I change, trying to shock my captor and break free, but that cold grip is like a riptide. I'm a fly in amber as darkness takes me.

In the distance, something beeps. No, not in the distance, next to my ear.

Wakefulness pulls me from dreamscape perdition. I open eyes crusted at the corners with dried bloody tears. Pulling the phone from its charger, I read the name of my savior.

Maya. She's saying sure, I can ask her anything I want. Is she flirting with me? I can't tell over text, so I figure a call might be in order, even if I'm totally out of her league. But I have to check on Frankie first. The last thing I want to do is stomp all over the poor guy's damage by asking point-blank questions about magicians where he can hear. If he's too messed up to talk about them coherently, he's too traumatized to listen to that yet.

Frankie's still out like a light, but he isn't snoring anymore. He's moved, too, as though he had a bad dream at the same time I did. To play it safe, I head into the bathroom and close the door before calling Maya.

"Tino, good to hear your voice." I imagine her smiling, the white of her teeth and fangs like a crescent moon in the dark sky of her face. Yeah, I think I've got it bad. "What did you want to ask me?"

Ways to ask her out litter my mind like stars in a clear night sky. But I won't make any assumptions on how she thinks of me, not over the phone anyway. And I have to figure out how to help Frankie. Right. That was the reason for my call in the first place. Maya's great, but she sure is distracting.

"I'm trying to learn about magicians who aren't alchemists. I got a new case, and this poor guy from a magic family needs serious help, but none of his relatives will even talk to him. Do you know anyone besides Raven who's got knowledge or experience with magicians and their ways?"

"Wow, Tino." Maya sighs. "Well, I've got good news and bad news."

"Lay it on me, good news first."

"I only know a little, but I'll tell it all to you."

"That's amazing, Maya." And it really is, because she didn't mention a favor exchange at all. "Thank you. You're the best. Now, what about that bad news?"

"There's another vampire who's in the know about magicians, but you aren't going to be happy when you hear who it is."

"The king?" I can't think of a scarier vamp in the entire state of Rhode Island.

"No. Whitby."

"Shitballs." I sigh. Whitby is a powerful vampire from maybe the Middle Ages with a handful of followers chained to him by blood or debt. Or both. Maya's one of them, and she's made it very clear she's not happy about that. I suspect Whitby's involved in crimes against both the vampire and human communities. On a personal level, I like Raven way better than him, but so far I don't owe him anything. If his price for information is too high, I have the right to refuse the deal.

But there's one factor to consider before making a deal with the proverbial white-suited devil.

"Okay, Maya. Tell me what you know. I'll investigate what I can on that before deciding whether to go into Whitby's debt."

"Sounds like a plan. There are Alchemists, Spell-Singers, and Theophiles."

"So, what do they all do?" I already know a pretty respectable amount about Alchemy but want to hear Maya's take. My pen is against a blank page in my notebook, ready to jot down everything she says. I'm forgetful, okay? At least I'm doing my best to cope with it.

"Alchemists make stuff. They do magic by crafting and always need materials and a little bit of time to prepare. Spell-Singers don't have to make music, but their words have literal power with almost no preparation. They need to be careful with what they say, or they'll risk an accidental cast. And Theophiles get their magic by paying tithes to magical or divine creatures in exchange for power and good fortune."

"Divine?" I blink. I'm Catholic, so the idea of gods doesn't play nicely in my head or heart with my beliefs. "Like classic Greek and Roman mythology? Zeus? Or is it monsters?"

"I'm talking about the stuff of myths and legends here, Tino." Maya sighs. "Not Zeus. Not hybrid people like us or the werewolves, either. More like Yokai or Dryads. It's been a long time since the majority of humans believed in those creatures, but magicians do, and that's what counts. Because the only other thing I can recall about Theophile magic is this; it only works if the head of the family believes the pact is valid."

"Wow, Maya. Thanks, that's incredibly helpful." And it is. Because she's awesome. But I don't say it because she'd probably rather hear that from someone cooler than me. Which is practically every other vampire in Providence.

"You coming to the Blood Moot tonight?" The event she's talking about is a monthly vampire gathering endorsed and enforced by King DeCampo.

"I am now."

"Good!" She sounds happier about that than I expect.

We say our goodbyes. Maya hesitates over the farewell though I'm not sure why. Once I hang up, I tell Siri to set a series of alarms so I'm not late to the Blood Moot like last time. After that, I settle in for another attempt at sleep. This time, no daymares plague me.

# CHAPTER SEVEN

The sound that wakes me up this time is not the phone. It's a hollow thud followed by a short muffled scream. I open my eyes to see Frankie on the floor by the bed, tangled in the curtains and blankets. His arms pinwheel, flailing wildly as he sits up. In half a moment, I'm at his side.

"Frankie, cool it, man." I put one hand on his shoulder, feeling its heat. Was I this warm when I was still really alive?

"Tino?"

"Yeah, it's me." I grin. "Your friendly neighborhood vampire guy."

"God, I thought—" He hangs his head. "It was like being back there. I'm sorry."

"Nothing to apologize for." I help him up, back to the edge of the bed. "Nightmares are normal, under the circumstances. Or daymares."

"Is that what you call them?"

"Yeah." I pull a section of blanket out from where it's twisted under his arm.

"You're a good guy, Valentino." Frankie yawns.

"That word. I don't think it means what you think it means." I gesture back at the bed.

"It's not inconceivable for a vampire to be a decent person."

Frankie curls up in a ball with his head on the pillow. He looks so young that way, not like the newly adult man he is, more like a Freshman in High School.

"Yeah, well. I try." I tuck the blanket around his shoulders.

"Thanks for that." His eyes close. "It's more than my parents ever did."

I listen to his breath and heartbeat until they're at a pace to indicate he's sleeping. After that, I look at the clock. It's one in the afternoon now, and I'm wide awake, so I figure it's time to do some checking on the information Maya gave me. I use the terms in the notebook for some Google searches. Most of it is fiction, but that's what you get when you look up vampires, so I expect it to be the same for other supernaturals.

I end up finding one site that looks like it actually has legitimate information. I read the About page and see that it's still a fictitious website. I mean, no factual page would claim to be authored by a real Sasquatch who interviews cryptologists and their subjects, right? But anyway, the site's a blog, with posts on cryptids from Chupacabra to Yeti. Baba Yaga's even listed, but I leave that entry open in its own tab for now.

Each post I look at has information about the featured creature, including human legends. The difference between this site and others with similar subject matter is the sympathy for the monsters. Usually, websites about the supernatural don't humanize their subject matter, and often give advice on how to harm or kill the creatures in question. Not so here. The writer actually cares about giving a fair description.

That empathy is what kicks off my hunch that this is the real deal. Or at least as real as these things get on the world wide web.

So, I select a few entries with the idea in mind that at least half of the content is true. It takes a while even with a mug of blood at my elbow so I can read at high speed. Eventually, I find it tucked away at the end of an article about Domovoi.

In case you've never heard of them, the article says Domovoi are house-elves. Well, not really elves exactly but spirits who look like little old people and appreciate good housekeeping skills. But the part that interests me isn't the fact that they're from a Russian legend, it's that they're known for following families.

Even with his *Crocodile Hunter* style enthusiasm and clear appreciation for his subjects, the blogger doesn't slack off in the research methods department. Sasquatch lists citations and credits at the end of all the blog posts. There's a name for this article, a very familiar one. Leora Kupala.

"Well, I'll be a bat's brother." I shake my head. "Even the internet's a small world when you're from Rhode Island."

I lean back in my comfy chair, laptop across my thighs. If the kid talked to a blogger who dresses up like Sasquatch, she's definitely no ordinary 'tween. Or maybe she is. Leora seems to be at about the top limit of the age where most people stop believing in imaginary things. According to Maya, belief is a big deal for magicians and their kin, so maybe that makes a difference for mundanes who sit down to toast and jam with Baba Yaga, too.

The phone beeps, and this time it's Kayleigh. The message says yeah, she'll help me track the kid down. I give her the phone number that called us last night and a description of Leora, leaving out the part about her interview with the Sasquatch. If this blogger is really what he claims to be, the last thing I want is for him to end up in the Killarney family crosshairs.

I drink down the last of the blood in my mug and go to get more. High-speed internet searching is thirsty work when you're a vampire, and part of that speediness moniker has to do with using a blood-burning ability. I'm jotting down what I hope are useful notes from the website when the phone beeps again.

Kayleigh has found Leora's record of enrollment in Alan Shawn Feinstein Middle School. Apparently, she's just finishing eighth grade already, so maybe she's older than I thought. And from Coventry, where it's a little bit country and a little bit crunchy. Well, nobody's perfect.

My ex says she's on like *Donkey Kong* for the recon. Yeah, she actually uses those words. Our time in high school was spent in the geek crowd, and while I was into theater like Maury, Kayleigh was a gamer. Maybe still is, actually, considering her favorite titles back then were *Halo* and *Call of Duty,* and she's an expert sniper.

I send back a thumbs-up emoji. Yeah, okay, I'm a creature of the night, but I'm still a Millennial. Of course I use emoji in text messages; I'm not an undead relic yet.

Settling back into the comfy chair seems like an exercise in precarious Feng Shui. I move everything over to the breakfast table except for the fleece throw, which I end up staring at longingly every time I woolgather after reading one of Sasquatch's articles.

This is taking forever, but the blood has finally perked me up enough to do the sensible thing. A site search. I look for articles that include the word slime. A handful pop up, and I have a browse through them. I read the entry on Deep Ones seven times. After that, I get up and stand over Frankie, watching him sleep.

I'm not sure whether I'm on the right track or not because there are inconsistencies. But the similarities chill me to the bone despite Rhode Island's warm early summer weather. Deep Ones make contracts and mate with humans in exchange for relics from the sea. They're immortal creatures, tied to unnamable entities they worship as gods. And the families they tether themselves to become prosperous and stay that way. I get the impression that even kindly old Sasquatch didn't like them much.

Stephanie was right. As much as I want to hate that, the desire to help Frankie takes priority over getting angry at her for giving me creepy homework. I shut the laptop down, plug it in to charge, and take my mug of blood back over to the comfy chair where I take my sire's advice.

I read *Shadows Over Innsmouth* while I wait for either the next text messages to come in or sunset. And it's just as disturbing a read as I expected. The Deep Ones from Lovecraft's imagination are true monsters, treating their human allies like livestock needed to produce their hybrid offspring, and the humans get the short end of the stick every time.

Esther's text comes first. It says to call her, so I set Lovecraft's disturbing book down, head to the bathroom, and tap her number on the screen. It rings only once before she picks up.

"That tracker was a bitch to make, Tino. It's not my usual, either."

"What do you mean?" I stare at my empty collar in the bathroom mirror.

"I mean, you've got to drink this shit; mix it in soda or water or whatever. And it won't even fucking work for bloodsuckers."

"It figures."

"Also, I'm not fucking taking it."

"What?"

"Doesn't fucking work on magicians, either. Don't be an asshole and ask more stupid questions when I've got a date with my pillow."

"Okay." This is why I have two partners. "When can I get it?"

"Dropped it in your mailbox already. Now I'm going the fuck to sleep. This bitch is tired."

"Thanks, Esther. I owe you one."

"No. We're even. Thanks for helping with that other fucking thing." She's talking about her uncle without naming him. I'm getting the impression that she's not allowed to help him or even say too much.

"Ah. You're welcome." There's a list of questions I want to ask her about magicians, so the entire situation's a bummer.

I let her hang up and look at the clock. It's getting late, so I stay in the bathroom and take another shower. Yes, *Shadows over Innsmouth* and the fact that Deep Ones are real and also really horrible is literally making my skin crawl. The shower helps.

When I'm done, Frankie's awake. He's rummaging around in the fridge looking for food and coming up empty, of course. I open the closet and get out the stash of Myoplex bars I keep here for when Scott gets hungry. I also grab a duffel to stuff the evidence bags into. I snag my jacket too, because pockets are important when you need to carry blood around.

"Sorry for poking around in there," Frankie jerks one thumb at the refrigerator. "And thanks for the bars."

"No problem." I get some of my blood bags and stock my jacket. "We've got someplace to go in a few minutes."

"Will there be more food there? No offense, but—" His stomach rumbles.

"I'll find you some." I don't think the Fitzpatricks will feed someone they can't stand the smell of, but my folks have a fully stocked fridge right next door, and we're Italian. They expect me to eat when I go to their house.

"Where are we going?"

"I've got to talk to some werewolves."

"Oh, no." Frankie takes half a step back, the counter stopping him when he bumps it with his hip. "They'll want to kill me."

"These are good werewolves, Frankie. Friends of mine and my sire's from way back. I'll explain how I'm helping you, and they'll back off."

"You don't understand. It's how I smell to them now; it'll enrage them. I can't go into a werewolf's den."

"That's why we're only talking to one, and our meeting is outside."

"Outside?" Frankie's shoulders relax a bit. "Okay, so they've thought this through."

"Yeah, like I said, they're friends. Neighbors, actually. Grew up next door to them."

Frankie seems mollified by this new piece of information. He's still making with the nervous tics, like picking at his thumbnails. But that's understandable. I stash my notebook, and we head out. I grab Esther's tracking powder out of my mailbox on the way.

It takes less than ten minutes to get from my side of Cranston to the neighborhood to the west where my parents and the Fitzpatrick family live. Rhode Island is small in a geographical sense. This means it doesn't take more than forty-five minutes to get anywhere unless the traffic sucks. It also means you can tell who grew up here by what they consider a long trip to be.

Anyway, before we know it, we're there. I park around the corner, though, because I don't want my folks to see my car and think I'm avoiding them. Sunday dinner still happens, but aside from that, I haven't been over here since Ma mistakenly decided that all my weird behavior since getting turned is because I'm gay, not a vampire. Bringing Frankie by will only reinforce that idea since I'm not allowed to tell her the truth.

But it turns out the house is dark. I finally remember that this is Ma's and Dad's date night, which means my folks are up at what Ma calls "Stinkin' Lincoln" casino. They'll be out until well after midnight. I could have parked there after all.

We're walking up the side of the Fitzpatrick house, which is one of those ranches built into a hill. The basement is covered in the front but exposed at the back of the building, which is where we go. A wooden gate, one I can all too easily imagine falling and staking myself on, probably deters most vampires from visiting. Well, that and the odor.

Werewolves smell like a High School locker room to vampires. Whether it's because of the speedy healing they can do or some sort of weird wolfy hormone, I'm not sure. But they're probably the last creatures any vamp wants to put the bite on unless we're in a hunger rage. Which happened to me once in the not too distant past, but that's a whole other story.

Inside the fenced enclosure, there's a gazebo all strung up with little white Christmas lights. It's got a hand-cobbled path leading from the steel back door of the basement to the screen and wood one on the gazebo. I remember looking down from my bedroom window as a kid, imagining myself walking up to it, discovering a magical creature inside. And now, here I am facing that gazebo. But I'm not alone, and I know that the seated figure at the center isn't magical, not exactly.

Werewolves and vampires are hybrids. They were all human at one point in their lives and then changed, either by their DNA in the case of the wolves or by somebody's deliberate choice for vamps. Because it's just the way my brain works, my thoughts jump to a question. Can a vampire turn a magician? I already know they can't turn werewolves because Stephanie told me. It doesn't work and only results in one seriously pissed-off wolf. Next time I see her, I'll ask.

I'm standing on the path just steps from the gazebo because I literally stopped to think. I'm not even sure whether I should bring Frankie in with me or ask him to stay outside. I see a silhouette inside, seated. So he's in there, but do I knock, or what? And then, a voice from behind the screen tells me exactly what to do.

"Enter, Valentino Crispo and Frankie Pickering."

We both step forward because with an order like that from the oldest and wisest werewolf in this territory, what else is there to do?

# CHAPTER EIGHT

"I never thought I'd see the day." Grandpa Fitzpatrick chuckles and winks one cataract-marbled eye. "And come to think of it, I didn't."

"Sir—"

"Don't sir me, sonny boy. I've known you from diapers to Dracula, and you're still not done growing up. It's Fergus like always, and if you call me 'sir' again, this meeting is over."

"It's your house, Fergus."

"From the mouth of babes." Fergus nods. "Now, you're wondering why I've asked you here."

"Yes. Especially Frankie. From what he tells me, people like him are eternally shunned."

"Nothing about the boy is eternal unless he gets turned." Fergus leans forward, putting some of his weight on the shillelagh he's holding between his knees. "And as you're demonstrating now, the magician tradition's not totally universal."

"That's just because I don't know any better."

"You've got that dead wrong." Fergus gives us a doggy grin. Dad jokes aren't good enough for him, he's got to make grandpa puns. "As a vampire, you're not bound by anything you haven't explicitly vowed to do, Valentino. No one will censure you for helping or for having a great big heart."

I can practically hear Frankie's jaw drop.

"So it's not some kind of supernatural effect that's turning everyone off?" I ask while looking into Frankie's misty eyes. "Just a set of rules?"

"There's no just when it comes to binding supernatural rules, boyo. Except for the true mundanes and your kind."

"Yeah, that seems to be an unfortunate pattern."

"Mark my words, Tino. Magic needs patterns. Even the limited amount we wolves get from our ties to the moon has its regulations."

"You remember how I was on the force." I snort. "All those do is trip me up."

"Ain't that the truth?" Frankie finally gets himself together enough to speak, but he slaps his hand over his mouth immediately. I try not to imagine the kind of punishment he got for speaking out of turn while growing up.

"You can speak here, Frankie Pickering. But only while we're still in this fancy-pants gazebo of mine. It's neutral ground."

"Oh." Frankie lets out a sigh bigger than most yawns. "That's a relief."

"You were saying?" The old man turns his finger in the air, a sign for Frankie to continue his line of thought.

"My family's rules are brutal. The Lambs have no say in them like some other families. Deep Ones want to know who they're getting the second we're tested for magic. I was doomed before I was weaned and raised knowing it. We're literal scapegoats over at the Pickering house. Tino and his great big heart? It's all a big fat mistake. You called us here to stop him from helping me, didn't you?"

"I did no such thing."

"Wait, what?" Frankie takes the words right out of my mouth.

"You're here to get the official and unfortunate news that my wolves and I must stay out of this. My clan can't help you this time, Valentino. Not even young Scott."

"Well, thanks anyway, Fergus." There goes my idea about giving Frankie's phone to Scott.

"Don't thank me yet, boyo." He clears his throat. "You're also here so I can say we're staying out of your way.

"What does that mean?" Frankie scratches his head.

"That means if we see you, Tino, or any other allies you might gather toward the goal of breaking the Pickerings' rules, we look the other way, and mum's the word. If they ask us directly, we claim ignorance. All of my people are on board with me about this."

"Are you serious?"

"Deadly."

"Wow, Fergus. Thank you." I know what refusing to talk can mean for vampires, and it ain't easy. I've tried it. It might be different for werewolves, but probably not much. And magicians are powerful, too, which is clear even though exactly what they can do remains murky.

"Don't mention it." He winks. "Get it?" There's no chuckle this time, just a full-on guffaw. And now I see why he leans on the shillelagh. It keeps him from toppling out of the chair.

"So, is that it?"

"Almost."

"Okay, let me have it."

And he does. With both barrels.

"You can't go on like this with your faith and your folks. Something's got to give, Valentino. And if you're not prepared for trouble on those fronts, it'll break you in the long run. I might not live to see that happen, but I definitely do not want Scott to have to put you down when he's in this seat decades down the line."

"Um." I'm not blinking from surprise. My eyelids are trying to hold back a bloody deluge. Grandpa Fitzpatrick might be blind, but his insight's keen as a razor, and he cut right to the heart of my matter. I walk around every night with a vague sense of moral danger, like a brushfire off in the distance. Fergus just pointed out something I should have known already. Even slow burns consume when left unchecked too long.

"Si— Uh, Fergus." Frankie steps forward. "Tino's not alone. He'll have help with his family and everything else besides."

"Vampire debt won't do a thing on these fronts, Frankie. They're matters of the heart, not something to resolve with the payback for a vampire's favors."

"No. I'm telling you that *I'll* help him with it. Not because I owe him since there's no debt. Because he's my friend. You have my word, for whatever that's worth."

"I'll take it."

"You. You will?" Frankie blinks. "My family says my word means nothing."

"Your family isn't typical for Theophiles. And you're not the first to rise above the Pickering family this way either, though according to our tales, it was ages ago. But that's another matter I've promised not to mention outside my clan. You'll have to stumble across it on your own."

"That's fine by me." Frankie actually grins. "I'm pretty good at stumbling."

"Now this meeting's over. Shoo. Scram. Get outta here!" Fergus brandishes the stout wooden walking stick in sham menace.

I head through the gazebo's door, Frankie in tow. The sensation of being watched, even listened to, persists the entire way through the yard, out the gate, and down the path to the street. We go back to my car so I can move it and get the stuff we need to give to Maury, since Esther's tracking powder is practically useless. Scott's banned from helping me until we fix Frankie's problem. And that's when I get a bright idea.

"Hey, Frankie?"

"Yeah?"

"How do you feel about Alchemy?"

"Esther used to let me help her with all her gear after she got home to recover from the Iraq War. I'm cool with it."

"She gave me this stuff." I shake the envelope. "It's to track someone down, maybe a missing kid. But magicians and vampires can't use it, and Fergus said Scott—"

"I know what you're going to ask. And I'll help you, but only if I'm not going to have to fight anything. I suck at that."

"There shouldn't be any fighting, no. Just the tracking is enough. If it comes to blows and you want to bug out, I don't mind."

"Cool."

Once we get out of the car, I get the side door open, and we head into my mom's kitchen. The only light comes from the fixture over the stoop. So once we're inside, I flip the light switch.

It's never Better Homes and Gardens in Ma's kitchen. She's got one side of the sink piled with a pair of plates, forks, knives, and glasses. The dishwasher magnet is set to empty. A box of pastry from Solitro's Bakery sits on the counter, red and white strings slack and untied, a dusting of powdered sugar beside it. God, I miss their bismarcks. Best in Cranston. Have one sometime and think of me while you do.

I move the box away from the sink, setting it in front of Frankie, who eats everything left inside it. Can't blame the kid for being hungry. And I get to smell the pastries, which is what I've always imagined as heaven's fragrance. My parents will notice they're missing, but they'll think I deserved them in exchange for tidying while I dropped by.

I brush the sugar away from the formica surface, then start rinsing dishes and loading the dishwasher. I want the sink clear so I can mix up the tracking powder for Frankie. It's quick work, washing up after a meal for two people with vamp speed. I also realize it's truly an endless chore, like laundry. Vampires still drink and wear clothes, after all.

The envelope has instructions written on it. Fortunately, I know where Ma keeps the measuring cups, and there's plenty of water. I get a glass down and set a spoon beside it. Once the red and green granules are sitting at the bottom, I stuff the envelope in my pocket since the last thing I want to do is leave supernatural info in plain sight on Ma's counter.

I measure exactly seven ounces of water like the instructions say and then stir until the concoction looks exactly like the iced tea

Maury and I used to make from a Lipton canned drink at our sleepovers.

I'm about halfway back to the table where Frankie is waiting to bring him the magic beverage, when there's a knock at the door. I can already tell it's Maury by how he smells, which is of illness and chemicals. He doesn't wait, just walks in. Decades of familiarity will do that.

"Tino! You're a mensch! How did you know I'd be thirsty?"

Before I can speak up, Maury Weintraub chugs every last drop of the beverage, which is definitely not iced tea. That's right. He accidentally drinks the tracking potion it took Esther all day to make. Because, of course, he does.

When he's done, he sets the glass on the table and heads straight for the evidence bags on the kitchen table. He pauses, one hand over them, and lets out a long, gurgling belch.

"Excuse me." Maury grins benignly at Frankie. "Hi, I'm Detective Weintraub. Tino might have told you that I'm his PD contact. You remind me of someone. Do you have a cousin who's an Enby, by any chance?"

It's like watching a train wreck. I can't look away or even move, but my brain's not frozen. The Enby Maury mentions is Raven, who apparently had a connection to Edwin Tierney, who worked with the dead partner whose funeral Maury and I attended last month. Along with Scott. And a mystery person in a long, black veil. Who was kid-sized. Oh, shit. Could it have been Leora? Was that why she decided to hire me? But I've got no time to skip down that mental path.

"Uh—" Frankie's watching Maury like a hawk. I don't blame him since that's what I'm doing too. We're both waiting for the tracking potion to have some kind of visible effect.

I flare my nostrils, a sense of foreboding setting in. Maury must have been at a chemotherapy appointment earlier that day. He's got lung cancer, which he's fighting, and he had better beat it, or I'll kill him. But if the chemo drugs in his system cancel out or otherwise alter that tracking powder, Leora might end up suffering for it.

And the worst part is, I can't say word one on the subject. Maury's not in the know, and I pledged to King DeCampo at my Trial that I wouldn't tell humans about the supernatural. But my best friend Maury has serious investigative instincts, and our staring at him has them going off like fire alarms.

"What?" He puts his hands on his hips and gives me the same glare he used in our high school musical review *Les Mis* number when he sang Javert to my Valjean.

He's all hollowed out now, but it's still the same. I'll never forget it even if he dies. No, not if, when.

Because he will. And I won't. That's what Fergus meant about coming to terms about my folks. I close my eyes, stricken with preemptive grief, unable to answer. If I open my mouth, all of it might come pouring out like Valjean's eventual admission of guilt.

"It's just, um, Mr. Weintraub?" And it's Frankie for the Hail Mary.

"Yeah, kid?"

"That wasn't just tea in there."

"No?"

"No, it's also medicine. That drink was for me. See, Mr. Crispo was helping me out. I haven't been eating right after everything that happened, not enough fluids. I'm blocked up."

"Oh. Well, shit."

"Um." I open my eyes. "Yeah. You might feel like, maybe a sense of urgency. Like you've got to be somewhere else. It's a side-effect."

"That doesn't sound like Ex-Lax."

"It's not. It's a prescription from the kid's doctor. Has some of his other meds in it too. Right, Frankie?"

"Right!"

"Oy vey. Well, before it kicks in, tell me about this evidence."

I explain that one bag contains the clothes Frankie wore during the assault. The other one has my shirt since I think evidence got on it, maybe. That's good enough for Maury. He scoops up the bags and heads out the still-open door. We follow, and I burn some blood to lock up quickly while my old friend's back is turned.

Once Maury puts the evidence in his car, he gets into the driver's seat. I can see something on the passenger side, another evidence sample sitting inside an unzipped cooler. It's blood, and I can read the name Kupala on the label.

I open the passenger side and start getting in. It's the natural thing to do, what with Maury unwittingly tracking Leora's mysterious guardian while under the influence of an alchemist's potion. Also, I want a taste of that blood. Sure I'll puke my guts out, but maybe a couple of my zillion questions will finally have an answer.

But Maury's having none of it. "Tino, what the hell are you doing?"

"Uh, bringing Frankie down to—"

"No. What you're doing is getting the hell out of my car. I'll call you when I hear something, as usual. For now, I've got the feeling I have to be somewhere. Like, yesterday. Thanks for that, by the way." He rolls his eyes.

And just like that, I have to let him go. Trying to get in was a gamble, but if I push the issue, Maury will start poking his nose into supernatural business I'll only have to stop him from getting involved in. I don't even wait for Maury to get out of the driveway before dashing toward my own car, dragging Frankie along with me. We get in.

"Follow that car!"

"You're the one driving!"

"Yeah. Okay. I knew that." I crank the ignition and throw it in reverse.

My nervous excitement at the prospect of a high-speed chase vanishes when I realize Maury's driving like Grandma Moses. Which makes sense because if he's on a tracking potion, he doesn't exactly know the way as much as he has to sense it. At least, that's what Esther's instructions said.

I'll have to trust them for now and take it on faith that the stuff actually worked.

# CHAPTER NINE

In the car, my phone rings. Like an idiot, I never set the Bluetooth up when I got in, and Rhode Island's hands-free driving law just went into effect last month. Well, I was in an unmerited rush, okay? I don't dare pick it up because then Maury could just pull me over, chew me out, and write me a ticket. The potion in his system might stop him from doing that, although I don't want to take any chances.

But Frankie steps in again. He's picked the phone up, put it on the charger, tapped the button to answer the call, and put it on speaker. The kid's a freaking hero. What's up with these younger adults and their awesomeness? Well, they'll save the world someday, I bet.

"It's Maury," Frankie whispers.

"Heya, Maur." I grin and keep my eyes on the slow-moving bumper in front of me. Not to keep up, but so I don't step on the brake too late and hit it.

"Tino, I don't feel so good." He stifles a small burp. "More than usual, I mean."

"Yeah, sorry about that." And I am. The last thing I want is to make my oldest and best friend feel worse.

"Look, I was gonna tell you to stop following me, but now I think I'll let you." He snorts. "Got a hunch I should."

"Where are you headed?" I'm hoping maybe he's been to wherever this potion leads before and knows the answer to this question.

"I dunno what to tell you, man. Just I've got to be there. It's the weirdest freaking thing."

"I hear you."

"And I have this enormous headache coming on." Yeah, that's one of Esther's listed possible side-effects.

"Oh, man, Maury."

He's been driving down Park Avenue, heading east toward the coast. We pass Roger Williams Park, where he slows down, and I breathe a sigh of relief when he doesn't stop there. I bet who or whatever we're tracking has been in the park recently, though. It's just a hop, skip, and a jump from my office. But I know next to nothing about the Kupalas or Baba Yaga. For all I know, the legendary old hag hangs around in parks.

And this is where I kick myself because I finally ask myself the question you must have had on your mind for half this story. Why didn't I look Baba Yaga up online when an article about her was right there on Sasquatch's cryptid site? Because I'm a scatterbrain who forgets almost everything I don't write a to-do list for, that's why. And I read about the stupid Russian house-elves instead. Nobody's perfect, okay?

We get to the end of Park Avenue and bang a right on Broad Street, heading south down the coast. There's no view because buildings block it, but we pass Rhodes on the Pawtuxet and then all the awesome restaurants I can't eat at anymore. Go have a crepe at Schastea in my honor or something if you're ever in that neighborhood.

And there we are, crossing the border with Warwick. Maury pulls into the parking lot at Pawtuxet Park, spitting distance from Cranston. He gets out, leaving all his evidence in the car. And the door open.

As he walks toward the water, I pull on my gloves and grab the bag with the blood in it. I can't just take the vial I'm holding, so I open it instead. Now is a bad time to have a gulp, puke to the point of starvation, and trance out into one of my vision things. I look around in Maury's messy car for another option.

There's a Dunks iced coffee cold cup nestled inside a hot cup. I separate them and put the cold cup back in the holder, then tip the blood sample sideways over the empty styrofoam container. About a third goes in, and that's plenty. I cap the vial, put it away, and head back to my car with the ill-gotten evidence.

Frankie's already headed out to follow Maury, so that's where I go next. We find him standing at a wall that holds the water back at high tide, right at the border between the two towns. Maury turns and walks along that barrier toward a tree. Under it is a bill, smeared with red. He reaches down and grabs it, peering intently.

"Is this blood?"

"Raspberry jam."

"What?" Maury blinks, then levels his gaze at me. "If I didn't have the biggest headache in the history of cranial pain, I'd be on your case forever, asking how the hell you know."

He peers at the serial number, and I can practically see the wheels in his head turning. Unlike me, Maury's got a brilliant memory. And I know exactly what he's doing. Checking that number against the ones I gave him over the phone from the cash Leora paid me.

"It's sequential, Tino," he says, finally. "The kid's either complicit, or whoever gave her the cash for your fee is. I'm not sure which." Maury closes his eyes and rubs his temple. "Don't know how CSI missed it. Probably because Raph wasn't on shift last night."

The tide's in, but around five in the morning, it wasn't. I realize I can't get at the actual crime scene now because it's underwater.

"Wait, is that the crime scene?" I point down at where the sea covers the edge of the Cranston side.

"Yeah, Tino. This was where we found the kid's mom. Down there." He jerks his chin at the water. "Barely inside our jurisdiction in front of a Cranston Water overflow pipe." That rings a bell but not loudly enough.

"Hey, guys," Frankie's standing completely still, pointing one finger at the grass by the corner of the barrier. It's on a little hill, beside a spot where the park planners left space for people to be at the edge of the water, chosen because the tide won't flood it out except during a hurricane.

I power-walk over there. Even as a human, I was faster than Maury, and I blow him out of the water now, of course. It always amazes me how complimentary our skills still are even now. It's what made us good partners as beat cops. And we were supposed to continue that as detectives, too, until the supernatural world sank its fangs into me and divided us.

But the item Frankie's pointing at banishes all that wistful nostalgia from my mind. The thing he's found strikes me to my knees in fear. Because there's no way he should have been able to see it. And it shouldn't have been discarded by the water in the first place.

I'm talking about the amulet all vampires ever tested and recognized by a vampire king wear every night of their unlives. This is a Lazakhar, the red vampire jewel, and it's set in a familiar Greek key-embossed frame. This amulet should be around my sire Stephanie McQueen's undead little neck.

Unless it's been severed from her body, that is.

No. I fucking refuse to stop hoping because I'm a Rhode Islander. We might be misfits, but we never give up. There's one more reason Steph's Lazakhar would be here. She left it on purpose, so any vampire who sees it would know she's gone missing and where it happened. My gut tells me I'm on the right mental track. Something's familiar about this place, too, but I'm not sure why just yet. I have faith it'll come to me.

I scoop the amulet up in my hand, then stow it in the front pocket of my jeans. I'm going to the Blood Moot later, so I can bring this directly to King DeCampo. But there's still one piece of information I don't know what to do with.

"Frankie, how did you find this?"

"Uh, I saw it?"

"Hmm." I glance at Maury because I can't talk openly about this in front of him. What I see makes me dash to his side.

Maury's knees are buckling, and he's holding his head with both hands. His face is pale as a sheet, too. I catch him as he topples over and find that his center of gravity is all messed up. Like Frankie's was last night, only to a lesser degree. There's something slimy on his shoe.

"Maur, you okay?"

"Gotta sleep it off." The end of the last word resolves itself into a snore. I try not to end up on the ground while reaching for Esther's can of levitating powder. Frankie snags it from my pocket and sprinkles some on Maury's head.

As we get the sleeping detective to my car and into the back seat (seatbelts are awesome for anchoring levitating people in case you didn't know), I can finally talk to Frankie, well, frankly. I close the car's door just in case Maury is only out of it instead of truly asleep.

"Humans can't see vamp amulets unless we're turning them. And you pointed it out to me. So what gives?"

He follows me over to the detective's car, where I lock it up. Once we're somewhere safe, I'll use Maury's phone to text the PD and have it towed back to the station. I know enough to say that he ended up needing to investigate on foot and doesn't want to leave the car where it is.

"I don't know. I didn't expect to see anything. But I had a nightmare about this park, and when I went to the spot that seemed most familiar, I saw something shiny."

"Are you psychic?" Some humans have sixth senses, and they vary widely in strength and type. Kayleigh's dad can sense supernaturals, for example. Maybe Frankie has prophetic dreams.

Or maybe he tapped into mine somehow. And yeah, that hill is familiar, could have been the one near the drainpipe in my dream. There was something else here, too. A building. And it's gone, which should be impossible. It's coming back to me now, how some creature snatched what felt like a shapeshifter. But if this is Stephanie's amulet, that means she's—

The alarm on my phone goes off. You know, the one I set so I won't be late to the Blood Moot? Again? I don't have time for this. That's a recurring theme I'm not fond of. It's like I've pissed off a Time Lord or something.

"Never mind. We've got to get you and Maury someplace safe. I've got to go out, and you guys can't come along." I open the driver's side door on my car.

"Why?"

"It's vampires only. Don't worry, I'll take you and Maury someplace safe."

"Oh, okay." He shrugs and gets in the passenger side.

I take them to the studio. One reason for that is, it's close. The other reason is, Esther's there. She made it clear she'd prefer not to have Frankie around, but if it's for Maury, maybe she'll tolerate his presence.

Wait. Esther doesn't even know Maury.

Well, it's too late to worry about that. I'm in the parking lot. I look up at the windows and see that the lights are out at the weirdo factory on the second floor, but they're on in my office directly above. We head in and up to the third floor. I bring the cup containing the Kupala blood with me.

When I open the door at Sentry Vanguard Sleuthing, Esther jumps up from the futon we've got in there next to the Shoji screen she sold me last month, which has reverted to its original shabby appearance. One glance around the room tells me everything else looks like the office's original College Hill dumpster-dive decor again. The Alchemy that made it all swanky was only temporary. Bummer.

Esther's black hair is mussed on one side, and she wipes away a trail of what looks like drool from the bottom of one angular cheek. I'm not sure why the alchemist is sleeping here instead of in her lab. But she's not at her apartment because of the slow renovations. Don't look at me, she destroyed her own place. Anyway, that's a story for another time.

"What's with the fucking cop?" Esther looks from me to Maury, eyes skipping over Frankie entirely.

"He needs a safe place to sleep off your tracking potion." I walk over to my desk and get out one of the vials and corks I keep in it for blood samples. The stuff I nicked from Maury's evidence goes in there. Once it's sealed, I put it in my jacket.

She saunters over to Maury. I can't decide if she's checking him out or using some kind of magic to see if he's okay. Esther reaches into his jacket pocket, pulls out his wallet, and opens it. Her left eyebrow raises.

"Weintraub? This is your fucking PD contact you expect me to babysit?"

"Frankie's got to stay here, too."

"This is absolute fucking horseshit, Tino."

"I know, but it's not my horseshit. There's vampire business in my immediate future, and I can't bring them."

"A girl can't get her goddamned beauty rest in this crappy fucking place."

"I mean, you could. If you set up your wards like in your lab. Maury's going to be out for a while, and Frankie's tired." I turn to have a look at what he's doing and see he's raided the mini-fridge, which is fine. Bismarcks are amazing but not exactly filling.

"Why can't you leave them at your place, then?"

"Because Frankie's been attacked, and Maury's been investigating the thing that did it. Or did you forget how fucked your uncle was last night?" I can't help it. I'm angry with her. Traditions or no, she should care about a kid who did nothing but look up to her when his parents treated him like shit.

"You know jack and shit about what happened to my uncle, asshole."

"Look, I found out he's from a Theophile family, and he's part of their pact-making. It's pretty easy to understand, really. They get their powers from their Faustian deal, his sacrifice, and your silence. So yes, I maybe know some shit, even if it's not of the jacked variety."

Frankie drops the bottle of Gatorade he's holding and freezes. Thank God they come in plastic bottles now. Only his eyes move. He blinks, gaze moving from me to Esther and back again. He looks like someone who's been caught out. And that's true in a way because I got details about the heart of his damage behind his back.

"Sorry, Frankie, but I had to do some digging so I could help you."

Frankie's silent, but not Esther. She drops Maury's wallet, grabs me by the jacket, and shakes.

"What in the ever-living fuck do you think you're doing, you shit-brained undead moron?"

"I…I…Investigating!" I try to pull away and get her hands off my shirt. But only one of them feels warm and supple enough to pry off. The other one's like a vise of the metallic variety. "Sexual assault is a crime, no matter how high and mighty the perp is in the supernatural department, Esther."

"Rape." Frankie's by my side, the unstoppable shaker of levitating powder open and hovering over the immovable object of Esther's hand. "At least give me that much. It was rape, and Mother and Father agreed to let them do it the minute they learned I was mundane."

I look him in the eyes. They're dry but rimmed with red. The gleam of baleful fire in them is evidence he's moved out of despair and into the anger part of grieving.

"There's nothing I can fucking do about it, Frankie. No matter how much I want to, I can't make any difference."

"That's wrong, and you know it. You're the only relative who ever showed me kindness back then, Esther. Tino's the only person now who's willing to help me. Don't fight. What is it you used to say, back when you holed up at my parents' house and got this?" He jerks his chin at her arm.

"You've got to fight someone back for everything they take in this shitty life, but you only ever start one with a real fucking enemy."

"Tino's not your enemy. Neither am I. I'm just fighting back like you taught me."

"Never fucking taught you a goddamned thing, kid." Esther's voice drops a notch in pitch. She lets go of my jacket. "Not on the record, anyway."

My alarm beeps again, signaling my ten-minute warning for the start of the Blood Moot. "Are you two going to get along while I'm out?"

They both nod, and Frankie closes the levitation powder and puts it in his pocket. They might not be best chums, but they seem copacetic enough for now. I smooth my shirt and head out the door.

I've got a date at the vampire club.

## CHAPTER TEN

The place where they hold the Blood Moots and conduct all vampire business in Rhode Island doesn't have a name that I know of. But that's probably for the best since it's easier to keep a secret club from getting outed if it doesn't have a title to blab on accident. Or under coercion because that's also in the realm of more unfortunate possibility.

I walk up to the door and do the secret knock. It opens, and I'm surprised to see Maya, her face flat and unsmiling. I blink because there's definitely something wrong if neither of the king's enforcers are in charge of vetting the secret knocks.

Maya steps aside and lets me by, then shuts and locks the door behind me. I lean against the wall instead of heading down the hall to the room where all the politicking happens. Because right now, I don't care about that. Maya has taken priority over everything else for the time being. Her eyebrows dip down, face a dusky mask of troubled thoughts.

"What's wrong?"

"Everything." She sighs, her frown deepening. "And nothing I can put my finger on, either."

"How can I help?"

"I'm not sure. But it's like that movie Invasion of the Body Snatchers in there. Nobody's acting completely normal. And I can't tell who's really off the wall and which ones are only nervous about the others."

"I think you're on to something, Maya." I lean closer, trying not to stare at her lips because the last thing she needs is for me to randomly plant one on her for the first time when she's upset. "Something's fishy in the state of Rhode Island."

But I need to get as close as I can because if even half the old and powerful vamps in the building are off their rockers, I don't want them seeing this. Letting my jacket hang open, I flip up the flap on one of the interior pockets. Stephanie's Lazakhar catches the overhead light. Maya's eyes widen, then flicker up and to her right for the barest of seconds.

"Oh, God, Tino." She grabs my jacket by the lapels and turns my world upside-down.

That's right. Maya kisses me, and yes, it *is* that mind-blowing, thank you very much.

How exactly is one kiss so amazing and powerful? Well, it's all got to do with some of the special abilities vampires have. They vary on an individual basis, but it's clear what Maya's is. She must be an empath, able to share thoughts and feelings with someone through intimate contact. How do I know this? She's telling me right here and now and confirming that the little crush I've got on her is mutual.

Some of my thoughts and feelings leak past that barrier, too. We mingle in the most literal sense of the word, but only just barely. Not like a bottle of vinaigrette where the oil and the balsamic split into tiny bits that combine to make a delicious whole. More like when butter goes on hot toast and it's only just started to soften. Even with the cuisine analogies my brain conjures, I don't even care that I can't eat food anymore.

It's like Maya stopped the world, and I melted with her. I try sending that corny sentiment her way deliberately. It must work because in my mind's eye, I see her head shaking, tightly coiled curls a fascination of bouncing. I get the idea she needs me to focus on the important message here, one crucially dire piece of information. And just about the only thing in the universe that would make me willingly let our lips part at that moment.

Stephanie is behind me, and she's got the king's enforcers flanking her. And she's fake.

I know for sure she's not the real thing, because that amulet in my pocket would be glowing like the daystar if she was, trying to reunite with her. The Lazakhars are bonded to their vampires and are one of the few ways to know who's truly who. I don't think the fake Stephanie knows this because her expression is one of smug superiority under a thin veneer of benevolence.

She's smiling gently at me in a perfect replica of that benign face she puts on when she wants something from me, like the night she turned me and destroyed my life. Except this isn't really my sire. It's something else, a creature unknown to me. And if it's here impersonating Steph, which means it wants to take a bite out of vampire society from the inside, like a worm in an apple.

"Hi, Steph." I flap my hand in a goofy wave. Don't worry, this is my way of playing it cool at the vampire club. They all expect me to act like a spaz because I'm new. "Kind of busy right now, if you don't mind."

"You ought to be in the main room, Val." Ugh, that nickname. How does the body-snatcher know I hate it? Does this mean it has all the information Steph does or just some recent surface thoughts? If it's the former, we're all screwed.

"Well, Maya and I are having a private—"

"Necking session. Or at least that's what I think you modern vampires call it." She shakes her head and the bridge of her otherwise smooth as china nose wrinkles ever so slightly. "But part of full membership in our society is proper attendance at the Moots. You can't call it mingling if you only see one person."

"Oh." Playing dumb comes easily. And again, this is classic Stephanie. Everyone around will have no reason to suspect it isn't actually her without concrete evidence.

And yes, I know. The proof is in my pocket. But you don't just trot out another vampire's Lazakhar in people's faces. Especially not King's Enforcer type people. Because usually, the only way for one vampire to get another's is by murdering them. If I whip it out, Shadow and Hargrove will have every reason and right to stake and ash me right there in the hall. I can't help but gulp like the guilty fish I am.

"Come on, Tino." Maya grabs my hand and brushes past the toughs and the fake Stephanie, dragging me in her wake. "I've got some people to introduce you to."

Her tactic of acting like she's annoyed we got interrupted works. I'd never have thought of it because I was assuming the worst-case scenario about Fake Stephanie's power and knowledge levels. It's a testament to how much the unknown body-snatching foe scares me. But Maya's never been afraid of anything the entire time I've known her. Which isn't long, okay, but I like to think I'm a decent judge of character.

I practically stumble after her into the main room where nobody notices because they're all going about their own business. I was worried about it, though. Life as a new vampire is a bit like being a teenager that way. The constant worry is that the bigger, cooler fish in the blood-drinking pond will notice you in a bad way.

Maya stops us in front of a trio of vamps I haven't seen since last month's Blood Moot. They're Maya's people, the ones who showed up the same night she did. Well, actually, that's not entirely correct. They're Whitby's people. Yeah, that includes the girl I just spent the last few minutes lip-locked with. Bummer.

Whitby's the tool I suspect offed both Stephanie's vampiric bestie and the guy he had working for him at Cranston PD. Which is one of the reasons I didn't want to ask him about magician family drama. And now I'm definitely not going to. Because with Fake Stephanie running around and my gut telling me he's mixed up in this somehow, that's the opposite of a good idea.

But these vamps Maya's introducing to me might decide to flip on Whitby. I decide to play nice for now. All three of them are the sort of vampire that stands out in a mortal crowd like sore thumbs. I get it.

Blood Moots are gatherings where we can be ourselves without any mundanes present. But some of the wardrobe choices here could have come from the closet of Captain Obvious's cousin, Captain Conspicuous. I can only hope they don't dress like this on the nightly.

"Hey, guys." Maya's smiling and waving. "This is Tino."

"Oh, cool!" The guy in the tan trench who's frequently seen leaning on nothing and talking to himself stands up straight and grabs my hand for a shake. I hadn't been holding it out, either. "I'm Peligro, nice to meet you."

"Um, dude." I let him shake my hand because the motion is too vigorous for me to even think about pulling away without accidentally smacking someone. "Your name means danger?" Yeah, I took High School Spanish.

"You should hear his last name," says the towering woman wearing a bullet packed bandoleer.

"Um." I finally get my hand back and stare at it like it's been out past curfew. "Okay?"

"Cabeza!" And just like that, Peligro Cabeza's got my hand again, shaking like a leaf on the wind.

"Help," I mouth at Maya. But she's chatting with the gunslinger gal and taking sneaky side-eyed glances across the room at the fourth member of her little cabal.

This is a vampire I've at least heard of. Her name is Mrs. Kent, and she does some kind of record-keeping. She's built like a linebacker but dressed like a librarian, complete with cat-eye glasses on her solid skull and a pink cardigan over her massive shoulders. But tonight, she's missing the satchel of books she usually carries. And she's practically glued to Whitby's side when usually she's avoiding him.

That sneaky white-suited bastard catches me looking at the two of them. He tips his hat like the world's biggest asshole, showing off his long, blond, douchey ponytail. Yeah, I guess it's pretty obvious I don't like this guy. That's okay, I'm in good company on that front.

Raven is watching us and shooting sharp glares at Whitby. The attaché is sitting on a straight-backed wooden chair in front of the dais that the king's throne is on. And DeCampo's there, too. In the shadows that cover most of his torso and his entire face, something silver gleams. I figure it's the ring that all Vampire Kings supposedly wear. They give off light at times though I'm not sure exactly why yet.

"And this is Annie." Maya's taking Peligro's monopoly on my hand as a matter of course. But then, since they're part of the same cabal, that must mean this is normal behavior for him.

"Howdy." The gunslinger smirks down at the longest handshake ever.

I'm starting to feel like one of those lucky cats you see in Chinese restaurants. Except not lucky at all, at least with this mode of greeting. Why can't the guy exchange bows with me instead? I try pulling my hand away. At first, I think it works because his grip loosens. And then, Peligro smiles like a pageant contestant and pulls me into a bro hug.

"Uh, yeah. Good to meet you, too, pal."

Was I seriously worried about Whitby and his crew? Annie, Peligro, and Mrs. Kent seem like cartoonish walking stereotypes with fangs. But there's got to be a reason he keeps them around despite that. Or maybe he uses them as distractions. At least Maya's normal. Well, besides the fact that she's perfection on two legs with fangs.

Pulling back from the hug is way easier than the manic handshaking. Peligro Cabeza's gone back to a relaxed state. Well, sort of, for people who think leaning in and whispering to an imaginary friend is a good way to chill out.

"Mr. Crispo, a moment of your time." It's not a request. Whitby's practically in my face now, making demands. He's got one hand out, pointed at a set of unoccupied wingback chairs in a corner.

My eyes narrow and I feel something pricking the inside of my lips. Yeah, those are my fangs. And this is the beginning of an anger Rage. I take a deep breath I don't need and let it out slowly, trying to stave it off. I'm pissed at Whitby pretty much all the time, but that emotion got provoked by Peligro, who was clearly distracting me on purpose so his boss could get the drop on me.

"Sure. Because I've got so much time to waste."

Whitby's expression stays flat as if my words are below his notice.

Everything about him is lukewarm and average, from his tone to the apparent expense of his wardrobe. I'm not sure what that brand of mediocrity implies, and I don't really care. He's clearly trying to take the lead over to the seats, as though it matters to him who sits first.

I plunk my ass right in the nearest chair before he can and give him a grin I hope is snide enough. Yeah, I know I worry all the time about pissing off my elders and betters, but as far as I'm concerned, Whitby's only one of those things. Guess which.

"What do you want?"

"You truly are as uncouth as they say."

"Your moment's almost up."

"Stephanie told me you were as direct as they come. Very well. I'm here to negotiate a price for the information you want about magicians."

"Excuse me?"

"I'll accept five major favors."

"No."

"Very well then, four."

"I'm not haggling."

"And I'm not supplying any infor—"

"Don't need it." I cut him off because I'm well aware it's the height of disrespect to an elder vamp.

"Oh, yes, you do." His smile reminds me of a shark's, wide, toothy, and eternally predatory. "I'm well informed about current events on the border between Cranston and Warwick police jurisdiction. And your personal connections to them."

"You don't get to tell me what I need. I don't let my sire boss me around why should I let you?"

"Stephanie, your child is a cocky little toe-rag."

I blink. "She's behind me."

Whitby nods, that smile only widening and settling in for a nice stay on his bland face.

"Shitballs."

"Valentino, I think you'd do well to bargain with Whitby for this information. You're going to need it."

There's no way in hell this is the real Stephanie. She never tells me to give in like this.

"No, I don't. I already told him, and you're not the boss of me. Not since I honored the Compass in my Trials last month."

"Don't rely on what your little friends say, or you'll end up a pile of dust and ash. You might have passed that Trial, but you know less than you think you know."

I stand because I can't abide what she's saying or how she's saying it. Because my real sire always believes in me, even when she's got no good reason. Fake Stephanie is fake, and it's got my blood boiling. Guilt skewers me, pushes me further.

"You bitch."

You know how, when you're in a room full of people off having their own little conversations, there's always this sort of masking white-noise? Then you've also experienced the strange and sudden lulls that occur when the stars align just so. Well, that's exactly what happened when I called this fake Steph an itch with a b in front. Bad luck, thy name is Tino.

Every vampire in the room is staring at me. Some of them have hands on weapons under their coats or hold their fists up in postures conducive to combat. They're right to react that way to my outburst. I'm as close to Raging as I was that night in Esther's apartment when I actually bit a heinously scented werewolf. Except, this time it's not hunger getting my goat. It's anger. How dare this bitch pretend to be my sire when Stephanie's got more class in a toenail clipping? I'm ready to fight to the death, and everybody knows it. I'm grossly outnumbered. I'm going to die for good this time.

My salvation comes in the form of a throat clearing.

"King DeCampo demands a moment of your time, Valentino Crispo."

The formal tone is delivered in less than polished syllables. There's an accent too, though faint, of some lyrical romance language I can't readily identify. But I know the voice, its speaker. The last person I expect has stepped into this lion's den, prepared to walk through slings and arrows to get me out of it.

"Whatever you say, Raven." I do my best to get the words out past my elongated fangs. When we Rage, they make an impressive display that hinders coherent speech. But the king's attaché understands.

"Come along, Mr. Crispo."

And just like that, I rebel against the growing establishment and take the side of decency.

# CHAPTER ELEVEN

I follow Raven up on the dais and past the now-empty throne. There's a door behind it, which I suppose plenty of the other vampires here must have known, but of course they never told me. Why would they? Until I passed my Trial, for all they knew I'd be dead in weeks.

The door leads to a cozy study appointed with a few cushioned chairs and a table, and floored in herringbone parquet. Everything is awash in shades of earthy brown, sepia like an old photograph. Even though it's summer, there's a small fire burning in a grate. That's probably for intimidation factor. Even though all vampires fear fire, it's far enough from the chairs and small enough not to be a bother unless the king wants to make it so. Overall, the main effect here is one of calm.

This damps down my Rage, backing me away from the edge of irrevocable action in the midst of vampires decades or even millennia older than I am. I take the middle seat opposite the one King DeCampo occupies.

"Majesty, you wanted to see me."

"Yes, Mr. Crispo." He nods slowly, the coils of his twisted locks slithering against his suit lapels like ivy vines in winter. King DeCampo's presence carries a breath of winter despite warm weather. This makes sense because great age for vampires is associated with that season.

"May I ask what for?"

"You may." The corners of the king's full lips tilt ever so slightly upward, accenting his wide nose.

"So, Your Majesty, what can I do for you?" Indulging him in the formalities that go with his station comforts the part of me that wants to Rage. Either that or he reminds me of the real Stephanie.

"There are pretenders in our midst."

"I know, your Majesty."

"You are in a better position to investigate with impunity than I am."

"I'm already taking advantage of that, sir." I wince. "I mean, Majesty."

"Please, Mr. Crispo. For the sake of brevity, be frank for the duration of this meeting."

"Okay, sir." I'm still going to watch my mouth, but knowing I don't need to dot the Is and cross the Ts while minding my Ps and Qs is a relief.

"What have you discovered so far?"

I tell him about the crime scene in Warwick, the blood vial in my jacket pocket, and Steph's Lazakhar. Taking them out, I even hand them over. King DeCampo holds them up, lets each catch the banked fire's light. The sight of waning light reflecting off Stephanie's amulet chills me to the bone. What if she's met her final end? What will I do without her? I don't like contemplating the possibility of vampiric orphanhood any more than the mortal version. And I know what I'm talking about here since my dad was in Intensive Care just over a month ago.

"There's more, though, Mr. Crispo." The king knows what's up. The least I can do is appreciate that by spilling almost all the beans.

So I give him everything Maya told me about the Theophiles and include a names-redacted version of Frankie's assault. And then, partly because the king's authority demands it and also because I love me a good woolgathering session, I extrapolate.

"So, I think the Theophiles just up and pick one kid from every generation to neglect or even abuse before throwing them to the figurative wolves." I hang my head, eyes reddening with imminent tears at the unfairness of it all. "And then, if they survive, the families act like they never existed."

"Not all Theophiles."

"That's bullshit, Your Majesty, and you know it." Raven's strident tone startles me. They've never spoken like that before, hoarse and high-pitched at the same time. No, that's not entirely true. It's just that the last time the attaché sounded like this, I mistook it for laughter at first.

The king doesn't even blink. He's sitting still as a pond on a crisp autumn morning.

"This is my MeToo moment, Your Majesty." I don't know whether Raven's digging their grave here. But I'm going to let them speak. I'm even willing to object if the king tries to interrupt. A wave of something like relief washes over me. I'm not sure where it comes from because I'm not the one taking a huge leap of faith in an absolute Monarch and an untested neophyte in the same breaths. This is Raven's moment. The fact that I'm letting them have it shouldn't be as big a deal to me as it is to them.

"Nobody talks about this. Not even the other two kinds of magicians. The Lambs are their dirty secret, a walking symbol of the evil they're willing to do for power. The only reason some Theophile families don't shun their Lambs has more to do with the terms on the magical creature's side of the bargain. But the ones the Pickering family trucks with use us up and then throw us away."

"And how do you know this, Attaché?" King DeCampo's eyebrow rises in a bold arch, like something out of a cathedral paneled in mahogany.

"Because, back before they changed their name, when they were busy escaping the Spanish Inquisition, I was one of them, all because I wasn't born with magic like my brother. Yes, my mortal roots are the same as Tino's new client. We're from the same family, which operates no differently even after all this time."

"What does this have to do with Miss McQueen?" There's no way the king doesn't already know. All he's doing now is leading the relatively younger vampire down deduction's thorny path.

"It doesn't. But I believe Valentino is right. The Stephanie working the other room is a copy. If it were really her, the Lazakhar would glow in her presence, so that means another vampire has a contract with the Pickerings' monster friends." Raven closes their eyes. I've only ever seen another vamp look this weary when Stephanie exhausted herself helping the king last month.

"And all we've got to do is figure out who, I guess. Right?" I feel like it's my personal responsibility to bring some energy back to this room. It's what we younger vampires are supposed to be good at, after all.

"No. That part of the mystery has a clear answer." The king's stare is focused on his attaché. I know what it's like to be on the receiving end of that. Not like he's looking through you, but into you and at every secret in your mind and heart.

"It's my brother. Whitby. But I can't imagine why he'd do this. I always thought he liked Stephanie."

"He killed her best friend, and you think he likes her?" I blink. Three whole times because that idea seems so beyond the pale. "Begging your pardon, Your Majesty. I should have asked for permission to speak so freely on an unrelated topic."

"I'm willing to entertain the idea that perhaps these matters have a connection, Mr. Crispo. And your police training gives you insight into how some minds work differently. Please continue, both of you."

"Whitby's a sociopath. By his logic, Tierney's death means no competition. And somehow, I've got a hunch that Whitby's got a use for Stephanie or her special talent. Something only she can do." I shake my head. "I can't imagine anyone wishing ill on Steph. She's like everyone's favorite aunt or something."

"I'm not getting into my brother's proclivities here and now." Raven rests one hand on their chin. "But come to think of it, he always did gravitate toward the type of woman who valued chastity. We ought to bring the impostor in here before she does any more damage."

"More?" I try not to take a step back in alarm.

"Yes." The king nods. "She's been out and about, pushing whatever agenda the monsters have here."

"Can they make contracts with vampires?" I direct this question at Raven.

"Yes, but only if said vampire was born into the family. The contracts are for life, but terms can be changed if both parties agree that circumstances have changed drastically enough."

"So Whitby might be negotiating toward commanding an army of these things?"

"In theory. But they can't exist for long outside of the water."

And suddenly, it all makes sense.

"Your Majesty, I know you want to call Stephanie in here, but let me drink this first." I point at the vial. "It's going to be messy, but we might get vital information."

"Proceed, Mr. Crispo."

I uncork the vial, down its contents, and prepare for the worst, but it turns out not to be so horrible after all. Maybe the more I use this awful ability, the easier it gets. Or perhaps not. My stomach cramps like someone's kicked me in it with seventeen steel-toed boots. The pointy kind. And just like that, I'm trying to avoid upchucking all over King DeCampo's sensible wingtip shoes.

Remember Maya's telepathy, achieved with close contact? Nice little special ability, pleasantly used. Mine's the opposite. Blood from a dead person isn't too nourishing, and the expired bags Hargrove gets from his hospital connection sometimes come from a person who's also exceeded their "best by" date. For most vampires, all this means is it's like junk food. They've got to have twice as much to sate their hunger.

But it makes me puke almost to the point of self-harm. Which would utterly suck if it didn't have an extremely helpful side effect. I get to see through the eyes of the person that blood belonged to.

Pretty spiffy for a private investigator who happens to be a vampire, huh?

I lose count after four heaves, which is the point where only ashes come up. By the time I stop puking, I've had the whole vision. And it's a doozie. I can't talk sensibly until I've had some proper nourishment, though. Raven hands me a blood bag. I open it, take a whiff to make sure it's not some other poor dead sap's blood, and drink it down. I can feel the lining of my stomach and throat knit back together. They hand me a second bag and after that, another.

"Sorry about the grotesque performance art, Your Majesty." I look up from the floor as I try sweeping the ashes I've regurgitated into a pile with my bare hands. "I should start carrying a trash bag and a hand-broom."

"I've seen others with similar abilities, Mr. Crispo." He waves a hand at the mess. "I'll have someone clean it up later. Now, what did you see?"

"That the real Stephanie's being held prisoner." I include details from my dream, which I understand now was some kind of psychic connection to my sire while she went through this. I get to my feet. "She got captured outside a moving house when Leora Kupala's mother died, right before dawn. The kid's a Lamb, working for Baba Yaga." This explains why Esther didn't take that tracking potion herself. She's probably banned from interfering directly and couldn't even tell me. Magicians are weird.

"Lucky kid." Raven smirks. "Baba's Lambs get all the perks."

"Like what?" I'm thinking about Sparky, how she said he was the most important thing ever. And I remember the kid-sized figure in the long black veil attending Larry Nelson's funeral.

"No trauma. They run errands, travel the world, and get to meet all kinds of interesting creatures." Raven shrugs. "That's all I know."

"I think I've got all the information you need to detain Stephanie, Your Majesty. The main thing you want to make sure of is not to let her touch you or your allies. There's an attack they can use that messes just about anyone up." I glance down at her Lazakhar, still dangling from its chain in his hand. "But I need to talk to the Pickerings if you want any more information about this invasion of the body-snatchers. And I need a way out of the building that's guaranteed to take me past Whitby without any trouble. He'll try to stop me."

"I'll need you to do more than get information, Mr. Crispo." King DeCampo's eyes aren't focused on anything in this room. It's enough to make me wonder whether he's got a vision-granting ability of his own.

"What?" I freeze because this time, blinking's not enough.

"You'll have to confront these monsters and rescue your sire."

"Okay. But can I bring Hargrove and Shadow?"

"No. I'll need them here."

"Your Majesty, I will go with Valentino, with your permission, of course."

"Granted." The king tilts his head at his attaché. "May your efforts bear the fruit you need, Raven."

"So, how are we getting out of here?"

Raven turns their head and smiles. "Through the front door. Together."

And that's exactly what we do. On the way out the door behind the throne, we pass Shadow and Hargrove, hands on Fake Stephanie's arms, her clothes providing a barrier against skin-to-skin contact. She's got a baleful gleam in her eye, which is pinned on me like a bug on a card. I flap my golf wave at her again.

Whispers and stares usher Raven and me through the room full of vampires. We must make a strange spectacle. The only one smiling is Maya. For the first time, it occurs to me that after a mere few months' stay in Rhode Island under his belt, Whitby may have compromised or replaced more than just Stephanie. But the more reasonable explanation is, he only made himself look better than me. An easy enough feat.

There's nothing I can do about it besides worry, and there's too much on my plate for that.

In the hall, I try to express those concerns to Raven. They shush me until we're in the car, tires rolling.

"I already thought of that." They lean back in the passenger seat.

"We have to rely on the king's personal prowess. He's got to be at least twice my age. If anyone can fight a room full of body-snatchers, it's him."

Raven can't be wrong about that. If they have reservations, they're not showing. And I get the feeling neither of us would make one bit of difference if we turned out to be the only ones defending King DeCampo, anyway.

## CHAPTER TWELVE

We could go straight to the Pickerings' house, but the minute we get in the car, there's a text from Kayleigh. She's got Leora and is on her way to my office, so that's where I bring Raven first.

"Maybe you should wait in the car."

"Excuse me?" It's a question, but Raven doesn't mean it that way. I can tell because they're already out of the car. For a vampire named after a bird, they sure have a catlike demeanor.

"So much for not meeting the hunter."

"Tino, if you think I've never been in the same room as a hunter before, you're disappointingly naïve." The king's attaché strides through the parking lot.

"There are Mafia guys in there, too." I'm trotting to catch up.

"Been there."

"A police detective."

"Done that."

"A mean alchemist?"

"Hmm." Raven stands in front of the door, staring at the lock. It's not propped open anymore. "That's a first. Sounds interesting."

"The door's locked."

"Not for long." They reach out, grab the handle, and glare. I hear a click, and they pull it open. "You coming or not?"

I bend down and stick a loose brick in the doorjamb. "Now I am."

We go down the hall, into the stairwell, and up one flight before I ask, "Are you telekinetic or something?"

"Something."

"Can I learn to do it?"

"That information's too expensive for the likes of you."

"Oh."

We're at the door to my office before I fully realize that I've been following Raven all this time. Old vampires are reputed to be powerful so I'm not sure whether there's some blood-related ability in use or if the king's attaché is simply disturbingly well-informed. I watch them open it.

Frankie's eating a square sandwich at my desk on the customer side. Maury's still snoring on the futon. Esther looks up from something she's drawing, eyes wide. And that's when I remember the wards.

"Raven, wait."

"Hmm." They peer at empty space. "Wards. Good idea, but bad news if we cross them."

"Um, Esther?" I gesture at what looks to me like thin air. "Would you mind?"

Esther rolls her eyes and tears up the paper in front of her. A faint shimmer of green falls from the top of the doorway, then she waves us inside. I take a deep breath I don't need and let it out. Old habits die hard.

We walk in just as Frankie pops the last bite of his tuna salad sandwich into his mouth. He looks up at Raven, blinking. They saunter over and sit in my chair. One thing I can say for Raven, I expected a ton of snark and attitude about my office's shabby unchic decor. But they don't say a word about that.

"Um, Raven. That's Frankie. This is Esther. And the guy sleeping off the potion is Maury." I shrug, unsure exactly how to introduce my unlikely ally. Time to keep it simple. "Guys, that's Raven, a way more experienced vampire than me."

"Charmed." But Raven doesn't look charmed at all. More bored than anything else.

"And the lady on the way here is Kayleigh. She's bringing Leora to us. That other Lamb I mentioned."

"So, it's you, me, this Leora, and Frankie going over to talk to the Pickerings?"

"No way." Frankie has his hands flat on the desk now. "You don't want me there."

"Actually, we do." I lean against my totally occupied desk, which is better than having to sit in the customer side seat, I guess. "This is an intervention."

"Yeah, the Pickerings have a serious addiction to power at all costs that's gone on way too long." Raven locks gazes with Frankie. "I know from long experience. It's time to encourage them to renegotiate their contract with the Deep Ones."

"You assholes don't know what the fuck you're getting into, going over there." She crumples up a piece of paper and throws it into the trash.

"Letting us know would be great, Esther." I grin at the angry alchemist, sure she isn't somehow ordering us not to go. "Thanks for offering to do that."

"No fucking problem." She's smiling widely enough that I wonder what she's hiding. Maybe Esther's just happy we're not telling her to quit swearing in front of the kid. "You need to go in there armed like a motherfucker. Not with some shitty guns, either. You need fucking swords and knives."

"I think I've got something." I head to the Shoji screen, reach behind it into what used to be some college kid's umbrella stand. I bring out a rapier.

"You're a swordsman?" Raven snorts. "Give me a break."

"He was in the Fencing Club." The voice from the door defends my reputation. "Won a few awards, too, unlike that poor sap on the futon." Yeah, fencing was the one thing I was better than Maury at. Go figure.

Kayleigh Killarney stands in the doorway, trying to block Leora from entering. But the kid squeezes under her arm. She heads right over to me and looks down at the sword. "Cool weapon, Mister Crispo."

"You can call me Tino like everyone else does, Leora."

"Thanks!" She pats the pouch strapped to her chest. I notice a charm bracelet around her wrist this time. It's got a mortar and pestle charm hanging from it. "Sparky says hi."

"Hello again, Sparky." I wave at the pouch even though it isn't open. Who knows, maybe the magic lizard can see me. Amphibian. Whatever.

"You're not going to fight real enemies with that thing, are you, Tino?" Kayleigh's frowning at my rapier. "It's not a good idea to use those in actual combat, even the theatrical kind."

"Well, you're the tactical expert."

"You're using that fucking thing on wards and magical shit, Tino, not people." Esther's got a stack of Post-it notes, pen poised over it. "I can reinforce that shit. Bring it the fuck over here." I do, and she sharpens my rapier. The edge gleams, and it looks more solid, Feels better in my hand, too.

"Well, I guess your fighting style and the magic enhancement will have to do." Kayleigh shrugs. "At least that's not your old practice foil. Anyway, what's Maury doing here? Thought he was in the dark with the rest of the mundanes."

"He is." I shake my head. "But he had an accidental brush with some magic, and he's sleeping it off."

"Well, do you want me to get him out of here?"

"Um, excuse me for asking, but why is a hunter helping you?" Raven's eyebrow raise could give the real Stephanie's a run for its money.

"You can ask me directly, you know."

"Okay, fine. Why are you helping? It makes no sense."

"My higher-ups told me about these Deep Ones making menaces

of themselves. Bigger fish to fry. And I've got my own arrangement with these three, anyway." Kayleigh gives Raven a bright smile. "You know how important deals and debts are, of course."

"Wow, you're cheeky." Raven shakes their head, then smiles back. "But sensible."

"Damn straight." Kayleigh walks over to the futon, unfazed by Raven's fangs. "I'm taking Maury back to his place."

"Okay, thanks." I hand her his keys from my pocket, where I stashed them earlier. After that, I move to help her, but she waves me away. "I don't want him waking up here if I can help it, and it'd take a chunk of time from my night to do it myself."

Kayleigh carries Maury with no problem. Sure, she's strong for a human, but also Maury's lost weight. I know she notices it, too, although she doesn't mention it. We say goodbye as she heads out the door.

"Well, that was interesting." Raven leans back in my chair. "You've got a way of collecting strange and unusual friends, Valentino."

"Yeah." I belt the rapier around my waist. It's okay to carry it around in Rhode Island like that. Open-carry for bladed weapons is legal here. Told you it's a quirky place. "So, let's go visit the Pickerings."

"Wait a fucking minute." Esther's been scribbling on the Post-its this whole time. She hands them to me.

"Uh, my hands will probably be too full for these, but thanks anyway."

"Fucking delegate that shit, dead man." She rolls her eyes. "Not to the kid, either. She's packing enough magical heat already. Give it to the guy. You know, the one with the thing. I can't say who." I peer at Leora and notice a shimmering red and white glow around the charm bracelet. It's probably a trinket from Baba Yaga. What was it Raven said about the witch's Lambs running errands?

"Oh. Okay, then." I turn and hand the magical papers over to Frankie, who's got the least power in my little troupe of misfits. "Let's get out of here."

We leave the building and get into the car. It's maybe a fifteen-minute drive from the address I got off Frankie's ID yesterday. It feels like it's been a whole week instead of a day.

We pull up and park on the street in front of the big green gambrel at 66 Ocean Drive. Frankie's looking at his feet instead of the house, and I can't blame him. I'm not too surprised when Raven pats him on the shoulder or when Leora takes his hand. These three are all survivors of a similar set of trials, set on them by their families without choice or even consent.

And now they're following me into another one. At least they're making their own decisions about the danger they face this time.

# CHAPTER THIRTEEN

I walk right up and ring the doorbell, then draw my enhanced rapier. Leora pats the hand holding it, and I see a shimmer of red and black surround the blade. Double magic, cool deal. Her smile reminds me of flecks of white skin peeping out through holes in a lacy veil. The kid doesn't smell like anything at all. I realize this means she's not normal.

Well, for that matter, neither is the lady who answers the door. She's middle-aged, with touches of gray at the temples of her bound up chestnut hair. Frown lines punctuate her mouth and the space between her eyebrows. Her skin's sallow with a faint greenish cast. She's wearing a long gray dress, with long sleeves and a high neck that's something between mock and actual turtleneck height.

This woman is not happy to see us. At her breast is pinned a green-backed cameo with a white urn in bas-relief. Her hands move through the air with the fingers pressed together as though she's swimming in water instead of standing on land.

The overall effect has my brain so far back into my read-through of Shadows over Innsmouth, I almost fail to defend my group.

My sword comes up just in time, executing a block my muscles remember from college. Red blade clashes with sickly green magic, producing a shower of black motes that dust the mat in front of the door before vanishing.

"We're here to talk."

"You're not invited." The woman in gray holds her hands up again. "Begone, vampire, and take your Renfields with you."

"They're here by their own volition. And that's not how this works." I sigh and shake my head.

"That's not how any of this works." Raven steps forward, hands on their hips. "We don't need invitations, and even if we did, this is technically my house. Step off, witch."

"Hey!" Leora pouts.

"No offense, kid."

"I can't imagine why you'd say that." The woman hasn't set her gaze on Frankie yet. Which apparently he was counting on. "This house has been in my family for generations."

"What a funny little coincidence. Mine, too." Raven pushes past her and into the hall, sticking one of the Post-its Frankie slipped them on the front of the woman's dress. She freezes like a statue, one that blinks.

Leora tags along after Raven. Frankie follows her. The woman looks right through him, ignores his muttered " Hello, Mother," too. I bring up the rear, eliciting a glare that could wither an entire apple orchard.

"Gather the rest of your family." I put on the old glad-handing face and voice that went with my stint selling Cutco door-to-door back in High School. "We're here to tell you about something that's going to change your lives."

She either can't or won't answer. I follow my allies down the long hallway. One door near the back has that same sickly green light coming out from under it. Raven pushes through it and into the room. We enter, one by one, including the lady of the house who can apparently walk, at least.

Envy rears up and strikes me in the heart like a viper. This room is covered on every wall, from floor to ceiling, with books. There are too many for me to count even if I wanted to turn on vampire speed. I promise myself that somenight, I'll have a library like this. But I'll come by it honestly, not from literally selling my family members to degenerate body-snatching Deep Ones.

Raven takes the most prominent seat, acting like they own the place. Which, apparently, is what they're here to claim. I admire their audacity, and the tactic definitely has at least the lady in gray off-guard. She pulls a bracelet from one sleeve and blows on the whistle attached to it. The notes from it take me all the way back to our middle school production of *The Sound of Music* and the whistle Captain Von Trapp blew to summon his too-obedient children.

Leora sits in one of the chairs, feet kicking the air as they dangle. But Frankie remains standing behind me and to my left. It's a good position for a non-combatant expecting trouble, so I let him stay there instead of inviting him to sit down.

My rapier's still got that reddish glow, too. I keep it unsheathed for now. As strange as it seems in a room full of people with way more experience in supernatural affairs, I turn out to be the enforcer. Well, maybe I'm the only one with conventional combat training here. And sometimes, that makes all the difference when dealing with supernatural people used to relying on their powers to make up for lack of tactical prowess or even awareness.

One by one, more of the home's residents file through the door. There's a man who looks about the same age as the lady, though he's dressed much more conventionally and his skin's a healthier pink. And then there are two kids, a boy and a girl. They look to be in their early teens, like Leora. Only the boy looks at her though he doesn't return her friendly wave. He spares a glance at Frankie, too, but the girl elbows him, and he stops.

I figure this must be Levi, the brother Frankie mentioned last night. From the looks of things, the three of them are siblings. The girl next to him takes one look at my sword, then steps around Levi so he's between her and me. I give her a smile, and she shudders. Her hands light up with that same greenish glow that was around the woman's when she attacked earlier.

"Cool it, kiddo." I hold my free hand up, palm out. "We're here to talk, not fight."

"But you brought the Lamb back. And you're a vampire. You're not supposed to do that, and you're not supposed to be here, either."

"He's here because I brought him." Raven leans on the arm of their chair. "And believe me, I belong to the Pickering family."

"You might have while you lived, which would entitle you to have a say in our household matters." The man shakes his head, then reaches out and plucks the Post-it off the woman's dress. "The compulsion's off you now, Mother. Let's determine whether this vampire's claim of family ties is true."

"Thank you, Father." She reaches down and clasps his hand for a brief squeeze. Do these two actually call each other Mother and Father? Weird. "I know we refused to talk to the lady vampire on our doorstep last night. She had no magic. But this one used some on me, and might well have been a Pickering before getting turned." She pulls a monocle from a pocket on her dress and hands it to the man. "Have a look."

The man puts the glass to his right eye and shuts his left. After that, he nods. "Yes, you're right, Mother. He's Pickering, through and through."

"It's they, not he." Raven bares their fangs. "I'm non-binary."

"But old vampires are supposed to be traditional, not obsessed with all these new gender things." The woman sticks her nose up so high in the air she could have gotten a nosebleed.

"Back in my mortal days, there were more than two genders." Raven rolls their eyes. "So I am technically more traditional than you. But considering you're family, I'll let it slide this one time. Now, we need to have a talk about your Lamb, Frankie, and his future."

I figured out what Raven's playing at here, and it's a good plan. They're pretending to be Whitby, as though their identities and fates were reversed back in the Middle Ages. With the Post-its letting Raven do something that looks like magic, we might get away with this charade, too. But only if Whitby hasn't been here and proven himself first.

"There is no future for him. It's as it was since we became Pickerings and first came to our agreement with the Deep Ones."

"No, it's not." Raven shakes their head. "My generation's Lamb was cast into the waves but was returned, like your son. And you ought to embrace him, because without him, your contract would have broken."

I can see where Raven's going with this, but if I can tell their story includes some serious omissions, so can the odd couple. But before they can point that out, the Pickering girl speaks up.

"Yeah, why can't he come back?" She finally stops glaring at me to look at Mother, who is clearly the most powerful member of this family. "He's not dead like you said he would be. And I'm sick of doing his share of the chores when I could be practicing my magical studies, Mother."

"Mind your tongue, Sarah." Mother clucks her tongue. "And that elder Lamb of ours may still be breathing but just look at those eyes. He's dead inside, you see. We must have angered the Deep Ones in some way if they returned him to the land and the light."

"It's not anger," Raven says. "When one of their Lambs live, it's because they've found him of particularly potent virility and intend to use him again."

I blink. No wonder Raven went and got themselves turned at such a young-looking age. I would too if I had fish people I wasn't attracted to all hot and bothered for my bod.

"This is what your brother told you?" Father's peering at Raven through the monocle. I get the feeling this is an extremely dangerous game of choosing and using the correct words.

"Exactly that."

Mother and Father Pickering give each other a set of matching looks that make me want to vomit in my mouth a little. It'd be cute and romantic if they were anyone else, but these are people who pimped their teenage son out to monsters, so no. No sympathy here for them, at least not from me. But Frankie himself is another story. His brother and sister, too.

The three Pickering siblings practically simper. Which of course, they do because this has been their lifelong example of what love is, and all three of them probably aspire to something like it. Frankie's only just started to get the idea that there are other ways to be. And a big part of the reason I'm here is to give him that chance. Now, I want the other two to have the same.

The tip of my sword lifted with these thoughts. Let's call the motion accidentally on purpose. Raven sees my implied threat and immediately knows how to exploit it. That's one brilliant vampire.

"Now that I've demonstrated who and what I am, it's time to talk about renegotiating our family's grossly outdated and patently unfair contract with the Deep Ones." Raven stares directly at my raised blade until every pair of eyes in the room is on it, too. "I'm willing to fight alongside my allies for that right, if necessary."

"I think we agree you are part of our family," says Mother.

"And you are the oldest of us," Father continues.

"But we have no new advantage to negotiate with," Mother finishes.

"You'll have to trust me when I tell you I've got something they will want."

"We can abide that if you include one of us in your negotiation process."

"I'm not sure how either of you will survive at the bottom of the ocean." Raven leans back in the chair with a gleam in their eye that tells me this was an unexpected wrinkle.

"I can." Mother pulls away the long collar on her dress, revealing a set of gills along each side of her neck under her ears.

"Very well, then." Raven rises from their seat. "We will return after sunset on the day the new agreement is finished."

Mother Pickering leads us through the door with Raven on her heels. I let Frankie and Leora go ahead of me. On her way out, Leora gives Levi a grin, pulling one of her lower eyelids down with a finger and sticking out her tongue. He snickers, a blush forming on his cheeks. Cute.

Not much is for the remainder of the evening.

# CHAPTER FOURTEEN

There's no way everyone will fit in my car. But Mother Pickering has a van. Raven practically orders her to let me drive, but she's cooperative enough now for me to think that was overkill, maybe. But I can't blame Raven for laying it on thick. What happened inside the Pickering study feels like nothing short of a socially manipulated miracle. No wonder King DeCampo chose Raven as his attaché.

The entire meeting with the Pickerings only took forty minutes. We'll have time to chat with the king about everything we've managed to do before heading off to rescue Steph.

I drive us back into Providence and park the van in the shadows under a bridge near WaterPlace Park. It's not far from where I caught Sparky at the beginning of all this mess, either. I get out alone, letting the others wait while I go back on foot to report to the king at the Blood Moot. As I walk, I try calling Maya, but she's not answering. I pocket the phone and do the secret knock, and there she is, at the door looking over her shoulder like all hell has broken loose inside.

"Tino, we have to go." Maya's got a duffel filled with lumpy cargo slung across her body. I take a whiff. It's weapons, so my guess about hell was correct. Shitballs.

"What?"

"Shadow came out of the king's back room and dropped like a rock. Dead sleep."

"Holy shit!" It takes vamps either decades or loads of blood to get out of a long sleep like that. I try to go past her, but she blocks me successfully. "Let me go in and help!"

"You can't, Tino, and we have to go now. I'll give you the whole story while we walk."

I do what she says, more because I'm worried about someone hurting her if vampires are Raging back there than anything else. True to her word, she gives me an update by holding my hand as we power-walk away from the building. It's not as intense or as fun as the kissing earlier, but I get the picture through Maya's eyes. Literally.

I see Shadow appear from out of nowhere beside the king's throne, hand over his heart. An iron rod sticks out of it. He topples to the floor, sprawling halfway off the dais. And I'm running on Maya's legs with a crowd of other vamps toward that door behind the throne.

Through the doorway, I make out three heaps of ash and a jumble of stakes. The air in the room smells thick and musty, like something ancient and wet was in there recently. The fire in the grate is out, and the metal cover twisted and tossed aside. The king's Lazakhar is entangled with Stephanie's, while Hargrove's is nowhere to be seen.

Maya and I both know that the reason for Steph's amulet being in that room isn't because she's dead. It's because the king had it on him. But then, I see Maya's delicate brown hand reach down and snatch both amulets. I feel their combined weight in her hand and then her pocket. She hunches and elbows her way through the gathering crowd of vampires, trying not to make skin contact with any of them. She succeeds.

She pauses to listen to the jumble of voices while she tries to think of something to do with the Lazakhars. There's got to be a place to hide them. But then, the last thing she wants to hear meets her ears.

"If you're claiming the throne, Whitby, we need to do the Test of Ages on everyone here to make sure you're the oldest."

No. Maya knows it's bad to be here for that test. Her thoughts grow distant and incoherent after that. I realize she's hiding the reasons for her fear about this from me. I ease off a bit and give her thoughts some room by focusing on the memory's physical surroundings.

Racing through the room is easy because it's mostly empty now, but as Maya leaves, Peligro steps in her way.

"It's dangerous to go alone." He's holding a stuffed duffel bag in his arms like it's a baby.

"No, Peligro. Not now."

"Take this!" He pushes the duffel at her.

At the front door, She hears the secret knock and opens the door, and I see my own face.

"Wow, Maya. Well, Raven and company are in the van. I bet they're older than Whitby, so no problems there."

"Those two are the same age, actually."

"Oh." It figures. "They're twins?"

"Yeah. The others will back Raven, though. So whatever adventure we're going on, protect that attaché at all costs."

"We?" I shake my head. "No, Maya. You shouldn't get mixed up in this."

"Don't worry about me. Why do you think Whitby keeps me around?"

"Um, the telepathy thing?"

"No. I'm his muscle."

"Wait, seriously?"

"Absolutely. Annie's a gun-bunny, Peligro's psychic. Mrs. Kent's a walking archive, and I sprout claws and spikes."

"I can hardly believe it."

"Well, you will if things get bad enough for you to actually see it." Maya chuckles, but the sound cuts out like it was on a radio someone shut off. "Wait a minute. Was that your van?"

"What do you mean, was?"

And she's right. The ex-van is sitting there in literal pieces. I don't smell any blood, but that blackish slime is everywhere. And thanks to drinking Mrs. Kupala's evidence sample, I know exactly what that stuff does. It looks like the Deep Ones decided to start their negotiations without me. Forcibly.

What a bunch of assholes.

---

I warn Maya not to touch the icky ooze. We follow the slime trail down some cobblestone steps until we get to the waterside. At a quarter to three in the morning, there aren't any people in this part of town. The slime leads down the tunnel Scott, Esther, and I went down while chasing Sparky. I shake my head and snort.

"What?"

"It's just, I was here last night after a kid's lost pet. And now, I'm chasing after monsters way above my paygrade."

"Well, you take the good, you take the bad."

"I guess that's life."

"Unlife."

"Yeah. At least we've got weapons."

"Hello?"

Maya and I look at each other, then all around, trying to figure out where that tiny creaky voice came from. And that's when I notice what looks like a tent left up way after WaterPlace closed for the evening. I move in for a closer look and see that it's actually thatched and made of wood and mortar. There are two windows with geraniums in boxes below them, and a door which are all higher off the ground than I'd expect. The foundation's raised.

"Tino, look." Maya's pointing at the bottom of the structure. Well, not really. She's pointing at its legs and feet.

Yeah, I said the little thatched house has legs and feet. Chicken ones, to be exact. I might not have read Sasquatch's Baba Yaga article, but I sure do remember the illustration. And guess what it is? Ding! You win a prize! It's a cottage standing on chicken legs.

The door's open and I can see the light of a fire inside. Something's cooking in a pot over that, but all I smell is sandalwood. I step closer, trying to see the face of whoever called out to us. Could one of our friends have escaped into this strangely located tiny house?

"Mister Crispo!" Leora's head peeps out from one side of the door jamb.

"Leora! What happened?"

"She wants to talk to you."

"She?"

Maya elbows me, then leans over to whisper in my ear, "Baba Yaga."

I whisper back, "Well, that makes sense. Leora's working for her." I turn my head to speak to the kid. "Can you tell her I'm short on time?"

"She knows. Don't worry, she says you'll get to where you need to be in time."

I look at Maya. "So, what do we do?"

"We go in." She's already stepping into the dark goddess' house. I can do nothing but follow.

Saying it's untidy in there is like saying the ocean is wet. Dust bunnies big enough to be Great Danes live in each corner. The sourness of gone-over meat comes from crumbs littering the shelving to the left side of the fire. And a stink of unwashed flesh emanates from the crooked figure on the three-legged stool in front of the blaze. One wiry arm emerges from a nest of hair and faded red rags, a wooden spoon in its hand to stir the pot.

"Baba, your guests are here." Leora gives a little curtsy. I see that the wrist that wore the bracelet earlier is now bare.

"Inna minute." Baba Yaga finishes her cooking task, scraping the sides and bottom of her cauldron. When she withdraws the spoon, a fish head tries to come with it. She shakes it off, and it falls back into the stew with a fat plop. "Whaddaya want?"

"I figured you'd be the one telling us, ma'am." I give her a slight bow. Not because she's considered a deity by some but out of respect. Baba is a maternal word, and I was raised to respect mothers in general, even the non-Italian kind.

She cackles. I'm not sure whether she's thrown her head back or not because of all the hair covering her face and most of her body. But

I'd bet you dollars to donuts she has. And I can't even eat donuts anymore.

"Love that one. Gets 'em every time."

"Baba, you know we're worried about mortal time." Leora's tone is almost chiding but gentle enough to be mistaken for a plea, reminding me of how Ma used to talk to my grandmother at the beginning of her Alzheimer's.

"'At's right."

Something creaks as she gets up. I'm not sure whether it's the stool or her old bones. There are a table and benches built into the wall to the right side of the fire. She hobbles over to them and takes a teacup from the saucer sitting there. It vanishes under the steel-gray of her hair. In moments, she straightens. The hair deepens to a rich white-streaked auburn, and her figure goes from withered to matronly in less than sixty seconds.

"Valentino Crispo and Maya of Macedon, I welcome you for the time being." Baba Yaga's voice is the same, but her accent and inflection have changed entirely.

"Thank you." Maya copies Leora's curtsy.

"Thanks." I smile. It doesn't faze Baba Yaga one bit, of course. But I'm on the defensive because of the word Macedon, which is ancient. But Maya can't be that old. Maybe the witch meant Macedonia, which I happen to know is a country just north of Greece where Yugoslavia used to be. I paid attention in Geography, okay?

"Now. I hear that you're fighting back against the fishes."

"The Deep Ones. And yes, we're after them. They stole my sire, killed Leora's mother, and raped two other friends of mine."

"I saw what they did while you went on your errand of mercy for the Pickering Lamb, Sir Crispo. This child's mother was one of the mortals under my protection, among other things. We have the same enemy. Will you accept my assistance?"

I'm about to answer with a simple yes, but Maya takes my hand. I keep my mind's eye peeled and let her show me what I need to see.

It's Leora. She's outside the studio where my office is, getting into the same house we're currently visiting. And then I see her again, coming out of this house in a field behind what looks like a school. She's ugly-crying. I realize that this must be right after she found out her mother died. I watch Kayleigh approach her, and their conversation becomes audible.

"No. You're a hunter, and I'm not going with you. I'm getting the guidance counselor to find me a group home."

"Look, kid, I know you're the old lady's Lamb, but I've got no beef with either of you. My family's not against magicians, anyway. I'm just helping a friend find you because he wants to talk."

"Which friend?"

"Valentino Crispo."

"Now him, I'll talk to."

The scene fades. I grip Maya's hand tighter, preventing her from letting go. Why was she following my friends and me? I need to know. No word of excuse or explanation comes, but I feel her regret, like an undertow threatening to drag her down. And she gave me all the information to handle this talk with Baba after all. Our mission now is more important than past actions, especially if we want to rescue the others and keep Whitby from taking the throne uncontested.

We unclasp our hands. Baba Yaga is stirring her stew again, back turned to us.

"I understand you're used to making contracts, Baba. Arrangements with mortals."

"Yes, but you aren't one." She turns her head, so I see her in profile. "I don't want tithes from you. Vampire law will do." Awesome, that's exactly what I wanted her to say.

"Baba, here is what I offer in return for you and yours obeying my orders regarding the Deep Ones and the Pickering family."

"Continue." She turns her back again, stirring.

"Leora Kupala has no guardian—"

"I am guardian enough."

"Here? Absolutely. I'm not questioning that." I shake my head. "But I've heard you don't get out much. The mortal world is different. It's hard enough to navigate when you're anything other than human. And Leora isn't even an adult yet. She will face more hardships than other kids her age, going it alone on your business. That is unless you arrange for someone out there who knows what they're doing to help her."

The spoon goes still inside the pot. "And all it takes for you, an honorable vampire, to accept this responsibility, is my obedience in one single fight?"

"No, Baba. You will obey my orders regarding the Deep Ones and the Pickering family. Until they both cease to exist."

"And your intention is to destroy all of the fishes."

"No. Only the ones who don't accept the Pickerings' new agreement."

"Ah." The witch turns, brandishing the spoon. A rivulet of stew trickles inexorably down the handle and toward her hand. A long tongue with gray splotches darts out, catching the droplet, marring that matronly image by reminding me of the crone on the stool. "But there will be death? Bloodshed?"

"I'm almost ninety-nine percent sure that kind of thing will be happening."

"Then I accept your offer. Let me ready your most important weapon."

"That's okay." I wave a hand at Maya's duffel and my rapier. "We came prepared."

"No, you didn't. I've got someone better than that." She drops the spoon in the pot, then gets a ladle and scoops out a dipperful. "Sparky!" She whistles. "Get out of there!"

And the last thing I expect happens. From the whitest part of the fire in the hearth, a shape emerges, red and rimmed with black. As it crawls out of the heart of the fire, Baba lowers her ladle, and I recognize that shape as the salamander. He holds his sticky little feet up toward the food Baba's offering, but she moves it away to slosh it in a bowl. She places that on the stool. That's when Sparky starts to warp and grow in front of my eyes.

He still looks lizard-y, but this is a kid, sort of. He's definitely not human, although he's got a similar-enough anatomy to pass for one if he wears a hat to cover his lack of ears and total baldness. His skin has a yellowish cast, and his eyes are a dark enough brown to look almost black.

"Um, you said something about weapons, Baba?"

"Yes." She jerks her suddenly very wrinkled chin in Sparky's direction. "He's it."

"Okay." I can't imagine how I'll use a salamander in combat, but I've kept my mind open since becoming supernatural, and it's served me well so far. Might as well leave it that way.

"Hi, Sparky." Leora sits next to her friend and hands him a spoon. He starts slurping down the stew like it's the most delicious thing in the world. It's steaming so much I'd stop Leora from having any until it cooled off. But Sparky just literally walked out of a fire. So he's okay. But just because her friend is doing it doesn't mean Leora should. Oh, God. I'm starting to think like my parents.

Well, there's a first time for everything.

## CHAPTER FIFTEEN

"How do we find the Deep Ones, anyway?" I ask Maya the question Baba seems either unwilling or unable to answer. She's back to her stinky old crone self, the tea having worn off, apparently.

"I'm not sure."

"I know." Leora peeks at the duffel bag. "But I want to see what's in there before I tell you."

"Okay." Maya unzips it, then whistles. "Wow."

"Didn't you know those would be in there?"

"No. But that's because I didn't pack the bag. Peligro did."

"Is Peligro your dog?"

"No!" Maya laughs. "He'd think that was pretty funny if you said it in front of him, though. He's another vampire I work with sometimes. Well, I'm not sure why he gave this to me. Peligro knows I can't use those in combat."

"Well, you said he was psychic." I shrug. "So maybe they're for someone else."

"Nobody I can think of. But that's okay. Better to have them and not need them than need and not have, right?"

"Truth." I give Leora what I hope is a stern enough look. "Okay, you saw. Now you tell."

"All we do is walk out the door."

"Really? That's all?"

"That's how Baba's house works. It shows up where it's supposed to."

"Well, what are we waiting for?"

"Sparky."

I watch the salamander kid finish his stew by picking the bowl up and drinking from it. I have reservations about taking one kid into combat, let alone two. But Baba Yaga must know what she's talking about. Unlike the way Frankie and Raven discussed the Deep Ones, Baba seems to genuinely care about her Lamb, and even the rest of the Kupala family. Or maybe this is all that's left of it, and she wants revenge for that. She did seem awfully bloodthirsty.

Whatever her reasons, I'm glad for her help. And I think the agreement I struck would make Raven proud. It really roped her into helping us without being able to turn around and mess with the Pickerings later, including Raven and Frankie. And it keeps her from ever going full-on genocidal on Deep Ones. Which, I mean they *are* creepy fish people, but no group deserves that fate.

Sparky burps, giggles, then wipes his mouth. He holds his hands out for a hug and Leora gives him one, mortar and pestle charm bracelet gleaming on her wrist. They definitely have a sibling vibe going on there. I'm sort of sad my folks never had another kid, but what can you do? Make family, I guess. Like I did with Maury.

The salamander kid morphs himself back into a regular-looking amphibian and gets in the cross-body pouch Leora's still wearing. After that, she stands and goes to the door.

"You guys coming or not?"

Maya zips the bag closed again and slings it over her shoulder. We're all about to leave when Baba's voice sounds behind us.

"Knock 'em dead!"

As much as I'd prefer not to, I think we'll be doing plenty of that. And when we step out that humble little door, I have a bigger suspicion that death exits Baba Yaga's house with us. We're deep inside a pipe so huge it feels like a tunnel. With the light from the door and windows inside the hut, it's easy to see that there's water in the bottom, but not much. We'll get our shoes wet, not our ankles.

It's close quarters, and I'm actually sort of grateful it's not the entire group from the van in here. I'm not claustrophobic, but I think almost anyone would get a little bit tweaky in this place because there's no light. I see better than a human in the dark, but it's still disconcerting. Everything is gray. And then, Leora opens Sparky's pouch.

It's like she turned on a flashlight. Warmth comes back to my field of vision, and it makes all the difference. Even as a vampire who gets severely burned by the sun, I still love light. Maybe that has more to do with what's in my heart than the state of my body.

As we advance, I hear echoes of speech up ahead. I don't want to burn blood, even though I've still got a full stash in my pockets. Who knows what we might need? So I wait until we're farther along and I can make out what's being said with regular vampire hearing. That happens sooner than I expect because something's lining the ceiling farther in, damping the echoes that distorted the voices before.

"We need more of them. They're so durable, no dying when we're out."

"Not many more in this city."

"We get this new one to turn its friends."

"After this, there's Boston."

"Too many there. No Pickerings, no Lambs."

"Caution, then. And after that, New York."

"With New York, we'll have the world."

I realize that these Deep Ones are talking about vampires. Snatching us and stealing our appearances. And Providence is just the beginning. They want the world, or at least the coastal parts of it. We have to stop them here and now. One glance at Maya tells me she's on the same page. I still would rather not kill them if I don't have to.

If I can find Raven and give them time to negotiate, maybe I can stop an all-out war. But it's a long shot. I can't think of a way to locate our friends, although I do have two other clues. The Lazakhars.

I pull them from my pocket and loop one of them over each arm. The best thing is, they're both glowing. Faintly but definitely lit up from within. That means both King DeCampo and Stephanie are still alive somewhere nearby, or as alive as undead people can be, I guess.

Sparky sticks his nose out of his pouch and sniffs, then has a look at the glowing amulets. He winks at me, which I don't doubt now. I think my ability to roll with the supernatural punches is better than it was last month. Which is good because that was abysmal before. I hope I wasn't too much of an asshole.

I make a fist and raise my hand, signaling everybody to stop. We're near a corner, and I've got a feeling we'll run right into the Deep Ones if we just keep going. I take a mirror out of my pocket, which is usually completely useless for me. But this time, it's exactly what I need. I tilt it so I can see around the corner. And sure enough, there are two of the froggy fish people. They've got a line of people bound to each other by some moldy old rope. One of them is wearing my gym shorts. Frankie.

It's time.

I put the mirror away, then draw my rapier. When I drop my fist, I start the charge, wordlessly. Behind me, I hear my friends following, feet splashing. As we round the corner, the Deep Ones turn. They hiss when they see us. Then, they rush.

We clash. I don't see what happens right away. A flash of red-tinged light to my left means Sparky and Leora have attacked. A pained hiss tells me they didn't miss.

The Deep One rushing toward Maya on my right stops and takes a step back. I don't blame him. She's a horror of spike and claw, snarling and baring her fangs. And still perfect. Like a lioness, the ideal predator. She ends up having to chase hers down the pipe and past the prisoners. Her prowess is such that she cuts them free with a rake of her claws as she passes.

The third Deep One keeps on coming at me. That's fine because he's unarmed. But I forget about the slime until the last possible second and duck out of the way just in time. My rapier slash misses by a hair. But it's better than getting hit by the bad-luck goo.

The Deep One's slime does something to probability, making it work against whoever's been smeared with it. That's how Leora's mother Katerina, a formidable fire magician, got herself killed. It's also how Stephanie got snatched. Mrs. Kupala saw the whole thing as she died, watched her vampire contact be captured while trying to seek revenge. First comes the slime, then the bad luck. I have to avoid getting touched at all costs.

I step back again but hit the wall this time. So I've got just one shot at this. I feint left and right, then right again. The Deep One buys it. I slash left. It drops. I step over it and sheath my rapier to help my friends get the rest of the way free. The rope's been cut, but they still have hoods over their heads.

I pull the one off Raven first. They wrinkle their nose, and I don't blame them. The cloth is filthy and reeking. I'd rather sit next to Baba Yaga on a ninety-degree day at the beach than wear that thing. Well, no, not really because vampire plus beach equals perma-death. But you know what I mean.

When they see the duffel, Raven's eyes light up. They open it, and I understand. The throwing knives are for the attaché. Peligro must have foreseen this. I wonder what else he saw, but it'd be no use asking someone as incoherent as him about visions, even if he were here.

More hissing means I have to stop my rescue mission for now. Maya's taking three of the newcomers on, but that's only half the attackers. Leora and Sparky blast one. It rushes at them, and they blast it again. It finally drops. But two are headed straight for me, and my rapier's still sheathed. A knife handle blooms between one pair of eyes. Raven's got my back. The last of this new set drops with one of the projectiles in its left eye. The attaché retrieves their blades. I move to free Frankie.

His eyes are wide, rolling, and panicked, but when he sees it's me taking the bag off, he blinks. He's still got his peepers peeled, but they're not frantically moving every which way. He pats his pockets, and I remember that he's got Post-its and Esther's levitation powder. Thank God. All the same, I motion for him to get behind me and reach for the hood over Mother Pickering's face. Once freed, she nods, then re-secures her hair in its clip. I don't blame her. The last thing I'd want is to die from hairdo malfunction.

We hurry through the pipe where the ceiling is getting closer by the pace. I look up. By the light of Mother's magical hands, the Lazakhars, and Sparky, I can see they're bubbles. Big ones, like person-sized. And they are all black. Mother sees where my gaze is and nods. I take it as an invitation.

"What are they?"

"I can't pronounce the word for them. But those are what they put people in when they want to impersonate them."

"Earlier, the Deep One said something about them dying when they're out. What's that about?"

"The people in those black ones are dead because being without water that long kills them. It takes a couple of days, though. It's how Deep Ones find mates when there aren't any of our kin in the area."

"Oh." I don't want to hear more about this, but Mother's not finished.

"That's what happened to my brother. He was a Lamb, and they only sent him back after he died. In one of those."

I'm about to let her have it with a giant tirade, but I can't. There's a fresh wave of Deep Ones coming at us. They look smaller and more feral than the others we fought so far, and there are more of them this time. I use my anger up, fighting them. And I see the gleam of tears on Mother Pickering's cheeks as she lights up her hands with green fire and roasts the foes.

It's been a long time coming, but I think maybe she's learning.

I still won't forgive her until she apologizes for everything to Frankie and gets help. But that's not my concern right now. I check and see that all my friends are standing. Frankie's been behind me the whole time, and nobody who traded blows got slimed so far. It's a good time to check because we've fought our way through the pipes and into some new scenery.

It's a round room where the pipelike tunnels all intersect. In some ways, it reminds me of an old-fashioned railway roundhouse. In others, it's like the rotunda at the Rhode Island State House. Either way, it's lit up.

"Come forward and swell our ranks!" The king's voice is every bit as authoritative as it was during my Trial.

The bubbles are here, too, far above our heads, afloat at the high ceiling. They're shiny and bear different hues. None of the ones in here are black. At the center of this circle are Fake Stephanie and also King DeCampo. I think he's a fake, too, but I can't be absolutely sure. Both Lazakhars are glowing like stars. The real Stephanie must be on the ceiling. Unfortunately, I can't reach those bubbles to break some and find out. But we've got ranged attackers. Raven's already taking aim at the one nearest to them. The knife flies through the air but bounces off.

"Frankly, I'm sick to undeath of waiting." Fake Stephanie rushes straight at me. I ready my rapier, but she's got an honest-to-God saber, and I can tell she knows how to use it. The best I can hope for is to hold long enough for the others to figure out how to free the real Steph and everyone else up there.

King DeCampo's locked eyes with Maya. She screams in wordless challenge. As they rush toward each other, I try not to worry. She's even more outclassed than I am. I watch the king pop claws of his own, but instead of spikes, his skin covers over with something chitinous. They clash, and I'm thanking God that copying a vamp seems to mean copying our abilities. He's either not able or willing to slime Maya. I hope the same holds true for Stephanie.

We lock blades, and even though my greater height and weight gives me an edge, she's by far the superior fighter. I try to use leverage in my favor, but that effort is only just keeping me from getting myself beheaded. Fortunately, I hear my allies discussing things in the background.

"Needs magic to break them." Mother looks at her hands. "Opposite kind."

"Why can't Sparky fly?" Leora's wringing her hands.

"He can fly with this." Frankie holds up the levitation powder. "Is that okay, Sparky?" Yes, my buddy Frankie is asking a lizard for consent. Salamander. Whatever. I'm proud of him, okay?

"Go for it!" Leora gives Frankie the thumbs-up, and after a few shakes and even fewer seconds, the salamander's rising toward the bubbles on the ceiling.

Maya and the fake king break their grapple. The fake king sees what's happening and points a magically glowing finger at Sparky. Maya closes with him again and knocks his arm to one side.

The blast hits Leora instead.

## CHAPTER SIXTEEN

I see my future ward faintly inside the new bubble, fists banging on the side. We've got to get her out of there, but I don't know how, besides waiting for Sparky to do his thing. I'm barely holding Stephanie back. She's fighting with a fury that makes little sense unless it's personal, but I can't imagine why it would be. Well, there's no harm in asking.

"What's your problem, anyway?"

"You are, Val."

"Hate that name."

"Hate your attitude."

"Yours is worse."

"Restraint is vital to a long existence."

"You're not my sire. You don't have that kind of experience for real."

"Yes, I do. We're as immortal as you vampires."

"She admits it." I cackle.

"No."

"Not a vamp." I blow Fake Stephanie a raspberry. It's a good thing I don't have to breathe. "Got you!"

"She regrets turning you."

"No shit." I try to pretend that doesn't hurt. Which is impossible. I convert all the pain to anger.

The Deep One grunts, blocking the attack that comes after my feint with ease.

"My attitude sucks." I strike. "I'm homesick." Again. "I whine." This time I feint. She doesn't take the bait. "And I'm no good at vamping."

Fake Stephanie gets past my parries and her saber runs me through the gut, which isn't as bad as it sounds because of the whole being undead thing. But it still hurts like a bastard. She pulls the saber out and I just keep on going, using method acting techniques to try to ignore the pain.

From the corner of my eye, I see Maya. She's looking a bit tattered from grappling with the fake king. Basically, they clash, sink claws into each other, then break it off to start the cycle again. It's brutal. I'd never have survived even one of those.

Which leads me to wonder why these Deep Ones attacked us the way they did. It'd make sense for the brawler to tackle the stage-trained swordsman and the finesse fighter to take on the brute with no armor plating. And that leads me to think about how the whole body-snatching thing must work.

Because the person they're wearing has to be alive in the bubble for them to keep on walking around looking like them, so that must mean there's a psychic link. And one thing I learned tonight from Maya about those is, they go both ways. So Stephanie and King DeCampo are both up there, and they're doing what they can to help us by controlling the information the Deep Ones get. I decide to send them a message.

"Hey, Fake Stephanie!"

"Oh, shut up and die already, Val." She tries to run me through again. This time, she aims for the heart.

I parry her blow. "You know, I like the real Steph. Want her back."

"Hogwash." The fake snorts and tries a slash.

"No, really. She's bossy, but the girl's got real class." I parry. Is it getting easier?

"You try to get rid of her." Fake Stephanie lunges.

"Because she's too awesome. I feel like a moron around her." I dodge.

"She wishes you were Tierney." This time, Fake Stephanie's attack is totally obvious.

"Don't blame her one bit." I smile as I block. It's working.

"You hate her." The fake snarls and rushes at me.

"No way. Love her like a sister." I just stand there, smiling because I just saw the fake's eyes change color from storm-gray to sky-blue. It's almost over.

Fake Stephanie drops the saber, jaw slack. Her hands twitch. Something drops from the ceiling. No, someone.

Before I know it, the real Stephanie is sweeping up the dropped saber. She uses it to behead her double in one fell swoop. Told you she was awesome.

The head reverts back to its Deep One appearance before it hits the wet concrete. Stephanie is about to put down the saber, seemingly oblivious to everything else going around us.

"Heads up!" One of Raven's knives flies past us. I manage to track it and see it bounce off the fake king's hide. Still, he hisses.

"Oh, my." Stephanie blinks and casts her gaze around the room. Then she looks at my rapier. "You need to get up there."

"But Maya—"

"I'll help her. Your sword's got magic on it."

And she's right. And without that red and black energy blazing along the metal edge, I'd have died for sure. Baba Yaga's making good on her end of the bargain, so at least something is going right.

I sprint toward Frankie and skid to a stop, almost smacking into him. "Hit me with the flying powder, buddy."

"Okay."

But just as he does, I feel a trickle of something that's too thick to be water on my leg. I look down. My right leg is covered with slime. The splatter pattern makes me think Fake Stephanie got me with it when she was going down. A parting shot.

I open my mouth, about to tell Frankie never mind and hand my sword off for someone else to go up in the air. But it's too late. He's sprinkled me seven times already. So, there I am, flying in a glorified wastewater treatment hub with bad-luck slime all over my pants.

And I thought the undead life would be eternally boring.

Flailing around in the air sucks. I don't know how birds do it, honestly. Probably without bad-luck slime. I see Sparky dog-paddling. Or salamander-paddling. If the little guy is trying to get through all that space and break bubbles, the least I can do is help. Leora's in one of these. I take a swing at one with the saber and it hits, cutting through like butter.

The occupant falls like a star. It's Leora.

"Catch her!"

The last person I expect responds to my call for help. Mother Pickering. She pauses in her spell-casting to do it, too. And I realize that the whole time, she's been holding off hordes of Deep Ones, keeping them away from Maya and me as we battled the body doubles.

Leora crashes down on her, and they both go down in a tumble. Because of this, a Deep One finds a way through and slimes them both. Mother pushes Leora away and gets swarmed by a mob of angry Deep Ones. She doesn't stand a chance, and there's nothing I can do.

But Leora's got an ace up her sleeve. She grasps her charm bracelet and calls out for Baba Yaga.

In the meantime, I slash open another bubble. It's no one I recognize, but they sure look weirded out. I don't blame them for hiding in a corner until this is all over. Sparky pops another one. And this time, I definitely recognize the person inside, who must have gotten snatched that very night.

"Kayleigh!" I call out to my ex. "Heads up!"

She doesn't land on her feet exactly. More like on all fours. But the hunter recovers fast and does what her daddy trained her for—taking out monsters. She's got guns, so having her join the fray doesn't turn the tides of this battle, but it makes up for Mother Pickering getting slimed.

I take a stab at another bubble, but I miss this time. Stupid slime. Looking down, I see that Maya's flagging. Stephanie's been helping, but my would-be girlfriend is just no match for even the fake King

DeCampo. Well, there's a good reason he's the vampire king of Providence, after all. Even his copy kicks serious ass.

The bubble I was trying to get open comes in range again. I slash but don't have time to look because a scream from below pierces me in the heart. I have to see what's going on down there.

It's Frankie. He's slapping Post-its on a gaggle of Deep Ones who broke through while Mother was down and before Kayleigh joined the fray. Leora's there with backup, swinging what looks like Baba's wooden spoon. It glows with red and white light and decimates every enemy in front of her. The hut's here too, now. And so is the person who fell from my last bubble.

It's Father Pickering, and he looks to be in rough shape. That bubble I got him out of was turning brown, too. Which probably means he was almost dead. It also means the guy I dealt with back at the house was a Deep One, and we left Levi and Sarah with him. Of course. That's how they knew to look for Mother's van. And why there are more bubbles up here than I expected. As Father falls to earth, I scream, "Incoming!"

Baba's hut spins, the motion carrying it sideways just in time to break Father's fall on its thatched roof. The poor man sits up, and the first thing he sees is his wife, covered in slime and fighting anyway. He looks up at me, then points to two new-looking bubbles.

I get the message and slash at one. Sparky understands too, and he has more success. The first bubble bursts, and Sarah sails through the air. She keeps her head and uses her magic to push off the ground, so she lands gently. Sarah Pickering sees her mother and screams, defiant as an eagle.

Jets of sea-foam light shoot from her hand, blasting with more power than anyone else in the room. She's still screaming as she walks forward. Deep Ones scatter in her wake. Sarah's a prodigal talent in the magic department. But all she wants right now is her mother, as dysfunctional as that lady is.

I know from long experience as the stable friend that loving someone, especially a parent who is that toxic, will only hurt in the long run. But you can't tell a person in the throes of that kind of love what it is and how to manage it. It's like with addiction; only the affected can effect their escape. So I let them be and try for another bubble.

This time, it works. I free Levi. The kid touches the ground in an unprotected patch.

Frankie is now screaming because this is his worst nightmare come to life. Levi's in exactly the danger Frankie sacrificed his sanity or escape to keep him out of. He's sprinting toward his brother, getting in front, between him and the Deep Ones. His hands are empty, too. I want to be down there, but it's no use. I forgot how Esther turns this stuff off. And even without the levitating powder doing its thing, I've been slimed. I'd just klutz out.

Leora throws herself in front of Frankie. She screams out for Sparky, who's changed into humanoid form in mid-air next to me. He holds out his hands, but their glow is still building because he used half his mojo on shapeshifting. He won't have his blast ready in time.

Raven acts. They just stride up, full of purpose and the promise of doing major harm. Nobody else sees, but I have a special vantage point. It's all bluff, even more so than back at the Pickering house. Raven's out of throwing knives. They're unarmed and defenseless, but willing to give up eternity to protect their fellow Lambs from yet another set of abuses.

My face is wet, my eyes so bleary I almost don't see Mother and Father Pickering give each other that look again. You know, the one that made me sick before. Mother's got her magic back, but it looks paler now, faint and underpowered. Father's as unarmed as Raven and in twice as rough of shape. I see Sarah's mouth form the words, "Mother, no," but if she stops casting she'll fall, and she knows it. That kid has a tactical mind.

The Deep ones meet them, and the couple is overwhelmed. I realize they'll never get a chance to make amends or apologize.

But no. I understand. This final act is their apology. Sacrifice. And with it, at least in my book, damnation. Suicide ain't painless when you're Catholic. I've got no idea what the Pickerings believe in this day and age, but my own faith compels me to stop them. Not in spite of how awful they've been in the past but because of that. They'll never find redemption for any of it if they go out like this right here and now.

There's nothing I can do. The betrayal made by former loyalists incenses the Deep Ones to new heights. Their bloodlust is tangible, even from up here. Frankie, Levi, and Leora cling to each other. Raven stands in front of them like an eternal shield. Mother and Father Pickering get torn to pieces. I glance at Maya and Stephanie, horrified to find that they're on the cusp of suffering a similar fate.

Something bumps my arm. I turn my head. It's the last bubble. My sword slices through it with ease, and the real King DeCampo lands on the ground in a superhero pose, the back of his suit tearing as he flexes his muscles. He roars like a lion and smites his double with one clawed hand, cleaving the fake's head in two.

The hordes of Deep Ones stop in their tracks. Of course, their leader took on the guise of ours. I should have known. And if I'd only acted sooner, there wouldn't be four orphans down there instead of one.

Guilt washes over me, tainting all my senses. It muffles Raven's words as they negotiate new terms for the Pickerings so the family won't lose their access to magic. I even hear them all agree that Lambs will only go to the Deep Ones if they consent, and any family member can choose to act as one, not only those with no magic.

And the guilt reddens my sight as I gaze down on Stephanie and King DeCampo, standing closer together than I'd ever have expected to see them get. Their Lazakhars glow on the ground where they fell during my duel. She picks them up, and he sets hers around her neck. Stephanie returns the favor.

Something dips in the air at my left. It's Sparky. He's starting to drift downward. I hope that means I'll start descending soon, too. Except I already am down, in the emotional sense. There's nothing I can do about it, either. I'd talk to a priest, but that's impossible. The weight on my heart is so heavy I'm absolutely certain nothing can lift it, not even if I unlive for a million years.

## CHAPTER SEVENTEEN

When I touch ground again, my first impulse is to curl up and stay there. Vampires have the ability to sleep for ages, waking in new times. And at that moment, there's nothing I'd rather do.

A hand drops on my shoulder.

"Tino, come on." The warm voice reminds me of waking up on a Saturday morning in my old bedroom. "It's time to go home."

"I don't deserve to, Maya." Yeah, it's her. She's the only one here who has that kind of effect on me.

"We're all responsible. Anyone could have jumped in and saved them."

"I was the only one doing nothing."

"Nuh-uh, mister." I turn and see the salamander kid tugging on my sleeve. "Me too."

And he's right. I don't want him to be. And he's only a kid. I could just ignore him, but someone else won't let me. A pair of shoes, scuffed all to hell and clearly second-hand, appear in my field of vision. The socks on the feet inside them came from my wardrobe.

"Hey, Tino." It's Frankie. "This really smart dude told me a thing. It changed my life. You wanna hear it?"

"No."

"Well, I don't care. I'm gonna say it, anyway. You're not alone."

And I can't stand it. My head sinks into my hands, shoulders heaving with sobs as blood tears stain my face and palms. Because I *should* be alone. I think that's what I deserve. But if people only ever got what they think they deserved, if they treated people according to their worst experiences the world would be hell. If no one acted with compassion and mercy, everybody would be alone for a darker eternity than any vampire ever endured. And yeah, both the oddball kids are right. I can't argue with the truth, so I don't.

Instead, I let Maya take me home.

Well, she tries, at least, but it doesn't work out the way we'd both like it to. Leora and Sparky get in Baba's hut but pass us the message that the witch can't transport us into any vampire's lair. Something about territory and incompatible magic. And it's daylight outside. At least I know the kids are safe. Baba Yaga is scary, but she'd never harm those two.

Kayleigh and the sun-resistant Pickering siblings can leave, but all of us vampires have to wait out the rest of the day. And we're hungry, of course. I pass my blood bags around, and we pass the time together. Just me and my girl. And my vampire mom. And our socially adept friend. And an ancient vampire king. Hey, I never said this life was normal.

It's not so bad, hanging around with all of them. King DeCampo used to scare me so bad I thought of him as King Decapitate, so while we're all there, I come out and tell him that.

Stephanie practically has kittens over that until she realizes the king's laughing. Yeah, that's right. He thinks it's funny. And for months, she told me he'd likely Rage at the nickname. As it turns out, the vampire king of Providence is a pretty cool guy.

Raven really came through in all of this. On the night I met them, I tried very hard to come across the right way and be respectful to the king's attaché. But I made assumptions, mostly by thinking of Raven as someone with a cushy job who'd never get their hands dirty to save their own life. I couldn't have been more wrong.

Also, I discovered that I consider my sire part of my family, like the older sister I never had. She's the perfect vampire for me to look up to, a role model who's been nothing but a good example and a source of support. I might not have chosen the vampire unlife if given the chance to refuse it, but Steph makes this easier than it would be without her. Her choices were limited too when she turned me, and she's got more than enough compassion and decency to make up for that.

And then there's Maya. What can I say? She's amazing. Sure, her past is a complete mystery, and the few hints I've gotten don't look anywhere near simple. But I'm taking a chance because she's more than worth any risk.

Sunset comes, then dusk. We venture out into the streets of Providence, making our way toward that building on Weybosset Street. But something feels off, and I'm not sure what it is. King DeCampo steps up to the door and uses the secret knock. When the door opens, Shadow narrows his eyes.

"Who the hell are you?"

King DeCampo holds up his hand, showing the ring that tells anyone in the know that he's a vampire king. Shadow nods.

"And which city should I tell our king you're visiting from?"

"Warwick." Raven steps forward. "Please address all questions and concerns to me. My king is weary from recent events."

Before I can put my foot in my mouth and tell Shadow that this right here is the king of Providence and he'd better take a fucking knee, Maya takes my hand. She shows me the edges of cliffs, snakes with rattling tails and fangs dripping venom, bonfires, the sun. I send back a giant question mark. She responds with the business end of a knife meeting a back. Finally, I get it. We've been betrayed.

We're let inside and led down the hall. And just like that, we're presenting ourselves like we're strangers. And actually, we are. None of them recognize us, though I don't know how, and Maya is just as mystified.

Peligro eyeballs me warily, like he's trying to remember who I am but can't. Mrs. Kent stands on the edge of the dais, turning her nose up at Stephanie. Annie puts her back to Maya. Other familiar vamps I haven't met fill the room. I look up at the throne and the figure sitting in it. Instead of shadows, it's all lit up, bright enough for greasepaint.

"King Whitby will see you now." Mrs. Kent steps to one side, and we see his face. And Whitby? He knows who we are, for sure. He stares at Stephanie, her body, not her face, gloating.

Maya and I hang back as Raven makes our formal introductions. We saved the entire city, not just for vampires, but all the supernaturals and mortals. Maybe we even saved the world. But none of it matters because our own people have no idea.

Nobody remembers. At least, not here. It's so bad, they're denying us pretty much any of the respect we've earned. It's not so bad for me, who didn't have much to begin with. But for King DeCampo, Stephanie, and Raven, it's awful. And Maya's got no friends now.

Against the odds, I got a group together, and they came out with the upper hand against an enemy that outclassed us. I thought it was a huge, important accomplishment, too. Well, I guess we all did. In the big-picture sense, we were right. The Deep Ones were a true threat, and we weren't wrong to fight them.

But all along, Whitby had his own agenda—taking the throne. We ignored him in favor of chasing a more immediate danger, and he accomplished a feat with fundamentally more impact. We might have rescued a couple of powerhouses in one battle, but Whitby won a war we didn't realize he was fighting and used a mysterious power we must learn to counter. His prize is this city.

We mingle, like vampires do when they're visiting. The entire time, I'm overhearing whispers, mostly stuff about how this new guy can't be much of a vampire king if he's declared himself in a place like Warwick. A couple of times, they say King Whitby would have every right to attack us for setting up shop right on his kingdom's border if we make any trouble.

This tells me that Whitby's charade isn't too well established, at least not yet. There's no detail in the new background he somehow inserted into the brains of Providence's vampire population. Raven must have guessed at that and chosen the Pickering House's city as our territory because nothing was mapped out for it yet.

"He made some mistakes." Stephanie's leaning in to deliver this information like she did with DeCampo and Raven before getting to me.

"Really? I only see one." I tell her my best guess.

"Good deduction, Tino." She grins. "He didn't make Providence his personal territory with the entire state as his declared kingdom, and that leaves us room to operate."

"Why wouldn't he do a thing like that? It sounds like the way to go."

"Yes, and it was the way King DeCampo set things up. But there are two reasons I can imagine for Whitby to make this mistake in particular. Hasty ignorance, or misinformation."

"I'll take misinformation for five hundred, Alex."

"I beg your pardon?"

"Just a joke. It only means I think it's because someone gave him the wrong details while he planned this coup."

"Raven disagrees. Their brother's always been the sort to put the cart before the horse."

"Well, maybe it's a little of both." I shrug. "How is all of this going to affect the other projects we've got in the works? The Mafia and that supernatural hit list they're probably still shopping around after Kayleigh quit? And Leora."

"That remains to be seen." Stephanie turns and heads toward Maya, no doubt, to share these same ideas.

I wait for King DeCampo to stand up and challenge Whitby to the throne. He's absolutely going to outdo him in a Test of Ages. But even with the bagged blood we drank, he doesn't. I wonder why but don't want to ask where the walls have ears. There's a solution to that problem. My office.

Once I reach DeCampo's side, I suggest a change in location. He agrees and gathers the rest of the group. We head back to the dais where we go through the motions of civil farewells. Mrs. Kent gives us the phone number for checking in any time we cross into the Providence city limits. She tells us we can contact Shadow to arrange for blood bags and gives us that number, too.

And just like that, I'm saddled with a handful of vampires who lost everything.

Out in the street, I realize we don't have a car. We walk away from the immediate area, back toward WaterPlace park. The remains of the Pickerings' van are gone; only a few shards from busted headlights are still there, glinting under the LED street lights. I take out my phone, which is intact, thank God. I dial Esther.

"What the fuck do you want?"

"You still using the office?"

"No."

"Okay. I'm bringing a few vampires over there."

"Well, la-di-fucking-da."

"I don't have my car."

"Tino, you're killing me here."

I cover the phone with my hand and ask permission to give some details. DeCampo nods.

"No, the old vampire king says that the new vampire king will kill us if we don't get out of his city in the next fifteen minutes."

"Shitballs." Esther's stealing the catchphrase she always rolls her eyes at.

"You said it this time."

In ten minutes, she pulls up to the curb. Fitting all five of us inside even the mid-size sedan, Esther drives would be a comic exercise if it weren't for the depressingly dire circumstances. I notice as she helps us inside that her left arm and right leg are moving more smoothly. No wonder she's in a less grouchy mood than usual.

That does nothing to cheer anyone else up, though. Inside the crowded car, it's like we're in Glum City at the border of Despair Town. But before we can all fall into an irreversible funk, Esther's music comes on.

She favors '90s bubblegum pop. Last time I rode in her car, she played *Barbie Girl* by Aqua. This time it's the Spice Girls singing

*Wannabe*, a fitting anthem for down-and-out elder vamps trying to get everyone to remember how powerful they are and the assholes who deposed them in the first place.

"I'll tell you what I want," I mumble. "The right to change this music." Nobody answers. But I really, really want that, as a matter of fact. I know from previous experience that Esther will zig a zig my ah if I even ask. Dammit. I forgot how catchy this song is, the type of earworm that digs into your brain. It's taking over my headspace, but at least it ends when she shuts off the ignition in the parking lot. Finally, I get to stop being a Scary Spice zombie. Yeah, Scary was always my favorite. Don't tell anyone I said that.

Esther heads for the bathroom on the first floor to take care of human biology the rest of us don't have to worry about anymore. I bring everyone upstairs. Raven's seen it already, but I give everybody else the grand tour, for what it's worth. We share the bags of blood in the mini-fridge. I realize something. Well, more like someone.

"Hey, did any of you see Hargrove tonight?"

Nobody has. I think back to the piles of dust and ash Maya shared with me before the whole mess. Well, some of that was the remains of my vision pukefest, but Stephanie and DeCampo weren't dead. Maybe Hargrove isn't. He definitely wasn't in the Deep One's body double bubbles. Try saying that five times fast. Wait, don't. I'm wool-gathering here.

We could look for Hargrove, see if he's still got the real memories in his noggin like we do. And then, I also remember Peligro. He helped us before, definitely against Whitby's wishes. He's psychic as well, so we might have a decent chance of getting Providence's real history restored if we can leverage his ability in that direction. I don't tell everyone all of these ideas. Instead, I'm jotting them down on some paper from my desk. Remembering is at an all-time high on the scale of important things to do.

"Hey, guys, there's still hope." I set my pen and paper in the desk drawer, done writing for now. "We've got to keep on keeping on. Otherwise, we'll lose the will to make things right again."

"That's easy for you to say, Tino. But there's a reason we elders like it when the younger set runs around and gets things done for us."

"Yes. We're tired." DeCampo leans against the counter running down one wall of the studio space I use as an office. "With a change like this, perhaps the best option is to sleep for a while and let Whitby have his short-sighted run at being king."

Maya's standing there silent, eyes wide as though his words are a physical blow. Maybe she saw something in the king's memories while she fought the fake, or she might have remembered some detail about Whitby's plans after coming to power. But I think those are both wrong. The expression on her face looks like someone reliving their own experience, long forgotten. My mind's ear hears an echo, Baba's voice saying Maya of Macedon. But a real voice, front and center in the present, derails that train of thought.

"No, Your Majesty." Everyone turns to look at Raven, who's been sitting in the pink saucer chair in front of Scott's desk. "We're going to get everything back the way it was."

"But how?" Maya's hands clasp in front of her chest.

"I'm taking a page out of Tino's playbook." Raven stands. "Last night, he showed me how much of a difference alliances with other supernaturals can make. It's a powerful tactic, and something my brother will probably never bother doing himself. He's too proud for that."

Raven's at the door, hand on the knob.

"Where are you going?" Stephanie blinks.

"I've got a family of teenage magicians to manage. Their parents just died. They need their dear old dad's ancestor and the head of their family to help them through that loss and focus the energy grief generates in a constructive direction. And I think we can all agree that Whitby had something to do with the Deep One uprising."

"That's right." I nod. "He's a Pickering, too. And with magic."

"Yes." Raven turns the doorknob but stops short of opening the door. "He didn't go to the mortal family, opting to drop information to the other side of that contractual agreement I renegotiated last night. Whitby doesn't make real alliances; never has. He prefers duping people into letting him exploit them."

"So all we've got to do is make or reinforce our contacts?" Maya grins. "I can do that. So can you, Stephanie."

"Yeah, aren't you friends with Fergus Fitzpatrick?" I pat my sire on the shoulder. "I hear he's in charge of all the werewolves."

"Yes, I am."

"Go have a meeting with him. And I'll talk to Leora."

"Who is that?" DeCampo asks.

"The girl with the salamander. She's Baba Yaga's Lamb, and recently orphaned. Last night I volunteered to take responsibility for her. You know, all the mortal paperwork. It's part of an agreement with Baba. So I've got an in with her."

"Perhaps there is hope after all." DeCampo straightens, finally beginning to resemble the vampire I faced during my Trial last month.

"Come on." Raven beckons to their once-and-hopefully-future king. "There's room at the Pickering house for all of us."

"If it's all the same to you, I'll stay at my apartment in Cranston." I yawn with good reason. It's been too long since I really rested.

"Yes, Valentino." Stephanie grins. "And I'll stay there, too." There she goes, inviting herself again. Except this time, I don't mind at all. For now.

"Just don't give me any more reading assignments by H.P. Lovecraft, okay? Those daymares suck."

We have a nice chuckle over that, then follow Raven out the door. I use my phone to summon a Lyft. The driver drops us all in front of the Pickering house. My car is still there. Frankie opens the front door, listens to Raven's brief explanation about temporary guests, and nods. He welcomes them all inside the big gambreled house by the sea. Before shutting the door, he waves at me.

Steph and I get in my car and head home. I get a message from Raph Paolucci, but the crisis he was investigating has passed, so I let it wait until tomorrow.

Stephanie curls up in the comfy chair under the fleece throw that goes with it. She's small enough to fit there comfortably. I climb into my bed, which I have sorely missed. After I shut off the light, I stare up and into the darkness, and I smile because together, we can weather Whitby's storm.

We will take back our city.

# COUNTING COSTS

## SUPERNATURAL VIGILANTE BOOK THREE

*There's no fortune in favors owed.*

*After saving a king but losing a kingdom, Tino's up to his fangs in debt. But he doesn't owe money. A vampire's word is his bond. When a rival, a witch, and a hunter all call in their markers at the same time, Tino's suddenly got a metric ton of promises to keep.*

*To keep his vows, Providence's newest vampire must find missing memories, adopt an orphan, and cure a comatose fiancé. Sounds easy, right? Wrong. The Mafia's in his way at every turn, and the holes in his own recall are a total roadblock.*

*Meeting obligations is impossible if they're forgotten. Can Tino pay his debts without cashing in his unlife?*

# CHAPTER ONE

I owe Baba Yaga, big time.

All I wanted to do with her borrowed power was to rescue some friends. Instead, I helped foil a world-domination plot. And I lost a kingdom in the process. At least that last part wasn't completely my fault.

No, I'm not the protagonist in some Eurocentric epic fantasy novel. I'm Valentino Crispo, Private Investigator. Also, I'm a vampire. Which kind of sucks, but I'm getting used to it. The kingdom I mentioned before is a secret vampiric one, and yeah, there's a king. Was, because he's deposed now and the new guy is a nasty piece of work. But brooding about my unlife is a bad idea now. Sitting in this office is like being on display. And it's all part of paying back that favor I mentioned earlier.

I'm applying as a foster parent for Baba's servant Leora Kupala, who also happens to be an orphaned minor as of last month. Yeah, I'm trying to convince a Rhode Island Social Services caseworker that I'm dad material. Good thing they know nothing about my so-called undead life.

So I'm sitting across from the nice lady in the drab beige office, listening to her list all the paperwork in my immediate future. It's a fairly straightforward process. But from what she's telling me, I'll have to submit something the size of an Epic Fantasy manuscript in order to pay off my debt to the notorious witch. Keeping vows is part of being a vampire. We can't go back on our word without serious consequences.

All in all, it's not too atypical that I owe Baba Yaga a favor. Last time I made a deal like this with a non-vampire, the homework was helping formulate a cure for a comatose hunter with a werewolf and an alchemist. That's only almost done, though. Yeah, my life is pretty strange. Or unlife. Whatever you want to call it.

Here at Rhode Island Social Services, it comes as little surprise that this process is just one huge knot of tangled red tape to cut through. Since I'm an ex-police officer, following procedure shouldn't be too difficult. It's the tower of forms she's putting in the expandable folder that makes me nervous. For some reason, it reminds me of fire, which no vamp in their right mind likes. How flammable is all that wood pulp, anyway? Something she says catches my ear.

"Excuse me? Could you repeat that, please?"

"I said, you'll need to schedule a home visit so your caseworker—that's me, by the way," she drops me a wink, "can ensure your living space is an adequate and nurturing environment for a young teenage girl like Leora. We always do this when someone applies as a long-term foster parent."

Shitballs. Fortunately, I don't say that out loud. I close my mouth, though, because it's hanging open. Don't worry, my fangs aren't noticeable unless I'm angry or hungry. Which I'm not, because it's the opposite of smart to go meet with the living on an empty stomach.

"Oh. Yeah. Of course. Can do." No, I can't, but this nice lady doesn't need to know that. I will need super-sized help in an itty-bitty time span in order to find anything resembling an "acceptable environment." I can't think about failing either because I'm not going to like Baba Yaga when she's angry. I also can't abide the idea of a girl like Leora living out of a trash bag in a group home with non-magical kids. Yeah, the state makes them carry around all their possessions like garbage.

"That's great, Mr. Crispo." The lady smiles, stands, and holds out her deep olive-complected hand.

I get up too, extending my much paler one, expecting a handshake. But that's not what's going on here. Instead, she's got a business card which I didn't notice because my brain craps out on me sometimes. I glanced down and pinch the edge between my thumb and first finger. The name on it is way too familiar. Gina Paolucci. Yeah, that's right. The caseworker for this foster application is the kid sister of the best CSI at Cranston PD. Did I send him something sensitive to analyze just recently? Yes, I did. So I just might owe him, too.

Finally my memory jogs. I've met Gina before, at one of those police charity mixers. Even danced with her there. How did I not recognize her? Oh, yeah. That lousy memory of mine. For whatever reason, my brain is like a sieve. Has been for as long as I can remember. Anyway, maybe she forgot me, too. She hasn't done the typical Rhode Island name drop that usually comes with prior acquaintance in this quirky little state.

"Thank you so much, Gina, for all your advice, help, and this." I nod, smile, and pick up the overstuffed folder she's finally finished filling. "I'll make sure to have this back to you in the next week."

"Make sure and get some help with that. If you need it, I mean. From what Raph always tells me, it was Maury's name on all your paperwork during your days at the precinct."

"Yeah, Maury sure liked putting his John Hancock all over everything." I try to stifle the nervous giggle aching to escape my throat. I fail. Yeah, she remembers me. Maybe leaving off the name-drop was some sort of test.

"Just make sure you get it in as soon as possible, Mr. Crispo." Gina's emphasis on using a formal address instead of my given name tells me all I need to know about how seriously she takes her profession. She won't make any exceptions just because her brother worked with me for a few years. If she thinks I'm not a good guardian for Leora Kupala, she'll deny my bid for custody.

Good for her. Government agencies need more people like Gina, inconvenience for yours truly notwithstanding. I'll just have to do everything I can to make sure I pass her standards.

"Will do, Miss Paolucci."

"I mean it. We process first-come, first-served." I don't like the way she raises her eyebrows and looks over my shoulder. But I don't turn my head and look through the glass pane in her office door. "Don't wait around on this."

As I head out, I wrack my brain, trying to think of where Leora can stay if I get custody. I call my studio apartment the Belfry. It's pretty much one room with a bathroom. I sleep inside a closet with the doors removed. Gina might not hate my place, but she won't consider it nurturing. And I can't show her around Baba Yaga's hut with all the bones in the corner and the salamander living in her fireplace.

There's a reason the witch enlisted a vampire to navigate state bureaucracy on her behalf. We're supposed to be the experts at this kind of thing, blending in, while witches are the rebels of the supernatural world. I suspect Baba's at least a couple of centuries behind on the mortal times and seems to suffer from a form of supernatural social anxiety. And potentially agoraphobia.

I take the elevator to the ground floor. It's dark out, so I don't have to worry about going up in flames by walking outside. Luckily, this office has night hours, like the Family Court. The fact that modern-day employers have flexible schedules at all hours sucks hardcore, but it means government services have expanded to keep up.

I get in my car and set the stack of paper in the passenger seat. As I pull out of the parking spot, a horn blasts. After turning my head hard enough for a mortal to get whiplash, my vampire reflexes manage to avert the impending accident.

Slamming on the brakes, I see the car come up behind me and swerve to one side, rubber streaking the asphalt and stinging my nose. The driver blasts his horn again and waves a fist, his mouth an angry rictus, spouting off profanities in Italian I recognize from my late grandfather's repertoire. I know this guy. He's usually acting as the slumlord in the converted mill building where I rent office space, but tonight, he's a driver. For someone important.

I recognize the people riding in the back of the black sedan. Caprices. Not the car, the crime family, which is Rhode Island's biggest and best. Supposedly, they've gone mostly white-collar this decade. But that hasn't stopped them from ordering hits on people in the supernatural community very recently, myself included. Big mistake. On their part or mine, it's too early to tell.

The kid pressing his face against the window is the Mafia Prince, Sebastian Caprice. He's maybe fifteen and wearing clothes with that distressed look, which means they're brand spanking new, are artificially weathered, and typically distress the contents of the wallet paying for them more than anything else.

The woman sitting beside him is his mother, Francesca. She looks like she just stepped out of a salon, the kind that believes everything should be straightened, buffed, and polished to a high gloss shine. I wonder what people in their income bracket are doing coming out of the Rhode Island Social Services building. I hope it's court-ordered supervision.

Francesca flashes me a malicious little smile, her eyes filled with a competitive gleam I don't like. She's not technically the Boss of the crime family she married into. But rumor has it the real power lurks behind the Caprice Family throne, a space she absolutely inhabits. Gina's words about first-come, first-served return to me now, although I can't fathom why. Stupid memory is stupid.

I try to forget about crime families and focus on making one, sans the felonious part. Pretty much alone. Because the only romantic prospect on my radar is another vampire who I haven't gotten around to expressing my affection for. Yeah, I ought to change that. But you know, we've been a bit busy, saving the world from body-snatching creatures and all.

When you're stopping hunters from assassinating your friends and family or fighting evil beings in the catacombs under Providence, there isn't much time for romance. So sue me. Nah, don't bother. I'm broke. And I'm pretty sure Maya looks worse on paper than I do. She just got into town this year, and succeeding in Rhode Island is all about who you know.

I finally drive away, not bothering to stop by the building in Providence I always think of as the vampire club. Now that Whitby's in charge instead of DeCampo, I don't respect the office of vampire king enough to bother with optional formalities. I passed my Trials, I do what I want. Full members of vampire society are still required to check in every time they visit the city, but I don't care. Take that, Whitby, you usurping bastard!

As I approach the highway and take the on-ramp, I think again about who could help me fill out this paperwork. I'm going to need a wingman, but Detective Maury Weintraub is right out of the question. He knows nothing about the supernatural world, and I'm not allowed to tell him. That means even though he speaks fluent bureaucrat, I can't give him the information I need to be translated. Can't ask my parents for help either for the same reason. I'll tell them about my family expansion when it happens, though. They're in the dark about vampirism and all the other things that go bump in the night too. Ma knows something's different about me but assumes I'm in a more mundane sort of closet.

Maybe I can ask Old Man Fitzpatrick for help. That's my good buddy Scott the werewolf's grandpa. But the fellow is blind, and will need me to read everything on each paper to him. Potentially more than once. It's my bad, not asking for a set of braille instructions. I'll never get this filled out in a reasonable timeframe unless I look elsewhere for help.

Maybe Raven could help. They're undead like me, nonbinary, and still consider themself DeCampo's right-hand vamp. I already owe them loads of favors, though. I suppose I could ask to cancel some of my debt, considering I helped Raven wrangle control of his magical yet mortal family away from his power-hungry brother. Then again, said brother is Whitby. Yeah, the guy who usurped DeCampo, which, as I mentioned, was partially my fault. Maybe Raven will decide I owe them my life over that mistake.

Stephanie might have some ideas about how to proceed with this.

She's my vampire sire, which is sort of like saying she's my mom friend with fangs. Maybe she'll get a kick out of becoming a grandma friend on paper. And she'll want to help me honor my debt to Baba Yaga, because if anything happens to me, she might end up saddled with my debt. That's the way vampire favors go. No such thing as bankruptcy or forgiveness upon death.

I head back to my apartment because that's where Stephanie's been staying for the last couple of nights. It's only been that long since we got back from stopping the Deep Ones from taking over the world. Seems like forever. I swallow reflexively, trying not to contemplate how long ago things will seem once I've had my centennial.

There's another thing to ask Stephanie about, some other night when I'm not saving the world from Whitby. Or even just one high school freshman from living in a group home. My sire and I have lots to discuss, so bringing home a stack of paperwork the width of my palm is probably acceptable. Maybe. I hope.

# CHAPTER TWO

"Hey, Stephanie, I'm home!" I do my best impression of Ricky from *I Love Lucy*, which is to say I sound pretty terrible.

Either she doesn't get the reference or something's wrong, because there's no answer. Of course, my instincts go to the latter. It's way too quiet in here. A vibe I don't recognize sets my enhanced vampiric nerves humming. So even though I don't technically need to, I reach for the wall plate and turn the lights on.

I'm a new-enough vampire to still take comfort in illumination. From what my elders tell me, that changes with time. Or maybe growing up mortal with sunless and fire-safe light sources has more to do with my feelings on the subject. I don't know and for once, suspect they're sailing along in the SS *Ignorance* with me. Flipping that switch negates my apprehensions. And then gives me a whole new set. Thanks for that, Tesla and Edison.

Stephanie's sitting up on my bed, which is inside what used to be a closet until I took the doors off and replaced them with light-blocking curtains. This doesn't bother me in and of itself. She's slept here before to coach me through the changes that came with the business of getting turned. Also to recover from a harrowing night or two at the vampire club. But my problem isn't with her directly. It's that

Stephanie's not alone, and it's impossible to tell whether her companion is a friend or foe.

I can make out a humanoid figure in the bed behind her, but not that person's identity. I know better than to assume the genders of unknown vampires. At least, I think it's another vamp with Steph. I can't hear a heartbeat, and all the supernatural people I know say zombies don't exist. So, that's the simplest explanation I can think of. But my first-hand experience of supernatural beings is still limited, so take my theory with a grain of salt.

"You're early." My sire's deadpan response is probably designed to deflect my interest in the identity of her guest.

"Yeah. The nice lady gave me a huge pile of homework, and I need help with it, Mom." I don't wave the jam-packed folder in her general direction because a blizzard of Xerox would be mighty inconvenient right now. Instead, I just hold it up. "See? This paperwork could stop a bullet or even a stake."

"That's nice, Valentino." She stretches her arms above her head, then out to either side like she's just waking up.

"No, it's not. This stuff's an obligation. Part of my formal vow to you-know-who." I don't mention Baba because there's no way to tell if the other person here should be privy to the facts of my unlife. "It's due yesterday, and won't get done without help."

"Raven's the person for that sort of job." She tilts her head and leans on one arm, a posture that blocks my attempts to peek behind her at whoever else is in my apartment. "Take those down to Warwick."

"Well, it's parental in nature, so I thought of you first." I make with the puppy dog eyes that still work on my mortal mother. "Please, Stephanie."

"On one condition."

She has me here. Vampires don't do anything for free. At least we shouldn't, because our promises restrict us and last indefinitely unless we specifically state otherwise. There's almost always a formal catch, and when there isn't, unspoken quid pro quo lurks in the shadows of all our interactions. Like the other occupant of my bed.

"Okay, Steph. Whatever you want."

"Go into the bathroom, close the door, and don't come out until I open it for you."

"Is this where you do your disappearing guest trick?" Yeah, I snark off to her. She didn't make me agree to good manners, at least. "Because, just saying, the execution is as amateur as a five-year-old kid's neighborhood magic show."

The only responses that zinger gets are rolled eyes and a tapping foot. Stephanie's conditions make the price for her help a bargain-basement deal, though. It could have been way worse, and we both know it. She didn't say I couldn't try investigating who she's with later.

I realize now that my sire leaves these loopholes on purpose. She's done it the entire time I've known her, so maybe she's actually fond of me or something. I try not to smile too visibly, then set the folder on the tiny breakfast table, head into the bathroom, and close the door.

I don't run the water. It's like a game of Simon Says, and Steph didn't say I had to mask any sound. So I put a plastic cup against the wood and enhance my super-powered hearing. Yeah, I refer to my unholy blood fueled powers like it's a spidey sense.

Vampires aren't generally thought of as superheroes but maybe I'll bust some stereotypes. Anything to cope with all the changes. And it makes unlife a Hell of a lot more positive to imagine myself juggling great power and responsibility instead of a vampiric curse.

I'm frustrated in my efforts at eavesdropping, though. Stephanie's way older and exponentially wiser than I am. Neither she nor her guest say a word, but they can't do jack or squat about the Belfry's creaky floorboards. Thank God for old apartments and the landlords who rent them. The sounds aren't much for human ears to write home about, but to my undead eardrums, there's a music to the mysterious guest's passage.

They're bigger than Stephanie, which isn't too unusual because she's tiny. But the guest is well over twice her size judging by their tread, large enough that I'm glad my mattress is foam instead of breakable springs. I can also tell that said person isn't wearing shoes. I didn't see any by the door or the bed besides Stephanie's. What's more, a faint muffled tapping tells me they have calluses that'd give a podiatrist a coronary. So, whoever my sire's been entertaining probably goes barefoot daily. Interesting.

I dig in my pockets, searching for something to jot all these details down with. It's not a problem at the moment for some reason, but I'm used to having a memory that sucks. I write everything in a notebook, but it's kept at my bedside, not by the toilet. Somenight I should run down to CVS and grab a pack of pocket notebooks. If I don't forget to remind myself to do that, of course.

My nostrils flare, and I take a deep breath in order to let out a dramatic sigh in honor of my swiss-cheese brain. And what I smell reminds me vaguely of wet dog. Not fell-in-the-pool pooch, or even drenched-in-record-rainfall rover. More like doggie-in-a-light-drizzle.

Before you go second-guessing my senses, Stephanie's guest isn't a werewolf. They're way stinkier than whoever's currently walking out my front door and smell like both human and wolf, not wet hair. I'd have recognized that odor when I walked in the building and assumed my buddy Scott was over. I've never smelled this particular type of biped before. But whatever he is, it's not human or canine.

Oh, yeah. That's another clue my nose gives me. Testosterone. I can tell who's got that as their majority hormone. Really alive people, anyway. Other vampires mostly smell genderless unless we take pains to artificially scent ourselves.

Somenight, I'll try a frivolous perfume just for kicks. There's a whole line of unusual cologne, everything from soup to old books. I smile, imagining the reactions I might get from the ancient vamps if I walk around smelling like a library. Maybe one or more of them will weep for Alexandria.

Anyway, I hear my sire's guest exit before she shuts and locks the door behind him. I tap one finger for each clue I learned and repeat them under my breath in an effort to remember them long enough to jot everything down in my notebook.

When Stephanie opens the door to the bathroom, I dash out like a cat who heard a can-opener. Pouncing on my bed, I reach for my latest composition notebook and flip to the first empty page. I fumble the cap off my pen and scrawl the following: *male, huge, barefoot, hairy, not a werewolf.* Well, I write it in Latin like everything else of a sensitive nature, but I'm translating it here in the interest of clarity and sanity. Don't say I never do anything for you, okay?

"Are you through?"

"Yeah, just about." I sit up and smile.

But Steph isn't smiling. She just shakes her head and sighs in the massive folder's general direction. After that, my sire heads directly to the fridge, where she gets a bag of blood to warm up in the coffee maker I keep for that purpose. It's a good idea. Since her attention's occupied, I'm able to snag my favorite mug before she does.

Stephanie has a way of making all the little things a touch more annoying than they have to be. Sort of like the opposite of my flesh-and-blood mother, who makes creature comforts a little better all the time. But Ma doesn't really come into this story. For now, it's just Steph and me tackling something bigger than a compilation of every high school homework assignment I ever had to complete.

"It's not as bad as it looks, you know." Stephanie peers at me over the now open folder. "Many of these pages hold instructions for filling the others out."

"Huh." I lean my chin on one hand, reading the top sheet upside-down. "So, Gina Paolucci's psyching me out."

"How do you mean?"

"By making sure I'm nice and intimidated by this whole process."

"As you should be."

"But you just said the paperwork—"

"I'm talking about the witch's avatar." She turns her head, tawny hair cascading over one raw silk-clad shoulder. "Becoming the responsible party for another sentient being is a process which should give anyone pause."

"Um." And Steph's got me there. The mundane aspect of parenthood is scary enough. But Leora sometimes has Baba Yaga's consciousness riding along in her body, even though most of the time, she's just a normal human girl. It's part of how she assists the witch. "Well, but Gina doesn't know anything about Baba or the other supernatural stuff."

"Really?"

"As far as I know."

"So no, not—" she makes with the air quotes, "'really.'" She gazes at the papers, sighing. "Honestly, all these modern regulations are quite perplexing."

"I don't see what's so mysterious about them." I shrug. "I mean, there must have been formalities to follow in your time, too. Right?"

"They differed greatly in nature, Tino." She lets out a motherly cluck. "A pity you can't simply make a declaration on your honor, for instance."

"But that's what these are." I flip past a handful of pages filled with instructions in three different languages. She's right, of course. "Honor's just something they want you to show in writing nowadays, is all."

"Strange times."

"Yeah, okay." I let Steph have her get off my lawn moment and try not to judge. Who knows? In a handful of centuries, I might have the same attitude.

I sit down with my sire, and we begin reading all the paperwork. We get through about twenty-five pages before I hear the theme from Inspector Gadget.

The phone rings. Because of course, it does right when I'm already busier than a bee in summer. It's on the work line. The number has no name attached but looks familiar. So I answer it. What else can I do?

---

"Valentino?"

"Holy shit! Zack Milano!" I smack my face with my palm. "Dude, I'm so sorry. It's just, haven't heard from you in how many years?"

"I know, I know." The voice on the other line sounds tired, maybe even a little strung out. And that's not typical at all for this old frenemy of mine.

"So, where have you been anyway?" Zack is something of a local celebrity. He loves being seen out and about doing things because of course, he does. I knew Zack Milano back during high school. He wasn't at Cranston West because his parents sent him to a fancy private school in Warwick. Instead, we ran into each other at Thespian District and State competitions every year. Where he trounced me soundly every time we entered in the same category.

Zack takes his time before answering. And that's another difference from what I remember of him. He's had a quick wit and been an insufferable chatterbox the entire time I've known him. I shut my eyes and rub my temples, cursing my shady memory. Something nags at the back of my mind, an extremely recent event. Something to do with Zack Milano. But I just can't place it. Worst PI ever, right?

I feel something cold and soft touch my forearm. When I open my eyes, I see Stephanie, her face a mask of concern. Do I somehow look like I've been mortally injured while trying to recover from a brain fart? If that's the case, I'm going to have to do some practicing in the mirror and fix it. No, wait. I can't do that, because vampires have no reflection. It sucks to be undead.

Finally, Zack speaks. "Sort of underground, I guess." He lets out an ironic little chuckle, something more high-pitched than his usual fare. So he's had problems. I grin, which makes me feel like a tool. Thank God he can't see that.

And now I feel like a sorry sack of manure. Nobody's perfect. But Zack was the kind of guy who had everything in the world going for him. I mean, to some people, I might appear that way too. Or at least before I got turned, anyway. Still, I can't escape feeling a little vindicated by an old rival's distress. I'm only human. Sort of. At least I can tell when I'm being a jerk and try to correct it.

Good old Zack Milano pulled crazy amounts of performance talent from seemingly nowhere in every competition. Because of that, I never placed higher than silver at state level, and, I never got to national. Not even with my best performance, courtesy of Maury and our scene from *Rosencrantz and Guildenstern Are Dead*.

"So what can I do for you?" I'm dying to know, or I would be if I wasn't already sort of dead.

"I hear you're in the PI business." So that's how it's going to be. I'm a contact, the "guy" this locally famous Rhode Islander knows. Zack Milano's one of the last people I want to help at this point in time, but his money's still green, and I'm trying to become a dad. Maybe working on his case will reveal whatever memory landmine lies buried in my subconscious. And it won't hurt my foster application to have more in the bank account than I expected.

"You heard right. I'm in the investigation business. And I've got time if you've got something for me to do."

"Boy, do I ever." Zack sighs. It's heavy, like somehow the air coming from his lungs is radioactive, Chernobyl style.

"Well, then, lay it on me, man."

Before Zack speaks again, Stephanie is shaking her head, pointing at my bookshelf. I turn, trying to see which book she's indicating. Stephanie's literary choices always mean trouble for me later. Or maybe she knows bad news is coming, and that's why she gives me reading assignments. I can't figure out which. Hopefully I won't take a hundred years to suss her true motivations out. But anyway, it's clear my sire thinks Zack's little job means big trouble.

"This problem of mine might be a little close to home for you, Tino." I hear him swallow something on the other end of the line. "I'm missing about a week's worth of time, with no idea of what I was doing. Except there's proof. I was on the air." Zack's an anchor on Channel Forty-Two news. "You get how hard that is, right?" There's a strain in his tone. Desperation. Stephanie's probably right, dammit.

"Yeah, I understand." No, I don't. As far as I'm aware, I know nothing about missing an entire week from my own memory. But then again, my recall is so bad, maybe Zack knows something I don't.

"So I need you to help me figure out what really happened. Do you think you can do that?"

"Well, tell me where to start, and I'll see what I can find out for you." Stephanie pulls her wallet out of her handbag, points at it, then points at the phone. Her intention is abundantly clear. She's helping me remember to ask for payment. "I get half my fee upfront."

"Okay. Do you take PayPal?"

"Yeah, I'll text you an invoice." I'm going to charge him top industry rates, of course. News anchors are well-paid in Rhode Island.

"And I'll text your starting point. Thanks. I really appreciate this, Valentino."

"It's what I do, man."

"Who'da thought, huh?"

"Dunno." I chuckle. "Probably Maury. The man knows everything."

Zack laughs with me. There's something in his voice this time that I don't like. That chuckle comes with a compulsion, something that makes me want to head out of my apartment and start right away on his case instead of waiting for the payment to post. What's worse, it reminds me of something. But once again, I can't put my finger on what it might be. I just agreed to take this job, and unless Rhode Island's most popular news anchor somehow lacks the funds to pay me, I'm on his hook. We say our goodbyes, and he hangs up first. Because of course, he does.

"What a cocky son of a bitch." I shake my head.

"If that's how you feel, why are you working for him?" Stephanie's eyebrow is as arched as her tone.

"Well, I'd say I gotta eat, but you and I both know that's impossible. I've got rent to pay on two places, so I guess that counts. And Leora needs food."

"I don't like the sound of that goose chase he's got you on." She lowers her eyebrow. "Still, he doesn't sound like an utterly horrible person."

"He never does at first."

"Interesting."

I swallow even though I don't have to. It's reflex, part and parcel with hearing what sounds like bad news. Stephanie's idea of interesting is usually pretty scary. She looks harmless enough, but the kind of trouble she chases is definitely not. At least I'm fairly confident I won't have to rescue her from body-snatching Lovecraftian horrors this time.

"So, should we get back to this?" I tap the remaining stack of paper with one finger.

"I believe we are stuck at this part." She indicates a line labeled home address.

"I mean, why can't I just put down the one for here?" I know the answer to this, of course. I just don't like it.

"Because these instructions say they will ensure your living space is suitable." She waves a hand around her head. "The mortal authorities won't condone this one-room apartment for a fourteen-year-old girl and her completely unrelated single male guardian."

"Yeah." I shake my head. "And they won't like my studio space, either. I think I've got competition for custody, too." I tell Stephanie all about the Caprices.

My sire sits back in the chair, listening as she drinks warmed blood from my second-favorite mug. Her eyes narrow at my account of the near-miss accident outside Rhode Island Social Services, too. Once I finish my tale, she's drained her mug. I refill it and hand it back before she answers. With a question, of course, because she's Stephanie McQueen.

"That does complicate matters. I don't suppose your income is at a level where you can afford a third residence?"

"It's not. Not even if Milano pays me five times the industry maximum."

Stephanie is flipping through the papers at the back of the stack, some recommended guidelines. She holds one up.

"It says here they favor environments in which the child has their own room and access to the company of other children near their own age."

"What are you, a speed reader or something?" I blink. There's still a lot I don't know about Stephanie.

"As a matter fact, I am. However, I am no expert on good environments for children in this day and age." I don't dare ask about other days or ages. If I do, we'll be here all night.

"So, what do you think I should do?"

"I just said I'm no expert."

"Well, you're the best I've got."

"I'd suggest calling your mortal and modern associates and asking what they know about foster care."

Stephanie has a point. Scott's a werewolf who also happens to be a teenager. Maybe he knows some foster kids from school. And if he doesn't, I could ask Frankie. He's not supernatural himself, but he belongs to a magical family, somewhat literally. In fact, he and his siblings were orphaned just days after Leora's mother died.

Wait a minute. Frankie is legally an adult. Maybe he's dealing with a similar situation right this minute. We could help each other. I watch my sire's lips slowly pull up, just enough to dimple her left cheek. And she's practically glowing. It's like she's been watching my entire thought process somehow. But as far as I know, she's not telepathic.

"Stephanie, I'm so sorry."

"Yes, generally, you are." She breaks into a full grin, which I've come to learn means she's waxing sarcastic and not intentionally being a megabitch. "So you finally realized that *you* have more knowledgeable connections than little old me."

"Yup." I stand. "Thanks for all your help so far, and the moral support while I was talking to Zack Milano." I wrinkle my nose.

"Don't mention it." Stephanie stands too. I wonder whether she means to say you're welcome or if I should take that statement literally and not mention that she was helping me with paperwork. I figure it probably doesn't matter in the long run. "By the way, I highly recommend having a look through The Waste Land by T.S. Eliot. It's dense but a valuable read."

I open the door for Stephanie, and she walks toward it. She's the sort of person you feel the need to do that for. It's something like a vibe she has, maybe part and parcel with her age and experience. But it's possible she's always been like this, even back in her mortal days. Whenever that was.

"Hey, Stephanie?"

"Yes?" She's stopped and turned, her heart-shaped face tilted up.

"You don't have to answer, but I always wondered. How old are you?"

"I'm not at liberty to reveal that detail." She touches two fingers to her breastbone, which is completely covered by her blouse. "But I can tell you I spent my mortal days in mysterium. My vows after my last sunset prohibit me from saying more than I already have. All else, you must discover elsewhere."

"Thanks." It's all I can do to keep from diving for my notebook, but I suppress that urge and wait until she's out the door.

After she leaves, I grab a pencil and jot that down. I pick up my phone to google mysterium and realize I've forgotten to send the invoice to Zack. I rectify that, and shortly afterward he gives me an address, a date, and a time. I should start working on his case, but first I do the search.

Wikipedia says it's a term used by ancient Greco-Roman mystery cults. Awesome. So my sire's an ex-priestess of something. But what? I jot down another note, realizing the second question doesn't bug me as much as the first.

With that inquisitive itch mostly scratched, I need to make more progress with Leora's application. So I call Frankie. He tells me to go ahead and bring the paperwork down to my office so he can meet me there.

I set that up for tomorrow night because it's getting late and I'm tired. Frankie's yawning on the other end of the line, so it's a good call for both of us. I should get a good day's rest. And somehow find time to do Stephanie's reading.

I put on my pajamas and settle into my comfy chair to read as much as I can before heading to bed. But I don't get much past The Burial of the Dead before I zonk out right there in the chair. That's why I got a comfy one, of course. For falling asleep during Stephanie's boring homework assignments.

When my alarm goes off the next evening, it's clear I slept later than intended. If I don't leave soon, I'll be late to meet Frankie. After changing into some normal clothes and slathering on the greasepaint

I wear to keep from looking like the invisible man in mirrors, I focus on collecting the paperwork, my notebook, and the slim volume of T. S. Eliot's poetry. What would I do without my friends, anyway? Exact details are unclear, but I don't need to be a rocket scientist to realize I'd be completely screwed without them.

# CHAPTER THREE

My office is on the third floor of a shabby old converted mill that stands at the border between Cranston and Providence, near Roger Williams Park. The window gives a lovely view of the parking lot, which is practically empty in the middle of the week. Most of the other tenants have bands, and they practice on weekends.

Because of this, the hallways are uncharacteristically quiet tonight, though I can still hear the sound of a bass guitar, it's player is plucking and slapping out notes on the other side of the building. I can't place the song this particular bassline is from, but whatever it is, it's putting a spring in my step.

I'm bopping there outside the door, sticking the key in the lock, turning the knob. A deep and raspy voice sounds behind me, one I should have expected. But I don't like expecting creepy dudes who shake me down for money. I manage not to jump, but it's a near thing. Instead, I turn around with my heel in the door, propping it open while blocking the view inside.

"Your rent's due." The man speaking does so around a cigarette tucked in the corner of his mouth. He's always got one lit up even indoors where that's mostly banned and generally frowned upon. He's also got his hand out, the nicotine-stained fingers sticking up like the legs of a dead spider. Yeah, my landlord gives me the creeps. He should, he's in the Caprice's Mafia.

And the night I made the rental agreement here, he killed a guy. He'd be in jail, but the only reason I know he's a murderer is because of my vampire senses. There's no evidence for me to point the police at. But I'll get him someday, for sure. I'm willing to bet he's done way more than the crime Scott and I supernaturally witnessed. So for now, I give the man what he wants.

"Sure, just a sec." I put my keys in my front pocket and reach for my back pocket. But my wallet's not there. Because of course, it isn't. I stop and try to remember when the last time I paid rent was. Maybe I don't owe; this asshole could be hustling me. My memory sucks, and so does my luck, apparently.

"Hey, Tino!" It's Frankie, walking up behind my sleazy land/crimelord.

"Hey, buddy!" I don't quite meet his gaze, mostly because I feel like a complete idiot right about now.

But Frankie is one perceptive dude, almost uncannily so. Living as a nonmagical guy in a family of magicians practically makes observation a survival skill. He takes out his own wallet, attached to his front belt loop by a chain, opens it, and fishes out two fifty-dollar bills.

"I got it this time." My pal hands the money over to the piece-of-shit landlord, a wide plastic grin on his face. I realize Frankie likes this guy about as much as I do. Which is not at all. Yeah, you know this already, but trust me, it bears repeating.

Like I said, Frankie notices almost as many details as I do. Even though he wasn't in this building the night of the murder, he can tell there's no love lost in this hallway. It reminds me of how some people trust their dogs to make character judgments. Great. My friend thinks of me fondly, like a golden retriever. And I'm not even a werewolf.

"Have a good practice." The landlord turns his back, stuffing the bills in his pocket and flicking a plug of ash in our general direction as he goes. I can't tell whether the rasp in his throat afterward is a laugh or a cough, but I let it and him go because I can't even deal with him right now.

I push the door open and gesture with my hand for Frankie to walk in ahead of me. He does, and I follow, closing and locking the door behind me. Once I hear the landlord's footsteps reach the bottom of the stairwell down the hall, I speak.

"Thanks, Frankie." I shrug. "Got no idea where my wallet is."

"That sucks." Frankie shakes his head, then leans against my desk and raps his knuckles on it. "Have you looked in here?"

"Nah." I open the top drawer, and there it is. "Woah, dude. Thanks!" I'd suspect him of teleporting it in there, but Frankie's got no powers at all. And he won't unless someone turns him, which probably won't happen. There are rules about that.

"No problem."

"No, I mean it. You're a godsend." I take the wallet out and stuff it in my back pocket. "The last thing I need is to make a million phone calls over a lost wallet."

"So, where's this paperwork nightmare you need help to get through?" He eyes the stack of stuff I'm carrying.

"Right here." I drop the folder full of paper in the middle of my desk, where it lands with a hollow thud. My notebook and the T. S. Eliot chapbook topple off it to one side. "It's like the size of the entire *Harry Potter* series."

"I don't know." Frankie paces toward my desk, eyeballing the stack. "It can't be as exciting as a series about a magical school. More like *Dianetics*, only way bigger."

"Hey, thanks for coming out to help me with this."

"It's the least I can do." Frankie grins, which looks good on him. When I met him a week ago, he was on the verge of suicide. And now, even if he's not completely okay, at least he's functioning. I pause to have a listen to his heartbeat. It's a little elevated but not enough for him to be hiding some kind of panic mode. Good.

"So, what do you think I should do?" I flipped to the page about addresses and home visits that stumped Stephanie.

"Hmmm." His eyes move from left to right as he reads the text and peruses the blank spaces on the page. "This is something like what I have to fill out for Sarah and Levi."

"Oh. Too bad you didn't bring yours over, we could have worked on them together." Like I said, Frankie and his sister and brother are orphans. But at least they're related, and he's a legal adult.

"I did." Frankie fishes a few folded up pieces of paper out of his back pocket. When he opens them, I see that it's approximately four pages out of this gigantic mountain I've got in front of me.

I do just about the only reasonable thing possible in a situation like this. I laugh. I laugh so hard and for so long that if I were still mortal, my sides would hurt. But undead people don't have that problem. Thank God for small favors, right?

Frankie is wiping tears from the corner of his eyes as he bends down to pick up the paperwork he dropped. That's another cool thing about Frankie; we've got the same morbid sense of humor. Or maybe he's an empath. No, I'm wrong on both counts. The strain around his eyes and how he's laughing too loud tell me it's more than that. Coupled with that heart-rate elevation, I guess at some sort of nervousness. Maybe anxiety? The least I can do is reassure him.

"Hey, Frankie, I just want to say I'm so glad you decided to stick around. You know, in spite of everything."

His eyes widen, eyebrows trying to hide in his hairline. I shocked him, and I wonder for maybe two breaths, whether I've made a mistake. But after he blinks, I realize it was what he needed to hear. Maybe it's a little too soon, but in this case, that's got to be better than too late.

"I will never think you're anything but a great guy, Valentino Crispo."

It's not the first time he's said something like this. And I know he means it, too. We stand staring at each other, the air between us holding an energy that's familiar yet baffling at the same time. It's like being outside during the moments between thunder and lightning. Something's charging the air, and you know that once it passes that exact energy will vanish forever. But I'm not sure what to do with it, and neither is Frankie.

The edges of the paper in his hand crumple slightly; I'm not sure whether from nervous reflex or as some sort of grounding method.

Grounding is probably a good guess. Yeah, let's go with that. I pick up the residence page, walk over to Frankie, and hold mine next to his. We compare them like college kids from two different sections of the same course going over notes.

"Huh, it's exactly the same." Frankie scratches his head. "I guess I get the short form because I'm trying to get custody of my siblings."

"Yeah, I've got no line of relation between Leora and me. So I'm not sure whether I'll even get a shot at keeping my promise to Baba Yaga." I shake my head.

"Do you even know what happens to vampires if they can't keep their word?" Frankie asks with a wince.

"No, I don't, but it's got to be the opposite of fun." I sigh. "Especially if I end up failing a witch whose primary magic is fire."

"You sure do have a talent for understatement, Tino."

"Yup." I shrug. "Well, this sucks."

"I got an idea, but you might not like it." Frankie isn't looking me in the eye, but I can't figure out why. So far all our interaction has been more straightforward than anything else since I've been turned. I decide not to overthink it or pry.

"Lay it on me."

"I don't think either of us really stands a chance on our applications." Frankie fidgets with the papers in his hand. "I mean, I don't have a job, even though I've got this great big house. Mother and Father had me listed on the deed, but there's no fund in my name like there is for Levi and Sarah."

He doesn't mention the fact that his parents planned on his death at the hands of the Deep Ones they promised him to. Neither do I. Frankie's the only one with the right to broach that topic. He clears his throat. "And you have no house, but you've got an income, and a sterling reputation."

"Yeah, hence the whole idea that making this foster application sucks."

"Well, together, we look a lot better, as far as these things go." He reaches up to tug on the collar of his T-shirt. "So maybe, instead of just you or just me filling these out, we should both apply."

"It makes a lot of sense, Frankie. But how do we do that?"

"Easy-peasy." Frankie's laugh is high-pitched, nervous. His finger trembles as he places it next to a line labeled spouse or domestic partner. "This right here."

The poor guy's heartbeat has got to be at least one hundred beats per minute at this point, and now I understand. I'd have a hard time looking my relatively new friend in the eye if I were about to suggest we pretend to be a couple in order to fill out legally binding paperwork. It's like the plot of *Will and Grace*, only completely different. You know, because there are kids involved. And I'm a freaking vampire. But he's right.

"Do you really think they'll buy it?"

"We won't know unless we try."

"Good point."

Frankie stands there, almost as unmoving as a vampire even though he's definitely not one. He's got some stake in this, one I don't understand. Is there something I've forgotten about him? I am, and I know it. Some crucial and personal piece of information I should remember. I can't check through my notebook either, not while he's right in front of me, trembling like a leaf. But it seems like he's hanging on my response for whatever reason. I need to do something.

And that's why I lean over my giant stack of paperwork, pick up a pen, and write the name Francis Pickering in black ink in the blank beside spouse or domestic partner. I mean, what the Hell, right? My mother already thinks I'm gay because of all the vamp stuff I've got to hide from her. Why not let Gina Paolucci think the same thing?

The change in Frankie is immediate. His heart rate declines to a more normal seventy beats per minute, and he lets go of a breath he may not have been conscious of holding in. His grip on the papers in his hand eases. And instead of a military worthy posture, he falls back into the broken-hip stance I usually see him assume.

"So, we will finish all of this together." I flashed him a smile, and even though there was more than a little bit of fang in it, Frankie smiles back. Well, that's what I get for running out the door without drinking my breakfast. I head to the mini-fridge behind the shoji screen I bought off a surly alchemist and grab a bag of blood.

"I'd better tell Raven." Frankie shakes his head. "They've got their hands full with DeCampo and Maya staying in the basement."

"Oh, boy." I roll my eyes and tug the tubing on the blood bag. "Because I'm, like, Raven's favorite person, of course."

"Cool it with the sarcasm." Frankie chuckles. "They may not make it obvious to you, but I can tell Raven regards you pretty highly."

"Wow." I blink. "Okay. That's the last thing I expected to hear, but I guess I should be flattered." I wrinkle my nose and bite down on the tubing, opening its sealed end to use as a straw. Plastic pretty much tastes like dirt to vampires, which makes sense. It's made from dead dinosaurs, after all. Eew.

"I'm not sure why you're surprised." He shrugs. "I mean, you only gave them their family back and let them right centuries-old wrongs against same."

"You've got such a point, it could cut through metal." I smirk.

We laugh again, this time with less falling paper. The energy between us has changed to something less ominous but still somehow electric. I think maybe there was a point this evening where I could have become an enemy of the entire Pickering family. I can't pinpoint when it was or how it would have gone down, but it doesn't matter. It's been avoided, right? I can breathe easy. Figuratively, of course.

There's nothing so satisfying as solving a problem you didn't realize you had. We still have to fill out mountains of forms, which might take us most of the night. But that's only one hurdle jumped over with ease in my quest to obtain guardianship of Leora Kupala.

The cagey Caprice family is a whole different story.

## CHAPTER FOUR

We're just about done with the paperwork, and it's almost two in the morning. A key rattles in the lock and the door opens, revealing Esther Solomon. She's my other partner in this PI business, but definitely not teenage and most certainly not a werewolf. Esther's an alchemist. And besides the fact that she's an adult, I've got no idea how old she is. But Frankie does. She's his niece.

Magician families are weird. By some strange accident of birth, Esther's uncle is younger than her. Apparently, this sort of thing happens all the time. Magical families are said to be less like family trees and more like family wreaths. At least I've never heard of one being his own grandpa. Yet.

"I thought I'd find a couple of assholes fucking around up here." Esther leaves a glittering green residue of some magical substance on the doorknob. It's sort of like the color of her casting energy only more translucent. Most people can't see it, and I've only caught fleeting hints of it before. I'm not sure whether seeing magic energy is something any vampire can just do or just my own special ability. Our powers vary so maybe this is the start of another rare talent for yours truly. Joy.

"Wipe that off geez." I shake my head and point at the doorknob.

"The last thing we want is some client sneezing for five hours, or feeling like they need to go off on a wild goose chase because your last concoction gets all over their hands." Which happened before when Maury accidentally on purpose drank one of Esther's concoctions. But that's another story.

"For fuck's sake. You think some desperate asshole is going to walk in here looking for help right now?" Esther ignores my request and closes the door behind her without locking it. "Nobody's up or out in the middle of the week at this fucking hour except for you two sons of bitches."

"Don't be so sure." I shrug. "I mean, you're around. And vampires like me, and who knows what else."

"You're full of shit, Tino." Esther laughs. Well, she lets out what passes for a laugh in her book, anyway. The alchemist is like two parts whiskey and one part irony, shaken not stirred. "Like a fucking waste treatment plant."

"Yeah, but I'm so much fun." I roll my eyes.

"He's got a point, you know." Frankie's smile is almost manic, but not quite. He still feels a little awkward around his niece, which makes sense since she broke serious rules to show him how alchemical gadgets work. Pretty much anyone who does can use a finished potion or device. But that all turned out okay in the end, so it shouldn't be a big deal anymore.

"Fucking point or not, this is a goddamn fucking place of business." Esther saunters toward her desk and pulls open the bottom drawer. The item she grabs clanks and sloshes. "We make money working here and shit."

"Been one of those nights, huh?" I jerk my chin at the bottle of amber liquid she's produced.

"You could say that." Esther pats the satchel hanging at her hip. "Should finish the damn cure for Killarney's man this weekend. Still got my ongoing research, which drives me batshit-crazy."

"Oh." Frankie looks down at his hands, studying his bitten fingernails. "That."

"What research?" I know nearly nothing about the part of Esther's past that doesn't involve Frankie. Eventually, I'd like to find out, but she never talks about it and clams up when I ask. I cross my fingers under my desk, hoping for a change in the trend.

"Nothing that's any of your motherfucking business, fangface." Esther sits in the shabby chair at her desk. She leans back, placing her combat booted heels on its surface. The tilt of her head and the soft gaze she gives me before glaring at the bottle cancels out the harshness of her vocabulary.

“Open says me.” She snaps her fingers.

Exactly like magic because that’s what she’s using, the screw on the bottle of liquor comes off. More mundanely, the neck of the bottle meets her lips, and Esther Solomon guzzles at least five gulps of pure whiskey without even taking a breath. I wonder where the signs and sigils that power her alchemy are on that fifth of Maker’s Mark. All the magic alchemists can do are prepared in advance, but I don’t see any inscribed spellwork, powder, or potion that might be levitating that bottle. Maybe it’s under the label, but how she got it on there, I’ll never know.

“Um.” I try to relax my facial muscles, which threaten to pull my mug into a mask of extreme worry. Magician or not, Esther’s still pretty much human, and alcohol poisoning is no joke. I'm the blood-drinking creature of the night, but she's the one scaring me right now.

“Go um yourself, dickhead.” Esther narrows her eyes at me and then levels the same gaze at Frankie. “If this fucking night had an asshole, I’d rip its head off and stuff it up there. I need a pause that fucking refreshes, okay?”

"Okay." I don't ask why she's up here instead of drinking in her lab, which is on the second floor directly below this office. Probably, she ran out of whatever stash she's got down there. Or maybe she just wants to be around people right now for whatever reason. There can't be anything behind my gut suspicion that she's not alone down there, right?

I try not to flare my nostrils as I breathe through my nose. Esther likes her privacy, and she knows enough about vampires to recognize when we’re using our extra senses to get information. But whatever demented angst bug has bitten the alchemist, it's enough to keep her from paying much more attention to me.

I'm relieved that my nose finds no sign of illness in her scent, though I expected some sort of liver toxicity. Bad attitude and drinking habits aside, Esther's health is practically perfect. Maybe she brews and uses some kind of detox potion. If she sold something like that on the internet, she'd make a mint. For all I know, she does. Esther complains about lots of things, but money isn't one of them.

"What are you two assholes up to anyway?" Esther jiggles the bottle in Frankie's general direction. "Anything you need to share a beverage over, Uncle Frank?"

"Just going over this insane application." Frankie points at the stack of finished paperwork, which is hefty. He smiles.

"Why do I only see one of those?" Esther fixes me with a gaze that could pin a bug to a card in an entomology lab. I haven't been undead long enough to escape the reflex to swallow the lump currently forming in my throat.

"Well, we're sort of applying together, kind of." Frankie's not looking at Esther or me. His hand comes out of his pocket, bringing a chrome-plated object with it. It's etched with alchemy sigils, all right. He flips it open and closed, and I realize it's a Zippo.

Frankie's eyes dart around even more than all the filler words in his speech. "You know because, well, I'm kind of a deadbeat with a big old house and an in at a nice private school. And Tino has a job but, uh, itty bitty living space." Frankie puts an awful lot of hem in his haw when he's nervous. This is a guy who should never play poker with real money.

"The only fucking way to apply for that kind of shit together is if people are fucking. Or fucking married. Or married and fucking. So what the hell, dude?" The bottom of the whiskey bottle hits the top of the desk so hard I'm afraid it will shatter. It doesn't. "You can't fucking marry a vampire, Frankie. They can't even walk into a goddamn house of worship."

"Um, we're not getting married." I give Esther the sidiest side-eye that ever sided. "Look, it's just so we can take care of three kids easier.

I mean, do you want a bunch of red tape to get in the way of magical kids growing up in a magical house? Because otherwise, they could end up placed in a group home with mundanes, getting in trouble all the time. I mean, Leora and Levi might blend in, but Sarah? Can you picture her as a ward of the state? The last thing we want is the Pickering family to unmask supernatural everything because Frankie doesn't look good on paper as a legal guardian." And neither do I, but that goes without saying. Probably.

"You're fucking right, Tino. You asshole." Esther does not look happy about this little development. She probably downright hates the whole tangle of trouble we're in. But I guess I shouldn't be surprised. Alchemists have to play by rules and follow directions. She's told me before that if she screws up, people blow up. It makes her something like a helicopter parent when it comes to anything supernatural, except she's not a mom. As far as I know.

"The whole thing was my idea, anyway." Frankie leans his chin on one hand and glares at his niece. "So stop busting on Tino, okay?"

I guess the whole overprotective thing runs in their family. Which of course, I should've already known. Part of the reason I met Frankie in the first place had to do with him trying to keep his little brother Levi out of harm's way.

"As awkward as all of this is right now, I think in the long run, it's for the best." I blink at my own words because I sound just like Stephanie. Blood, even the vampire kind, is thicker than water apparently. And I guess the Solomons and Pickerings aren't the only families traits like this run in.

"So if you're gonna fucking do this anyway, tell me how the hell I can make sure it doesn't go tits up."

"Thanks, Esther." That's really a phrase I should say way more often than I do. It's hard to deal with the alchemist's mannerisms, but her talents have gotten us out of some seriously terrible predicaments. And I have a feeling she's going to be even more important to our success in the future. She might look and sound abrasive, but she's proven several times over that she cares.

"You're God damned fucking welcome, asshole." Esther picks her whiskey up with her hands this time and proceeds to make her way through another quarter of the bottle. Her lips glow green with a magical shimmer as she wipes them with the back of one hand.

Yup. Her command of magic is absolutely the reason she doesn't smell sick or even terribly drunk. For the first time, I wish I'd been an alchemist instead of a vampire. Well, maybe not. I might not have the discipline for it, and I definitely don't have the memory. I might have burned down my whole neighborhood.

"I'm not sure what you can do to help right now. Unless you know of anyone at Child and Family Services who's in the loop about supernatural stuff."

"Nah, no one there. Just someone down at Cranston PD."

"Really?" I blink. But honestly, I shouldn't be surprised. Rhode Island's a small world. "Who?"

"Can't say."

"Oh." My brain's running a mile a minute, sorting through everyone I can think of who's still on the force.

"I might be able to tell you if Frankie hands over Father's lighter." Esther stares at the shiny object and smirks. "Powerful stuff for a Lamb to carry around." The nonmagical kids in Theophile families are called Lambs because they're often tithed to supernatural creatures. Theophiles make pacts in order to keep magical power in their families. Like I said, in the supernatural world, word is bond.

"The will says it's Sarah's when she turns eighteen." Frankie levels a gaze at his niece, unflinching. "I'm holding it for her until then."

"Fine. But fucking be careful what kind of shit you do with it. I'd say you owe me, but since you're in a fucking partnership now, Tino can run the errands to get me some of the shit I need for this motherfucking potion." Esther pulls a piece of paper from her desk, folds it into a paper airplane, and throws it at my head.

The paper projectile sails on a current of glittering green wind beneath its wings. Yeah, Esther magicked her alchemical ingredient list. Even though I duck, it hits me square between the eyes. It might be annoying, but magic is still novel enough to me that I'm more fascinated than ticked off. Once its flight ends, the paper airplane drops into my waiting hand. I unfold it and read.

"Shitballs." I shake my head. "I used to have some of this stuff, but it's gone now."

"Ugh!" After reading over my shoulder, Frankie recoils, stepping halfway across the room with his arms wrapped around himself. "No way. Why would you want something that horrible?"

"My research." Esther sighs. "It's important, Uncle Frank. You know why."

I'm blinking like there's a bucket of sand in my eyes and not just from surprise. The air between us all stings as though we're standing in a sandstorm instead of a studio. Because Esther's speech without all the cuss words peppering it has honest-to-God power. It's tangible, like a strong wind ahead of an explosion or the leading edge of a Nor'easter. And it's nothing that fits with an alchemist's skillset.

"Yeah, Esther. I know." Frankie shudders, one hand over his mouth. "But keep me out of gathering that—" He's shaking so hard he can't finish the sentence. And I don't blame him one bit.

One of the things Esther wants is a handful of scales from Deep Ones. They're inhuman body-snatching monsters that live under most of Providence and the coastal parts of Cranston and Warwick. You know how Leora's family made a deal where she's serving Baba Yaga as part-avatar and part-assistant? Well, Frankie's family made a deal similar to that with the Deep Ones, except Deep Ones don't want liaisons in the mortal world.

They want breeding stock from magical families. I met Frankie practically right after he'd held up the Pickering's end of that bad bargain, and I promised him it'd never happen again. And my vampiric ally Raven ensured it by renegotiating the terms. But they're going to be the stuff of his nightmares for the rest of his life.

Now it's my turn to shudder, but I've got to shake it off. My friends need me.

"Look, Esther." Walking over to her desk, I set the paper on it. "I didn't throw the scales away. I sent them out along with some other stuff to be analyzed. But I can ask to have it back when Raphael Paolucci is done testing."

"Wait one motherfucking minute." Esther closes her eyes. "You mean to tell me you sent it to Cranston CSI?"

"Yeah. I hoped the results would come back before now but—"

"Raph ain't sending any fucking results back."

"He's not?"

"No fucking way. Not to you."

"Why?"

"Because he doesn't fucking know you're a damn vampire."

"Shitballs." I shake my head. Raph Paolucci is Esther's in the loop contact. "I can't believe this."

"Figured it the fuck out, huh?"

"Yeah." I grin. "So you can ask him for it then. And everything's hunky-dory."

"He won't give me shit."

"Uh, why?"

"Because Alchemy fucks shit up, and he learned that the hard way. He'd stop me from doing my fucking thing forever if he could. Only reason he hasn't is it'd take a bullet in the fucking brain to keep me from my magic. Raph promised he'd never put one there out of respect for—" She drags a chalk-stained sleeve across her cheekbone. It comes away wet, leaving pale green dust behind. "Never mind. Long fucking time ago. When shit was different."

"Wow, Esther." There's nothing else left for me to say. "I'm sorry. If I'd known—"

"Well, you fucking didn't, and now you fucking do." She shakes her head. "My own goddamned motherfucking fault. Shoulda fucking known you two assholes had ties, you being an ex-baconator and all." She's swiveled the chair around, putting her back to Frankie and me, but I still see her shoulders and elbows rise and fall as she wipes her face a few more times.

"All right." I don't even bother with rolling my eyes at the pig-related remark. Esther's not okay right now, so a little tolerance for her slang is the least I can do. “I’ll get them back and send the sample over to you, then.”

“Good fucking call.”

“Do you think he’d give you the lab results, though?”

“That asshole?” She turns the chair back around, raising an eyebrow. “Not unless I had an equivalent fucking exchange. But maybe I do have some shit to give him.” She sneers at me. “Yeah, bet your fucking undead ass I do. I'll give him you. Solves all the goddamned problems.”

“Thanks, Esther.” Don't be surprised I'm grateful. Esther's actually doing me a favor by looping Raph in. I’m not allowed to reveal my nature to humans. But if they figure it out on their own and let it ride, it’s all good. The same goes if someone they already know isn't strictly human outs you. Esther's actually giving me something like a professional reference. At least that’s the gist of what I learned from Stephanie.

“What the fuck ever, Tino.” Esther rolls her eyes. They’re bloodshot and salty with unshed tears. “Just get the fucking scales.”

Yeah, those are some pissy words, but Esther’s tone is one of relief. With the air finally somewhat cleared, Frankie eases back on the anxiety, too. He tucks the Zippo back in his pocket, saunters over to my desk, and sits on the stool in front of it.

"So, what do you want to do with this now that we're finished?" Frankie gestures at the stack of paperwork.

"I told Gina I'd have my paperwork back in by the end of the week." I can’t ignore the knot forming in my gut as I say her name. The fact that Gina is Raphael’s sister can only be a coincidence, right? Maybe my gut instinct’s acting up for some other reason.

"Well, I told her I'd have mine in tomorrow." Frankie shrugs. Either Frankie doesn’t know or doesn’t care that they’re related. Maybe he's got the right idea. "It looks like you'll be early and I'll be on time, then."

"At least it seems like something's going right for us for a change." I grin.

"Why in the hell did you have to say it out loud, shit for brains?"

Esther's teeth actually grind. Yeah, I can hear that. "Don't you fucking know what a goddamn jinx is?"

"I'm a vampire." I scratch my head. "Thought I didn't have to worry about that kind of thing since I'm not technically alive."

"You're mixed the fuck up in this with two fucking Lambs, two magicians, and a regular kid." Esther takes her boots off the desk and gets to her feet, clutching the neck of the nearly empty bottle in one hand. She swipes the lid from the top of the desk, then kicks the drawer closed with her foot. "I gotta get the fuck back to work and then call Raph at zero dark fucking thirty in the damn morning. You guys have fun with your fucking fake ass marriage paperwork bullshit."

"Thanks, Esther." Frankie waves as she exits, smiling brightly. "See you later!"

I'm not sure which oddity bothers me more, the suddenly shiny-happy Frankie or the plain-speaking Esther. It almost feels like I'm in some sort of alternate universe, but those don't exist, right? If they did, I'd have to go find the one where vampires are all millionaires, able to eat garlic inside a Church, and can go to the beach at high noon. Yeah, I seriously miss a ton of stuff, being a creature of the night and all.

I put my signature on the last page of paperwork. After I lean back, Frankie does the same. I'm about to slap him on the back and jokingly congratulate him, but when our eyes meet, I realize my error in judgment.

Frankie's eyes practically have stars in them, and I recognize that look. It's like hero worship, the kind I remember from when little kids came up to me while I was in uniform. But I'm worried there's more to it than that. I hope I haven't just led Frankie on because if I break his heart, Esther will fracking kill me.

# CHAPTER FIVE

I say goodbye to Frankie, who leaves with more of a spring in his step than any mortal at two-thirty in the morning ought to have. I'll have to make it clear to him that I only want to be friends. I'm not gay, but even if I were, Frankie Pickering isn't my type. Everyone I've ever had a thing for has been competent, assertive, and female. My romantic relationships tend to be few and far between, for whatever that's worth.

At any rate, there's still plenty of time before sunrise to do some legwork. I decide it's a good idea to check on the lead Zack Milano gave me for his case. You know, the stuff I get paid to do. I kind of need money for rent, internet, and investigation supplies. And even if I don't need groceries anymore, Leora will.

I enter the address from Zack's text into Google Maps before I head downstairs. Once I'm in the car, I put the phone on the hands-free clamp. Rhode Island has laws about holding communication devices while you're driving, and for some reason I think it's ultra-important the police don't pull me over in the near future. I found my wallet, so it isn't that. Oh, yeah. A moving violation will look bad with that foster application.

After I click start, I see that the Warwick address is across the street from a hoity-toity private school. Stout Academy is the institution of choice for wealthy people who want an Ivy League-level prep school without all the parochial elements for their kids. That's where Sarah goes. Levi will join her this year. Maury almost went there, but his dad lost a bunch of money in the dot-com bust. Yeah, that's right. Good old faith-neutral Stout Academy brings in the Jewish families. And, I'm beginning to suspect, most of the magical community as well.

The exact address Zack gave me is the storefront for a music shop, the kind where you can buy or rent an instrument and then get lessons on it in the back room. A display in the window features the usual run-of-the-mill orchestral and marching band instruments, not electric guitars or even Casio keyboards. We're talking clarinets and saxophones here. There are also several fliers in the window with tear-off strips furred along the bottom advertising the available lessons.

I walk past the music shop just to see what's next door. It's a cafe, the kind that serves all the espresso drinks plus a variety of classic Italian pastries. I'm surprised at first that I can't remember having been to this one. Before I got turned, I loved checking out places like this. But one look at the name on the sign leaves me shaking my head. I roll my eyes at the silhouette of a goat beside curlicue lettering.

"Caprice Cafe?" I snort. "Yeah, big freaking surprise I avoided this joint."

"Probably a front, boss."

I look around for whoever just said that and see nothing. At least not until a shadow next to one of the music shop's fliers catches my eye. But the sign itself drags my attention away. It's got a huge graphic with a microphone, advertising voice lessons.

Somebody short and slight stands in front of it. I blink at the half-grown fellow in the baseball cap because he's wearing it turned forward. Atypical for his age demographic, but nothing's normal about the person addressing me. Yeah, I know this kid. Well, he's sort of a kid, but not really.

"Hey, Sparky, what are you doing out in the middle of the night?" I put my hands on my hips, trying to project a paternal vibe. Which is probably a good thing to cultivate, all things considered.

"I got no curfew, boss." Sparky the salamander, sometime minion of Baba Yaga, calls me boss for some reason. I don't even want to know why. I'm not the boss of him. Maybe it's because I offered to be his bestie's dad.

"You might not, but the police will disagree." I glance at the street, hoping not to see the hut on chicken feet that Sparky inhabits with the most powerful witch in the world in the middle of it. "Uh, where's the, um, house?"

"Oh, don't worry, boss, it's invisible to the norms." Sparky jerks his chin toward a small historic cemetery at the end of the block. Rhode Island is full of those.

"Because invisibility automatically makes everything okay." Oops. There goes my inside voice, coming out when I really don't need it to.

"I just needed one of these, boss." Sparky tears a scrap of paper from the bottom of the flyer advertising voice lessons. "I'll go wait by the house now."

"Baba Yaga wants to take voice lessons?" I blink. Stranger things surely have happened, but I can't imagine the witch leaving her hut, even if it's just to go into some retired opera singer's parlor and run scales. "And what do you mean, wait?"

"No, not lessons for Baba." Sparky smiles like a pageant contestant and jerks one thumb at his chest. "This guy."

"Uh, I kind of know my way around vocal training, kid." I shake my head, trying to fathom the idea of a salamander getting formal vocal training.

"I know." Sparky's smile dims, twisting into an impish little grin. "Been a fan my whole life."

I try not to ask the million questions that come to my mind. One of these has to do with what or whoever Sparky is waiting for in Warwick at almost three in the morning. But the query that escapes my lips isn't so useful. In fact, it's downright conceited. But I've never met an actual fan before, so my reaction is more disappointing than surprising. The kid actually stops me from asking more about what kind of appointment he could possibly have at this hour.

"You've seen me perform?" I blink.

"Yup."

"But it's been like ten years since my last show." I'm side-eying him now. "You'd have been a baby."

"You'd think that." The salamander kid winks, then turns his back on me and starts hightailing it toward the cemetery. I let him go because I don't want to deal with the fallout if the police come and ask me why I'm hanging out with what looks like a teenage boy in the middle of the night.

Sparky looks like he's maybe twelve. Could he be one of those magical creatures who ages slowly? Maybe. Can't ask him about it now, since he's vanished from view. If only I knew an expert on critters of the supernatural variety, I could find out for sure. But the specifics of salamanders aren't a priority right now. Zack Milano is.

It's time to continue my investigation and information gathering session. I take one of the little spiral pads out of one pocket and a little golf pencil out of another. I love pockets. Thank goodness I'm not female, because I hear they have either tiny or nonexistent ones in the clothes designed for them. Someone ought to change that, but dammit, I'm a PI, not a fashion designer. If I meet one, though, they're getting a piece of my mind about pockets.

I scrawl out some words in Latin about Cafe Caprice, along with its address. I want building and business records on that and the music shop, which is called Muse-icality. I close my eyes for a moment, sending a silent prayer that the whole Muse thing isn't literal. The last thing I need are Greco-Roman mythological figures springing to life around the Caprice crime family, who are Italian, the modern version of Roman. Like me. Shitballs.

It's probably smart to get as much information as possible while I'm here about the local scene. So that's why I jot down the names of the music instructors from each flier. And all of them seem to be either Italian or Greek. Maybe I'm lucky, and one of them is even the shop's proprietor. I also make a note to ask someone how old Sparky is in mortal years. After that, I look around for anything that smells or sounds supernatural in the immediate vicinity, and there it is. Something I never want to experience again, even if I unlive for a million more years. Deep Ones.

The amphibious creatures who snatch bodies and impersonate whoever they can grab also drop slime. That doesn't sound so bad until you realize the stuff's literally full of bad luck. I had the, um, privilege of experiencing that effect first-hand in the very recent past, and I don't want an encore of that performance. It should come as little surprise to you that I hightail it across the street and back into my car, but I don't want to leave the vicinity since I'm not done investigating yet. I decide not to let those slimy assholes chase me away. In fact, I drive toward the slimy scent.

I pull into the parking lot behind the music shop. Sure enough, half the spaces are labeled Music Store Parking Only Violators Will Be Towed" and the rest are for the cafe. I manage to see that through some unexpected and annoying fog back here. I'd be suspicious, but it isn't sparky or green, and this shop is in coastally-located Warwick. The ocean in New England likes to breathe out pea soup every now and again,u bt this bank of fog is starting to clear up. I roll the window down and take a whiff. Yup, the Deep One's slime smell is way stronger back here, and I immediately discover why.

A set of bulkhead doors squat at the back of the building between the music shop and Cafe Caprice. There's no lock chain or other apparatus to keep them closed, either, so that can only mean one of their tunnels is under here. Body-snatching inhuman creatures or not, they've got to get around, and they don't exactly blend in. I don't know whether any other supernatural denizens of Rhode Island use passageways like this, but I am absolutely sure the Deep Ones do. Or maybe did because Raven's renegotiation on behalf of their family also laid out rules against impersonating people without consent in the future.

Last week was well before that new agreement. So I figure Zack Milano either got snatched deliberately because he's a celebrity or he went poking around on some journalistic quest in the tunnels and stepped in bad luck slime. That would explain where he'd been but not why he doesn't remember. Certain inhuman creatures have mood or memory altering effects on mundane mortals. If they didn't, everyone would know all about them. Secrets are important in the supernatural world, especially of the identity variety. But anyway, people remember Deep Ones. The memory whammy has to be something else. But I've got no idea what does that. Neither do the old vamps I hang out with. If they did, we'd know exactly how to counter Whitby's takeover of the vampire club. That's right. He did it with some kind of memory-wiping effect.

Glancing up at the rear signage on the Caprice Cafe makes me consider a third possibility. Zack's a reporter. Well, sort of. News anchors often get their start that way, and the habit of investigation dies hard. Maybe my old rival tangled with the crime family and got himself dumped in this basement. After that, he'd be easy prey for the Deep Ones using it as a passage above ground. But it's unclear why body-snatchers would want someone like Milano. Maybe who or whatever wipes memories has their own agenda. Or maybe Zack has dirt on the wrong person, place, or thing.

As far as I know, he's a regular plain old mortal. Then again, I had no idea I lived next to a family of werewolves my whole life. Even I hide my supernatural details in plain sight. So maybe I'm wrong about Milano, too. But there's nothing I can do besides flat out ask him. As you learned during my whole Raph Paolucci conundrum, that gets dangerous real quick. Asking around, however, isn't a bad idea.

I'll need to chat with some of the older supernaturals I know, see if any of them have heard the name Milano bandied about in magician's circles. In case magical heritage comes from Zack's mother's side, I jot down a note to find out her maiden name and ask about whatever that is, too. All that'll take is a phone call to Ma. She knows everybody's business, including the Milanos'. Yeah, I guess I got all my curiosity from her side of the family.

I look at the clock, throwing its blue-green light from the dashboard of my car. It's now almost four in the morning. I check the weather app on my phone that tells me what time the sun rises. Thank

God for technology. I think I'd probably have burned up in the sun if it weren't for this app. Like I've said so many times, my memory sucks big blue donkey balls. That goes double for knowing what time it is off the top of my head like my friend Maury can do. And anyway, the app tells me it's too late to go spelunking. Which is a good thing because I'm sick of subterranean tunnels lately. At least I've got stuff to research while my curiosity keeps me up all day.

I throw the car into reverse and step on the gas because nobody's here at this hour and this vampire has a need for speed. A thud causes me to apply my shoe right back on top of it, making a rubber-scented squeal and probably the skid-marks to match in the parking lot.

I throw the car back in park and get the fuck out of my car to see what the hell just happened. And I already said I can't afford to get a traffic ticket right now. Forgive my Esther inspired vocabulary, but when you get in a vehicular tangle, it's hard to refrain from colorful metaphors.

"Shitballs." I definitely hit something. No. Someone.

# CHAPTER SIX

There's a humanoid figure laid out behind my vehicle. It's taller than the average person and seems to be wearing what looks like a fur coat at first. As soon as my brain's gears catch on to the reality of who I hit with my car, I turn on the blood fueled speed and hightail it over to make sure the fellow on the ground is okay. And yes, I know it's a fellow absolutely for sure because I'm a huge fan of his blog. Practically everyone who reads it loves the guy. It's Sasquatch. I fucking hit Sasquatch with my goddamn car.

I stare down at the supine form of the supernatural world's equivalent of the Crocodile Hunter. If he dies or gets permanently injured, everyone who's not a regular human will hate me forever. I try to get my hands around his wrists, searching for a pulse. But his thick hide and even thicker pelt prevent that. One glance up at his neck tells me I'll have no better luck there. Sasquatch has a furry ruff almost as thick as a lion's mane. Who knew?

Sasquatch's descriptive blog on the Internet was invaluable to me during my last case, probably saved a lot of lives at other times, too. I owe this guy big time, and I might've killed him. See what I mean about my luck? But at the moment, I'm way more worried about the creature I hit. If he was checking in with the Deep Ones back here, he might have been slimed with the bad luck wooj, which means I could absolutely have killed him. And for all I know, he's an endangered species or something.

I'm about to start flailing, flopping around like a fish out of water, which is ironic considering I'm next to the entrance to a fishlike race's lair. An angelic voice I believe truly might have been inspired by the heavens sounds behind me and heralds my hopefully imminent salvation. Well, its tone of calm confidence definitely chills me out, at any rate.

"Stand back, Tino. I've got this." I stand aside and let the woman go through. Well, technically she's a vampire, but who's counting?

I'm clenching my hands into fists so tight my nails dig into my flesh. I'd bleed if I were still mortal, but I'm not, which is a good thing, considering whose company I'm in now. In case you haven't heard me wax poetic about her before, I'll cut right to the chase. Maya is the most amazing being I've ever met. She's comfortable in her skin, adept at navigating both combat and social scenarios, and has a smile that's the closest thing I'll ever see to the sun again.

Right now, she's got her hand directly above Sasquatch's nostrils. The nod and smile she gives me trigger a profound sense of relief as I realize she's detected breath. Then Sasquatch wiggles a toe or two, and I realize everything's going to be okay. I don't know if that says more about Sasquatch's constitution or Maya's ability to work miracles. Probably the former because the latter is just my bias.

I turn around because my physically unneeded but emotionally essential sigh of relief threatens to bring tears to my eyes. I'm not sure why I'm so emo all of a sudden, but I stop wondering in ten seconds flat. Because my car, the back end at least, is a hot mess.

Maybe it says something about me, the fact that I worried more about Sasquatch's well-being than the damage to my vehicle. For most of the supernatural world, my reaction says nothing nice. Strike that, reverse it. It says too much nice. Not everybody who isn't human is a piece of shit, but most of them have a selfish streak a mile wide. You sort of need it when you need to lie through your teeth to most people on a regular basis.

Apparently, I'm too much of a nice guy to be a bloodsucker. So what else is new? It still doesn't prevent me from wincing at the bumper currently falling off my car, with a Sasquatch shaped dent caving in part of my trunk. I can't even take the bumper off and put it inside, because I don't think I can pop the trunk without the Jaws of Life at this point. I can see the inside of the latching mechanism. Yeah it's bad enough that I don't think it'll ever open again. At least not without some serious help in the form of a blowtorch.

"Oh, man." The voice is a warm tenor, not what I expected at all. "Dude, I'm so sorry. Your car's totaled. Look, if you need help with repairs, I'm happy to throw you some green."

I blink, not sure what to say, or whether I even want to turn around and face a guy I hit with my car, cryptid or not. But I have to. This is worse than adulting, something I avoided for as long as possible while still mortal by living in my parents' basement. But that's another story and trust me it's way more boring than this one.

Anyway, I do turn around. Sasquatch is sitting up, rubbing the back of his head. When he pulls his hand away, there's nothing on it. For whatever reason, I expected some kind of blood or gore, but he's unscathed. Thank God.

"No, I'm the one who should be sorry. With vampire senses, you'd think a guy like me could look where he's going." I extend a hand downward. Sort of. The intention is to help him up, but Sasquatch is built like a linebacker. I'm almost reaching straight across toward him.

"Wow, thanks." Sasquatch grips my hand in his, completely engulfing it in his furred mitt. He doesn't pull on me. It's more like he uses my offer of assistance for balance instead of leverage. The world would be a fairer place if the people in it were more like Sasquatch.

"Don't mention it." And I honest-to-goodness hope he won't. Mention this whole fender-bender, that is. To anybody. Like I said, Sasquatch is extremely popular. He gets along with anyone and everyone. I don't know how he manages it. Maybe he's Canadian.

"So Maya," Sasquatch grins. "Aren't you going to introduce us?"

"Sorry, Sass. It seems I dropped my manners in the rush to make sure you were okay." Maya grins back. "Tino, this is Sass. He writes a blog, which is really cool. You should check it out. And Sass, this is Valentino Crispo. You know, the new vampire I told you about? He's Stephanie's."

"Wow!" Sasquatch claps his hands, which makes a sort of muffled flapping sound instead of the usual sharp slap.

"Wow?" I'm not sure why everybody's favorite neighborhood cryptid is so excited to meet little old me.

"Yeah. Maya told me all about the whole kerfluffle between the vampires and the Deep Ones." I can't believe the words coming out of Sass's mouth. I mean, who says kerfluffle anymore?

"Really?" I raise an eyebrow. If I had a heartbeat, it'd be going a mile a minute because he just said Maya actually talks about me.

"Oh, yeah, she did. And then they told me about it themselves." Sass brushes something off his fur, collecting it in his hands. "I just came back from getting an update and they're way more well-behaved than they used to be, so thanks."

"Uh, well, Raven's the one who actually convinced them to play nice." I shrug.

"I know. But they wouldn't have negotiated in the first place if you hadn't gotten involved." Sasquatch shakes the ick off his fingers like Taylor Swift shakes off haters.

Whatever it is splatters to the ground to glisten in the orange-toned glow of a streetlight. I'm not sure I want to hear what my very recent enemies have to say about me. But it looks like I have no choice in the matter, so I have a gander at what fell off Sass's coat.

It smells like Deep Ones and looks like a handful of their scales. Score! But no. They're covered in the bad luck slime. Well, at least that explains why the fender-bender happened. I rummage in the pocket of my big opera cloak for some crime scene supplies and find some gloves but no bags. I'll have to improvise then.

"Um, sorry. I space out sometimes." I realize I've left the big guy hanging, so I stop trying to collect samples for now. "You were saying?"

"The Deep Ones said if it wasn't for your meddling, they might've taken over the world." Sasquatch shrugs. "That wouldn't be good for the magical ecology, you know what I mean?"

"Um, no, not really." I shuffle my feet. Awkward Tino is awkward.

"That's okay. Not everyone is into cataloging supernatural creatures, after all."

"That's right." Maya smiles. "Some of us are supernatural vigilantes instead."

"Uh, I wouldn't put it that way. I'm a PI. You know, private investigator." I shrug but punctuate it with a grin. "I'm not Batman."

"Supernatural vigilantes has a nice ring to it, though." Maya chuckles, a velvety sound.

"Well, maybe that's too high-brow for someone like me. I'm just a busybody, Maya. Nosy Parker, at your service." I make a little flourishing bow.

"Well, I'm a Nosy Parker, too, I guess." Sasquatch chuckles. It sounds like claws scratching tree bark. "Journalists and investigators. Next-door neighbors to Nosy Parker, for sure."

This time when he chuckles, I'm right there with him. I guess it makes sense for a big hairy guy who seeks out interviews with even the most inhuman supernatural beings to have a good sense of humor. Hopefully, he has better luck than I do, though the whole car accident implies otherwise. At least he's more resilient than I am.

My mirth tapers off when I realize that Maya must have called, emailed, or otherwise chatted with Sasquatch only hours after we finally got out of the tunnels. She's got him on speed-dial or something. Either that or he was already in the area for some reason. My gut tells me that second guess leans toward the truth. Sass was here visiting somebody. But who?

"How long have you two known each other, anyway?" I'm trying not to sound like an envious jerk, but it's a losing battle. Because I am actually jealous. Of a big hairy dude. Who Maya probably could take in a fight. Yes, she is almost a literal beast in combat, but that's beside the point.

"Oh, yeah, we go way back." Sasquatch gives Maya a pointed glance. I'm not sure what that look in his eye means, and I get the impression Maya doesn't either. Could she have memory problems too? Older vampires are rumored to need some help with that when they come out of hibernation. But then again so do I, and I'm the youngest.

"I can honestly say I can't remember a time when I didn't know Sass." Maya's eyebrows draw nearer to each other. Either she's trying to remember and can't, or she's got some sort of vampiric obligation not to say too much. I'm familiar with that sort of evasiveness from Stephanie, so I take it in stride. Maya doesn't make a habit of vagueness like Steph, at least.

"Cool." I swallow the green monster threatening to rise up from my throat. There's no time for jealousy right now. Or really ever. It's better to just talk about stuff like that.

"So, are you on a new case Tino?" She changes the subject. Like I said, Maya's wise.

"Yeah. For an old, um, friend. From my high school days."

"Your Hunter contact?" Maya is talking about Kayleigh Killarney, my ex-girlfriend turned Hunter, who I still happen to owe a favor to.

"No, a guy from a different school. Used to compete against each other all the time." I'm not sure I want to mention Zack's name. These two probably know who he is. Even though he didn't specify a need for privacy, I know I wouldn't want strangers poking into my business if I'd lost a week. Hey, I try to be professional while working a case, you know?

"Okay." Maya lets it go. She's cool that way. Well, in every way, but who's counting?

"Well, I was here trying to track someone down for an interview. New rare creature seen here a few months back, in the company of Baba Yaga."

"Shitballs. Now I have to apologize again, Sass." I shake my head.

"You're looking for Sparky. I sent him running home. Maybe the hut's still in the cemetery across the way."

Sasquatch takes a few strides that cover the ground between the parking lot and the sidewalk. With one hand held up to his brow like he's shielding his eyes in bright sunlight, he peers at the graveyard. I wonder whether he's nocturnal, and if so, whether the moon makes a glare that gives his eyes trouble. Or maybe he's diurnal and just can't see in the dark.

I pace up to stand at his side, wondering whether I ought to offer him a favor to make up for ruining his interview. Because of course, I already know Baba's hut is gone. Vampires have eyes made for seeing in the dark after all. Apparently, Sasquatch doesn't.

“Is it really Sparky you want to talk to?”

"Yeah, the salamander kid. So you know him?"

"Sort of." I grin. “I might be able to help you get in touch with him again. He comes around pretty regularly.”

"Oh, yeah, that sounds great! Next time you see him, drop me a line at my blog. I'll be in Rhode Island all month."

"Will do." I nod and extend my hand. We shake again, and this time it's less weird than before. I guess handshakes with Sasquatch are something you can get used to. Who knew?

“If you don't mind, Sass, it's getting close to sunrise." Maya gestures at the sky, which is still thankfully dark. "We've got to run along to someplace sunless, you understand."

"You bet I do." Sass nods. "I'm sorry about your car. Don't worry, I'll make sure you're compensated for any repairs. It might take a few weeks, though."

I'm about to open my mouth, refuse his help and tell him I've got it covered. It's not like I don't have insurance. Rhode Island sort of requires that. No, not sort of. I was an officer of the law; it absolutely does. But before I can say anything, Sasquatch claps his furry mitts together again three times, and the next thing I know, he's gone. I flare my nostrils, trying to catch a scent. Which works, but it's getting fainter by the second. I don't know if Sasquatch has a teleportation ability or some sort of invisibility. I put my money on the latter.

I saunter back toward my car. Something shiny on the ground catches my eye. It's the slime and scales. Good thing I'm seeing them again now or I'd forget to pick them up. I still can't remember exactly why I want them, but it'll come to me eventually, I guess.

Putting on the nitrile gloves is second-nature for me. I scoop up all the Deep One goop in my right hand, then turn the glove inside-out while taking it off with the left. After that, I take off the left glove and bundle them together, with the full one inside. I stick them back in my pocket and hope I remember them before they leak any slime. For good measure, I brush my hands off on the outside of my cloak.

"Well, he seems like a salt-of-the-earth kind of guy." I shrug and shoot Maya a lopsided grin. "Uncanny for some reason I can't put my finger on, but I can see why everyone's cool with talking to him."

"Uncanny?" Maya throws her head back and laughs. "Yeah, I guess you could say that. It's probably because even we vampires can't hear Sass's heartbeat."

"Wait, what?" I blink, thinking back to walking in on Stephanie. "Sasquatch is undead?"

"Not one bit." Maya rubs her sides like all that laughter isn't something she's used to. "Thick fur and thicker hide just make it impossible to hear."

"Hmm." I'm wondering whether Sass was the mysterious guest in my apartment last night. But Steph seemed awfully cagey about that whole evening. Even though I could technically ask Maya what she thinks of my wild idea, I know for sure that my sire wouldn't appreciate it.

Even though the silence between us persists, it's not awkward. Being with Maya is easy, and probably the most uncomplicated interaction I've gotten since becoming a vampire spending much of my time with same. Whether that's as mundane as personal compatibility or some sort of power Maya has, I don't know. At any rate, I sure do appreciate it. And the only way I can express that without acting like a total douchebag is with words.

"Hey, Maya?"

"Yeah?"

"Thanks."

"For what?" She blinks.

"Just being yourself, I think." I stare down at my thumbs, which are circling each other as they act out one of my nervous tics. "You make everything feel almost normal."

This time, the silence feels longer than it probably is. Still more comfortable than not, though. I don't dare look up and risk breaking it. I'm Catholic, so confession is something I'm more accustomed to doing without the other party seeing my face, after all. But she doesn't tell me to say the rosary or any Hail Marys. Instead, she asks me a question.

"Where are you headed, Tino?" There's more to her question than plain old geography, but it's unclear exactly what else is there. I make the mistake of looking Maya in the eyes as she speaks.

"Um." I'm lost. Gone. Tumbling in the depths of her gorgeous brown eyes. I forget what she even said. Do vampires get amnesia? Apparently, I did as a mortal, so maybe it's just me.

"Tino?" Her eyebrows rise in tandem. "Earth to Tino?"

"Sorry. My brain went on a little jaunt." I grin. Can't help it.

"Are you sure you're okay after that accident?" She peers at my chest. "Nothing in the car broke off and got you near the heart or anything?"

"No?" I look down, pat my chest a few times. "I think I'm unharmed. Maybe? I'm not sure?"

"Why don't you come back to Warwick with me?"

"Do you think Raven would be cool with that?"

"I don't see why not."

"It's just that I'm hesitant to ask them for any more favors."

"I know. But hospitality isn't a favor between vampires." She grins. "It's an obligation. Do you want to come with me or not?"

"Oh." I hope my grin isn't as sheepish as it feels. "You know, I'd forget my head if it wasn't attached. I'm glad you're around."

"I think you need to be with people, not alone." She nods, as though answering her own question. "You're staying the day at Pickering House, just to be safe, Tino."

I don't say anything after that, just nod and let her get in my car. I drive half the posted speed limit. It's three and a half miles to the house on Ocean Avenue, which used to belong solely to the living members of Raven's family. Now it's theirs in every way except the name on the deed, which makes sense. They are the oldest member of the Pickering family, after all.

# CHAPTER SEVEN

I park the car around the back, hiding its damaged rear end by backing in beside the garage. The last thing I want is for somebody to knock on the door looking for me in the middle of the day because they think I hit a deer, or possibly a great Dane. Or an escaped lion from the zoo, which is more Sass's size anyway.

Maya walks right in through the back door, almost like she owns the place. But almost doesn't count. The main thing is, she's there as one of King DeCampo's allies. Which I guess also goes for me, all things considered. He's staying here, too. Even though our goal is to get him back on the vampiric throne and owning everything undead, he's not the boss of the Pickerings. Raven is.

When I walk into the kitchen, I see the king sitting at the round four-seat table, his head bowed over his amulet. It's called a Lazakhar, and every vampire who's become a full member of our society has one. They're how we identify each other, verify that any given vamp is who they say they are. During the body-snatching incident, Stephanie's went missing. Finding her Lazakhar was how I figured out her body double was actually a fake. So those are useful even though I don't know the full extent of their properties and powers. At least not yet.

Right now, I'm wondering why the king has his out. Most of the time our Lazakhars remain hidden when we wear them. The way he stares at it, how his lips move, forming words in a language I don't recognize, is disturbingly familiar. It's how I look while trying to remind myself of something. For the first time since I heard he existed, I'm concerned the king has problems he can't handle. Since he's basically a good guy, and the rightful leader of all vampires in the state of Rhode Island, I'm not happy about that prospect.

"Hey, Your Majesty. How's it going?" I stand beside one of the empty chairs at the table. Technically, I could sit down, but it's probably better to wait for permission.

"As inexorably as time itself." Hey, I said the king was a good guy. Not that he wasn't overly formal and too wordy most of the time. Age and experience do that to vamps, apparently.

"Anything I can do?" No, I'm not brown-nosing. I genuinely want to help King DeCampo. Like I said, he's the rightful king, and I want him to get his throne back one of these nights. Besides, the guy currently on it is a conniving twatwaffle.

"I believe you're already doing as much as can reasonably be expected of such a young vampire, Valentino."

"Thanks, King DeCampo." I stare at my shoes because it's the only place my eyes will go at the moment. "Just seems like I should be making more of an effort, you know?"

"I absolutely understand." The king clutches his amulet, curling all ten of his fingers around it so he looks like he's holding his heart in his hands. For all I know, maybe he is. Or something at least as important, anyway.

"Your Majesty, do you think it'd be okay for us to spend the day here?" Maya's voice is gentle, the placement of her hand on the table within the king's field of vision is as decisive as anything else I've seen her do. And I watched her hold back a doppelganger of the king in full-on blood-fueled armor for an entire battle so that's saying something.

"This house's hospitality is not mine to give." The king sounds weary, like he needs an extra-long sleep. Vampires can do something like hibernation, not just sleep during the day when we can't go outside. According to Stephanie that sort of thing can last for decades. My sire took a long nap in the middle of the twentieth century. I'm hoping King DeCampo doesn't have an extended siesta in mind.

"Oh. It's you." The girl standing in the doorway flips a wavy lock of long dark hair, nearly blue with how black it is, over her shoulder. After that, she points her nose firmly in the air.

"Good evening, Sarah." Maya nods in a gesture of more respect than I'd want to give this little twit, but like I said, she's got grace. And Sarah is Raven's great-to-the-umpteenth-power grandniece.

"There's nothing good about being woken up after three in the morning." Sarah sniffs. "I'm sick to death of you vamps coming and going at all hours of the night while I'm trying to get my beauty rest."

"And I'm sick to death of hearing complaints from whelps like you." Raven looks down their nose from the other doorway to the kitchen, meeting Sarah's upturned gaze solidly halfway. Now I see where Sarah got her chutzpah.

"Whatever." Sarah rolls her eyes. Her attempts to out-snark a vampire with centuries of experience at slinging insults floats like a lead balloon on Lake Michigan. Because of course, it does. At least I'm not the only person getting outclassed on the regular by their own family. Along with this observation comes the knowledge that I'm not angry or bitter at Sarah. With this much in common, we might end up as friends someday for all I know. Yeah, I'm an optimist. So sue me.

"If you need sleep, I suggest you get it before your alarm rings and you head out to those lessons you're so fond of in the morning." Raven's leaning in the doorway, clearly enjoying the little family spat. When it comes to arguments, Raven tops the leader boards practically every time. The only person they don't bother initiating one with is King DeCampo. Considering what I've seen of his combat skills, I don't blame Raven one bit.

Sarah turns and shuffles off toward the stairway. I watch her go until the door closes on her retreating, bathrobe-clad back. Once she's gone, Raven steps into the room to take the seat across from King DeCampo. They reach out with both hands, laying them palm up on the table, cupped. The king only gazes at them longingly. I think. It's hard to suss out any emotional tells with him. He's so stoic most of the time, I'm surprised to witness even the faint trace of melancholy he's revealing this evening.

"Valentino, unless things change spectacularly for the worse, you always have my hospitality." Raven doesn't look up as they speak, but the gravity behind their words carries the full effect of an honest-to-goodness vampiric vow. The one vampire I owe the most favors to has given me a permanent pass into their living space. So that's a thing I never expected.

"I'm not sure how to thank you, Raven."

"Continue to serve our King. That's thanks enough."

"Okay." I nod. "So, I don't want my stay to be one-sided. Is there anything I can help either of you with while I'm here?"

"As a matter of fact, some troubling news has come to my attention." The king looks up as though hanging his gaze on me. It's leaden. "A youthful perspective would be much appreciated."

"I've got that. What's this about, then?"

"Please have a seat." The king gestures at the one to his right. As I lower myself into it, Maya takes the one on DeCampo's left. "Let me show you what I've seen."

The king places his amulet in the center of the table and murmurs a few words in that mysterious language again. My eyes widen as it lights up, projecting a red-tinged display of images. Along with them comes a tinny soundtrack, reminding me of the AM radio my dad listened to back in the day. I see a series of numbers; dates and times on a television screen. And there, reporting on a story about photo evidence of a superhuman being, is my client Zack Milano. Here's his on-air appearance during his missing time, then.

The images shift, showing a dusky-skinned man with silver-tipped dreadlocks and claws on his hands, like Wolverine from the X-Men comics. The film quality is grainy, not even close to high-definition. All the same, I know exactly who it is. King DeCampo. My mouth drops open as I listen to Milano's voice-over.

"Are there superheroes in our midst? How about villains? Which is this vigilante? Did this superpowered man intervene on the side of the law or the criminals during an Organized Crime investigation?"

King DeCampo waves his hand and mutters again. The images zoom in on the ticker at the bottom of the screen. I blink, then rub my eyes to make sure they're working properly and I'm actually seeing this. Then, for final verification, I read them out loud.

"Suspect in the murder of Detective Larry Tierney found dead on Oakland Beach." A square to the right of the ticker shows a picture of a wiseguy whose murder I witnessed during a dead-blood vision, and DeCampo definitely isn't the killer. My skeezy landlord at the studio is. I shake my head. "Shitballs."

"Someone's using us to deflect attention from their own crimes." DeCampo shuts down his little hologram show and lets the Lazakhar rest against his shirt again. "Or perhaps, toward some end still unknown to us. And I've no idea who or how."

"But—" I drag my notebook out of my satchel, the one I brought out of my apartment at the beginning of all this. "Your Majesty, can I speak frankly about something we discussed privately back in June?"

The king's mouth hints at a grin and his eyes downright twinkle, belying his formal speech. "You may. Proceed."

"Good, because I think their ends aren't as mysterious as you believe." I flip through pages until I find the notes I want. "You got framed in the vamp community for Edwin Tierney's death, which happened before he could turn me. And now, the mortal news is making you out to be some kind of comic book vigilante—"

I clear my throat, glancing at Maya because something's bugging me. "And all because of claws supposedly only you have. But we all know your power isn't unique. Someone else knows, too. A vampire who's connected to the crime family mentioned in that news report. I'm sorry, Maya. I don't want to make assumptions, but I'm ninety-nine percent sure you have another piece of this puzzle."

"It's cool, Tino." She reaches across the table and puts her hand over mine to take me on a trip down her own memory lane. Before that talent of hers blocks out all sight and sound in the present, I see the king and Raven add their own hands to the pile.

And there's Maya standing outside the triple-decker in the Stadium neighborhood of Cranston that used to belong to Tierney before it burned down when he died. Because it's all from her perspective, I know that down in the basement, Edwin is already a pile of ash. Whitby is with her, holding her by the wrist, forcing her to clasp hands with good old Detective Larry, who was a mortal in the know.

In their combined grasp is something we never get to see. But since Maya's touching it, I know the thing is living and warm, humming with magical energy. Maybe it's a person's hand, but the spot they'd be standing is obscured by thick, gray smoke. The object's identity is less important than how it makes Maya feel. And I feel every emotion coursing through her heart at that past moment. We all do.

Blinding rage. With a thick coating of guilt.

The feeling is so familiar I almost mistake it for my own. It's how I felt when I couldn't stop the older mortal Pickerings from suicidally leaping in front of a pack of Deep Ones. And this vision comes with more context. We all learn that someone, possibly Whitby, forced Maya to do more than what we're seeing. Whatever whammy he had put on the vampires in Providence to make them forget DeCampo is their rightful monarch, he managed to pull it on Larry too. With Maya's unwilling help, Larry reported the mocked-up version of the murder back to Stephanie.

When we all return to the present, Maya's shaking. I don't blame her. I'd put my arm around her if the king wasn't sitting between us. But DeCampo surprises me by doing it himself. She leans toward him, too. Hides her face against his chest like Ma sometimes does with Dad when there's a tear-jerker on television.

I blink. You would, too. An honest-to-goodness vampire king outclasses yours truly every day of the week and twice on Sundays. Raven's shaking their head. I can see them from the corner of my eye. I'd rather look at them right now, so I do. And Raven's face tells me everything. The raised eyebrow and the smile fighting for dominance on the attaché's features holds no irony or trace of pity for my plight.

Instead, they clearly find my knee-jerk assumption amusing. Which raises my thoughts to a much more optimistic level.

Maya and DeCampo aren't a thing. They're related, although I'm not sure how at this point. It's clearer now that this isn't like Dad embracing Ma; it's like one of them comforting me after a nightmare. Which leads me back to the facts as I've just seen them. Whitby forced her to provide a false version of events, contributing to the truth being overwritten by whatever that other power in the object was. And he did it to harm one of her family members, depose him, maybe even get him killed.

Fuck Whitby.

I grab my notebook, flip to the first blank page, and scribble all that rage and the details surrounding it down on paper in my Church Latin. I press so hard the nib of the pen threatens to break through the top sheet. But I don't care about that. All that matters is getting this down so I never forget it. Because if I can only remember, I can gather the rest of my supernatural gang together and do something about it.

Raven's been watching me the whole time, their face back to inscrutable for now. But I know they'll back me because we saw the same thing. And when DeCampo looks up, I know Hell can't match the fury he's carrying around now. The woman scorned has that too, but she's not alone in this anymore. With folk rallying around her now, Maya's all but guaranteed victory.

I stand up, practically toppling the chair as I push away from the table. The time to act is now, dammit. Whitby's shit has gone down too long as far as I'm concerned. But the others don't even lift a finger, let alone stand up. I blink.

"What gives?"

"Excuse me?" Raven just loves answering my questions with more of the same. I'm almost used to it.

"Aren't we going to march into Providence and kick Whitby where it counts?"

"No." Maya leans back in her seat, unentangled from the king. "We still don't have everyone and everything we need."

"But he's a monster, and we all know it now."

"We're just as outnumbered as we were the night we came out of that tunnel. And it's almost sunrise."

"Oh."

"We'll also need harder evidence than a collection of incomplete memories." King DeCampo sounds wearier than a hollow Bristlecone Pine. For all I know, he's got a five-thousand-year lifespan like one of those, too.

"I'm going to go out and get that for you." And I will. Nobody should go through what Whitby did to Maya. And I'm also investigating Milano, who I happen to know was missing when that news report aired. For all I know, the two incidents are connected in more ways than even I suspect. And it all comes back to what or whoever added the memory-altering mojo to the mix.

"Good. But wait until tomorrow night."

"Will do." I'm not going to wait. Not really. Old vampires forget about the internet. But there are tasks, preparations, and knowledge to gain, and I have methods.

I reach down for my notebook and see something I entered not long ago. It's about the Deep Ones and how they're related to both Raven and Whitby, who are brothers from back in their mortal days.

Both of them have a claim on the Pickerings' traditions and arrangements, but while Raven made it their goal to become head of the magical family, Whitby went straight to the monsters. Even though he was the one who inherited magical ability. Raven was mundane until they got turned.

My notes are only confirming the conclusion my gut wants me to follow. Whitby's not resting on his laurels or his stolen throne. He's still working against us, putting DeCampo's image out there to limit his activity. He used footage from the Deep One's copy of the king, but that means he was prepared to lose their help eventually. Whitby must have other magical creatures on speed-dial to do his dirty work, make it harder to trace things back to him. And for now, we don't know what's in his arsenal, only who he's trying to screw over with it.

"Listen, Your Majesty." I gulp out of reflex at my audacity, addressing him with what sounds like an order. I'm subordinate to him in every imaginable way and vampires can Rage when insulted, so this is riskier than it sounds. "You need to stay in. No going out for anything. I know we're short on blood, but the others will just have to bring it back for you."

"I'll see what we can do tomorrow." Stephanie's voice from the open doorway isn't entirely unexpected.

"It's about time you got here." Raven taps the watch on their left wrist. "Let's go and do our busywork."

My sire and the king's attaché stalk through the kitchen and into the parlor, which has been tweaked to let no light in. They remind me for all the world of a pair of cats. I don't bother asking what work the two of them are doing, either. Because I've got more than enough to keep me busy.

I bring my notebook and the pen with me as Maya leads the king and me down into the basement. A short hallway with four doors off it is at the bottom. I'm shown to one of these. Behind it is a small, Spartan space with stark gray walls, a threadbare recliner, and an old school desk with the chair attached. The belly of the desk holds markers, Post-its, string, and tape. This place is a conspiracy mapper's dream. A gooseneck lamp is clamped to the side, bowing its head over the smaller than average workspace.

I'm used to tight quarters, though, so this doesn't bother me. Not having my laptop does. But the electrical outlet has room for my phone charger so I can use that if I need to access the web. I plug it in to let it charge up, then begin looking over all my notes on the supernatural, starting with the entries from the night Stephanie turned me.

At least Leora's paperwork is already done. It's going to be a busy day.

## CHAPTER EIGHT

The room I'm staying in is windowless and has no clock. The notes I make take so much of my attention that I lose all awareness of time's passage. I know it sounds impossible, but it's not. When you remember that I'm undead, it makes sense. There's a reason the lore says vampires get distracted by details.

My feet don't fall asleep, I don't need bathroom breaks, the urge to yawn doesn't derail trains of thought. Fatigue is not an issue. I'd say I don't get hungry, but that's not exactly true. Nothing I do in that room, from reading Latin to writing and tacking up sticky notes to connecting them with string on the wall, requires using blood.

There's an infrequently mentioned part of the vampire mythos that comes to mind. The whole thing about getting absorbed in a task to the point of obsession is absolutely true. Most frequently, this supposed trait of ours involves the need to count things. Maybe categorizing the facts is close enough. Staring at the diagram I've made on the wall, I'm practically in a state of hypnosis. Nah, that's too clinical a term. It's more like a reverie.

That's why the knock at the door startles me so much.

"Honestly, Tino." Stephanie's voice drowns out the minuscule squeak from the door's hinge that follows my little scream. "There's no need to shriek like a bat."

"Sorry." I shrug, closing the notebook at my side. When I turn I see Stephanie's holding another one. Of course. She always hands me some reading material though it's usually just once in any given fiasco. Didn't she already give me homework? Oh, yeah. *The Waste Land*. But I reach out for the tome she's carrying, anyway.

"No, this book is not for you." Stephanie tucks the volume under her arm, then crosses the room and sits on the edge of the cot.

"Thank God."

"Well, if that's how you feel about it, I won't make any more reading recommendations in the future." She sniffs, then gives me a sideways glance.

"That's not what I'm saying. It's just that every time you recommend something for me to read, I get in trouble."

"Correlation does not equal causation." Stephanie sniffs again. If she were human, I'd think she was allergic to something in here. But she's not. Actions she takes that are normal for the mortal set are usually deliberately left hints when it comes to her. Subtext. Unspoken messages, probably ways around communicating something she's bound by some vow not to say with words.

Unfortunately for Steph, I'm too dense to get most of them. So I do the only reasonable thing. Make a pop culture reference.

"Have you been watching *Star Trek*?"

"Not recently, no." She raises an eyebrow, then smirks in an all-too-familiar fashion. "Mr. Spock is one of my favorite characters, however."

"Geez Stephanie, just when I think I've got you pegged–"

"Pegging notwithstanding," She clears her throat. Yeah, that subtext is brighter than a neon sign. "I hear your application is done. Congratulations, by the way."

"Are you making fun of me?" I extend my finger as though I'm the parental figure and about to scold her.

"I came here for a reason." Did her smirk just get perkier? I'll take things I never wanted to know about my vampire mom friend for five hundred, Alex.

"Okay, then." I let the dig or whatever it is slide. I can figure out the whole implication that I smell funny go for now, too. "Lay it on me."

"We've got a little mission to do this evening."

"Oh?" I blink. Not because I'm surprised she's got work for me but that the day passed so quickly.

"Yes. It's important. King's business."

"I'm sort of kind of working on that high-paying case right now." I jerk my chin at one cluster of notes. "And some of my own King's business. Can it wait?"

"No. This is far more time-sensitive than your project." Stephanie sighs. "I can assure you, however, that it will take very little out of your evening from a temporal standpoint."

Leave it to Stephanie to overstate what could be said with extreme brevity. Shitballs. I'm doing it now, too. But this is my story so you'll have to deal with it.

"Well, then," I stand up. "Let's go and get the thing over with. Whatever it is."

Stephanie only nods, then leads the way out of the room, down the hall, and up the basement stairs. I sometimes wonder why she needs to phrase practically everything with five hundred SAT words. But of course when she learned them, there was no such thing as standardized testing. Sometimes I feel like us newer vampires got the short end of the stick. Modern conveniences are convenient mostly for living people, not the undead. Especially when it comes to education.

"See you later, Tino!" It's Frankie, sitting at the kitchen table with his sister Sarah and his brother Levi. They're having what looks like mutton stew for dinner, and it smells heavenly. One of the things I miss most about being really alive is food. Sometimes I wish I had Maya's telepathic talent, simply because I'd be able to experience food again just by touching somebody who's eating. But even without that ability, I give Frankie's shoulder a friendly pat on the way out of the kitchen and through the back door. I don't want things to get awkward between us, no matter what happens. He's a good guy, just trying to do the right thing by his family. We've got a lot in common that way.

Once we're outside, Stephanie lets me walk down the steps. She closes the door behind us, locks it, then stands and waits. I wonder what for until I remember that Stephanie doesn't have a car, doesn't even drive. This is probably why she needs me with her this evening. As a chauffeur. Although she's always managed to get herself to vampire gatherings without me in the past, I don't have any idea how. I'm sure it's not Lyft or Uber, though.

I thought I had it figured out at some point, but I can't for the life of me remember anything I discovered about my sire off the top of my head. It's all in the notebook, and I left that downstairs. Because of course, I did. Considering where we're going, that's probably for the best, though. The last thing I want is Whitby or his people getting my notes.

I take a look at the damaged trunk and bumper. There's a set of bungee cords wrapped around the detached end, anchoring it to the caved-in trunk. I definitely didn't put them there, so it must have been one of the daywalking Pickerings. Probably Frankie, but maybe Levi. I can't imagine Sarah doing MacGyver-style auto repair, although I've seen stranger things.

After I get to the driver's side door and open it, I'm about to sit down when I notice Stephanie standing next to the passenger side, examining her fingernails. I shake my head, walk around the car to open the door for her, and wave vaguely at the empty seat inside. She's way too formal about stuff like this, but maybe she's got her reasons. Judging them is beyond me.

"I invite you into my vehicle, Stephanie." I waggle my eyebrows like I'm in a Groucho Marx short because that's how I feel. Like a total clown. I know we don't need invitations, there's no compulsion for that like there is for us to drink blood. But older vampires tend to stick to some of those legendary rules folks assume are absolute truths in an existence like mine.

"I'd tell you not to be a fool, Tino, but that's a useless admonition." Stephanie buckles her seatbelt. After I close the door on her, she peers at me through the window, grinning. Maybe this is her attempt at a sort of dry humor. She's definitely not as clueless as the angel in the trench coat on that show with the monster-hunting brothers. If only my car was as cool as theirs.

Once I'm in the driver seat and belted in, I pull out of the driveway and on to Ocean Avenue. I can practically drive with my eyes closed to the building in Providence I like to think of as the vampire club. I've only been undead since mid-spring, but there are some things that just stick with you immediately. Knowing where I have to go in order to follow the basic vampire laws is a good thing, and I'm thankful it's not just another victim of my crappy recall. Too bad I can't use whatever that is to make everything else stick in my memory.

I find us parking on Weybosset Street, which isn't surprising given that Thursday is still a weeknight. Downtown Providence is kind of a ghost town after dark unless it's Friday or Saturday night. I hope it's not a literal ghost town because the idea of poltergeists scares me. Imagining invisible people watching every single embarrassing thing that happens to us is truly creepy. But that's another story. Stephanie gets out of the car all by herself, closes the door, too. I practically want to give her one of those stickers that says, I adulted today. As we crossed the street, I chuckle at the stray thought.

"You'll need to tone it back, Valentino."

"You really think King Whitby is going to be that pissed off if I bust out laughing?"

"He'll never let you know it until he decides one of your actions is an offense punishable by death."

"Well, you know the guy better than I do." I shrug. "Is he really much worse than I thought DeCampo was?"

"Indubitably."

"Awesome." I nod. "Thanks for telling me."

"Just follow my lead, Tino. We are here to request a small monthly blood supply from the court's reserves. If we give Whitby any reason to deny a request that reasonable, there'll be no salvaging this endeavor."

I shut my trap and make a motion like I'm locking it up with the key. I wish it was real, sort of. The last thing I want is a padlock hanging from my lower lip, but it's the thought that counts. I need to keep my mouth closed so my foot doesn't end up in it. If Stephanie thinks we can't get enough blood to feed five vamps on our own, she's probably right. We need this court's help, and it's clear Steph thinks we're unlikely to get it just by asking our sworn enemy politely.

Stephanie makes with the secret knock, the taps of her knuckles echoing against the weathered wood of the door. It opens on a familiar face, Peligro Cabeza. I don't smile at the goofy precognitive vampire even though I used to like the guy. Probably still do, but if he's hanging around with Whitby, he might be an enemy no matter how amusing his antics seem. Then again, he might be in the same predicament as Maya used to be. I decide to be civil unless Peligro gives me a reason to act otherwise.

"Guests!" His mouth drops into a little round o of feigned surprise. Yeah, I know it's fake because his eyes don't match his mouth. Reading people is like watching oncoming traffic. The turn signal might be on, but if the wheels don't move to one side or the other, the car's going straight. So I think Peligro isn't turning. That information would be a Hell of a lot more valuable if only I knew which side he was on in all of this.

"May we enter to visit his Majesty?" Stephanie's tone does nothing to indicate her disdain for Whitby or her disbelief in his claim to the title of King. Which is as it should be. Steph's not just old, she's experienced in high vampire society and knows all the proper manners to go with it.

"Yes! *Si! Ja! Da!*" Peligro stands aside and waves us through. "Mazel Tov!"

Everything's different now. Whether Whitby made changes for aesthetic reasons or in the hopes that redecorating would reinforce whatever whammy plagues the memories of the vampires in Providence, I don't care. I hate this crappy frigging place now. Which is a shame because I used to like it here. If it's one thing I can't stand, it's old buildings that get renovated out of their character. And boy howdy, this historic register worthy place now looks like something out of Martha Stewart's living, circa nineteen ninety-two.

Everything's white. Last time I walked down this hallway, the walls were highly polished, warm cherry-stained wood. And this pretend-y king-time asshole had someone cover everything in here with something like five hundred gallons of whitewash. I find myself wishing I could vomit up a bowl of Fruity Pebbles, a good old technicolor yawn like I used to have back in my food days, just to brighten the place up a little bit. But that's a lost cause. The best way to return this place to its former glory is to depose Whitby and put DeCampo back in the seat he rightfully owns.

When Peligro leads us to the main gathering room, I find that the new decor choices are everywhere. But what am I going to do? Cry about it? Of course not. Tonight, my job is to position myself meekly behind Stephanie, follow her instructions, and let her do her thing. Whatever that is.

She approaches the dais and its brand-new throne. It looks like somebody brought Dr. Frank-N-Furter's chair from that creepy old mansion in The Rocky Horror Picture Show into a WhiteOut factory and dunked it in a vat of correction fluid seventeen times.

I'm pressing my lips together because it's hard not to smile at the images my manic brain is creating. I figure looking stern for this entire little charade is for the best. I can manage that much with my old acting experience, at least. Even though I don't know if my chosen fake demeanor is entirely correct, and at this point, I don't care. I'm basically an accessory of Stephanie's right now, anyway. Like a nice, humanoid handbag or something. She'd better not call me Louis Vuitton, or I'll get even scowlier.

"Your Majesty, King Whitby of Providence, I greet you." Stephanie curtsies deeply enough that even in her typical Hepburn-inspired boat neck top, she's probably flashing at least a little bit of cleavage. This makes sense because the going rumor is that Whitby's got a thing for her. Eww.

"We greet you in return, with similar sentiment." I should have known Whitby would use the "Royal We" like the asshole he is. It would've been nice to be pleasantly surprised, but nothing about this guy has ever been above the level of borderline tolerable.

The woman to the right of Whitby leans and whispers something in his ear. Because we're vampires, Stephanie and I hear every word she says. This is typical and expected in vampire courts. Even DeCampo and Raven whispered to each other, knowing perfectly well everyone in the room could hear what they were saying. This is why they often speak in a sort of code, or at times in languages I don't recognize. But Whitby and his attaché, Mrs. Kent, do no such thing now.

"Sire, show them no hospitality they wouldn't give *us*."

"I'll show them exactly what I feel like, no more or less, Kent."

I close my eyes to hide the fact that the verbal venom between the two of them shocks me. Blinking is my usual response to that emotion, but I can't give my feelings away in so obvious a fashion. Well, at least not without Stephanie's express permission, which she hasn't had a chance to either grant or rescind. Crap. Now I sound like her. But that doesn't matter. It's more important right now to pretend my face is made of Botox.

"What brings you here this evening, Miss McQueen?"

"A simple and routine request, Your Majesty. If I may have a moment of your time?"

"If your request is, as you say, routine and simple, then a moment in private is not necessary." Mrs. Kent taps her foot, and I see it now. The green monster, envy. She's jealous of Steph. Well, what else is new? So am I. She knows practically everything, and never makes a mistake. But I think there's an extra dynamic between them that comes from competing for Whitby's, uh, attention.

"We meet as we please, Attaché." Whitby remains seated, yet somehow still manages to look down his nose at Mrs. Kent. I hate the guy but have to admit he's a grandmaster of condescension. Not that it's anything I'd aspire to.

"Merely a suggestion, your Majesty." Mrs. Kent takes a step backward, the force of Whitby's disdain harsh enough to make her stagger. Or at least that's how I view her movement.

"Miss McQueen, approach the throne."

Stephanie navigates the two steps up the dais. I make as though to follow, but Peligro's hand on my arm stops me. I still myself, despite all the alarm bells going off in my head and heart. The pit of my stomach drops with uncustomary fear for Stephanie. It wasn't long ago that I came to appreciate how important a figure she is in my unlife. The last thing I want to do is lose her in any sense at this point.

But it doesn't look like I'm losing Stephanie. As she approaches Whitby, his eyes widen and his nostrils flare, as though he's trying to take in as much of her presence as possible. It reminds me of the sting operation Maury and I went on at a strip club two years ago. The corrupt banker in the VIP room looked at the topless dancer entertaining him with a similar expression. For the record, we arrested that banker. The dancer had done nothing wrong after all. The biggest difference between those two situations is the balance of power. In that case, the banker had it all until we walked through that beaded curtain. But tonight, Stephanie is ascendant.

I'm not sure whether she's using a vampish power or not. The older a vampire gets, the more abilities they can develop. It's something about the length of time they've existed and the activities they've engaged in throughout the decades. Nobody's been able to explain it to me exactly, but I know that the reason the oldest is given the throne is that they literally have more power than other vamps. Also, they're less free to act directly because they've made a ton of vows over the years.

It's no secret to me that Stephanie McQueen is older than Whitby. The rest of the vampires here, however, are under the effects of that unknown memory-altering magic. They've got no idea the guy they're following isn't the oldest vampire in Rhode Island, and I realize that Stephanie is using this dynamic to her advantage. None of them move to stop her, or even seem to suspect she's using vampire wooj on their monarch. Why would they? As far as they know, Steph's not much older than I am.

The hand on my arm squeezes. Maybe Peligro knows something's up, too. He is psychic, after all; according to Maya, he's precognitive.

Either he's seeing something of note happening in the future, or he has seen this before and is getting a major case of déjà vu. I don't dare look at him to try figuring out which. Stephanie said not to make any waves, so I'm staying her course. But I do back down and stand next to Peligro like a good little vampire.

"I'm here to request a monthly allotment of blood from Providence's reserves for me and mine."

"And you aren't finding your own in Warwick where there's a hospital? Why?"

"You and I both know who the real power is here." Stephanie lifts her chin in a gesture I can't interpret. That's probably by design. Exposing the throat is either a sign of challenge or one of submission, depending on context and setting. I realize exactly how out of depth I am in the situation, and I'm glad I didn't try coming here on my own at any point in the recent past. Which I might've done if I hadn't been so busy with everything else, a point I'm sure is not lost on Stephanie.

"And what will you offer my court in return?"

"The services of my childe, Valentino Crispo." And just like that, Stephanie throws me under the Whitby-shaped bus.

The gravity in the pit of my stomach switches over to fire and Rage. I'm about to speak, and possibly even rush the dais and my sire. It's nothing personal, I swear. Rages are just one of the more inconvenient parts of being a vampire. Usually, they're brought on by fire or hunger, but in rare cases, a dire enough insult will do it. As you see now by my reaction.

Unexpectedly, Peligro Cabeza has got my back. Or he's holding me back. Or both, maybe. This could be what he saw coming earlier, and why he never broke contact with my arm. His intervention gives me the few moments I need to calm the hell down, probably saving my life in the process. Attacking a king publicly is grounds for immediate termination. I'm talking public execution here. I'd thank Peligro, but don't want everyone to know what just happened. Subtlety is par for the course in vampire courts.

"And what value do your childe's services carry, Miss McQueen?" As if Whitby doesn't know already.

"He has visions related to dead blood, which I believe you'll find useful. In specific, this evening."

I close my eyes again and take a deep breath I don't need. I hate my special vampiric power, mostly because it comes with an extremely embarrassing and painful side effect—vomiting. Now do you see why I'm no big fan of this whole vampire gig? Maybe in a hundred years I'll feel differently, but I don't have that kind of perspective right now. And there's no guarantee I ever will.

"Yes, I do believe that will be extremely useful. Your request is granted."

Mrs. Kent escorts Stephanie to the left of the dais, toward the area I remember from DeCampo's reign reserved for selecting bagged blood from the supply kept for court vamps by the king. I'm about to follow, but Peligro steps in front of me, shaking his head with his arms crossed over his chest. I'm about to disregard his nonverbal warning, but another far more dire one makes its point behind me. Literally.

I flare my nostrils taking in a breath. The scent of aged oak emanates from between my shoulder blades, where what I can only assume is a stake presses. If only that were a nice rib-eye instead of wood, but what can you do? Nothing, not with my luck anyway. With Whitby in front of me, Kent with Stephanie, and Peligro at my side, there's only one other person who could be on the other end of that wooden death stick. I go with my first instinct and do the only thing I possibly can in the situation. Snark off, of course.

" Hargrove!" I put my hands up palms out. "Good to not see you coming." I chuckle, hoping I don't sound like as much of a lunatic as I feel at this moment. But that probably doesn't matter. I've already made my first impressions, and they are the opposite of good. "You've reminded me how much I miss Shadow. Have you seen him?"

"Move it, whelp." Hargrove's steely voice sounds from slightly to my right, telling me he's a southpaw. A detail I probably noticed before but just don't remember, because of course I don't. One of these nights, I'll have to ask Steph if there's any way to fix my memory. "Shadow's none of your business," he hisses in my ear.

Hargrove was one of King DeCampo's enforcers, and it appears Whitby has recruited him to serve in a similar capacity. This makes sense because Hargrove stands about six foot three and is built like a linebacker. Vampires get extra strength, speed, hearing, and sight by burning blood, but it never hurts to start from a position of natural-born power. Maya could probably take Hargrove in a fight, but I sure can't. My only hope in a direct confrontation would be to outrun him. I'm pretty speedy even for a vamp. But of course, this isn't the time or place for that.

Stephanie sold my services to Whitby, and Hargrove is only making sure I keep her side of the bargain. I close my eyes and think of DeCampo, and how he appeared so deflated in the Pickering kitchen last night. And Maya. I'm doing this to get him back in charge here, or at least help us all hold out until we can manage that. A vamp's got to do what a vamp's got to do, so I open my eyes again and step forward, letting Peligro and Hargrove lead me back behind the throne.

# CHAPTER NINE

I've been in this hidden meeting room before. Last time I was here through one of Maya's psychic link things. She showed me Whitby discovering a pile of ashes where everyone expected King DeCampo to be. That was the night he got body-snatched by Fake Stephanie and her Deep One allies during the whole debacle that got Whitby on the throne in the first place. If only they'd kidnap Whitby, they'd spare us all a heap of trouble. But the new treaty protects everyone including usurping assholes, so them's the breaks.

I consider texting Leora and asking if we can summon Baba Yaga's hut directly into this room, but this building is a vampire-only zone. Baba's a witch with godlike powers, and Leora is the last surviving member of a family of mortal magicians. The last thing I want to do is start a war between the magical sect and vamps just because I hate the idea of making visions for Whitby's amusement out of dead blood and an upset tummy. Besides, I promised Steph I'd help her, and this is what she wants me to do. So blah, blah it is.

The sound of leather-soled wingtips on marble taps behind me. Hargrove herds me into a wingback chair using the stake he didn't need to threaten me with. But he does anyway because he's a sadistic son of a bitch and that's just how he rolls, apparently. I would've gone and sat down without that kind of incentive. Yeah, I respect Stephanie's judgment that much. I guess I'm a mama's boy. So sue me.

Whitby approaches with a bag of blood in his hand. He passes it to me, and I take a moment to glance at the name on the label, which says it's courtesy of Rhode Island Blood Center. It's Michael Angelone, a name I don't immediately recognize.

"Can I get a cup?"

"Just sink your fangs into the plastic and drink, whelp," Hargrove snarls.

"Now now, no need to be so brutal with the childe." Whitby shakes one finger at Hargrove like a mother admonishing a misbehaving kid. I'd be relieved, but dammit, I used to be Cranston PD. I know a good cop-bad cop act when I see it. I also know how to navigate that sort of dynamic.

"I'd really like a cup if it's possible. Even just paper is fine, nothing fancy." I ease my lips into a gentle grin that's entirely fake but at least convincing, if all my effort at theatre rehearsals still means anything.

"I'm terribly sorry, Valentino, but we haven't got any drinking vessels on hand at the moment. You understand."

"Oh, yeah, totally." And I do. Whitby wants to humiliate me, but look like he's being a nice guy while he does it. What a piece of shit.

To a vampire, food tastes like cardboard. Stuff that isn't food and isn't blood tastes even worse. That includes the plastic encasing the dead blood I'm being socially strong-armed into drinking right now. It's like biting down on decaying bones, stuff that's been stuck under a swamp or bog for maybe a thousand years. Sounds gross, right? That's because it's what plastic actually is. The fleshy bits of dead dinosaurs, long gone. Eww.

But at least the blood tastes relatively normal. There's a slightly more metallic element to it than most, a flavor I've begun to recognize as the hallmark of blood from a person who has since passed away. For most vamps, blood like this is a little less nourishing, like junk food. For me, it's got a less-than-nifty side-effect, which is why Whitby's feeding it to me in the first place. I swallow it, finishing the entire bag. The best way to weather my allergic reaction to dead blood is drink as much as I can of it. Take that sub-lingually, homeopathic doctors!

It might seem counterintuitive to drink more of what makes me sick in the first place, but it isn't the blood that causes my massive vomiting, it's occupying the memories of the poor sap who died. I never tripped on acid, but it reminds me of the bad sort of vision-thing folks I know who have tried it describe. Drinking the entire bag of blood will actually help me recover from the process of puking my literal guts out. Yeah, it's that bad.

I topple out of the chair as I feel the effects of my vision begin. That's for the best as far as the upholstery is concerned. When vampires vomit, it's messy, dusty, and tends to stain fabrics. This room is still decorated in DeCampo's style, and the last thing I want to do is sully the true king's last remaining decorative elements. Regurgitated ashes are messy.

On the floor, I curl into a ball, hugging my knees to my chest. I throw my head back, relying on gravity to carry any debris away from my mouth. It's not a technicolor yawn, more like red and gray. Like I said, it's disgusting. Thankfully, the memories of Michael Angelone carry me away from the gory scene of my vision-having vampire self.

I'm in a dining room, the formal kind. The table has a clear glass top, supported by baroque marble carvings of dolphins in a wannabe Renaissance style. Mirrors line one wall, while the other is stucco, pale pink. The decor here is Nouveau Mediterranean circa 1999. I turned my head, catching a glimpse of my reflection in the mirror. It's a bit of a relief to actually see one, all things considered. However, it's not the face of Valentino Crispo glancing apprehensively at me.

Michael Angelone was about my height with my coloring, but he sported a goatee and shoulder-length wavy hair, sun-streaked like a surfer's. He had a tan, too, and a wiry musculature that a certain sort of woman favors. One of said women sits at the head of the glass-top table. I recognize her immediately. It's Francesca Caprice.

"You'll do everything you can to get information on Miss Kupala and her family situation. I have it on good authority she'll need a home in the extremely near future, and I intend to be the one to provide it."

"Yes, ma'am." Michael shifts his weight from one foot to the other instead of leaving to do her bidding like the good little Mafia soldier he's supposed to behave like.

"What is the problem, Michael?"

"I can't figure out why, ma'am."

"Yours is not to reason why, Michael. Don't make me finish that sentence."

"But I thought—"

"You're not as special as you've been led to believe." One of Mrs. Caprice's blue eyes drops a wink that strikes a healthy measure of fear into Michael's heart. I feel it pause, then continue on at a hastier clip than before.

"All right, I'll do it. Where do I start?"

"With the good old Coventry School Department. Be sure to get there before either the magicians or the vamps. If you don't, our little understanding will come to an end, among other things. Capisce?"

"Perfectly, ma'am." Michael turns toward the door and takes two steps in that direction.

"Oh, and Michael?" Her voice stops him, one foot in the air.

"Yes, ma'am?"

"No more fraternizing with those Irish hunters. I don't care if one of them is engaged to your cousin." She clears her throat. "Look at me, Michael."

He does.

"You will obey me." Francesca smiles again. "And you'll succeed. If you don't, I'll let Carmine have his way with you."

Michael swallows past a huge lump in his throat. Part of my experience of his memories are his surface thoughts. In his mind's eye, I see a young man I don't recognize and a woman I'd know anywhere. Kayleigh Killarney, my ex from high school turned hunter of supernatural creatures like me. He's afraid for them. Not for their lives, but for their souls. And his own. Whoever this Carmine person is, he's a harder case than Michael the boy-toy.

The next thing I know of Michael's experience is being outside at the edge of Tiogue Lake in Coventry. It's sometime in the early morning, just as the sun's tinting the horizon cotton-candy pink, and he's screaming because there's so much smoke surrounding him. It's not a fire; there isn't any heat. Instead it's downright clammy, like an autumn fog.

But it doesn't behave like fog. At its center is a humanoid figure, making me start with recognition that's almost immediately swept away. That thick slate smoke barrels down his throat, up his nose, and wherever else it can get in. And it consumes the guy, scrapes him clean like soap scum from tile. Michael dies, of course. All he can manage with his last suffocating breath is a name. Carmine, of course. My own mind returns. Shitballs.

I come out of the vision, realizing I said that last word out loud and hoping Whitby isn't offended. Oh, who am I kidding? I don't give a rat's ass whether my language pisses off the pretend king of Providence, but now I have to think fast about what to tell him I saw. I definitely don't want to give him the whole truth, and realize Stephanie made no restriction on whether I can lie as part of her agreement. I can protect Leora and Kayleigh and my debt to both of them. It's all fair game from here.

"What did you see?" The fake king of Providence leans over, his face all I can see under the thin brim of his ever-present Trilby hat.

"Mi-Mi-Michael" I pitch another hurl, inwardly lamenting the fact that I sound like GLaDOS from those *Portal* games. If Jonathan Coulton also writes me a theme song, I won't mind feeling like that so much.

My spectacular display of the physical effects of my psychic powers puffs out instead of slopping to the floor. Yeah, it's all ash this time, which means part of the lining of my stomach came up. Whitby scuttles out of the way just in time to avoid getting any on his suit. Dammit.

"Stand back!" Peligro bursts into the room, both hands up and out like he's commanding a trio of velociraptors as he steps between Whitby and me. "Give him blood! Air!"

"Your welcome in my Court is wearing thin, Mister Cabeza." Whitby's eyes narrow as he glares at Peligro. I'm actually concerned for the kooky guy's safety, but I can't do anything but remain indisposed.

"Your Majesty," Hargrove rolls his eyes. "The idiot's got a point. Crispo can't talk if he can't stop—" He jerks his chin, wrinkling his nose. "Whatever he's doing."

"I suppose you have a point." Whitby turns his back on me, then issues orders with a wave of his hand. I'm getting sick of that gesticular bullshit from him. "Get him some fresh blood."

Hargrove jerks his chin at Peligro, who scuttles around to the side of the room I can't see. I hear a clink of glass and catch a whiff of something that just might be the nectar of the gods. Which is to say, blood. It's the only thing that smells this good to a vampire like me. I grok why Peligro Cabeza's on Whitby's shit list, too. His antics reveal that there were drinking glasses here all the time. I try to snort out a laugh, which gets flooded by another gout of ash from my gut. Whitby is so full of shit, he could be a day-old colostomy bag.

It's Peligro who sits me up, dabs at my mouth with a bandanna, and holds the cup of sustenance to my lips. As bad as my memory is, I won't forget this kindness, even if he didn't dare deliver it before he got his orders. Self-preservation is only common sense, after all.

I realize the precognitive vampire has stayed at Whitby's Court even after helping Maya, surrounding himself with enemies deliberately. Yeah, I know he's not specifically my ally, although I have no idea whose side he's on. Maybe the guy's got his own, but I can't ask or assume right now. Acknowledgment of common decency will have to do for the time being.

"Thanks," I mutter. My voice sounds harsh and raw. I won't be winning any karaoke contests this evening, which is fine since it's been almost a year since the last time I tried one of those anyway.

"Don't mention it. Really. And take my wife. Really." Peligro's eyes roll, but not in an ironic way. They remind me of the one time I saw a pig slaughtered before a block party in my neighborhood. The trussed-up animal's eyes rolled like that as the blade approached its throat. I realize Peligro's in mortal danger every minute he's here, and

I make myself a silent promise to help get him out of it as soon as I possibly can.

"Now." Whitby lays down a handkerchief before perching on the edge of the wingback chair, as though he thinks it's filthy. I sat in it, and can assure you it's not. "What did you see, Crispo?"

"Michael Angelone. He got some orders from the Caprice Boss the night he died."

"What kind of orders?"

"I don't know," I lie, and then omit. "He got them before the vision started. But he called that meeting to complain about them, so he didn't like his job at the end. Oh, and the Boss told him to stay away from the Irish hunters and the magicians."

"So." Whitby stands, leaving the handkerchief behind on the edge of the chair seat. Hargrave picks it up and tosses it in a wastebasket next to the chair. "The crime family is in the know."

"Sure seems that way. Which sucks." I attempt a grin, which turns into a grimace. My stomach still hasn't settled. I take another sip from the glass of blood.

"Your opinions are not my concern. What else did you see?"

"The room they were in was super-swanky. Marble everywhere, glass-top dining table; had to cost a fortune to decorate that place."

"Interesting." I don't like Whitby's smirk. "And what was the overall mood?"

"Michael was scared, which is saying a lot, considering he's a Mafioso, and the way they were talking, he's at least a step above Enforcer." I decide to take a page out of Raven's book and phrase part of my answer as a question. "Do you know if he's a hitman?"

"I know who Angelone was. However, the fact that his employer's orders disturbed him is enlightening." Whitby stands, then turns his back on me. One of these nights, I'll be in a position to stab him in it, but I recognize now is not the time. My elders were right when they told me as much back in the Pickering kitchen. "Thank you for this evening's services, Crispo."

"This evening's?" I can't help it, my voice squeaks. I hope Whitby thinks it's just part of recovery from all the throwing up and not a display of the apprehension I'm failing to hide.

"Yes. Expect to hear from me again next time I've got this sort of lead."

"Oh." I can't think of anything else I can reasonably say in his company without losing limbs or my unlife. Or both.

"Send him back to his sire after he's decent again." Whitby stalks out the door, closing it behind him firmly.

Hargrove retrieves a broom, dustpan, and trash bin from some dark corner while Peligro helps me to my feet. With those implements, plus a set of brushes and cloths, they clean up my mess and my person. Hargrove empties all the detritus into the trash can, picks that up, and heads out the door with it. Peligro escorts me back to Stephanie, a mask of benign vacancy on his face. But I know better. I need to get all of us out of our current situations as soon as I can.

# CHAPTER TEN

Stephanie hands me two heavily insulated satchels and shoulders three of her own as we leave the building. Yeah, she's smaller than me, but stronger because she's older. She insists on stowing the bags in the trunk, which makes sense to me since I'm sure they're full of blood. That's a challenge because the latch is jammed shut thanks to my fender bender with a cryptid. We're saved by the folding side of my back seat, however. That opens just fine, and we manage to get the blood inside.

Transporting blood around town like this is tricky. Even though it's all official and labeled from the blood bank, any police officer worth his salt who sees this much donated blood inside a garden-variety passenger vehicle will want to investigate. If we're going to do this every month, I ought to hit Vistaprint for some courier magnets, or even apply for a bona fide Department of Motor Vehicles permit to drive human materials around. I can always say the courier thing is my side hustle.

The headache involved in getting sustenance legally must be a doozie. I wonder how the older vamps do it. It's something I'll need to look into if I ever have time between crazy occurrences and cases.

Hopefully, I'll survive that long. I drive, careful to go the speed limit, as we make our way back to Warwick and the Pickering house.

"What did you see, Valentino?" Stephanie examines her nails, which are flawlessly polished, of course. "In the blood vision, I mean."

"You too, Steph? Jeez, can't I get a break?"

"Surely, you're aware I made this agreement so that we have access to a fraction of the information Whitby has in abundance."

"Yeah, I get it. But I do have other tasks this evening if it's all the same to you. And now I'm a cold mess." I pat my dusty jacket with one hand, kicking up a puff of ash. "I need to change clothes, wash up. Rhode Island Child and Family Services won't give me the time of day, let alone custody of a kid, if I walk in there to drop off paperwork looking like this, no matter how good my application is."

"Oh, so you completed it?" She arches an eyebrow. For once, I don't blame her. She knows how bad that paperwork was.

"Yeah, with some help from Frankie Pickering." I clear my throat, unable to mention the full extent of that situation.

"Good. I'm glad to see the two of you working together. You seem to get on famously." Steph's grin makes me think she already knows about the domestic partner thing. "But back to my original question. What did you see?"

I make like I'm on the witness stand and tell Stephanie the whole truth and nothing but the truth. All of it, including the inappropriately unbuttoned blouse on Mrs. Caprice to Michael Angelone's too familiar address at the start of my vision. Stephanie is a social prodigy. She'll pick up on any subtext I might not have initially grasped. But that doesn't mean she'll tell me all about it until she needs to. She raises her eyebrow a few times and chuckles once. But Steph goes quiet after my description of smoke and fire and the sound of hooves. Either she finds that more compelling or more disturbing than the mafia-speak. After Whitby's reaction to my abbreviated account, Stephanie's silence is nothing short of a relief. We arrive at the Pickering house.

"No need to come in, Tino." Stephanie steps out of the vehicle, then leans and pokes her head back in through the car's door. "I'll take the blood inside and sort through it. And I'll send Frankie out, too. Then you can head back and go about your other business. But return once that's through, would you?"

"Sure thing Stephanie."

I sit, waiting in the idling car as she removes all the satchels from the trunk through the backseat and heads into the house. A mortal woman her size might have struggled, but vampires are always stronger than we look. One thing the fangy life has taught me is to never judge anyone by their appearance. It's something I struggled with during my career as a cop, which might be why I came up short and didn't make Detective.

A few moments later, Frankie emerges from the front door. He's wearing a button-down shirt with a sport coat along with the darkest and neatest pair of jeans I've seen outside a Macy's Men's department. He usually dresses scruffily, but it turns out he cleans up decently. He'd still never make the cover of GQ but probably Rolling Stone. Frankie's holding the folder full of paperwork, too. Which is a good thing because I would've forgotten it. I'm about to ask him to go back for my notebook, but he has that too.

"Wow, Frankie. I ought to hire you as a secretary at the agency."

"I've kinda got my hands full with my siblings and all, but it's good to know you think I've got useful skills. You know, for the future." He grins, but in a less manically bright way than the previous evening. Whatever cloud he was on that night, he's coming down from it. Which I suppose is for the best. Maybe I'm not the only one getting an education in assumptions just lately. Or maybe I had it wrong and Frankie felt just as awkward as me, and also wondered how to broach the topic of keeping things platonic. His chill level changed after Maya brought me here last night, after all.

"Okay." I wave a hand at my ash-stained attire. "I've gotta change before I freak the mundanes, so if you don't mind, we'll stop at The Belfry on the way to Providence."

"Sounds good." Frankie frowns at my grubby face and attire, but he doesn't pry. With his history, he probably avoids asking too much on purpose. "You look a little pale. I'll put some blood on while you get cleaned up."

I nod and point my car in the direction of Rolfe Square, where my apartment is. It only takes about five minutes, because in Rhode Island, everything is near everything else. Forty-five minutes and an iced coffee will get you from one border to another. It's one of the things I love about this quirky little state.

On our way up the stairs, I hear creaking behind the second-floor door. My neighbor down there has always been a little too nosy for my tastes, but there's nothing I can do about that unless I somehow win the lottery and manage to rent the apartment out from under whoever lives there. Or maybe even buy the entire building. That's something to discuss with Stephanie in the future. Buying the building, I mean. I'd be able to move out of the attic, where fear of a broken window letting the sunshine in is always a concern.

Once we're in the apartment, I shower and put on clean clothes. Decent ones, of course. I sigh at the suit I wore out earlier, realizing it'll have to go to the dry cleaner. Hopefully, they won't ask how it got covered with ashes. Frankie's bustling around the kitchen, pouring blood from the bags in my refrigerator into the coffee maker I use to warm it up. He knows the drill. Frankie was a Belfry houseguest for a couple of nights.

I take extra time to apply greasepaint to my face, coloring over my features so I'll pass for an appearance-obsessed human in case I walk past a mirror. Maybe I'm a little too paranoid about that. Stephanie and the older vampires don't seem to worry or take any precautions like I do. But maybe it's simply because they're from an earlier time when mirrors were less common.

For a moment, I consider the Roaring Twenties and Art Deco. How vamps stayed secret through that is anyone's guess. Maybe it has something to do with cocaine and morphine being in common medicines and beverages instead of locked inside a pharmacy. I ought to seriously consider encouraging them to at least put on a little bit of Maybelline because vampires aren't born with it in any way, shape, or form.

I chuckle as I watch my face materialize in the mirror, remembering how in May I ran all over town with gray greasepaint covering my mug because I ran out of the tube that matches my skin tone. Events were so hectic I didn't have time to buy cold cream to take it off for four days and nights. Those were the days. Nights. Whatever, I got through it. What doesn't kill you makes you stronger, right?

Finally, I'm done. I can't sit in front of a mirror for more than a few minutes and expect people to think I look strictly human, but if I have to walk by one, I'll pass muster. My eyes are empty, but I'd look almost as weird wearing sunglasses to cover that.

I consider adding contact lenses to my ensemble, but that'd mean a trip to an eye doctor because I can't remember where I put them last time I took them off. Optometrist equipment uses mirrors, so that's out of the question. I dyed my hair, so it's also visible. Thank God that works, otherwise I'd have to wear a hat. I hate those.

When I'm done, I head out into the main room, where my notebook and a pencil sit on the breakfast table beside my favorite mug. That's full to the brim of blood from the coffee maker, still steaming. My opera cloak hangs off the back of my chair, which is good, although I can't exactly remember why. I need it for something later. Not the application drop-off, maybe a meeting with Esther. I ought to set up Google calendar, but I'd need to enter everything in euphemisms and double-speak so I don't out the supernatural to an unwitting tech worker.

Frankie sits in the seat across from me with a cup of chamomile tea, which I don't have in my apartment. I only have Earl Gray because Stephanie brews it for the bergamot scent. I blink but then shrug my puzzlement off. He must have brought it over with him. Or maybe I did pick some up and then forgot about it. My memory's worse lately, and I might never find out why.

"I figure you want to write everything down that happened over at Vampire Central." Frankie gestures at my phone, which is on the charger next to my comfy chair. "Do you need me to send any texts or make any calls? You know, to Scott or Esther?"

"Yeah, hold on." I open my notebook and jot down a few details about Whitby's new decorations, Stephanie's agreement, and my dead-blood vision in Latin. Then I add a few lines about wanting to help Peligro. I read it out loud, translating into English as I go. I add one last bit at the end. "Francesca Caprice is making a supernatural power grab. Tell Scott about that and my vision, the whole thing including the stuff about the Irish hunters. Make sure you lay it right out that the Caprices are talking about the Killarneys. He's not one for subtlety."

"What about Esther?"

"Just tell Esther that the crime Boss knows about the supernatural, and that they want Leora. Don't mention Kayleigh specifically to her, though. Esther hates her guts."

"Sure thing, Tino." Frankie leans back in the chair, texting like a maniac.

I finish drinking my blood and think about what sort of chance I'll have to get custody of Leora if my theory is correct. I saw the Caprices outside Rhode Island Social Services. Now I finally know why. They were there picking up the same application I've got sitting filled out on my table. I can only hope their reputation affects how they look on paper. I've got little to nothing to offer financially compared to them. Well, the Pickerings probably do consider how valuable their house is. But the name Caprice has a truck-ton of clout, even if it's unsavory.

This is Rhode Island. Everybody knows a guy, and they've all heard of the Caprice family. There's nothing official on the books against them specifically, but known associates of theirs have circulated around the criminal justice system like dollar bills around a greasy spoon's waitstaff.

Most of it's white-collar crime like fraud, but a handful of their henchman have gone on trial for crimes as heinous as aggravated assault and murder. Surely that's got to count against them, right? Maybe not. In Rhode Island, guilt can't run by association. If it did, more than two-thirds of the state's population would be suspect. It's a small world here, after all.

"Hey, Tino?" Frankie's phone beeps and he studies the screen.

"Yeah?" I'm betting either Scott wants to gossip about the vampire club details, or Esther wants me to fetch her something.

"Esther says she expects us to be on time meeting at her lab tonight after we're done dropping the papers off."

"Yippee." I wave my pointer finger in the air, a gesture meant to convey irony. Frankie chuckles, and I can't tell whether he actually thinks I'm funny or gets my real meaning.

"Are you ready?"

"Is anyone ever really ready to be a father?"

"Been there, done that. Sort of. Okay, not really because I'll never have responsibility for any of those." Frankie stares into his mug of tea.

"Oh, shit. Sorry about that, Frankie." Technically, Frankie's already a dad. Or, if not, he will be in the extremely near future. Biologically.

Part of the Pickerings' agreement with the Deep Ones includes reproduction, ensuring the continuation of that amphibious race. And before Raven's new negotiations with them, Frankie had to meet the terms in the most traumatic way you could imagine. Yeah, subterranean amphibious creatures don't know how to set up a sperm bank. Maybe they'll have the motivation to get with the times now that they're limited to consenting family members.

"Don't be sorry." Frankie looks up, his eyes only slightly pink instead of red-rimmed at the painful memory. "If it wasn't for you and Raven, nothing would've changed. But now, no one else in my family has to go through what I did. I'm the last."

"I get it, Frankie." And now I'm the one trying not to cry. I can't afford to do it now, at any rate. It'll smudge my greasepaint. "You know, you're one of the bravest people I've ever met. And remember, I was a law enforcement officer."

"I don't know what to say, Tino." Frankie's looking me in the eye, exactly as he did the first night I met him. But this time, instead of heartrending despair, there's an equally touching emotion occupying the air between us. Maybe it's hope, but that's almost too soft a word. My mind refuses to name whatever it truly is, but my heart knows it's faith. We believe in each other. Implicitly.

On that other night, we sat at this same table across from each other, our positions reversed. He held my arm while I told him he could have a future, promised I would help. And he showed me the scars, attempted escapes from the life and expected fate that was his by accident of birth.

And I guess he's right. Maybe I did good, the right thing by him and his family for generations to come. Probably I tend to go too big on heroism. Maybe it's because I can't truly go home. My parents aren’t in the know, and if I can help it, they never will be.

"Well, my ears are always open. I'll be around when you've finally got something to say. Even if it takes forever." I jerk one thumb at my chest. "Vampire. Immortal. Forever. Get it?"

"Oh, man, Tino." He shakes his head, giving me a lopsided grin. "We haven't even submitted this stack of paper, and already you're making the daddiest dad jokes to ever come out of a dad."

We say no more, only stand and hope we’re prepared to deliver the completed application.

# CHAPTER ELEVEN

"Well, Mr. Crispo, Mr. Pickering. Everything seems to be in order." Gina Paolucci smiles across the desk at us. "I do have one question, though."

"Oh?" I raise an eyebrow.

"Yes. This address in Rolfe Square, this isn't your primary residence, is it?"

"Oh, no." I shake my head. "It's just, I signed a multiyear lease. So, since I'm stuck with the apartment, I'm using that address for my private investigation business."

I'm not lying under pressure. That's all premeditated. I didn't put the address down for my studio space where my office actually is mostly because it's under the table but also happens to be in a Caprice-owned building. Anyway, I knew I'd need to explain the address I have a real lease for. So, when Frankie and I filled out the paperwork, we decided to designate The Belfry as a business address.

"We'll be housing Leora at my house on Ocean Avenue." Frankie smiles. "She's the same age as my brother and just a year younger than my sister, so she won't be lonely there. And I'll be able to enroll her at their school."

"Oh." Gina's eyebrows lift, forming pleasantly surprised arches above glittering brown eyes. "Private school? That sounds lovely."

"It is." Frankie grins. "I graduated from there myself, and it's a great school."

"I see your income is listed as a trust fund, Mr. Pickering. But it's in your siblings' names."

"Yes. It's money my grandparents put aside for them." Frankie says nothing about why there's no fund for him, and he doesn't give Gina time to ask. "But Tino's managed to get his PI firm off the ground at a profit instead of a loss. The school has a sibling discount, so he'll have no trouble affording school for Leora if everything goes through."

"I'd like to set an appointment for a home visit next week." Gina smiles like she thinks we're a couple of saints. I feel okay about that. Our intentions are definitely good, which is more than I can say for Mrs. Caprice's. Despite the thoroughly awful vision, those are unknown to me.

"My schedule is flexible." It isn't. I'm a vampire, for crying out loud. I can only meet her at night, of course, but with the listed profession and income information, there's really nothing else I can say.

"Since I'm on the evening staff, I'd like to make my appointment with you at dinner time. When is that in your house?"

"Seven-thirty." Frankie gets out his phone and opens his calendar app. "We do chores and some reading first, and Sarah likes to practice her vocal exercises after that. Yeah, I know it's summer, but my parents stuck to a routine. I'm continuing that because it's what mom and dad would have wanted."

"Would Monday work for you?"

"Sounds great." I grin because I don't dare give her a full smile. Fangs suck most of the time.

"I'll see you then." Gina smiles, then stands and holds out her hand in Frankie's direction first. Frankie stands, and they shake on it.

"Thanks so much, Miss Paolucci." I get up, and then it's my turn to shake hands. Thank goodness it's warm, so my room-temperature hands don't shock her.

As we're leaving, we elbow each other, nodding and smiling but saying nothing as we navigate the crowded hallway. Emerging from the office across the hall are Francesca Caprice and her teenage son, Sebastian. The lady in the office they're emerging from looks just as smiley as Gina, so I guess their application for Leora's custody looks at least as good as ours. Or maybe smiling like that is office policy. The voice of the other caseworker calls out from inside the office.

"Your appointment's with Gina on Sunday night, nine o'clock sharp, Mrs. Caprice."

Glancing over my shoulder, I try to catch a glimpse of the lady's name on her desk placard. All I manage to see is she's got no alphabet soup after her name, which explains why Gina's doing the visit. Frankie has turned his head, too. Maybe he saw the full name, so we can see if she's got any Caprice connections. He's more likely to remember it since he doesn't have my memory issues. It's good to have a partner again, even if this is a totally different dynamic than the one Maury and I shared on the force.

And then I notice Frankie's got his hand in his pocket, the one with the alchemical Zippo. He eases it out, points it in Francesca Caprice's general direction, and flicks out a flame. I hold a breath I don't need, but despite a faint smell of singed seaweed and a spark of blue I suspect nobody else can see, nothing happens. Mrs. Caprice shoots Frankie a wink. Something that feels like a small boulder drops in the pit of my stomach.

I steer Frankie toward the stairs because the Caprices are waiting for the elevator. At least Sebastian seems oblivious to everything that just happened. He's finished screwing his earbuds in. Faint music emanates from them, but I recognize it. My vampire ears tell me he's listening to the *Sweeney Todd* soundtrack. Not the movie, the original Broadway cast recording. Sebastian Caprice is a theatre geek. Who knew?

I set that thought aside and hurry down the steps. Frankie follows after. Instead of getting into the car, I try to stick to the shadows near the exit. Waiting for the Caprices to leave doesn't take long. I watch them go, and they seem oblivious to my presence. Frankie's, too. Once they're gone, I count to sixty, waiting a full minute before we leave the shadow of the building.

"What's that about, Frankie?" I gesture at the pocket where he's stowed the lighter.

"Just figured any edge we can get is a good thing."

"I have a mundane but probably still practical idea. Avoiding the competition for now." I pressed the button to unlock my car doors, and we get in. "I just found out this evening that the Caprices are in the know. We've got no idea exactly why they want an orphaned Lamb in their house. I'll look into that later, but for now, we need to meet Esther at her lab. Let her know we're on our way."

"Sure thing." Frankie texts while I drive. He's either writing a novel to Esther or handling more than one conversation at the same time. I don't pry. It's not my business who he's texting, and if it's something important, I can trust Frankie Pickering to tell me, right?

---

Frankie and I hustle up the stairs, heading straight for 219, the studio space where Esther does all her magical tinkering. I'm not sure exactly what they are, but they involve alchemy, one of the three disciplines magicians like her can learn. Or are born with. Or both, I'm not sure exactly how that works. At any rate, I've never met a magician who can do more than one type of magic, but my experience with them is limited. Anything beyond that kind of basic info is going to have to come from an actual magician. I'm just a vampire and a new one at that.

Before I knock, the door shimmers green. I don't dare touch it now. That hue means Esther's warded the door, which could be dangerous. Who am I kidding? You know that saying about not angering wizards? You know that other one about not liking the green guy when he's angry? Esther just happens to be both magical and constantly pissed off. I think I've seen her smile once, and that was when I broke Kayleigh Killarney's back. So yeah, I don't knock. I just stand there and wait.

I'm rewarded for my patience by my werewolf buddy Scott opening the door and letting us in. He smiles as he steps aside, his entire attitude a distinct contrast with the surly magician bent over the workbench in the middle of the studio space. She's got what looks like a chemistry set covering the entire black enameled surface. I always wonder whether she went to a defunct high school's yard sale to get half her equipment.

Beakers, flasks, stands, and test tubes of different heights and width compete for my attention. Some are filled with a liquid that bubbles on its own, others appear to contain sludge, but the vast majority stand empty, or lean because they sit in crooked racks. The entire rig looks so haphazard, I'm amazed she hasn't burned down, blown up, or otherwise decimated the old mill building that houses all the studios, including our office directly upstairs.

"Hey, Esther." I speak softly, attempting to keep from startling her. The last thing I want is a chemical spill. Or a magical spill. Or both.

"Just a fucking minute." Esther waves her hand above her head as though shooing my greeting away like it's a fly or a pesky mosquito.

I keep my trap shut and turn away from the bench. I can't bear to watch. Being here while she works on this particular project feels like that one time I had to watch the bomb squad defuse a device down at Cranston Savings and Loan. I like suspense, but only in fiction. Unfortunately my life hasn't followed a peaceful course. Them's the breaks, I guess.

When I turn, I see Sparky and Leora sitting in the corner, giggling over a smartphone. I'm not sure where either of them got the device. Baba Yaga is the opposite of tech savvy, and I didn't lend them any burners. I side-eye Scott, guessing correctly that he's responsible for their little upgrade. Which makes sense. Scott's mostly a kid himself, considering his sixteenth birthday was last spring.

I saunter over and peer at the phone. There's a flash animation I can hear even though Sparky and Leora are splitting an earbud. Vampire hearing rocks. As I watch animated sharks of different sizes, colors, and in modes of whimsical dress bounce along through a turquoise rendered ocean, I can't help but smile.

Sparky is a shapeshifting salamander, born in a magical hearth. Leora frequently carries Baba Yaga's consciousness with her. But they're still kids, and this is still the modern era. Of course, they want to have fun, engage in activities their mundane peers take for granted. And I think they're right. So I smile and say nothing, let them have this rare normal moment.

"I need your fucking contributions stat." I turn, watching Esther brandish two syringes. One is labeled with my name, and the other with Scott's. Of course.

"Sure thing." I roll up my sleeve and hold out my arm as I cross the room. Scott says nothing but mirrors my action.

Esther's concentration makes sense now. She's working on the potion that's going to heal Kayleigh Killarney's fiancé and bring him out of the coma he's been in for the last six months. And pay her for quitting as the Caprices' freelance hitwoman. Magically, Esther's already told me this potion is serious business. I don't like to pry which is why I haven't asked for further details. But I should, probably. I know for sure that Kayleigh has no such reservations about getting in the middle of other people's personal details. She hasn't asked me for an update, at least not yet. But that trend won't continue.

Since we bought Kayleigh's promise of nonviolence with the creation of this alchemical coma-ending tonic or whatever, it's important that we deliver it as soon as possible. Medical bills suck, and the Mafia pays. Esther needs my blood and Scott's as ingredients, and who knows what else. Well, Esther Solomon knows. Other alchemists might, too. Or maybe not. Considering the rarity of miracle coma cures, I'm inclined to suspect she's got an uncommon recipe.

As Esther draws blood from my arm, I notice Frankie leaning against a bookshelf on one wall. He appears to be whispering something over there, but I don't bother listening to what he says. The only thing I know for sure is he's not on the phone. I can't hear an open line. But I let him keep his one-sided conversation private for now. I spot something on the shelf and understand what he's doing. It's none of my business what Frankie says to Esther's creepy doll. I want nothing to do with that thing ever again.

Yeah, that's right. The alchemist has one of those faux-Victorian porcelain dollies, the kind with ringlets and a rosebud mouth. In case you're wondering, it's no ordinary toy. I've tangled with that creepy thing before. Esther's got some way to make it come to life in a giant-sized version of itself, frilly dress and all. The last time I saw it off the shelf, that doll made like the good fairy in that Bunny Foo Foo rhyme and bonked me on the head.

You might wonder whether that was really necessary. If you've been following my stories at all, you'd know it was. I was trying to eat my friends. It wasn't pretty. Hunger rage never is. So thank heaven for little girls and their giant freaky dolls. I still won't touch the thing unless I absolutely have to.

Frankie's conversation with the doll almost seems two-sided, except I can't hear a thing coming out of the painted-on porcelain lips. I wonder, not for the first time, whether Esther's doll is sentient or just a construct loaded up with the magical version of a computer program. Is alchemical AI a thing? Whatever. That's not important now.

"Are we all set?" I raise an eyebrow.

"Not fucking yet." Esther drains the syringes into one of the test tubes, mingling my blood with Scott's. They don't seem to react, which is a little anticlimactic, but something I should have expected. Vamps and werewolves aren't supposed to put *the* bite on each other, but nothing much happened that one time my fangs actually got a mouthful of the wolfkid's wrist.

"What else do we need, then?" I rolled my sleeve back down.

"A motherfucking impossibility is what we need." Esther taps a line in a small leather-bound book. I can't read it, it's in Hebrew.

"Does said impossibility have a name?" Sometimes conversations with Esther are how I expect the ones with Scott should go based on his age. But he's not intractable, doesn't make me feel like I'm pulling teeth to get information out of him, even if he is obliged to stay mum on werewolf matters.

"No one's gonna find any God damned fucking Sasquatch hair in the middle of suburban sprawl central like Rhode fucking Island, Tino."

"Um, Esther." I shuffle one foot against the concrete floor. "I might have some."

"How in the fucking hell did you get something like that?"

"I might've hit Sasquatch with my car the other night." I look everywhere in the room except at its other occupants. "Totally by accident, I promise."

"Holy shit, Boss!" No, that expletive did not come from Esther's mouth. Sparky dashes to my side, pulling on my sleeve. "No way, Tino! You didn't! I'm supposed to talk to him."

"I'm sorry to say I did. But don't worry," I clenched my fists then unclench them. "Maya checked him out, and he's fine, just hurt his dignity is all."

"You don't do things halfway, huh, Tino?" Scott's shaking his head, but he's grinning.

"I'm sort of a glass-all-the-way-full kind of guy. Or overflowing. You all know that."

Almost everybody gets a chuckle out of that, except Esther, who's putting on her jacket. I glance at her benchtop and its volatile contents, then back at her.

"I'm going the fuck down to get the goddamn hair off your motherfucking bumper." Esther rolls her eyes than chuckles. I know there are no hard feelings here, just Esther's typical profanity peppered vocabulary. "Chill."

"Okay. You want the keys?" I scratch my head, wondering why I think there's something else inside my car that she'd want. But that idea flies the coop. I shrug. "For, um, some reason?"

"Yeah, Esther." Frankie glances over his shoulder at his niece. "Get his cloak thingy from the backseat. Just keep it away from me." He shudders, then turns back to his conversation with the doll.

"Fine. Remember not to touch any goddamn thing in my fucking lab, or I'll rip your heads off and shove them up your asses." She smiles like an angel. The avenging kind.

"I won't forget, Esther." Except I've been forgetting practically everything lately. Even more than usual. And I don't know why.

She heads out the door, stomping her feet but closing it gently behind her. I still haven't quite figured out whether Esther actually likes us or just tolerates our presence like a cranky old cat. I prefer to believe the former.

But what can I say? I guess I'm some sort of optimist. It makes little sense, considering everything I loved about being human I can't do anymore as a vampire. And of course, so many things I try go wrong. Sometimes I wonder whether the Murphy who wrote that cockamamie law isn't a disembodied supernatural being, watching us all and waiting for the best time to mess with us.

But then, I look at Sparky and Leora sharing a device that just fifty years ago would've been considered magical and unbelievable. Humans made it anyway. Regular people, no spells, blood abilities, or wolf shapes required. There's more good in the world than we think. Even though I can't go to church anymore, that's what they taught me there, and I'm sticking to it.

When Esther returns, she's got my cloak over her shoulder and her right hand up, thumb and middle finger pinched like she's about to snap them. Except I hope she doesn't because I spy a clump of off-white hairy fur between them.

I give her plenty of room to approach the bench, which is a good idea because Esther stomps right over and drops the hair into a beaker. It's got an unlit Bunsen burner under it. In fact, none of the flame-producing equipment in the room is actually lit. I take that as evidence that Esther wishes me no ill will. She drapes the cloak over an empty chair.

"We want to know when you'll start brewing that." Leora's voice sounds flatter than usual. That, coupled with the use of "we" instead of "I," tells me Baba's watching through the kid's eyes.

"Why does the witch care about curing a hunter's fiancé?"

"That's none of your business, alchemist." Leora isn't even participating in the conversation now; I can tell it's all Baba all the time. So can Sparky. He's staring at her intently, as though he sees something I don't or maybe can't in her face.

"Well, it's sort of my business." I almost slap my hand over my mouth. Challenging the most powerful witch in the world is the opposite of a good idea. Who am I kidding? That's an understatement. But on the list of bad ideas is also reneging on one of my vampiric vows. "This cure is one of my obligations, just like the foster paperwork is. I'm sure you understand that, Baba."

"Let's just say we've got a common interest in the Killarney family's business, Mr. Crispo." Leora's flat voice would give me chills if I were still alive. I manage to play it cool, thanks to my undead anatomy.

"Good enough for me." My mind races ahead, splitting its focus among tangents, threads to investigate connecting the Killarneys with Baba Yaga. Come to think of it, I'm pretty sure Leora was the kid under the veil at Larry Tierney's funeral. So I ought to investigate that, too.

Of course, I'll probably forget all about this in five minutes, or the next time something shiny dangles in front of my nose. And I left my notebook behind. Dammit. I sigh deeply enough to shame an emo kid.

"Hey, Tino, whatsamatta you?" Scott waves his hands, completing his mimicry of talking like a stereotypical Italian. Yeah, that's right. We talk with our hands. Get over it.

"This whole memory business sucks." I shake my head. "And it's getting worse. I can barely remember a thing."

"You need a to-do list." Scott shrugs. "That's what works for my mom, anyway. She has a pen and paper practically glued to her at all times."

"Yeah, but lists of chores or shopping aren't as sensitive as the stuff I need to jot down."

"Maybe you need a magicked notepad." Scott points at Esther's back, which is bent over her vials and bottles of ingredients.

"He can just go the fuck down to the magic store and buy one on his own dime."

"Hey, I wouldn't ask you for something like that when you're this busy." I scowl at Scott. "Adulting ain't easy, kid."

"How about putting it in your phone?" Sparky waggles the one he's holding in my direction.

"Again with the security issues." I shake my head. "Besides, I'm kind of old school when it comes to investigations. Just ask Maury. Oh, wait. Please don't, he's got no idea salamanders, witches, or even vampires exist."

"Just trying to help." Sparky shrugs.

"What?" Leora blinks, and I can tell it's only her this time.

"Nothing much, kiddo." I point at my head. "Just trying to come up with secure ways to make notes on the fly and coming up short."

"Oh." Leora stands up, pulling a small notebook out of her pocket. It's shabby, one of those fifty-page deals you can get for a dollar at CVS. There's a tooth-marked golf pencil stuck through the spiral at the top. "You can use this until you think of something better. Why not just write in another language?"

"Duh." I hold up my right hand, extending my thumb and forefinger, then apply it to my forehead. "Church Latin to the rescue."

Leora and I cross the room, meeting in the middle. She hands me the notebook, which I flip to the first available page. It's blank, but I can tell a few have been torn out, leaving only faint impressions of what she wrote on them. I let her have her privacy and scrawl my ideas on investigating the Killarneys, the Tierneys, and Baba Yaga.

It sounds strange, but the act of getting those thoughts out of my head and onto the paper soothes me. They'd been running around like panicked children, frantic in my head, and I've tucked them in for the night so I can take care of them tomorrow. It's not catharsis. With hanging investigations, that's impossible. But this is as close as it gets for now.

"Better?" Frankie pats my shoulder. He's got one hand in his pocket, but it's not the one with the magical Zippo inside, so I let it ride.

"Yeah, thanks, Leora. And you too, Frankie." I glanced up at Scott, who is studying his fingernails. "Good idea, Scott."

“I need you all to get the fuck out of my goddamn lab.” Esther's holding up the bundled gloves from the pocket of my opera cloak.

What's in them again? Oh, yeah, Deep One scales. She tosses the garment at me. "You fuckers don't have to go home, but you sure as hell can't stay the fuck here."

"You heard the lady." I waved toward the door.

"More like a sailor with the way she talks." Frankie drops a wink.

We head out the door and toward the stairwell, intending to reconvene in the PI office. But that's not what happens. Because of course it isn't.

# CHAPTER TWELVE

I'm in the stairwell on the way to the third floor when I hear the voices. No, not the kind some people get in their heads when experiencing schizophrenia. I'm talking about voices coming from down the hall, exactly in front of my office door. I raise a hand, making a fist to indicate I want everybody to shut their yaps.

Scott joins me at the stairwell door, leaning with one ear turned toward it. His hearing is almost as good as mine out of wolfy form and probably better in. Oh, God. I hope he doesn't decide to shift right here and now. The last thing I need is a wolfman-thing running wild through the halls.

But he does no such thing. Scott is sensible, at least. We just stand there, listening while Frankie and the kids huddle behind us. I hate this part of renting in a Mafia-controlled building even more than I hate my personal private space getting invaded like it is right now. But there's nothing I can do about that. They've got keys, and I've got no formal lease. Possession is nine-tenths of the law.

"I'm telling you boss, the guy paying for this place said he had a band. I don't get it." This voice belongs to Cigarettes, the wiseguy who collects the money I pay for the privilege of being here. I happen to know he murdered one of his associates in this very building, but I've got no evidence except my own supernaturally enhanced senses because of course, I don’t. They’re the Mafia, not a pack of rabid weasels.

"I don't get it either." This new voice is warmer, and definitely not raspy. I flare my nostrils and take a breath, verifying my suspicions. This second speaker doesn't smoke, and probably never has. But I do smell an undertone of something chemical through the decidedly hoity-toity cologne he's wearing. Pain medication, maybe, or a less legal substance. Something mood-altering rides his bloodstream like a surfer on Narragansett Bay.

"What’s the big deal, Dad?" A teenage boy's voice comes out in a bored northeastern drawl.

"Pay attention, Sebastian. This is your family business, whether you like it or not."

I try to imagine the hand gestures that go with Alfredo Caprice’s words. Hey, I'm Italian. I know better than anyone how much we talk with our hands and how important those gestures can be in context. But without seeing them or met the speaker, I can't glean that without opening the door. And I'm definitely not doing that right now.

"Whatever." The teenage mantra almost makes me laugh. As it is, Leora and Sparky stand behind me, hands muffling mouths trying desperately not to giggle. They lean against the walls, sides shaking, while Frankie mimes zipping his lips at them.

And I get an idea. The boss and his murderous employee will definitely go on the offensive if Scott and I walk through that door. But a couple of kids? Not as likely, especially when one of them is the girl they’re applying to foster. Baba Yaga would step in for Leora and Sparky if shit went sideways anyhow.

Mrs. Caprice knows about the witch and the vamps, but that doesn't mean her family does. But even if father and son are in the know, they're probably not packing anything to take down magical amphibians or witches. I figure Leora’s got the best chance to cut in on the dance going on outside my office. Call me crazy, I don't care. It just may be a lunatic the situation is calling for.

I reach out with both hands, tapping each kid on a shoulder. Once

I have their attention, I point at the door. Sparky grins, and Leora nods. They head over and push through. I watch them step into the hallway. I hold Scott and Frankie back, who both blink at me as though I've suddenly become the sun. Yeah, they think I've gone batty.

"Dude!" Leora's voice carries, ringing through the hall clear as bell. She's got serious projection skills.

"What..." Cigarettes voice squeaks out the word at a higher than usual pitch. She surprised him. Good. "What are you two kids doing here?"

"Just getting my homework." Leora sounds about as bored as the mob boss's kid. "Summer school sucks, but turning in work late is even worse." She lets out an honest-to-God laugh. "You understand."

"Um yeah, actually I do." The mob boss's kid sounds startled and alarmed, almost like Leora shocked him in some fundamental way, possibly for the first time. Oh, shit, he's a goner. Crush at first sight, most likely. These kids today and their hormones. Exactly like they were back in my day. If I had a lawn, I'd tell you to get off it.

"Hey, buddy," I practically hear Sparky's grin as he speaks. He might be funny-looking, but the salamander kid has charisma in spades. "You let us in, okay?"

"Sure." The boss clears his throat. "Open the door, Carmine. Now." Finally. Mr. Caprice has given me an actual name for Cigarettes. I jot that down in the notebook.

"Boss, I don't think that's a good—"

"I said, now." Alfredo Caprice doesn't raise his voice, but his tone conveys an air of authority inherent in just about every dad I've ever had the privilege of listening to. I still think Mrs. Caprice's mom-voice game is stronger, though.

Nobody else says a word, but my ears pick up a key rattling in the lock and tumblers falling into place. I don't hear the door open because last time it creaked, I had a go at it for a few rounds with a can of WD-40. Leora and Sparky hurry into the room, their footsteps' echoes decreasing as they exit the hall.

I hear the door close, the lock turn again, and then the chain I installed inside rattle home. Clever girl. And she doesn't even need help from Baba Yaga for that. I grin, proud of her. Like a dad. Shitballs, I'm going to be one to a kid more competent at that age than I ever was. God help me, especially if I ever need to impose a curfew on her.

Now it's my turn to put my hand over my mouth and stifle laughter. Scott does the same, and we're like echoes of Sparky and Leora's behavior earlier. I'm struck by how symmetrical this all is, like fate is at work here. But as far as I know there's no such thing. At least not in this universe. Anyway, Frankie breaks the mood by elbowing us both in the ribs. That's probably for the best because of what happens next.

The sound of footsteps headed toward the stairwell puts me into a panic. I glance at Frankie, who's just slapped a Post-it note on himself before dashing down the stairs. Alchemy speed boost for the win, I guess. Frankie and I can make it down a flight and halfway across the building before they get in here, but Scott won't. So I do the only thing that makes any sense at all. Yeah, that's right. I burn blood to get my speedy on, then pick him up.

Dashing down the stairs with a werewolf in my arms isn't something I ever imagined myself doing, but this is happening anyway. Frankie pushes through the second-floor door and we hotfoot it toward Esther's studio, then make a left. The hallways in this building are one massive rectangle. So, if we make it to the other long side, we can get into the opposite stairwell and head back up.

Our mad dash takes us there in what amounts to a span of four breaths for a living person. Or at least that's how many Scott takes in the interim. Maybe werewolves breathe slower, but I don't know or care about that right now. Frankie pulling the door open slows us down a moment but once inside the other stairwell we're heading up, Frankie and I both scale three steps with each stride.

Once we hit the third floor again, Scott gets heavy, and my frantic pace slows. I trot around the corner, stopping in front of the door to room 319. The index card we put in the holder beside the door still reads SVS, the abbreviation which now has a triple meaning, thanks to Maya. I set Scott down, then fish around in a pocket for my keys.

"Duh." I roll my eyes. "Leora, you can open the door now. They're gone."

The chain lock rattles, the door opens, and we step inside. I take a deep breath, about to praise the kids for their quick thinking under pressure. But I'm an idiot. Because the mob's not all gone. I make a fist to keep from smacking my forehead in frustration.

"Good evening, Mr. Crispo." It's the kid. What kid, you ask? Sebastian. The kid with power. What power? Power of the Mafia, apparently. At least he's not king of the goblins. If those even exist.

"No, it's not good, actually." I lean on the door frame, just far enough inside that Scott and Frankie can scuttle through. "I didn't invite you here. Leave."

"Can't do that, Sir." Sebastian Caprice shakes his head like it's heavy.

"I don't give a good goddamn how polite you're being, it doesn't make up for barging in here uninvited." I step away from the doorframe, about to go parental on this kid, Mafia Prince or no.

"I invited him." I don't need to turn around and look Leora in the face to know she's not speaking alone, but I can't fathom why Baba Yaga wants Sebastian hanging out with her servant and her salamander. Maybe she thinks it's none of my business. She'd be mistaken, and we've got the agreement to prove it. But now is not the time to haggle with a literal hag.

"Okay." I put my hands on my hips. "I'm the adult here, and I'm uninviting him now. My office, my rules."

"Um, Tino?" Scott taps me on the shoulder. "Technically it's *our* office, and I'd like to hear what he has to say." This is my turf, according to vampire laws. But I'm only part-owner. Scott's got a point.

"You've got exactly sixty seconds to deliver your message before I throw you out." I point at the clock on the wall. Yeah, I know I sound harsh, but dammit, vampires, and hospitality are thing. I didn't extend it, and Baba pushed serious supernatural boundaries by making that offer on my turf.

"Mr. Crispo, my mother would like to have a conversation with you. Parlay. She says you have a common interest."

"Go on." I point at the wall clock, reminding Sebastian that his time is limited.

"She said you'll know what I'm talking about." He crosses the room, away from Leora and toward my pals and me.

"I don't. Spell it out for me." I stand beside the combination hat, coat, and umbrella stand. My magically enhanced rapier is in there, still charged up since I used it battling Deep Ones. It'll be enough to scare one snot-nosed teen, Mafia Prince or not.

"She's put in a foster application almost exactly like yours." Sebastian's eyes cut to Frankie, whose hand is in his pocket. He gulps. I guess he's right to do so; we probably look pretty dangerous.

"I figured as much." I shrug, trying to break the tension, but it's like trying to cut bone with a butter knife. "Tell me something I don't know or get out."

"Don't shoot the messenger, Sir." Sebastian looks at Scott, his eyes honeying. Apparently, he thinks the werewolf's the good cop here. Maybe he's right. "Please. Look, Dad is the Boss in name only. In practice, it's my mother." He deflates, all his vitals decreasing. Exactly how hopeless does he feel about the lady who birthed him? And why do I suddenly care? "You don't know what it's like, working for her."

"Yeah, and I'm sure she sent you here because she knows I'm a softie when a kid's got a problem." And she's right. "But I've got a long list of business to take care of, and if you ever get on it, you'll be at the bottom. So get to the point."

"My mother wants you to drop your application." He pronounces the maternal word like it tastes bad. "Let us take care of Leora. We've got the resources, and look better on paper than a gay couple."

Scott inhales and takes a step back. I guess that domestic partnership thing wasn't in any of Frankie's texts. Oh, boy. I almost don't understand the implication that Sebastian knows what's on my application when he shouldn't.

"It's okay to be gay, and our personal details are private." I snort. "You want me to believe the state will view the home of a notorious crime family as a better environment for any kid?" Yeah, it's a low blow, but the kid's reaction tells me we agree.

"Listen, sir, I didn't make this world. I was just born into it." Shit. That sounds familiar. I realize why when Frankie takes his hand out of his pocket and lowers the intimidation factor. I see the semicolon tattooed on his wrist. Same shit, different family. "I've got no power to change anything."

"Get some. And then be better than that." I narrow my eyes. Frankie needed an open door, but this kid Sebastian might do better to realize that doors exist in the first place. "You might already know this, but my caseworker happens to be connected with law enforcement, just like I am. You tell me whose application looks better now."

"You make some good points, Sir."

"I'm glad you agree with me, so go back to that mother of yours, and tell her I said she can drop her application instead."

"She has something that'll hurt you. Your boy Frankie, too. Something that'll mess you both up if she points it in your direction." His eyes move from me to Scott, then to Sparky. When they land on Leora, two spots of red form high on his cheeks like he's got a fever. "Knowledge and connections might not be fangs, claws, or spells, but they still have power. My mother's not afraid to use it."

"She wouldn't dare tell the world about us. Every supernatural community would have her head. And if she isn't scared of that, she'd be here herself." Yup. When I see a bluff, I call it. Except that when I fail, I fail big.

"That's not what she means." Sebastian's eyes move down to my frowning lips. "Sir."

"I'm not afraid of anything she or anyone she knows can do. Get out."

"She told me you'd reply like that."

"Did she give you a plan Z in case I did?"

"Yeah. She said, and I quote, he'll remember nothing." Sebastian's as still as Meshanticut Lake on a calm day. The phrase reminds me of something I read recently. Oh, no. The Waste Land. "Trust me, you don't want to take what she's got to dish out."

I don't speak. I can't, because he's right. And I don't miss the genuine fear in his eyes or voice every time mentions or quotes his mom. Daily life with Francesca Caprice must be like navigating a minefield. She's got me over a barrel and all because of my cockamamie memory and its inconvenient holes. But I'm not the only person with that kind of problem. It can't be a coincidence that Zack Milano hired me to investigate the sinkhole in his recall. Maybe there's a way to fight back.

"Your sixty seconds are up." Scott saunters to the door and holds it open, waving his hand from Sebastian to the open portal. I don't like the tightness around his eyes or crispness in his limbs. Scott's usually relaxed and slouchy until things get dangerous. "Leave. Now. Don't make me ask twice."

"See you later, Sir." The kid actually snaps me a salute, like he's been to military school or something. For all I know, maybe he has. It takes Frankie stepping up behind him to actually get Sebastian moving, but he finally turns to step out of my office.

The tails on his flannel shirt tremble, which means this whole business rattles him more than he's let on. I can't afford any more sympathy, so I try closing my heart to Sebastian Caprice. I fail, of course. The kid's got a raw deal in his home life and doesn't deserve it. But I already gave him my best advice. There's nothing else I can do for now.

Scott closes the door behind him. It's so quiet I hear a pin drop. Literally. Because a pin drops. It falls out of the item in Leora's hand. A doll. It's not creepy and porcelain-like Esther's. Instead, it's made of straw, burlap, and twine, marked with dabs of ink. And still freaky.

"Voodoo? Really?" I shake my head. "Leora, you're not an alchemist, theophile, or an evocator. You're a Lamb. So why have you got that doll?"

"It's not voodoo. It's sympathetic, and anyone can use these as long as a real witch makes them." She stares down at the object in her hands, shaking her head. "But she didn't. I keep it to freak mean people out. It's harmless, I promise."

"That's not really the point, Leora."

"So what is?"

"The place for magic that might backfire, explode, or otherwise go awry is Esther's lab, not this office."

"Sorry. But I figured since that guy was in the know, dragging this out might help scare him away." Her eyes tilt up, her gaze piercing. "And he threatened you guys."

"So let's think about what we learned from this experience, okay?" I sigh, running one hand through my hair. "Did Sebastian threaten us, or was it really his mother?"

"No. It was his mom."

"Did your own threat actually work?"

"No."

"Could it have given Sebastian information he'll have to report back to our enemies?"

"Crap." Leora studies her shoes. I know the feeling all too well.

Suddenly weary, I sit in the closest chair and promptly regret it. Why did it have to be the pink and fuzzy one? Oh, yeah. Because I haven't had time to upgrade our office furniture from curbside chic to something reasonably professional. But that's lower on my priority list than just about everything at this point.

"Yeah, that's a good word for what we're in." I shake my head. "Anything else you can think of?"

"Magic doesn't scare him as much as his mother does."

"Bingo."

I'm afraid of Francesca Caprice, too. God help me.

# CHAPTER THIRTEEN

The office phone rings. It's not anything so archaic as a landline, just a dedicated cell, but I still jump out of my pink, furry seat when it makes a noise. All five of us stand there, staring at it. Sparky and Leora immediately press their fingers to their noses. I'm fast enough to follow suit in a fraction of a second. Frankie looks like he was already scratching the bridge of his. Which is why it's left to Scott to roll his eyes and answer the damn thing already.

"SVS, Scott speaking." He listens while I try not to. "Oh, Mr. Milano, Tino's out working on your case. Uh-huh. Okay, I'll get that message to him as soon as I can. Thanks. Okay, I will. Bye."

"Shitballs." I pull the pad of paper from my pocket and flip through it. "I've done almost nothing on Zack's case. I'm a shitty PI. Thanks for the cover, Scott, but you probably shouldn't have."

"Thank me by getting back to it." Scott shrugs. "Do you have any leads at all?"

"Yeah."

"Need help?" Frankie's holding a handful of Post-it notes. I realize he might have put one on Sebastian a minute ago. Between that and the thing he did with the alchemical lighter at Rhode Island Family

Services, I ought to sit him down for a chat. But there's no time for that.

"I don't think I need any with Zack's stuff, but if you could bring Leora back to the group home and Sparky to Baba's that'd take a huge load off my mind."

"No way, Boss." Sparky folds his arms over his chest. "Baba told me to stick with you tonight. No matter where you end up."

"Um." I blink, unsure what to say. So I look at Leora.

"Yeah, that's right." She nods.

"Did she tell you the same thing?" I blink.

"Nope." She holds one hand out toward Frankie. "Sparky has to ride along in either your car or your pocket. I'm cool with Uncle Frank taking me back to the group home."

"Did you just call me—" He stops in his tracks on his way to the door.

"Yeah, I did. Esther dared me to."

"Okay." He shakes his head. "Gonna have a chat with my niece in the near future."

I still hear Leora chuckling as they close the door and head down the hall. Behind my desk, I rummage in the drawers. My crime investigation supplies will fill half the space in my opera cloak's pockets. At the mini-fridge, I grab the last few bags of blood and stow them in the rest. The flip-top notebook goes in the back pocket of my pants.

By the time I'm done gathering supplies, Sparky's changed from kid-shaped to lizard. Amphibian. Whatever. He's little, four-legged, and has a long, curly tail. His skin's also red with spots. The salamander crawls into my outstretched hand. When I try lifting him up to get on my shoulder, he shakes his head.

"What do you want from me? All my pockets are full, kid."

Sparky points his nose at my chest. Oops. Guess I forgot the shirt on my back has a chest pocket. I put my hand there and the little guy gets inside. With the cloak and everything on top, nobody will notice I've got a ride-along. Though they'll think I'm a weirdo for sporting outerwear in summer. But what else is new?

"Ready?" Scott's got his hand on the doorknob.

I'm about to reply in the affirmative when the door jerks out of the werewolf's grasp. It opens on Esther, who smells like death and has got what looks like a thermal food pouch slung over her leather-jacketed shoulder. At least I'm not the only one wearing warm clothing in summer, then.

"You sons of bitches are coming with me."

"Huh, what, where?"

"To the fucking hospital. It's time to wake Killarney's man the fuck up, assholes."

"Now?"

"Hell yeah."

"Can't it wait?"

"No fucking way. Already told the hunter bitch to meet us there."

I can't argue with paying an overdue debt to a family with the knowledge and tech to kill me and all of my friends. In our sleep, even. So instead of going directly to take care of Zack's business, we head out with the lady.

---

The near-constant beeping makes it hard to focus on anything for more than a second and a half. And the smell of antiseptic has my other senses numb. But I shouldn't complain. I'm standing idle. Esther Solomon is the one doing all the hard work here, after all.

She sits at the comatose man's bedside, bent over him as though grieving. And, as far as any of the nurses bustling or the doctors pacing the hallway outside room 520 in Kent County Hospital can tell, she is. But we all know better.

Esther's activating her alchemical potion.

I'm standing in front of the window that covers half the wall, blocking the view with a little help from my next-door neighbor the werewolf and my ex-girlfriend the monster hunter. Yeah, my unlife is complicated. At least I'm not a medically trained zombie like that white-haired chick on the CW show. Well, maybe I am a little. I bet we could chat over drinks about disturbing visions of dead people.

Anyway, I dropped the ball on just about everything else I've tried to do this week. At least this coma cure is actually happening.

I say a silent prayer thanking God that the monster hunter isn't trying to put a stake in my heart or shoot my pal Scott with silver bullets. About four months ago, Kayleigh Killarney made a truce with us. We promised to cure Calvin, the poor sap in the bed. Scott and I only donated blood. Esther did all the hard alchemical mixology work like some kind of top-marks wizard school student.

I'm uneasy. Not because I'm worried about this cure going sideways or even the rope-and-sticks bridge of truce between Kayleigh and me going up in flames. It's all about Esther and the massive amount of work she does. From pulling all-nighters making tracking potions to siccing some kind of giant creepy doll on me while I rage, Esther's saved my immortal ass on more than a few occasions. I wouldn't still be unliving without her around.

I'd make a mental note to thank her profusely, maybe get her a series of nice little gifts. Except mental notes just aren't working out for me now. I forget to do practically everything I don't write down. For all I know, this is something I thought of before. Probably, you know more about that than I do.

A stench like the pig farm halfway down Scituate Avenue all but smacks me upside the head. I'm wrinkling my nose while Scott's trying not to gag. Kayleigh's rolling her eyes so it must smell like practically nothing to her. Good thing. Because the doctors won't suspect anything either. Unless supernatural doctors are a thing. I cross my fingers under my opera cloak and pray they aren't.

"There." Esther omits her usual colorful language from the brief statement. She stands and takes a step back, joining the line we make in front of the window. I almost let out a manic cackle, wondering whether we look like a witness ID lineup.

Nothing happens.

I'm not trying to be anti-climactic here, but that's the truth. We're standing there for at least ten minutes, doing nothing. Esther's watching Calvin like he's the series finale of her favorite suspense drama. She's taken out a little notepad and golf pencil from a pocket, making spidery-sounding scratches with it against the paper. Which makes sense. She brewed the potion, of course she wants to document its effects.

Like the song says, waiting is the hardest part. I realize I'm tapping my foot out of boredom and stop it right away. Scott actually yawns. Then sneezes. All the conflicting odors in here must get to his nose. It bugs me, too, but in a good way. None of the blood I currently smell makes me remotely hungry with that bleachy undertone floating around. Maybe I can use that. I take out my own notepad and jot something down.

"Not you too?" Scott shakes his head and huffs out a sigh. Then sneezes again and covers his nose. "Ow."

"What? My memory sucks, you know." I roll my eyes and manage to catch Kayleigh giving me a guilt-stained glance. Before I do any obvious double-takes, Scott replies.

"Too bad I can't help you fight it."

"I've got to do something about it. If I can remember this thing." I tap the paper with my pencil.

"Yeah, sorry." He catches Esther's eye. "How much longer?"

"No fucking clue. Shit shoulda worked by now." Esther's still taking a million notes. She must see more than I do, which is next to nothing. Tiny green sparkles show up against Calvin's skin, between all the freckles, and on occasion, in his coppery hair. I wonder whether there's any risk of our little alternative treatment revealing itself to mortal eyes and tests.

But I figure, if there were, Esther wouldn't have offered this cure. I mean, sure. Our lives were directly at risk when she did that. But every supernatural group has exactly one rule in common. Don't freak the norms. In other words, don't let them know anything besides non-magical crap happens.

And magical crap finally starts happening in here.

That infernal beeping gets faster. Which means the potion is finally doing something. But Calvin Kelley doesn't move, and Esther's still holding her breath. One glance up at the screen to the left of his head tells me exactly nothing. I'm a Private Investigator, not a Doctor.

Scott and I exchange glances and shrug. Esther rolls her eyes. Kayleigh clasps her hands in front of her breastbone, and I don't blame her. She's engaged to the guy we're trying to wake up, after all.

Alarms start going off on the other side of the glass behind us.

Next thing we know, nurses and doctors sprint into the room, pulling on cords, tubes, and limbs. We watch them work until a whip-cord-thin woman with her hair tied back in a shaggy steel gray pony-tail herds us out of the room, her clogs tapping and squeaking against linoleum like hooves on snow.

"Wait out here." She points one thin finger down at the linoleum, then peers keenly at me, wrinkling her long, crooked nose. "You. You've been in my ICU before. Under my care."

"Um, okay?" I squint at her name badge, which is silver and pinned to a lab coat. She's got MD plus a whole host of other two- and three-letter acronyms behind her surname. Which I don't remember. Along with ever being here before.

"Hi, Doctor Maris." Kayleigh steps forward, extending her hand. Doctor Maris looks at it like it's a fish.

"Killarney." She shakes her head. "You're bad luck for the men in your life. Keep them out of my ICU in the future."

After that, Dr. Maris spins on the heel of her Dansko clog and trots back into the room she just extracted us from, braying orders to her team like some kind of medical Drill Sargent.

"What does that mean?" I'm blinking at my ex because there's no way Esther or Scott knows anything about what Dr. Maris just said. Except that, as it turns out, they do.

"I can't believe you don't remember." Scott reaches out with one hand and pats my shoulder. Awkward city.

"It means little miss huntress got you fucked up enough to put you here, shit for brains." Esther crosses her arms over her chest and gives Kayleigh the stink-eye. "Bitch."

But when I look at her for any sign of anger, answer, or apology, Kayleigh's got her back to all of us. Her hands are pressed up against the glass separating us from her fiancé and she only has eyes for him. Oh, yeah, she's got it bad. Which is a good thing considering, she's supposed to marry that guy. I remember that look, too; this exact expression of hers, a combination of hope and guilt. Even if I'm not sure where said memory comes from.

"Shitballs."

"You remembering anything yet, Tino?" Scott's amber eyes practically drip with some soft emotion I can't identify.

I grit my teeth, telling myself it's genuine concern and not condescension. Like I said, my memory sucks more than a Dyson on high speed. Both of my friends know it, too. We've even been bitten in the ass by it a few times. But Scott's a good kid who I've known his whole life. He doesn't mean anything by that look except maybe empathy. Nothing to be angry at, right? I take a deep breath and let it out slowly.

"Nothing important."

"Everything's important, Tino." The voice comes from behind me. Which is not a good place to be around a vampire on edge. But I know this voice almost as well as my own mother's. I should. Been listening to it practically since I was born.

"Maury." I turn around slowly, controlling every movement so I can face my best friend. He doesn't have the slightest clue that I'm a vampire or that magic even exists. But at first, I don't see him. I blink, then look down. And there he is. In a wheelchair with a tube sticking out of his left arm. He smells more like death than Esther's concoction. Which makes an unfortunate kind of sense. He's fighting lung cancer.

"Yeah, it's me. In the irradiated flesh." His eyes sparkle with the smile his lips don't quite muster. "I'm here for chemo downstairs and the captain pings me with news that I need to check on a material witness."

"Um."

"It looks like he's still indisposed." Maury shrugs. His eyes are on the scene playing out through the open door. I have a gander myself.

Calvin Kelley is surrounded by medical professionals. A cart with supplies sits untouched, and that's because he's got his sleep-crusted eyes open. One nurse has a stethoscope on his back, while another's checking all the connections on his IV tubing. Doctor Maris shines a pen-shaped flashlight in one eye, then the other.

"Impossible." Dr. Maris' declaration hits everyone in the room's blast radius, pausing all that medical hustling and bustling.

"No." A cough chases Calvin's refutation. His lips form words he can barely utter. "Who does seven impossible things before breakfast?" His smile's framed by raggedly chapped lips as he hooks two thumbs at his chest and winks at Dr. Maris. "This—"

A nurse pats his back as Calvin doubles over coughing. Dr. Maris wags one spindly finger in her direction and she stops, withdrawing her hand slowly.

"Get bloods." The doctor stands, her figure somehow stolid, imperious, and larger than her slender frame suggests against the already forbidding ICU room. "I want a full panel. And where's that Killarney girl?"

"I think that's our cue."

"Fucking-A." Esther jerks one thumb over her shoulder. "Skedaddle City, assholes."

"Okay." Scott nods.

"I'm staying." Kayleigh takes a step back toward the door.

"Same deal." Maury wheels after her, then pauses to glance over his shoulder. "Nothing personal, Tino. But call me."

"Okay, later!" I throw one hand over my head in a lazy gesture of farewell.

I take the stairs instead of the elevator, going down at a regular human pace even though vampires can move much faster than that. But I saw the security cameras across from the door and on each landing and wasn't born or even unborn yesterday.

I keep my head down because the greasepaint on my undead face will only hold up to the barest of scrutiny. Cameras and mirrors don't flatter vampires. Which is to say, they don't show us at all unless we're covered up and colored in somehow. Which I am, thank goodness.

"No good." Scott's keeping up with me, but Esther's having more trouble.

"What?"

“Maury sticking his nose in.”

“Damn-fucking-straight.” Esther’s voice echoes from maybe the fourth floor. We’re on the second. "Deflect his ass, Tino."

"Okay." I turn around and head back up with the intention of helping her down. And she’s got her right hand on her left arm, which dangles at an odd angle. After a click and a glimmer of green, it’s righted. She heads past me down the stairs and I’m left wondering why.

Descending the stairs more slowly this time, I’m wondering why Esther’s rogue limb reminds me of something. And it’s not coming to me until I catch up with Scott. That’s right. I noticed this in the truck, the night I met Sparky for the first time.

“You think she’s an amputee?”

“I fucking heard that, jizztrumpets. I don’t fucking talk about that shit.”

“Shitballs.” My palm has a meeting with my forehead because saying that twice in the same night at the same location is bad news.

I get to the ground level and catch sight of a sliver of night sky as the door swings closed behind Esther. Jogging to catch it is as futile as resisting the Borg. It’s too late. She’s hightailed it out of there without an explanation or even a goodbye. I lean against the wall, rolling my eyes. I notice there's no camera down here at the bottom of the stairwell, just a set of holes where one used to be mounted. And I can smell drywall. Odd.

“It’s okay, Tino. We’ll catch her tomorrow.” Scott’s solution to practically every problem is assuming the best and acting accordingly. He gestures at the door marked exit.

I shrug but don’t make any moves toward it. It’s almost like I’m wearing concrete overshoes. Which could happen if I keep crossing the Caprices. “I hope.”

“Well, at least we live in the right state for that, huh?” He grins as he leans against the doorjamb. “Hope, I mean.”

All I can do is shake my head. It’s the Rhode Island state motto, so there’s nothing much to say to that even if I had the energy to argue. I only want to go back to the Belfry and sleep everything off. But I can't because I've got to work on Zack Milano's case.

"Um, Tino?" Scott's wrinkling his nose

"I'll never get any of it, you know. Not the foster stuff, not my memory back, not Zack's case." I hang my head. "I mean, is it so wrong in the grand scheme of things to wanna help other people first?"

"Not wrong, just unusual for a vampire."

The voice at my back makes the hairs on the back of my neck stand up. I swallow and turn to face the person calling me on the carpet.

"Valentino Crispo, oddball. At your service."

"Not at mine. You're the one who needs some help." Doctor Maris tosses her head. At the same time, she swishes her tail.

Yeah. I said tail.

Doctor Maris is a centaur. Who knew?

The beams of shimmering light behind her reveals the horse half of her body. I also notice Scott's wolfy attributes where the illumination hits him. But the stairwell only has those annoying buzzing fluorescents. I blink, then my eyes widen as I finally understand what's going on here. This unrelenting flood of golden light from an unknown source shows the truth.

I don't have to wonder how a person with hooves snuck up behind me. She didn't.

Doctor Maris stands in front of a hole in thin air. I'm not talking about one of those cartoon deals that the Road Runner uses to outwit the Coyote, either. This is like a doorway made of moonlight.

"Um." My erudite expression of realization isn't impressing the doctor one bit. "What is it?"

"Bigger on the inside?" Scott chuckles. "Get it!" He slaps a knee. "Doctor. Sparkly gold stuff. Who does that remind you of?"

"It's not a TARDIS, and I'm a centaur, not a Time Lord. That's the Vault of Memories." Doctor Maris steps aside, her rear half seeming to vanish as it moves out of the beams emanating from the light source inside the portal.

"I have to ask. Why are you showing me this?"

"You, Mister Crispo, are the lucky winner of one trip in and out."

"Woah." I blink. "And I can take whatever I want?"

"You can bring one item back out with you." She crosses her arm and paws at the concrete under her front hooves. "That's not my rule, but it applies to anything sentient that enters here. And we can tell if you try to cheat the system."

"Why me?"

"Because this is the only way to clear a debt to your sire." She grins. I don't. People keep making a habit of paying debts to my elders through me, and they can't possibly like it. "My mistress doesn't like owing favors to night creatures."

"Mistress?" I blink. Are centaurs fans of *Fifty Shades of Gray*? Oh, my.

"This is a limited-time offer." Doctor Maris taps a hoof. "Mnemosyne doesn't let me open this door any old time, you know. You've got ten minutes before it closes again."

I close my eyes, trying to remember who Doctor Maris is talking about. I'm a new vampire, but I've had an education. The name Mnemosyne and the fact that it's linked to an honest to goodness centaur reminds me of something from school. Sophomore year literature. Bulfinch's Mythology.

"Dude." Scott elbows me. "Take the deal. Go in there."

"I'm getting a little tired of offers I can't refuse." I open my eyes, finally remembering. "But yeah, okay. I don't want to offend the mother of the Muses."

I'm not going to look this gift horse in the mouth. Taking a breath I don't need, I step through the portal, which now resembles a door on a bank vault. I mean, you only unlive once, right?

## CHAPTER FOURTEEN

The vault door closes behind me with a ringing echo. I watch the pegged wheel spin at its center, round and round like it's a roulette table. And I freeze, panic kicking in to stick me somewhere between the fight and the flight reflex. But I'm not hungry. There's no fire or chance of sunlight in a windowless vault. And nothing's making me angry. But I still feel like the tips of my toes stand on the border of a vampiric rage.

The going theory is that rages are an outdated survival instinct. Even vamps as sophisticated as Raven and as old as Stephanie consider this next-door to fact. Standing here in the Vault of Memory, I'm not so sure. There's nowhere to run. Making like a statue isn't doing jack or squat to up my chances of survival, and neither will tearing this place apart.

Because there's not much here. The walls are lined with shelves. Between those stand endless rows of stacks, like in a library. But unlike one, There's not a book in sight. The shelves all hold urns. The pottery kind, with scenes on them. Friezes, I think they're called, a Grecian thing. Because with a centaur granting access on behalf of Mnemosyne, of course, it's Greek and archaic. I'd investigate, but the whole knee-jerk gridlock thing cramps that style.

I'm not sure how to go forward here. Vampires can't go to church; I've got no angel on my shoulder. And I don't play poker, so there's no ace up my sleeve. Fortunately, there's something I forgot. Well, an entire truckload of things, actually. But one in particular springs to my rescue. Or maybe crawls is a better verb.

Something stirs on the left side of my chest. No, my undead heart is not miraculously beating all of a sudden. The movement comes from my shirt pocket, where a red and shiny head pokes out of the top. It drops a wink with one of its black eyes before scuttling down my shirt and then the left leg of my pants.

I watch the creature's legs lengthen, joints bending at impossible angles as they morph from amphibious quadruped to humanoid. The tail vanishes, and that ruddy skin pales to a dun color. The grin on the face grows human-shaped teeth at an alarming rate.

"Okay, Boss." Sparky reaches out, grabs my left arm with his right hand. "You can unfreeze now."

A warmth washes over me, calling back a foggy memory from the night I got fersnickered on Dad's limoncello with Kayleigh Killarney. Muscles seized up tetanus style unclench, leaving me struggling not to flop to the floor. It feels like I just dropped something heavy or maybe said item was lifted off of me. Or like someone broke my neck a couple of minutes ago and then healed it.

"Gaah!" My eloquence in unexpected situations is usually second to none. This isn't usual. Not even for me.

"Come on, Boss." Sparky reaches out and taps my wristwatch. Yeah, I still wear one of those anachronisms. Bad memory, worse sense of time's passage.

"Yeah, okay." I nod. "I get it. Limited time offers are limited."

My feet are still feeling half-full of pins and needles, so I shuffle over to the nearest shelf and have a gander at the friezes on the urns. A wavy-haired brunette with pale skin brandishes a pistol at a figure with sharp, bloodstained teeth. They fight over a swaddled infant. I squint at the markings under the picture. It's all Greek to me for a moment until it resolves into Latin I can make sense of.

"Who's Judah Black?" I scratch my head.

"Not you, boss."

"Well, like, duh." I tap my temple with one forefinger. "Even if it is a dude's name, and that's clearly a lady."

"Wrong section." Sparky jerks his thumb over one shoulder. "This way."

"How would you know?" I follow him anyway.

"Ancient Salamander Secret." Sparky barks out a laugh.

"You're no ancient."

"Right, boss. But we're born knowing about some stuff."

"Whatever you say, kid." I shake my head. Someday, I'll ask Sparky exactly where baby magical salamanders come from. I'm pretty sure it has nothing to do with a mommy salamander and a daddy salamander loving each other very much. But now is not the time.

"Check this one." Sparky points at one of the stacks.

"Hmm." The urn I look at this time shows a guy busting his way out of a coffin, only to emerge on a street in New York City. In front of a tiger. The Greek letters do their mighty morphing thing, and I shake my head at the name that comes up. "Can't tell if this title is the dude's name or his predicament."

"Huh?"

"Graves. Vincent Graves. And see where he came from?"

"You tell me, Boss."

"A grave." Normally I'd laugh, but something about what I'm looking at gives me a sense of foreboding, like this dude's going to go horrible places and see terrible things.

"Oh." Sparky squints at the urn. "Thought it was a photo booth at first."

"Whatever works for you, kid."

"Anyway, it's kind of cool you're in here somewhere, too."

"Yeah. Cool. Right." I don't say that I think there's no common thread between me and the two badasses I've seen so far. Which is a good thing because I realize I might be wrong. I recently fought against creatures who devour innocence, and maybe the guy in the coffin is undead like me.

"Next stack. Over here."

I follow again and find one with a girl tossing her pills in the garbage. She's got a raven on her shoulder, and on the bird's back is a fairy with mangled wings. I read the name and instantly know it's got nothing to do with me. I don't know any Megan O'Reillys, and there's no such thing as fairies.

We move along. Finally, some of the figures start to look familiar. There's one that's clearly of King DeCampo, though he's got a different name. Makes sense, since he's standing in a work camp over the prone body of a man with a whip, breaking copper chains off slaves. On the horizon squat three pyramids, uneroded.

A second urn on this shelf shows a whip-thin figure, dressed all in black. Their hair is shorn almost to the skin over their skull, making their bared fangs all the more frightening. They hold an iron cudgel, brandishing it at figures in red habits as a handful of men in tallis and skull caps flee through the open door behind them. The caption tells me this is Raven. They appear to be fighting a squad of Inquisitors during the Spanish Inquisition.

After that, it's Maya. I don't even need to read the script below the frieze to know it's her, either. She's next to an old oak tree beside a bridge, with an empty noose hanging from one gnarled branch. And Maya's with Sasquatch, dumping a figure in white robes and a hood over the railing on the bridge's side. There are a few more urns featuring her there, too. They all look at least a few decades older than this one, and Sasquatch isn't in them.

I shake my head, wondering how I'll ever even be near the same league as any of my friends. They're all older than me, stronger, more resolute in the face of evil. Even those heroes I didn't recognize on the other shelves seem larger than anything my life or unlife could measure up to.

Just who do I think I am, anyway? What right do I have to be here?

"Boss, try this shelf." Sparky jerks his thumb at one to my right.

And that's when I see them. The first thing I notice is just how many there are. Urns with my image and name on them, I mean. As it turns out, my mind isn't a sieve. It's like a bucket without a bottom.

"These are all mine, kid. All of them."

"Looks like it." Sparky's eyes resemble melted obsidian. Except I don't know whether obsidian can melt or not. I'm a PI, not a geologist. "Sorry, boss."

Clearly, he is though I can't imagine why. None of this could be his fault. I turn back to gaze down the long row of memory urns with my goofy mug on them. One in particular catches my eye. For maybe the first time, I don't take a breath out of habit.

It's like when I was still alive and had the wind knocked out of me. It happened only one time, although I don't know how. When was that, exactly? I can't remember. And then one of the urns catches my eye and knocks loose the veil shrouding that section of my memory.

I'm standing between Kayleigh and a hooded figure. Whoever's under that dark swath of fabric has a finger outstretched. Slate-gray smoke curls from it like a forgotten cigarette in an ashtray. That wispy tendril is making contact with my temple. The picture of my body in the frieze stands rigid, unnaturally stiff, like I'm getting electrocuted or turned to stone.

That image prompts what comes to mind next. Full frontal contact with the asphalt strip behind Cranston West High School, part of the Meshanticut Bike Path. That memory never made sense to me before. But now I know why Doctor Maris admonished Kayleigh in the ICU. I took a supernatural hit to protect her while I was still mundane. And I'd bet an unlife of favors Calvin Kelley did something like it himself.

Because the next thing I remember after taking that fall is waking up to Ma telling me I'd been in the hospital. And nobody ever told me how seriously bad a condition I was in, either. Not even Maury or Kayleigh though she'd broken up with me that day.

"What is that thing?" I point. The question's mostly rhetorical because I don't expect a kid like Sparky to have any answers, salamander or not. He surprises me.

"Lethian." He shakes his head. "Nasty things. That explains a lot."

"Well, that's going in the notebook." I flip to a blank page and jot it down with the golf pencil. Sasquatch's blog might have information to look up later. Then, I consider all the urns with my stolen memories in them. "Hmm."

“Five minutes left.”

And just like that, I’m almost out of time. Why am I here again? Oh, yeah. To solve an impossible case for Zack Milano. And his memory is the one I need for that, not any of my own. I stuff the pad and pencil back into my pocket and pace quickly down along the stacks.

Sparky’s footsteps tap along rapidly behind me as he trots to keep up with my longer stride. A glance at my watch makes up my mind to burn some blood. I’ve got bags in my pockets to drink later for exactly that reason, after all. But I grab Sparky’s arm first. Don’t want him to get lost in here.

Doctor Maris told me I can only bring one thing out. She never said what. Since Sparky isn’t a thing, exactly, and he came in via my pocket, he’ll have to leave that way, too. But there’s one huge fact I don’t know. The only way to find out is to ask an awkward question.

“Uh, Sparky?”

“Yeah?”

“When you change into, um, an amphibian, can you bring stuff with you?”

“Sure can!” He pats his chest. “It goes under my skin until I shift back.”

“Cool.”

Unfortunately, I ask this too late for the kid to go back and grab that first urn of mine. But my stolen memories are so numerous I’m only just getting to the end of them. Several more sit on the shelf next to me. I stop, about to ask Sparky to just grab one at random. Before I speak, I glance across the aisle and see Esther’s urns. There are only four, but I don’t look at three of them. Because the first is like a picture of Hell.

And now I understand why she’s surly, where the artificial arm and leg come from, and why she keeps that creepy doll Frankie chats with. I blink, something cold wetting my face so suddenly, I glance up. But there’s no leak in the ceiling. I’m crying. For Esther fucking Solomon, of all people.

She’s in Army battle gear, out in a desert. And her uniform’s got more stripes than I expected. A Lethian has its arms outstretched and what looks like fifty fingers of gray smoke curl out from it, connecting to everyone in her platoon. Shattered bottles litter the ground at her feet as though Esther's already thrown every potion she had at it. Her right arm is translucent, along with her left leg.

Beside her stands another soldier, this one with short but unruly jet-black curls peeking from under her helmet. The women hold hands, mouths open like they're chanting some incantation. The name on her uniform's patch says Solomon, too, and her body's disintegrating, fading away from the ground up. A child's discarded doll lies prone on a flagstone between them, a glowing green thread stretching between it and the woman who's got to be related to Esther.

I go with my gut.

"Sparky, take this urn right here."

"This one with Esther on it?" The salamander blinks. "You sure, boss?"

"Absotively."

"Okay."

And just like that, I blow my chance to bring anything of my own back. But Esther needs this more than I do. At least my instincts say she does, and she does so much for the rest of us without asking for anything. When Sparky snags the pottery jar, the mood in here lifts. It's as though Mnemosyne herself approves of my decision. Though why a Greek goddess cares about a pair of Jewish alchemists, a salamander, and a Roman Catholic vampire is beyond me.

In twenty paces, I see Zack's section. It's nowhere near as big as mine, and less disturbing than Esther's. And most of his urns depict nights of getting blackout-drunk than anything else. Except for two. One glance at the first has me dropping my jaw.

My old rival's getting punished by his father for taking home a silver State Thespian Festival award instead of gold. Punished so hard this memory got lost.

I stare at that frieze, notice a ruddy glow splaying out at Zack from his father's mouth. My brain puts that together with the smoky Lethian tendrils and the green glow of alchemy from Esther's wartime scene. It's magic. The Milanos are magicians, and Zack's having the memory of his second-place win removed by dear old dad. Possibly because he used magic to compete. Or maybe because he didn't use enough of it to get gold.

Zack's shouting, too. But the magic coming out of his mouth is directed back on himself. It's not shielding him from what his dad's doing. I've got the impression it's literally changing Zack's own mind. So, Milano's a magician. The spell-singing kind, just like his father. But he doesn't remember.

In the second urn full of serious business, Zack's getting handed over to Deep Ones, which I expected. What surprises me is who's making the trade.

Instead of Francesca Caprice, it's Mrs. Kent leading my bound and gagged client. Carmine is with her, gray smoke wreathing his head even though he's got no cigarette. I wonder why, but the frieze holds no clues. Zack's got his mouth covered, of course. Magicians who do magic with their voices are dangerous without a gag. Even though Zack doesn't know his own magical strength, the others do.

So, Whitby's had his henchwoman working with the Caprices as well as the Deep Ones. And hers is a longer game than I'd have ever imagined. Mrs. Kent gives Zack to the Deep Ones in exchange for another prisoner.

It's Sasquatch. Maya said something about the cryptid missing memories, too. I glance over my shoulder and immediately see Sass's section. A very similar urn rests directly across from this one of Zack's. Except it's from a different perspective, one that shows a hungry gleam in Carmine's eyes.

Zack isn't the only one who needs the memories in here. Practically all my friends and allies do. But Zack's is the focus.

When I pick his urn up, it sloshes. Of course. Memory, oblivion, and water are a thing in Greek myths of the underworld. Mnemosyne's got a river of memory there. And didn't Hades also keep a river of forgetfulness? What was that called again? Oh, right. The Lethe. Maybe these things aren't quite as mythological as I originally thought, what with a centaur running the ICU at Kent County

Hospital. Anyway, I snag a bag of blood from my pocket and guzzle it. That makes room for me to tuck Zack's urn in there.

"Okay, that's it," I announce to nobody in particular. "Got what I came for and need to find the—"

"Look!" Sparky points at the end of the stack we're in. He starts shifting immediately, then scuttles up my leg and torso to return to my shirt pocket. The urn he's carrying goes with him, showing up as a large black spot on his shiny salamander back.

The round steel-reinforced door appears. I glance at my watch, realizing we've got maybe thirty seconds left before we're shut in here forever. I burn blood and hightail it toward the open portal. It's a long way, but I make it before the door clangs shut again. Just barely.

No pressure, right?

# CHAPTER FIFTEEN

I walk out into a firefight and immediately thank God because it's not flames Scott and Doctor Maris are dodging. It's bullets. Silver ones. Those definitely kill werewolves, but I'm not sure about centaurs or salamanders. I pause, worried about the kid. Sparky must be reading my mind because he scuttles down from my pocket and away from my feet, leaving me free to conduct Operation Vampire Shield.

Don't worry. I got this.

And just like that, I'm intercepting projectiles faster than the human eye can track. My speed surprises me because it's increased since the last time I did something like this. I'm quick enough to knock back the rest of my blood bags while I'm at it. Which is more than necessary. It's dire.

I don't bother healing the bullet holes riddling the parts of my flesh uncovered by Kevlar. Yeah, I vest up ever since Kayleigh came at us in Esther's apartment. Being shot stings. I also don't want to know what happens when too many unhealed holes add up in my midsection. But I need my speed now more than unblemished flesh. Priorities suck, but blood is a limited resource for vampires.

Dodging into the bullets instead of away from them gives me perspective. Not about life, about the direction they're coming from. And it's above, farther up the stairwell. So, I shoo my trio of friends as far off to the side as I can. Outside would be better, but the exit is right in the line of fire, and a skinny guinea like me isn't enough cover for a horse-sized lady and a wolfed-out teenager.

Anyway, I see the shooter now that I'm standing in the stairwell's box. They're wearing a hoodie with a ski mask on underneath. It's eerily similar to the night Kayleigh shot my dad. Yeah, she did that. Thought he was me. It's nothing personal, she was doing it to pay her fiance's medical bills, and we fixed that. At least, I thought. Is this attacker another hunter?

I take a breath in through my nose and know right away this isn't my ex-girlfriend. It's a dude, though too slight in build to be her father. Hunting is a family business. The tinny odor of antiseptic and tang of saline remind me of the ICU room. I blink, drawing a conclusion that makes little sense.

Could this be Calvin? He's also a hunter, which gives him reason to shoot at shifters and a vamp like me. I know he was just in a coma. But then again, maybe Esther's alchemy is extra powerful. The urn Sparky stole seems to imply that, anyway. But is it enough to return a coma patient back to fighting trim in thirty minutes? If so, Domino's alchemy more than delivers.

"Parlay!" At least that's what I try to yell.

But no sound comes out of my mouth. I feel my throat vibrating with the words, though. And that's when I realize the gunshots are making no sound, either. Nothing is, or has been since I came back. It's silent as a Chaplin flick in here. And of course. I realize this can't be Calvin Kelley even if he's all better in a medical sense. He's been in a coma for so long he'd have no idea Scott or Doctor Maris are anything but human. The same goes for my vampirism.

At this point, the guy's identity isn't important. A pause in the gunfire means he's reloading. I dash up, clearly faster than he expects judging by the scent of adrenaline. I'm almost to him when I realize he's stopped moving. His eyes dart to a spot just above the second-to-last step. And it's definitely a doozie I'm too late to save myself from. Speed has its downsides.

The wire trips me and I go down, arms pinwheeling. One of them knocks over what looks like a gray mushroom with blinking blue lights studding the top, and sound returns.

"Shitballs!"

Scott's howl rings out in counterpoint with my exclamation. He's dashed up the stairs behind me, leaping into action and tackling the shooter. Kid should play Lacrosse or something. Nah. Too cliché.

I hear the metallic snick of a blade being drawn. It glints silver under the fluorescent lights. Even with my speed boost, there's no way to get in between Scott and the masked man. My only weapon is my voice.

"Stop!" I struggle to my feet, stepping over the wire that tripped me up earlier.

The manic laugh from under the mask doesn't match my recollection of the recently comatose man's cracked voice, though it is raspy. Because I was right. It's not Kayleigh's fiance. This is someone who's plagued me for years, judging by all my urns in the Vault. Carmine, the Lethian.

"Die, son of a bitch!" Carmine jabs his knife, missing Scott's midsection by millimeters.

"My dad's the werewolf, dumbass!"

I laugh at Scott's exasperated battle-cry. I kick at Carmine's knife hand, but it's not where I expect it to be. Instead, he's flipped the blade, and it's coming straight for my side.

At first, I wonder what the mafioso hopes to accomplish with that move. But when I hear the crunch of shattering pottery and feel a gush of water, I understand. He's destroying Zack's memory urn. How did he know it was there? Oh, right.

"Scott! Get out! Carmine's a Lethian!"

As I shout, my hands dart into my torn opera cloak, where the remnants of the urn clatter in the left pocket. A shard slices my finger, and because I'm only a new vampire, I put it in my mouth. Along with the water. Which turns out to be a good thing, actually.

In the blink of an eye, Zack's full memory comes back to me. The detail's more vivid than my blood visions and without all the ash-puking side-effects. I could get used to recalling like this. I smell things, hear conversations the frieze on the pottery couldn't convey. So I try to focus, needing to remember this so I can tell it all to Zack. And I start to think maybe I will. The vision's just that evocative. But there's a price for even such a brief moment of clarity. Always is.

Bone shatters, ash erupting from the new wound in my shoulder. A machete's lodged there, socked into the heart of my rotator cuff by Carmine. I blink, not surprised over the fact that he attacked me but at how. I bare my fangs and hiss only partly out of hunger. Mostly, I'm vamping out to cover for the side-eye I'm throwing at the mafioso.

He's not using his weird Lethian smoky powers to whammy my memories. My vampirism can't be preventing him because I'm pretty sure he's been there and done that after I got turned as well as before. No. It's got to be something about the water from the urn. If only I could figure out why and how to use it against him.

I'd better think faster, because Carmine's finally back to reloading his guns with silver bullets. Scott managed to dodge the memory-sucking attack I sensed before but smacked into the wall hard enough to knock the wind out of him. He's currently gasping for air right in the Lethian's line of fire.

Hunger decides for me. I've got no idea whether Carmine bleeds like a human while pretending to be one, but he's got a pulse, for sure. I leap at him, fangs out. The machete's hilt knocks into the elbow of his firing arm, making him drop the gun with a wince that has too much grin in it.

My shoulder's wrecked, but I don't care. The only thing that matters now is that pulse, its beat driving me forward without hesitation. Pushing his head to one side with my still functional arm is easy with Carmine up against a wall. Too easy.

"Keep your fangs off him!" Doctor Maris's footsteps are bipedal now.

"Huh?" At this point, I'm as close to salivating as a vamp can get. burning that much blood on our powers makes us hungry. I'm close enough to a rage that my give a damn's selective. Still, I hope somebody stops me because I know that what comes next ain't pretty.

Scott snarls, pushing off from the wall. He knocks me away from Carmine, holding me back. I'm reminded of the showdown with Kayleigh in Esther's apartment again. I bit Scott that night and then promised I'd never do it again. Famous last words, right?

Carmine pulls off his ski mask and pushes through the stairwell door, escaping without a scratch on him. And he'll get away without any issue, too. If anyone sees him, he'll make sure they forget about it unless he needs an alibi.

But I've got no time to worry about that. The machete falls from my healing shoulder, clattering to the floor. An alarm sounds from somewhere in the hallway outside the door. Carmine pulled the fire alarm. Because of course, he did.

So what happens when a centaur, a werewolf, and a hungry vampire get caught by security with illegal weapons in a stairwell?

Fortunately, something hits me on the head, and I never find out.

---

Everything's dark. At first, I think I'm dreaming. Having a nightmare, actually, because of the smell. It's that rank and salty aroma from under Providence. That's right, folks. My nostrils are getting the Deep Ones treatment for the second time in as many weeks. Because that's just my luck.

Sure, I didn't want Carmine the Lethian wiping my mind or for security to catch me vamped out in a hospital stairwell, but this is worse. I already beat the Deep Ones. Well, my friends did, anyway. And besides, there's a truce now. Raven negotiated it so the agreement's airtight and in our favor.

I try to open my mouth, protest this treatment. But there's something in it that tastes like old socks. Eww.

Wait a minute. Zack was gagged in the frieze on his urn. Which shattered in my pocket. Right. So it's not me with Deep Ones. I'm finally able to experience what Zack Milano did in his missing memory. I open my eyes.

Sure enough, there's a trio of froggy-looking, slime-scaled, big-eyed bastards. Literally bastardly, too. They mate with humans and definitely don't marry them before or after. But that's another story.

Poking into my back is what feels like the barrel of a gun. A small one, but it's at close range against my spine. No, not my spine. Zack's. This is his memory and his body. And since the urn's broken, this is the only chance I've got to investigate the mystery he hired me to solve.

If only I remember this whole thing once I'm back to experiencing my own unlife. I can't take notes here, so this whole experience might be useless. Like me.

There's no time for self-deprecation. Glancing to my right, I see Carmine. He's got no smoky tendrils around him like I remember from the frieze. But that makes sense now. The pottery art was only trying to tell me his true nature, not failing to illustrate a cigarette. Unless he wipes it from my mind, I'll probably never forget he's a memory-stealing Lethian.

Anyway, I know for sure now that it's Mrs. Kent holding the gun on Zack. She's also got hold of one of his arms, her grip cold and steely like the vise in my dad's basement workshop. Some feeling emanating from her hand radiates sluggishness, like when you open the door on a day when the wind chill's tens of degrees below freezing. I guess she's got some kind of paralyzing power.

The Deep One's voice echos like water dripping in a vast underground cavern, even though we're in a small concrete tunnel.

"Where's the human behind this agreement?"

I blink, unsure whether the flutter of shock I feel in Zack's chest comes from him or me. But of course, it's his. I already know Francesca Caprice is the villain of this piece. The fact that Zack doesn't realize this, even with her henchman standing right there, speaks volumes. He might be a magician, but my old rival seems woefully uninformed about criminals in the mortal community.

"I'm here as her representative." Carmine inclines his head toward a large shadow across from us, behind the two Deep Ones. "Release your captive."

"Not to you."

"Fair enough." Carmine's chuckle echoes with a rasp like flint on steel. "Give the yeti to the vampire. This agreement's with her coven, too. I'll handle your magical celebrity guest."

"Wipe him." Mrs. Kent shoves the barrel of the gun harder against Zack's back as she speaks. "Before I lose my grip on him. This one's particularly dangerous even if he doesn't know it yet."

"I've eaten magicians for breakfast since before you were born, Kent." Smoke blooms from Carmine's fingertips.

"Not like this one."

He ignores her warning, generating more smoke. It lengthens into thready tendrils that reach toward Zack. Four stream out to circle his ankles and wrists while a fifth and sixth curl and unfurl toward his head. Mrs. Kent drops his arm.

I feel Zack make one last desperate attempt at escape, struggling to spit out the disgusting rags he's gagged with. And he does it, but winds himself in the process. Sucking down an enormous breath, I feel his diaphragm engage like he's about to sing *Ave Maria* or something. Which is close to the truth because Mrs. Kent's words jogged his memory. He knows his voice has literal power now, even if he's unsure how to use it.

A hot rush of hope floods through Zack, or maybe it's magic. I wouldn't know how casting spells feels after all. But it outstrips the sensation of burning blood. Whatever it is, that rush is powerful, more so than any ability I ever engaged in my short unlife.

And for a minute, I think he's going to do it. Despite the fact of the urn's existence proving otherwise. I'm convinced Zack's going to get away.

Except Carmine's way too experienced and too well prepared. Zack never stands a chance.

That fifth smoky tendril closes around his neck, cutting off Zack's impending utterance before it can meet his voice-box. His gaze cuts to one side where he sees Sasquatch getting the same treatment. Carmine smiles, his teeth as stark and hungry as a shark's. And then the last smoky tendril wreaths his temple, and Zack's caught out of time and mind.

---

"Is he gonna bite us when he wakes up?"

I try to answer, but nothing on my face moves, not even my eyelids. It's like my body's under a ton of cement or lead blankets. Maybe both.

"Dammit, kid." Doctor Maris snorts. "I'm a centaur, not a vampire. Use your brain. What do you think transfusions are for?"

"Putting blood back in."

"So, what's your hang-up?"

"I dunno. It's just that I've seen him have, uh, a bad reaction to blood."

"You're trying to tell me this vamp has an allergy to blood?"

"Not all blood." The dry sound of Scott Fitzpatrick scratching the patch of hair behind his hair is unmistakable. "Just some of it. But I don't know why or what kind."

Doctor Maris snorts. I want to get up, pull out the IV. At least I don't feel hungry now. But I'm still like a lead brick for whatever reason, drowning slowly. Yeah, that's melodramatic, but I need to write down the info I can still recall from Zack's memory, or his case might go unsolved. I can't afford that, and neither can he. My struggles against whatever's wrong with my body reaches a crescendo I can't maintain. Luckily, I don't have to.

"He can hear you, doc." The salamander kid to the rescue.

"Hmm." I feel icy fingers press against my lips. Cold hands, warm heart. What could the centaur possibly be feeling for? "Well, he's not out of the woods yet. But he'll recover. I can let him up now."

Something tugs against my pinkie finger, like when you realize there's a hair stuck in your glove after you already started shoveling snow. I feel a tingle, then a snap. Whatever has a grip on me releases, and I sit up slowly with a wobble, like Frankenstein's monster rising from his slab for the first time.

"Paper. Pen. Now." My voice is creaky, but the words come out okay. Sparky picks my pocket and hands over the goods. I jot down everything I can remember from the vision. Unfortunately, that's only something about Deep Ones, which I already knew. I hang my head.

"What's wrong?" Concern pulls Scott's eyebrows down.

"Strike one." Swinging my legs over the side of the stretcher is easier than I expected. When I stand, it's like the weight of the world's bobbing behind me like a lead balloon. "But there's no time to worry about that."

It's the bottom of the ninth, and I've got one more swing before this vampire debt-reduction game is over. My interview with the social worker is tomorrow, and I haven't done a single thing to spruce up Pickering House.

As I walk toward the door of what turns out to be a hospital room, something crashes behind me. The aroma of blood meets my nose. When I turn to see what happened, something tugs and itches at the crook of my elbow.

"Sorry, Doctor Maris." I sigh over the exploded bag of donor blood, my eyelids unexpectedly prickly with a fifty percent chance of tears. "Sorry."

"Don't go Canadian on me, Crispo." She reaches out and pulls the tape and needle from my arm, which stings just enough to snap me out of all the fatalism. "And don't cry over spilled blood. Just get out of my hospital and fix all this."

"I can't. Urn's broken."

"So what? So's your brain. Doesn't stop you from sticking your nose in where it wasn't invited. You always find a way. Now get out there and mind everyone else's business. You already had enough to drink. Go know things. Even if you forget them later." One of her feet clomps against the linoleum. "Doctor's orders."

"Um, okay."

I head out, Sparky and Scott following along. Because I get the idea that arguing with a centaur doctor might be hazardous to my health.

# CHAPTER SIXTEEN

After dropping Sparky at a park where he can call Baba Yaga, I head to The Belfry and pick up the outfit I'm wearing for the home visit. That's because I'm spending the day at Pickering House. When I arrive, Scott's already there, unloading some garden equipment to spruce things up on the outside of the house. His dad's beat-up blue pick-up is parked at the curb. I back into the driveway and get out, slinging my bag over my shoulder as I close the door and lock it behind me.

I put my hands on my hips and sigh. There's nowhere I can possibly park my car without the social worker seeing it later. Even though all of Sasquatch's hair has been removed from the bumper, clearly, it's been in an accident. Unreported, too.

"What's wrong, Valentino?" Stephanie steps out of the shadows beside the garage.

"Everything." Usually, I'm not this candid with her, but my inside voice is just as busted as my give-a-damn.

"I'm sorry to hear that." She strides toward me, looking more like a coyote pacing toward a wounded rabbit than a concerned parental figure. But that's Stephanie for you. Matronly isn't a word that'll ever apply to her. "How can I help?"

“I dunno. Turn a good mechanic? Or stick me in the ground for fifty years.”

“Tino.” She shakes her head. “Surely, you’ll think of something.”

“That’s the problem, though.” I tap my temple like my finger’s the barrel of a gun, and wonder whether that’d kill a vampire. Now’s not the time to ask, and I’d probably forget anyway. “My thinker’s not working right, and after tonight, I’m not sure there’s anything I can do about it.”

“What happened?”

I tell her everything I can remember about my trip through the memory vault, including the fact that Carmine’s a Lethian. I also mention how I’m not even sure exactly what that means.

“Well, this is a wrinkle I did not expect.” She sighs. “I should have been with you. Then, I could have gotten the urn myself. But I had no idea things would play out quite this way.”

“Really? Because your little reading assignment kind of gives me the opposite idea.”

“I’m not infallible, Tino.” Stephanie sighs. “Those books I caution you with are based largely on guesswork and limited by what I'm allowed to reveal.”

“Woah.”

“Yes, I imagined you’d have that reaction.” She turns her head, gazing at me like an appraiser judging the worth of a diamond. "Especially considering you don't seem to remember asking me a question I gave that necessarily limited answer to a handful of nights ago."

“My mind’s blown like a slashed tire.” I shrug. "I don't remember half of anything half the time. Which is like a total handicap."

“I understand what you mean, more than you know.” She leans against the car, resting one hand on top of the trunk. “So, what will you do about it?”

“I’m not sure.” I shrug. “But I’m starting to get the impression that most of us are flying at least half-blind. The ones with the best intentions, anyway.”

“Ah. Wise words from one so young.”

“I do my best. Even though it’s never good enough.”

"I disagree."

"And we're on a tangent." I kick the tire. "Lethians, Stephanie. What do they do?"

"They feed on memories."

"Okay. But that doesn't make much sense. If what they eat ends up in Mnemosyne's vault, what's the point?"

"The point is prolonging their lives. They use the memories for fuel, but water only ever changes state. Eventually, all of it condenses in the urns. Carmine's far older than he looks, though he's still technically mortal."

"Huh." I scratch my head. "And he's running with the Caprices, who seem to have limited knowledge. Okay, let me ramble for a minute here."

"Proceed."

"Francesca Caprice is the real Boss in the crime family. Her son all but said so. She's trying to adopt Leora for her connections to Baba Yaga. Francesca wants more power, the supernatural kind. But as far as I know, the Caprices aren't magicians. They only know magic exists and maybe have the idea that making pacts with supernatural beings is one way to get it. But from what Raven and Frankie say about theophiles, magic's in the blood as much as in the contract. So Francesca's efforts are going to be futile. Carmine's presence practically confirms that, because he'd have made a deal with her for sure by now. So, why does she want Leora, then?"

"You just said it, Tino." Stephanie crosses her arms, standing with her feet shoulder-width apart now instead of leaning on my busted up car. "Blood. Francesca wants her family to have magic even if she doesn't get to see it in her generation or even her lifetime. Leora's got the blood of theophiles in her veins. She's the last surviving member of the Kupala family. And if she's under the same roof as Sebastian Caprice, well, they're both teenagers with hormones. What do you imagine Francesca hopes will happen?"

My nose wrinkles as my upper lip curls back in a snarl. A low growl comes from somewhere. Not my chest, either. It's on the other side of the stockade fence between the front and back yard. And it's familiar.

"Scott?"

The growl goes silent. I dash toward the expanse of wood, tempted to jump it and confront my wolfy pal, but the risk of staking myself on the pickets at the top is too high. I sigh and shake my head, letting Scott get back to cleaning up the yard ahead of Gina Paolucci's visit.

"I'd worry more about the witch than the wolf for now, Valentino." Stephanie's hand comes to rest on my shoulder, its light touch like a moment of reason in a rapidly maddening night. "Baba Yaga will want Leora to procreate sooner rather than later. And she'd prefer a regular mortal for her Lamb over a werewolf."

"So you think Baba's on Francesca's side?" I turn, looking my sire in the eye.

"Not exactly." Stephanie shakes her head. "But either way, you've got to leash your assumptions about your future ward's romantic interests."

"Huh?" I blink.

"Leora's going to develop her own thoughts and feelings on who she cares for. You must let her have them. They'll color the witch's influence and allegiance."

"Well, that's a relief. She hates Sebastian Caprice."

"Really?" Stephanie's eyebrow arches so high I think it's shooting for the moon.

"Um, well, she sure gave him a lot of lip during the chat in my office."

"It's been ages since I was Leora's age, Tino, but one thing never changes about teenagers."

"And that is?"

"They're contrary to a fault. Tread cautiously where her heart is concerned."

"Okay, I'll try to do that." I sigh. "On top of the list of things I need to fix up in this house in less than twenty-four hours."

"Don't worry. We're all handling that."

"Really?" I jerk my chin at the nearest window. "It's not just Scott Fitzpatrick's Yard Service here?"

"It's the least Maya, the king, and I can do in exchange for Raven's hospitality."

"Well, let me get in there and help, then." I don't bother asking why Raven cares whether my outstanding debt to Baba Yaga gets paid. I owe them more than I owe the witch, so it's a good investment on their part to keep me from getting roasted, I guess.

Stephanie's silent on the matter. But she beckons as she makes her way along the side of the house and up the front walk. I remember the first time I came here, brandishing a rapier in Mrs. Pickering's face. It was just over a week ago but feels like ages. I wonder whether older vampires suffer from even more time-dilating weariness than I already deal with or if it's just part of my memory trouble. Maybe I'll find out somenight. If I survive long enough.

Inside the house, I find vampires working. It's not as mundane a sight as that phrase might conjure to mind. Maya's engaged in the relatively simple task of vacuuming. But she's got enormous earmuffs on. I immediately understand why when I wince at the wall of sound smacking against my eardrums.

Luckily, I can copy the smart people. Stephanie's taking another pair off the coat tree in the hall. I do the same. We put them on, and the noise goes from insanity-inducing cacophony to annoying but tolerable. Now I understand why cats hate the instrument of this chore so much. I never thought I'd have this much empathy for the feline condition, but here I am.

There's only one machine of auditory apocalypse in the house, so Stephanie arms herself with a feather duster and goes to town on the shelves and mantel. I leave the parlor, understanding on a fundamental level that as a fellow Italian, Gina Paolucci's going to care more about the state of the kitchen than anything else in the house.

King DeCampo's in there, but he's not doing any work. Instead, he's listening to Sarah Pickering prattle on about the food in the fridge. Which makes complete and total sense. DeCampo's literally ancient and doesn't know the first thing about modern food preservation.

"You don't want to throw any of it out," she's telling him. "It's all still good enough for us mortals to eat."

"But that's going over." The king points at half a chocolate cake.

"No." Sarah's in his way, blocking his path to remove the aging dessert.

And DeCampo's right. I can smell how it's gotten past its prime. There's no visible mold on it yet, but the spores are there. The old vamp's stance tells me he's about to burn some blood and dart past the teenage magician in his quest to clean out the refrigerator. I put a hand on his arm before that happens.

I notice Sarah's lip trembling. This isn't just a cake to her. There's an emotional connection, one that's still raw. I don't know which of her dead parents baked it, but tossing the confection in the trash will do more harm to her heart than the minimal mold will do to her stomach.

"Hey, why don't we put it in the freezer?" I step forward, and the king lets me. I think he understands now though his owlish blink says he's drawing conclusions slowly.

"The freezer?"

"Yeah, Sarah. It's what they do with all kinds of celebration cakes and totally normal as far as the opinion of a social worker goes."

Her grin is grimmer than I'd like, but it's present. I think this compromise is going to work out. Which is all for the best because the last thing we need in this house right now is a knock-down-drag-out between an ancient vamp and a young but powerful magician.

Sarah pulls the cellophane-wrapped bundle from the bottom shelf, then closes the fridge. As she unwraps it, revealing the remaining lettering, I'm reminded of how recently the senior Pickerings died. And it's a birthday cake. Sarah's own, for her sixteenth. No wonder she's willing to defend it with her magic.

I'm rummaging through cabinets and drawers, searching for a suitable container. But I've got nothing, of course. This isn't my parents' house, after all. I don't know where anything is. But that's got to change if I'm pretending to live here tomorrow evening.

"In here." King DeCampo points at a door beside the dishwasher. I blink, and he responds by tapping his nose. Of course. I should have thought of that.

And I've hit the jackpot. Rows of plastic containers and rolls of various food wraps stand at attention inside the cabinet. I know just the thing because a few months back, we put the remainder of Dad's retirement cake away exactly like this. I burn some blood and wrap it with vampiric speed because I can't think of a good reason not to.

Once that's done, I get out of Sarah's way. She puts the container away in the back of the freezer, behind two tubs of ice cream. The way she sets it down is gentler than anything else I've seen her do. The Pickerings were horrible to Frankie, but to Sarah, they were different because she had magic. She doesn't grasp that yet though someday she will understand. But sometimes, the first step toward the truth is through your emotions, no matter how problematic they are.

With the near-miss supernatural battle behind me, I'm free to explore the kitchen and see what needs tidying or adjustment. And it's a good thing I do because I find a number of stored bags of blood in the fridge up here instead of the one in the basement. I shake my head.

"Your majesty—"

"I know." The king lowers himself into one of the chairs at the kitchen table. "That blood in there is my fault."

"How so?"

Before he can answer, Stephanie's through the door, earmuffs and all. How she managed to hear DeCampo over Maya's vacuuming is beyond my comprehension. But she must have because my sire's first action is to put one delicate finger over the king's lips, and the next is dashing to the fridge to retrieve the bags from the top shelf. In the blink of an eye, she's gone, the door to the basement swinging shut behind her.

"What are we doing about that?" I jerk my thumb over my shoulder at the cellar door because the last thing I want is for Gina Paolucci to go down there and discover a colony of elder vampires.

She's mundane and out of the supernatural loop, and I bet her brother Raph likes it that way.

But Sarah and the king have no idea, judging by his shaking head and her one-shouldered shrug. I scratch my head because I've also got nothing. At least until I notice the familiar stack of Post-it notes sitting on the counter. Frankie's had that since the night we dropped off the application. It's one of those that's cut into the shape of a poop emoji. The pad's thicker than usual, but that's because it's not brand new out of the package. The entire thing's been inscribed with alchemical symbols. But they're not in Esther's writing. I blink just as Frankie walks through the door from the hallway and scoops them up.

"Oh, hi, Tino." My friend turns, and I notice a wire leading from an earbud in his left ear down to his shirt pocket. "Just a sec."

Frankie pulls another earbud out of his pocket and holds it out toward me. Faint green-blue light comes from inside. I pinch the wire between my fingers like I'm holding a mouse by the scruff of its neck. I can hear what's coming through perfectly fine. He's spying on the Caprice's home visit with Gina Paolucci. Well, it hasn't started yet, but I hear Francesca barking orders.

"Holy shit, dude." I blink. "How did you bug their place?"

"Not their place. Sebastian. Alchemy notes plus the Zippo." Frankie pulls his pocket open, and I can see an iPod Shuffle with the lighter, a Post-it wrapped around both of them and rubber-banded together. "Handy, huh?"

"Illegal." I drop the earbud, letting it dangle by Frankie's side.

"Look, they've done worse is all I'm saying. We don't want Leora living with them." He's right. And I hate it.

"And where did you get this idea?" I put my hands on my hips.

"An old friend."

"Does Esther know you've been pinching her stuff?" I'd like to pinch Frankie's ear and drag him off to exile in his room right about now, but I don't.

"This isn't Esther's."

"How many alchemists do you know?"

"Enough." He picks the earbuds back up. "I'll be hiding the basement door and the damage on your car with these, too. Are you going to listen in or not?"

I shake my head, deciding not to touch Frankie's illicit magical spyware. Heading through the hall door, I realize I'm about a hairsbreadth away from going full-out rage at my on-paper domestic partner. I need to cool off somewhere, alone, if possible. But of course, that's not happening. Light footsteps behind me and a tug on my sleeve have me whirling around faster than a dervish. If those even exist.

"What do you want?" I bare my fangs at Sarah.

"It's just, I got a look at those notes." She stands her ground, even facing an angry vamp. Girl's got more guts than some of the guys at Cranston PD. "You helped me, so I want to help you now. And there's something you should know."

"What?"

"That's Ruth's writing." Sarah shakes her head. "Esther's sister. But she's been dead since 2003."

"Wait a minute. Let me check my notes." The puzzle I'm presented with takes me down from the edge. It's like those old legends, where mortals stump the vampire by throwing a handful of rice and making them count the grains. I need my notebook, so I take that out and flip it open. "No. I need the other one."

It's in the basement, so I head down there, Sarah following me. I really don't want a tag-along kid, but I guess teenagers following me around is something I have to deal with. For whatever reason, vampires are awfully popular with that demographic. Anyway, I go into the room I used yesterday to escape the sun down here and find it on the desk.

When I flip through the notebook, I scan the entries for Esther's name. Practically every time I mention her, there's something about the creepy doll she keeps around all the time. And there it is, wedged into a margin. The description of the doll. And it's familiar, but I can't be sure because of my stupid memory.

"Sarah, is there a picture of Ruth somewhere in the house?"

"Yeah, hold on. I'll get it."

She's back in under a minute with a dusty photo album. After flipping about halfway through it, Sarah turns it around then points at one of the pictures under the cellophane. It shows two women in military uniform, standing outside Pickering House. Their faces are impossibly young, and they look quite similar except for their hair. The one on the left has hers pulled to the side in a long braid, while the other's curls peek out from under her hat. And of course, I recognize that first girl, though it takes a moment or two. Because this is the only time I've seen Esther Solomon's face wear a genuine smile. And then my eyes home in on Ruth.

"Curls." I glance back at my notebook. "Like the doll's."

"But that's impossible."

"Are you an alchemist?"

"Well, no, but people can't be dolls."

"Surely you've heard of golems before, Sarah."

Stephanie's voice surprises me, but it downright startles the kid. She takes a full jump toward me, then scuttles to the side, putting me between herself and my sire. Well, I'd better get used to it. I'm supposed to be a guardian. So I nod slowly, letting the kid compose herself.

"A golem, huh?" I shake my head. "Not what I expected—" I blink, setting the big notebook aside so I can get the little one out again. I peer at the page where I described the frieze on Esther's urn, which Sparky's still got.

"You're drawing conclusions, Valentino."

"Me too." Sarah's looking over my shoulder. I guess she can read my pidgin Latin.

"Yeah. Okay, so, Ruth got herself disintegrated, and Esther put her in the doll as a golem. I can buy that." I shrug.

"But a golem who can do alchemy on its own?" Sarah shakes her head. "Implausible."

"Except it's happening." I glance back at my big notebook. "It's been happening. To me, even. I've encountered alchemy that wasn't

Esther's before, but it's all the same color and has a similar feel. So it makes sense to me, anyway."

"But it goes against every rule of magic I've been taught."

"I don't know much about what you magicians do. I'm a detective. So my bread is deductive reasoning and my butter's Occam's Razor. Have you learned that in school yet?" I give Sarah a sideways glance, but she shakes her head.

"The simplest explanation, no matter how implausible, is probably true," Stephanie lectures.

"And what's simpler than an exceptionally powerful alchemist keeping her powers even after becoming a golem?"

As I find out later, not much. Everything else I discover about Ruth Solomon ends up at a downright Gordian level of complexity. But that's a story for another time.

# CHAPTER SEVENTEEN

As it turns out, I can't escape the show put on by Frankie's magical Post-it note spyware. It's as futile as trying not to watch the Super Bowl at a sports bar. No matter where I go in Pickering House, it's there. Like a fungus, the play-by-play grows on everyone's lips but mine. My supernatural hearing and the simple fact of daylight hours conspire against me. I'm literally a captive audience, listening in on the daywalkers from the sun-proof basement.

Yeah, I'm a Negative Nelly about this, but I should be. Because the whole home visit at the Caprices' house is going well. Way too well. And Frankie's method of listening in is just that. Audio only. So much is missing from the context, and it's not doing my attitude any favors. But apparently, hopeless situations are Frankie Pickering's glory. Or something.

He's taking more notes than a college student shooting for Valedictorian. As he scribbles them down, he paces from room to room, noting down ways to improve each one so Gina Paolucci will like it more. And he's talking to Levi and Sarah, giving them tips so they can outdo Sebastian's little performance as potential foster siblings. Levi only smiles and nods, making me think he'll be a natural. But Sarah's sounds like a knight and some dishonorable cur just threw a gauntlet at her.

I'm not one to shrink from a challenge, either. However, I know from long experience that going into an interview with the emotional equivalent of cement overshoes is the opposite of ideal. I've got to do something to get my mind off of how awesome the Caprices are making themselves sound and back on track. So I get out my phone and make a call.

"What the fuck do you want?"

"Hi, Esther. I'm just checking to see if it's okay to call Raph Paolucci yet."

"Why in the name of Satan's fucking crotch rot would you want to do that?"

"Because we talked about it the other day." Was it really such a short time ago? Unlife's going too fast and too slow all at the same time.

"You got me the scales. No need to call."

"Uh." I'm sort for words because she's right. "Well, I might have other business involving him in the future."

"Whatever." I can practically hear Esther rolling her eyes on the other end of the line. "But it's need-to-fucking-know, asshole. I don't just give all my damn secrets the fuck away."

"I'm your secret?"

"Your undead ass status is valuable information, fuckfangs."

"Well, okay, then."

"I'm so fucking glad we had this useless ass conversation. Adios, motherfucker." And Esther hangs up, tying that loose end off.

I smack my head, remembering I should have told her about the urn. But I don't have it anyway. I make a note to tell Sparky to bring it up to her lab once all the custody stuff is done. But I can't escape the feeling there's more to do.

I count off the debts I'm trying to pay ASAP. Already cured Calvin Kelley, so no more owing Kayleigh. We're working on helping Leora for Baba Yaga. And what else? Trying to remember reminds me of something. The feel of a bullet shattering pottery against my chest.

But why does my mind conjure that image? Now I remember. The dropped ball is for a paying case—Zack Milano's. I've got no memory of what I did wrong, but I happen to have a psychic friend. I grab all my notes and walk out of my room, trying to locate the vampire I'm always looking for.

Instead of heading into the sleeping room I use during the day here, I head all the way down the hall. Yeah, this basement has one of those. It's completely finished and converted into a sunless living space. Anyway, we end up in what used to be Mother Pickering's laundry center. I say center because it's got the machines, a table, chairs, and even an old sofa to sit on while waiting to take clothes out and fold.

Someone's put a load of laundry in the dryer, I'm not sure who and right now I don't care. The fresh scent of clean, drying clothes soothes all my senses. And I need that right now because I'm about to admit, to perfect Maya no less, that I screwed up an investigation. Big time.

"Maya, can I get your help with something?"

"Anything." She sets the book she was reading down on the sofa.

"Made a breakthrough in the Milano case."

"Oh? Sounds like you should feel great." She doesn't smile. It's as though Maya's well aware there's always another shoe about to drop when I get this serious.

"I don't."

"So, what happened?"

"I'm not sure." I tell Maya about trying to leave the hospital and how Doctor Maris stopped us and paid off an old favor to Stephanie by giving me a pass inside the memory vault. I tell her about the stranger's urns, the temptation to take one of my own, and how I ultimately didn't. But that's where my memory fails. "All I remember after we got out is breaking some pottery and losing something important that was inside."

"Hmm." Maya pulls a battered case from her pocket. There's a phone inside. She taps and swipes. "Sounds like you might have tangled with a Lethian. More than once in your life, too."

"A what now?" I know I should recognize that term. Didn't I have a conversation earlier about something that starts with the letter L? But my mind's blank.

"They're sort of like vampires, after a fashion." She turns the screen so I can see it.

"Wow." The hooded and smoke-surrounded figure in the drawing reminds me instantly of Carmine. "So they can't go in the sun, have garlic, or go to church either? Like us that way?"

"No. A Lethian's power is rumored to come from the goddess of forgetfulness, Lethe, and the river she's named for. They're almost always either of Greek or Roman descent and don't have the same drawbacks we do. But they don't get any extra powers like ours, either. And as long as they steal memories, they get to live indefinitely. And they have total recall."

"Maybe I remember talking to Stephanie about this. Or figuring some of it out. Or both." I clutch my head between my hands. Something's in my head, a sound like bees, disrupting my ability to remember anything. "Ugh. Why is the memory like looking through frosted glass?"

"Because Lethians wear away your knowledge of them. Individually and generally. Lose enough to one of them, I could tell you what they are a million times, and you'd still forget."

"Hold on. Before you say anything else." I take my own phone out, click on a voice recording app, then set it between us on the sofa. Maya repeats the information she already told me because she's just awesome. And then she continues.

"Thankfully, these Lethians are rare. But you've had this memory loss problem the entire time I've known you. I talked to Scott, and he says you've been like this ever since you and Kayleigh Killarney broke up in high school. So my guess is, you tangled with a Lethian back then. And now, every time you meet the same one, this affliction of yours gets worse."

"Makes sense." And it does. More than Maya could possibly know. "Is it safe for me to show you, or will you start losing memories, too?"

She doesn't answer with words. Instead, she holds out her hand. I think she means it'll all be okay. At least that's what I hope. But there's only one way to be sure, and it's not by being an impulsive jerk and taking what she offers without another word.

"Maya. Is helping me this way going to mess with your memories, too?"

"No, Tino." She taps one temple. "Sasquatch helped me put down the particular Lethian who did this to me years ago. This other one can't touch me, not through you or even directly. I'll be fine, thanks for asking."

"Okay." I reach out, holding my fingers a few millimeters above hers. "Thanks for helping."

Our hands touch.

All perception of my past since junior year in high school changes.

When we return to the present, I know exactly what to do for one brief shining moment. But I have to choose whether to record as much as I can or act. Maya chooses for me. She calls Zack Milano, tells him the address here, leaving me free to jot down the current essentials.

It looks like I've solved his case, after all.

I text Frankie so he's expecting Zack's arrival at some point during the day to get his case report. I listen to Stephanie, DeCampo, and Raven settling in for the morning in their basement rooms. And Maya and I stay in the laundry room, reading The Waste Land to each other while we wait.

---

At around noon, my phone beeps. Maya's fallen asleep on the sofa, so I grab a blanket and cover her up before checking the message. Zack won't be over until seven o'clock. But I shouldn't be surprised. The man's got a job, after all.

I scratch my head, wondering why this is might not be so convenient. Anyway, I can't figure it out right now. Instead of getting angry about my memory, I go into the basement's bathroom and have a shower.

There's soap in here, shampoo and conditioner too. Washcloths and towels sit on a shelf next to the relatively spacious stall. Terrycloth bathrobes hang from a rack on the opposite wall. There's no mirror, which doesn't bother me, of course. Something else does. Something's missing.

I've got a change of clothes here. One of the robes will cover me until I get to the room where I can put them on. My notebooks are here. I've got my phone. And I'm batting two of three here. My debt to Kayleigh is paid, and Maya will use her psychic powers to help me give Zack's memories back. The appointment with Gina is a half-hour after Zack's, cutting it close but still okay.

So what's my problem? What did I forget?

"Clothes, phone, notebooks, Kayleigh, Zack, Gina."

I shake my head. Maybe it's nothing. Turning around, I stick my head under the water, letting it flow over the top and back of my head. Then, I tilt back and let the spray wash over my face.

"Shitballs," I splutter through the deluge. My face. I don't have my greasepaints to make my appearance mirror-friendly. And there's one right over the mantel in both the dining room and the parlor, the only two rooms big enough to accommodate all the kids, Gina, Frankie, and me.

With Frankie taking Sarah and Levi out shopping for school uniforms today, there's nobody to run to The Belfry and get my supplies so I can literally put on my face. Scott's got exactly the same errand today over at Cranston West. And I'm not asking Esther, not with Frankie's stash of alchemical gadgets lurking who knows where in this house. No, I'm up Mirror Creek without a reflection.

Showers usually invigorate me like coffee used to. But this time I get out feeling like a slowly leaking helium balloon. I'll just have to be careful not to sit where I'll be seen in a mirror. But that's a lot to think about along with everything else. And who knows what kind of mental shape I'll be in after helping Zack.

I dry off, then drop the towel in the hamper and wrap myself in a robe. The hallway floor feels almost icy under my shower-warmed feet. It used to be a far less novel experience, having cold feet in the literal sense. But figuratively, it seems I'm always having reservations.

Good thing they aren't at a fancy restaurant because I can't eat food anymore anyway.

Now I'm getting down in the dumps again. This always seems to happen at some point no matter what fine mess I've gotten myself into. I pull on my clothes anyway.

At least I can multitask in my misery.

# CHAPTER EIGHTEEN

"You're cutting it close, Tino." Frankie raises his eyebrows, giving me a concerned look as he opens the door for Zack Milano.

"I know, but don't worry." I hold my hand out, welcoming Zack in with a gesture. "Maya and I will have this all set in time for our home visit with Gina."

"Home visit?" Now it's Zack's turn to raise his eyebrows. But he looks like a GQ model when he does this, unlike Frankie, whose charm is more quirky than anything else.

"Yeah, that's right." I shrug. "It's kind of what you gotta do when you're trying to get custody of an orphaned high school freshman."

"Wow, Tino." Zack shakes his head. "Now I've seen everything. You? A dad? Who'd have thought, huh?"

"Oh, I'm not one yet. We'll see how it goes."

"The second you're done down here, come back up." Frankie taps his foot on the top step of the basement stairs. "I need to do something about this door before Gina gets here."

"Will do." I realize Frankie is being cautious, not mentioning the supernatural in front of Zack. Which makes sense. Zack is a magician though he doesn't remember it yet. And if something goes wrong, we can't exactly tell him anything we wouldn't say in front of a regular mortal.

Frankie swings the door shut. I take that as my cue to lead Zack down the hall and into the laundry area where Maya sits waiting on one end of the sofa. I gesture at the middle cushion. Zack glances at Maya, then at me, and blinks. Clearly, he's wondering what I'm doing with a looker like her, but it's none of his business. No, I'm wrong. It's totally his business, or it will be once we get started with the psychic transfer of his missing memories.

"Have a seat." I'd forgotten that Zack Milano doesn't take hints very well. Either he doesn't get them, or he's one stubborn calabrese son of a bitch. My money's on the latter.

"Okay." Zack hitches up the legs of his khaki pants before resting his rear on the solid yet shabby sofa. "So you found someone? Is she a witness?" He jerks his thumb over his shoulder in Maya's direction.

Maya throws back her head and laughs. She's holding her sides, not merely giggling, but letting out an honest to goodness guffaw. I smile, feeling my face stretch to the point of a faint ache. Maya's laughter is a thing to behold, possibly one of the seven wonders of the world. Well, at least that's my biased opinion, anyway.

But it looks like Zack's got a similar mindset. He smiles too even though I know for sure he's not in on the joke. But Zack was always the kind of guy to take a good laugh wherever he found it. It's one of the reasons I never could hate him despite our long rivalry.

"Okay. That's enough from the peanut gallery." I shake my finger in Maya's general direction, grinning as I take my seat. "Let's get this show on the road."

"So, where was I? What was I doing?" Zack leans back on the sofa, clearly waiting for some sort of long-winded explanation from yours truly.

"I was going to tell you, but I think it's better for you to see it yourself."

"What's that supposed to mean?"

"It means I've got some unconventional methods that you don't understand right now. But don't worry, you will in the next few minutes." I smile, trying to reassure Zack and maybe myself. There's no guarantee this will work, after all. But I overdo it because of course, I do. He sees my fangs.

"Um, no." Zack leans forward, his heart rate increasing. I can tell his flight reflex is about to kick in.

"Yup." My arm darts out, my hand closing around his upper arm to keep him in the seat. "I'm honoring my commitment, whether you like how I do it or not. Trust me on this, you absolutely need this information back, and this is the best way to do it."

"What the fuck are you, Tino?" Zack's voice is higher-pitched than usual, tight and strained. By now he's realized the strength in my grip is inhuman.

"Don't worry." Maya's voice sounds soft and low, like she's singing a lullaby to a child. Maybe she is, after a fashion. "It won't hurt, I promise."

As her hand closes over Zack's wrist, I feel a thread. No, it's more like a presence. Some small part of Maya's consciousness runs through Zack and into me, then back toward her again. It's like she's strung all our psyches on a thread like beads. With Maya's special power, our minds connect, three parts into a whole. I never thought I'd be opening my consciousness to Zack Milano, of all people. And definitely not in this literal a fashion.

I sense Maya's presence the way you'd feel someone playing with your hair. It's gentle, yet firm. She all but tells me she's searching for something. The memories I absorbed from Zack's urn, of course. It takes her some time, and I feel her help me break through more than one smoky gray barrier of resistance. As the two of us move past that fog of forgetfulness, I realize it's not isolated to this one memory, which makes sense.

"Was this damage here from Carmine?"

"If that's what the Lethian plaguing you calls himself, then yes."

"And what about this?" I indicate another patch of scratched-off impressions.

"Yes. All the tampering in here comes from the same creature."

I've got nothing. Because from what I can sense with Maya's guidance in this section of my mind, the damage is extensive. Is this how a dementia patient feels when they see a scan of their brain, with areas misfiring and plaques interfering?

Was I terrified of the potential to outlive my friends before? No. Not compared with the idea of walking the earth indefinitely, unable to remember any of them. I feel a deep and compelling urge to walk back into the sun-proof room, lay down, and sleep forever.

"No, Tino." Maya's voice is like that feeling you get when you walk into your house after a long day.

"Why not?"

"There's plenty of time for that in a decade or three. Stay with me, please."

"Okay." If it weren't Maya asking, I might not have had the strength to resist the urge to hibernate. Or whatever it is vampires call it. But she wants me around whether I remember everything or nothing. That's more powerful than a room full of magicians preparing for war. Not that I've ever seen anything like that. Or want to.

Moments later, Maya finds what she's looking for. I recognize it, wondering how I could ever have forgotten. It's Zack's memory, the one I got from Mnemosyne's vault. And a little something extra, too.

I'm moving away. There's no other way to describe the sensation or what's happening. I'm going out of myself, and not like those crazy kids in the Flatliners movie. I'd freak out, maybe even rage, but Maya's there. She's the one taking me on this crazy trip.

And it's definitely a vacation that I hope doesn't turn permanent. Because the destination is Zack Milano's head. Or his memory, to be exact.

I thought this would be simple, the scenes from the urn transferred through Maya and over to Zack. Maya senses my unspoken question and answers it with an image of people talking on the phone. And I get it. It's already secondhand for Zack because I came between the urn and him. Too much might get lost if it's filtered a third time through Maya.

The inside of Zack's head is clearer than mine. I expected this because along with the memory from his urn, I also recall how few sat on the shelves from his psyche. Lucky bastard.

The abstract setting turns into a visualization of the three of us on the sofa in our bodies. Except I know this is imagined. We're sitting in a row, exactly like our corporeal selves except for one difference. I'm holding the urn. I wait for one of my companions to do something. But finally, I realize it's my turn to act. I hold up the vessel in my hands and offer it to Zack.

He reaches across Maya, and when his hands touch the earthenware surface, we're all thrown into the memory, exactly as I witnessed it while unconscious after the battle with Carmine. For me, it's just like watching an instant replay of a sporting event. But that isn't the case with Zack.

It changes his mind. And later, his life.

---

"Let go."

My hand and Maya's both drop from Zack's person at exactly the same time. I'd given it no thought, hadn't even realized what was happening until the movement is complete. But Zack does. He stands, turns, extends his hands. He looks like a preacher at a pulpit.

"Zack's back, folks." He's grinning like a lunatic. No, like a megalomaniac. Is he one? I hope not. Because we just gave him back an enormous and rare power.

"How does it feel?" Maya tilts her head, the way she does when she suspects one of the Pickering kids is lying.

"Amazing." Zack reaches down with his right hand, offering it to me. "You weren't kidding, Valentino."

"So, you understand now." I'm not asking him a question because I already know the answer. I'm only looking for confirmation, and maybe if I'm lucky, some sort of reassurance that I haven't gone out to help an old friend and brought back a monster.

"Oh, yeah. Absolutely." He jerks his hand once, asking with the gesture for me to take it again. I figure I'd better oblige. I don't want to wait and see if he'll make me by using his magical voice.

Zack helps me up but doesn't extend the same courtesy to Maya. Once I'm standing, he reaches in the pocket of his sport coat, bringing out a smartphone. He taps, swipes, taps again, and then my own phone beeps. I realize what just happened. He's paid me the rest of my fee. Which is as it should be. The last thing I want to do is haggle with the spell-singing magician. That seems like it'd be an effort in futility.

"Thanks, Tino." Zack tucks his phone away. "You've got no idea how much this means to me."

Before I can respond, there's a knock on the basement door. Frankie, of course. I glanced down at my watch and see I've got under a minute to go before seven-thirty.

"Okay, guys, it's time for me to skedaddle. You too, Zack."

"What about your lady friend here?" Zack waggles his eyebrows, clearly indicating he thinks Maya and I are an item.

"Oh, basements are my natural habitat. I'll just sit here and read." She grins. "I'm glad we could help you, Mr. Milano. See you around."

"I hope so."

I head down the hall, and my ears tell me that Zack is following me. As we head up the stairs and push through the door into the kitchen, we walk past Frankie. As soon as the door closes behind us, he slaps a sticky note on the cherry-stained wood surface. The door doesn't vanish, exactly. Instead, it changes color, texture, and shape to match the wall.

"Neat trick, kid." Zack smirks at Frankie. "Especially for a Lamb."

"Oh, cool, you got your memories back." Frankie smirks back at Zack, then punches him in the arm.

"You guys know each other?"

"Oh, yeah, sure do."

"That's news to me." I'm looking at Frankie, but Zack responds to my statement first.

"Yeah, it's news to me too, even if it's technically a little old." He grins. "But news is my business."

"The more things change, huh, Zack?"

"Yup." Zack opens his mouth like he's about to say something else, probably some snarky centuries-old inside joke that the Milanos might have had with the Pickerings for all I know. But the doorbell rings.

"Are you going to get that?" I put my hands on my hips and look at Frankie.

"Nope." He shrugs. "that's Levi's job."

"Okay." Zack may have gotten his memory back, but mine still sucks. I know Frankie must have told me the game plan at some point, but I can't for the life of me remember. "I think I might have to wing this, Frankie."

"No problem," Frankie says. "I kind of figured. And I planned for it, too."

"You really do think of everything."

"I know. Because I'm awesome."

The sound of sensible shoes echoes down the hall leading to the kitchen. I know what's coming, memory problems or not. Our interview. And I'm utterly clueless. The best I can do is follow my heart.

The door from the hall swings open, revealing Levi leading Gina Paolucci into the kitchen. He pulls a chair out for her at the large table there. I look down and noticed it's set for dinner, party of six. Shitballs. I'm going to have to sit through an actual meal with a social worker.

Before any of that happens, Gina spots Zack. Her eyes go wide and her expression changes from one of bored observation to starstruck in five seconds flat. I can almost hear the internal fangirl squee she manages to contain.

“Excuse me, but aren’t you Zack Milano?”

“Yes, I am, Miss?” He holds out one hand.

“Paolucci.” I nod, smile, and make with the introductions like the good Italian boy I am. “Gina Paolucci, this is my old buddy Zack Milano. Zack, this is Gina. She’s the sister of the best CSI in Rhode Island.”

“Pleasure to meet you.” When Zack takes her hand, he doesn’t shake. Instead, he lifts it and plants a kiss on the back of it. No, he's not into her. I know Zack's acting when I see it, and this is it.

"Oh, I never expected to—" Gina's blushing like a sophomore getting asked to the senior prom. "Um, I mean, how do you two know each other?"

"Theatrical competitions, mostly." I grin.

"Yeah." Zack nods. "Tino here was the only guy I ever worried about beating at State."

I'm about to go off on a long tangent about how that's not true, how we actually kind of hated each other. But Frankie passes by with the stack of spoons he's setting on the table and elbows my ribs. I take the not-so-subtle hint and keep my trap shut.

"And you still keep in touch after all that time?"

"Well, he's the first person I thought of when I needed help. He just finished working a case for me."

"Hmm." I practically hear the gears in Gina's mind start working again as she shifts back into Social Worker mode. "How did he do?"

"His services are outstanding. In fact, I'm not sure anyone else could have gotten me the information Tino did."

"If you don't mind my asking, what was the job?"

"Missing property." Zack pulls his sleeve up, revealing his Rolex. "I gave him two weeks, hired him three days ago, and the job is done already. He deserves a speedy delivery bonus, I think."

"Oh, definitely." Gina smiles, tucking a lock of long dark hair behind one ear.

If I were still alive, I'd be blushing by now. I'd also feel like I just got whiplash. Did Zack really go from frenemy to fan club manager in ten minutes, or am I missing something here? I stare at Zack, trying to figure out what just happened. Maybe nothing. Maybe I finally just know a guy who's kind of a big deal.

Sarah enters the room, an apron tied around her waist. Zack watches her over Gina's shoulder, still making small talk with the social worker. He's not looking directly at Frankie's sister but at her hands. Can he see that she's got magic? I keep forgetting to ask whether magicians can see that sort of thing and I've got no way to write it down now.

A buzzer goes off on the stovetop. Sarah puts on a pair of oven mitts and pulls a large Dutch oven out of the actual one. At least I don't need to stick my highly flammable arms in there. Sarah sets the hot dish on top of a trivet in the middle of the table, then takes the lid off. A heavenly smell rises up from the brisket, of potatoes, carrots, and brussels sprouts inside.

Now before you get on my case about thinking a non-Italian dish like beef brisket smells amazing, you gotta remember that my best friend Maury is Jewish, and I'd go to his house for dinner as often his he came to mine. This meal was a main feature on the Weintraub menu. Memories from my time coming up in Western Cranston flood my mind. A sort of peace comes over me as I remember how good I had it as a kid and how much I want that for Leora too even if I'm late to her particular party.

When I open my eyes and see Leora walk out from behind Gina, I smile. I thought the home visit would just be a glorified interview with the social worker. But watching Leora walk through the door to the kitchen at Pickering house, approaching the table to sit down for dinner, makes this place feel like home.

I almost cry. Yeah, I know it sounds lame, but I can't help it. Months ago, I used to imagine getting married, having kids, someday. But there are only somenights in my future as a vampire and definitely not any biological children. Homegrown parenthood isn't in my cards. This is my shot, I'm not throwing it away.

But it's not over yet. If I didn't think it would count against me with Gina, I'd kick myself. Why didn't I take Frankie up on his offer to eavesdrop on the Caprice's home visit? Oh, yeah. I've got a code, and I'm sticking to it. This entire evening would sit much easier with me if I had that inside information, though. But I don't, so all I can do is get through this interview by being the best man I can at this point in my existence.

"What a beautiful house," says Gina. "Very charming. Are these the original cabinets?"

"I wish. But no," says Frankie. "Here, let me show you."

Frankie and Gina chatter away about the woodwork and other features in the kitchen as though this meeting is with a realtor instead of someone from Rhode Island Family Services. Frankie is so natural at this sort of thing, it's almost uncanny. But that's as it should be. He was raised specifically to keep magician's secrets and ultimately carry out family business even if it meant his demise. Which it almost did, but that's another story. At any rate, he's not just an asset in this situation, he's a virtuoso.

Sarah joins in on the architectural discussion and love fest. She also has an air of practiced calm about her. This makes sense too, but for different reasons than Frankie has. Sarah is a powerful magician, which means she's grown up learning self-control along with the use of the power she must leash every day for her entire life. Of course she's kicking ass and taking names during this interview.

Levi's another story. He's a kid after my own heart, standing back and taking everything in before acting. The youngest Pickering child is also the most perceptive of the bunch. He notices everything, from the way Gina Paolucci tugs at her coat sleeves to the fact that Leora has no idea which seat is hers.

"Sit next to me, Leora." Levi pulls a chair out from the table and waves at it, smiling at his hopefully future sister. "I missed you."

"Thanks, Levi." Leora grins, sits on the seat, then lets him push it in. She's got excellent table manners for a kid who hangs out in a chicken footed hut with a salamander most of the time.

"Miss Paolucci, can I take your coat please?" Levi's smile won't win any beauty pageants. His front teeth show a slight overbite, and one of his bicuspids tilts to the left. Though his smile lacks symmetry, it's genuine almost to a fault.

"Oh, thank you." Gina can't help but smile back. "Yes, please." She shrugs off the garment and hands it over.

As soon she does, I realize this was a test. Nobody needs a coat in Rhode Island during the summer. Yes, the weather is unpredictable here, but not by that much. She wore a coat on purpose to see if anybody here had the empathy to offer to take it, and Levi helped us pass this test with flying colors when we otherwise might have floundered. Probably, he cares too much. I understand now why Frankie sacrificed everything to protect this kid.

As we all take our seats, I realize the flaw in all our planning. It's me. Let me explain because it might not be immediately obvious. This is a dinner meeting. We've got a delicious meal prepared to perfection. We've got a homey dining area with plenty of smiling faces. And we have a vampire who can't eat a single thing. Now do you see what I mean? Yeah. I suck.

"Don't think I forgot you, Tino." Frankie whisks the plate at my seat away, settling it on the stack inside the cabinet with the rest of the dinnerware.

"Um, okay?" I try not to blink. Everything should look normal. Real families are supposed to work well together, fit some sort of pattern or routine we haven't fallen into yet. So I have no idea what's going on.

"No brisket for you tonight." Frankie pulls a bottle of cranberry juice from the fridge rater. "I know it's hard when this is your favorite meal, but you've got doctor's orders."

"Oh." Gina's eyebrows make concerned little arches. "Have you been ill, Valentino?"

"Norovirus." Frankie shakes his head and clucks his tongue. "I told you to be careful with that case on the cruise ship."

"Yeah, no more spousal surveillance at sea, I guess." I shake my head, then look down at the glass Frankie's filling from the bottle. It's not cranberry juice, of course. It's blood. "Thanks Frankie."

"Recovering from a stomach bug doesn't mean getting left out at family mealtimes." Frankie smiles then takes his seat.

I had no idea how this meeting would ever work. But now, I think everything's going to be okay. And when Gina tells us Leora's hearing is the next night at eight, I'm confident it'll go well.

# CHAPTER NINETEEN

The Family Courthouse in the state of Rhode Island doesn't look like the ones you see on TV. Which makes sense since this isn't a criminal trial. All the same, I half expect to see the Caprices acting nervous when they show up. But they're not shaking in the seats they occupy. Of course, that probably has more to do with the fact that it's just Francesca and Sebastian with Carmine instead of Mr. Caprice. I'm wondering why he's absent but I probably won't ever find out. At any rate, their confidence does nothing to bolster mine.

I don't like wearing suits. You probably think that's weird. Especially coming from a guy who wore a police uniform for a handful of years. But uniforms are somehow both more comfortable and comforting than a jacket, dress slacks, shirt and tie. The uniform almost feels like it could stand on its own, with its authority stitched right into the fabric.

There's something I'm forgetting too. An item that goes with a uniform. But anyway, suits feel like every inch of material exists to hide an awful truth. One glance at Carmine shows me an exemplified idea of how respectable clothing can hide a monster.

I'm hiding plenty, myself. So I tug at the sleeve of blue gabardine draping my arm. Frankie picked it out, of course. I would have worn tan but apparently that's a borderline fashion faux pas in situations where you want to project an image of trustworthiness. Since my on-paper domestic partner seems to have a better handle on this sort of thing than I do, I go with his advice. But I still can't shake the feeling that I forgot something when I got dressed.

Our case is last on the docket. As I sit waiting through the custody adjustment hearing ahead of ours, I wonder if my unease in the courtroom contributed to Cranston PD passing me over for a promotion. Newly minted Detective Maury Weintraub is brilliant on the stand. I'm the opposite.

I know it sounds weird that someone with a big theater background like I have has trouble speaking in public. But there's a huge difference between pretending to be somebody else for entertainment and telling the truth, the whole truth, and nothing but the truth, so help you God.

I say a silent prayer thanking my Lord and Savior that this isn't a common occurrence for me. Being in court that is. Sharing space with enemies known or unknown unfortunately happens all too frequently. In my recent past, I've had the good fortune for some of those enemies to become either neutral or tenuous allies. My gut tells me that's unlikely here, no matter what happens.

Sitting in the row with me are Frankie, Levi, and Sarah. Zack showed up too, but he's seated behind us, clearly there for moral support. Or maybe he's got a crush on Gina, who definitely has one on him. In front of us, the social worker sits with Leora, who she's brought from the group home. Another woman, older than Gina by maybe twenty years sits halfway down our row of chairs.

This lady runs the group home. She looks exhausted from managing a house full of teenagers full-time. On her other side sit three other girls, all of them older than Leora. They had their hearings earlier this evening. The group home lady petitioned to extend custody from short to long term for these three girls. This woman provides temporary homes for kids in transition and then went long-term with these three. She's a bigger hero than I'll ever be.

I squint, peering at the three teenagers. Nope. Nothing magical or supernatural about any of them that I can detect. The sidelong glances they give Leora make sense, then. She's been in and out of the group home, bouncing between Pickering house and the Caprice's the entire time she's been staying there, after all. But there's more to it than that. I know envy when I see it.

The other three teens must wonder why the newest girl in their group home has two prominent families fighting over her. I wonder how long they've been in the foster system themselves. It makes me feel guilty, wish I could foster them all. Especially after Leora told me that foster kids keep all their stuff in black plastic trash bags, like the state as a whole thinks they're garbage.

I close my eyes, realizing that if I were still mortal right now tears would be running down my face like the river in the underworld where Carmine's power comes from. Maybe that's a form of wishful thinking. I'd like to be able to forget these three silently jealous girls and all the other children like them in the state of Rhode Island and beyond. But of course my big undead heart won't let me even if there's absolutely nothing I can do to make their lives easier for even a second.

When I open my eyes, I notice Sebastian Caprice staring at me. I stare back, intending a withering defiant glare. But I fail at that, of course, due to my soft emotional state and his youth. It's a good thing too. Sebastian's face could almost mirror my own. He's like the sympathetic eye of the storm, surrounded by the cold calculation of his mother and the brutal sundering nature of her Lethian henchman. The poor kid is just as much at risk as the displaced children in this courtroom. Having no home for your heart is just as destabilizing as having no home for your body.

"Miss Leora Kupala, approach the bench." The judge, an ebony-skinned man with pearly white curls circling the back of his head below the temples, beckons.

"It's your turn Leora, sweetie." Gina pats the girl's arm.

Leora stands. I watch her shoulders square then lift as she takes a deep and bracing breath. She sidesteps to get out from behind the table in front of her, then practically marches straight up to where the judge sits. She has to look up, not just because the bench is higher by design, but because she is still just a youth. When I'm working with her, Leora almost seems larger-than-life, but here she's dwarfed as though the court and its processes could swallow her whole if she isn't careful.

I can tell by the set of her shoulders and jaw that Baba Yaga is not with her in any capacity this evening. But that makes sense. I'm the one who promised the old witch she'd have no need of magical help in situations like this. It's up to me to be here for her through this and any other mortal protocols and processes until she's an adult with her own legal autonomy. I'm protecting and serving again, though in an entirely different capacity now.

I only hear bits and pieces of their conversation. Mostly, the judge asks questions and Leora answers them. She makes her declarations with a tenuous sort of confidence. But one exchange does stand out, mostly because I don't see it coming.

"And what do you think of the Caprice's house, Miss Kupala?"

"It's a beautiful place." Leora smiles. "Sebastian seems to have almost everything and anything he could possibly need." She glances over her shoulder, her gaze connecting with the Mafia Prince's.

"What do you mean by almost, Leora?" The judge raises one salt-and-pepper eyebrow. It's clear he's just as surprised as I am by her answer.

"I guess I mean that needs are important but what you want matters, sometimes. You know?" Leora glances down at her shoes, then back up at the judge, looking him full in the face. I know that stare of hers, have felt its weight and power firsthand.

"That's quite perceptive, young lady." The judge notes something down on a paper in front of him. "I suppose this whole conversation has circled the most important question. Since your space, companionship, and even your schooling would be equal either way, which house you want to live in?"

"If it's all the same to you, Your Honor," Leora glances over her other shoulder at me before continuing. "I'd choose Pickering house."

"And why is that?"

"Because of Valentino Crispo. He helped me when a lot of people wouldn't have. And also Frankie Pickering. I think they'll be fair without going too easy on me." Leora closes her eyes, shakes her head and sighs. When she opens them, tears stand at the corners. "They just want me to learn and work hard. Like my mom."

"I see. Thank you Miss Kupala." The judge waits for Leora to take her seat again, then beckons to Gina. "Miss Paolucci, approach the bench."

"Yes Your Honor."

The two of them put their heads so close together, I don't have any hope of hearing without burning blood. Because I'm in a room full of mostly humans, I don't want to do any such thing. I had a decent breakfast of blood warmed in the coffee maker, but Carmine's presence prohibits me from using it on what might be a frivolous endeavor. After all, we'll know in mere minutes what the judge's decision is whether I eavesdrop or not.

I glance at Carmine, wondering if my memory issues will resolve on their own with his demise or if I need to take other steps. Maya's mention of defeating her own Lethian gave me hope, though I don't have enough details to even make a plan let alone act against the creature who messed my mind up.

Waiting on the decision should be harder than it is. But the time passes far faster than I would have thought if you asked me two weeks ago. Maybe my immortal status is catching up with me. Or this could be at another symptom of my supernatural memory loss issues.

Movement catches my eye as Gina turns away from the bench. I watch her walk toward Leora, holding a hand out. Leora stands, shifting her weight from one foot to the other. I totally understand. If I were standing I'd fidget too. You could cut the tension in here with a knife but it would snap back and hit everyone in the face if you did.

"The court grants long-term custody to domestic partners Valentino Crispo and Francis Pickering."

The rustle of paper, clothing, and shuffling feet echo in the courtroom as Sarah and Levi get up and reach out to hug Leora. Frankie slaps me on the back, then pulls me in for a hug. I hug back, of course then stand and reach out to the girl who's been released from the embrace of her new foster siblings. I don't make out Francesca Caprice's murmured words. As our fingertips touch and I clasp Leora's hand, a cloud of slate gray smoke covers the lights overhead.

Carmine's unleashed his Hell. And it's every bit as terrifying as you might imagine.

The air fills immediately with gray fog. It's everywhere, covering everything like a burial shroud. I can't even see Frankie anymore due to its obfuscating effects. Sure, vampires can see in darkness but this isn't the same. The Lethian's smoke isn't the absence of light, it's a collection of small particles refracting it. And bent light isn't so easy for vampire eyes to handle. It dampens scent, too, so I can't even tell where anyone is with my nose.

I burn blood and rely on my ears instead. The good news is that works. But there's bad news. I haven't studied for this situation. It's like that time I sat for a final exam in college and the strung-out adjunct professor accidentally administered a test from the next level course. I'd heard of the material before, knew the basics of how it worked, but never experienced it.

The first thing I hear are the doors behind me opening, the ones from the hall. A set of footsteps patter in, familiar ones clad in high-heeled pumps. That's Stephanie. And another squeaks through on sneakers. Scott? And one more comes with an uneven tread and a murmured four-letter word. Esther.

After that, the doors slam shut. The lock engages with a sharp snick. Yeah, some of the cavalry made it inside. But that means they think this already fubar situation's about to go even further south in a supernatural sense. And there are way too many mundanes at risk here for a handful of supernatural vigilantes to protect.

Yeah, that's right. I only count Steph, Scott, and Esther. Sure, Zack and Sarah are magicians. But one of them doesn't remember how to be one and the other's currently crying on her little brother's shoulder. I can hear her. So it's up to me and my rag-tag band of misfit supernaturals to stop a dude who can wipe everyone's memory and change the outcome of this hearing. Because of course it is.

# CHAPTER TWENTY

I'm not even sure where anyone besides Leora is anymore. The fog's thickened enough to muffle sound so I've got no choice but to keep up by burning blood. I pat the front of my jacket with my free hand, then shake my head. My extra blood is sitting in the refrigerator back at The Belfry. Steph might have brought some but I can't get at it for now.

"Tino?" Leora's voice comes out all shaky. Her hand trembles.

"Right here, kiddo." I squeeze her hand.

"You've got to stop him."

"Okay." Of course she's talking about Carmine. Who else could she mean?

Despite Leora's confidence, I haven't got a snowball's chance in Hell of beating Carmine. The guy's used my brain as a punching bag for probably a third of my life. I'll never get the upper hand and I don't know how. Maya's not here and she's one of the only people I know who's defeated a Lethian. I'm flying as figuratively blind as I am literally.

And yeah, you heard me right. I'm flying through the air now. Someone pushed me but I don't know who. A friend might have pushed me out of the way. Maybe a foe's trying to kill me. But no, it's neither. I got knocked over by accident. At least I manage to hold on to Leora. She tumbles on top of me so I roll over, shielding her from the trampling feet coming toward us.

The three girls and the lady from the group home panic. I don't blame them because that's what I'd have done four months ago. Supernatural shit freaks mundanes like nobody's business and these poor girls and their guardian already have enough past trauma to cope with. The last thing they need is more. Of course they bolt for the judge's chambers.

"Oof!" My breath huffs out as a booted foot crushes my left shoulder. A second sneakered foot scrapes all the knuckles on my right hand. What feels like a loafer conks the back of my head, setting it spinning in a whirling vertigo. The last set of feet stomp my ribcage on the left, crunching bones. At least I don't have to worry about breathing with a punctured lung. I focus on not healing the broken bone or anything else. Because I need to reserve my blood for other stuff.

I burn some and speed up, which makes me faster than even the older vampires I know. They tell me it's another special talent of mine, like the vomiting visions only cooler and less painful.

I'm on my feet before I finish those thoughts. Yeah, I learned to kip up in a stage combat workshop. This puts me between Leora and the danger, which is more considerable than I originally thought.

The conjunction of oil and powder in my nose tells me someone in here is packing heat. Which is usually no big deal because regular bullets don't hurt me. But I also smell wood along with the usual scent of a loaded weapon. Expensive-smelling wool, Chanel Number Five, and leather back it and I know now who's holding the gun loaded with wood shrapnel rounds.

I thank God. Francesca Caprice can't see any better than I do right now and has no other supernatural senses to help compensate. And I know exactly where she is and I can tell she's moving her firearm in an arc like she can't get a bead on me.

So I dash straight at her.

Nothing significant is in my way. I leap the chairs like they're nothing. My hand wraps around her wrists like a pair of undead manacles. She chuckles, pushes up. I realize what I forgot this evening. My Kevlar vest. The gun goes off.

I fall backward, rigid as a pine board. Staking sucks.

"Carmine." Francesca's voice rings through the fog, more piercing than the bullet in my chest. "Here."

My mouth doesn't budge when I try to snark off. But I should have known. Stephanie warned me. Staking equals full and total paralysis.

I'm going to die. Or effectively cease to exist if Carmine eats the rest of my memories. And I'm not even going to go out with a biting meme-worthy insult.

The touch at my temples is both foreign and familiar. I'd shudder or struggle, probably both. But the stake stops me. At first.

My shoulder's shaking, hitching up and down in time to a tune someone's humming from what feels like a million miles away. And my forearm's twitching, too. I'm practically screaming at my arm with my inside voice, telling it to slap at the smoky tendril I can't see but know is here to drink my entire identity away.

But my brain doesn't save me. It can't, not against this enemy. This unexpected music does.

"Tarantara, tarantara!" The humming's expanded, grown into a number from Pirates of Penzance.

I blink.

"All right, we go," Zack's warm baritone fills my ears. "Yes forward on the foe—"

My forearm lifts off the floor.

"Yes, forward on the foe—"

I sit up, my jaw moving, voice joining his. I'm not doing any of this.

"We go, we go!"

And I'm off the ground now, fangs out in the fog. I see the tendril now, a thicker rope of smoke in the miasma leading straight to the Lethian attacking me.

"Yes forward on the foe—"

I'm not moving or singing on my own. I'm like a marionette and Zack's voice is my string.

"Yes, forward on the foe—"

"We go, we go!"

And I stumble into Carmine, bat his hands away with movements not my own. He gapes, eyes and mouth wide, like a fish. Zack repeats the refrain and I slap, kick, punch in time to Arthur Sullivan's bygone tune.

Italian moms always threaten their kids with the wooden spoon though my mom never actually used it on me. Right now, with the way Zack's brandishing me at Carmine, I feel like that spoon. But no. I'm too floppy. More like a loaf of crusty bread.

I want to laugh but can't unless Zack makes me. He doesn't. Instead, we repeat half the refrain. I wonder what my old rival's tactic is. He's not the combat type so I seriously doubt his choices right now. I take my ears off the catchy song and finally hear what's happening in the rest of the room.

The rest of the bystanders are escaping into the chambers behind the bench, including the judge, Gina, Levi, and Leora. Sarah protests, insists on staying to help. Esther argues and I hear them scuffle by the door.

I think about what I'd shout if only the damn stake wasn't next-door to my ticker. A moment later, Zack belts out a "we go" with me and my heart throbs twice. The paralysis eases enough for me to move my face and neck. And I can talk. Finally.

"Sarah, leave!"

"But—"

"Now!"

The door slams behind her. A shimmer of green flashes in the fog. By its light, I see Esther spraying it with a re-purposed Windex bottle.

And the fog's been dissipating since Zack started using me to attack Carmine. But he's not the only one who's been fighting the all this time. Scott's grabbed Francesca, has her by the arms so she can't reach for any more of the guns holstered under her suit jacket. She's dropped the one she used on me.

Stephanie's moving her arms in a syncopated, almost ritualistic pattern. And then, she adds her voice to the impromptu performance, kicking backward to an earlier verse in the piece and directing it at Carmine.

"Go to glory and the grave!"

I'm dismayed to learn that though Stephanie can carry a tune, her voice is nothing special. That doesn't stop her from adding the song to whatever she's doing. My sire's been negating the Lethian's memory-stealing energies. I can see it now though her energy isn't like what my magician friends do. Instead, it reminds me of the lighting back in the memory vault.

Maris said Mnemosyne owed Stephanie a favor, paid it off with my ticket into the vault. And here she is, earning herself another one. She opens her arms, sweeping them to indicate each of her allies in this room. Everyone picks up a line.

"For your foes are fierce and ruthless," Scott snarls.

"False, unmerciful, and truthless," Frankie waves the open Zippo like he's at a rock concert.

"Young and tender, fucking toothless," Esther spits a colorful improvisation.

"All in vain their mercy crave." That's a voice I haven't heard lifted in song before. But I recognize it anyway.

Sebastian Caprice.

Before Zack can utter another line in the song, we hear a thud behind Carmine, like an ax hitting a log. The Lethian throws his head back, Adam's apple bulging until I think it'll burst. And it does, with the copper-tinged blade of a punch dagger protruding from it. It's absolutely as gross as you might imagine. Worse, actually.

Black water erupts from the wound which reminds me of the time I put a soda can in the freezer and forgot about it. This mysterious Lethian liquid smokes like something toxic. And maybe it is. I know right away it's nothing like blood. Everyone gets out of the way, avoiding the spray. Except for Sebastian.

He steps around Carmine, standing directly in front of the dying monster. And he holds his hands out like he's a kid running through a sprinkler on some nicely trimmed lawn in the suburbs, gory dagger still in hand.

As the water or whatever it is gushes out of his neck, Carmine shrivels. At least, his skin does. What happens to him is something like watching time-lapse photography of a jerky dryer. Except strips of meat for jerky don't have a skeleton, aren't still trying to stand upright. The Lethian's flesh can't hold his bones together and he topples. His limbs scatter across the floor like tree branches after a windstorm.

Sebastian's on the floor, hands in the water, as though he's trying to touch every drop he can. At first, I don't notice that he's oblivious to the smoke rising from it. I only grok what I'm actually seeing when I notice who else can see what I see. Stephanie. But not Esther or Zack.

I lock gazes with my sire. She's got a lot of explaining that she'll never end up doing. I'm sick of that. I narrow my eyes, about to cut loose on her now that the most imminent danger has passed. But she shakes her head and points at the twists of lost memory curling through the air.

More than half of it is coming straight to me. My eyes widen and my jaw drops. Some enters my mouth, fills my nostrils. Flashes of past days and nights fill my mind. But trying to isolate them is like trying to grab dandelion seeds after they've blown off the stem. Almost as soon as they hit, they're gone.

No. Not gone. Assimilated. And there's more coming.

I smile. Finally, no more mind sieve. I try to remember the night before Kayleigh broke up with me when I would have woken up in Doctor Maris's ICU. But the memory's still gone. My face falls harder than cement overshoes in Narragansett Bay. I drop to my knees, more because Zack's attention isn't on animating a partially paralyzed vampire than anything else. But the shards of dashed hopes don't help.

"Oh, Tino." Stephanie lifts my head, rests it in her lap. "I'm so sorry."

"No." Zack's shaking his head, which is surrounded by more of the smoke. But I see what's wrong. It's reversed direction. "Come back. Why didn't it work?"

"It did." Sebastian Caprice stands up, the smoky memories that belong to us flowing into him. He brushes off his hands.

"What did you do?" Francesca struggles in Scott's grip again, almost breaks free, too. Because this is a mother's fury right here and not the protective kind, either. "Sebastian! Answer your mother!"

"I did this for you." He blinks. "To make us powerful."

"How dare you!"

"But this is what you wanted!" Sebastian's voice cracks, his shoulders trembling. "You wanted magic in the family and I got it."

"Not like this." She hisses out the last word. "You fucked up. You're worthless to me now."

Sebastian's silence twists his face into a mask of despair. I mean, what do you even say to something like this, even if you've heard crap like that all your life? And the poor kid absolutely has, too. Our conversation in my office makes way more sense now.

"No, you fucked up, lady." Frankie snarls, brandishing his Zippo. "Prepare to be worthless, bitch." His other hand holds the remainder of the alchemical sticky notes. I'm worried he'll throw the book at her.

Because Frankie's own abusive parents said shit like this to him. And for all intents and purposes, they killed the person he once was. Saying this situation triggers him is an understatement. He's got murder in his eyes, blood on his hands will follow. And I can't move a muscle. Well, maybe I can. My voice isn't magically enhanced like Zack's, but I've got another kind of power. Friendship.

"Somebody stop him!" I glance up at Stephanie, over at Zack, toward Esther, then Scott.

The werewolf is the only one who responds. Which makes sense. Scott's young enough to lack Stephanie's obligations, Esther's fatalism, Zack's indifference. The kid's all heart. And he doesn't have a stake in his ticker like I do. He drops Francesca's arms, gets between her and Frankie.

I forget about Sebastian. But I'm trying to save Frankie Pickering, not Francesca Caprice.

Before Scott can enact whatever he's planning, kid Caprice raises his hands. It's the same posture all the Lethians took on the urns in Mnemosyne's vault. Slate gray smoke shoots from his fingertips, wrapping around his mother's head like a laurel wreath. She screams like it's a crown of thorns.

"You're working for me now, Mother." Sebastian squints like he's taking a difficult exam. His arms tremble and sweat beads on his forehead. His lips thin down to a pressed white line. The moment she succumbs to his new powers, her eyes roll back in her head and she stops screaming. But the tension in his pose remains.

This isn't easy for him. Becoming a monster never is.

Scott takes a step toward the mother and son. Thank God, someone's trying to stop this. But Frankie slaps a sticky note on the werewolf and he freezes. I grind my teeth.

The door unlocks and opens. Not from the Judge's chambers, from the hall.

"Sorry we're late." Raven saunters through the room, Maya following behind them.

"Uh." I glance from the newly arrived vampires to the scene playing out in front of me. "Help?"

"Sebastian Caprice, let's make a deal."

"In a minute."

"No, now. Before your new minion there turns into a husk." Raven's smile shows off all their fangs. "Trust me, you don't want what's behind door number one."

Maya's hand sprouts claws.

"Oh." Sebastian finally eases back on the memory-drain. The fog around his mother dissipates, though one thin tendril remains, like a leash between a dog and its master. "Okay. I'll deal."

Raven waves Maya and Frankie away. They both back down though it takes Frankie a moment longer than I'd have liked.

One thing I can say for this kid, he knows his priorities. I'm not sure I can ever trust him as an ally without whatever iron-clad agreement Raven's currently cooking up. But I think that's going to be a moot point. Raven and Sebastian hunker down in the corner with

Francesca Caprice sitting insensibly nearby. I hear them mention hunters, Providence, vampire courts and school.

Before I can burn more blood to listen in better, I'm distracted by Maya.

"What's wrong with him?" She sits on the floor beside Stephanie.

"Staking rounds." Steph gestures at Francesca, then the hole in my shirt. "He needs help I can't give him."

"Yeah, that fucking bitch can go suck a tailpipe." Esther squints at Maya's clawed hand. "You ever do any fucking surgery with that freaky ass thing before?"

"No, not really." Maya smiles up at the alchemist. "But there's a first time for everything."

"Here, use this fucking shit before you start." She holds out a baggie filled with green ointment.

"Okay." Maya doesn't take the bag. Instead, she pierces the plastic with her claws. They come out with a green and gold tint.

"Wait." I try squirming out of the way as I realize what's about to happen. "Surgery?"

"Just a simple unstaking, Tino. Don't worry." Maya's smile lets all the tension out of my neck and most of my face.

But my jaw clenches hard enough to shatter my teeth. I'm still on the verge of freaking out. I might have the biggest crush on her ever, but the last thing I want is for Maya to literally touch my heart with the business end of those claws.

"Shh." Stephanie rests her fingertips on my temples. "Don't think about what's happening now. Remember."

And I do.

---

The memory scraps that escaped me rest in a tattered pile like autumn leaves. A handful of them rise, lifted by a stiff breeze. As they fly toward me, I understand. These are the ones with the most substance left. The ragged pieces still on the ground are tattered beyond recognition.

This is happening in my head but it's absolutely real. I don't get much back but it's all precious. A prank pulled on a bitchy stage manager with Maury in college. Ma's face as she opens a Christmas gift. Scott and Esther, yukking it up at the office. Leora and Sparky in Baba Yaga's kitchen, daring each other to put ghost peppers in the stew.

The largest threadbare remnant drifts toward me, restoring the last of my stolen memories; it's Stephanie herself, telling me a plain and simple truth.

"I'm not just a vampire, Valentino. I serve a higher power. If you survive these early nights, you'll do the same."

"What if I'm not worthy?"

"You are. Remember, everybody is until they prove otherwise."

"What if I forget?"

"I'll remind you as many times as I must, though my means may be frustratingly cryptic. It's no more or less than my duty to do so."

---

When I open my eyes, Maya's sitting beside me, holding wooden shards and a metal slug in her now normal hand.

"Hold him."

"Is he raging?"

"No."

"Here."

My chest gapes and stings, the pain draping most of my body like an agonizing sheet. The world is anguish until something cold but sweet passes between my lips. Blood. I swallow it all and there's a sensation like it's flowing into my chest, numbing the hole next to my heart.

I sleep.

## CHAPTER TWENTY-ONE

"So Sebastian's the new Boss?" I wince as Maya pulls away, dropping the tiny wooden particle into a metal bowl.

"Yeah. Not the same as the old boss." Raven shakes their head. "Thank God for small favors, right?"

"Right." I try to shrug but it hurts too much.

"He's a Lethian now, but he's got a conscience, unlike his mother and that Carmine creature." Raven sighs. "Even if it's for the best in the long run, I'm conflicted about the whole transition there."

"Yeah, me too. That's why Zack and me didn't get everything back like you and Sass, right Maya?"

"Right." Maya nods. "The Lethian's power has to die with it. But Sebastian stole it instead, along with memories Carmine hadn't fully digested yet."

"Well, you can ask him to return the more recent ones once he's fed." Raven twirls a pencil between their fingers. "The details of those negotiations are yours to make, however."

"Uh, that sounds risky," I say, like Maya's continued open chest surgery is safe as houses. It's not.

"It would be under average circumstances." Raven drops a wink.

“My negotiations are a cut above. The details of our contract muzzles Sebastian to an extent. He can’t feed on any of us.”

“By us you mean who, exactly?”

“Everyone in Pickering house.” Raven holds up a finger for each name. “Stephanie. Zack, Esther, and Scott. All their families. And your parents, Tino.”

“Wow, Raven.” I blink. This is so huge there’s got to be a great big catch. “Thanks. How much do I owe you?”

“Consider it insurance. I’m protecting my Valentino-shaped investment.” Raven chuckles. “And I want to hire you.”

“Oh?”

“Yes. I’ve got a problem with my brother.” They sigh and shake their head. "It's about time we got proactive where he's concerned."

“Whitby.” Maya rolls her eyes, then drops another wooden shard into the basin.

“Tino’s already got an excuse to associate with him, thanks to Stephanie.”

“Things are going to get complicated.” Maya’s claw shrinks down, merging back into her finger.

“As long as it’s not shot with wooden shrapnel rounds levels of complexity, maybe I’ll survive.” I stare at the bowl.

“You always do.” Maya wipes her hands with a pre-moistened cloth from my first-aid kit.

“I mean, I’ve got things to do, people to help.” I snort. “Kids starting high school.”

“You have help with that.” Raven grins. “Besides, Leora’s got her head on straight. She won’t give you much trouble.”

“I hope those aren’t famous last words.” I turn my head to look at the person stepping into the doorway.

“Hey, nobody’s allowed to get this morbid without me.”

“Hi, Frankie.”

“Hi yourself.” He takes one glance at my open rib cage, then cuts his gaze away. “I’m not gonna ask whether you’re comfortable, but can I get anything for you from the office or The Belfry?”

“Nah, I’m good once the sucking chest wound closes all the way.”

"Why hasn't it, though?" Frankie raises an eyebrow at the wall which is really the only place he can look and not see gore.

"I'm still checking for shrapnel and removing any I can find." Maya hasn't taken her eyes off me this whole time. She's the opposite of squeamish.

"Oh." Frankie gulps. "Why?"

"We can't let it heal over and leave even the tiniest sliver of wood. Otherwise, Tino's staked instantly if he gets hit the wrong way."

"Makes sense."

I'm not exactly comforted by the fact that Frankie now knows this bit of vampire lore and instantly ask myself why. He's seen some shit and survived it, has been nothing but helpful to me and my friends. But tonight's adventure proves he's not okay no matter how much he promises. Attacking an enemy who's already contained crosses a line none of the rest of us would consider.

I understand now. My on-paper domestic partner needs professional help and can't exactly go out and randomly pick a shrink from his health plan's recommended list. But I've got an idea and for once I don't instantly forget it.

"Hey, no offense Raven and Maya, but I kind of need to talk to Frankie in private for a minute or three."

"Do what you must." Raven extends the crook of their arm at Maya. She takes it and they leave the tiny cell, shutting the door behind them.

"Okay, I flipped out back there at the courthouse." Frankie hangs his head. "I'm sorry, Tino."

"Listen, thanks for the apology. But I don't want that."

"Uh, then what is it?"

"Give me my phone."

"Why?"

He hands it over with the question, at least. I'm relieved. He still trusts me. Which is a good thing because I'm alone in the room with him literally baring my heart.

"I'm helping you." I Google the number I need, then dial. It takes seven rings but she answers.

"ICU."

"Doctor Maris, hi. It's Valentino Crispo."

"What do you want?"

"I've got a friend, the type who knows all about my trip through the vault. He needs help, the mental health kind."

"No."

"What?"

"Doesn't work like that. He's got to be the one wanting help, not you."

"Gimme." Frankie holds his hand out. I drop the phone into it.

"Make it snappy, friend of Crispo."

"Doctor, my name's Francis Pickering and I need a psych eval. Probably outpatient treatment, too. I'm taking care of kids and I know my parents didn't raise me normally. I need help."

"I'm transferring your call. Doc Young's unconventional but you can tell him everything."

Frankie waits on the line, then makes an appointment in September. I can't believe the summer's going by so fast. But I guess fighting hunters, Deep Ones, and Lethians, paying three debts, and coping with the aftermath of a vampire society power grab makes the time pass. Or something.

When he's done on the phone, Frankie hands it back. He says nothing, just nods and avoids looking at the hole in my chest before leaving the room. We don't need to speak. I just demonstrated how I won't let him fall farther than he already has. And yeah, I get it now. Frankie needs a constant reminder that someone sees him and cares. Once he's out, Maya and Raven come back in.

"Stephanie fixed this for you." Raven's holding my favorite mug from The Belfry. It's full of warm blood with a reusable straw sticking out on top, elaborately twisted into the shape of a smiley face.

"Oh, send her in. I want to thank her."

"Can't, she left already." Maya sits beside me, peering into the pit of my chest.

"For what?"

"She's on a date."

"Really?" I blink, finally understanding what my sire was up to in my apartment when all this started. Restoring memories. "With Sasquatch?"

"No." Raven's laugh is nothing nice and I don't blame him once he drops the name. "Whitby."

"Shitballs."

"Drink some of that, Tino." Maya points a finger, the claw extending down and out from its tip. "I think I'm finally getting the last piece."

"Thank God." I gulp blood down, then set the cup aside and close my eyes.

And I've actually got loads to be thankful for. As Maya works, Raven gives me a full account of what transpired while I slept my injuries off.

Sebastian Caprice teamed up with Stephanie to cut and splice memories of Carmine's attack from the mundanes present in the courtroom. They doctored other supernatural details, too. Esther used a potion, making me invisible for long enough to get me back to Pickering House. Sebastian took care of Carmine's remains and brought his mother home.

Sparky never showed up at court or here afterward. That's okay because I couldn't have asked him to deliver the urn with Esther's missing memory to her anyway. But for once, this task isn't a debt I owe. Instead, it's a kindness from one friend to another, just like all the little things Esther's done for each of us. I can make sure she gets it after I recover.

Sarah and Levi got Leora settled in upstairs. All the kids will be down sometime tomorrow because we've got to talk about school. Which will give me maybe the next four hours to rest and heal. Something tells me nothing about their high school experience will be normal. But that's okay. I'll handle it.

I always do.

# COUNTING STARS

## SUPERNATURAL VIGILANTE BOOK FOUR

*Undead stars still burn.*

*Still adjusting to recent changes, Tino Crispo, vampire PI, saddles himself with a new case. An ailing friend charges him with investigating a series of mysterious assaults.*

*Rhode Island's youngest vampire has to balance his work life and new domestic responsibilities. With his extended supernatural family counting on him, he'll need help. Which is in short supply.*

*Tino's biggest advantage is his circle of friends. But the threads he follows in this case seem connected to some of his closest allies. Who can he trust?*

# CHAPTER ONE

I'm at the Belfry, which is what I call my apartment, getting ready to head out for the evening. The shower I take is piping hot, even though we still have dog-day summer temperatures at the beginning of September in Rhode Island. There's method to this madness.

I want to feel as alive as possible.

Before you go thinking I'm depressed or have some kind of nerve disorder, you've got to understand that I'm not technically what qualifies as a living creature anymore. I'm Valentino Crispo, vampire private investigator. But tonight, I'm just a man on a mundane and personal mission. Which is why I'm also singing in this shower.

Yeah, I've still got it. I'm talking about the pipes in my throat, not the ones delivering the fine spray warming my undead flesh. No, don't tell me that everyone thinks they sound like Ed Sheeran when they're either drunk or in the bathroom. I've got over a decade of experience and training as far as performing arts go, which is more than I can say for being vamped.

Too bad there aren't any meetings for the newly turned. Getting up in front of a room full of sympathetic strangers to say, "Hello, I'm Valentino, and I'm a vampire," might make me feel worlds better. But the supernatural is secret, so that's impossible. It's also why I'm preparing to do the next best thing. Acting.

Well, hopefully. I'm auditioning for a production of *Nine* with the Cranston Community Troupe, the only Community Theater production with a rehearsal and production schedule that fits my nocturnal nature. So, there are no guarantees, but I'm gunning for at least a spot in the ensemble. Nah, who am I trying to kid, here? I want the lead role. And if that's going to happen, I need to get out of the bathroom and get dressed.

I'm toweling off, not bothering with the mirror. Can't see myself in it anymore, which was a huge shock at first, but something I'm getting used to after four months. Going anywhere in public where there might be mirrors and mortals means I need to wear a full face of makeup. Even though I've had all the theatrical practice with applying the stuff, it's not so easy to put it on when you can't see yourself. Technology helps. Digital cameras don't have the whole mirror problem for people like me.

I wrap the towel around my waist and head into the big room that makes up the rest of my apartment. Seconds later, I'm back inside the bathroom, pulling on the pajamas I discarded before getting in the shower. Because I've got an unexpected guest in my apartment. Again.

When I emerge, Stephanie McQueen is still sitting at the tiny breakfast table, drinking warmed blood from my favorite mug with the local news rag The Cranston Call in front of her. Typical behavior, not surprising. I really should expect her to turn up more often, especially after she lived here on and off when Rhode Island's entire vampire court got deposed this summer.

And before you get the idea that she's my girlfriend or something, ew. She's definitely not. Steph is the vamp who turned me and more like an eternal mom-friend than anything else. Well, if mom-friends were mysterious, highbrow, and five foot nothing.

"Tino, what in the world do you think you're doing?" And judgmental. Should have mentioned that part.

"Um, trying to get a shower, get presentable before going out." I shrug then head to the dresser to get my clothes. "You know. In my apartment. With privacy, like a normal person."

"Oh, goodness, no." She shakes her head, looking up from the newsprint under her dainty hand. "I'm referring to this." One manicured nail taps a circled entry in the Classifieds.

"Um." I definitely haven't forgotten what it says, but I pretend to be in one of my brain-fart modes anyway. "Huh?"

"Valentino, vampires shouldn't put themselves in the literal spotlight like this. It only leads to trouble in the long run."

"I'm more than a little magnetic as far as trouble's concerned, Stephanie."

"All the more reason to refrain from activities like this." She curls her hands around the mug of blood.

"Look, you definitely know how boring things can get for us. I only want to stop that from happening." I'm lying.

"Oh, Tino. I wasn't turned yesterday." Stephanie makes that clucking noise. You know the one—the disappointed mom sound. Yup, even the ones with fangs do that, and it makes you feel just as lousy, too. "You've still got guilt over everything."

I have a choice here. Accept that she knows better and confess my true intentions. Or keep right on lying because sometimes Stephanie's got the wrong idea about modern times and how to navigate them. It should be an easy choice, but ever since the night down in the catacombs under Providence, followed by helping create a literal monster in the courthouse, I have trouble deciding much of anything.

But refusing to reply is a choice, too. I set the clothes on top of the dresser, fill my second-favorite mug with blood from the coffee maker, and sit across from my sire in my pajamas. Her eyebrow is sky high, but instead of commenting, I just drink my breakfast.

"Are we having a conversation here?"

"It's too early in the evening." I feign a yawn.

"So, it's a regression back to your adolescent years." She sounds like a shrink from the Freudian era. Which she might have actually been, for all I know.

"Whatever." If she's going to treat me like I'm sixteen, I'll play along and act like it, dammit.

"Be aware that this is dangerous." She taps the circled listing again. "For you personally, among other things."

"This is what I love about you, Stephanie." I try smiling, but my mouth rebels and makes it a sneer I hope comes across as ironic. "Your plain and simple yet shockingly cryptic warnings of imminent danger."

"You shouldn't need the details, Tino." She shakes her head and picks the newspaper up, folding it. Then, she sets it aside to reveal something in the middle of the table. "But if you insist, read this."

And of course, she had a book hiding under the newsprint. I know the basic story, which is why I never actually bothered reading the dog-eared and yellowing used copy I've owned since middle school. Any theater geek worth his salt knows the one about the guy in the mask. *Phantom of the Opera* is a classic of late twentieth-century musical theatre as well as classic literature.

"Every time I play along with your surprise book club suggestions, something bad happens."

"Have you considered that perhaps it's your actions that predicate my suggestions?"

"Can't you ever give me a straight answer about this kind of stuff?"

"Most of the time, no." Which is some of the plainest speech out of Steph's mouth the entire time I've known her. Because of course, it is.

"Okay." I shake my head and grab the book. "Look, I need some privacy, and then I'm going out."

"To your audition."

"Yeah."

"I'm not stopping you from making your preparations." Her hands curl more tightly around the mug, slender fingers failing to cover the theatre mask design on its sides.

Stephanie's gazing down into the red liquid inside the cup instead of at me. Which, I suppose, must be her idea of giving me privacy. But I'm Catholic and too modest for that, so I bring my outfit into the bathroom. I try not to be too put out over her refusal to take my hints and leave. I need the mirror in there to apply my makeup anyway.

With four months of practice, the whole routine takes about fifteen minutes to literally put my mirror-friendly face on. Flesh-tone greasepaint fills in the visage that wouldn't otherwise show in the mirror. I make use of an eyebrow pencil and mascara that match my hair. A bit of contouring with other shades out of my stage makeup kit gives me the finishing touches I need. My hair's already been taken care of with dye. With Just For Men, no one can tell you're a blood-drinking creature of the night.

Most vampires I know avoid actual mirrors as much as possible. And that's fine for them, because things like shiny cars don't give us a problem. But mirror-loving me needs help in this department. Yeah, that's right. I've always been more than a little vain, and I like looking at myself. Nobody's perfect.

When I get out of the bathroom, I catch Stephanie doing the weirdest thing I've seen from her. She's bent halfway at the waist, rummaging in my fridge. Half a pot of warm blood is still in the coffee maker, too. I clear my throat and she slowly rises, turning her head until she's giving me the frostiest fish-eye ever. But I'm not falling for the shame game this time.

"What gives? Whitby's court not giving you enough for DeCampo and the rest?"

I'm talking about the deposed vampire king, our friend Raven, and Maya, who all unlive with Raven's mortal-yet-magical family in Warwick.

"You know how much they give me, Tino." And she's right. We get a supply because of an agreement she hoodwinked me into paying for, after all. For two months in a row.

It's important to stay on the good side of the vampire authorities for a number of reasons. One of these is, there's some kind of age test to determine who's the king, so it's almost always the oldest and most powerful vamp in the area. Which of course means you don't want to piss that person off. But the other reason is being able to get enough blood to survive without freaking the mundanes.

Feeding directly from people is seen as barbaric nowadays because it pretty much blows our cover completely. Back in the day, Vampires used to have human allies in the know they fed from in exchange for knowledge and aid, but modern times are different. Someone in Providence has an understanding with the blood bank, so we get donations the hospitals can't use for whatever reason. Or at least, the court and the king do.

Us rank-and-filers need to offer favors in exchange for a monthly allotment. And that's where things get tricky. DeCampo and Raven don't dare attend the monthly Blood Moots because they're both older than the guy who stole the throne. They used to be the head honchos so hanging around with the new king and his brainwashed entourage is a risky proposition. Besides, they can't exactly beg for blood when De Campo's claiming to be king of Warwick. Technically, he is, I guess, because the five of us are the only vampires there.

Whitby and his enforcers only invite Stephanie and me to attend meetings if Whitby wants something. They do let us pick up a reasonable monthly allotment of blood, however. Eventually, the pretender to the throne will have to invite us to all of the Providence shindigs. Vampires are supernaturally bound to follow the rules, and the new guy's about to run out of excuses for barring me and my sire entry on what's supposed to be a blanket invitation. We won't be biding our time for much longer.

"Hey Steph, can you maybe wait until after my audition before we hit Whitby's fake court up for more blood?"

"It's not that simple, Tino." Stephanie pauses. It's one of those stops where I can tell she's finding the right words. "How do I put this? We need another source that better fits certain needs."

"Okay." I shrug on a sports coat over my t-shirt and grimace. The role I'm going for is a guy who'd wear that kind of thing, but I'm definitely not. In case you couldn't tell, I'm not a fan of method acting. But I'll dress for the part I want if it means getting my foot in the door.

"'Okay' is all you have to say?"

"Well, I can go to Kent County Hospital later. Ask Doctor Maris if we can make a deal, maybe."

"Maybe isn't good enough, Valentino." She gazes at my fridge like it doesn't contain the long-lost family member she'd been searching for. "This is too important."

"Look, I'm new. Not sure what to do or how to finagle it anyway, but at least I'm willing to try."

"You do have a point."

"Right. So give me some tips on what to do and I can help, okay?"

"I'm afraid I can't do that, Tino." She shakes her head. When Stephanie says she can't help, she means it. "But perhaps Maya can. I already arranged for her to meet you."

"What?"

"Valentino, I know your ears work perfectly." She taps the newspaper, then drinks the last of the blood in my favorite mug. "She'll find you here. I'd best be off. I've got obligations of my own, you know."

"Uh."

"There's not much more I can say."

And she's out the door. Stephanie's cryptic speech is the real reason I have a hard time dealing with her. But my mind goes back to something Old Man Fergus Fitzpatrick said to me a couple of months ago. Vampires are only bound by the vows they make. So what demented cat has got my sire's tongue this time?

I'm not sure I want to find out. But with my luck, I'll probably have to wrangle with it in the near future anyway.

# CHAPTER TWO

I pull my car up in front of the playhouse that belongs to the Cranston Community Troupe. It's dark out, thank goodness. The streetlights outside are the new LED kind. No weird sodium orange coating everything, which is a nice touch. Rhode Island loves its arts community, so these lights are probably courtesy of some grant or other available to talented individuals or creative organizations in the state.

There's a sign pointing the way to the stage door, so I head in that direction. It's not the first time I've been to an audition here, though the last time was during the summer between high school and college. I got in, and *Grease* was supposed to be my last show. But here I am again.

I stop walking in the middle of the parking lot. Maybe Stephanie's right, and this isn't a good idea. There are so many things on my plate right now, how can I find time to play the lead in a show like this? I mean, I'm a foster dad to three kids, technically. What if Leora, Levi, or Sarah have some kind of emergency right before I've got a performance?

"Tino?" I turn at the sound of the unexpected voice.

"Zack. Old pal."

No, he's more like a situationally benevolent frenemy. I am not happy to see this guy right now. Yeah, we just buddied up and mended fences after I did a case for him. But he can only be going up against me for this role. And every time we compete, he wins just about everything. Zack Milano's not an asshole, he's just more talented than I am at performing arts. And supernaturally. Yeah, he's a magician. The most powerful kind, too.

"You're seriously auditioning for *Nine*?" He chuckles. "Aren't you a bit, uh, rusty for that?"

"Yeah, it's been years since my last appearance. But I practice all the time. So I figure why not? It's only one of the most challenging roles for a baritone. It'll be a piece of cake."

"Same here." Zack flashes his perfect bleach-whitened smile. Okay, maybe it's not bleached. He always had uncannily good looks. Which is why he's Rhode Island's favorite news anchor, of course.

"Cool." It's not.

"See ya inside!" Zack Milano paces away, throwing a wave over his head as he goes.

"Well, this is frigging great." I roll my eyes at no one and nothing. If only Maury was here. We always used to have a laugh or three about Zack's uncanny good luck to make ourselves feel better. Which would have been mean, I guess, if the dude wasn't so pompous about it all.

But Maury's at the hospital, getting chemo. I hang my head and stare at my shoes, watch them pace the rest of the way over cracked and tarred asphalt. My best friend's fighting for his life and I'm having catty thoughts about Zack Milano. One of these things is more important than the other. Fuck cancer. I'd punch it in the face if I could.

I look around for Maya before pulling open the door because Stephanie said she'd be there, and my sire hasn't lied to me yet. But there's a first time for everything, I guess. Or maybe Maya didn't want to come and watch a bunch of borderline amateurs belt out tunes on cue.

But when I follow the signs leading from the green room to the audience seating, I see her sitting in the fifth row, a reasonable distance away from the mostly female crowd waiting to audition. And of course, Zack is sitting in the fourth row, completely turned around and chatting away like they're old friends instead of acquaintances who met one time over the summer.

I tell myself that Maya, definitely an older vampire than I assumed at first, isn't going to fall for a mortal guy, magician or not. But Zack's so…well, how do I put this? He's pretty. His dark hair sits neatly in glossy waves without a hint of early gray or receding hairline. The traces of laugh lines around his eyes have near-perfect symmetry, like the rest of his face. He escaped the fate of the classic Roman schnoz, and his skin's that healthy olive mine used to be in the summers before I got turned. Maya laughs at whatever he's saying, too.

Once again, Zack Milano's positioned himself to make a play for who and what's important to me. Which, to be fair, he's used to getting. But I just went through trying to avoid that from another direction in my supernatural life. Yeah, I'm going for this role and this show as a form of escapism, so no wonder I almost turn around and leave.

"Tino! Hi!" Maya stands up, smiling and waving as she navigates the row to move toward me.

We meet in the middle, and she takes my hand. Which is sort of a big deal because she's got touch-telepathy. The image she gives me of Zack as a vainglorious peacock having a bucket of water dumped over his head is just too funny. I bark a laugh, even though the real deal is stepping up behind Maya.

"I was just telling Maya here that she'd be a perfect Carla." That's about the smarmiest backhanded compliment he could have given her.

Zack's talking about the lead role's mistress, who does a literal strip-tease on stage and is the reason this is an evenings-only production.

"And I said I'm not here to audition."

"Well, you ought to."

"Can't carry a tune in a bucket."

"Carla's a dancing part anyway. And you've got the figure for it." Ew. Smarmy, like I said.

"Two left feet, too." Which I happen to know is a blatant lie. Maya's got more grace and physical coordination in her pinkie than I do in my entire body. And I'm a fencer, so no slouch in that department, either.

"Oh, well." Zack glances along the rows of other ladies there to audition, rolls his eyes at me, then saunters off in their direction.

He's got a smirk that I think I know all too well. I guess he's going to hit on one or more of them. Except for the gal with the asymmetrical haircut who looks like she's falling asleep in her seat. But my gut says there's more to the woman's drowsiness than that, maybe something magical. I shake it off because more than likely, I'm just jealous of Zack and trying to distract myself from confronting that emotion. Again.

"That guy, seriously." Maya shakes her head. "Incapable of taking a hint."

"Captain Oblivious?"

"Pretty much, yeah." She peers toward the table set up in front of the first row, where the directors sit. "Great magical power, itty-bitty emotional intelligence. You going for the same role as him?"

"Yeah. This show's only got one part for a guy." I jerk my chin at the clipboard sitting on the edge of the table, pen perched atop the paper on it. "I'd better sign in."

"Well, break a leg."

"Thanks." I wave at her as I saunter down the aisle toward the table in front.

I print my name on the paper in the column for men right under Zack's. He's the only other guy here, too. That's common with community theater since it's not for pay, and acting still isn't considered a manly man's hobby. But I never cared about that. It's fun and challenging and worth the effort.

My watch says it's eight-thirty on the dot. I'm about to sit, ready to wait through all the ladies auditioning. And then, the director gets out of his chair and claps his hands. Practically right in my face.

"Okay, Guidos first!"

I don't take this as some kind of crass insult aimed at Italians like yours truly. The lead role in *Nine* is a dude named Guido Cantini, a film director experiencing a professional and personal crisis. Which, if you've been following my stories, you'll know I relate to in spades.

"Let's hear you first." The director points one fleshy finger at me then glances down at the clipboard. "Crispo. You're up."

I've got my song practiced and my music prepared. There's no orchestra pit here, or even a piano because they only do one musical per year. It's a file on my phone because Cranston Community pipes all of its backing tracks in digitally.

The director jerks his wobbly chin at a mini USB cable, so I plug my phone into it. He picks up a pencil and a legal pad to take notes on. After that, I turn my back, instantly second-guessing the act of taking the three steps up to the theater's stage. And that one spark of doubt lights me up with an internal inferno of mental self-harm.

I close my eyes and stand there, waiting for the director or one of his peers to tap play on my phone, trying to act natural. But nothing's natural about how I feel at that moment. My lizard-brain turns on, its voice hissing at me from the dark cavern of my self-doubt. *Who are you to get up here like this when Zack Milano's in the front of this house, waiting his turn? You were nothing compared to him back in high school. He's a local celebrity, and you're nothing now. He'll get this role. Don't embarrass yourself.*

The worst thing about that sickening voice in my darkness is, I agree with all of it. I'm about to walk back down those steps, hustle my ass the hell out of Cranston Community Playhouse, and never return to this theater or any performance art ever again. But the only thing that could stop me from doing that happens.

The music starts.

I open my eyes, wanting to see who's condemned me to perform up here like the hack I am, tormenting the eyes and ears of everyone present.

It's Maya. Her finger hovers maybe an inch above my phone's screen. And I can't even be mad at her because the tiny smile she gives me banks down the flames of my shame until my flickering nervousness is a warmth I can work with. She makes a half-turn, then takes the nearest unoccupied seat.

The director and his assistants catch a glimpse of her face, and their expressions soften. Sure, I freaked out and forgot to press play. They almost all noticed. But Maya's special. She makes every gesture, no matter how small, look like the most natural thing in the world. And she's on my side.

They must all think I planned to have her do this. For all they might think, it looks like a demonstration of method acting. And perfectly in line with both the musical I'm auditioning for and the song from another show by the same composer I'm about to perform.

And that, my friends, is one way to stomp on the neck of impostor syndrome. With help.

*Where In The World* is a song from the other musical about the *Phantom of the Opera*. Not Weber's version, Yeston's. Who, as I said earlier, is the same guy who wrote *Nine*. It's all about how Erik, the Phantom, seeks the one perfect voice in the world.

Vocally, it's almost an exact match for my range. I always nail this song in that way, but I've never been able to capture the feeling, that desire for something as intangible as a voice that just might finally put an upswing on an otherwise dismal life. Until now.

My ears are better than a human's, but nowhere near as discerning as the Phantom's are described to be. A beautiful voice is nice, but there's no way it counts as the epitome of anything in my book. Fortunately actors don't need to be quite so specific with our inspiration as, say, illustrators or poets. The script or the lyrics aren't ours to play with. The emotions are another story.

The words I sing from Erik's perspective are next-door to desperate. Because he doesn't want a pretty sound to soothe his ears. He's had every iota of peace stripped away from him, and in the opera's absence, Erik realizes he wants more than mere existence. This is the first time in all the years I've mouthed this piece that I've understood the truth about the Phantom of the Opera's truest fundamental motivation.

He wants salvation.

As I sing, my truest feelings spill out with the notes. Recent ones. Because I can't get relief in that department, as a Catholic vampire. An old werewolf warned me about this eventual development, telling me that coping with the divide between faith and my new normal is a do-or-die proposition.

And now, this song brings a light into the catacombs where emotions surrounding our misadventures with the Deep Ones and a kid's turn from mundane to monster lie buried. And they're doozies. Because of course, they are. Guilt over preventing two suicides and a fall from grace isn't something a good Catholic guy can find absolution for on his own.

But you don't have to take my word for how profound an effect the matters of my undead heart have on my performance. Neither do I, because energy on stage is a two-way street. The audience reaction is all I need. Maya, who's in the know, puts one hand to her cheek, eyes widening. Something changes in the air between us as our eyes meet. I'm not sure what that means yet, but it's clear she's touched.

The director is nodding, having dropped his pencil in order to just sit and listen. His assistants have followed suit. Most of the ladies waiting their turn grin, and a couple begin to give me the eye. I don't care, because I saved the best reaction for last.

Zack's jaw looks practically unhinged. He's heard me sing probably hundreds of times and this specific song at least a dozen. I must have really kicked it up a notch. Or maybe plural notches. Before he starts catching flies in his open mouth, my old rival shuts his trap. He's grinding his teeth hard enough for me to hear them over the music, too.

Not that most of the other folks in the room have that problem. Vampire ears for the win.

The director stops me after thirty-two bars. Which is good because usually they only let you do sixteen. I descend from the stage in better shape than I stepped up to it. My feet barely feel like they touch the ground. Unplugging and picking my phone up off the table feels natural and easy. I think I have this role in the bag.

Zack side-eyes me as he heads along the aisle to take my place up there. There's a look on his face that I don't like one bit. But I get to sit next to Maya, so I don't care. She's clasped my hand in both of hers, something that lets her share thoughts, feelings, and experiences with me. She doesn't do any of that vampire woojie power stuff this time. Instead, we just sit there together, almost like a regular mundane couple.

Zack's music starts, and I can hardly believe my ears. He's doing the big audition no-no, singing a piece straight out of the musical itself. Yeah, it's *Only With You*, which the show's main character sings at all the women he's known. Biblically.

And he's nailing the shit out of that motherfucker. Excuse my Esther-inspired language here, but there's really no other way to describe Zack's performance. Yeah, okay. I improved a lot due to time, experience, and perspective. But over the seven-odd years since I competed against him, Zack's moved light-years beyond even that. Rediscovering his vocally-based magic powers means he'll never lose a role he wants again.

Was I feeling cocky because the director let me squeak out double the amount of usual audition time? That feeling dies on the vine. He lets Zack finish the entire song. And afterward, the guy gives my old rival a standing ovation and asks him to stay and give feedback while the ladies try out for their roles. After that, he calls a break and approaches the seat where I'm frozen in a mortified state of shock.

"Nice job, Mr. Crispo." The director extends one hand. "I'd like you to come back next year. I think the show we're considering then will have a more suitable role for a fellow with your particular talents."

"Um, thanks?" I reach out and make a grab at his hand with my free one. I almost miss.

He shakes while I just go along with it. The grip and motion are firm, reassuring. I think he's being honest. Maybe. But all the same, I'm being dismissed, and it stings like a nest of wasps. He lets go and heads back down to his little coterie of assistants. Politics in the theatre world for the lose.

# CHAPTER THREE

I don't remember getting up under my own power, but I am fully aware that Maya's the one escorting me up one aisle, along the side of the seating, and back out through the stage door. Because of the connection between our clasped hands, I feel her match my exasperation, but something in the flow of her emotions peels away all of my embarrassment at losing to Zack. Again. Once we're in the parking lot, she lets go of my hand and speaks.

"Tino, I'm glad you didn't get that role."

"Huh?" I lean against my car. She joins me.

"From where I sit, that Guido character is a nasty piece of work. Let the other guy have it. The role fits him, not you."

"Hmm." I cross my arms. "But it's acting. I could have pretended to be more of a jerk than I already am."

"Yeah, but you're one of the best people I know. For someone like Zack, playing a part like that isn't much of a stretch."

"You barely know the guy."

"Right. But you do."

"Oh." Right. That psychic touch stuff Maya does works both ways. She must have gleaned some of my old memories while we watched Zack's audition. "Well, thanks, Maya."

"Any time, for you Tino." Her smile's brighter than the stars but pales in comparison to the light in her eyes.

I let my arms down and lean in slowly, putting one hand on the car between us as I turn toward her. I raise my eyebrows, about to speak. She reaches out and takes my free hand, letting me know in no uncertain terms that the answer to all of my unspoken questions about us is yes. Her chin tilts up, and we kiss for the second time since we first met. And this time, it's real, not a sham to put Whitby off both our cases.

Tonight, there's no imminent disaster looming over us, no vampire court waiting for us to be formal and stiff and proper, no obligations for at least another hour. We get in the car, drive the five minutes back to the Belfry so we can spend that time together.

---

I put a bag of blood on because when we get to my apartment, we realize we're both hungry. Maya's sitting sideways in the comfy chair, barefoot, with her denim-clad legs draped over the arm she's not leaning on. I hand her a mug of blood, which she holds in one hand while flipping through Stephanie's little homework assignment with the other.

Yeah. We're vampires, and one of the drawbacks is getting distracted by anything puzzling. But that's okay. We've potentially got eternity to explore romance, after all.

"Interesting."

"Oh, no." I grin as I pour myself a cup. "You said the i-word."

"I'm going out on a limb here and assuming your sire told you to read this."

"Yeah." I shrug. "No point, though."

"Really?" Maya blinks.

"Really. Not gonna do it."

"Why?"

"No point, like I said." I shrug, taking a seat at the breakfast table. "I know both of the musicals backward and forward."

"I'm not a theatre geek like you, but this is one of my favorite works of fiction." Maya takes three long gulps of blood. "There's a difference between Leroux and Weber, Tino." She shakes her head. "Even Yeston didn't get everything right. Erik and Raul aren't the same men in either musical that they are in the book."

"That's what they tell me." I gulp some blood. "But I want to save my time for more important things. Like you."

Maya leans one hand against her cheek, flipping pages with the other as though looking for something. After a moment, she finds it and runs one fingernail along the lines of text as she reads.

"But you would have lots of fun with me. For instance, I am the greatest ventriloquist that ever lived. I am the first ventriloquist in the world!" Maya rolls her eyes. "What a catch." She snorts. "But seriously. Does Erik sound stable and logical to you?"

"Well, no."

"Not exactly the tortured but calculated genius from Weber, or the sensitive savant from Yeston."

"Okay." I shrug. "So what is this about Raul?"

"In Weber, he's a hopeless romantic. In Yeston, he's a clueless but harmless dude-bro. But on the page, he's just another judgmental little toe-rag."

"Read me something about that?" My eyebrows go up as I take a smaller sip from my mug.

"Okay. Here." She clears her throat.

"*Alas, madame, alas,*" Maya puts the back of one hand on her forehead and rolls her eyes. "*I believe that Christine really does love him! But it is not only that which drives me to despair; for what I am not certain of, madame, is that the man whom Christine loves is worthy of her love!*"

"That's just a little melodrama."

"Oh, but then Christine says," Maya recites, "*It is for me to be the judge of that, monsieur!*" She sighs. "Poor liberated woman. I say this because Raul goes into full mansplaining mode."

"Can I see that?"

Maya nods and hands over the book. I scan the page, reading about how Raul up and assumes Erik's romantic gestures mean the

Phantom's a villain and Christine's a fool. As though real men don't do romance, and women aren't allowed to make up their own damn minds about who they prefer to spend time with.

"Wow." I blink.

Maya makes an ironic little cluck. I totally understand why.

"They cut that the hell out of both musicals." I shake my head. "What a douchebag, Raul."

"Right." Maya grins. I'm not entirely sure why. My best guess is that she's dealt with that sort of attitude from a man before. Men plural if she's this sick of it, probably.

"Hey, I promise not to talk at you or make assumptions about your own feelings, okay?"

"Thanks." She chuckles. "You're a prince."

"As long as I'm not that guy," I point at the book. "Call me whatever you want." I waggle my eyebrows like a total geek.

"It's okay to say thanks, Tino."

"Okay, then. Thank you, Maya. You're amazing."

"Thanks!" She chuckles. "See? It's easy. Am I right?"

"Always."

"Anyway, really." She closes the book and taps the cover. "You should read this when you get the chance."

"I'll do that." I check the clock. "But it's time to start heading to the hospital."

"Oh?"

"Yeah. I'm going over to see Maury. He wants to talk to me about something, says it's important. Also, I want to have a chat with Doctor Maris." I finish my tepid beverage and start filling the pockets of my coat with stuff I'll want for the rest of the evening. That includes an extra bag of blood, my phone, and some plastic bags with gloves, because I don't have my PI certificate for nothing.

"Couldn't you leave that stuff in the car?" She eyes the bagged blood.

"No way. Scott's picking me up from outside the auto shop in about twenty minutes. It's about time I dropped it off for repairs." I shrug. "Should take a few days to fix that, er, damage."

"Yeah." Maya doesn't bring up the reason it needs work. I hit everybody's favorite supernatural blogger with my car.

"I'm glad he's okay." And that's true. Sass seems like a stand-up cryptid, even if he occasionally spends time with my sire on the down-low. Alone. In dark rooms, for reasons I don't understand. But that's none of my business.

"Nothing much can harm Sasquatch, Tino." She smiles.

"Right." I'm not sure about that. But she's right when it comes to physical harm.

"What's up with Doctor Maris, anyway?" She drinks the rest of the blood in her mug. "You told me she's a centaur, and that she's got something to do with the goddess Mnemosyne."

"That's right. And also all I know." I pause, not sure whether Stephanie's kept Maya in the loop about whatever the blood supply problem is. "The plan is to go in and ask her for help."

"With your memory?" She raises an eyebrow. On our last adventure, I got most of my memories back. There's still a little damage, just enough to be annoying instead of downright debilitating.

"No, I'm not going to see her for myself. This is more like actual mundane doctor stuff. Because someone important to us has that problem."

"Yes." She sighs. "DeCampo. With the blood."

"Stephanie says she can't tell me what's going on."

"Neither can I." She hangs her head. "I would if I could. I think you'll be able to figure it out anyway, Tino, but I made a stupid vow to keep that secret."

"Oh. I understand." And I do. For a vampire, word is bond. I might be new at the fangish life, but I'd never ask Maya to break her word just because I'm a curious cat. I've got sleuthing skills, and I'm not afraid to use them.

"Do you want me to come with you guys?" Maya's eyes tilt up, peering at me from beneath her lashes. "I've got all my usual business done."

She's talking about helping out around Pickering house. A building inhabited by a mix of vampires and magical teenagers tends to need more than a few small repairs and Maya's handy.

"Nah, I'll meet you back at Raven's place." I point out a duffel I packed full of costuming and supplies. "And bring this over there too. I'm staying through the day in the basement again to help Frankie and the kids with stuff. We can hang around too, watch the laundry dry. Maybe read more of this." I wave the paperback.

"Good call." Maya stretches, then downs the rest of her beverage.

I could stay here with her all night, and our psychic touching earlier means I know she's of the same mind. But vampires get hyper-focused. We'd distract ourselves out of keeping the rest of our obligations, and other people are counting on us.

"How's everything going over there with DeCampo anyway?" I keep the conversation going. "He's kept himself scarce every time I've been over lately."

"You'll see for yourself when you get there, I guess." She turns her back, then heads to the sink and rinses the now empty mug.

"That doesn't sound good." Watching her perform such a simple task with her supernatural grace softens what she's implying. That the king's not all right.

"It is what it is." She rinses the soapy mug along with her hands.

"How's Raven holding up?"

"Stephanie didn't say anything about them?"

"Really, Maya?" I watch her set the wet drinking vessel on the drying rack. "Answering with a question?"

"Back at you."

"Okay, I understand." And I do, after everything I went through at the end of August. We vampires are bound by our word. Literally. And since Maya's older than me, she's made more promises than I have. Finally, something occurs to me. "Hey, Maya?"

"Yeah?" She turns, adjusting the golden bangle on her right wrist.

"Does Steph give me all this reading to do because she can't tell me what's up directly?"

"Yes, that's exactly right." She reaches up, drying her hands on the towel hanging above the rack.

"Oh, boy." I shake my head, then lower it into my hands. The corners of my mouth twitch.

"What's wrong?" Maya's hand is on my shoulder. I place one of mine over it and look up.

"I'm just trying to imagine what I'll have to do if I ever turn someone in the future." I snort. "Probably make them a mixtape. Or a YouTube playlist. Maybe tag them in a series of memes on social media."

"We use whatever method works." She tucks a stray lock of hair behind my ear.

"Makes sense." And it does. "'Whatever Works,' the motto of House Crispo."

"It's served you well enough so far." She smiles, then crosses my one-room apartment to grab the bag of gear I asked her to bring with her from the coat tree by the door.

"Which isn't saying much." I shrug and rise to my feet. "Maybe it should be 'Too New To Know Better.'"

"Valentino." She shakes her head, but she's smiling. "You're landing on your feet most nights, even if you don't always realize it."

"Thanks." I smile back, striding over to put my arms around her. "For everything."

We kiss. Maya slips her hands into my back pockets, and I chuckle at the quirky, affectionate gesture. After we part, she hoists the bag over one shoulder before heading out the door.

It's not until I've dropped my car at the body shop and climb into Scott's rusty blue pickup that I notice my girlfriend left a gift in my pocket. It's one of those flip-top notepads, the kind mildly forgetful people like me ought to carry around. I've got a few of those, but this one's different. It's fancy, with its own refillable mechanical pencil, refillable pad, and a moleskine cover that snaps shut.

I hope I can remember to make good use of it.

# CHAPTER FOUR

Scott waits in the elevator with me, the pit of my stomach dropping as it rises to the fifth floor at Kent County Hospital. I'm here on business with Dr. Maris, but first I need to see Maury Weintraub. He needs to see me too.

When you're in the hospital for a weekend of chemotherapy treatments, it's probably reassuring to get a visit from your best friend and his tag-along kid neighbor. But that's not the only reason we're here. He called me asking for a favor, and I love Maury like a brother, so I'm here.

The elevator dings and the doors open, rolling back slowly to reveal a white hallway, atypically calm. But I know the visual impression of peace here is only that. My ears pick up an auditory account of the true chaos on this oncology unit.

Nurses argue with doctors about bedside manner. Family members of all ages huddle tearfully in the all-denominations chapel, giving vent to thoughts and feelings they don't dare express in front of their ailing kin. And I recognize one of these voices. It's Mrs. Weintraub, Maury's mother.

I take a left instead of a right, heading away from all those faithful-yet-distressed voices and toward the end of the hall where Maury's room is. I probably should visit the chapel myself. It's religious but not consecrated, which means maybe I can actually go in there and get my prayer on.

Being a Catholic vampire sucks, although I have to admit I don't know what it's like for vamps of other faiths. Maybe they can go into their houses of worship, or maybe not. It's possible some of the undead set have established alternate and structured ways to worship. I won't know unless one of them decides I'm worth telling about it. Anyway, I'm more concerned with captaining my own faith. And I can visit the chapel some other time.

I knock on Maury's door even though it's open. It's a courtesy, and something I wish more medical staff would do. Even with debilitating or life-threatening conditions, people deserve a basic level of privacy and respect for same. I don't like the idea that anyone on the payroll here might not extend that to my best friend. But, I can either assume the worst or hope for the best. After everything I've been through recently, I prefer the latter.

"Come in." Maury's voice is louder and brighter than it was last time I spoke to him. He must have gotten some rest, then. Good.

"Hey, buddy." I step through the doorway and up to Maury's bedside. Scott shadows me, saying nothing. "How you doing?"

"I can't say I've been much worse than this." Maury shrugs. "But what do you expect? It's cancer, not a trip to Disney World. You know what I'm saying?"

"Yeah, I get it."

"So, what's up with you?" Maury squints, peering at me from behind the horn-rimmed glasses he usually replaces with contacts. "You look different. Like something happened over the last couple weeks."

"Auditioned for *Nine* at Cranston Playhouse." That's all I can tell him. Maury's not in the know about my undead status, and I'm not allowed to tell him.

"Oh, yeah?" Maury grins. "How'd you do?"

"Zack Milano was there."

"Shitballs." Maury pouts briefly, then lets out a chuckle to let me know he's goofing around. But the laugh turns into a cough. "Dammit," he croaks.

I pat Maury's back while Scott heads over to the bedside table, pours a glass of water, and hands it to him. I keep rubbing my friend's back, waiting for the fit to subside. Before I can say anything, another voice rings out from the hallway.

"Slow breaths, Maur." The light click of heels accompanying the raspy flat-voweled voice is like a traffic signal, telling me to move over for Mrs. Weintraub or risk getting run over.

"Mama," Maury sips water from the cup in his hand. "I'm okay."

"No, you're not. Not yet." Maury's mother is a tiny woman, just an inch or two over Stephanie's height. Somehow she manages to be thinner and more birdlike than my vampire sire. I always wonder how Mrs. Weintraub managed giving birth to a baby who grew up to be six foot two.

"Mama, we talked about this."

"All the books say you gotta keep a positive attitude with cancer." Mrs. Weintraub shakes her head, a gesture that contradicts her words. "You'll never beat it if you start thinking you can't."

"Whatever you say, Mama." Maury's expression is familiar. It's the one he always wore when our captain down at Cranston PD wanted more paperwork after we already turned in our reports. I get the feeling he's been through this conversation with his mother, or one almost exactly like it before. It's turned into a routine, and not the knee-slapper kind you see on *Saturday Night Live*, either.

"Such a mensch, my boy is." Mrs. Weintraub looks up at me, smiling. "But you already know that, Valentino."

"Hi, Mrs. Weintraub." I lift my hand and waggle my fingers at her, feeling like I'm about ten years old again. Hanging around with your childhood friends and their parents tends to take you back in time. Scott stands there silently, possibly feeling like a preschooler, for all I know.

"Hey, Mama, can you go down to the cafeteria and maybe pick up some snacks?"

"Oh, you have an appetite?" The light in Mrs. Weintraub's eyes goes from a feverish and desperate gleam to a glassier variety of warmed-over hope. "Of course, I will."

"Get yourself something too while you're there, okay, Mama?" Maury grins, but the expression stays on the lower half of his face, getting nowhere near his eyes. "I can't remember the last time you had anything to eat."

"All right, kiddo." Mrs. Weintraub turns her back and walks halfway to the door, then looks over her shoulder and smiles. "Love you."

"I love you too."

I listen to her heels click away down the hall. Mrs. Weintraub overdresses for pretty much every occasion. She always says that if you dress better than you feel on a crappy day, circumstance improves, and then you feel better. Maury's mother is a Jewish woman of faith, which means she's a big believer in the power of positive thinking, being the light you want to see in the world, and doing good wherever you can.

It's a mindset you can't blame her for clinging to under the circumstances. That last part is already built into my psychological architecture anyway. For a moment, I consider adopting it for Maury's sake. Because more positivity can't hurt, right? But the werewolf stops me.

"Tino, we need to talk." Scott taps me on the shoulder. His nose is so wrinkled up I'm worried he's going to vomit right there on the floor.

I breathe deliberately through my nose, letting my vampire senses tell me what Scott shouldn't and Maury won't. A positive attitude can hurt in this case.

The cancer is terminal.

I close my eyes and exhale, holding in the bloody droplets forming at the corners of my eyes. I can't focus enough to make human-seeming tears like Maya taught me. Not at a time like this.

"No, we don't need to talk, Scott." I open my eyes and turn, leveling a withering glare at the teenage werewolf.

"But Tino—"

"Don't 'but Tino' me, or you can take your butt the hell out of here." I put my hands on my hips. Scott is one of my most reliable friends, but Maury's my oldest and best. I'm going to defend him, no matter what or who threatens him or in what way. Giving him a diagnosis the doctor hasn't yet is no better than walking up and slapping him across the face.

"Okay, boss." Scott steps back, but he rolls his eyes. Then he leans one shoulder against the wall, crosses his ankles, and stands waiting. For what, I don't know.

"What's up with you guys, anyway?" Maury's glance moves from me to Scott like the ball in the tennis match.

"We've been working together too much on all the PI stuff, is all." I shrug. "A little time and distance might be in order if we can ever get a break."

"So business is booming, huh?" Maury chuckles. "See? I said you were a natural."

"Yeah, and if only the chief thought so, we'd have stayed partners."

"That's the way his cookie crumbles, I guess." Maury's lopsided grin carries me back to days spent in the tree fort back behind the ball field we never played on.

"I don't know, Maury." I blink, banishing the bygone image. "I miss working with you."

"Yeah, me too. The plan was womb to tomb, right?"

"Yeah, but *West Side Story* doesn't have a happy ending, so I don't know why we expected the whole career thing to go any differently." I lock gazes with him. "And now this cancer."

"You're too smart, Tino." Maury looks away, staring at the analog clock hanging across the room from him high on the wall. I wonder what he's using it to count right now.

"Yeah, but you're a freaking genius."

"Stop complimenting me so much, or my ego will grow to Zack-sized proportions." Maury closes his eyes, resting them for a moment before continuing, "Anyway, working together is why I called. Or working, anyway. I want to hire you."

"Huh?"

"There's been a series of…I guess you could call them assaults. In

Cranston and the surrounding." Maury closes his eyes, tilting his head. "Weird stuff, women waking up with no memory of how they got where they are, and they're not filing reports." He opens them again. "You understand."

"I'm sure the PD has someone good on this, though, Maury."

"They do but not a genius like me." He drops a wink. "Or even a too smart guy like you. So I want you to look into this serial whatchamacallit."

"You should be focusing on getting better, not sending me out on an investigation with no charges filed."

"Like I said, it's weird, Tino. Hinky."

"Oh?"

"Yeah. The victim last night was Kayleigh Killarney. She holds grudges like a pitbull with lockjaw." Maury gestures at a manila envelope sticking out of his satchel. "Everything I've got on it is in there."

I realize that the only way Kayleigh, who grew up in a house full of psychic hunters, wouldn't let the police do their job is if she or her family think the crime or the criminal is supernatural in nature. This problem that Maury dropped in my lap is literally one of mine. But there's no way he could possibly know about my new undead lifestyle, right?

This has to be handled delicately. At least here and now with Maury's knowledge of the situation. Whoever's mucking around in the memories of a bunch of supernatural folks won't get handled with kid gloves. And I'm already suspecting that this is the work of Providence's newest and youngest crime boss, Sebastian Caprice. Who just became a memory-stealing monster a couple months ago. So, of course, I'll take this case.

"Well, if it's this important to you, then it's a priority to me."

"Knew you'd say that." He taps his temple. "What did they call me at the precinct?"

"Mind-reader Maury." I reach down and take the envelope, stuffing it in the interior pocket on my sport coat.

He always debunked anything supernatural with logic every time someone applied that moniker. I let out a chuckle before the sob in my throat can escape. None of this is fair. Maury gets promoted, I get turned. Our frenemy happens to be a magician, and the neighbor kid's a natural-born werewolf. But Maury, who we all thought had every advantage growing up, gets the short end of a metastasized stick.

Out of all of us, Maury deserved to have power over his own destiny. But fate decided otherwise when it gave him lung cancer. Zack ended up with major power, Scott with equal amounts of strength and responsibility, and me with this deathless existence of eternal obligation. Now I feel utterly unseated, like the world flipped upside down and then turned itself inside out just for good measure.

But I could fix fate's wagon. I could turn Maury's tables right back over again.

All I'd have to do is vamp him.

# CHAPTER FIVE

At first, I don't think I'm storming out of the room. It feels like I'm striding with purpose, direction, and the sense of justice that has been a constant companion my whole life, only a day longer than Maury's been in it. I can't imagine losing either that or him. And that's why I'm leaving the hospital, or at least attempting to.

"Tino, wait up, man."

"Ain't nobody got time for that, dog breath." Yeah, I snarked off to Scott. It's not the first time, and it won't be the last. I know he means well, but I'm in a hurry.

"You can't do this, dude." Scott grabs at my shoulder, his fingers catching on the polyester-blend fabric. I'm fast when I want to be, even without burning any blood.

"There's no law against asking DeCampo anything I want to." I snort. "Including this."

"I'm no expert, but according to Gramps, he doesn't have the authority right now." Scott's voice cracks. "He's king of nothing," he clears his throat. "Supernaturally speaking."

"Shitballs." Scott's right, and it's damned inconvenient. I almost turn around and bare my fangs at him, but that would only give any vampire king worth his salt grounds to refuse my request. So I don't vamp out in the hospital hallway, even though I want to. But I do keep on walking.

"So stop already. Or at least slow down." Scott's sneakers squeak on the linoleum as he works to keep pace with me. " We're supposed to see the doctor."

"Yeah, but she can't help me with what needs to be done."

"Slow down." Scott's not even panting, although the average Joe would be. And for the first time, it's pissing me off that he's got powers because I don't want him to make sense of this mess when I just want to act.

"Better yet, stop and think." Scott's voice is low enough so mortals won't hear it. "You're helping DeCampo by seeing the doctor, or at least trying to. You want him to owe you, right? Have some sense, man."

"You kids today with all your facts and your insight." I stop short, feet dead-flat in the middle of the hall.

Scott bumps into me, of course. Yeah, I slammed on my brakes out of spite. Which is wrong, and why I immediately turn around, help him up, and apologize.

"I'm sorry, Scott. This just sucks, you know?"

"No, I don't really know exactly," he shrugs. Thank God, Scott Fitzpatrick isn't some know-it-all. "Nobody in my family ever had cancer. But I understand why you're freaking out."

I can't think of anything else to say. I'm struck silent by simple facts. Scott's right again. He does understand, because if he didn't, he'd be filling the silence with a bunch of inane and ill-thought-out sentences and phrases, pretending sympathy. But he's better than that.

Usually, I don't pay much mind to the common platitudes that go with disaster and grief. I was a cop, so I've used them, and know why they work in general situations of shock. But an ageless vampire and a disease-resistant werewolf beginning the process of grieving for their cancer-stricken mundane friend is different. It's certainly nothing general, and definitely not something the police academy or my years on the force prepared me for.

I turn around, my back to the elevator, then hang a right down the hall leading to Dr. Maris's ICU. I know she's here tonight. On the way over in Scott's truck, I called and asked. But then again, I didn't leave a message. I start thinking maybe she'll be busy, and I can just leave and have my chat about Maury with DeCampo instead.

Going to the king empty-handed, however, is probably not a good way to make as enormous a request as turning my best friend when I'm still so new myself. I'll only get one shot, too. Decisions about someone becoming a vampire are always final.

I can't even make a good case that Maury would be useful. He's got almost the same skill set I do, so the others wouldn't think he could help us retake Providence from Whitby. I have to hope Dr. Maris is willing and able to give us access to the thing Stephanie thinks we need to cure the king's ailment, whatever it is.

As I walk through the hallways in the Intensive Care Unit at Kent County Hospital, I turn my head left and right to peer through the glass that fronts each room, separating critical patients from passersby. Probably protecting them, too. I don't see Dr. Maris in any of those.

A door with her name on it is at the end of the hallway. I walk straight up to it and raise my hand, about to turn the knob and open it. Or not, if it's locked. Scott grabs me by the wrist.

"You never know what's behind the door when centaurs are involved."

"How would you know? You met her the same night I did."

"I've had way less to do than you over the last handful of weeks, and Gramps has lots of lore he's happy to share with me."

"Good point." I bow my head out of respect for my dearly departed free time. "Thanks."

"You're welcome." Scott raises his hand and knocks. Which was what I should have done in the first place because it's just polite.

I hear the tap and squeak of Dansko clogs on linoleum tile from the other side of the door. Yeah, she's in there. The knob turns and the door pushes out, almost hitting me in the nose. I step back in time, thank God.

"Crispo. Don't tell me one of your friends is currently a guest in a room down the hall."

"No, I can honestly say none of my friends are occupying beds on your ICU."

"They'd better not be in the emergency room, either."

"Nope, none of my pals are down there, either."

"Well, you'd better come in and tell me why you're here already. I figure it isn't something to discuss out in the hall." She steps aside, making room for me and Scott to enter her office.

"You figure right." I walk in, Scott following me.

"Always." Dr. Maris doesn't sit behind her desk or offer us the chairs in front of it. Instead, she closes the door and leans her shoulders against it. I hear the snap of a pushbutton lock that she engages behind her back.

"I hate to incur any more debt than I'm already in, but I need your help if it's possible."

"I'm not opening the vault for you again."

"That's fine. I'm not here for that. Somebody else needs help."

"Oh, so you're taking out new debt to pay off the old, then?"

"No, actually. I'm doing some research for a friend."

"Is this the type of friend who also drinks blood?"

"Yes, I tend to have a lot of those. Funny, huh?" I smirk. I can't help it. Dr. Maris's assumptions are almost absurd, and it's been all I can do to keep from laughing to break some of my tension anyway.

"Like a clown." She looks at Scott, clearly done talking to me.

"Don't look at me. I'm just here for moral support."

"Now I've seen everything. An emotional support werewolf." She snorts. "Give me a break."

"Look, all I want is to ask if Stephanie McQueen can have a look through your spare blood, if there even is any at Kent County."

"Stephanie? Why didn't you say so in the first place?" Dr. Maris rolls her eyes, tapping the toe of one clog-clad foot on the tile.

"I don't know."

"That was a rhetorical… Never mind." She tosses her head as

though to clear it. “Sure. If Stephanie's got the time, I've got some supply. But there's one problem."

"Okay, lay it on me."

"Most of it is dead blood."

Her words start what feels like a tornado in the pit of my stomach, even though I'm reasonably sure all the blood I drank tonight came from living people. Great. Now I'm getting flashbacks to my dead blood vision episodes. Well, it's not great, actually, but maybe you don’t know or remember what I mean.

Let me refresh your memory. Each vampire has a signature ability besides the usual extra hearing and sense of smell. Most of us even get more than one, which I learned very recently. My first and worst one is having visions. Why worst, you ask? Because there's a catch.

I have to drink a substance it turns out I'm allergic to in order to get those visions. Yup, you guessed it. Dead blood. For other vampires, it’s just not very nourishing, like junk food, but it makes me spectacularly ill. The one upside to all the pain is I get to see how the person the blood belonged to died. This has helped me on more than one occasion, because supernatural deaths are mysterious. But my bad reaction is a bitch and a half.

Some people’s allergies cause hives. I'm not so lucky. Dead blood doesn’t just make me vomit. When vampires get sick, it ain't pretty. Not everything that comes up is blood. After a certain point, I start sicking up the lining of my stomach, and then parts of the organ. If someone doesn't snap me out of it, I could die by puking. Definitely not the way I want to go out for good when it's time.

So that’s why I surprise myself by not immediately rejecting Doctor Maris’s gift horse. I shock her, too, because she knows about my allergy. But maybe you’re in the same boat as Scott and not too surprised. He says I’m an altruist, even though I don’t agree.

“Well, that might work, I guess.”

“Do you know what she’s looking for, exactly?”

“No, not at all.” I shrug. “She says she can’t tell me about it. Beyond what you just heard.”

“Here.” Doctor Maris plucks a business card from a wire mesh holder on her desk. "Tell your sire to call me at least ten minutes before she comes in."

"Will do."

"Is that all?"

"Well—" I'm about to ask about Maury and whether she knows his oncologist.

"It's got to be. I'm out of time." Doctor Maris points at the door. "Now get out of here."

I raise my hand like I'm back in school.

"Skedaddle."

"Okay."

"Scram."

"I said, okay!"

I'd say she didn't have to tell me twice, but apparently impatient centaurs have a knack for repetition. Or at least that's what I assume until I open the door.

Leaning against the wall outside alone is a fifteen-year-old kid. You might wonder why a teenager younger than Scott is loitering in an Intensive Care Unit at an hour when most of his peers are doing their homework. Don't ask me, because I've got no idea. But unfortunately, I know this particular urchin. He's not what he appears to be in more than one way. And that's why I step backward instead of heading out of the doctor's office.

"Mr. Crispo."

"Mr. Caprice."

"You can call me Sebastian."

"Thanks, Mr. Caprice."

"Tino, come on. Give the guy a break." Scott actually tugs on my sleeve. He hasn't done that since he was eleven.

"No." I pull my arm away from Scott, then cross my arms and scowl at the other kid.

Yeah, I'm being hard on someone who's acting friendly enough. But Sebastian Caprice only happens to have decent manners. His mundane connections are all Mafia, and his supernatural ones are even worse.

He recently became a type of creature that's going to haunt my nightmares for a century or more. And that's no surprise. There isn't much out there that can eat a vampire. Sebastian can. He's a Lethian, also known as a memory-drinker.

I've still got holes in my memory, and my short-term recall will probably be on the fritz for decades because of a creature like Sebastian. Stephanie tells me it'll improve somenight, but one of them fed from me for years, literally messing with my mind.

Like I said, it's supposed to get better, but only if another Lethian doesn't come along and think I'm a tasty snack. So, of course, you understand why I'm not happy to see the Caprice kid here, there, or anywhere.

"Give him a break, Tino." Scott elbows me in the ribs. "He's new. You remember what that's like, right?"

"Yeah, no thanks to someone like him."

"Get out of the doorway." Doctor Maris stamps and snorts, making me wonder whether she's about to charge through and knock Sebastian over.

"Maybe I'm protecting you."

"From my student?"

"Wait, what?"

"You heard the good doctor, Tino." Scott nudges me again. "Move it."

I step aside, and Scott follows. I watch the werewolf give Sebastian a sheepish grin. Yeah, that's a prime example of irony right there.

"Sorry about my partner." Scott shrugs. "But really, even if you want to blame him, you can't be surprised."

"Maybe you're right." Sebastian shakes his head, then looks at me. "Mr. Crispo, I'm trying to do the best I can with this whole thing. It's why I asked the doctor here to help me learn to control myself. I don't want to make more enemies than I already have, but I couldn't let things stand the way they were with my mother in charge, either. Some part of you has to get that, right?"

I freeze in that wide beige hallway, silent. I can absolutely grok where this cocky kid is coming from, and hating every second of empathy I've got for him doesn't make either emotion vanish. His situation is familiar, and his words even more so. But I can't shake the idea that trusting him could be a big mistake. Not every anti-hero gets a redemption arc, and the odds are against him.

"Do what you've got to. But stay away from me and mine."

Sebastian blinks. Why are his eyes so wide afterward? How could he be surprised by my reaction to him? He's a monster now, chose to be one, went out of his way to steal his power from the Lethian who preyed on me.

I watch him walk into Doctor Maris's office. She reaches out and shuts the door in my face. That's fine by me. I do an about-face and start striding down the hall, Scott at my heels. I don't want to be cruel, just cautious. But that idea sits on my heart like a lead weight the moment it enters my mind.

Caution has never come with such a steaming heap of guilt before.

As we stand outside the elevator, waiting for its ascent, an unwelcome thought occurs to me. Maybe Sebastian only struck his predecessor down because I told him to take power over his life. The shame from that night already drags on my conscience, though I wasn't aware of its exact nature until now. I open my mouth, about to make a confession of sorts to Scott right there in Kent County Hospital's fifth-floor hall.

But the muffled sound of Sebastian ugly crying in Doctor Maris's office silences me.

There's no room for words in the echo of a Lethian's tears.

# CHAPTER SIX

Outside the hospital, I slip Maya's spiffy new notebook out of my pocket. After flipping it open, I jot notes about the stuff Maury wants me to investigate. Scott stares at my jacket, where I tucked the manila envelope, then gestures at it, his eyebrows gaining altitude.

"Hey, thanks for reminding me I've got that, and sticking with me through that whole embarrassing episode." I put the notebook away again, the notes finished. After that, I hold my right hand out toward my buddy. "Sorry about storming out of there, and for losing my temper. I was a dick."

"Nah," Scott snorts. "More like a prick, you know, because of the fangs?"

"Nice dad joke, kid." My chuckle turns into a sob.

"What are we gonna do?" Scott sniffles, dabbing the corner of his eye. "About Maury?"

"This case, to start with." I hold my hand out to let him pass the folder over to me. "After that, it's going to depend on what happens with DeCampo."

"Have you thought about asking the other guy?" Scott stares at his shoes. "Whitby?"

I freeze. Which looks pretty disconcerting on a vampire because we don't have to breathe or blink. But I can't really stop myself from stilling. I'm utterly shocked by Scott's idea. I take a moment and try thinking about the situation from my enemy's perspective.

I'm a major inconvenience for the fake King of Providence. The fact that my friends and I won't join up with his court and acknowledge his rulership makes his position unsteadier than he probably likes. But my mind refuses to take the next step along this speculative path without verbalizing.

"Would he negotiate with me? Accept my vow to stay out of the struggle for the throne in exchange for Maury's life?"

"I don't know, man." Scott shakes his head, which is still tilted down.

"I could find out, though."

"They can't stop you, right? Steph and the others, I mean. From going downtown to see him?"

"No. I'm a full member of vampire society now. I can go where I want unsupervised. It's dangerous to go in there alone, though."

"Why?"

"I might never come out again. I'm not important enough to the right people. My vampire etiquette skills are practically nonexistent too. That makes me both intolerably obnoxious and expendable."

"Sounds like a gamble for sure. Are you going to take it?"

"I think my plate's full enough without a heaping helping of whatever Whitby's serving." I shrug. "Besides, asking him seems too easy and not in a good way. What did that old wizard say?"

"Not all those who wander are lost?"

"Nah, the other guy."

"The one about choosing between what's right and what's easy?"

"That's the one."

"So, I guess you've got a lot of hard work to do then."

"Starting with Maury's case."

"Hmm." Scott finally looks up, scratching his head. "Don't tell me, I think I've got this. If one of Whitby's people is causing this problem that the mundane police are looking into, then you have ammunition."

"Right." I nod, then clear my throat. "Dealing with Whitby alone definitely seems way too easy. And he doesn't like me. I'd probably come out of any one-on-one meeting with him in a vacuum canister."

"Ugh, Tino." Scott takes a step back, his nose wrinkled and his eyes wide. "Don't talk like that."

"Sorry for that graphic little interlude, dude." I take a deep breath that feels like a crutch. "Neither of us is an expert, but do you think Maury has time for you to do this the hard way?"

"I'm no expert, but I managed to get a look at the folder next to Mrs. Weintraub's jacket."

"What did it say?"

"Here."

Scott shows me a picture he took with his phone. It's of a medical document.

"You know this breaks all those HIPAA laws, right?"

Scott only shrugs. I read the words in the image.

"We've got some time. According to this, he's still getting chemotherapy."

"How long, do you think?"

"Six weeks of the chemo at least. Who knows, after that. So I'd better hustle my bustle."

"Did you want to go and talk to Kayleigh now?"

"Yeah, let's do it. I'll skim this on the way over. And thanks for driving."

"No problem."

We get into the beat-up old truck and buckle in. Rhode Island is a click it or ticket state.

Looking through the file is interesting. The fact that Kayleigh and other women like her haven't filled out reports or filed charges should result in just a page or two inside. But my old flame was found by a beat cop in Roger Williams Park. The victim before her had an off-duty Cranston officer literally trip over her during a morning jog.

There are three victims in all, each found three days apart, and in places they don't remember getting to. Each was unconscious with steady vitals, not rousing until at least five minutes after being found.

The women vary in age, with my ex smack in the middle. The oldest is sixty-seven, and the youngest twenty. I only recognize Kayleigh's name.

One other detail jumps out at me. The women all have bruising around their right wrists like someone grabbed them and pulled hard. As much as I'd like to suspect a Lethian, specifically Sebastian Caprice, that bruising doesn't match that monster's modus operandi. The memory drinkers don't have to touch their victims.

"We're here."

Scott's putting the clunky old truck in park out in front of the duplex Kayleigh moved into with her fiancé Calvin.

"Hey, Scott. Thanks for all the rides and stuff."

"It's all good."

"You don't have to go in with me."

"I'm gonna anyway."

"Thanks again."

"No problem, my dude."

I find the mailbox with their name on it, then ring the bell beside it. Shortly afterward, I get the impression we're being watched. A glance upward confirms my suspicions that Kayleigh's put a camera on the front porch. Another over my shoulder tells me Scott's got a wolf friend hiding at the edge of the wooded strip between the street and a walking trail.

Supernatural people and the mundanes who hunt them are paranoid.

It makes complete sense, but I sigh anyway. Our tentative truce with the hunter group Kayleigh belongs to ended when Esther, Scott, and I gave Calvin the potion that woke him from his months-long coma.

You'd think folks would be more grateful.

The lesson here seems to be that it's easier to make a lasting deal when it's vamp to magician or werewolf to salamander. But vampo-a-mano is rarer than hen's teeth.

Kind of drives home the importance of keeping mystical shit secret.

Bolts sliding and locks tumbling tell us we don't have much longer to wait. The door opens a crack, and I'm looking Kayleigh in the eye. Well, sort of. There's a silver chain between us. That'd keep Scott from busting in. The scent of wood and garlic means my ex is packing anti-vampire heat.

"What do you want, Crispo?"

"Hi, Kayleigh."

"Can it and answer."

"It's more like what Maury wants. He's hired me for a case and has me doing a little legwork for him. Official. It's about your lost time in Roger Williams Park."

"He's only paying you because he doesn't know about your new and unimproved health condition."

"Well, that and our decades of friendship, of course." I hold up Cranston PD's folder. "Can I come in and talk to you about this?"

"No."

"Not a good look, Kayleigh." Scott's shaking his head. "You know the whole vampire invitation thing is a myth."

"It's not about the myths. It's more like I've got a lot of things in here the both of you are severely allergic to."

"Oh, okay." I nod, the corners of my mouth tilting up. "So where can we talk in private about this? My office?"

"No."

"Hold on." Scott's texting at supernatural speed. His phone bleeps, bloops, and chimes. "Gramps says you can hang out in his gazebo."

"Meet me there in five. If you're late, I'm gonna jet,"

"Thanks, Kayleigh."

"Whatever." She doesn't exactly slam the door, but it doesn't close gently either. The locks engage almost immediately, too.

"Let's go." Scott strides off the porch and toward his truck. I follow, trotting to keep up.

"Why are we in such a hurry?"

"I've got to do a quick chore for Gramps before we use the gazebo."

"Okay."

The ride over is short, barely two minutes. Even still, I wonder how Scott's going to do anything before Kayleigh's deadline. But I'm not left in the dark for long.

Once at the side of the Fitzpatrick's house, Scott stops under a window. When I say under, I mean two stories down. He picks up a pair of pruning shears. There's a tree between my parent's house and theirs, one that's gotten severely overgrown over the last summer.

He squats then leaps straight up into the air.

"Think fast, Tino!"

I dash out of the way as I realize the nature of this chore, which is extremely dangerous for a vampire. But I'm fast, so I get out of the way with plenty of time and space to spare before branches start dropping on the spot where I stood.

You might wonder why I'm not freaking out. And yeah, any other vamp might think Scott wanted to paralyze or even kill me. But I know better. Okay, strike that. Maybe I don't. Maybe I'm dangerously trusting and absurdly naïve. I might be a fool.

But if I am, at least I won't end up a paranoid mess like Kayleigh. Trusting in friendship and love is the way to go.

At least, it is for me. My mother raised me to have faith, and I'm sticking to those guns like an entire factory of crazy glue.

I pace through the gate to the backyard where Gramps has his gazebo. The structure back there is a real showcase of talented craftsmanship. It's also the only supernaturally-enhanced neutral ground in the state of Rhode Island. The Fitzpatricks are the most important and longest-standing werewolf family here, and from what Stephanie's told me, it's the alpha werewolf's duty to maintain such a place.

Kayleigh's already standing inside it because she's practically a ninja. I change my power-walk into a saunter, knowing she can't attack me while she's within the boundaries here. But then she raises her arm and taps her watch.

I sprint.

"Hi again." I set Maury's folder on the picnic table on the far side of the gazebo.

"I have to sit for this?"

"Yeah, it's probably a good idea."

"Fine." She takes one side, then gestures at the other.

"Relax, Kayleigh. I'm not interested in biting you. Or anything else besides helping figure out what happened to you."

"Really?" She's lacing her fingers together, then slipping them apart again, something she always used to do when she was nervous.

"Yeah."

"I mean, this is always extra awkward because we were a thing back then. And I love Calvin."

"I'm seeing someone." The smile I can't hide when I think of Maya tells Kayleigh it's serious.

"Oh, my god!" Those lacing hands clap together instead, three times in rapid succession. Her blonde side ponytail bounces as she makes a little squeeing noise. "Who? Is it the cute guy with the tattoos?"

"What, Frankie? No. I'm straight, but whoever ends up with him is gonna be a lucky guy."

"Then who? Not the alchemist?" She makes a face.

"No. She's a vampire like me. Except totally gorgeous."

"Wow, congratulations!"

"Thanks." As I come down from new-relationship euphoria, I realize my ex is procrastinating. "So. Last night a beat cop found you in Roger Williams Park?"

Kayleigh sighs and shakes her head. "Ugh. I can't do this. Told Maury the same thing."

"I know. But you can tell me things you can't say to him."

"That'd be a good point, but I don't remember anything except waking up."

"Can I look at your wrist?"

"Sure." She holds her arm out, palm up. "But don't touch."

"Okay."

I examine it as best I can with my eyes, which is actually not a bad thing. I notice something I might have missed if my hand had been on her arm.

"Well, I can tell you for sure that you didn't get whammied by a Lethian."

"How?"

"They leave traces behind, but never bruises, so your injury there doesn't match up. But that's not all I see, either."

"So, what did this?"

"I'm not sure." And that's the God's honest truth.

"What else is on me, then?"

"I'm only telling you that if you promise to share anything you know about this stuff." I point at the area around her wrist, right above the bruising.

"Only a vampire for a summer, and you're already wheeling and dealing."

"Not for myself. There are three other victims, Kayleigh. So far. And Maury won't have a clue how to help them. Neither will the PD."

"Raph Paolucci might." Everybody in the supernatural community apparently knows the head of CSI is an ally.

"But he can't see this with his own eyes any more than you can."

"Good point. But maybe I'd be better off talking to him instead."

"I know how to send him an official consultant's evidence report that might let Maury go after the perp if we can find mundane grounds."

"And I know people who can take care of said monster on their own without getting the police involved."

"How do you know it's a monster?"

"Anything that's stealing time and God knows what else from random women has got to be one."

"It can't be an accident? A misunderstanding?"

"Just the way they have to feed?"

"Good point." I shake my head. "But I can't help wondering whether I'd be in that boat. If the vamp who made me hadn't stuck around, I mean."

From the other side of the rosebushes, Scott snorts.

"You'd have ashed while sunbathing or died of garlic poisoning on the first day."

"You know me too well. All the same, I'd appreciate any information and time you can give me." Kayleigh knows I prefer the carrot over the stick.

"You know me well too, Tino. So you'll understand that, regardless of my preference, I can't do much to help you."

"Your dad already knows about this, huh?"

"Yeah."

"Shitballs." My face meets my palm. "Is it the time or the information you've lost control of here?"

"Time. Daddy's already on the prowl for baddies."

"Okay, so what's the intel you're willing to share?"

"Two things."

"Not even enough for a charm?"

"You'll have to do the arithmetic on your own, sorry."

"Should have paid more attention in Algebra, huh?" I let out a chuckle she adds to.

"Something like that." She sighs. "Anyway, the first thing about the night in question is what I remember from before waking up in the cruiser. It was a voice."

"Okay. Tell me more."

"I can't." She shrugs. "I was walking down the sidewalk after leaving the bike path. It was across Cranston Street from Meshanticut, about a block from home. And then from maybe a dozen paces behind me I hear this voice. Loud. Commanding, even. But it also had a sort of music to it."

"What kind of music?"

"That's your thing. I'm tone-deaf, remember?"

"Nobody's perfect, Kayleigh. Anyway, what was it saying?"

"Can't remember." She taps her temple. "But I have the idea that I wouldn't have understood the words anyway."

"And you didn't feel anything on your wrist?" I point at the fading marks.

"Nope."

I finish jotting her account down in my notebook. As I sit tapping the end of my writing utensil on the page, I wonder whether this could be the work of a magician. An alchemist could prep a potion to do just about anything, even make a sound like a voice. But it also reminds me of something I encountered more recently.

"Do you remember any other time you heard a voice like that?"

"Um." Kayleigh's looking everywhere but at me. "Yeah, once."

"Are you going to tell me about that?"

"Tino, ixnay, ixnay."

"Scott, I don't speak Pig Latin."

"He said nix." Kayleigh finally looks me in the eye. "There's a night I promised never to mention."

"Ah." I nod. "I'll quit on that."

Kayleigh's talking about that time I got whammied by something evil and ended up with an entire week lost from my memory. Nobody will tell me exactly what happened that night. Well, none of my friends, anyway. That bastard Carmine was there, and I'm still trying to sort the truth from the fiction in his tall tale.

"Okay, so you said there was one other thing you remember about last night."

"Yeah. When I go out running, I always bring the hip bag Dad gave me when I finished hunter training. It's got all four of my cans of mace inside."

"Four? Isn't that overkill?"

"Not really. Only one of them has pepper spray in it."

"Oh, okay. I get it. One with holy water, one with silver nitrate. But what's the fourth?"

"Garlic."

"Vamps are that dangerous?"

"No. The holy water's not for vamps."

"Some night, I'd love to sit down with you and discuss tactics."

"You and every other thing that goes bump in the night."

"Fair point. So. You had four mace cans when you went out."

"Right. And in the cruiser, I had none." She shakes her head. "But I was out of it in Roger Williams Park for who knows how long. Anyone could have taken them."

I rub one hand over my mouth, trying to hide the smirk I'm surely making at the idea of some garden-variety human spraying water at another, waiting for the eye burn. Which is maybe the most benign fate my imagination can come up with for Kayleigh's misplaced weapons.

"Have you been out to look for them?"

"Yeah, with Calvin earlier today. But we didn't find anything."

"Hmm."

"So, what do you think did it?"

"No idea."

"Bullshit."

"Didn't we already have this conversation but reversed?"

She huffs out a hostile breath, crossing her arms over her chest.

"Look. You must have at least a theory."

"Yeah. It must be bunnies."

"Don't go quoting Whedonverse at me."

"Well, what do you want from me, then? A target? Because I can't give you any."

"Quid pro quo, Valentino."

"Hannibal Lecter is not a good look, Kayleigh."

"You don't want to owe hunters. Bad for your health."

But I also happen to know it'd be even worse for my health if anyone found out I put Kayleigh or her father on the trail of some other poor supernatural sap. Theorizing with her is dangerous, especially here on neutral ground where the werewolves can hear. Not that I think this string of crimes has anything to do with them.

Another hazard to my health is my prime suspects. Magicians can put holes in walls and turn folks into puppets. Centaurs and Lethians are masters of knowledge and memory. Vampires have all sorts of powers, verbal commands included. I have the suspicion that Stephanie can manipulate memories, too.

Half my friends fall into one of these categories. I am not pointing a loaded hunter at anyone I care about.

For vampires, there is one eternal way out of any social predicament. I take it.

"I took vows. Breaking them is similarly hazardous."

"Well, thanks for nothing, Tino."

Kayleigh rises and stomps away, making a big show of anger and frustration at the direction our conversation took. But my vampire ears hear her heart beating at a pace too slow for that. It's still elevated, but in a way that makes me think she's mildly excited.

Not like that. Get your minds back up into the gutter where they belong.

My ex looks back at me over her shoulder, and the sly grin on her lips makes me understand what's happened. My refusal to name even creature types gave her enough to go on. The rest of her deductions about my unspoken theories come from our shared history. She knows that my suspects include the people closest to me.

I'd better solve this one before she does, or the blood or ash is on my hands.

---

Scott leaves me in awkward silence on the way back to the Belfry. Fortunately, after a couple of minutes, he decides to break it.

"Look, Tino." Scott glances at me, then back at the road. "I've got to keep things copacetic with Sebastian."

I don't answer, only blink. This is the last thing I expect to hear out of the werewolf's mouth. Last time I checked, he had some territorial issues with the monstrous Mafia prince. I want to keep my mouth shut, but the timer runs out on my curiosity.

"Why?"

"You know how Gramps transferred me from Cranston West to Stout this year?"

"Yeah." The whole thing was Scott's idea. He wants to keep an eye on Leora. For more than one reason, if the teenage werewolf's past behavior is any indication. It's totally my business since I am her legal guardian. But my opinion of Leora's romantic prospects isn't as important as her own. So I stay mum on that part of it. At least it's nothing I need to be curious about.

"Well, I need a tutor for Geometry, and they assigned me to Sebastian. The kid's some kind of math whiz."

"Okay." I sigh. Math isn't something I can offer him help with, after all. "I'll lay off while you're around. Make it look like you're making me chill out."

"Thanks."

After that, I get a text. That's why, instead of bringing me home, Scott drives us to the old converted factory that houses our private investigation office, nestled in with the typical art and music studios. And one alchemy lab, courtesy of Esther, of course. But it's the office we want because that's where Leora is. Also, Esther's most recent alchemy project is creepy with a side of gross, and I'd prefer not to see it.

She's sitting at my desk, head bent over notebooks and a pre-algebra textbook, doing her homework as promised. Like I said, good kid. But her bestie Sparky the salamander is a distracting little fellow I've come to seriously consider banning from my office during homework sessions.

He's decent enough most of the time and a great ally in a fight, but he gets bored easily and always messes with Leora's books and papers. He's currently sitting on the floor between Leora's backpack and my duffel full of investigation supplies, playing with whatever he can get his hands on.

How much trouble is a salamander? According to the books in the Pickering house library, not much, normally. But nothing about Sparky is normal, from his interest in World History to his nosiness about all of my cases. Right now, he's in his almost human form, bipedal with opposable thumbs, yet totally hairless. Mildly atypical, like the book says. But his looks are no problem as far as I'm concerned.

A nitrile glove farting proudly past my nose while deflating is.

"Sparky, what the hell?" I pluck the flying glove between two fingers and shake it like a Polaroid picture.

"Sorry, mister." The amphibian kid hangs his head.

"Why, dude?" I toss that glove in the trash because it's ruined now. Sending Salamander DNA to the CSI lab is not a good look, even if my contact there is in the know.

"Dunno. Got bored." Sparky blinks his big, muddy, lashless eyes. "Sorry."

"Hey, Sparkmeister." Scott holds up one of the controllers from the Nintendo 64 he got at Reality A Games last week. "Come and smash some bros with me, fam."

"Yeah!" The kid forgets all about my stuff and runs off to do some retro gaming. Thank God.

I drag my duffel over toward my desk, take the seat in front of it, and begin repacking my supplies. I must be making my annoyance too obvious because Leora looks up from her books and raises both eyebrows.

"Look, I need this stuff to solve cases." I shrug. "You know, help people?"

"Yeah." She taps the page she's been scrawling equations on. "I know."

"What's wrong?"

"Can I just be home-schooled?"

"Wait, what?"

"You've got vampire ears. You heard me."

"Okay, so maybe why is the better question."

"They want us to pick an extracurricular activity, and I don't want to."

"Well, those are fun, though."

"Really? Because they all seem like, too public, you know. I mean, for someone like me." She holds her hand up, letting the mortar and pestle charm that links her to Baba Yaga dangle and catch the light. When I say links, I mean the teen talking to me is permanently tapped as the witch's meat-suit any time she needs to leave her chicken-footed hut.

"Look, Scott runs track at your school. He did it back at Cranston West, too. And he's a werewolf. The whole reason you're going to

Stout is that it's for folks like us. We all have our ways of reining things in."

"I don't want to do sports."

"Um, why not?"

"Because you can't come and see me." Leora's looking down at her paper, cheeks reddening. "You know, competing and stuff. All of the sports at Stout happen in the daytime and outdoors. Or in the gym where they have windows."

"Oh." She does have a point. She wants me around because I'm her dad. Not biologically. I went to court and petitioned for Leora's custody with my friend, Frankie. It's a long story, told elsewhere. "How about Drama Club? Don't they have one of those at fancy-schmancy Stout Academy?"

"Yeah, but I wasn't sure if it's a good idea to go out for it." She takes a deep breath and spills the beans before I can ask why. "Because that's Sarah's activity."

"I see." I nod, totally understanding what she means. Sarah Pickering is one of Frankie's siblings, and her foster sister. The girls are a year and a grade apart. And Sarah's a magician, meaning she's got mojo she was born with. Leora's got no powers of her own, only when Baba feels like channeling them. "Absolutely get the picture. You don't want to make a frenemy."

"Yeah, Tino." She looks up, meeting my eyes. "How'd you know?"

"Because that was exactly what happened with Maury and me back in the day."

"Really?"

"Yeah. We thought we'd compete for every role all the time." I shake my head.

"What happened?"

"We didn't. We'd get cast as the buddies, together for the most part."

"Why?"

"Because our looks and talents were different enough. Like yours and Sarah's."

“Oh, wow.” She shakes her head as though it never crossed her mind that hair, skin tone, and stature would figure into auditions and casting. And that makes sense. Most people don’t who haven’t been there. “So, the two of you got roles all the time?”

“No, not always. Because I did happen to have a dude who looked and sang almost exactly like me. Only better.”

“The cookie.”

“Shut up, Scott.” I put my hands on my hips. “We don’t talk about our past clients that way.”

“No, I can’t remember his name for some reason.” Scott blows a raspberry in case I couldn’t tell he’s being extra sarcastic. Sparky gives him the TKO on Smash Bros. With Dr. Mario, ouch. “It was right on the tip of my tongue. Like a cookie.”

“Jeez.”

But now Leora’s giving me the eyes. You know, like a sad puppy dog but ten times worse. She’s an orphaned teenage kid with a refreshingly mundane problem, and she’s actually got a sympathetic parental figure to ask about it. That’s rarer than trace elements or noble gases or whatever. And I’d be a shitty dad friend if I blow her off. I decide to fess up.

“Yeah, I lost half the roles I went up for to Zack Milano. Including tonight.”

“Holy shit!” Leora immediately slaps her hand over her mouth, then winces. She should have put the calculator down first. Now she’s got a fat lip.

In a flash, I’m out of the chair, dashing to the mini-fridge for something cold to put on the inevitable bruise. I hand over the item I grabbed way too hastily. Which is a bag of blood because of course, it is. I need a t-shirt that declares me Worst Vampire Dad Ever.

But Leora’s not bothered by what I’m holding, or even the idea of using it as an ice pack. Which maybe shouldn’t be so unexpected. Baba Yaga does some pretty grody things to make her magic.

“Sorry, Tino.” Her voice is muffled behind the blood bag.

“Dude. I mean, Leora.” Can’t I ever get it right? “The stuff Esther says is ten times worse. Just don't talk like that with your teachers or whatever." Yeah, being a dad isn't awkward at all. Why do you ask?

"But Zack Milano was your Drama Club rival? Like, seriously?"

"Yeah." I shrug. "What's the big deal?"

"He's the volunteer vocal coach at Stout. Practically everyone he helps wins everything." Leora knocks over the chair and bounces on the balls of her feet. "And you're as talented as he is. I could die!"

"Uh, please don't."

From in front of the game console, the werewolf clears his throat. "More talented."

"Scott!"

"True story." He drops his controller then pats Sparky on the head. "You got me good, short and scaly. Anyway, the only reason Tino here didn't go to Nationals with musical theater and monologue his junior year is because he was in the hospital. We all were rooting for him, too."

"Oh, my God! Tino, you've got to help me! If I'm gonna do this, I need to get audition pieces ready. We've got a musical revue coming up this fall!"

"Just. Finish that math first, okay?" At this point, I'm giving up on denying it all. Or trying to remember the hole in my junior year, because that doesn't matter. I know why the memories are gone, even if the contents are still missing. You can take the geek out of the theater, but not even a memory-eating Lethian can take the theater out of the geek.

And now Leora's bouncing around the whole room practically, having left the calculator and the bag of blood on my desk. I reach across and grab the latter item, open it, lean on one hand, then pour the blood into the cup sitting in front of me. If only it were whiskey, neat, and I was alive enough to fully appreciate it.

I understand now why so many moms drink so much wine.

Before I can even take a sip, my phone rings. I tap the answer button and put it on speaker.

"Tino, get down here." Raven's voice comes in like a wrecking ball. "We're having the problem again. And he's evading Maya this time."

"Shitballs." I stand, gazing down at the untouched blood like I'm Humphrey Bogart, and it's Ingrid Bergman. "Okay, kids. You've got to do your homework and retro gaming in Warwick for the rest of the evening."

"It's DeCampo, isn't it?" Sparky's at my elbow, wagging a travel container in the general direction of my mid-evening snack.

"Thanks, kid." I transfer the blood from one vessel to the other and screw the lid on. "Let's go."

Leora comes down from her starstruck cloud and packs her books up. Scott's at his desk, shuffling through some documents. I see map printouts of Roger Williams Park, with marks where victims were found. I take the file Maury gave me out of my sports coat and tuck it in with the other papers for him to bring.

"Thanks, Scott."

"No problem, boss."

"Dude, stop calling me boss. We're not those guys. We're wiser than that."

"Okay, Tino." He sticks everything in the satchel I keep on the coat rack, then slings that and the CSI supply duffel over his arm. "We can go now."

Leora glances at Scott without saying a word to him. Her cheeks almost match the red highlights in her chestnut hair, and I hear her pulse speeding up when he smiles back. Looks like my ward and my sidekick have a little mutual crush going on. Oh, boy. I'll take things I'm not ready to have dad conversations about for five hundred, Alex.

"Hmm." I'm side-eying Sparky before opening the door because he only almost looks like a normal kid. Also because I can't make that face at Leora or Scott without invoking the spirit of teenage rebellion that might make everything a million times harder down the road.

"Wha?" Sparky grins and puts one hand behind his head.

"You can't go out looking like that, kiddo."

"Don't wanna shift."

"Can't we let him stay? Please?" Leora's batting her eyes.

"Not like this, we can't." I gesture at the top of his head, indicating his nonexistent eyebrows.

"This good?" Sparky pulls a folded and well-worn blue ball cap from his pocket and puts it on his completely bald head. It's got five symbols on it. Rock, paper, scissors, lizard, and a hand making a gesture made on Star Trek. Even salamanders watch television, I guess.

"Fine." I put my free hand on the doorknob and gesture at Sparky with the mug of blood. "But you keep the hat on the whole time we're outside on both ends of this trip and in the car, too. Don't want people doing a double-take at your almighty hairlessness and getting in a wreck."

"Okay!" Sparky's grin turns into a smile that reminds me of the sun. In a good mortal memory-lane way, not a fright-fest like the day star typically is for vampires. The kid is strange but still good overall.

I can't help but smile back. And it's sort of a big deal to me that I'm standing in this room with honest to goodness breathing live people who don't freak out over my fangs. Back when I got turned, I was pretty much alone with my inconvenient undeadness. I guess maybe things improve if you have an open mind and just keep on moving.

So that's what I do. Keep on going through the music-filled hall, down the echoing staircase, and toward the dinged-up front door of the studio. I've got my hand stretched ahead of me, about to push out into the night.

"Rent's due." The voice at my shoulder comes complete with a flat-voweled drawl that's too familiar for comfort. I know it's Sebastian Caprice's father, who's been manipulated into running this building's under-the-table rental racket. He drops a stubby cigarette butt on the floor, then stomps it out with his heel.

"Yeah, sorry." I drop my hand to my pocket, grab my wallet, pull out five twenties, and turn around to pay the Mafioso behind me. And then I resist the urge to hold my nose because I hate cigarettes.

"Those kids ain't in your act." The new landlord's not asking, he's telling. And I manage to remember he thinks we're a band, not an investigation outfit.

"Nope." I pat Leora's shoulder. "My sister's kid. Just started at Stout Academy."

"What about this?" He jerks one nicotine-stained thumb at Sparky.

"Exchange student." I can't say from where, of course.

"He got all his papers?"

"Excuse me?" I blink the second I realize that he's not talking about the kind with five pages that get turned in to the English teacher. Caprice is talking about Sparky as if he's a dog or something instead of an actual person. Because of how he looks. And dammit, he's a sentient salamander, not some kind of animal.

"You heard me."

"Yeah, I did. But the school keeps track of that. I'm just the cool uncle with the Emo band, remember?" I shrug. The chicken footed hut Sparky lives in with Baba Yaga doesn't have a legal address or issue photo ID. But this guy's a Mafia enforcer, not the government kind so that stuff's none of his business.

"Whatever." He snorts. "Keep 'im out of trouble while he's here."

"That's the plan." I take a risk and turn my back on the guy, even though I'm one hundred percent sure he's a murderer and just as confident he's a bigot now, too. I've got zero evidence that would hold up in court or even convince Maury of the first part.

Sebastian's the only member of his family with powers. Nothing the elder Mr. Caprice can do without an ax or a sword could kill me at first blow. My nose tells me he isn't carrying either of those, so he doesn't scare me at the moment.

The landlord lets us go without further comment. Out in the fresh air with the smoke scent clearing, I realize he should smell like Maury but doesn't, and also why. He wasn't a smoker before. Last time I saw this dude, he was on another guy's case for the nicotine habit. So he only recently started. Sebastian's influence maybe isn't so benign as he tried pretending at the hospital.

I stop walking, shut my eyes. Thinking of the hospital makes me remember how I need King DeCampo to get over whatever's been ailing him and back on the throne so I can ask his permission to turn Maury. Because I'm not doing a heel turn and going to Whitby with this. Yeah, the plan's complicated as all get out. But it'll be worth it if I can pull it off.

"Get the fuck out of the road, ya asshole!" The man's voice booms in the flat r-dropping accent residents of the Ocean State are known for. Yeah, that's right. I'm getting chewed out, Southern New England style. And I deserve it because I was standing in the middle of the street like a yahoo. Being easily distracted is a real vampire weakness, even if it's invisible most of the time.

"Fine, jeez!" Trotting across the street at a regular person's pace is hard at the moment. If my heart could still beat, it'd be going a mile a minute after that startle.

Leora and Sparky lean against Scott's truck, doubled over as they shriek with laughter. Kids these days, with their morbid senses of humor. Well, I can't blame them for sharing a trait with me. I chuckle my undead backside all the way over to the passenger side. Scott unlocks the truck, and we all get in.

Leora's tapping her phone, but I know she's not being anti-social. She's setting up some Bluetooth tunes. Which would be fine with me if she weren't at that phase most kids her age land in for maybe a year or three. I remember it well myself—the favorite song on repeat stage.

I figure anything that helps her cope with the loss of her mother and what she's been through since then is a good thing. But she's not blasting out anything you hear on Pandora stations or internet radio. Instead, it's *Take Me As I Am* from Jekyll and Hyde. Yup, the theater bug really has bitten her. And Sparky, too.

The almost-human kid's singing every word, with feeling. He's got one of those signature voices, the kind that can't exactly be called beautiful but will stand out in a chorus as instantly recognizable. He's got a character actor's tone and timbre.

Leora's smile stretches as her voice joins her friend's. And hers is everything his isn't. It's a challenge to keep my mouth from dropping because this is talent with a capital T. Powerhouse territory. Yes, I'm still going to coach her through whatever she wants, but I have to seriously consider getting her some more experienced and professional instruction down the road. Because even though I'm a vampire, her voice is giving me chills.

Scott drives to the old green gambreled house on Ocean Avenue in

Warwick. We all head in because the Pickering home is full of my allies and a couple of friends. Leora's and Sparky's, too. This is where she goes after school but before the sun sets, and also where she sleeps every night Baba doesn't need her help. It's a strange parenting arrangement, but she's no typical kid.

I wouldn't want it any other way.

## CHAPTER SEVEN

We park on the street and get out. I'm in such a hurry I have to run back and wait for everyone else to get out of Scott's truck. Yeah, I'm just that nervous and that fast, too. King DeCampo is formidable even at the best of times and especially when he's having these new fits of his. Apparently, there are hardships that come from being an extremely old vampire, along with all the prestige and power.

I send Sparky and Leora upstairs, where Frankie's two younger siblings wait for them. Magical Sarah rolls her eyes at me, although her lips tilt upward at one side. Mundane Levi grins and gives me a wave tiny enough to fit in at a country club party. Leora and Sparky carry their books, the Smash Brothers game, and a sense of liveliness up to the second floor with them, thank goodness. Scott hangs my bags in the hall and follows me.

Pickering House is one of those places with an element of gravity and emotion to it. When you walk inside, the air feels heavy and clammy, like a classic New England pea-soup fog. I'm not sure whether it's due to the history associated with this family and its magical connection to Deep Ones. Maybe it's just the fact that the backyard's directly on the water.

At any rate, Leora and Sparky always serve to brighten the place up a notch or three. Maybe it's because of their connection with Baba Yaga. From what Frankie's told me over the last few months, Baba's magic sits on some sort of metaphysical diagonal, balancing those creepy frog people. Yeah, I just equated Deep Ones to frogs even though they're nothing like Kermit. But they still haunt my daymares. Everybody has their favorite ways to cope, I guess.

I head back toward the parlor, expecting to see the same tense scene that's become all too common over the last month. And I'm almost right. On the other side of that doorway, the once and hopefully future vampire King of Providence stands, surrounded by his three closest allies as they try to calm him. But one thing is different this time.

They're barely managing to hold him back.

King DeCampo is short but as solidly built as the Great Pyramid. Probably as old, too. My first memories of him are dominated by authority and gravity. Even in Mnemosyne's Vault, the lost pieces of his history held a theme of sacrifice and justice. But tonight, he's like a destructive storm on slow-churn.

His long dreadlocks hiss through the air like snakes, tipped with silver beads. The sheer length of his fangs tells me he's close to some form of vampiric Rage. Strong brown hands reach, fingers splayed. He hasn't activated the ability that turns them into claws capable of cutting diamonds. At least not yet.

Words flow from his mouth, rounded syllables and harsh consonants I can't comprehend. They sound nothing like my childhood church Latin, the most ancient language I know well. The closest thing I've heard was Maury's bar mitzvah Hebrew. But even with that slim linguistic insight, I've got no idea whether the true King of Providence is currently issuing blessings, curses, or warnings.

And even though his ravings are, unfortunately, nothing new to me, they still leave a hollow in my chest. Something like grief, but closer to desperation. Because according to Stephanie, we can still save him if we manage to get what he needs in time. Something that's been missing from his blood supply since he lost his throne.

Unfortunately, none of them can tell me specifically what that is. Not even Raven, who has worked with DeCampo for a couple of centuries. The old vamps like their secrets. There's just one thing that helps now—Maya's psychic talent. But it only works if she can manage to touch him without losing her arms in the process.

For a few beats, I watch them. Stephanie and Raven flank the king, their movements at either side giving him pause every time he tries to turn and head for an exit. Maya attempts to make skin-on-skin contact with him. Her hand passes through the air, trying to grab at one of his. Once. Twice. De Campo evades her each time.

Maya is graceful, strong, and absolutely brutal in combat. But she's too slow to catch the king.

I'm not.

I'm like the quick and the dead all wrapped up in one newbie vampiric package. And I'm also, by vamp standards, a hotheaded idiot. So, I do the job like only a speedy kid who mostly doesn't know any better can.

I burn blood to dash down the hall, through the doorway and into the parlor, right behind DeCampo. And then it's just one giant leap for vampkind up to his back. I hang on for dear unlife.

The king's arms pinwheel, sawing through the air. And now he's got those wicked claws out. I can't do a damn thing to dodge out of the way, either. I close my eyes and repeat a mantra I'm not entirely sure is true. Vampires regenerate.

When DeCampo's claws mangle my left arm, it hurts. Take me down to understatement city where the verbs don't describe all the stuff that's shitty. I'll do better this time.

It's like getting pinched by tongs straight out of the fireplace. I think because that's never happened to me before. But almost as soon as the pain comes, it's gone. I smell ashes. And I flop on the king's back like a fish out of water because there's nothing to anchor my left side to him anymore.

"Tino!" Maya's eyes gleam, red-rimmed with impending tears.

I already know how much she cares, but the actual impact of her emotion even across the room hits me like a follow spot. It's all I can do not to freeze at this crucial moment, but years of performance experience and conquering stage fright helps me now.

"Just get him!"

She nods and lunges, coming in under DeCampo's arms. I'm not sure where or how she manages to get her hands on him, but she does it. The king slumps sideways, hitting the floor but luckily not with either of us under him.

Letting go with my right arm is easy. Standing up, not so much. I'm off-balance, of course, though it doesn't hurt physically. Unimagined benefits of being undead, I guess. And it's not bothering me much mentally, either. I'd be more pissed than an alley behind a bar on Saturday at three in the morning if anyone else had taken my arm off. I guess King DeCampo has a significant spot in my beatless heart, after all.

I pause, wondering why we're all so loyal to this ancient ex-King. The logic-ruled detective part of my brain concludes that both Stephanie and Raven are older than Whitby, and their existence still gives us a chance to take back Providence without the slowly maddening DeCampo. But my big old heart cuts that analytical line off.

The king shocked me with his gravity when I first met him. I didn't understand the weight of vampiric unlife and the vows we make back then. And sure, he just wounded me pretty badly. But DeCampo's in worse shape than I am. Not physically, but sometimes, an invisible malady is just as debilitating as the ones everybody can see.

His eyes are closed, and I'd think he was asleep or knocked out, except he's trembling like a leaf in a hurricane. A series of tones come from his throat, musical somehow, even though I recognize them for what they are. Whines; desperate and primal and frightened as a child's in total darkness. All concerns about my missing arm fly like spooked sparrows.

Maybe this is one of his powers, the kind vamps accumulate with age. The power to endear.

I almost laugh because snark is my shield, and DeCampo's noises remind me of an intro from a musical number I did years ago. One sideways glare from Raven and a headshake from Stephanie kill my nervous giggles. But music soothes the savage beast. Maybe that even applies to undead berserkers. When I open my mouth instead of laughter, the song comes out.

Raven and Stephanie blink, so much in tandem they could have been choreographed. Maya only smiles. Every musical number tells a tale, and *Not While I'm Around* from *Sweeney Todd* is no exception. As my song-spun words unwrap the story about a doomed boy promising to protect his sinister foster mother, the king's terror calms.

My audience grows, too. Four sets of eyes peer at me from the doorway leading to the hall. The kiddos, down from upstairs, of course. I feel someone else watching at my back, and the tiny noise of sympathetic comprehension reveals his identity. Frankie Pickering, who got a similar form of help from me just a handful of months ago.

As I utter the song's closing notes, Frankie is there, stooping over the pile of ashes that used to be most of my left arm. He's sweeping them into a dustpan, though I can't imagine why. He's the closest thing to a good housekeeper this odd family has, but this is hardly the time to tidy up.

Raven and Stephanie move in, helping the owlishly blinking DeCampo to one of the wing-back chairs near the empty fireplace. He sinks back against the tufted upholstery and splays one hand maybe six inches in front of his face, palm out.

"I'm so sorry, Valentino." His eyes tilt up toward mine but turn aside a moment before our gazes meet.

"Hey, it could have been worse." I give him a sideways grin and shrug my now-tattered sports coat off to drape it on an ottoman. Thank goodness I didn't like that old polyester rag anyway. "Vampire arms grow back, right?"

"It takes several weeks." Raven shakes their head. Yeah, I used a pronoun many people think of as plural, but Raven is one person and nonbinary. They/Them is their preference, and I'm sticking to it. Even if they're delivering me some pretty awful news.

"At least I'm not a southpaw, then." My smile fades despite the optimistic phrase.

"We'll need more blood than we currently have access to if you're going to heal that at all, Valentino." Stephanie's at my side, pushing back the remains of my sleeve to examine the stump. "If you are deficient for too long, your missing limb might become a permanent issue."

"Maybe I can get Danny Rand or Tony Stark to foot the bill for a prosthetic." I chuckle because really, there's nothing else I can think of to do in front of all these people. So do Frankie and the kids. The vamps don't get it. Well, Maya does. We binged all the Defenders shows with Frankie a couple of weeks ago. But she's not laughing, just trying to hide a grin.

"This is serious, Tino." She shakes her head, then goes about the process of removing the blood bags from my now-ruined sports coat. "This means someone's got to go to Providence and see if we can increase our allotment from the people in charge there."

She doesn't mention Whitby's name. None of them do, even though that's who we need to get around if we want more blood. Either that, or go another way with this.

"Look. We're telling all the vamps in the city that DeCampo's king of Warwick. There are hospitals outside Providence City limits, like Kent County. Doctor Maris said she has some extra dead blood she'll let Stephanie have. Maybe if we offer her more favors, she can wrangle some of the good stuff too." I hold the card out to Stephanie. "She said you could call her and have a chat."

"It's not that simple." Stephanie takes the card and tucks it in a pocket. Then she leans against the king's chair and glances down at him. "You can't use anything from a dead person, Tino. You'll get sick. The hospitals haven't got a surplus of fresh blood. Hargrove was our procurer. He's got connections locked down at Rhode Island Blood Center, which is the only living donor source in the state. That's why Maris's surplus will be mostly from the morgue."

"Would it help if I got a job at, like, one of the Providence hospitals or something?" Frankie's putting a twist tie on the bag he's dumped my arm's ashes into. He looks up at me. "Nobody in the vampire club up there knows who I am. I might be able to snag expired stuff from living donors on the sly."

"Do it." Raven's quick answer takes me off the spot. Which is good because I'm the farthest thing from an authority compared to the other legally adult people in the house. "I'll make sure you look good on paper when you apply."

"Okay." Frankie heads out the door with the bag of ashes before I can ask him what he intends to do with them. This is a guy who suffered unspeakable supernatural trauma at the beginning of the summer, and now he's picking up my pieces. Literally.

"Thanks!" I project from my stomach, using stage techniques to make sure Frankie hears the belated expression of gratitude. My sharper-than-human ears pick up a faint acknowledgment from the kitchen. It's good to have friends in the know.

"Even with this new plan, a visit to the Providence vampires is in order." Stephanie looks up from her assessment of my arm. Or what used to be my arm.

"I'm not going." Raven crosses their arms.

"No, you're not. Neither is His Majesty." Stephanie gives me a faint smile. "We are."

"Ain't no vampire got time for that." I shake my head. "I've got to go find Esther. I kind of need her help. Let's just say, she might be able to give me a hand with something."

I shrug my armless shoulder, then waggle my eyebrows. Nobody laughs.

"Yes." Stephanie nods. "I understand the importance of seeking a temporary replacement for that arm. But this visit takes priority, at least for now."

"How about I go find Esther for you, Tino?" The voice in the hall doorway is unexpected enough to catch everyone's attention.

"Thanks, Sparky, but that's way above your pay grade, as well as past your curfew."

"I'm a salamander in the employ of a teleporting witch. Who else is gonna be better at tracking down magicians?" The kid smiles. "And

Baba never gave me no curfew. You're legal guardian-ing Leora, not me."

"Kid, you've got a funny way of saying stuff that makes sense."

I try passing this buck by looking at the king, Raven, and Stephanie. None of them return my glances. Maya does them all one better when I try catching her eye, putting on the adviser hat.

"I think it's not a bad idea, letting Sparky do his thing." She nods at the almost-human kid. "I believe in him."

"Thanks, Maya!" Sparky turns his blue baseball cap around on his head, accentuating his lack of eyebrows. "I'll track her down, wherever she is."

"If you're really going around in public, you need to fix your face." Everyone blinks at Sarah, the middle Pickering kid. Because she barely ever bothers actually talking to any of us.

Sarah Pickering's sort of a mean girl. And her powers are nothing nice. As the last surviving member of her family to have actual magic, she's also a little scary. It doesn't help that none of her snark has an ounce of warmth in it. I can't blame her, though. She's a product of an elitist upbringing, after all. But Raven's told me before that they intend to lead their descendants into a healthier dynamic even if it kills them. Maybe some of that effort is paying off already.

"What do you mean, fix my face?" Sparky's turned around to stare her down. Maybe having the mercurial salamander around has helped counter Sarah's snotty attitude.

"So what if you're not born with it? We can use Maybelline. Come on upstairs, and I'll get you looking more than halfway human." She snorts, but I get the impression it's meant ironically instead of with malice. Or maybe that's my hopeful streak talking. The unlikely duo turns away from the door, and I hear their footsteps on the stairs moments later.

"Are you going to be all right, Tino?" Leora's steps forward, her eyes on my stump. "Being around all those other vampires like that, I mean?"

"Piece of cake, kiddo." I reach out with my right arm and ruffle her hair.

"Just come back, okay?"

"I will, I promise." But Leora's blue eyes stare out of a face pale with fear. I can hardly blame her. Maybe her mother said something like this the night she left Baba's hut to meet her doom.

"He won't be alone, child." Stephanie drapes my opera cloak over my shoulders. At first, I wonder how she got it, then remember she was at my place earlier. Judging by the weight, she took some time loading its pockets up with the blood Maya got out of my now ruined sport coat. "Valentino is my responsibility as far as Whitby's vampires are concerned, as you are his in the eyes of mortal authorities. I'll keep him safe for my own reasons. And because I owe you quite the debt, Leora Kupala."

Stephanie's words ease the tension in Leora's shoulders but do nothing to move her grave expression. Levi's hand on her arm does that job instead. The kid just turned fourteen, but he's got more emotional intelligence than some of the adults I know. Just like his big brother, Frankie.

"Come on, Lee." He gives her forearm a gentle tug. "Let's go watch my big sis put your bestie's human cosplay on."

"Okay, Lee."

I catch the ghost of a smile settling in to haunt her face in the sliver of time before she turns and heads down the hall after her friends.

Kids are resilient. Let's hope that goes for me too, because I'm basically the vampiric equivalent.

# CHAPTER EIGHT

We stand outside as I watch Stephanie look for my car, which is at the shop since I just left it there this evening. I blink, totally confused myself. The Pickerings had a van once upon a time, but it got literally taken apart by Deep Ones. Steph, Raven, and DeCampo don't drive, which means I've been like that friend people only keep around because he has a car.

Except, like I said before, I don't right now.

"Need a lift?" Scott walks down the front steps.

"Yeah."

"If it isn't any trouble, young man." Stephanie gives Scott a polite grin.

Well, at least I don't have to drive with one arm. Scott takes back streets instead of the highway as I direct him through Pawtuxet Village, the South Side of Providence, and finally downtown. As I ride along in the crowded cab, I think about my sire, wondering what her agenda is tonight. The last time we visited Providence together, I got the impression we were only welcome on a quid pro quo basis. But that sort of thing never bothered Steph. Not at my apartment or even down in the Deep Ones' domain under the city. She's an equal-opportunity wheeler and dealer.

Stephanie has a habit of making herself welcome. She always looks both totally at home and completely out of place anywhere she happens to be. I've only been stupid enough to ask her true age once. Believe me, you wouldn't dare do it at all if you met her yourself. But my point is, even though she works harder at keeping up with the times than any other really old undead person I know, my sire never quite passes as thoroughly modern.

It's easy for me. I'm a product of the gap years between two centuries. I've got no idea how old Maya is, but she makes fitting in look effortless, probably because of her touch telepathy powers. Raven knows how to pick a counterculture, in their case Goth, and stick with it. Even DeCampo manages to avoid the issue, helped by some force of personality laced with wicked gravity.

Stephanie's charming, don't get me wrong. She's got class but little in the way of style in modern terms. Her figure and the polish she puts on it with posh wardrobe choices would make any other woman appear to be either on the prowl for a partner or predatory in a corporate way. Steph comes across as neither.

It might be her stature. She's five foot nothing, and I've lifted her before. She can't be more than a hundred pounds. Combined with her round cheeks, wide eyes, and button nose, my sire is cute. Her dark, wavy hair and light-olive Mediterranean complexion fit right in here in the Ocean State, too. She could be any woman in a legitimate business, but I happen to know she's nobody to cross if you don't like being cut into ribbons. Yeah, I mean that literally. Steph's an expert swordswoman.

If this makes her sound too perfect, don't worry. She's not. Stephanie's overconfidence got her hoodwinked and captured by a body-snatcher. It also made her easy enough to imitate that I was the only one to realize she literally wasn't herself when her doppelganger rubbed elbows with all of the other Providence vamps. Her arrogant and snide delivery of just about any piece of useful information has made her more enemies than the usual coterie of vampish frenemies. And like many overachievers, her apparent competence makes her an easy target for jealous assholes.

Scott drops us off in the parking lot behind the Arcade, which is closed now. We get out, thanking the werewolf again, and watch him drive away. Stephanie takes a couple of mincing steps toward the building we're heading for, but I put my only arm out and stop her by taking her hand.

"How are we playing this?" I stare directly into her eyes, hoping it's clear that I'm not cool with her making me wing it this time. And I'm right to do so. Last time, she pimped my abilities out to Whitby without so much as a wink in the way of warning.

"I'll make a deal with Whitby this time. Alone."

"Why am I here, then?"

"You'll need make sure we get out of there once he's finished."

"This sounds, um, not good, Steph."

"It isn't." She doesn't break our eye contact. "But it's the best I can do, and still less than DeCampo deserves."

"Can you tell me what, exactly, you're giving this guy?"

"Precisely what he thinks he wants."

"And that is?"

"None of your concern."

"Stephanie."

"We're done discussing this."

"No, we are not." I grip her hand tighter. "Look, my imagination's going places, especially with everything Frankie went through. With the Deep Ones, and how they hurt him."

"It's nothing like that, Tino." She squeezes back. "I'm not closing my eyes and thinking of jolly old England in there if you catch my meaning. I'm vestal, a spinster, abstinent. One variety of what your generation terms asexual, and Whitby's aware of that."

"Is this something to do with your special power?"

"I can't answer that."

"Okay." Vampires are bound by their word, and Stephanie's given hers too many times for her to ever speak with absolute freedom. "Will it make taking the city back for DeCampo even harder?"

"Yes. And no."

"What do you mean by that?"

"I can't tell you, but Raven may be able to." She slips her hand out of my grip. "After we do this deed."

"So, what do I do while you're, um, indisposed, anyway?"

"Mingle as usual." The left corner of her mouth turns up. "Learn what you can from whoever you manage to observe."

"You're not giving me much here, Steph." I get my new notebook out, flip it open, and lean it against a stone windowsill. I make a note to check on Maury's mysterious assaults. After that, I'm ready to jot down more notes in Latin. "I'm an investigator. But having a goal helps."

"I'm not looking for the latest gossip. But I would like to know who seems discontented with the current administration."

"Should I lean on anyone in particular?"

"Let me think." She closes her eyes. "Peligro."

Stephanie can speak Spanish, but I know she doesn't mean literal danger. It's a vampire's nickname.

"Any reason you mention him?" I'm only asking because he came in with Whitby in the first place. And as far as I know, Stephanie's not privy to the fact that he's helped me before.

"So did Maya, Tino. And you know where her loyalties lie."

"Yeah, good point."

"But Peligro's a seer. He gets impressions of truth from people and things. If anyone left in that den of snakes can see a bigger picture of this situation, it'll be him."

"Anything else?"

"Ask around about Shadow." She opens her eyes. "Last time, Whitby told me he died, but that rumor may be greatly exaggerated. I've done some rather extensive searching in my free time, and his Lazakhar still hasn't turned up."

"Yeah, he's probably not an ash pile." I tap my pencil on the paper. "And he went missing before Whitby's memory whammy. So I can see why you want to find him." I don't mention that he isn't likely to do me any favors because the fact that we weren't friends is not important.

"Ask Hargrove about him." Stephanie glances at me, raising her eyebrow.

She knows Hargrove doesn't like me, and the feeling is mutual. But any port in this storm is better than none. Still, something bothers me when I think about Shadow. Almost like I've seen him recently. But my memory is notoriously faulty. I jot a few sentences about the pair of enforcers down in my notebook to check against my larger records from June and July.

"Ask Hargrove about Shadow. Got it." I flip my notebook closed and tuck it away.

"Perhaps Shadow's in a long sleep. If we find him, we could get access to a wealth of useful information. Waking a vampire of his age won't be too difficult for me, and it won't hurt for him to owe us a favor." Stephanie glances at the court building again but raises an eyebrow at me before taking another step. "Is that enough to keep you occupied?"

"Yeah." More than she knows, but I don't tell her that. Now's not the time.

As we walk, I glance behind us. Scott's long since driven away. The building where all of the vampire stuff happens in Providence is across the street from the Arcade. I'm careful not to step in any mud puddles this time. Stephanie probably doesn't even need to think about stuff like that. Maybe in a century or two, I won't have to either.

There's a special knock everybody uses at the door, one designed to have nuances only people with vampiric hearing can discern. We get it right, so at least that much hasn't changed. But when Hargrove, the last remaining enforcer from DeCampo's time here, answers the door, we see that almost everything else has.

The hallway used to be wood-paneled with the real stuff, not that fake 1970s pressboard. Now it's all been whitewashed. This means there aren't any more dark corners for vamps to commune in, the way I did with Maya the night we rescued Stephanie and King DeCampo from Deep Ones. I roll my eyes at the crappy new remodeling job.

DeCampo's style was discreet, and shadowy yet warmly appointed. Whitby's isn't. It's also got more ornate decor in a baroque style that's chic minus the shabby. Cut-glass doorknobs match a trio of chandeliers. All the walls are white, and the crown molding is painted in gilt I'd see myself in if I wasn't a vamp with no reflection. These elements add up to a strange blend of Renaissance and art deco styles, with a finishing touch of chrome.

I hate it.

It's like expecting Hogwarts and getting the White Witch's castle from deep-freeze Narnia instead. I have to work at concealing my distaste. But Stephanie doesn't bother. She's even older than Whitby himself. And she isn't stooping to put on airs over it. Following her example is probably the best choice.

I watch her approach the throne, which is now a tufted affair with a back that would shame any self-respecting albino peacock. The buttons are all diamonds. Whitby takes foppishness to an entirely new and obscene level, apparently.

The vampire who gets in Stephanie's way is only a little taller than her but built like the love child of a brick shithouse and a linebacker. I'm talking about Mrs. Kent, the pink cardigan clad vampire. Usually, her ever-present sweater is unadorned. But tonight, there's a white ribbon pinned to it.

This means she is now one of Whitby's court officers. Also, she's an archivist. Whatever that means. Either nobody explained what vampire archivists do or I forgot. Probably the latter.

Anyway, it's pretty clear that Mrs. Kent is acting as King's attaché. Which is what Raven does for DeCampo. Did. The attaché is supposed to deflect social threats and handle business considered beneath the king's station. But Raven was lightyears better at this job than Mrs. Kent, who seems desperate to keep King Whitby all to herself instead of acting like she's too bored to care what the little people want.

Judging from the thorough eyeballing Whitby gives Stephanie, Mrs. Kent is right to be concerned. Stephanie wasn't specific about all her goals here tonight, but I suspect one of them is positioning herself to make a play for Mrs. Kent's job.

Speaking of occupations, watching Stephanie's personal drama unfold wasn't one of mine this evening. She's older and knows better, at least in social battles like the one she just started. After all, she's just gotten past the attaché and directly to Whitby's side. I lift my foot, about to turn away.

"Crispo."

# CHAPTER NINE

"Good evening, Mrs. Kent." I figure there's no harm in being polite, even if this is the vampire who sold Zack Milano's body, memories, and magical powers to the Deep Ones for a week.

"What's your sire's game?"

"Do you think she tells me any of that?"

"There must be some reason you're here with her, and I'll have it." Mrs. Kent's fists are balled up and resting on her solidly built hips. Archivist or not, I don't want our confrontation coming to blows. I'm a glass cannon in vampire terms. If she decks me, it'd be a TKO even without my stupid injury.

"Blood, Mrs. Kent." I lift the left corner of my opera cloak with my right hand and give her the most blatant and unimpeachable excuse. "She's here to help me get what's needed to grow this back."

"And you couldn't make such a request yourself?" She's tapping one loafer-clad foot against the white marble floor.

"I'm new, and you know it."

"Excuse me?" She blinks. Either Mrs. Kent's deception game is stronger than I thought, or Whitby's whammy also hit her memory. And here we thought he trusted someone enough to keep them in the light, so to speak. If I want more information, I'll have to look like a rube.

"I got turned back in April and did my trials in May, remember?" I shrug and give her that gee-whiz smile I learned from watching syndicated 1950s television at my grandma's house. "We don't want to offend King Whitby because the youngest vampire asks for a favor the wrong way. Well, at least that's what I heard Stephanie say, anyway."

"Fair enough." Mrs. Kent's still standoffish but seems to disregard me as a threat for now. "Off with you." She actually shoos me away.

I nod, smile, wait for her to turn back toward the dais. Once she does, I have a stroll through the room. It's unnerving, partly because I'm wearing a combination of red, brown, and black in a bright white room. I try to spot other vampires, but it's not so easy. They all got the memo about the decor and are clad in pallid outfits of varying shades like a pack of Pastel Goths.

Except for one man. Peligro. Peligro Cabeza, sometimes referred to as Roger. And since he's one of the vamps I'm specifically there to see, I head in his direction. Quietly, so I don't make too much of a spectacle or cause a ruckus.

Unfortunately, I forget that anything or anyone Peligro gets involved with becomes blatant in ten seconds flat. He sees me coming, raises both arms over his head to throw me double waves, then trots halfway across the room, so we meet practically in the middle. Not that there are any dark corners for us to chat in anyway.

"I think I missed out on the dress code announcement, too." I gesture at the black turtleneck and slacks he's wearing under the tan trench coat I've never seen him without.

"Good." Peligro's nodding so enthusiastically I worry about the integrity of his neck and its ability to keep his head on his shoulders. "Lets you have wings."

"Um." I stand perfectly still, unsure what exactly he means until Peligro grabs the lower corners of my opera cloak and flaps them like I'm some kind of fanged bird. "Okay, I guess."

He chuckles, rolling his eyes. The smile on his lips is strained enough to make me wonder what he's really at. I wait his episode out. The whole process reminds me of the kid who shoveled the driveway last winter for my parents on days I was working. Wally, who's on the autism spectrum. Peligro's actions now remind me of Wally when he's stressed and stimming. Maybe he's coping with more than vampirism and whatever precognitive psychic ability he has.

"Thanks, Lieutenant." Peligro's smiling. He looks like how I felt the night my dad came home from the hospital after being shot.

"No problem." I grin back.

He drapes one arm over my shoulders. "Everyone's looking at us, you know."

"Yeah, it happens."

"Where's your arm?" He's whispering even though other vampires can hear that sort of thing anyway. But I'm okay with playing along.

"Left it home," I murmur back. "Too much of a drag."

"It drags?"

"No, sorry." I've heard that autism makes it hard to take some stuff as anything but literal, so I explain. "I made a bad joke just then. My arm got cut off by accident."

"Oh, no *bueno*." He leads me toward a wall. All of the other vampires are hanging out at the sides of the room, even though there aren't any shadows to hide in, no matter how close they get. "Like all this. Like swimming in a fishbowl. I don't like it."

"Yeah, me neither." I cut to the only chase I can think of. "Hey, don't you miss your old friend Maya?"

"Maya. Right." He scratches behind one ear. "Sounds familiar, but I can't put my finger on her."

I'm not sure whether Peligro's actually remembering how things were before Whitby took over here or is just as clueless as everyone else. The finger on her comment might imply he's got some memory or at least information about my girlfriend and her special ability. On the other hand, it might have been a subconscious slip. But then he speaks again.

"She always made sense out of things." Peligro glances at the wall then back at me. "Where angels fear to tread, there goes the girl with all the armor. And scary hands. I can't see her now. But you can. And you do. How is she?"

"Okay, good." I nod. "She's hanging in there. Helping my own good friend, who also has armor and scary hands. But he's not doing so great." I figure there's no reason not to go for broke. "Do you know what he needs? Can you, uh, see it, I mean."

"See?" the upper half of Peligro's face scrunches like he's thinking hard. "Oh, yeah." He snaps his fingers. "Magic."

I'm about to ask him to clarify. He could mean anything by that, from Maya's technically psychic ability to the stuff Esther does in her lab. But I can't because a shadow falls over us. It's strangely comforting even though it shouldn't be.

"Is this guy giving you trouble, Peligro?"

I look up into the face almost half a foot above my head. It's framed by thick, amber braids, and looks about as aggressive as I feel when I think someone's messing with one of my friends. I know this vampire, too.

"Hi, Annie!" Oops.

She doesn't know I know her. Forgetting about huge memory whammies because your own memory sucks is a bad thing. Contrary to popular belief, it's not a good feeling when people who you don't know seem to have all your details. Even in Rhode Island, where everybody knows a guy.

"Stay away from my partner or so help me. I'll put a hole in your heart big enough to obliterate it. At range. When you least expect it." Annie the vampire gunslinger pats the scope-equipped rifle strapped to her back. Which is a ballsy move, considering she's not wearing the white ribbon on her chest that Mrs. Kent and Whitby were sporting.

"Um, okay. Whatever you say." I back away from Peligro, letting his arm slip off my shoulders. "Later."

Making myself scarce is next to impossible in there, but I do the best I can. It's not working. All the vamps lining the walls stare at me. So I do the only thing I can think of. Smile and wave, like Miss Rhode Island in a motorcade. Without the dress, heels, and crown of course.

It works. They stop staring and start whispering to each other instead. About me, but it's still an improvement. I'm a performance artist, but that doesn't mean I'm totally fine with being stared at while not on stage. That much attention at the wrong time has gotten people killed, after all.

I realize I've blown my purpose for being here. Find out Whitby's replacement version of events. But as the murmurs lamenting my newness and social faux pas continue, I start to get an idea that there's consciousness of a collective history here. One where I did my Trials with Whitby and barely passed them, and the Deep Ones never dared show their faces above sea level.

I have a look back up at the throne. Stephanie's sitting on one white-draped chair arm while Whitby is turned sideways as she chats him up. Everything about his posture says he's bored, but I know better. Power of observation comes with both acting and investigating. His eyes don't leave hers. She's got his full attention.

I realize I've got to divert mine or else risk losing track of everything I've discovered so far. Fishing my notebook out of a pocket is easy. So is flipping it open. But I can't write anything down without something to lean it on. Stupid missing arm.

"Allow me."

"Uh." I look up into a face I don't immediately place. I blink, then recognize the meanest fanged mug in my memory. " Hargrove, hi."

"Mr. Crispo." He holds one hand out and glances down at my notepad, then looks me in the eye. I notice the white ribbon pinned to his lapel almost immediately.

"Hey, thanks, but—" Before I can continue my protest, the intimidating vamp plucks the leather-bound paper stack from my only hand.

My stomach does an elevator dance as I wait for him to flip through it and read all my notes. Shadow's a polyglot. It's one of the first things Stephanie told me about him my first night here after getting turned. Shadow knows something like seventeen languages, Latin included. It's one of the things that makes him a good enforcer. Made. Right?

I blink, then shake my head like there's a bug buzzing in my ear.

This is Hargrove here. Shadow's missing, has been since the Deep Ones impersonated Stephanie and took DeCampo. Right? And of course, he's not really reading my notes. The bulky enforcer makes his hatred of books no secret.

"Well?" And he's holding the pad up, paper facing me. Hasn't so much as looked at the empty page it's open to, let alone the rest of it.

"Ah, thanks." I make my notes. He's not watching my hand or even my eyes. Instead, they're on the wall behind me. The enforcer's unexpectedly giving me privacy. After I'm done, he hands it back and is about to walk away.

"Hey, Sha—" I correct myself, but he's turning around anyway. Am I really this brain-damaged? Is he? "Hargrove?"

"Yes?"

"I really appreciate the help there, but I've got to ask why you'd do so much for a sore thumb from another town like me."

"Professional courtesy."

"Huh?"

"Clearly, you are one of the Warwick king's enforcers." He clears his throat emphatically. "I expect you'll use everything I've assisted you with in said capacity."

"Oh." I don't correct him. However, I do notice that he's still the only vamp here who could remotely claim that title under Whitby. And vampire kings typically have two or more. So it's possible that Hargrove's as concerned about his missing counterpart as all of us over at Pickering House are.

"Well, thanks again."

"Don't mention it."

I'm going to, of course. Stephanie will expect a full briefing after we leave. As I put the notebook away, I find a sticky note attached to it. Hargrove must have put it there while he held it for me. But it's blank. I attach it to the page I put my notes on and close the cover, a mystery to delve into later.

---

Stephanie does need an arm to lean on, which I give her until Scott arrives. Together, we help her up and onto the middle of the truck's threadbare bench seat.

It's late by the time we get back to the big house on Ocean Avenue. Well, not for me, but all of the children are sleeping. Frankie's turned in too, probably so he can work on the day job idea. A note on the kitchen table tells us that DeCampo's resting in his basement room, while Raven has gone to the twenty-four-hour Super Walmart with Esther to get more supplies for their projects.

My brain and notebook are full of questions with nobody to ask. I head downstairs, hoping to find Maya watching over the king. I find that she tried, but fell asleep on the sofa in the laundry room.

My first impulse is to lift her, carry her back to one of the vampire guest rooms, and tuck her into the bed in there. That's not happening with my one arm, so I do what real men do when faced with a beautiful slumbering woman. Find the coziest blanket in the linen closet and drape it over her sleeping form, of course.

After that, I grab a bag of blood from the fridge down here and drink it cold, then head into my room for some shuteye of my own.

---

I'm in the Temple to Music at Roger Williams Park, wearing what feels like the makeshift toga I had to don at a frat party during college. I'm also singing, but in a voice with a much higher register than my own.

In this dream, I've got a feminine stature and build. But that's beside the point and nothing new when it comes to blood-induced visions.

The words aren't comprehensible to me. The vowels and consonants ring out over the field in front of the amphitheater. Though nobody is visible out there, it feels like a full house is watching. It's as though they're on the other side of a veil or a wall, one that's thinning by the moment.

Something's around my wrist, but I can't turn my head. Red and white sparks shimmer at the corners of my eyes, blocking any other clues from my peripheral vision.

The last light of the sun squeezes over the horizon, hitting my face as the notes in my throat reach a crescendo. But my borrowed voice cracks, the sparks fade, and darkness falls as I drop to the marble beneath my feet.

I wake, expecting a mass of ashes on my pillow, desperate hunger, severe heartburn. But there's nothing. Which can only mean one thing.

The blood I drank wasn't from a dead person. I'm getting visions from the living now.

It's still midday, so I go back to sleep. As I drift off, my gut tells me to keep this new development a secret for now.

# CHAPTER TEN

I spend part of the next afternoon in my windowless basement room, transferring things from my spiffy new notebook into the battered composition book I compile everything into. Details about the assault investigation also go into an old Acer Netbook I affectionately call "the Craptop."

Internet searches on what kind of cryptid bruises wrists with a side effect of lost time give me next to nothing. I shoot off an email to Sasquatch, the only real expert on rare supernatural folk and critters. An automated reply comes back, telling me he's in the field. I knock on wood, hoping he'll have something for me within a week or two.

After the sun sets, I grab a cup of warmed blood from the downstairs coffee maker. Some other vamp is already awake, so I bring my breakfast upstairs.

All four of the kiddos are in the back parlor with a movie on, sitting around a bowl of what smells like caramel kettle corn. With cinnamon. If I wasn't already undead, I'd die of envy. Food is still the number one thing I miss about having a functioning digestive system.

"How'd it go last night?" The slender, cool hand slipping into mine is instantly familiar and comes complete with a deep undertone of curiosity.

"Um," is all I manage verbally. I give Maya the whole obnoxious experience at Whitby's version of the vampire club without saying another word.

"Wow," is all she says back.

"Yeah, Stephanie had it worse, I bet." I squeeze Maya's hand.

"She's with Raven, talking about blood and alchemy."

"Ah." I'd be staring out into space, but the images on the flat screen catch my eye. "Teenagers watching *Phantom of the Opera*. Brings back memories."

This time the kids hear me. Levi presses a button to pause the movie. Sarah rolls her eyes and elbows her brother. Sparky tosses me an idle wave. Leora's eyes home in immediately on my hand, intertwined with Maya's. She smiles and drops me a wink.

"You know, Maury and I did most of that show back in the day, for the Thespian Society Regionals. Even made it to State a couple of times."

"Well, it's what they're doing this fall at our school."

"Oh, really?"

"Yeah, we're watching it to get ready for auditions."

"When are those happening?"

"Next week."

"Cool."

"You know, Tino might be able to teach you a thing or two about that." Maya lets go of my hand and jerks her thumb at me. "He's got it down."

"I don't need help." Sarah flips a lock of dark hair over one shoulder.

"Well, I'll give it a try." Levi shrugs. "He knows more than I do."

"This is so awesome!" Leora jumps up from her seat on the floor and rushes me. It's totally unexpected, so I just roll with the spontaneous hug. Well, as much as one-armed little old me can manage while holding a half-full mug, anyway.

I'm her legal guardian, so acting at least a little bit paternal is something I should get used to, I guess. Especially after the court gave me and Frankie custody instead of the big money crime family. But that's another story.

"Hey, me too, man?" Most people would frame Sparky's question as a statement. Then again, most people aren't acquainted with magical shapeshifting salamanders. He's still a teen like the other three, even if he's not enrolled at their fancy private school. And I did catch him eyeballing a flyer advertising voice lessons a couple months ago.

"Yeah, sure." I flash him a grin because I'm still not sure whether my fanged smile bothers him or not. That kid's hard to read.

"Tino, you're the best."

"Nah."

That makes Leora break out of the hug. She steps back and gives me a grave look, the same one from the first night we met while sincerely thanking me for finding Sparky. I realize the whole self-deprecation angle isn't going to fly around my ward, so I'd better keep it quiet in front of her.

"Fine. I'm okay, I guess."

"I think you're better than that." Leora puts her hands on her hips.

Sarah Pickering lets out a snorting little laugh. "But not better than your new friend at school. Seb—"

I think she's about to say "Sebastian." As in Caprice, the Lethian. I open my mouth.

Leora blinks, then cuts Sarah off pronto. "So, do we start this performance coaching tonight?"

"Of course not, witchbait." Sarah grins at Leora. "We've got homework."

It's not the nicest expression, but it gets returned. I'm not sure Leora loves Sarah's snark or this nickname, but it doesn't seem she can't handle it, either. I decide to deflect the bout of foster-sibling rivalry the girls have going on instead of freaking out about their monstrous Mafioso classmate.

"You know, maybe I didn't really think this all through."

"You're not gonna teach us, buddy?" Sparky's mouth turns down into a pout.

"Of course, he is." Maya pats my shoulder. "You are, Tino." It's not a question. Apparently, my paramour is at least as big a softie for these kiddos as I am.

"My missing arm is kind of conspicuous." I clear my throat.

"Esther's on her way over." Sparky smiles. "She's got something you can use."

"Well, that's awesome. Thanks, kid. But there's one more problem." I clear my throat even though undead people don't generally get post-nasal drip. "How am I going to help you three out while I'm confined to the night shift?"

"You can help them in the daytime." Sarah shrugs.

"He can't teach us in the basement while the other vamps are sleeping." Levi sighs as though this fact should have been obvious to his sister.

"I'm not saying he should." Sarah sniffs.

"Well, where then?"

"At the regular time, right in Stout Academy's Theater."

"My sunlight allergy kind of prevents that, though." I jerk my chin at the early evening sky peeping through the parlor's bay window. "In the daytime, I get the worst sunburn ever."

"There's a tunnel, and theaters have no windows. As your generation likes to say, 'duh.'" Sarah taps one cheek with her first finger, making a fake dimple.

"Wait, what?" I blink, ignoring for a moment that the word "duh" is a Gen-X thing and I'm a Millenial. "A tunnel? Where?"

"Oh, they're all over this old place." She waves one hand toward a large oil painting of the ocean on the other side of the room. "You can get into the one I'm talking about behind that monstrosity."

"Huh." I shrug. "Frankie never told me."

"He didn't know. Us Pickerings are totally hooked up with the Deep Ones, including literally with tunnels. They run all under Warwick and most of Roger Williams Park. Some of Cranston and Providence, too."

"Wow. I had no idea." I get my notebook out, resting it on a table as

I scribble something down about the tunnels and the park. That's going to help me big-time in the assault investigation.

"Well, now you do."

"Thanks, Sarah."

"Oh." She blinks. I guess maybe she's not used to being thanked most of the time. And I get it. Went through a phase like that while I was a beat cop. Nobody likes you when you're writing them a ticket, believe me. And Sarah's more than a bit of a taskmaster. "Um."

"You're welcome!" Sparky belts out the line from that song in the Disney movie. Maybe the salamander kid is something like a shapeshifting demi-god, though not nearly as surly as Maui, and seriously lacking in the magical fish hook department.

It's enough to break the tension, so everybody laughs. Two more voices I hadn't expected join in from the other door to the parlor. I look up to find Frankie and Raven there. I peer past them, looking for Stephanie.

"Your sire took off." Frankie crosses the room, heading toward the painting. "I heard what Sarah said, and I'm boarding this up. Go do your other homework. Movie night is over."

The kids all grumble and groan, but none of them challenge their foster co-parent. Apparently, Frankie's the disciplinarian in this household as far as the teenagers are concerned. They gather up their pillows and blankets, then head upstairs.

Sparky goes with them, and I don't have the heart to tell him he should head back to Baba's. What's the harm in letting the salamander hang around with people he can relate to who know what he is and don't mind?

Turns out, I have no idea.

---

When I look back toward the parlor, Frankie's gone. I glance at Raven and then at Maya. They both shrug. When I hear the back door slam through the kitchen, I remember what Frankie said he'd do.

"You don't think he's really going to—" Maya blinks at the ugly old portrait.

"I hope not." I sigh. "But he probably will, even though limiting exits is a total fire hazard. Along with every other advantage these tunnels can give us."

"Don't worry guys, I got this." Raven steps out of the door from the hallway.

When Frankie strides back through the door from the kitchen, carrying a bundle of two by fours under one arm and a toolbox under the other, Raven stands in his way.

"Move it," Frankie snaps.

"No."

"You're not the boss of me."

"Yes, I am, Francis."

"Tino, back me up, dude."

"Sorry, Frankie. I can't."

"What?"

"You heard me. I promised the kids I'd help them practice, rehearse. You know, the coaching thing?" I reach out, grabbing one end of the off-balance toolbox. "And I promised to help Maury with a case. Those tunnels will help me help them."

"Shitballs. Vampire vows for the lose." He passes the box of hammers and nails over to me but keeps the boards, which I wouldn't want to hold anyway. Splinters and vampires don't mix well.

"Yeah, that's about the eternal size and shape of it."

"Times two." Raven gives Frankie a twisted grin. "I've got a whole pile of those between this family and the Deep Ones. Trust me, Frankie, you don't need to board up any of the tunnels. I've got our safety covered already."

"You actually trust those bastards?" Frankie's arms tighten, causing the wood under one of them to click and groan. He smells different right now too, acrid somehow. But this is nothing new to my nose. It's adrenaline.

"They're supernatural creatures, Frankie. They're not like magicians or werewolves. If they break the agreement and lose their powers, they die." Raven's statement makes me wonder whether that's what happens to vampires when we go back on a promise.

"And your new agreement stops them from just walking in here whenever they feel like it?"

"Yes." Raven places a hand on Frankie's shoulder. "I still have nightmares about them too. I'd never have agreed to a contract without a rule keeping them out of our house."

With clash and a clatter, the wood drops to the floor. Frankie's head bows. Raven pulls him into a hug, hiding his face against their shoulder. They stand, swaying like a couple slow dancing at a prom, except way underdressed. Before you get any icky ideas, this whole interaction has a definitively platonic vibe.

In this, the two of them are partners. Both of them went through similar abuse at the hands of those monsters from the deep. The hitching breaths Frankie takes, punctuated by the occasional sniffle, are the only indications this isn't just your garden-variety familial embrace.

"Are they going to be okay?" Maya nudges me with one elbow.

"Yeah." I go to loop my left arm around her. But of course, it's still missing. I turn to face her instead. "Sometimes you need a rock to lean on. Other times, a couple of trees in the same wind are just as good for each other."

"Wow. Zen." Maya tilts her head up and gazes into my eyes. "You ever write any haiku?" She smirks.

"Nah." I grin. "Limericks are way more fun. Let me demonstrate. There once was a man from Nantucket—"

"Do any of you have a bucket?" Sparky pokes his head out from the door to the hall.

Everybody stops what they're doing and turns to look at the salamander kid. We stand there blinking at each other.

"What?" Sparky shrugs, stepping into the room and glancing around. "We're cleaning up a massive boba tea spill. There's not one in here, is there?"

"No, kid." Frankie shakes his head, then points at the dropped wood and tools on the floor beside him. "Just a Lamb, dealing with his old Lamb baggage again. Bucket's in the kitchen."

"Oh. Sorry." Sparky strides over, bends down, and starts gathering the wood back into a bundle. "I got this."

"Thanks, Sparky." Frankie reaches for the toolbox, so I hand it over.

"Want some help bringing those back out to the shed, buddy? I'll get the bucket on the way back."

"Yeah, if you don't mind."

The strange pair walk into the kitchen, headed outside to put the unneeded materials and tools away. Raven steps forward, putting their hands on their hips. Maya and I give them our full attention.

"Before they get back, I wanted to tell you two where Stephanie went."

"Okay."

"She called Dr. Maris the second she got up this evening. By now, she's probably going through Kent County's stock of dead blood."

"That's awesome."

"Maybe." Raven shrugs. "I'm cautiously optimistic, but only a little. It's unlikely we'll find anything to help the king in there."

"Why?"

"I can't say exactly what he needs. Neither can Stephanie."

"That goes double for me." Maya shakes her head. "But I can tell you it's not likely to be found in supplies of dead blood."

"Can't I just ask DeCampo?" I shake my head. "I can't help if I don't know what he needs."

"You could try, but I don't recommend it." Raven's eyes are everywhere except on my face. I'm actually kind of freaked out right now. "Your arm's…" The rest of their words are so soft even I can't make them out.

"I'll take your word for it."

"Wow, Tino." Raven blinks. "You never give up on anything this easily."

"I'm not giving up, just preparing to explore from a different angle."

"I knew you were a fast learner." Raven turns their back, facing the kitchen door.

"Hold on a minute there, attaché." I chuckle. "I'm not done with you yet."

"Oh?" Raven doesn't turn around but stands still.

"I'm going to need either a tour through those tunnels or a map and a compass."

"Why?" This time Raven turns around and looks me full in the face.

"I promised to train the kids. Unless you guys want me to have them do scales in the basement while you all are trying to sleep every day."

"I don't, but that's a family secret, Tino. And you're not a Pickering, even if you are co-parenting with one."

"Okay, if that's not enough incentive for you, I need a way into Stout Academy on school days." And ways out of here in general, especially while my car's in the shop and I'm armless. Maury's short on time.

"Still doesn't give me good enough reason to share information this sensitive."

I need to give Raven a good reason, one that doesn't make them look over my shoulder the entire time I'm investigating Maury's case.

"Is Sebastian Caprice getting, er, friendly with Sarah and Leora enough incentive for you?"

"Valentino Crispo, you've got yourself a deal."

"A deal?" Frankie walks back through the door, Sparky trailing behind him.

"Yes." Raven nods. "Go get some graph paper from the study, Frankie. Some drafting pencils too. I'm making a map."

"I love maps!" Sparky claps his hands, almost dropping the blue bucket tucked under his arm.

"You're supposed to be somewhere else, kid. Go up to bed, or I send you back to Baba's."

"Okay, buddy." Sparky shuffles toward the hall and the stairway. "Whatever you say."

Frankie follows Sparky up shortly after with some sodas and school supplies. Raven and I work on the map for a while.

Esther finally arrives, coming in through the kitchen door instead of the front. The green glow of magic tells me she's either got an alchemy gadget that lets her unlock doors, or she's activating a ward on the way in here. She doesn't give me a chance to ask which.

"I heard some brainless twat-waffle got his fucking arm clawed off."

Esther stomps up to the empty chair beside me, then drops the large laundry sack off her shoulder. It hits the floor with a hollow thud. She turns the chair around and sits on it, leaning her arms on the tall wooden back.

"Yup, that's about right." I close the pad I was taking notes on and set the pencil down.

"Let's see that shit." Esther holds out one hand.

I shrug off my opera cloak, draping it on the chair, and turn toward her.

For once, Esther is speechless. Eventually, she manages a low whistle.

"Tell me you're not about to catcall my stump."

"What do you think I am, some kind of twisted shit-turnip?"

"Well, no." I stare at the sack beside Esther's booted feet to avoid looking anyone in the eye. "It's bad, huh?"

"I've been worse." She slaps the table. "Seen. I fucking meant seen."

"Look, I saw your urn." I'm talking about the one with the memory of how she lost her arm in it, from Mnemosyne's vault. "It's okay."

"No, it sucks hairy, wet donkey ass." Esther leans down to rummage in the giant bag. "But I'll stop acting like an ingrate turd-monger and pretending you don't know shit."

"You're welcome." Honestly, there's nothing else I can think of to say to that.

"Fucking-a, you are." She chuckles, then sits up. "Can't use any fucking wood on a damn vampire, so this fake plastic crap ought to do it."

Esther's holding what looks like a handful of drafting supplies.

She's got rulers, angles, even a French curve. I blink, looking from her to Raven to the graph paper map on the table.

"Uh, are you helping Raven with that drawing project or me with my arm?"

"Well, that's some coincidental fucking nonsense." Esther barks out a laugh. "This shit's not for them. It's gonna be your goddamned arm."

After that, Esther's so involved in her alchemical spellwork I can't justify interrupting her. Which is bad because I wanted to ask her about Hargrove's Post-it note. But a substitute arm is more of a priority for me at the moment. There will be time later on for the other stuff.

But I'm wrong. The arm rigging takes all night. It's practically miraculous how Esther took a collection of seemingly random plastic items and made them into a fully articulated limb. Even the fingers move like an actual hand's.

Esther's nodding in her seat at the table. She even snores a couple of times. Raven pauses in their mapmaking to settle the alchemist in on the sofa. Unfortunately, this all happens before she can attach the arm to my shoulder. On the bright side, it's a good time for me to get some rest as well.

Before turning in for the morning, I manage to find a magnetic compass in the parlor's sideboard. I also drop the heavy curtains over the bay window, making the room lightless enough for me to get into the tunnel behind the portrait the next day.

Finally, years out of high school, I'll get to satisfy my curiosity and see the inside of hoity-toity Stout Academy for the first time.

Missing an arm and vamped, but nothing and nobody in this world is perfect.

## CHAPTER ELEVEN

My footsteps echo as I walk down cobblestone-floored tunnels with walls made of pockmarked brick. Most of the human population knows that there are catacombs under Providence but not about the ones that stretch underneath Warwick Neck. I'm alone, so I don't need a light, but I have to hold the map and the compass in one hand. It's not easy, but it's doable.

Every now and again, I check my bearings against the lines on the graph paper. I'm almost at where the turnoff is for Stout Academy's theater basement, and there it is. A slab of granite juts up from the floor beside the corner I need to turn.

I bang a right and fold my map, then tuck it away in a pocket of my opera cloak before reaching out to try the doorknob. The compass clatters to the stone at my feet. I bend to pick it up, scooping it from the cold surface into my not much warmer fingers.

Instead of putting it in my pocket, I take the keyring it's attached to and hook it on my belt loop. You never know when you're going to need a compass while tooling around strange places without being able to see the sky. Not that I was ever able to navigate by the stars.

I step to one side and reach for the doorknob again. It's not where I think it will be. The right-hand side of the door is as barren as a scorched field. The door feels like maybe it's had that experience, too. Which doesn't make me happy because fire bad, vampire no like.

I stop and think, wondering how I'm supposed to get in, and what the point of a tunnel is when it's got doors with no knobs, handles, or latches. I know some of the Pickering ancestors had cockamamie ideas, but this is just plain ridiculous.

Leaning against the door, I contemplate my next course of action. Thinking doesn't do much. I'm uninspired because dammit, I'm a PI, not a contractor. Or whatever you call people who design secret underground doors.

There's a million-dollar question I always ask myself almost every time I'm this stuck. So I wonder what would Maury do, standing outside the door he'd already know how to just walk on through.

By Jove, I think I've got it.

I reach across my body to the other side of the door. Sure enough, there's a minuscule latch blending its bad self in with the old, scarred wood it's embedded in. A rocket scientist I am not, but that should come as no surprise to you at this point. I lift the latch with my hand, then push.

Nothing happens. Well, that's not exactly true. The latch moves, flattening down like one of those levers on the back of a garlic press. Except there's no garlic anywhere, unfortunately, and thank goodness. I simultaneously pine for its loss and curse its presence nightly. But anyway, the door doesn't move forward. So I take the next logical action. No, not busting boards. I'm not some door-kicking maniac.

There's this old comic, the kind that used to run when everybody read print newspapers. One frame, sight gag, often punny. I used to love those. Anyway, the one I'm remembering has a picture of The School for the Gifted and Talented. The kid outside leans on the door, pushing with all his might. And right above his head, in bold black lettering, is the word Pull.

Today I feel like that kid, and I'm supposed to be teaching a handful of teenagers. At least their lesson doesn't have anything to do with opening and closing doors. Because apparently, I could still use some more practice with that. Yeah, I'm a freaking genius.

I pull. It works. I step through.

The new room is a broom closet. Literally. I know this because I almost stake myself on an errant handle while bumbling around in there. Who am I kidding? I don't bumble, I flail like my mom when there's a spider in the kitchen. Well, as much as I can. It's a broom closet, not a ballroom, after all.

The door opens, and I'm face to face with the last person I wanted to see in the middle of the day at Stout Academy.

"Tino?" Zack Milano blinks, then throws his head back and lets out a rolling belly laugh.

I can't be mad at him, either. I'm literally wearing a mop on my head. I reach up and toss it aside.

"Guilty as charged." I shrug, knocking the broom that's trying to get too friendly with my ribcage against the wall behind me. "What are you doing here?"

"Volunteering. You?"

"Same thing."

"Ha!" Zack snorts, then looks down his nose at me. "If I let you."

"Wow. Really friendly talk, especially considering the solid I did you just recently."

"Oh. Yeah." Zack doesn't hang his head. Which, I mean, he should. I only gave him back his memories about being a powerful magician and all. But he averts his eyes, at least.

"Yeah." I put my hands on my hips. Nothing helps a vamp wax assertive like someone owing one of us a favor.

"Fine, then." He rolls his eyes, but he meets my gaze afterward. "Coming out of the literal closet?" He steps aside.

"Yeah, sure, fine, whatever." I walk right past him, unconcerned about his toxic masculinity jibe or meeting the sun. Because I already know Stout Academy has no place inside its theater where sunlight can reach, thanks to the kids.

"Hold on, Tino." Zack paces me as I stride through the broad passageway under the stage. "You can't do any volunteer work here without a pass."

"Okay." I glance at him. "Where do I get one of those?"

"The lovely and sunny front office."

The words I utter in Italian would get my mouth washed out with soap if my mother ever reads this. So I'm not repeating them here even if Esther might respect them. Zack's not bilingual, but he gets the gist.

"I'll bring you the form and have a student run it back after you sign it."

"Thanks, Zack. You're a pal."

"Does that mean I don't owe you now?"

"I went into a Titan's vault to get your memories back, and you think a little form-wrangling makes up for that?" Yeah, Milano is in frenemy territory, like Kayleigh Killarney. I can trust him to act in certain expected ways that benefit him directly, but not the same way I can rely on folks like Frankie or Maya.

"Well, you can't blame me for trying." His smile is toothy, with an eye twinkle his male-admiring broadcast news fans must swoon over. Me, not so much.

"So, you're coaching kids too?" Changing the subject is often the only way to keep things copacetic if you know what I mean.

"Yeah." He walks up the steps leading to the stage level.

"Okay." I follow him.

When we step out into the wings, I see the house lights are up. For some reason, I had a random and unfounded fear that working lights would be on and I'd get a follow spot the second I step on the apron from the wings. But that doesn't happen, of course. I glance up to see that nobody's even in the light booth and breathe a sigh of relief. Yeah, stage fright is still a thing, even when you're undead.

And right now, I realize that even without an actual theatrical performance happening in here, I still need to act. Like a regular human, I mean. My kiddos aren't the only ones around, and I don't want to be Mister Scary Vampire.

Breathing and directing some of my focus toward making my skin feel slightly warmer than room temperature are on my mind. But my thought train's forcibly stopped by something slamming into my midsection.

*"Oof!"*

"Tino! You're here!" It's Leora, of course. She would have knocked me over if she weren't on the small side for her age.

"Hey, kiddo." I pat her back until she lets me go and sits beside Sarah, who tolerates her presence.

"Jeez." And there's the Sarah Pickering I know, rolling her eyes at me from the edge of the apron where she's sitting.

"Attitude much?" Levi blows a raspberry at his older sister from the front row, where he's in the middle of a line of other students.

"What are you, eleven, still?" Sarah turns her nose up at her brother. A few of the others in the row titter, but most smile at Levi instead. He's outdoing her in the making friends and influencing people department. Good on him.

"Hello?" The feminine voice from up in the back row is musical and somehow familiar.

"Um, hi?" I squint, trying to peer at the figure back there, but it's pretty much fruitless. She's backlit by brighter lights from the lobby. "Valentino Crispo, vocal coach."

"Valentino, as I live and breathe!" The door closes behind her, and now I know who's in charge of all the adulting here. Another old theater friend from back in the day.

"Eunie?"

"Uh-huh!"

I absolutely know the woman walking up the steps at the side of the apron, arms laden with scripts. It's Eunice Terry, who was a senior when I was a freshman back at Cranston West. If she hadn't been there, Maury and I might never have joined Drama Club.

"Yeah, she ended up teaching." Zack's backhanded compliment pulls the corners of my mouth down. He's a firm believer in the old bullshit adage, "those who can't, teach." I'd elbow him in the rib for that, but he's gotten off the stage and into the front row. I decide to ignore his attitude and greet my old role model.

"How have you been, Eunie?"

"Well, technically, it's Dr. Terry now, but you can call me Eunie once all your paperwork's in." She shoots Zack a glare that hooks his attention back her way, then jerks her chin at the door.

"Hey, who's going to help me run paperwork for Mister Crispo here?"

"On it." The voice comes from behind me and to the right, from the wings I just left with Zack.

"Huh?" I blink, startled by my own utterance. Because Zack's little helper is Sparky

"Hey, b—uh, Mister Crispo."

"Hi." I blink again. The last person I expected to see here is the salamander. "How you doing?"

"Okay. Gonna help Mister Milano like usual." He adjusts the ball cap he always wears around mundanes, even though this is a school for supernatural folks, then beats feet to keep up with Zack.

It occurs to me that Zack Milano has been interfering in my life during the day when I can't do anything about it. I wonder how long this has been going on, and what his motive is. But Zack's just a bad friend, not a criminal. Right? The only way to find out is to ask some questions.

"Like usu—"

"This is good of you, Tino," Eunice pats the section of the stage's apron beside her.

"Uh, what?"

"Coming here to help at the school your kids are going to."

"Um, well," I drop into the old familiar seating arrangement as though it hasn't been over ten years since I shared a stage with Eunice Terry. "You know. Things happen. And Frankie's definitely not a performance artist."

"So Sarah tells me." Eunice hands the stack of librettos to my oldest and snootiest ward. "Hand those out, if you please."

For once, Sarah doesn't roll her eyes. Either she respects Eunice or fears her. I'm not sure what fright looks like on the girl because she's never shown it where I can see. Also, my opinion's a bit biased toward the teacher here, so I opt for respect.

"So how'd you end up teaching Drama at Stout?"

"They came looking for me, actually."

"Oh?"

"Yeah, but they hired me for more than this. My post-doctoral work caught their eye."

"Cool." I wait for Eunice to start telling me all about it. She always used to be a chatterbox, absolutely the friendliest extrovert I've ever met. But she only nods, watching the students flipping through their librettos.

The silence isn't uncomfortable, though there's something unsaid hanging in the air between us. I don't want to break it and risk whatever's unspoken catching fire and burning any bridges. Instead, I just let my feet swing.

It's novel, dangling your legs as a full-grown adult. The gravity between your feet and the floor makes you feel younger, remember the carefree assumption of invincibility almost everyone has up until a certain point in their lives. I close my eyes and Frankie's there in the red-tinged darkness behind my eyelids.

He wouldn't know this feeling I've got now if it smacked him upside the head. Because he never had the chance to experience something so untainted by horror. All he wants is for things to be easier on the next generation than how he had it, a sentiment we share.

And so, I'm here for his siblings and for Leora, trying to sweep whatever shards of innocence they've got left back together again. My phone buzzes in my pocket, so I open my eyes and reach for it.

Think of the Devil, and he shall appear. Frankie's texting me.

**Tino, I'm not sure I can do this.**

**Yeah, you can.**

**I'm at the door and want to turn around. I'm not going in there alone.**

He's talking about his appointment with the therapist, Doctor Young. Which he was supposed to go to after picking my car up from the shop today.

**Just walk on in, my dude. You've got this.**

**No, I don't.**

**You will. Reschedule for after sunset, and I'll come with you.**

**I'll do that. Thanks, Tino.**

I send back some emojis. Clapping hands, thumbs-up, and then end with a semicolon. He knows what I mean by that, but maybe you don't. It's a long story, told elsewhere, but he's got a tattoo of that on his wrist, covering some scars. Since he showed it to me, we've tossed the punctuation at each other in texts to show each other support.

"So, Frankie Pickering's the guy, huh?" Eunice grins.

"Uh, we're domestic partners, but platonic." That silence eases, and I understand Eunice in a way I never considered back in the day. "Corey. Your old pen-pal from Greece. She's the gal."

"Yes. We got married in 2013." The year Rhode Island made it legal for two women to wed.

"Congratulations." I hold out my hand.

She hugs me, complete with patting on the shoulder and everything. It's totally genuine, but Eunice has an ulterior motive for the friendly display of affection.

"Vampire, huh?" she murmurs. "It's okay. None of us at Stout are completely mundane."

"I didn't know you were a magician." I stiffen, but Eunice gives my shoulder one more solid pat.

"I'm just psychic, but it's all good."

"Okay."

There's really nothing else I can say to that. And at the end of the hug, I realize that's fine. Everything's hunky-dory because that's how Eunice Terry gives my introduction to her class. A few of the kids blink owlishly or stare with slightly out-of-focus eyes at me. I realize they're checking to confirm my undead status. But once they stop, each one either nods or gives me a grin.

My identity isn't so secret here at Stout Academy. Instead of the pit of dread I thought would form in my gut, my lips turn up. Sparky scuttles through the door with some papers. I fill in my name, address, phone, and driver's license numbers, then sign it. He hustles back out with it, nearly running into Zack on the way.

"Watch yourself." Zack snarls. A ruddy shimmer leaves his lips along with the harsh words.

Sparky says nothing, but his eyes are glued to his own feet.

"Ease up on the kid, would you?" I give Zack a side-eye. I've been literally jerked around by one of Milano's spell-singing incantations before and hated it, even if it did net us a win against the bad guys.

"He's not even enrolled here."

"Well, nobody's complaining except you." Eunice stands between us, hands in fists on her hips. "Let the orphans have their support salamander, Zack."

"I'm already doing them a favor, but whatever." This time, the utterance is silver. He's undoing the command. I hope.

As we get on with giving one-on-one advice about reading the script before choosing an audition piece, I come to a fundamental understanding. The three adults in the room are all here for different reasons.

For Eunice, it's simply that teaching is as natural to her as breathing. I'm there because my newly-extended family needs me. I'd bet dollars to donuts it's neither of those for Zack, and I can't even eat donuts. It'd be easy to assume this is his usual showboating, like at the audition for *Nine*. I could just chalk it up to him being a showoff, but my gut tells me it's deeper than that.

He's taking my welcome presence here way too hard, and I feel the long-static frenemy vibe turning into something more sour. Zack's got a reason for being here besides self-promotion. It's enormous and important, and I have no clue what it could be.

Maybe he can let it go and stick with the uneasy truce that's stretched between us all these years. Stretchy things have a bad habit of snapping back, though. Hopefully it'll only hit me if the worst even happens.

Of course, with my luck, I can practically count on that.

# CHAPTER TWELVE

Scott drops me at the main entrance. Seconds later, I'm walking up from the parking lot behind Kent County Hospital, heading toward the annex building and the office of one Doctor Young, Psychiatrist. A plume of smoke from under the bus shelter tells me Frankie's there waiting. And Raven's earlier text message said more; how my friend never came home after the canceled appointment.

Plastering a smile on my face is easy because I always had more reasons to grin than otherwise in my breathing life. The unlife is a whole other matter entirely. Maybe Frankie's not the only one who needs therapy.

He puts the cigarette out on the nearly smooth sole of his threadbare Converse All-Stars. I can tell right away he's been chain-smoking. My first impulse is to get on his case because I don't want him upstairs in the Oncology ward in a handful of years like Maury. But I don't. Some people have got to deal with the brain before the body. Frankie's neglected his mental health for his whole life, through no fault of his own. This is a legitimate emergency, he's in the middle of a potentially fatal medical crisis.

Whoever says mental illness is all in the head like it's somehow imaginary can just leave now.

Get out. I mean it.

Stop following my adventures and take a flying fuck at a donut. I'm not sorry if that sounds harsh because it's supposed to. The brain is an organ in the body, and it can get sick like any other. Just because it's in the head doesn't mean it's not real, like the subversive old wizard said. And Frankie can't ignore his disease without consequence any more than Maury can bail on chemotherapy.

Anyway, rant over.

"Tino, thank God."

"He's got nothing to do with it."

"Dude. You're too hard on yourself." Frankie chuckles. I've known him long enough to understand that it's actually a well-disguised sob.

"Come on, we're going in."

"You're awfully gung-ho."

"Well, yeah. I probably need this too."

"Huh." Frankie trots to keep up with me. "How?"

"I used to go to church when I had a problem." I pull the door open and step inside, holding it. "Can't anymore, you know why."

"Oh. Right." He takes two steps past me, then freezes in front of the door to the office.

Usually, we take turns opening and holding doors for each other as part of our platonic lifemates vibe, but not this time. Maybe it's something like a metaphor for our entire interpersonal dynamic. Or whatever is between Frankie and me.

"I can't."

"You can't, or you can't even?"

"Even."

"Okay, so odd, then. I'll even for both of us." I open the next door and stand aside. Because like it or not, I can't fight this particular battle of Frankie's for him. All I can do is be here so he doesn't have to do it alone.

He takes a deep breath, swallows, sets his jaw. Clenches it, actually. And then, he takes measured steps forward, mumbling.

"One. Three. Five. Seven."

Yeah. That's Frankie Pickering there, reciting odd numbers as a way to defy his anxiety. It's like he's got armor made of nonsense, which is better than nothing at all, I guess. And it's familiar. But for once, I'm not stuck wondering how. Because I totally recognize that he's adopted my own tactic.

"Proud of you, my dude."

I don't pat him on the back as he shuffles past me. Maybe it'd seem condescending or belittling. But mostly it's because I know a thing or three about nonsensical armor. It's brittle when you first start girding it on. Breaking it just when Frankie needs it most is not an option.

The woman perched behind the desk is plump, with straight hair falling to her shoulders in streaks of black and white. She tilts her head up, gaze lingering on Frankie as she nods in my general direction. There's something more than natural about her, which makes sense.

"We're here for our appointment with Doctor Young," I announce.

"Nineteen," Frankie murmurs.

"Go right in." She waves her hand at the door to her left.

"Thanks, uh," I squint at the small nameplate in front of her. "Ms. Chen?"

"Yes." The corners of her mouth tilt up.

I smile back even though Ms. Chen still hasn't looked directly at me. I'm unsure why, and even though my inquiring mind wants to know, it's a mystery for some other time.

Frankie fumbles with the doorknob. Just as I'm about to help him, the door opens, revealing a diminutive fellow with a fringe of dark brown hair ringing his mostly bald head. His orange and red plaid shirt is tucked into his sky blue chinos though he wears no belt. The breast pocket on his flannel sports a pocket protector containing several mismatched ball-point pens.

I'm not sure what to expect inside the office, but it sure as hell wasn't this. Every wall is hung with a different religion's icon. Dr. Young doesn't seem to be nondenominational like Dr. Maris led me to believe. Instead he appears to be poly-denominational. There is such a thing as too inclusive. I never imagined I'd think something like that, but there's a first time for everything. And I guess it's really not a good idea to say never. After all, I never thought I'd be walking into a therapist's office with another man, but here I am.

Frankie has a seat on one of the two single chairs. There's a couch, but it's small, loveseat-sized. The fact that he doesn't take it and invite me to sit beside him speaks volumes. Just a couple of weeks ago, I think our seating arrangements might've been totally different. Or maybe I'm just flattering myself, which is almost as bad an idea as saying never. Okay maybe it's a worse idea than that.

I sit in the middle of the loveseat, not giving a good goddamn what kind of statement that makes to Dr. Young. And it does make a statement. He's jotting notes on a clipboard he holds tilted away from us, supported by the edge of his desk. Dr. Young must have either a high office chair or some sort of booster seat. The front of his desk is solid, with a wooden panel over the knee space. Otherwise, I'd expect to see his feet swinging or supported on some kind of gargantuan footrest.

I just realized exactly how jerky I sound here. Dr. Young is in the business of helping people. Business. Helping. I don't feel comfortable with that, and I'm only realizing it for the first time. I roll my eyes, lean my elbow on one knee, and settle my cheek on my hand. The eye roll is from me to myself and I. Because I'm a total hypocrite right now.

"If neither of you wants to be here, the door is that way." Dr. Young jerks his wobbly chin at the door we just came in through.

"Jeez, Doc, you don't screw around." Frankie blinks.

"I'm one of two doctors in this very populous state who's in the know about what you people go through. I don't have time to screw around. Others who want my help are waiting."

"It's not that I don't want help." Frankie clasps his hands together, a gesture I've come to understand is his way of keeping them from shaking visibly. But my hearing is acute enough to discern the rustle of his sleeves against his twitching forearms.

"I understand that, but your partner there doesn't."

"I don't think you get it, Dr. Young." Frankie shakes his head. "Tino's just here because otherwise I couldn't have even set foot through the door."

"Some support system you got there, kid." Dr. Young's smirk isn't unkind until he turns his head and looks me in the face.

"No offense, but I'd rather see a priest." There's too much hiss on the S in see and priest. I feel my fangs pricking at the inside of my lips, but I can't figure out what about this time, place, and company has got me so close to a Rage.

"Well, I'm not one anymore, but I'm the closest you'll ever get now that you're vampire, Mr. Crispo." Dr. Young jots something else on his clipboard.

This is only the second time, and already I hate the gesture, wonder how anyone in therapy manages to cope with knowing everything they say is recorded and not even for posterity. In the church's Reconciliation booths, that's not an issue. I wish I was there, but it's not happening.

"I have a problem with that."

"When you're ready to talk more about your issues surrounding religion, you can make your own appointment. This one is for Mr. Pickering."

"Fair enough." Frankie is closer to a mental health crisis than I am.

"Now Mr. Pickering Dr. Maris tells me you want to talk about your life as a Lamb."

"She's got it a little bit wrong, Dr. Young. What I want to talk about has less to do with being a Lamb and more to do with some of the impulses I've been having."

"I have to ask, do you think you're a danger to yourself or others?"

"Yes, to both. But not in the ways you might think."

"Then enlighten me, Mr. Pickering. Exactly how are you a danger? Begin with how you're endangering others."

Now it's my turn to blink. In my experience with law enforcement, psych evaluators usually want to start with the potential for self-harm and then ask about endangering others as a way of easing the suspect onto the topic of potential or actual criminal offenses.

"This isn't a criminal investigation, Mr. Crispo. If you don't stop making toxic assumptions, I'll have to ask you to leave."

"But I need him here, Doc."

"You don't. Vampires make some of the best foul-weather friends, but if you ever want your atmosphere to reach a state of equilibrium, you'll need a less volatile role model."

"Okay, then. I *want* him here." Frankie snorts. "Is that better?"

"Much. It's a step farther than I thought you'd go from where you're starting."

"I'm not his Renfield, if that's what you're thinking." Frankie shrugs.

I make my expression as blank as possible to hide the fact that I don't know what he means by a Renfield.

"That's refreshing." Dr. Young is writing a novel on his clipboard at this point. I can't imagine why until he looks up at me. This time his eyes twinkle. "How long have you been a vampire, Mr. Crispo?"

"Since May of this year."

"Ah." He nods, his face easing out of its frown to assume a more neutral expression. "I'm beginning to understand."

"Understand what?"

"That this partnership between you and Mr. Pickering is not what I originally expected. Even doctors make mistaken calls. Now, sit still and let me do my work with your friend, Mr. Crispo."

I'm not repeating everything that transpired between Frankie and his doctor. This isn't because it's none of my business. It's because it's Frankie's business specifically, and it's up to him to detail the story of his struggle with this illness. Perhaps one day he'll decide to let you hear about it. But just in case he wants his privacy in the future, I'm letting him have it now. You can't untell a story, after all.

What I will say about the rest of this visit to Dr. Young's office is that, while he doesn't trust me, the doctor at least believes I mean well. He even invites me to make my own appointment with him. Which I do. I absolutely need his help.

It all goes back to what Old Man Fitzpatrick told me over the summer. My faith, my family, and my supernatural state are pulling me in three different directions, and I need guidance I can't get in a church.

Once the hour's up, Frankie and I head out of the building and toward my car. Leaning against it is the last person I want to see. Yes, you guessed it. Sebastian Caprice.

"Don't you have a curfew or something?"

"Technically I do, but as far as my mom's concerned, I'm keeping it." Sebastian's grin is genuine, but I still don't like it. I guess Lethians are even harder to like than vampires.

"Are you here for another lesson with Dr. Maris?"

"I just got out of one. Now I'm waiting for Dr. Young."

"Dr. who?" No I'm not talking about the man in the blue box. I'm playing dumb. The last thing I want is for Sebastian Caprice to know we go to therapy.

"Never mind. I want to talk about your friend, Mr. Weintraub."

"Maury's not your business."

"I know he's sick. Dying, even. And I want to help."

"There's nothing you can do. Unless somewhere in Carmine's old eaten memory there's a cure for lung cancer."

"There isn't. But I've got some information you might want."

"I'll think about it." I snort.

"Tino, you don't even know what kind of dirt he's talking about." Frankie rests his hand on my arm. "At least let him discuss it with you."

"Dude." I lean in to whisper in his ear, knowing Lethians like Sebastian don't have enhanced hearing. "Would you listen to a proposition from a Deep One?"

"No. But Raven would." The breath goes out of him like he's deflating. "Listen to a Deep One, I mean. They did it to protect me."

"Raven's not here."

"I'll talk to Sebastian for you if you want."

"It's risky, Frankie."

"Maury's your best friend, and he's in just as much trouble as me right now."

"If I fix DeCampo's problem, everything will work out without this piece of work's help."

"When there's a fire in a building, you can't always rely on the door. You need to know where the windows are too."

"What?"

"It means you always have a plan B, C, D. Sometimes the whole alphabet. Let me talk to him."

"I won't stop you." I lean against the car away from Frankie's ear. “But I'm watching your back.”

"I'm going to negotiate with you on Mr. Crispo's behalf." Frankie grins as he steps toward the boy mob boss.

"You?"

"Yeah, turns out I come from a long and storied family of expert negotiators."

They step away from the car, two feet of space between them as they stand beneath the amber light illuminating this half of the parking lot. I open the driver's side door, reach in, and turn on the ignition in my vehicle. Also, the stereo.

*The Music of the Night* from the Weber version of *Phantom* surrounds me, obscuring the details of the conversation between the Lethian and the Lamb. For once in my life, I'm not the least bit curious. If Frankie wants to check all the emergency exits because it makes him feel better, he's entitled.

We're in this together after all.

In the car, Frankie shuts off the music. He puts it in reverse, backs out of the space, then heads out of the parking lot and toward the road. Yeah, he's driving. My arm's still missing, remember?

"I don't understand why you'd put yourself in danger like that, Frankie."

"Sebastian's not as dangerous as you think he is." Frankie shakes his head, staring at his shoes. "He's new at all this, and still in high school, trying to do something with his life. Maybe he'll make better choices than Carmine did."

"You've already been victimized by one horrible monster, why are you getting involved with another now?"

"Because when you've got monsters living in your own head, it's almost easier to deal with ones you can fight or run away from. At least you know they can be killed."

I ride in silence for a few minutes. Because I'm a monster too. If I ever Rage out and attack him, he won't pull any punches. With the upper hand in a scenario like that, Francis Pickering will end me. And it's likely he'd come out on top. He knows every strength and weakness vampires have.

This isn't frightening. I know you're probably concerned, maybe worried about my safety or even my sanity. Ignoring clear and present danger is a warning sign for maybe a half dozen psychological ailments. Those inventories and diagnoses were all made with humans in mind. I'm not one anymore, no matter how much I wish I could go back and be my old self again. But I do know something about fighting internal monsters that my buddy does not.

"Frankie, you don't run from the stuff in your head."

"Yeah. Like I said. It's always there, slowly killing you. And there's nothing you can do to stop it, no escape." He stares straight out the windshield at the road ahead, foot planted firmly on the brake. "Not even love can do that."

"Not true." I stare at the red traffic light and square my jaw. "You don't run because brain goblins are monsters you stand and face. You fight them with the weapons folks like Dr. Young teach you to use. Love is one of them."

Frankie's wiping his face. Dammit. I didn't want to make him cry. He's the last person who deserves any more pain. And here I am giving him painful and shitty advice.

"I suck at fighting."

I have to swallow past the lump in my throat before I can reply. Because the psychobabble I'm spouting has two edges, and one of those is cutting me too. I want to protest, tell Frankie to shut up, say that he doesn't suck at fighting, that he's one of the strongest people I know. Because I want that to be true. But even if my gut is judging his character right, he won't believe a millimeter of that line. He's not ready to hear it, so I've got to wait to say it. Maybe forever. But there's something you can pretty much always say to a person in distress like this.

"That's okay. All anyone wants you to do is try."

I reach out, stretching to put my hand over his knuckles as they whiten on the steering wheel. He doesn't have to say a word for me to get the message because it's the same one between us since the night we met. Frankie's not alone because I made him a vow, so neither am I. That's absolute and at least as eternal as King DeCampo. And just as dangerous if we ever try to break this chain.

I have to face certain facts about my condition. I'm not who I used to be. Frankie knows this, fully comprehends the implications and impact my vampirism could have on the mortals closest to my heart. He'll know immediately if I lose touch with where I came from.

In a more literal sense, he also knows where I'm going right now. Which is over to the studio to meet Esther. A reasonably working arm is sort of important at the moment. I tell Frankie that he can hang with me, but he says no. He has an errand to run.

We say our goodbyes in the parking lot, with far less eye contact than usual. Which makes me wonder what sort of task he's handling. Maybe it's something to do with his new job and DeCampo's blood. I let that sleeping dog lie for now even though I'm getting that worried knot in the pit of my stomach.

Somehow, I get the impression that whatever my buddy's doing is dangerous. But after this appointment, I know better than to be a helicopter friend right now.

Dr. Young is right. I need my own appointment with him. Even though He's not listening to a vamp like me, I thank God I made one. Now all I need to do is get through the week ahead of it.

# CHAPTER THIRTEEN

"Hey, fuckwit!"

It's just another typical evening's greeting from Esther, nothing to write home about. Unless you've got a family full of drunken sailors, which I don't.

"Hey, yourself." I wave with my only arm.

She waves back with an unattached one.

I smile, bouncing on the balls of my feet. This seems like it'd be an odd reaction to a macabre situation if you didn't already know I'd give my left arm for, well, a left arm. I'm excited, okay? Cut me a little slack.

It's been seven days since DeCampo took my arm off.

As psyched as I am, hesitating at the threshold of Esther's alchemy lab is a habit I don't want to break. And it's a good thing I do because she saunters over to throw a shower of green, glittery powder at the seemingly open space in front of me.

No, she's not glitter-bombing me like some kind of one-woman Pride Parade. Esther's deactivating the ward protecting this place. The motes of dust crackle and fritter into nothingness, and the energy shifts from electric to unreactive.

"Get the fuck in here."

I follow that order. Alchemy is a potent form of magic, both versatile and also powerful in terms of raw destructive capabilities. The main drawback, according to Esther, is it "takes fucking forever to set this shit up."

The main takeaway is, never get on the bad side of an alchemist. Generally, I like to refrain from pissing off any magician but especially Esther's brand.

"So, the arm's done?"

"Fucking-a, it is." She smirks. Uh-oh.

"What's the catch, though?"

"You got blood?"

"Um. Upstairs, yeah."

"You'll need that."

"How much?"

"All of it."

I'm taking Esther seriously here because it's rarer than my dad likes his steaks for her to omit all the four-letter words. That's why I shuffle out the door, then head up the stairwell at the end of the hall into my office to fetch my stash.

I've made it down the stairs again and am walking back down Esther's hallway with the blood in a cooler when a high-pitched and breathy voice speaks behind me.

"Where's the party, tiger?"

"Huh?" I turn to face the speaker.

She's got shocking-pink hair with one side shaved, like Cyndi Lauper back in the eighties. She looks old enough to be said celebrity, too. I stand there staring at her like a total yokel, saying nothing with my mouth wide open.

Good thing I'm not hungry. Or angry. Otherwise, she'd have definitely seen my fangs.

"The party. You know?" She drops a wink then gestures at my cooler with a hand covered in enormous rings with semi-precious stones. "The one you're bringing all the beer to?"

"No, nothing so fun." I shake my head and also the cooler. "This is full of keto snacks. Perishable ones."

I'm not technically lying. Blood has no carbs.

"Oh." She smiles like a magazine cover model. "You look familiar."

Oh, great. The old Rhode Island song and dance of "where do I know you from" has begun. Exactly when I didn't need it. This is the smallest state, but it's got the biggest social network. Sometimes that's damn inconvenient. The only thing I can reasonably do is give her all my mundane deets as efficiently as possible.

"I went to Cranston West, graduated from URI in criminal justice, and worked at Cranston PD for a few years." I grin. "Maybe I pulled you over. But before you did your hair pink. I'd remember that."

"No, that's not it." Her smile widens, which I hadn't thought possible.

"Um, I was in performing arts?" I shrug because I've got nothing else.

"I don't think so." She taps one neon-pink nail on her cheek. One of her rings is missing from it, judging by the tan line. "I think it was in a picture. Have you ever sat for a portrait? One of those sketches?"

"What the fuck, Mom?" Esther's boot stomps the floor just outside her door.

I drop the cooler.

"Oh! So this is your—" she clears her throat over a word that could be vampire, "friend! He's cute! Just like a little wind-up doll."

"Shut your damn cakehole and get in here already, Mom." Esther points at me. "You too, asshole."

I pick the cooler up and follow Esther's mother into the lab, wondering exactly how much trouble I've gotten myself into here. Hopefully not as much as the time Maya had to use her claws to extract wooden splinters from my heart.

Once the door closes behind us, I breathe a sigh of relief. The usual disorganized clutter graces the lab bench, all of the chairs are of the folding metal variety, and there's nothing resembling an operating table in sight.

Shrugging off my opera cloak is easy. Hanging it on the row of hooks by the door, not so much. A pair of well-lined yet deft hands comes to the rescue.

"Thanks."

"Wow." Esther's mother flashes a smile. "A vampire with manners. I could almost start believing in unicorns, Essie. Is he always so refreshingly subservient?"

"What do you fucking think, Mom?" Esther rolls her eyes. "Tino's not one of those weasel-dicked fangmasters from the fucking Bronze Age. This son of a bitch was turned practically fucking yesterday."

"Oh!" Her mother actually claps her hands like an excited grade-schooler. "This is amazing! I've never met one of you people who was so *new* before!"

"Um, technically, we haven't been formally introduced, Miss—" I raise an eyebrow. She blushes.

Yeah, I'm laying it on pretty thick here, but can you blame me? This level of flattery doesn't come my way often, even if it's a bit infantile. I'm so amused by this whole interaction that I forget the one rule of supernatural folk.

There's always a catch.

"Oh, it's Mrs. I'm still a married woman, although I divorced Esther's father ages ago."

"Well, what shall I call you then?" I grin.

"You'll be calling her Queen Bitch of Nutsack Mountain in a minute." Esther's mumbling too low for her mother to hear, but my vampire ears pick those words up loud and clear.

"Oh, you don't get to call me anything at all, dear boy." Her eyes gleam in a way I don't entirely like.

Esther's mother taps the top of one of her gaudy rings. The gemstone top swings open on some sort of hidden hinge, releasing a plume of gray dust. Which lands all over me because of course, it does. She snaps her fingers.

And I can't move. Flashes of that horrible night when a wooden bullet staked and paralyzed me advance on my psyche like a conquering army. I can't possibly imagine how this could get any worse.

But it does.

Queen Bitch of Nutsack Mountain taps the tips of her fingers together, and my legs are moving without my consent. They march me over to a chair, where my rear end promptly rests itself. Forcefully enough to make my teeth clatter together like a bag of rocks.

There's so much I want to say right now. Words that usually come out of Esther's mouth, mostly. I can't, of course, because this mother has total physical control of me. It's worse than that one time Zack puppeted me toward victory against Carmine the Lethian. Because at least Zack let me sing in the big musical finale.

"Let's do the needful now, Essie."

"Stop calling me that fucking name, Mommy Dearest."

"Oh, Essie. I'll call you whatever I want. You're the one who needs me, after all." Her smirk is more poisonous than a basket of figs and asps.

"Like a fish needs a bicycle, mother." Esther's mouth twists into a smile that reminds me of flowers on razor-wire. She says nothing else but her actions speak volumes. My friend grabs a stick of green chalk and goes about the business of marking the floor with one of the geometric seals that help contain alchemical magic.

She works swiftly, making me think she's done spells like this with extreme frequency. I remember the handful of times I bumped her prosthetic arm and leg. She must use a formula like this one on herself periodically.

I want to ask Esther how she manages to tolerate her mother so often, but I can't. No wonder she's surly all the time. But then I realize that I've got it wrong. During the course of the bizarre ritual, I overhear plenty.

Esther's reference to fish and bicycles makes sense. She only needs Mommy Dearest this time because I'm undead.

Apparently, necromantic alchemy is a thing. And it involves a generous helping of gray, ashy-looking powder.

I've got plenty of time to consider this bit of information. The arm attachment process is painless but lengthy. It also itches more than I'd like.

I wonder whether Esther's mom is acquainted with Whitby. She controls vampire bodies utterly. And if she's eliminated my pain responses, she can affect us neurologically as well. It's no big leap of intellect to guess that she's capable of altering our memories.

I glare at my opera cloak, wishing I'd turned on my phone camera before taking it off. I'm a naturally curious dude. Even though I trust Esther when it comes to magic, it wouldn't have been out of character for me to make a recording. But I'll bet that's exactly the reason evil mom "helped" me with my cloak in the first place.

I turn my eyes heavenward, praying to God for the ability to remember my observations and conclusions here long enough to jot them down.

Wait. I turned my eyes. I start laughing on the inside and feel the corners of my mouth tilt up. It's a tiny smile, but persistent as a daisy growing in a pothole.

"Shit. Mom, your fucking dust is wearing off."

"It's because he's so new." She chuckles.

"What the fuck? You could have told me that fucking shit earlier."

This strengthens my suspicions about her potential involvement in Whitby's whammy. If necromantic alchemy doesn't last long on the newly undead, no wonder he pulled the trigger on his conquest while I was away from the vampire club.

And Esther didn't know.

In fact, this whole arm attachment exercise has spoken volumes. Just being present and aware for the duration is at least as valuable to me as the magical prosthetic that's now attached to my left shoulder.

I guess it's safe to say I gave my left arm to discover how DeCampo's court forgot all about him.

"Now, give him the blood, Essie."

Esther's already a step ahead of her mother. She's set the cooler at my feet and opened it, is in the process of tucking a bag of blood into my right hand. Since her back's to her mom, only I see the ferocious snarl on her face as she nods.

"We don't want him Raging when I lift the spell." Evil mom holds up her right hand, fingers poised and ready to snap. "Or maybe you don't want me to end the spell." She grins. "If I leave it to wear off on its own, you can do whatever you want with him for at least another hour."

Esther straightens, doing a snappy about-face worthy of the military veteran she is. Her hand's in her back pocket, where I can see a stack of Post-it notes.

She can blow holes in entire walls with those things.

"Fucking let him out of it right now, or so help me—"

"Done." She snaps and turns her back, striding toward the door. "Don't forget how much you owe me now, Essie dear."

"I forget fucking nothing, bitch."

I'm gulping blood from the bag, holding it over my head with my chin tilted up to get it down quicker. My fangs tear the thin plastic practically to ribbons, but I don't care. I'm no longer just angry for my own sake, but for Esther as well.

Tossing the empty sack aside is automatic, just like the motion I make with my left arm, bringing the second one to my lips. Except I miss.

The blood bag hits me in the eye. I try again and get my nose, which has me howling like Scott at a full moon and gnashing my fangs.

"Easy there. Slow and steady."

Esther's voice barely sounds like hers, but vamp ears don't lie. She's changed her tone and volume, softening the drawling vowels and slurred consonants of her Rhode Island accent.

I find myself following her advice, even though the Rage threatening to take over is still too close for comfort. The bag comes into view, I imagine myself making it float toward my mouth. When I bite down, she speaks again, this time facing me.

"Chill." Green sparks surround her mouth.

I do. And I also make shorter but less violent work of the second bag of blood. When I'm done, I come up for air.

"Shitballs."

"Tell me about it."

"Your mom needs a serious lesson about consent."

"No, she doesn't. She knows what that is."

"So, what's her problem?"

"She thinks the undead have got no rights. And legally speaking, if the world knew about vampires, you wouldn't."

I'm not sure what to say about that. Esther's probably right, and it sucks. There's no scarier monster than an enormous group of frightened and uninformed people.

Instead of contemplating this for longer than I have to, I gaze down at the new prosthetic. It's paler and colder than my own was, and that's a major difference from Esther's two replacement limbs. While hers feel like they'd been in the air conditioning while the rest of her was outside on a balmy day, mine feels more like one of those gel cooler packs that go in your kid's lunchbox.

The fingers flex, and my grip is almost as strong as on the right. Which isn't much different from usual, after all. I wonder whether the arm will show up in mirrors while the rest of me doesn't. It's probably a good idea to wear long sleeves and gloves now that the autumn weather will allow for it.

I stare up at my friend and catch her frowning as she dabs at the corner of one eye with the back of a hand. Esther's gruff and rough around the edges. Normally it seems like nothing ever really gets to her. But this time is different. Finally, I know what to say.

"I know this is usually your line, but what a fucking bitch."

"Fucking a." She holds out another bag of blood to me. "You need at least two more."

I nod and drink two more bags in a silence that's grown less awkward. When I'm done, I get my notebook out of my back pocket. But then my phone rings.

Esther hustles over to the hook where my cloak hangs and gets it. I blink but recover from my astonishment quickly enough to jot down a few lines about necromantic alchemy.

"Private Investigation, Valentino Crispo's phone, who may I say is calling?"

This time I can't help it. I drop my pen along with my jaw.

"It's a Doctor Eunice Terry." Esther places the phone in my still open hand. Then she silently mouths the words, "You're fucking welcome."

"Hello, Eunie."

"Hi, Tino."

"What can I do for you?"

"I called Maury, and he said I should call you."

"Oh, no." I shake my head. "You're missing some time?"

"Yeah, a chunk of the afternoon. He said that if I'm not going to press charges, I should call you." She clears her throat. "But I don't understand why? Unless—"

"There's no unless. He has me looking into things because we've been friends our whole lives, but Maury's totally mundane and not in the know."

"Well, that's a relief."

There are a million things I could tell Eunice. About Maury's health. About how I wish he were anything but mortal and fragile. About my unlife and all the troubles in it.

But part of being a good investigator is empathy. And Eunice sounds scared in a way that Kayleigh didn't.

"Let's talk. In person. Where can I meet you?"

"Down at Corey's shop. Muse-icality in Warwick."

"Oh, I know where Muse-icality is!" And I do, all right. It's where I hit Sasquatch with my car, which I still don't have.

"Great. Come by anytime in the next hour. We'll be there."

"See you then. Bye."

I'm closing up my notebook with my slower and clumsier temporary (I hope) left hand when I realize my mistake. Before I can say anything, Esther's grabbing her keys.

"I'll fucking drive you there, but you're walking your sorry ass back to the Pickerings' after."

I'm following her out the door and then waiting as she locks up and activates her wards. I understand way more about why she uses them now. Her lab is still pretty trashed, and I feel like a jerk because I was going to offer to help tidy things up.

"Thanks, Esther. For everything. If there's anything I can do for—"

"No. Don't fucking make anything remotely resembling a vow, asshole. Not to me, not ever." She strides off down the hall and toward the stairs. I trot to keep up. She's way faster than I am when I can't turn on the supernatural speed.

"But, um—"

"If you don't fucking understand why your sad shitsack ass can't owe jack, then you need a prosthetic fucking brain."

"No, I get it."

We get in her car, which she starts immediately. Her stereo blasts out *MMMBop* by Hansen, and as is usual for Esther with her quirky musical selections, she starts bobbing her head and humming along with the tune as she drives.

I'm a child of the nineties, so I can't stop my feet from tapping. Don't ever tell her I said that.

As she pulls up in front of Muse-icality, it occurs to me that vamps making promises to Esther is hazardous to our health. But I can make one to myself.

I'll do my best to keep all my limbs attached so she doesn't have to call Mommy Dearest any time in the near future.

It seems like the least I can do.

## CHAPTER FOURTEEN

The inside of Muse-icality is warmly lit, furnished with rows of shelves holding sheaves of sheet music. Instruments hang from padded hooks on the walls, everything from clarinets to a shiny silver triangle.

The counter where people purchase these items is almost an afterthought, tucked into a corner so as not to detract from the main focus here.

Muse-icality has nothing so mundane as a door marked Keep Out, No Public Restrooms, or even Employees Only. Instead, a collection of four doors line the back wall. Over top of them, someone's stenciled the letters of two beautiful words.

Welcome Friends.

I've been here less than thirty seconds and I can already feel the sentiment, as though it's a benevolent ghostly presence haunting the place. No wonder Sparky spends his alone time peering through the window outside.

"Tino, hi!"

A tall overall-clad woman with a mop of glossy chestnut curls and a rich contralto voice waves from behind the counter. Her accent reminds me of Doctor Maris's, which makes sense because Centaurs are Greek, and if I'm guessing correctly, this lady grew up in that country. She's in front of a denim curtain, which would explain why I hadn't noticed her before.

"Hello. Corey?"

"Exactly!"

"It's great to finally meet you. Eunice talked about you all the time back in high school."

"A mutual activity, to be sure." Corey chuckles.

"Eunice called."

"Uh-huh. She'll be out momentarily."

"So, how many of these do you teach?" I wave a hand at the nearest wall of instruments.

"All of them." She smiles. "And voice."

"Awesome!" I lean an elbow on the counter.

We chat for a few minutes about her shop; how she chose the location, the decor, about lunches at the cafe next door. I find myself considering how much of a difference kindness can make.

Manners are a veneer, trappings. Esther's mother had that act down pat, a technique to cover her fundamental cruelty. Corey Terry's polite, but instead of acting as a blanket over a bucket of ice cubes, her manners enhance her warmth.

Eunice emerges from behind the curtain, pushing it aside enough for me to see a set of stairs back there. As she greets Corey with a quick hug, she's practically glowing. I realize I'm looking at a true pair, a couple who's bound to be compatible for a lifetime. Like my own parents.

I'd be the biggest jerk in the world if I interrupted this moment with a bunch of PI questions, so I don't. Which is fine because I get to bask in this aura of contentment while it lasts.

Corey squeezes Eunice's hand, then lets go, pacing away from the counter and toward one of the practice rooms. She picks up a broom on the way, humming a waltz.

"Okay, Tino. I'm ready to talk."

"And I'm ready to listen." I put my notepad on the counter between us, holding it steady with my new left hand.

"Oh!" Eunice blinks, then points. "That's, um, different."

"What's wrong?"

"Nothing. Well, that's not true. I'm alarmed because at first, I thought you grew it back already, which would mean—"

"I didn't grow it back, if that's what you're wondering."

"Really? Because that much blood that fast is a scary thing to contemplate."

"Just bagged blood required after attachment. It's a magical prosthetic." I tap it with my pen, making a vaguely hollow sound. "One of my friends is an alchemist."

She leans closer, the pointing finger hovering over my fake plastic hand. "May I?"

"Sure."

Eunice presses the pad of her index finger against the back of my new hand. Her eyes widen before she withdraws it.

"Wow."

And just like that, Eunice is rubbing her hands with sanitizer she's gotten from somewhere behind the counter.

"That bad?" I shift my weight from one foot to the other. "You're the first person to see it, and—"

"No, there's nothing wrong with your arm. But I do psychometry. You know, where psychic impressions come in from an object."

"Yeah, okay. My friend had a not-so-nice person helping her."

"Valentino Crispo, that's the understatement of the century."

"Don't worry. I think the bad lady won't bother us anymore."

"I hope not." Eunice shakes her head. "Anyway, one thing I can say for sure is that she had nothing at all to do with my lost time after school today."

"Good." While I'd love to catch Esther's mother assaulting random in-the-know folk, I'm also glad Eunice never tangled with her. "So, what can you tell me?"

"Well, there are two things."

"Okay."

"I remember music." Eunice leans her chin on her hand, inadvertently showing off the bruise there. It's just like Kayleigh's. "A song with words I didn't understand. But it was a beautiful tune, an operatic duo in a language I've never heard."

"Do you know who was singing?"

"I was. But also the other person. You know."

"Right. I remember what a duo is."

In case you aren't aware, the difference between a duo and a duet is in how the song is constructed. In a duet, each singer has their own verse and sometimes a chorus to themselves. In a duo, both sing at the same time, often in harmony or on occasion in counterpoint.

"Anything else?" I'm expecting Eunice to say no and then move on to talk about some personal item missing. But she surprises me.

"He was a baritone."

"He? Are you sure?"

"Yes. I remember because it reminded me of our duet from *Into the Woods*."

"Oh, boy." I sigh. "And when did this happen?"

"The last thing I remember before the singing was walking to the car after school let out. So maybe four in the afternoon."

"Okay, and what's the other thing you remembered?"

"It's more like what I lost. The locket my parents gave me on closing night. I wear it every day I teach over at Stout. It's got some of my best experiences in it, which helps when I touch anything nasty. When the police officer woke me up, it was gone."

I'm writing everything down but trying to maintain some semblance of eye contact the whole time. Which is challenging, but really the best way to go about questioning someone about upsetting events.

"Thanks. Please call me if you happen to find or remember anything else."

Corey comes out of the now-clean practice room, sets the broom aside, then puts an arm around her spouse.

"Are you making any progress on this?" Eunice's hands are clasped in front of her collarbones.

"I think I will now."

"I helped?"

"More than you know, Eunie. Thanks again."

We all wave as I make my way slowly toward the shop entrance. I'll definitely have to come back here again, with Sparky and Leora. Hell, with the whole Pickering family, too. We'll bring the Terrys a basket of baked goods or something.

Outside on the street, I remember Esther telling me to walk home from here. It's a temperate evening, so I head east, toward Warwick Neck. About halfway to Pickering House, a memory from the less savory part of my night stops me dead in my tracks.

Esther's mother was missing a ring. She's about the same age as the first victim in Maury's file, too.

I take out my notebook, write myself a reminder to check the appropriate name, and make a few phone calls.

Back at home, the kids are already upstairs in bed. I head up to wish them all a good night.

Levi smiles and waves, his nose in a book I recognize immediately. *Frankenstein* by Mary Shelley.

"Homework or fun?"

"Both." He smirks. "Victor reminds me of Raul in *Phantom*, the book version. What a schmuck."

"I'm supposed to tell you to watch your language." I shrug. "Mostly, just keep it clean around adults."

"Which is practically all the time around here."

"Tell me about it."

He yawns.

"I think that's your fun homework's cue to get offstage and let you sleep."

"Yeah. G'night, Tino." Levi tucks a bookmark bearing the words Quitter Strip on its surface between the pages and sets the tome on his bedside table.

"Goodnight." I leave his door open just a crack, the way he told me those first few nights I spent here.

I peer into the girls' room, which used to be a point of contention. I can still see the marks on the wall and carpet where Sarah divided the room into two sides the day Leora moved in here, but the duct tape she laid down back then is gone now. And Sarah's still, sleeping in relative peace.

Leora isn't.

In fact, she's not in bed. I'm not worried because I can hear her moving around in the bathroom across the hall. I stand and wait, shuffling my feet loudly so she won't be startled by my presence.

When she emerges, I wave with my temporary left arm. She smiles at first, but the expression fades quickly. Leora's eyes are fixed on the magical limb, wide and full of an emotion I'm not comfortable with. Which makes sense when I think about it.

"You should have come to me, vampire." The dry raspy voice coming from Leora's throat isn't her voice. It's Baba Yaga's.

"Well, I figured you had more important things to do than undead orthopedics."

"You're in even more danger now."

"What else is new?" I'm getting kind of annoyed here. Baba Yaga is fully within her rights to call on Leora as her avatar in the outside world at any time. But growing kids need rest, and a magically possessed one is no exception. "Look, it's a school night here. Leora's future should be important to you."

"Our priorities for her differ. And may perhaps diverge if you aren't more careful."

"Okay. I already decided to avoid Esther's mother forever. So you don't need to worry about that."

"The monster in the hand is more dangerous than the one in the bush, young one."

"I'll remember that." I tap my foot, tired of waiting for the old crone to let my kiddo go already.

"Write it down."

"If I do, can I finally tuck my daughter in for a good night's sleep?"

She nods. Baba's voice probably feels strange coming out of a different set of vocal cords. Maybe that's why she always sounds cranky. I take my notebook out to jot down what she just said about monsters under the note about checking Maury's folder with regard to Esther's mother. My brain finally makes the connection.

What kind of being attacks and steals from a hunter, a mostly-harmless psychometry psychic, and a necromancer who sees magical creatures as things instead of people? A monster, of course. Someone who feels out of place despite their extreme power to command others. I can name exactly three individuals like that, and Baba knows it. Sebastian Caprice, Zack Milano, and King DeCampo.

"Shitballs."

"Yes." Baba's smirk looks too much at home on Leora's face for my comfort.

But why would any of them need their sentimentally valuable possessions? I'll have to look into that, but Baba Yaga has seriously narrowed the focus of my investigation.

"Um, thanks, Baba."

"Don't mention it." The smirk transforms into a feral smile. Thankfully, that expression fades in moments, replaced by an owlish blink. Big bright eyes gaze up at me as a small freckled hand rises to twist a hank of auburn hair.

"Hey, Leora." I grin, tucking my notebook away for now. "Just here to say goodnight."

"Okay," Leora nods and begins to shuffle past me on slipper-clad feet. She stops before stepping into her room. "Tino?"

"What's up?"

"Do you think I'll ever feel normal again?" Her shoulders droop.

"I don't know, kid." I place my right hand on one of them. "But I can promise you one thing. We'll feel like oddballs together, okay?"

Leora doesn't have the words to respond. Instead, she turns around and throws her arms around me. Her face is wet and her nose pokes me in the ribcage, but I don't care. The only thing to do now is hug her back.

An eternal moment later, we part. Her eyes are dry now, her expression wan. But her posture looks more tired than defeated now. As she closes the door behind her, I know she'll be better in the morning.

On the first floor, the house feels deserted. Down in the basement, the television's on. Probably Raven or DeCampo, trying to take their minds off things.

Tomorrow night is my appointment with Doctor Young.

I don't feel like socializing, so I leave notes in the hall and the kitchen, then make sure the parlor curtains are fully drawn.

The moment my head hits the throw cushion on the tufted sofa, I fall asleep.

# CHAPTER FIFTEEN

"Valentino!" The name comes complete with a hand on my shoulder, shaking me. "Get up. It's time to go downstairs."

"Huh?" I run a hand over my face, then open my eyes. "Steph? What's up?"

"The sun, almost." She shakes her head and taps her foot. "Honestly, you're too careless sometimes."

"I just didn't want to bother Raven last night."

"They're sleeping at this hour." She pulls on my right arm. "Come along now."

"Where were you?" I follow her, but figure we can multitask. She's got a lot of explaining to do. "I haven't seen you all week."

"At the hospital, mostly." She pulls the cellar door open, then waves me through it. "Being a squeaky wheel."

"Hanging around?" I wink as I pass her. I know all about her secret ability to turn into a bat.

"Something like that, but not entirely." Her feet make no sound on the wooden stairs behind me, no mean feat in those alpine-high heeled shoes she always wears. "I've made enormous progress, thanks to Doctor Maris."

"I want to run a few things by you. About my latest case."

"Just a moment."

In the hallway between sunless rooms, Stephanie moves soundlessly. She presses the fingertips of one hand against DeCampo's door and the other against Raven's. Her eyes go out of focus for a moment. When they're back to normal, she nods, then beckons me into the laundry area at the back of the basement. We sit on the old cozy couch there, and she scoops up the remote from the coffee table in front of it.

Once she's got Pandora playing nature sounds on the Smart TV, Stephanie begins to relax by kicking off her shoes. Then she lets her hair down, literally. After that, she unslings the fashionable snakeskin satchel she's been wearing cross-body all this time. My ears and my nose tell me what's inside.

"Blood? Is that the stuff the king needs?"

"Some of it. Enough to get him back to normal for a meeting in Providence." She shakes her head. "We're unlikely to get any more unless we take back the city. But Valentino, we need more information about Whitby before we can use this on him. How he managed to take over, for one thing."

Asking her for more information is a moot point. Steph has made so many vows, she probably can't say. Time feels shorter than it should, like something's cut off all its split ends. If the three Fates are as real as Mnemosyne, Baba Yaga, and all the rest, then maybe Atropos picked up some extra hours somewhere.

But that's all beside the point. I can cross the real King of Providence off my list of suspects. He's not competent enough to pull something like those assaults off.

But more importantly, I have new information that can help him and Stephanie. Knowledge is power, and having more of it at any meeting between DeCampo and Whitby increases our chances of winning the city back.

"We need the whammy question answered before going in, huh?"

"That would be a boon, certainly."

"Awesome. I've got a theory."

"I hope it's a miraculous one."

"Listen to what I've got, and we'll see."

I go into my room and grab Maury's file and my most recent composition book, then set them on the table with my notepad. After that, I spend some time with my sire, going over all the information on it and discussing my conclusions. I add Eunice to the list, and give Stephanie the known supernatural ties and abilities of each victim besides.

Turns out Esther's mother is the first victim in the file.

Her name's Gertrude Weiss. I use my phone to do a quick search and find that her husband Bradley owns an enormous mansion in Newport as well as a large estate on the East Side of Providence. Also, good old Brad is in his late nineties.

Bet you can guess why she married this guy.

"So you think this Gertrude woman helped Whitby by using her necromantic alchemy?"

"I'm almost totally sure." I scratch my head. "But there's one thing bothering me."

"Which is?" Steph is leaning back against the sofa, hands folded over her stomach. She looks like a doll. Which puts the last piece into place.

"Esther's related to Frankie. But indirectly."

"Is she now?" Stephanie blinks almost sleepily.

"Yeah. Both of them mentioned it. He's her uncle, even though he's younger than she is."

"And this concerns Whitby, how?"

"Gertrude's even more predatory than us vampires. But she's not highbrow and isn't exactly trophy wife material. Who do you think introduced her to this particular nearly-dead rich old man? And what does the name Weiss mean, translated?"

"White. As in Whitby." Stephanie's eyes twinkle, and she sits up. "So, Esther's mother married herself and her children into the power behind the Pickering family. Which indebted her to an old vampire."

"And puts all of us in huge amounts of danger."

"Tell me how." Steph says this in a way that makes me think she already knows what I'm going to say.

"The kids' money, the stuff in the trust funds. Frankie only handles the dividends until he's twenty-five. Who's managing those funds?"

I pace toward a file cabinet tucked away in the corner, opposite the washer and dryer. Inside, I find the file full of paperwork from mine and Frankie's foster agreement and flip through to the financials.

"Weiss Associates, LLC." I hold the paper up for Stephanie to see.

"Whitby's biding his time, then." She stands, slipping her shoes on. "Waiting for the moment he can pull the rug out from under us all."

"Pretty much, yeah."

"So, what's all this got to do with whoever's assaulted the women, including this Gertrude person?"

"That's the part I'm still not totally sure about."

"Do you think we can still confront Whitby without that part?"

"Probably? Maybe?" I shake my head. "I'm not too sure."

"Not sure about what?" That warm voice is exactly the one I most want and need to hear.

"Maya." I turn, smiling as she emerges from her room and then the hall. "Come and have a look at all this, please?"

"Sure." She ambles toward the sofa and sits down. "This is Maury's case. But who'd dare attack that woman?" Maya's finger trembles as it points at Gertrude's dossier.

"You know her?" Stephanie arches an eyebrow.

"I've seen her a couple of times." She averts her gaze. "Before we even came to Rhode Island."

"What was she doing?"

"Talking to Whitby. Something about her paying back an enormous favor he did her years back. We were all at Foxwoods Casino, down in Connecticut. Whitby asked for a demonstration, and she did something to Peligro. He hasn't been the same since."

A lump forms in my throat.

"Shitballs."

I tell the two most badass women I know about how my arm attachment went down. They both look shaken, like they think I'm in enormous heaps of trouble. I flip the pages of my notepad, ruffling them just so I can have something to do with my hands besides wring them.

And a paper falls out.

"What's this?" Maya plucks it out of the air.

Her eyes go wide. She flails with her free hand, so I take it in one of mine. The real one. Stephanie adds hers, like we're a team about to make a big play on some sort of sports ballfield.

Finally, I get the hidden message the vampire calling himself Hargrove wants me to see.

DeCampo's old enforcer Shadow is outside a triple-decker house on the edge of Cranston, not far from where my Belfry is. It's got to be at least four in the morning, judging by the street lights and the stars.

Gertrude Weiss steps in front of him and hits him with black powder from one of her rings. And then, right there in the street, Shadow's body begins to morph. He gets shorter, stockier, darker-skinned. Silver-tipped dreadlocks sprout from his buzzcut head, too. In moments, he looks exactly like King DeCampo.

Gertrude whispers a few words. Either Maya's touch telepathy only gets images clearly, or Shadow didn't need to make out the commands in order to be compelled. Regardless, the enforcer snarls while wearing his king's face, and his hands turn into claws.

Seconds later, he's rampaging up the steps and tearing his way through the door. All this while, Gertrude takes out her phone and makes a video. The same one that gave Whitby grounds to meet privately with DeCampo in the first place.

After all that, the scene changes. Shadow is in the round room where Stephanie's doppelganger let in the Deep Ones who kidnapped DeCampo. Gertrude is with them, too. She spreads ashes all over Hargrove, who dies while under necromantic compulsion, restraining the king.

And after I saw him in there, Shadow turns himself into his old comrade, an impersonation his unlife literally depends on. He came to me for help because I'm the only person who could have figured out his secret. The Deep Ones who saw Hargrove turn to ash died later that night, and as far as Gertrude is concerned, vampires are all the same.

"Shit. Balls." The words come out of my mouth as we exit the scene.

"I know, right?" Maya squeezes my hand.

"It's never simple, is it?" Stephanie shakes her head.

"We're vampires." I shrug. "Complex is kind of what we do when dealing with each other."

"Especially when it comes to Whitby the Drama King." Maya rolls her eyes.

"From the mouths of babes." Stephanie's smile is too bright, which means she's running out of patience. But something else catches my attention.

"I thought you were ancient, Maya." I chuckle. "Didn't Baba call you Maya of Macedon?"

"Macedon, New York." She grins. "The old witch likes giving people titles."

"So, you're not much older than I am?"

"Oh, I'm older. Just not by much compared to everyone else. My father worked on the Erie Canal."

"Oh."

Stephanie clears her throat.

"If you don't mind, I'd appreciate it if Valentino could solidify his theories into something we can work with." She's crossed her arms over her chest, too. Serious business. "And find out if we need to worry about whoever's assaulting ladies of power. Immediately."

"It's morning already."

She taps her foot, frowning. Even though the long hair framing her face makes my sire look Sarah Pickering's age, she's twice as intimidating. Which is saying a lot because Sarah put dozens of Deep Ones on her summer vacation. Literally.

"But I can set something up for tonight." I reach for my phone. "Let me send some texts and make some calls."

"Very well." Stephanie turns her back, then heads toward her room down here. After she closes the door, I hear her storing the blood from her cooler in the mini-fridge she keeps in there.

"Can I help?" Maya sits beside me on the sofa.

"Thanks, Maya."

We spend the day together, arranging everything.

# CHAPTER SIXTEEN

Once everything's set up for neutral ground, my phone chimes. It's a reminder about my appointment with Doctor Young, far too soon after sunset for someone who stayed up this far past sunrise.

I escort Maya to the room she uses here in the basement, right next door to mine. We kiss goodday, and through that simple gesture, I sense she's just as tired as I am.

When my head hits the pillow far too late in the afternoon, I fall asleep immediately. And then I dream about being somebody else.

---

*My heart's in my throat. Maybe that's why I push the door that's clearly marked Pull. Or that's just the way I get around Francis Pickering. Nothing like how I've been with the rest of the people who come and go from my life. Which, I suppose, is the reason he makes me want to change everything.*

*He's already there, sitting in the comfy chair near the fireplace even though it's warm for an early autumn day. He leans forward, back toward me and the door, watching the gas flames rising above the faux wood behind the glass.*

*As I turn past the counter, I tip the brim of my hat down and turn my face away. It's automatic; not a new habit, but one I still need. When I go out in public, people recognize me, and I'm obligated to act the way they expect me to.*

*That's not on today's agenda.*

*Francis knows this, too. It's the reason he greets me with a smile instead of calling my name in the sparsely populated Starbucks. Our eyes lock, the center of our universe as my orbit around the coffee shop decays in his direction. Only instead of our bodies colliding the way I want, I take the seat across from him.*

*"Hi, Z." It's what he calls me. Only him.*

*"Hi, yourself."*

*"Don't you want your Americano?"*

*I blink, long and slow. It's not an expression of surprise, just the predecessor to my exhale. If you've ever been around someone like Francis, you understand what I mean, and how this feels. There are some people whose presence is like sitting in a pool of afternoon sunlight in the middle of January.*

*"Yes. And thank you for getting it for me."*

*"No problem." The corners of his mouth curl upward.*

*"This," I wave a hand at our generic and all-too-public surroundings, "is different."*

*"Yeah." He picks his cup up and blows on the surface of the liquid inside. It's tea, something with mint. "Not our usual sort of meeting place."*

*Usual for us is either my place or the Biltmore, always when the sun's up. Usually the latter because we both have money, and I've got a disapproving father to avoid, as well as our mutual vampire acquaintances.*

*"Any reason for that?"*

*"That's fast, Z."*

*"Well, I thought you like it when I get direct."*

*"This isn't like any of that. It's different."*

*"I can handle that." I lean back, hands curled around the papery cup of coffee and water. "Take your time."*

*"Thanks."*

*Francis sips his tea, then gazes into it. If he weren't completely mundane,*

*I'd think he's scrying the future. But I know he must simply be collecting his thoughts. He's got the time and space for that, a luxury.*

*I turn the cup round and round, trying not to drink too much more of the caffeinated beverage. The last thing I want to do at this point is get impatient with him. Which is a challenge for me because the Milano family motto might as well be Think Fast, Act Faster.*

*The musical selection here is too sophisticated, even for me. Avant-garde tunes on wind instruments don't exactly annoy me, it's just that they've got no story to tell that I can get my brain around. I'm like many other Rhode Islanders. Simple things like coffee need simple trappings. But I suppose I should be grateful they're not playing talk radio. Ugh.*

*"Went to Doctor Young's three times this week."*

*"The shrink?" I raise my cup to hide my sneer. Another reflex, courtesy of the patented Milano Family upbringing.*

*"Yes. I mean, therapy is something I need right now."*

*"Go on." It's hard to accept a statement like that, especially when we've been meeting so frequently and clandestinely. His history's a horror show, but he swore he was ready to take a chance at happiness with me. It takes an insane amount of effort not to ask if I did something to hurt him.*

*"Z, I haven't been completely honest with you."*

*"About?"*

*"About being ready."*

*Everything that felt atmospheric, stellar, or heady between us drops. Including my heart. Into the pit of my stomach. It's like being on a plane in a thunderstorm, losing pressure and altitude.*

*"Doctor Young told you this?"*

*"No." He sets the tea down, leaning toward me as he does. On any other day, I'd take it as an invitation.*

*"So then, what happened?"*

*"I need you to support me in this, Z. In going to therapy and doing the work to be healthy again." He taps his temple. "Up here," then his chest, "and in here."*

*"I can get behind that."*

*"It's got to be bigger, though. Z, I need you to come in and do this kind of work too. For yourself."*

*"Are you saying you think I'm not okay?"*

*"I know you aren't." His gaze connects with mine like a slap. "You scream in your sleep, yet you never talk about your dreams."*

*"I don't remember any of them, Francis." I speak his name like a caress. My words carry literal power since I'm a spell-singing magician. While I'll never use my magic to coerce him, it does add a more tangible dimension to our conversations. Among other things.*

*"Doctor Young can help you. And he said he'd make room in his schedule."*

*"Why would he do something like that for a Milano of all people?"*

*Francis blinks. He forgets sometimes that my father's fortune and my own fame have not made me popular in the supernatural community. They tend to think I'm risking our secret existence just so I can be a news anchor.*

*Utter nonsense, but public opinion can be that way. Nobody knows that my entire career plus my life leading up to it was orchestrated by my father. But I conducted it, so it's me who gets the shame and blame that goes with it all.*

*"Because of this." Francis places his hand flat on the table between us. "Because of us."*

*"You're in there, defending me?" My voice cracks on that word, breaking on the pinnacle of Francis's misplaced faith in me.*

*"Always."*

*"You wouldn't be saying that if you really knew me. The things I've done."*

*"That's not important. Somebody told me it's more important what we do going forward than what's happened to us in the past."*

*I'm not sure whether to correct him or not. Part of me wants to make a list of all my sins and see what he thinks of what's behind the glossy veneer he's seen so far. But a Starbucks, even this relatively deserted one, isn't a place to speak frankly about dirty deeds of the supernatural variety.*

*And there's something else stopping me too. I'm ninety-nine percent sure that "somebody" he mentioned is Crispo. That dude has been the clearest and most present barrier to every task my demanding old dad has set me on. I've come up against him over and over, and each time he walks away intact. Even that time Dad hired the Caprices' pet Lethian and put him in the hospital.*

*Helping kill that time-stealing son of a bitch was one of the most gratifying things I'd done. It was also the night Francis first noticed me as more than a friend. So maybe I've got to forgive Crispo a little bit for all of his meddling.*

*"Z?"*

*"Yeah?"*

*"Are you all right?"*

*"That depends."*

*"On?"*

*"Is it over? Between us?" My voice is flatter than pancakes.*

*"Oh, God, no, Z. I just want you to get help."*

*"I'm not so sure I need it." I shake my head, hanging it in the process. "I lied about that. I do need help. But I'm not sure I can have it."*

*"Why?" Francis studies my face like we're having a life or death conversation instead of talking about seeing a shrink.*

*"It's dangerous."*

*"My experience with it says the opposite so far."*

*"You aren't a local celebrity."*

*"Oh. I didn't think about that. The stigma, I mean. But maybe Doctor Young can work something out, keep the fact that you're going a secret."*

*And he's got me pegged in an entirely different way than usual. Maybe Francis Pickering does actually know me better than I could have imagined. I find myself loving him even more for it. At that moment, I want to do this—get myself help, for his sake.*

*I already decided on our first date to do literally anything for him.*

*But I won't need to see this doctor if I can only finish my work. Neither of us will. I can't tell him about it or ask for his help. All I can do is keep him busy.*

*"Do you think he can take steps to hide my visits from a family of magicians?"*

*His eyes widen, and his lips part. Francis always looks shocked when he's thinking, a childlike quality that melts my heart.*

*"I'll ask him at my next visit. It's spell-singers you're hiding from."*

*I nod even though it's not a question. I'm a golden child and he's a scapegoat, but we both grew up under narcissistic parents. There are some things we'll never have to say to each other because of that, bricks embedded in the paths stretching out behind us that are nearly identical. There's only one thing to say to a person who truly understands this.*

*"I love you, Francis."*

*"Love you too, Z."*

*We reach across the table, hands intertwining over his tea and my coffee. Maybe Crispo has got the right idea. That the path going forward is more important than what's behind. But I've always looked at a bigger picture than him, lived larger, bore more with less support.*

*One thing's dead certain.*

*I'm going to save Francis, so utterly and completely that he'll never have been broken in the first place. The only way to do that is by repaving both our roads to Hell. I've almost got everything I need to do it, too. Two more chips to topple. After that, nobody can stop me.*

*Not even Valentino Crispo.*

---

I wake to my alarm in the twin bed with something draped over me. Not a blanket, a leg and an arm. It's Maya, who must have had some trouble sleeping with the way she clings to me.

By the time I finally get out of bed without waking her, I wonder whether her touch telepathy let her see my dream. One glance at the clock tells me there's no time to ask.

I've got a head to shrink. Figuratively speaking, of course.

I can figure out the parameters of this crazy dream later. Including why it's so much more vivid than my last daydream about being someone else.

# CHAPTER SEVENTEEN

Valentino Crispo, you just got out of a therapy session; what do you want to do now?

I'm going to Cranston, which is definitely not Disney World. But it does have the neutral meeting place I need in order to discuss a supernatural crime investigation. Plus my apartment, where I want to check on some things first. So that's where I stop.

I'm in my car, driving this time, and Frankie's in the passenger seat because he had the appointment right before mine.

My friend isn't surprised when we pull up outside the Belfry. This bothers me because I never told him any details about the investigation I've got running on Maury's behalf. Has he been spying on me?

Maybe this is just what happens when I spend so much time in a house full of people. Things get overheard.

Or my dream about him and Zack was true.

"I'll just be a minute, but you can come in if you want to."

"Okay."

He gets out of the car and follows me up to the third floor. I glance over my shoulder as I rattle my key into the door's lock, remembering how much of a struggle it was the first time he came here, insensible due to his time in the clutches of the Deep Ones. Frankie also floated that night, under the magic of one of Esther's levitation powders.

"You've come a long way, buddy." I give him a fangless grin. "Don't forget that."

"How can I, with you around to remind me?"

I turn back to face the door and shrug. There's not much else I can say. Practically every one-on-one interaction I have with Frankie Pickering comes with a heaping side order of the feels. He's just that intense. It makes him hard to take, except in small doses of time.

I can't push him away because that's exactly what everybody else does. And anyway, I made him a promise that I'd always have his back. As a vampire, I've got to keep to that. It won't be easy. But I've realized something after tonight's visit to Doctor Young's.

There's a worse fate than caring too much about a person as broken as Frankie. Being him, alone.

The weight of this promise lifts, morphing into something more like relief than a burden. Attitude isn't everything. It won't correct a chemical imbalance in the brain, replace missing limbs, or cure cancer. But it helps in other ways, sometimes. Especially for someone like me, who's taking care of friends with all of the above.

Inside the apartment, Frankie curls up on the comfy chair, reminding me of a scruffy stray cat. When he leans back, the chair rocks slightly. Leaving him to relax is easy because that state is so rare for him. The man's almost always tense, on guard, and it's not surprising. I hope someday he'll find a more perpetual peace than a newbie vampire's favorite reading chair can give him.

In the fridge, I rummage around for blood. I'm glad to have the replacement arm despite Gertrude's disturbing alchemy since my real arm still hasn't grown back. Maybe my body's craving more blood in order to start fixing things, finally.

I'm ridiculously thirsty, so I guzzle the first bag I get my hand on, even though it's cold. It hits the spot despite everything, so I have another. And then one more. Yeah, three bags of blood in under thirty seconds. Maybe it's some kind of record. I let out a huge belch.

"Dude!" Frankie chuckles. "Manners."

"Shitballs."

I'm not freaking out over being the butt of toilet humor. It's because of the sudden churn in my guts. One of those bags was dead blood. Because of course, it is.

Frankie blinks as I make a run for the bathroom. Yup. I'm about to pitch a hurl. But even though this is a tiny apartment and everything's just a few steps away from everything else, I trip and fall flat on my face before I make it there.

Warm hands dart under my home-grown arm and the waxy replacement one. Yeah, my buddy's dragging me to the bathroom. Just in time, he gets me through the door and over the toilet. The retching starts, but I only really parse a few seconds of it, thank God.

"You're going to be okay."

Those words aren't Frankie's. Instead, they come out of a woman's mouth, weathered lips painted in a magenta gloss that's settled into the fine lines. Her voice trembles, fearful as a mouse under a hawk's shadow. Whoever's memory I'm seeing loves this woman and wants to smack her across the face at the same time. They control the impulse more because of the pain in their left arm than anything else.

The pain stabs harder as whoever I am gasps for air, shooting down instead of up.

Great. I'm experiencing a second-hand heart attack.

"Move it, lady!"

The woman gets shoved out of the way by a whipcord-thin EMT with plugs in her earlobes and tattoos winding up her skinny arms. She turns her head, then places one side of it against the chest I only just realized is masculine. Moments later, she sits up, eyes wide and rolling.

"Defib, stat! We can save this one!"

Another EMT drops a case on the ground and opens it, pulling out paddles as the first rips the shirt off the person whose death I'm experiencing.

I want to tell them not to bother. That this dude's a goner no matter what they do, otherwise I wouldn't be seeing any of this. But of course, I can't. I'm not actually in the past, just having a memory with my allergic reaction. They keep on going as the woman, who I realize is vaguely familiar to yours truly, sobs on the driveway outside a nice house in the suburbs.

"Dad!"

I know that voice. It's Zack Milano. So, I'm watching his father, Zack Senior, kick the bucket here. Everything I've seen about the older Milano I'm experiencing this moment through helps me understand why my old frenemy isn't crying.

"I did it, dad. Everything you taught me. For love." His lips wear a frown, but his eyes are all mirth.

I'm gasping like a fish after the EMTs make their desperate attempt at a kick-start. All of the mortal sensations are somehow a relief, and horrifying at the same time. Because having visions like these prove that I haven't forgotten how to feel human, just that my undead body is incapable. I'm puzzled to feel the pain recede, like the medical folk have actually managed to save the day.

"You broke my heart, running around with that man," are the words coming out of Mr. Milano's mouth. "This is your fault." I practically taste power on my lips, magic he's trying to use on his own son. But he's too weak, and the sparks sputter and stall.

I blink, unsure at this point why Mr. Milano's thinking about Frankie Pickering. Also, not understanding why I'm throwing up. Dead blood means the donor has died, full stop. He couldn't have survived if I'm seeing this, right?

"Don't *let my dad die*." That first word is practically a whisper, but after that, Zack's voice booms like he's delivered a line onstage. But that's not the most striking thing about his utterance, at least from my perspective.

I'm watching Zack use his spell-singing. It's unclear whether this is my ability to see magic or Mr. Milano's. Except that I'm in his head. I'm painfully aware that he knows he's a victim of patricide.

Another wave of pain starts in my chest, tearing down my left arm. Mr. Milano can't scream or speak to work his magic. He hasn't got the breath for it. In fact, he's stopped respiration entirely. But his brain's still going like the Energizer Bunny on the last dregs of power in his titular batteries.

"Oxygen!" The tattooed EMT stays put while her partner jumps back into the truck.

As the light dims and the sound turns down on my borrowed senses, I come to the same realization as the dead magician.

Zack Milano just used magic to murder his own father.

---

I'm sitting in my shower stall, sipping warm blood from my favorite mug. Frankie and Maya talk together in hushed tones in the tiny galley kitchen just outside the door. Of course I can hear everything they say.

"I don't know." Maya shakes her head.

"Well, he does, but he's not talking to me about it." Frankie shrugs. "I was thinking, since he's gonna be okay, maybe you could do your thing?" He holds up one hand, palm flat.

"Not unless he agrees."

"I didn't know it worked that way."

"That's the only way I use it." She crosses her arms over her chest, side-eyeing Frankie. "Find another vamp with this talent, and maybe you'll get a different answer."

"Sorry." He cringes.

"It's okay. I get that a lot from folks." She gives him a tiny grin but doesn't drop her arms. "But you remember what they say about great power."

"Yeah, I know the saying." He nods. "Glad you're one of the good eggs. So how much should we give him?"

"We'll warm up one more bag and take a few more on the road with us." Maya leans to open the refrigerator. "I called to let them know he'd be late, but the Fitzpatricks won't wait forever."

I try to drink more from my mug, but it's empty. I set it down on the floor outside the shower stall, which has been swept. Yeah, I made a mess, and my friends cleaned it up because they're awesome. The only reason I know I missed the bowl at least once is because my shirt is covered with ashes. But there's one problem.

"Uh, guys?"

"Hmm?" Frankie turns his head to look over his shoulder at me.

"I've, uh, fallen. And I can't get up."

"Gotcha."

And he does. Maya's still making the blood, so it's Frankie who gets me off the floor. He also points out a clean shirt hanging from the hook on the wall where I usually keep my towel.

The gesture is oddly familiar. Am I getting flashbacks to the time I helped him clean up after his own supernatural disaster? Or is something else going on?

"Thanks."

"Just don't start telling me I'm one hell of a butler or anything cheesy."

"Don't worry, you're safe from that."

And it's true, mostly because I don't get his reference. When in doubt with the pop culture things, I always figure it must be from anime. I can't imagine anything more boring than a cartoon about a butler, but what do I know? I'm a musical theater geek, not an *otaku*.

Frankie closes the door and gives me some privacy. Which is sort of too little, too late, considering he watched me hurl my guts up to the point where he had to call my girlfriend. And now, the two of them are together in my apartment, plotting about how best to help me.

I change shirts, thankful that my pants are still passable for the places I've got to go and the people I need to see. When I'm done, I head out of the bathroom to find Maya and Frankie with their McPlotpants fully and properly on, although they stop talking abruptly when I emerge.

That's always nice.

Yeah, that's sarcasm.

I can't actually be waxing paranoid about these two, can I? I've watched enough sitcoms to know they're probably planning a surprise party and are not out to get me. My paranoia used to be reserved for people like Zack, which in retrospect, was a good call. So why am I so jumpy?

And that reminds me to go write everything I saw in the patricidal vision before it leaks out of my mind or I run into Sebastian Caprice again. Or Zack himself. I've got to assume my frenemy is behind those assaults now.

After the dream I had at the end of yesterday, I'm not telling Frankie what I saw. I don't know whether my day visions come from actual events, but one thing's certain. If my pal is in a relationship with Zack Milano, he's not going to take news that he's a murderer well.

As I write, it becomes clearer. Zack has never talked about his dad, only his mom. Probably he feared him. Bad enough to have a parent whose disapproving words can physically hurt you. Worse when they can control practically everything you do.

The only missing piece of this puzzle is a motive. Not for the murder, but the assaults. That's part of calling everyone down to neutral ground, of course.

"Hey, Tino?" My friends call me out in tandem like they're singing in harmony.

"Yeah?" I stop in the middle of shrugging on my opera cloak.

"We're late." Maya taps her wristwatch. Yeah, she wears one of those. It's not even digital. "Old Man Fitzpatrick's expecting you, remember?"

"Oh, yeah." I tuck the notepad away, and we all head out.

# CHAPTER EIGHTEEN

I park my shitbox Miata on a different street in case my parents are home. Don't start thinking I avoid them all the time because that's not true. Dinner with the folks still happens once a week, even if my weird hours and PI work made strict adherence to Sundays impossible. But I go solo because I haven't told them about Leora, let alone the other kids and Frankie. Which is one reason I don't want them to see me now.

There's no way to explain my new and unimproved arm without revealing the supernatural world to them. And that's Whitby's ultimate power-grab dream. Any unauthorized reveal gets all of us executed. "All" means me and Stephanie, plus Frankie and the kids, because mortal ties equate to vampiric responsibility. Which puts Raven and DeCampo on the chopping block, too.

So we walk to the Fitzpatrick house in a roundabout way that won't take us past the Crispo abode. But once again, all that paranoia is unwarranted. My parents aren't home. The car's gone, and the lights are out. But something flutters on the front door. I head up the driveway to check it out.

It's a note to my dad, thanking him for setting up the floral arrangements on short notice even though he's retired. The signature is Mella Milano, Zack's mother. Of course. Because Zack's dad is an extremely recent victim of patricide, apparently.

More recent than I'd initially thought. If this note is any indication, he died a day ago. And it also explains where my parents are. Down at Michellino's, setting things up.

"Looks like a funeral's in our near future."

"Huh?" Frankie and Maya both blink even though he's the one who speaks.

"Zack's father passed, according to this." I shake my head, deciding to let at least one fact drop. "Also my dead blood vision. Turns out, he donated blood down at good old Kent County Hospital recently, too."

"Oh, no!" Maya puts one hand to her cheek.

"Yeah." I sigh. "But we've got an appointment to keep. Come on."

I shamble down the driveway, then try to stop shuffling and pick up my feet. Maybe I'm undead, but dammit I'm a vampire, not a zombie. Time to start acting the part, especially since I'm representing the fanged set in a meeting with werewolves, hunters, magicians, and kid Caprice.

"The old man's expecting you, Crispo." The wolfish grin greeting me is a surprise. Because this is Jackie Cianci, my old babysitter. No, she's not related to the late, great Mayor, Buddy Cianci. And don't ask if you ever meet her. She hates that.

"Huh." I raise an eyebrow, then peer down at her, which is weird. Last time I saw her, she was taller than me. "Hey, Jackie. How's things?"

"Lively. Especially compared to you." She wrinkles her nose and tosses her head. An unruly lock of red hair flops against her forehead. "They said you'd been turned, but I didn't wanna believe it until now."

"Well, I'm glad to see you again at any rate." I grin. "Maybe you'll finally give me that rematch on *Super Smash Brothers*."

"Fat chance, Crispo." Jackie snorts. "They say you're the fast vamp, so I'm keeping that high score, thank you very much."

"Well, you can't blame me for asking." I shrug. "See ya!"

"Later, dude."

Meeting an old friend who seems to be doing well always puts a spring in my step. That was just what I needed to navigate this get-together after all the recent unpleasantness. Walking through the gate and down the stone walkway that leads to the gazebo is way easier now than it would have been just a few moments earlier.

Maya and Frankie appear relatively untroubled, of course. They're both used to playing things close to their chests.

"Hi there, Mr. Fitzpatrick!" I call out in the gazebo's general direction, lifting my arm to wave.

And I fail spectacularly because the arm's misbehaving. I lift the other one instead, then smack my alchemical replacement to show it who's boss.

"You may enter."

I realize that the delayed wave is no big flub, thanks to my opera cloak. Nobody except maybe Maya would know I had to use an alternate gesture.

Because of this, I don't reach out to open the screen door on the gazebo, leaving that to Frankie. A chuckle from inside tells me exactly how this looks. Like my friend is somehow my servant. Maybe even a Renfield, which I still haven't gotten around to asking about.

But having help is better that than walking with an obvious handicap into a literal den of werewolves and hunters. Even though the gazebo's neutral ground and I know almost everyone here by sight or better, it's more than a little unsettling.

"Fergus, good to be in your company again." I grin and give the elderly werewolf a respectful nod. Yeah, he's blind and can't see it, but the rest of the folks do. And that matters. "And Kayleigh, Calvin. Nice to see you two."

"Likewise." The old man smiles.

A throat clears behind me.

"Mr. Caprice."

"Thanks for inviting me, Valentino."

I can't respond to that without sounding like an even bigger jerk than I already do. Instead, I just nod.

"Now that everybody's here, we can have our talk." Fergus Fitzpatrick's grin is appropriately wolfish.

"So, what's this about?" Kayleigh Killarney crosses her arms over her chest. This puts the firearms slung over each hip out of reach, but I happen to know she's got sets of silver-tipped hickory stakes in arm holsters under her flannel shirt. That's my ex, never defenseless.

She's looking me right in the eye, and her expression is all business. She's waiting for my reply and disappointing her is a bad idea. As I open my mouth, Old Man Fitzpatrick speaks.

"I want to propose a perpetual agreement between our families."

Kayleigh and Calvin grin, along with a woman who looks like Calvin but is a few years older. The werewolves do as well, and Sebastian joins them. I start to smile too until something stops me. No, it's not my fangs. It's that other f-word.

"Family?" I blink, extending my hand back toward Frankie and Maya. "We vampires can't exactly be defined by that term the way everyone else can."

"I'm not here to teach you vocabulary, Tino." Old Man Fitzpatrick shakes his head. "But for all intents and purposes, you belong to a group that's bound by duty and works together toward common goals."

"I guess." I glance around. "But I'm still getting the feeling that one of these things is not like the other."

"Yeah, I'm not a vampire, for one." Frankie clears his throat. "Or a magician."

"And I'm not a werewolf, young Master Pickering." The figure on the other side of Fergus chuckles. It's Scott's mother. "Your point?"

"Oh. Well, I guess I haven't got one, then. Sorry."

"You come to this meeting with your domestic partner and your significant other and say you're not like Miss Killarney or me?" The werewolf to Fergus Fitzpatrick's right raises his eyebrow. Of course I know this guy. It's Sean, Scott's father.

"Uh." I glance at him and blink.

"Okay, Mrs. Fitzpatrick. I'll stop objecting, then."

"Good lad." She grins like she's about to serve everybody a plate of chocolate chip cookies. Which two of us can't eat, so I'm glad when she doesn't.

"So, about this agreement. Why now?" Calvin leans against the wooden beam behind him.

"We need an alliance to make sure things stay on the right path here in Rhode Island." Fergus leans forward in his chair. "One solid enough so we can trust each other with," he glances at me, "sensitive yet dire information."

"That's not easy with my father in the picture." Kayleigh sighs. "You know his views."

"And they're outdated. We discussed this." The third hunter tosses her head, her bobbed chestnut hair falling to the side to reveal a long, thin scar along the angle of one cheek.

"Yes, and that's why I'm here, Aileen." Kayleigh glances down at the sparkling ring on her left hand. "Even after the wedding, I don't think Dad will do things the Kelley way."

"It comes part and parcel with an alliance by marriage, though. He knew that before giving his blessing."

"He's hardheaded." Kayleigh sighs. "I'm not saying he'll immediately go out and break any agreement, but he's got other issues. Something that's going to affect him over the long term. He might not be able to remember what's in the past."

"If you're talking about his diagnosis, don't worry." Fergus clears his throat, probably trying to cover the collective gasp coming from the hunter's corner. "I've got my connections. And the right allies can help your father supernaturally."

"Ah. I understand." I tilt my head. "Members of my, er, family have talents and connections in the memory retrieval department."

"Exactly." Fergus's smile is bright enough to rival the fairy lights he's got illuminating the gazebo.

Taking a few moments to mull everything over isn't out of the ordinary during any negotiation. So I take advantage of the trope and stop to think. The first thing that comes to my mind is the fact that the only person I know who can reliably work with memories is Sebastian Caprice. And he's not part of my family. And the second is the question Raven would ask.

"What's in it for us, then?"

"We will help you with the investigation you discussed." Fergus grins. "You're not the only one with law enforcement connections."

"Okay." I turn my head, glancing at Sebastian. "So, what about him? The Caprices haven't always been the law-abiding type."

"I've got my own reasons for being here that have nothing to do with you, Tino."

"Let's hear them." Sean Fitzpatrick taps his foot.

"Listen. You all want my family to go legit. I can make that happen, but not without help." Sebastian gazes at his shoes. "New Lethians like me run out of energy. It's something only time can change. But I want to be part of this, to help and do better."

"Really? Because—"

"Let the kid ask for help." Frankie's hand on my elbow stops my impending tirade. I nod.

"I'm going to need help from other magicians. More specifically, Sarah Pickering." The boy's high cheekbones redden.

"Why my sister?" Frankie blinks.

"That water magic of hers has energy compatible with mine, according to Doctor Maris." Sebastian clears his throat. "With her help, I can keep working steadily instead of waiting weeks to make one little change."

"Rewriting personalities, you mean?"

"No. It's more like changing behavior."

"Like how you turned your father into a chain smoker?"

"I didn't do that. He's stressed."

"This isn't an interrogation room, Mr. Crispo." Fergus Fitzpatrick drops this info like he means business. "Be reasonable."

"So, you want a superpowered study buddy. But that'll be Sarah's choice."

"I'm okay with that." He nods, mouth a thin, pale line. "She can say no to begin with, and change her mind any time."

"Well, then I guess we're cool for now." I blink. "Sebastian."

"Thanks, Tino."

"So, can we all come together as a community for the greater good already?" I pull the notes I've collected out of my spacious opera cloak pocket. "There's a problem I'm just undying to get your help with."

Side comments, snorts, coughs, and other assorted side noises ring in my ears. I manage to make out one whole comment in all the din. It's Calvin Kelley.

"Who turned this guy, Mister Rogers?"

"He's always been like this," Kayleigh replies.

When the crowd settles down, Mrs. Fitzpatrick carries around an old hidebound book. Its pages are lined with printed names, paired with signatures. Some of them are old enough to be behind glass in a museum, too.

She brings it around to the hunters first. All three of them sign about halfway down the page.

At the top of the page she holds out to Maya is a familiar name. Stephanie Vasílissa-Adelphi. Right under it is Edwin Tierney-McQueen, followed by Sasquatch. None of those were written or signed with a ballpoint pen, so they must be at least as old as Fergus Fitzpatrick. More recent entries include Doctor Maris and Raphael Paolucci.

"I'm sure this isn't much of a surprise." She writes her first name, with her usual surname, Jones. After that, she adds a hyphen followed by DeCampo, then signs. Her next sentence answers my unspoken question about all the hyphenating. "I'm proud to list him as my sire."

"We're in good company, Maya." I point with the pen before going full John Hancock. Printing McQueen is way easier than signing it, but what do you expect on my first try?

The hunters gasp when I pass the pen to Frankie. He pauses, his eyes moving from side to side like he's watching a tennis match.

"Has a Lamb ever signed something like this before?"

"No." Fergus gives the answer I didn't have. "But there's nothing to stop you if that's your preference."

"Okay."

And just like that, Frankie makes history.

If only it'll stick.

# CHAPTER NINETEEN

Once they've all signed, Fergus Fitzpatrick gives me the floor. I launch into a brief description of my work on Maury's investigation, stopping short of naming the suspect. Once that's done, it's time to ask the important question.

"So, what kind of supernatural person commands folks with magical music, steals one personal item, and then leaves them with no memory?"

Nobody answers, but I can practically hear the wheels turning in their minds as they mull it over.

"Name those victims again?" Aileen's forehead is all scrunched up. "A magician named Gertrude, Kayleigh, and who else?"

"A psychic, and then this one I didn't meet personally." I read off the name. "Karen Battey. It says she lost a pair of earrings."

"I know Karen." Mrs. Fitzpatrick nods. "She's my cousin's wife. Got a role in that production of *Nine* over at the Playhouse, but had to back out because she's pregnant and will be showing by opening night."

"Oh. Then I did meet her." And so did Zack. Shitballs. "Do you happen to know anything about her earrings?"

"Yes, as a matter of fact." She looks confused. "They were my grandmother's. One of the werewolves on my side of the family."

"And is Karen a werewolf too?"

"No. My cousin is."

"I'll bet my life the child she's carrying will grow up to be a wolf. I believe I understand now." Fergus tugs his beard. I know this means he's not pleased with whatever he's about to say. "The collector is a magician, gathering the makings of a spell."

"Um?" Sebastian raises his hand with a sheepish grin. "Over at Stout, they teach us that alchemists use chemistry-type ingredients in their magic."

"This collector probably isn't an alchemist." Frankie's voice cracks, but at least it's not shaky. "I grew up watching magicians do just about everything. And the only time they need a bunch of stuff with sympathetic connections is when they're doing something big and collaborative."

"So, it's a group of them?" Kayleigh rubs her upper arms like she's caught a sudden chill.

"I think not." The voice comes from outside the gazebo. "May I enter?"

"Step forward, Stephanie McQueen."

Old Man Fitzpatrick's voice ushers her in. After that, I'm rushing to her side because she's a total wreck.

My sire looks like she's been in trampled by thirty to forty feral hogs and then went on to have a steel cage match with a bear.

I throw my opera cloak over her shoulders. It hangs down halfway past her thighs, which is good because she's suffering an imminent wardrobe malfunction. Once her dignity is restored, she waves me away.

"What happened?" Maya's eyes are wide, the rest of her face blank. I can't blame her. DeCampo was supposed to be with Stephanie. Raven too.

"That's not important." Her voice rasps. She clears her throat, swallowing something I hope isn't a chunk of ash. "It's one magician. I know because he tried commanding the three of us. It worked on your sire," she nods at Maya. "Tino, he took Raven's Lazakhar."

"Shitballs."

"Is Raven—" Frankie's eyes are red, a storm of tears threatening. "Are they—"

Stephanie shakes her head. "Still with us. Barely. I left them at your Belfry."

"Who did this?" Frankie's shaking like a pressure cooker about to explode. Which makes sense because Raven's the loving older sibling he never had. The man has a long fuse, but this isn't the first time it's nearly reached Detonation Boulevard.

Stephanie looks at me.

It's decision time. I could shrug or nod, give my sire a cue that I haven't figured this out. She'd bear the bad news, and I'd come out of this smelling like a rose. Which I need to do if I still plan on asking for permission to turn Maury.

Nobody's privy to the case's conclusion, not even Maya. None of them will blame me for making a mistake by insisting Zack was our ally, or not acting sooner. No one will know I'm lying.

Except for me.

I could fool everybody for a time, but I can't fool myself. Growing up Roman Catholic made confession part of my nature. I'll eventually go mad, keeping a secret like that. Because I can't even take it to the grave, a plague for eternity. And if I use a lie now to turn Maury later and he ever finds out, he'll never forgive me.

Never is forever when you're undead.

"The magician's a spell-singer," I say. "The only one of his kind to have knowledge of and access to all the victims. It's Zack Milano."

"Why?" Frankie's hands are fists so tight they smell bloody. He reminds me of the time I saw *The Running of the Bulls* on TV. Pushed to the limit and seeing red.

"I don't know," Stephanie answers. "But whatever spell he's prepared, he's casting it tonight. At the funeral home."

Frankie takes three steps before he's blocked by Scott. He tries going around, but Sebastian's smoky tendrils counter his evasion in a virtual game of "not touching you."

"Spell-singer?" Aileen reaches into a pouch on her utility belt.

"Everybody needs earplugs to put on before we go inside." She's got little plastic baggies holding pairs of foam earplugs individually wrapped.

"Except the vamps." Kayleigh shakes her head. "No offense, but your hearing's too good for those to block sound effectively."

"None taken." Stephanie shudders. "I have my own ways of resisting."

"You're in no shape to go back into the fray, Miss Stephanie." Fergus Fitzpatrick shakes his head.

"All the same, I must."

"Let us handle it, Steph."

"You're not ready for this fight, Tino."

"Ready or not, fate always seems to have me up against Zack Milano for something or other." I shrug. "You believe in fate, right?"

"You can't win this battle." Stephanie closes her eyes. "He's got a ring full of powder and is controlling King DeCampo."

"Been there. Fought that. Lost an arm." The sound I make is somewhere between a chuckle and a sob. "It can't get much worse, right?"

"What's to stop him from using that to control you?"

"I happen to know that stuff doesn't work too great on younger vamps like me." I point at my prosthetic. "I've already had the chance to diminish the returns."

"All the same, I ought to be there."

"Why?"

"This is too important. He's trying to end the world." When Steph's eyes open, they're too shiny, and also red. Like she's fighting tears.

"Well, that sounds pretty serious. Like you could die if you go and fight him the way you are now."

"This world is worth my giving up eternity."

"Let's say we agree to disagree on that." I take her hand. "Living forever without garlic scares the crap out of me. You actually like it. More reasons for me to go do this and give you a break."

She squeezes my hand. The hunters and werewolves watch this entire exchange, the latter nodding and clenching their jaws while the former blink and stare.

"Maya, talk some sense into him, please."

"Sure thing." She ruffles my hair. "You're right, Tino. Stephanie has to stay here." She turns to Mrs. Fitzpatrick. "Since we're allies, can you arrange a ride for Stephanie to Kent County Hospital? She needs medical attention from Doctor Maris, I believe."

"I've already called a Swyft." Stephanie holds up the phone I insisted she get. Thank God.

"I can do something else." Mrs. Fitzpatrick stands on her toes to whisper something into her husband's ear. He nods, then approaches.

"You will have our help. Jackie and Scott will go with you."

"Ours too." Aileen's offer comes out of left field. "It's sort of our job to negate threats like this, but you're taking point because you know the enemy best."

I'm blinking at Kayleigh as she stands shoulder to shoulder with her fiancé and future sister-in-law. She rolls her eyes but I catch the slight grin on her usually grave face.

"Wow. Thanks, everybody, for having our backs like this."

Something nags at the back of my mind. It's about the funeral. I pull the flier from my parents' door out of my pocket.

"Shitballs."

"What's wrong?" Scott's stepping up beside me, one of his arms looped around Frankie in a hold-back posture. Sebastian flanks them. They all peer at the paper with me, faces going slack. I read it out loud.

"With a special musical tribute by Zack Milano and two of Stout Academy's best Drama Club students."

"That's Sarah." Sebastian loosens his grasp on Frankie.

"And Leora." Scott's nostrils flare, but he manages to maintain control. He's been a wolf way longer than his peer has been a Lethian, after all.

"That's how he plans to collaborate and pull in the rest of the magic he needs." I shake my head. "The way he did in the courtroom. With a musical number."

It seems we're all going to a funeral. Hopefully, the number of deceased individuals won't increase during the course of the evening.

# CHAPTER TWENTY

Michellino's is relatively quiet when we arrive. I've seen the parking lot emptier than this on only one occasion. But this makes sense. If Dad set up flowers tonight, the actual wake is happening tomorrow.

I park and get out of the car while Maya and Jackie wrangle themselves out of the passenger side and the back seat. Frankie's in Scott's truck with Sebastian, while the hunters drove over in a Jeep.

"Shitballs."

My father's still in there. His van is out front, which means he's inside working. And Mom's helping. And here I am rolling up with a platoon of supernatural warriors.

"What's wrong?"

I wait until everyone's out of their vehicles and tell them the problem.

"If I go in and try getting them to leave, it'll blow our cover."

"And if you don't, your parents will be in the crossfire." Kayleigh chews her lower lip. "Ugh."

"Can't somebody else go in and take over for them?" Maya puts her hand on my shoulder.

"Does anyone besides me have experience with floral arrangements?" I cross my fingers.

A chorus of negatory statements is the response I get.

"How about music?" Sebastian's somehow managed to calm Frankie down. Probably not with any powers, either, or Scott would have bitten him. "As one of Zack's students, I've got the perfect excuse to go in there and delay him with coaching questions."

I'm not sure I should trust this to the kid. After the way we all got burned by Zack, it should be the worst idea in the world. But he's shown honor and good sense this evening, joining an alliance and jumping right in to uphold it. Don't I owe him for that?

The vow I took when I joined vampire society says as much. If any kind of supernatural will honor and protect humans, I've vowed vampirically to pay them back. Going against it is not an option.

"Kid, if your idea can keep my parents out of magical combat, go for it."

"And the girls?" Scott's forehead looks like a roadmap.

"He won't let them go." Sebastian shakes his head. "All I'm trying to do is stop him from doing his thing until they leave. Maybe they can help us once they know what's happening."

"Okay." I nod. "Get in there and do your thing, Sebastian."

He heads toward the entrance.

"So, we have to get in pretty much right after they're out." Aileen's nodding. "I know this building. There's a hearse entrance and a point of access on the roof. The crematorium, technically, but that's way too risky."

"He might be able to use it." Scott jerks his chin at a ball-cap-wearing figure leaning against the lamp post.

"Sparky!" I grin, waving as he turns around and jogs over. "Of course. That's perfect."

"Hey, boss?" Black eyes blink up at me.

"Yeah, buddy?"

"Is there trouble in there?" Sparky jerks a thumb over his shoulder.

"Will be in a few minutes."

"Shitballs."

"Language, buddy." I sigh. "Anyway, you know where the crematorium is?"

"Yeah. Want me to go in that way?"

"Exactly."

"Okay." Sparky sprints toward the back of the building.

"What is he, a dragon?" Calvin scratches his head.

"Something like that." I grin. "Useful but not so big. Still just a kid."

"We'll take the hearse entrance." Calvin puts on what look like infrared goggles. Aileen and Kayleigh don similar headgear. "We can leave the lights off back there and still get around."

The hunters follow Sparky at a full march.

"I'll take the roof." Maya cracks her knuckles.

"Be careful."

"Always." My girlfriend heads toward the side of Michellino's that faces away from the street. As she goes, I hear her activating her claws, answering my unspoken question about how she'll get to the top.

"Frankie, are you staying here or coming in?"

"I want to be here for you." He puts his hands on his hips. "Even though I can't do anything."

"I've seen you in fights before. You're nothing to sneeze at."

"I've got no Post-its this time, Tino. But that's not all."

"Frankie, there's—" I'm about to tell him everything, spill the beans on that dream about him and Zack. But he stops me.

"Look, I don't want you benching me." He shakes his head. "But it's time to tell you. I've been seeing Z. Romantically."

"Okay."

"Okay?"

"I totally understand what he sees in you." I nod. "The heart wants what it wants."

"I love him." Frankie deflates. "Even after all this." He gestures at the building. "And he says he loves me. So I understand if you don't want me in there with you."

"You're coming in."

"What?" Jackie snorts. "You can't be serious."

"I am, though." I grin. "Scott, tell her how we won last time."

"Musical number. Totally cheesy." Scott grins. "Also, by giving a shit."

"That's a simplified version, but it'll do." I reach out, put a hand on Frankie's shoulder. "I'm bringing you because if all else fails, Zack might listen to reason if it comes from you."

"Because he gives a shit, gotcha." Jackie nods, dropping Frankie a wink.

"I guess we're going in through the front door, which is perfect for wolfed-out shock troops, et cetera." Scott shrugs. "We'll have to stand nearby, but not close enough for Tino's parents to recognize any of us."

"Right, or they'll stop to chat." Frankie chuckles. "Not a good night to meet your parents."

"I know just the place."

I lead them through the front door and then to the right. It's a small alcove with a waiting area for people coming in to make arrangements. As the biggest funeral home in Cranston, Michellino's sometimes has customers waiting.

Scott's eyeing the coffee bar, which is laden with granola bars and other non-perishable snacks. Frankie shakes a finger at him, reminding the teenager to stop thinking with his stomach.

In the quiet as we wait, I try tuning my ears in to what's going on across the hall. My enhanced hearing doesn't fail me. Inside, Zack coaches Sarah and Leora through a rendition of *Wishing You Were Somehow Here Again*. Funeral appropriate, though not what I'd expect for a world-ending number.

He must have something else in mind, then. Some other song they'll all sing together while they work magic. I wrack my brain for musicals that include the use of magic. *Camelot's* too old. *Jeckyll and Hyde* has too few female roles. *Into the Woods,* then? *Puffs*? I wonder what excuse he'll give the girls for switching songs.

Either that, or I'm grossly misjudging his motives. If his reasons include grief, this number from *Phantom* fits. But something distracts me from my frantic theorizing.

The sound of a piano draws the corners of my mouth down. I

should have known Zack would go the whole hog with this and not opt for recorded music. The main thing I'm wondering is, who's playing? Because Zack Milano never has and never will do instruments.

Scott taps me on the shoulder, pointing at his ears and then his nose. I shake my head and make a lip-zipping gesture. Even if he learned something important, we can't afford to make noise and miss my parents leaving the building.

Jackie to the rescue. She's snagged a couple of Michellino's promotional items, a pad and pen. Scott snatches them and jots something down then holds it up.

*Doctor Terry and another lady inside.*

Because of course, they are. Just when I thought this couldn't get more complicated, the crazy coincidences pile even higher.

Stephanie walks through the door wearing fresh clothes and sporting a perfect updo, healed of all visible injuries. And she's got Whitby with her. He's wearing a white suit, complete with matching shoes. In a funeral home. Gross.

She didn't take the Swyft to Kent County, then.

My sire waits until her gauche companion turns toward the Milano family's room before glancing briefly at the alcove. Jackie puts a finger over her lips, but I don't need stage directions from a werewolf to know this isn't my cue.

I watch Whitby pull the door open, then step aside as my parents walk through. He greets my father, shaking his hand.

I blink, of course. After that, my vision's nearly obscured by the red tinge of imminent Rage. The last person I want anywhere near my parents is this fake plastic king. And Stephanie knows it.

If Scott and Frankie hadn't been there expecting this reaction, I'd have jumped the other two vamps by now. But they're being good friends as usual, holding me back.

While Whitby ushers my folks out of the door, my head clears enough to understand what's going on.

Stephanie was here earlier. She knew Mom and Dad had this job, and she came up with her own plan to get them out. Calling in a favor from that usurper to have him hire them for an under-the-table wedding, as evidenced by their conversation and the fat stack of cash he just handed over.

Once they leave, I'm almost ready to head in, only waiting on the sound of the van turning out on to Park Avenue.

But first, I pray that Stephanie doesn't come back in here.

God owes vampires nothing.

# CHAPTER TWENTY-ONE

I'm already on the verge of Rage when I rush through the door at four times a mortal's speed. This means everything else moves slowly enough for me to take it all in before the regular speed folks have time to react.

Inside, Sebastian hovers at Corey Terry's shoulder, peeking at the stack of sheet music in front of her. Eunice is about to stop him, frowning her displeasure.

King DeCampo sits in one of the seats, his arms slack, and his hands folded in his lap. From the way the girls disregard his presence, they couldn't have been privy to the battle between Zack and the elder vampires.

Or maybe I'm misjudging again. Sarah's looking right at Zack, who's openly wearing all the items he nicked off his victims. The earrings dangle from the strap on Kayleigh's belt of mace, and she can see the glow around them, plain as I can. Seeing magic is a talent the two of us share.

I hear the rending of clothes and the crack of bone as Scott and Jackie wolf out. I realize my own impetuous use of powers prompted them to go all-out. Oops.

Leora sees me. The werewolves, too. She stops singing and drops her jaw.

"Stop!" Zack holds out a hand, palm flat. The three of us halt as though a wall was suddenly in the way. It's not. Even Zack isn't that powerful. Yet.

"Fine." I snort. "Go on with your villain monologue."

"Villain?" Leora's voice rises. "Zack's the good guy. He's going to bring them back, Tino."

"What to the who, now?" I actually take a step back.

"Our parents," Sarah answers.

I can't argue. After risking everything to evacuate my own folks, that's impossible. And I'm an adult. Leora and Sarah are just a couple of kids who need parenting every day.

"No way." Frankie's pacing up the aisle between chairs, standing as tall as his wiry frame allows. He locks gazes with Zack. "Shit happens. People die. We're left to work through it. This spell is a copout, love."

"That's right." I nod, and Scott and Jackie join in.

"Maybe for you." Eunice puts her hands on her hips, facing us. "But if you had the kind of power they do, wouldn't you want to fix everything so love always wins?"

"Is that what he's trying to sell you all?" Sebastian blinks. "Because family ties and love aren't the same thing. Sare, you know this."

"Yeah, Bassey." She gazes down at him, like the angel statue in Swan Point cemetery. "That's why I helped him get Raven's amulet. Because he can change all that conditional crap we had to settle for, and make life better for our siblings."

"What does Baba think about this, Leora?"

"No idea." Her lips thin as she holds up a bare right wrist. "No bracelet, no Baba." She lets out a nervous titter.

"Not true!" Sparky's standing in the back entrance to the room. He brandishes the bracelet almost threateningly. The hunters sidle through behind him, flanking the performance area. "Don't help him, Leora. Don't make me stop you."

"I'd like to see you try."

"This is what I get for fixing everything?" Zack shakes his head. "So short-sighted, all of you."

"Back at you, dude." I snort. "You're meddling with reality. How do you know it'll all go the way you want?"

"My childe is correct." The second-to-last person I wanted to see speaks as she strides all the way down the aisle. "Reality has a way of balancing itself in ways you won't like."

"Finish that job, DeCampo." Zack points.

The former king of Providence leaps from his seat with his claws out, rushing Stephanie.

She's unarmed and stands still, letting him come.

I dash toward her. But all the speed in the world isn't enough.

Claws slash my sire, plowing furrows through her throat down to her waist.

Ashes bloom, gray flowers spreading across her body.

In seconds, Stephanie is gone. It's silent. Everyone hears her Lazakhar clink softly against its chain as it hits the carpet.

"I'll bring her back, too." Zack's lips twist into something too manic for a smile. "Just let us work the spell."

My face is wet; I smell blood pouring from my eyes. Those tears shake my voice like a 6.9 earthquake. My words do them one better.

"Like your father?"

Zack takes a step back.

"I saw it all, Milano." My nostrils flare. "You're nothing but an unrepentant murderer."

"You try my patience, Crispo." He gestures at Corey at the piano. "Valentino, why couldn't you have stayed calm instead of flying off the handle?"

She launches into an intro I can't place at first. The moment Sarah sings the opening line, I understand. By the time Leora trades off, joining the duet, I realize we might be too late.

Zack Milano is altering reality with *Defying Gravity* from Wicked.

On the first chorus, he sings along, adding a third part to the established harmony. All the items he's stolen begin glowing.

The universe holds its breath and stands still, but we don't. Maybe we can't.

DeCampo turns on the group of hunters. Wooden ammo bounces off his armored flesh. They go down in a tangle of limbs accompanied by tearing sounds.

Sparky rushes Leora. She upends a can of green levitation powder on her head, literally defying gravity. He leaps, swinging at her with the bracelet. Powder hits his arm and he floats up, but too slowly to catch her.

Jackie lunges at the piano. Corey keeps playing despite the angry wolf-woman. Eunice gets in the way, brandishing a silver Thespian Society trophy. It nicks Jackie, and she howls in pain.

Sebastian's got Sarah by the arm. I see him struggle to activate his powers through the sea-green glow of her water magic. Her voice continues on, nailing Galinda's next verse.

That leaves Zack to me. I burn all my blood on speed, letting Rage take over. My vision tunnels, and he's the light at the end, a bright bag of magic and blood.

He opens Gertrude's stolen ring.

My plastic arm rebels, punching me in the face.

I fall to the floor at Zack's feet. He stands over me, Kayleigh's holy water spray can in my face. The bastard's still singing, too.

This is how I go?

No.

Maya's dropped behind Zack, hissing like a basket of snakes. He whirls, spraying her right hand, which goes pale and limp, claws retracting.

She swings from the left, claws connecting, severing his wrist.

He sings at it. Bone, skin, and sinew come back together.

The second blast from the can takes out the rest of Maya's claws. She drops to her knees, screaming in pain as smoke rises.

I'm on my feet by now, but his can still sloshes.

"This is wrong." Frankie's there, stepping between us. Somehow he's able to talk over the musical magic. "Z. Stop. We'll fix this the regular way. Just you and me."

Zack wants all the pain in his lover's past erased. Raven's Lazakhar probably lets him change the Pickering family in fundamental ways, including who gets power and who mates with monsters.

But he's got no right. Not when Frankie himself says no.

Zack answers in song, harmonizing with Leora.

*"Everyone deserves the chance to fly."*

I fly at Zack, but Frankie's standing in the way. Rage won't let me go anywhere but straight ahead.

Scott howls, crushing Frankie down to the ground at my right. Bones snap. I trip over them, tuck, and roll.

Zack draws a silver knife.

I leap. My plastic arm splays out, throwing my balance. I miss.

Zack doesn't. The silver blade plunges between Scott's shoulder blades. He slumps forward, twitching.

And the song goes on, nearing conclusion.

I'll never stop him in time with a rogue limb, so I do the only thing I can.

Grabbing my left forearm in my right hand, I call on blood for the strength to tear it off.

Blood I don't have.

But something else happens. I feel power coming at me, fueling my undead muscles enough to pull the alchemical construct off my shoulder.

It's familiar. Gray. Smoky.

Sebastian.

He sends tendrils at Zack while I leap.

Everyone else is down. This is our last stand.

Music rises, racing us, racing time.

We lose.

On the final note, we're pulled out of space and time.

Everything changes.

---

I sit at the center of the Vampire Court of Providence, bored out of my skull. The figures to my left and right are so familiar I don't bother looking at either of them.

The line of waiting undead is longer than usual, and my patience shorter than ever.

Wasn't I just doing something else? Feats of strength? The most important task in the world? Perhaps even saving it?

Before leaning my left arm on the throne's cushion, I pause. Because my left arm is gone, torn off weeks ago. But how? I haven't fought since my last night as a mortal. The elders wouldn't dare put me in danger.

Fortunately, the night is young, and nobody will deny me time to find answers to these questions.

I am the vampire king, after all.

THE END

(Of the world as I knew it. It's not fine.)

# THANK YOU!

Thank you for reading! If you loved this book, please leave a review. You can find my other work by clicking the links below, going to my website or visiting my Author Central page.

Providence Paranormal College Volume 1

Providence Paranormal College Volume 2

A Change In Crime

Wiser Guys

The Longest Night Watch

Stardust, Always

Supernatural Vigilante Society

# CONNECT WITH THE AUTHOR

Find D.R. Perry Online

Website: https://drperryauthor.com/

Facebook: https://www.facebook.com/drpperry/

Twitter: https://twitter.com/DRPerry22

## OTHER LMBPN PUBLISHING BOOKS

To be notified of new releases and special promotions from LMBPN publishing, please join our email list:

**http://lmbpn.com/email/**

For a complete list of books published by LMBPN please visit the following pages:

**https://lmbpn.com/books-by-lmbpn-publishing/**

All LMBPN Audiobooks are Available at Audible.com and iTunes. For a complete list of audiobooks visit:

**www.lmbpn.com/audible**